# EAGLES
# OF FIRE

# EAGLES OF FIRE

## A NOVEL

# TIMOTHY RIZZI

DONALD I. FINE BOOKS
New York

Donald I. Fine Books
Published by the Penguin Group
Penguin Books USA Inc., 375 Hudson Street,
New York, New York 10014, U.S.A.
Penguin Books Ltd, 27 Wrights Lane,
London W8 5TZ, England
Penguin Books, Australia Ltd, Ringwood,
Victoria, Australia
Penguin Books Canada Ltd, 10 Alcorn Avenue,
Toronto, Ontario, Canada M4V 3B2
Penguin Books (N.Z.) Ltd, 182-190 Wairau Road,
Auckland 10, New Zealand

Penguin Books Ltd, Registered Offices:
Harmondsworth, Middlesex, England

Published in 1996 by Donald I. Fine Books,
an imprint of Penguin Books USA Inc.

1   3   5   7   9   10   8   6   4   2

PUBLISHER'S NOTE
This is a work of fiction. Names, characters, places, and incidents are the product of the author's imagination or are used fictitiously, and any resemblance to actual persons, living or dead, events, or locales is entirely coincidental.

**Library of Congress Cataloging-in-Publication Data**
Rizzi, Timothy.
    Eagles of fire : a novel / Timothy Rizzi.
      p.    cm.
    ISBN 1-55611-491-5 (alk. paper)
    1. Korea—Fiction.  I. Title.
PS3568.I835E24    1996
813'.54—dc20               96-6834
                                CIP

This book is printed on acid-free paper.

Printed in the United States of America

Dedicated to the memory of

# GENE GHERE

and his new beginning.

April 20, 1960–February 20, 1996

# ACKNOWLEDGMENTS

Without the assistance from the following people this novel could never have been completed. I wish to thank all of them for the role they played and the friendship along the way.

Laurel N. Holder and the staff at ITT Defense Electronics Division. The NVGs were a kick. I only got into trouble once.

Mr. James Clark for his unique insight, enthusiasm and no-nonsense view into the world of black combat aircraft, their systems and operations.

Thanks to Roxanne Coleman and her knowledge of Korean ground operations and the life of a grunt.

I mustn't forget the genuine Michael C. As always your observations were well thought out and very much appreciated. I hope you approve of the result.

Special appreciation goes to Jason Poston, my editor, and Don Fine. Thank you for the chance and sticking with me through the changes.

Roberta for keeping things in perspective and always having a sense of humor.

Brent and Janis—for being there during the process.

As always and most importantly . . . Diana.

# AIRCRAFT DESCRIPTIONS

**AV-8B HARRIER II**—Known as a "jump jet" for its ability to take off and land vertically this single-engine jet is used by the United States Marine Corps in the light-attack role. Designed to operate from a ship or near the battlefront on unpaved roads the AV-8B can carry an impressive load of weapons including AGM-65 Maverick precision-guided missiles or GBU-15 Paveway laser-guided bombs. The Harrier can also carry up to two lethal GEPOD 30mm gun pods as well as AIM-9M Sidewinder air-to-air missiles for air defense.

| | |
|---|---|
| Manufacturer: | McDonnell Douglas |
| Powerplant: | One Rolls-Royce F402-RR-408 turbofan rated at 23,800 lbs. of thrust |
| Accommodation: | One pilot |
| Dimensions: | Wing span 30 ft. 4 in., length 46 ft. 4 in.   13,968 lbs. empty; maximum takeoff 31,000 |
| Performance: | Maximum speed at sea level 662 mph, ceiling above 50,000 ft., combat radius 103 miles |

**E-3C AWACS**—The E-3 Airborne Warning and Control System aircraft is designed as a highly survivable and mobile command, surveillance and communications system that can operate in all-weather conditions. The airframe is a modified Boeing 707-320B which carries an extensive group of avionics including radar, IFF, communications, displays, mission avionics and navigational systems. The E-3's primary mission is to circle above a battle area commanding air operations from a safe distance.

| | |
|---|---|
| Manufacturer: | Boeing Defense and Space Group, Electronic Systems Division |
| Powerplant: | Four Pratt & Whitney TF33-PW-100/100A turbofans; each rated at 21,000 lbs. of thrust |
| Accommodation: | Standard crew of twenty-three including nineteen mission specialists |
| Dimensions: | Wing span 145 ft. 9 in., length 152 ft. 11 in., height 41 ft. 10 in.   335,000 lbs. gross weight |
| Performance: | Maximum speed 532 mph, ceiling above 29,000 ft., combat radius six hours on station 1,000 miles from base |

**F-15E Eagle**—The "E" model, or Echo, is commonly referred to as the Strike Eagle. The F-15E is considered the world's best all-weather air-to-air and air-to-ground deep interdiction aircraft. Designed to attack high-value ground targets inside enemy territory with the capability to fight its way back to friendly airspace. The E can carry up to 24,500 lbs. of ordnance. This includes a mix of AIM-9M Sidewinders and AIM-120 AMRAAM air-to-air missiles, AGM-65 Mavericks and AGM-130 precision-guided bomb. For precision attacks in adverse weather and at night, the Strike Eagle is equipped with a high-resolution APG-70 radar. It also carries LANTIRN (Low-Altitude Navigational and Targeting Infrared for Night) pods which includes a wide-field FLIR.

| | |
|---|---|
| Manufacturer: | McDonnell Douglas |
| Powerplant: | Two Pratt & Whitney F100-PW-220 turbofans; each rated at 231,500 lbs. of thrust |
| Accommodation: | Two: Pilot and WSO (Weapons System Operator) |
| Dimensions: | Wing span 42 ft. 10¾ in., length 63 ft. 9 in., height 18 ft. 5½ in.   81,000 lbs. gross weight |
| Performance: | Maximum speed Mach 2.5, ceiling above 60,000 ft., max range 2,765 miles |

**F-16C Falcon**—The pilots refer to the lightweight F-16 as "Viper" because of its ability to outmaneuver virtually every other aircraft in the sky. The Stage III Block 50/52 models have been equipped with powerful APG-68 multimode radar giving them increased range and advanced cockpit displays similar to the F-15E. Other improvements include wide-angle HUD and multitarget AIM-120 AMRAAM compatibility for air-to-air combat.

| | |
|---|---|
| Manufacturer: | Lockheed Martin Corporation |
| Powerplant: | One Pratt & Whitney F100-PW-220 turbofan rated at 23,500 lbs. of thrust |
| Accommodation: | One pilot |
| Dimensions: | Wing span 32 ft. 10 in., length 49 ft. 4 in., height 16 ft. 8½ in.   42,300 lbs. gross weight |
| Performance: | Maximum speed Mach 2 class, ceiling above 50,000 ft., max range 2,100 miles |

**MH-60G Pave Hawk**—A modified Black Hawk helicopter, the Pave Hawk is used primarily in the search-and-rescue and Special Operations Forces environment. Equipped with weather/ground mapping radar, secure SATCOM communications, window-mounted 7.62mm miniguns and integrated navigation system using INS, GPS and Doppler. The MH-60G is remarkably well suited for rapid response long-range missions behind enemy lines.

| | |
|---|---|
| Manufacturer: | Sikorsky Aircraft |
| Powerplant: | Two General Electric T700-GE-700/701C Turboshafts |

Accommodation: Crew: Three to four, eleven to fourteen armed troops
Dimensions: Rotor Diameter 53 ft. 8 in., length of fuselage 50 ft. 3/4 in., height 16 ft. 10 in.  22,500 lbs. max gross
Performance: Speed 222 mph, ceiling above 19,000 ft., max range 500 miles with auxiliary fuel tanks

**RC-135 Rivet Joint**—Affectionately known as "Super Snooper" the RC-135 is used to fly very close to enemy airspace for up to ten hours. Sensors aboard the aircraft allow it to record and analyze radar and other electronic signals. The aircraft has the capability to jam or interrupt an enemy's communications and secure data links. It is very common for this intelligence aircraft to be shadowed by enemy fighters while on a mission.

Manufacturer: Boeing Military Aircraft
Powerplant: Four CFM International F108-CF-100 turbofans; each rated at 22,225 lbs. of thrust
Accommodation: Crew of four with up to fourteen technicians
Dimensions: Wing span 130 ft. 10 in., length of fuselage 136 ft. 3 in., height 38 ft., 4 in.  322,500 lbs. max gross
Performance: Speed 610 mph, ceiling above 50,000 ft., range ferry mission 11,195 miles

**Antonov AN-72 (NATO "Coaler")**—A high-wing, twin-engine transport designed to operate from unprepared airfields or in ice and snow. This transport is primarily used for freight but can seat up to sixty-eight passengers or fifty-seven fully armed paratroops on folding seats along the fuselage and removable center seats.

Powerplant: Two ZMKB Progress D-36 turbofans, each rated at 14,410 lbs. of thrust
Accommodation: Crew of either three or four depending on mission
Dimensions: Wing span 104 ft. 7 in., length 92 ft. 1 in., height 28 ft. 4 3/4 in.  60,715 lbs. max gross
Performance: Speed 437 mph at 32,800 feet.

**Ilyushin Il-76 (NATO Candid-B)**—The Il-76 is the standard medium/long-range transport used by the former Soviet Union and its allies. Comparable to the USAF's C-141 Starlifter the Il-76 is designed with a rear-loading ramp/door and is capable of carrying 125 paratroops and their gear. The aircraft is designed for all-weather operations incorporating a computer for auto-landing approach and automatic flight control.

Powerplant: Four Aviadvigatel D-30P turbofans; each rated at 26,500 lbs. of thrust

Accommodation:   Seven including two freight handlers

Dimensions:   Wing span 165 ft. 8 in., length 152 ft. 10½ in., height 48 ft. 5 in.   374,785 lbs. max gross

Performance:   Can cruise at between 29,300–39,400 ft at 459–498 mph. Max range 4,195 miles.

**MiG-29 (NATO "Fulcrum")**—A twin-engine air-to-air fighter comparable in size to the Navy's F/A-18 Hornet. This fighter can track ten targets simultaneously with long-range look down/shoot-down radar out to sixty-two miles. Complementing this capability is a close-range laser rangefinder and infrared search/track sensor mounted forward of the windscreen. The MiG-29 was designed to carry a mix of short- and long-range IR and radar-tracking missiles, making it one of the most lethal aircraft in the sky.

Powerplant:   Two Klimov/Sarkisov RD-33 turbofans; each rated at 18,325 lbs. of thrust with afterburning

Accommodation:   Pilot only

Dimensions:   Wing span 37 ft. 3¼ in., length 56 ft. 9½ in., height 15 ft. 6¾ in.   43,450 lbs. max gross

Performance:   Max speed Mach 2.3. Mach 1.08 sea level. Ceiling 59,125 ft. Range on internal fuel is 945 miles

**Sukhoi Su-27 (NATO "Flanker")**—This fighter is considered by many Western experts to be on par or one step ahead of the F-15C in the air-to-air role. The Su-27's powerful radar can search for targets out to a range of 150 miles while tracking targets 115 miles away. Its four-channel fly-by-wire flight controls give the large jet the ability to turn with most other fighters in the sky. This fighter can carry a wide range of air-to-air and air-to-ground weapons including 130mm rockets.

Powerplant:   Two Saturn/Lyulka AL-31F turbofans; each rated at 27,562 lbs. of thrust with afterburning

Accommodation:   Pilot only

Dimensions:   Wing span 48 ft. 2½ in., length 71 ft. 11 in., height 19 ft. 5¾ in.   67,300 lbs. max gross

Performance:   Max speed Mach 2.35. Mach 1.12 at sea level. Ceiling 59,019 ft. Range on internal fuel is 927 miles

**Sukhoi Su-30**—This two-seat intercepter is designed for long-range high-priority missions. Built on the same airframe as the Su-27 the Su-30 can fly at low level to deliver high-precision guided weapons. Equipped with a Phazotron Zhuk-PH phased-array radar with the capability of tracking targets out to a range of 115 miles while detecting up to twenty-four targets. The Su-30 can carry up to 17,600

lbs. of weapons on twelve hard points for surface attack, including the advanced
KAB-500Kr TV-guided smart bomb.

| | |
|---|---|
| Powerplant: | Two Saturn/Lyulka AL-31F turbofans; each rated at 27,562 lbs. of thrust with afterburning |
| Accommodation: | Two: Pilot and weapons system operator |
| Dimensions: | Wing span 48 ft. 2½ in., length 71 ft. 11 in., height 20 ft. 10¾ in.   72,850 lbs. max gross |
| Performance: | Max speed Mach 2.02. Mach 1.03 at sea level. Ceiling 56,820 ft. Range on internal fuel is 1,865 miles |

# 1

Lt. Honh Sok Hyang slithered her slender body along the hard damp ground. The last eight hours had been spent crawling through a twisted maze of underground burrows in the dark. She had traveled a distance of 4.7 miles passing under one of the most guarded borders in the world, a dozen or so miles south of Pyongyang. Located in a heavily wooded region for optimum concealment, the tunneling had been rocky and unstable and it had taken years for her countrymen to complete the construction.

She was unaware of the loose dirt falling around her. Her mind stayed focused on the upcoming portion of her journey to the opening of the tunnel. Hyang had thoughts of the enemy waiting outside the opening, which was only a hundred yards south of the demilitarized zone or DMZ. The thoughts caused her well-conditioned body to stiffen and she stopped to rest a few seconds.

Several of the North Korean observation posts had sent word that South Korean acoustics experts had recently lined this particular section of the DMZ with underground sound detectors. This made her progress painstakingly slow to prevent creating an audible sound or vibration. Ironically, the detectors weren't put into place until six months after the completion of the underground passageways. The work had been finished uninterrupted but now it made the last fifty feet of Hyang's journey the most hazardous.

Pointing the underpowered flashlight ahead she saw the shaft was becoming much narrower. The lieutenant exhaled, seeing her white breath drift off, disappearing into the blackness. The temperature was dropping from cool to frigid. She closed her eyes trying to recall the mental strength it had taken for her to complete the seven months of *spetsnaz* special forces training. The silence brought back memories of her past.

Hyang's mother died before her fifth birthday and her father raised her the only way he knew how, with the discipline and structure of a military lifestyle. The daughter resembled her mother, having dark eyes and a slender face accentuated with high cheek bones, but the only character footsteps she had to follow were her father's. She joined the North Korean infantry at the age of sixteen, serving as a colonel's aide. Then at the age of twenty-two, she became an officer and three years later enrolled in the special forces as a second lieutenant, answering her country's call for a handful of

highly trained female specialists to be used in the infiltration of South
Korea. Hyang was the oldest member of her class and only one of three
females to graduate from the Special Operations Division frequently referred to as Unit 563. Now at the age of twenty-seven she was the senior
member of Unit 578, a squad of sixteen female commandos preparing for
highly sensitive missions.

The rigorous training had taken every shred of inner strength and will-
power she could muster to complete the program. The training, she knew,
had been modeled after the former Soviet Union's *spetsnaz* forces and
included command structures, selection process, day and night strike tactics,
infiltration and exfiltration, and of course psychological training. Out of
respect for their former Soviet instructors North Korean military officers
habitually referred to their own special forces as *spetsnaz,* a relic of the
Cold War.

Survival qualifications had been the most difficult during the intense cold
weather. Her team had patrolled the DMZ one night dressed in nothing
more than black cotton pants and a T-shirt, their faces and hands covered
with greasy camouflage paint. Several members of the team had frozen to
death and the commander's only reflection was that they would have survived the difficult conditions had they reacted properly to the situation.
Hyang would have quit then had she not realized the ordeal would be a
learning experience for future missions.

At least this time she was equipped with a forty-pound pack filled with
surveillance equipment, live ammunition, and enough food and water to stay
behind enemy lines for several days.

She moved again through the cramped hand-dug tunnel fully expecting to
see an American or South Korean patrol once she emerged. The lieutenant
promised herself that if this were the case, she would die like a warrior.


## HILL 17, SOUTH KOREA

CW3, Michael Q. Callahan Jr., thought it was a waste of his talents and
training to be lying on his belly nestled under a fallen dead pine tree just to
observe a North Korean tunnel. He had been doing this for a week—a long
cold week—and there hadn't been any activity.

Positioning himself fifty yards away from the tunnel's exit he had to make
sure his hide was well concealed to minimize his infrared heat signature. A
unique camouflaged Gortex-lined blanket, designed by Cabela's for use in
the high mountains of Colorado, covered Michael's 220-pound body. A
mound of rocks and dirt masked his head and rifle.

Before joining the army, the six-foot man's claim to fame had been basketball. Callahan had the distinction of being a two-time all-state guard for his high school in Sidney, Nebraska. He had plans for college ball, but two scholarships fell through because of his poor grades and hot temper. He joined the army thinking he could still get a free college education, while his parents secretly hoped he would at the very least learn a little self-control.

That had been fifteen years ago, the degree didn't matter to him anymore and his father would be proud of the self-control his son had now. The jumpy twelve-year-old boy noisily waiting for deer had evolved into a stealthy hunter.

American airborne infrared sensors had located the exit to the North Korean tunnel several months before on a routine sweep of the area. It wasn't a matter of if but when the North Koreans would launch a special operation. Michael hoped, even prayed, he would be on guard that night. Callahan had spent his nights during the week scanning the area with his night-vision scope, keeping himself awake by taking sips of strong coffee from a nearby thermos. He wouldn't eat, sleep or take a pee before sunup.

A sudden twinge in his gut made him wonder if tonight his prey would finally stir.

The yellow beam spread across the chilly mist, illuminating the jagged black walls of the crude tunnel. Hyang's flashlight cut through the darkness ahead. Every few feet dirty two-by-four wooden braces were imbedded, designed to keep the shaft from collapsing.

Hyang's orders were to penetrate the border before sunrise and make her way to the American surface-to-air missile battery located two miles south. Recent activity indicated the Americans had moved SAMs into the area. Hyang would set up an observation post on Hill 17 which overlooked the site. The North Korean Air Force would then perform their normal practice run at the border. If the Americans activated the site's radar as the Koreans hoped, Hyang would take pictures of the missiles, record any electronic emissions coming from the radar, and plot the site's exact location on a map.

The tunnel floor had become uneven, littered with broken tree roots and small rocks. Sliding from her knees to her stomach, Hyang checked the black tape covering the end of the two-port muzzle brake of her folding-stock AKS-74 assault rifle. She favored the squat lightweight AKS-74 to the standard AK-47 many of her companions carried. The assault rifle had been developed in the mid-1970s for Soviet airborne troops. The weapon fired a 5.45mm × 39.5 cartridge and had been fitted with a thirty-round plastic box magazine. The stock folded to the left at the pistol grip, making it easy to carry in the confines of a narrow tunnel. Her rifle, properly covered, would prevent any of the dirt from entering the barrel.

A large icy drop of water trickled from the tunnel's ceiling. It hit squarely on the back of Hyang's bare neck but she ignored it. In the distance the bottom rung of the ladder leading up to the opening had come into view. She squirmed determinedly the last few feet, thankful the hard rocks had given way to softer dirt.

Reaching out, Hyang grabbed the third rung of the ladder. She hesitated only a second listening for noises from above, then began pulling herself upward.

Several seconds later Lieutenant Hyang wrapped her dark gloved hand around the top rung of the ladder. Pulling herself up the last few feet her black wool watch cap, covering her head, hit the bottom of the wooden hatch.

She released a long breath, then felt around the plywood plank separating her from South Korean territory. The exterior of the inch-thick board had been covered with dirt, plants and small rocks for camouflage.

Hyang lowered her night-vision goggles (NVGs) over her eyes. She concentrated on her movements, blocking out any more thoughts of the enemy waiting outside the exit. Bracing her shoulder against the plank, Hyang used the muscles in her back, legs and arms to edge the board up slowly. Once a small crack appeared a few inches away from her face she stopped, listening and looking for movement.

The slight amount of moonlight streaming into the gap activated her NVGs. She pushed the cover, opening the trapdoor further. Peering out, the greenish glow of a nearby tree came into view. The texture of the bark appeared uneven and splotched. Hyang listened again for any noise and scanned the area for movement. She turned her head two full 180-degree arcs. There appeared to be nothing out of the ordinary, just shrubs and more pine trees.

Feeling the adrenaline surging through her, the lieutenant pushed the hatchlike door all the way open and scrambled up the last rungs. She was completely out of the tunnel and secured the hatch back into place. Staying low to the ground, Hyang scurried behind a nearby boulder sweeping the AKS-74 in a wide semicircle. Her heart beat wildly and she found it difficult to swallow.

"Bang . . . you're dead," CWO Michael Callahan mocked under his breath. He centered the greenish image of the North Korean soldier in the cross hairs of his starlight scope while brushing the trigger of his M16A2 assault rifle. The realization that he could have killed the person forced a smile. It was a power that helped the thirty-three-year-old Green Beret through the cold nights of surveillance.

Callahan liked what he did for a living. Sneaking around in the dark trying to catch bad guys was more fun than most people would ever have with their clothes on, in his opinion.

The chief warrant officer had cut his teeth during Desert Storm as a young weapons sergeant for Operational Detachment Alpha-57. His Green Beret team had been assigned to observe Highway 7 south of Baghdad near the Iraqi city of Nasiriyah. They were basically human trip wires. If the Iraqis had tried to reinforce their troops from the north, Callahan and the squad leader were to alert their commanders, allowing US air power to stop the ground assault.

Since the war Michael had honed his skills further. He was now a qualified free-fall parachutist, sniper, Ranger-trained commando and an expert in escape and evasion. He most recently cross-trained with Navy SEAL scuba teams on Coronado Island, California.

Through the scope he could see the Korean commando in a crouched position beside a tree, swinging his rifle right and left, then slowly turning 360 degrees. Michael could make out a backpack on the small frame of the soldier. The smooth outline of the head indicated it was covered with a cap of some kind and the bulky pair of NVGs shrouded the features of his face. Callahan swung the scope back toward the tunnel's exit waiting for another soldier to emerge, but none did.

*This guy plans to go solo,* Callahan thought, excited. *All right, one on one, and I've got home court advantage.*

Glimmering white stars filled the cloudless sky above and the tops of the trees didn't move in the icy night air. The surroundings were still and quiet.

Hyang rose up from her crouched position, remaining slightly hunched. She began to breathe more easily, absorbing every detail through her large NVGs. The ground was littered with patches of snow, fallen trees and boulders. She could see the broken contour of a distant hillside with glowing lights of a village to the south. Focusing on a nearby brush pile she decided it would be an acceptable hiding place if an enemy patrol happened to show up unexpectedly.

After briefly scanning the area once more, Hyang made her way back to the tunnel's exit. She was careful not to step in any patches of snow or spots of soft dirt that would leave footprints. She made mental notes of the hatch's location. At the base of a large boulder, the opening had been situated between several tall pine trees and was ringed with small leafless bushes. The lieutenant returned the loose rocks and dirt, being sure to cover the hatch completely.

Hyang checked her watch and had just enough time to reach Hill 17 to set up her observation post before the sun rose.

**2**

"You're going to need those, sir," Maj. Helen Erwin said, nodding towards a flack jacket, helmet and heavy winter parka. The stocky brunette had spread the items out in a neat row at the end of a gray metal briefing table.

"Are you expecting trouble?" Maj. Gen. Richard "Duke" James asked, half joking. He picked up the bulky jacket and looked at the army intelligence officer.

"I hope not, sir. The flack jacket is just a precaution. But you're definitely going to need the parka. We'll be in the air before sunup." The major put on her own flack jacket, adding: "Besides, it will help keep you warm. November winds can get nasty."

"I'm usually a hard target," James replied, slipping on the awkward bulletproof vest.

"I've heard that about you, sir." The army officer moved to the front of the room.

James adjusted the Velcro straps, securing the jacket properly before picking up the insulated parka. The thick coat had a wide fur-lined hood and seemingly weighed a ton. Draping it over his arm he shook his head and followed the major across the room. *With all this crap on I couldn't get out of the way of a slow-moving boulder.*

The briefing room, a poorly lit square chamber, was crowded with folding gray metal chairs and tables. Buried twenty feet under the ground, the room had been distanced away from the air base's main hangars and control tower. The moldy smell reminded Duke of his grandmother's basement.

James had spent the last three days with Major Erwin. She currently worked as a liaison officer between the air force and army, officially helping the two services integrate their needs to maximize mission performances. If both parties cooperated she could cut inner-service rivalries and misunderstandings and eliminate the routine squabbling that kept the two from communicating efficiently.

Erwin wore her hair cropped short, a pair of gold wire-framed glasses resting on her nose. Her physique resembled a high school athlete's, with her broad shoulders. She had a stern face with a clean complexion and deep dimples when she smiled—which, it seemed, was rare.

Duke made his way around the rows of chairs to the front of the room.

"As soon as you're ready I'll show you where we'll be flying today, sir."
Major Erwin tapped her pointer on the map waiting for him to be situated.

"Yes, ma'am," Duke grinned, still taking his time. *That helicopter isn't going anywhere till* I *get there,* he thought.

A three-dimensional wall map, patched together from high-resolution satellite photos, displayed the Korean peninsula in striking detail. James and Major Erwin stood next to each other examining it. Rivers, main highways and groups of buildings were easily recognized. Running through the center of the country was the DMZ, a thin strip of land containing very little natural growth.

"In thirty minutes we're scheduled to take off. Our destination is here." Erwin pointed to a section of rolling hills approximately forty-five miles northeast of Osan. The terrain looked steep and heavily forested.

"Where are the SA-5 missile sites?" Duke asked.

"Here, and here. We've located two of the Koreans' surface-to-air missile sites, both about four miles from the border. The sites contain eight launchers, each loaded with a single missile."

Duke let out a long sigh. "Why SA-5s?" he wondered out loud, knowing high altitude missiles would not be very effective in the mountainous terrain.

"That's what we'll figure out, of course," Erwin responded matter-of-factly. "The SA-5 is their best SAM system. In the past they've only deployed it directly around Pyongyang or other high-priority targets. In the last one hundred days or so we've detected a great deal of air traffic just across the border. A combination of choppers, MiGs and transport planes. We've protested but the North has naturally responded they're conducting training exercises."

"What's the CIA saying?" James asked.

"Not much." Erwin's dark eyebrows rose. Her eyes were green blue. "A month ago we responded with a Patriot battery to counter their SA-5s . . . it is placed here—" she gestured in the general direction with the pointer— "positioned a couple miles south of the DMZ."

"How convenient," Duke said. "Air training exercises within two minutes of the border complete with SA-5s, MiGs and attack helicopters. All they'd have to do is turn left and their air force would be halfway to Seoul before we'd know it."

"That's how we see it. Believe me, the North squealed like stuffed pigs when that Patriot site went up. But it's intel's opinion that one battery isn't enough. There are only sixteen missiles up there. We need the president's permission to triple that if the North is really going to take us seriously."

"I agree." Duke took a last look at the map, soaking in the details.

Six months ago Duke James had accepted the position of deputy national security advisor to the president of the United States. After sitting on his butt for a couple months playing Beltway politics and learning Washington ego stroking, James decided the job wasn't for him. He tried to resign, but his boss, National Security Advisor Bill Bishop, wouldn't let him.

Bishop had laughed his resignation off, saying if he wanted someone to sit around and push paper he would have hired an ex-congressman. If Duke wanted to get out of his office and into the field then he should do it. That was exactly what Bishop needed, a man respected in the military to tour bases and report back to him on the level. Duke was the right man for the job.

Besides, Bishop had reminded Duke, for Duke to get his third star the politicians and top brass at the Pentagon had to be polished like an apple. Colin Powell hadn't always enjoyed the spit and rub game either but he made it to the chairman of the Joint Chiefs of Staff. Like it or not, no good man can deny the urge from within to compete and reach the top.

Duke's first tours were to Europe and Russia, and now South Korea.

The president and other members of the National Security Council were anxiously requesting suggestions from James on how to defuse the situation. On the other hand the secretary of defense and the chairman of the Joint Chiefs had instructed James to recommend ways to send a clear message to the North Koreans that the US wasn't about to sit back and let them intimidate the South Koreans and Japanese. James knew the Japanese, in particular, were very sensitive about any military moves the North Koreans made. Japanese armed forces were structured for only regional operations and still relied on the US for strategic defense. With the powerful People's Republic of China's million-man army ready to back the North, the last thing Japan wanted was to be caught in the middle of a shooting war. James reasoned that the best way to prevent this was to let the North Koreans know, and immediately, that the US would continue to respond to the slightest provocation.

Duke had even given this assignment a code name: *Operation Eradicate.* He had borrowed the name from a classified air force mission during the Gulf War when a flight of eight F-15Es attacked a battery of SA-5 missiles north of Baghdad—the only difference now being that if the missiles were to be destroyed it would have to be by diplomacy.

Erwin checked her watch and interrupted the general's silence. "The chopper should be waiting, sir."

Duke slipped on his parka and zipped it up. "I could fall out and bounce back up with this much padding." Smacking the front of the coat, James attempted to get even a small chuckle from Erwin.

She didn't bother with a response.

Strolling out into the black night a blast of frosty wind stung their faces.

Duke quickened his pace, pulling his head down closer to the parka's fur-lined hood. Suddenly the heavy coat and vest didn't seem as cumbersome. He knew the major had been correct about needing the extra warmth as he stuffed his hands deeper into his pockets.

James was glad his trip to the SAM site would be the last to the DMZ. After meetings with the top brass from the army, air force and navy and the other jaunts to the zone his body was ready for Katie's warm arms and home-cooked meals. He felt comfortable with what he had accomplished in three days and had enough information to give Bishop and the president an objective account of the situation.

Sitting on the edge of the flight line, engines running, a special forces MH-60G Pave Hawk helicopter prepared for their departure.


HILL 17, SOUTH KOREA

Without taking his eyes from the scope; CWO Michael Callahan curled into a tight ball, pulling his knees up to his chest. Using his left hand he reached down and untied each of his boots before slipping them off. He then slithered out from underneath the protective warmth of his blanket and picked up the North Korean in his scope in less than four seconds.

The Green Beret had rehearsed every detail a thousand times in his head. He had prepared his equipment, ensuring it wouldn't budge or even rattle to betray his position during movement. The swivels on his rifle were bound with black electrician's tape and every gadget and bullet on his belt had been glued or fastened securely to be stationary. The two extra 5.56mm thirty-round magazines he carried were covered with soft black leather and the other metal items on his uniform had been coated with liquid latex. The bottom skin of his feet had become rock-hard from walking on any imaginable type of ground barefooted. Needing to camouflage his white feet, he chose to wear Gortex-lined black wool socks with leather bottoms keeping his feet dry in water or snow. The remaining skin on his body, including the insides of his ears, lips and eyelids, was covered with green and black greasepaint. Cut pine branches were taped to his helmet, belt and the tops of his arms.

Crouching down, he waited for the North Korean to make his move. Callahan would follow the intruder for a while to find out if he was planning to meet up with another *spetsnaz* officer or possibly even a small team. If not, his intentions would need to be determined, including the very remote chance this man could be trying to defect.

Callahan watched the commando hold his weapon out in front, hesitating before starting down the hill toward the gully. He rose up slowly and began to stalk his unsuspecting prey.

## MH-60G Pave Hawk

The rhythmic sound of the chopper's blades cutting through the sky and the surprisingly warm, somewhat comfortable interior was soothing enough that James could have taken a nap. The air remained calm for a change and the sky was free of the silvery clouds which normally hung low over the snow-covered landscape.

The general looked out the right side of the aircraft and watched the orange glow of the rising sun. The orange and yellow array of colors trimmed the gray canvas sky that was brightening into a deep blue. *The land of morning calm,* he thought to himself.

He wondered what his wife, Katie, and their kids were doing at home. Checking his watch, kept on East Coast time, he realized they were probably all in the car coming home from school. Katie had already put up their Christmas tree and they'd be running in to see if any new packages had been placed under it. He hoped she remembered to turn off the tree lights before going to bed each night. A smile crossed his lips as he thought of how it bothered her when Duke constantly questioned her about tedious routine duties on the phone. "I've managed to get by many years without you around, general . . . I'm not one of your grunts that needs to be told what to do," she would chide him.

Major Erwin sat next to James. The five other seats were occupied by members of the Second Infantry Division, or 2 ID, as they preferred to be called. They were the usual tough-looking bunch, their faces expressionless and pensive. Duke took notice of the low-visibility Indian head patches on their uniforms. Each was dressed in full combat gear carrying M16s with extra magazines of ammo clipped to their belts. He wondered how many times the young men had made this trip. It was obvious they took it very seriously.

Major Erwin poured coffee in two metal cups, handing one to James.

"You'd better drink that fast, General," the senior sergeant interjected. "The North Koreans generally like to start screwing around with us about now."

Erwin cut her eyes at the man for calling her judgment into question. Then she turned to James and pointed out the window. "There it is, sir."

Duke took a quick gulp before glancing at the ground. Two thousand feet below he could see the pale outline of the DMZ. It looked as if someone had plowed a strip of land through the center of the country. Every few hundred yards there were bright spotlights and guard towers. He could see foot patrols with dogs on both sides of the barbed wire. The rest of the countryside was covered with dark green pine trees with long sloping hills intermingling with steep rocky ridges. The valleys between were areas of open land used for farming. It reminded James of the Black Hills of South Dakota.

Duke's family's summer cabin was located in Spearfish Canyon. In the month of June he planned to take a couple of weeks off for fly fishing and relaxation. Katie insisted they not put a phone, fax machine or television in the cabin. It made it rough on her without modern conveniences, including a dishwasher or washer and dryer, but she knew it was the perfect place for Duke to get away and recharge his batteries.

James spotted a road lined with army trucks and hummers making their way south. He breathed a short sigh, thinking he'd better put his mind back to business.

Turning to Major Erwin he focused on the square laminated topography map resting on her lap. She had snapped on a miniature flashlight and inspected the area before looking back out the window.

"I'd say we're about ten minutes out." Erwin held the map up for Duke to see. "That puts us right about—"

Duke's body suddenly slammed into the bulkhead as the chopper banked left, heading for the ground in a steep dive. A loud shrill filled the air. The engine wailed as the pilot began jinking the chopper right to left.

Nosing over, the heavy helicopter picked up airspeed. At the same time Duke's arms flew up with a jerk and the rest of his coffee landed in Major Erwin's lap.

"Damn." The major brushed at the hot liquid stains soaking into her neatly creased pants. She slipped on a headset and keyed the mike to the flight deck. "What the hell's going on?"

Duke looked at the grunts seated around him. The senior sergeant and the rest of his squad weren't trying very hard to hold back their amusement. *The major's rigid attitude must get under everyone's skin,* he thought.

"They're looking at us, sir," Erwin explained to James, taking off the headset.

"Say again," James shouted over the sound of the engine.

"The North, sir. They're tracking us on radar. The pilot decided to take evasive action. Nothing to worry about, though. We'll be on the ground in eight minutes."

James nodded and glanced toward the senior sergeant again. The man waited a second for Erwin to look away. He held up three fingers: "Three minutes," he mouthed silently.

Duke raised his eyebrows, then tightened his lap belt, just as the Pave Hawk banked sharply to the right, decreasing its altitude one more time.

"Damn it!" Erwin muttered again, sliding in her seat and reaching for a bar above to stabilize herself.

*I think I'm going to listen to the grunts more often,* he thought, smiling in acknowledgment to the sergeant.


## HILL 17, SOUTH KOREA

The route Lt. Honh Sok Hyang took from the tunnel had turned out to be quite easy. Her mission planners had done their jobs well. Once reaching the bottom of the hill she followed a rocky ridge south to the edge of a burned-out area. The blackened trees stood like weary guards in the night, not caring about her presence.

Hyang stopped, rechecking the surrounding area for anyone tailing behind. Feeling reassured, she skirted the burnt ground to climb over a series of small rock outcroppings. Scaling a steep bank to the top of Hill 17, she came to rest on an abrupt point with only a few scattered pine trees growing on the southern rim. With the cover of night still in her favor she scouted the top area, looking for the best place to hide her observation post.

Two large rocks supporting a large fallen tree, its branches spread out, was the site she chose. The surrounding mixture of dried brown leaves, dead pine needles, green plants and charcoal-colored rocks blended well with her camouflage. She added debris to cover most of her body and the natural foliage also helped keep her warm.

Being sheltered from the open, her extremities beginning to warm from the winter weather, Hyang relaxed and her heart rate slowed. She placed her AKS-74 rifle next to her side, unfolding the stock and leaving the safety off. The compact backpack lay open only a foot away. Holding a pair of green rubber-coated binoculars to her eyes, she began to sweep the area.

The lieutenant could make out quite a few details with the glowing sunrise. Five hundred yards away, slightly below her, Hyang could see the American missile battery. It appeared about to be the size of three or four tennis courts. The trees that had been removed were piled in stacks on one end of the clearing next to a single-lane dirt road.

The command van appeared to be nothing out of the ordinary. It was the size of a school bus and the outside had been painted in standard NATO camouflage with streaks of black and beige running through several shades of green. Hyang noticed ten radio antennas scattered on the roof and could see steam curling out from the front vent. The steam told her the inside was being warmed and the van was occupied.

Spread out in front of the command van four launch vehicles were parked. They resembled giant insectlike robots with four pointed legs and awkward, box-shaped bodies. Each launcher contained four dark green rectangular canisters pointing north. She knew the canisters held high-speed missiles designed to intercept and knock down aircraft or ballistic missiles.

In the center of the clearing was a flat-paneled phased-array radar fixed to the front side of a square trailer filled with electronics. It didn't appear to be operating but Hyang couldn't be certain. Off to the right of that were three gas-powered generators and one large fuel tank. A trace of smoke corkscrewed up from the farthest generator and she could barely hear the soft hum of the motor echoing up the ridge. *The American missile site wouldn't be complete without those,* the lieutenant thought, spotting three hummers and a large canvas-draped trailer in the rear of the clearing. The Patriot site appeared to be well stocked and fully operational.

Sweeping the binoculars left, Hyang suddenly stopped. Eight soldiers, she couldn't tell if they were American or South Korean, were grouped together near the command van. One of them was smoking a cigarette and they seemed to be taking a break. They were, however, carrying black automatic weapons, probably M16s, and dressed in full combat gear.

Lieutenant Hyang removed the Japanese-made Nikon F2 35mm camera from her backpack. A flash of light caught her attention and she looked up just as the low-pitched thumping of an approaching helicopter swept over the area. Twisting her head right, the image of an American chopper appeared over the missile site. Hyang raised her camera and clicked off several frames.

## COMMAND POST KANSAS, SOUTH KOREA

"We're coming in from the south, sir," Major Erwin hollered. "We'll be setting down next to the command van."

James nodded, not taking his eyes off the rugged terrain. The rising sun cast long shadows across the broken hills making the pine trees appear taller than they were.

"The men call this place Kansas."

"Kansas?" James asked in disbelief, picturing the wide-open corn and wheat fields of the Midwest.

"When the shit's hitting the fan there's no place like home . . . Kansas."

Duke laughed, shaking his head. There had been many times in the last week he wished he were home.

Duke could feel the chopper bank to the northeast. A half-mile away he caught a glimpse of the Patriot missile site nestled among the trees. The equipment sat atop a barren mound, but was bordered by two higher and steeper ridges. There was one road leading into and out of the area and nothing else was around for miles.

"We're two miles south of the DMZ. You can see why it's critical we get more missiles up here. If all hell breaks loose we wouldn't be able to react fast enough," Erwin said. "The North could overwhelm this place in a couple of minutes if they wanted."

"How many crews do we have assigned now?"

"Four. The crew and the guards rotate into and out of the area every twenty-four hours. We haven't built any permanent structures, hoping the North will withdraw their SA-5s and it won't be necessary. But I can tell you it's starting to look like a pipe dream."

The chopper circled the Patriot site once before coming level and starting its descent. With an abrupt double thud the left and right skid bars hit the frozen dirt.

## HILL 17, SOUTH KOREA

"There you are," Michael Callahan whispered under his breath, locating the North Korean again. It was now light enough that he didn't need to use the night-vision scope on his rifle.

Through a standard pair of military binoculars he stared at the camouflaged figure 130 yards above him. The intruder appeared to be lying on his abdomen on the ridge facing south toward the Patriot command post. Only the topmost portion of the black skullcap was visible. Michael was impressed with the soldier's skill in covering the rest of his body with the natural surroundings. Nothing appeared out of place. Anyone else would most likely walk right past the North Korean, never spotting him.

The chief warrant officer sucked in a long breath and exhaled slowly. His initial exhilaration was wearing off and he wanted to keep his head clear. Kneeling down at the base of the hill behind a dense clump of brush, Callahan rubbed the stubble of his day-old beard. So far he had done everything by the book, staying a minimum of a hundred yards behind the North Korean, stopping whenever he stopped and, most importantly, not creating a single noise.

Callahan breathed deeply again to stay alert. The game was still in his favor, but now that the Korean was settled in the gap was closing.

James stepped out of the MH-60G Pave Hawk as the chopper's rotors slowed to a stop. A sharp-looking army officer strode toward him across the frost-covered ground. "Good morning, General, I'm Captain Westport. Welcome to CP Kansas." The officer saluted in Major Erwin's direction, acknowledging her presence also. His cheeks were beet red from the cold and his skin had started to look chapped. They all shook hands briefly, then the captain pulled on gloves to cover his hands.

"Let's begin, Captain Westport," Major Erwin prodded, "we have a schedule to keep."

"Yes, ma'am. This way, please." Westport turned toward the command van located in the center of the compound.

Duke surveyed the area, trying to get a feel for the exact layout. The perimeter had been surrounded with rows of barbed wire and armed guards patrolled just inside the interior edge.

"How long have you been operational?" James asked.

"Fifty-eight straight days," Captain Westport replied. "In that time we've tracked at least a dozen different types of North Korean aircraft approaching the border."

"Anything unexpected?" Duke asked pensively.

"Not really, sir. Primarily fighter patrols . . . a mix of MiG-21s with an occasional MiG-29. We've also tracked a few helicopters. They know we're here and they know we're looking at them."

They climbed up the stairs and Captain Westport opened the command van's door. Duke entered first with Major Erwin behind him. She spoke while checking the time on her watch. "I've asked Captain Westport and his men to prepare a short demonstration on this system's capabilities. It should only take fifteen minutes but you'll come away with a much better understanding of what we're up against."

Duke moved to the center of the van. The compartment's low ceiling caused him to hunch slightly. The inside was dark and the walls had been painted a dull medium gray. A greenish glow of computer screens and various multifunction displays of the communications equipment lit the van's interior. The place was cramped, forcing the three new additions to stand shoulder to shoulder. James didn't mind the crowding and, feeling warmed, pulled the parka's hood down to scratch his head.

A couple of army sergeants affectionately referred to as scope dopes, were seated behind two round four-color displays. Duke folded his arms to keep them out of the way and waited for Captain Westport to begin the demonstration.

"What you're about to see is a simulated air attack on this missile site," Westport stated. He touched a sergeant on the shoulder. "Okay, let's get started."

## Hill 17, South Korea

"Don't move," was whispered in perfect Korean.

Lieutenant Hyang's body froze while her insides rolled over. Her eyes instinctively shifted to the AKS-74 lying within reach. The safety was off, but she'd have to let the binoculars drop first.

"I said . . . don't move," the voice repeated as if reading her mind.

Hyang heard the faint click of metal. Whoever it was had waited to snap the safety off their weapon—a professional, not some gung-ho soldier making a lucky catch.

"Put your hands on top of your head one at a time and slowly turn around."

A ball of fire moved up from the lieutenant's stomach to her throat. She swallowed hard, her mind racing. She had done everything right and yet managed to shame her country and family. She lowered the binoculars before placing her gloved hands on top of her head. She then obeyed, twisting around to the sight of a burly American special forces soldier. The man's face hid behind smeared black and green camouflage paint. He was pointing a 9mm pistol at her head.

"Keep your hands on your head and stand up." The man's voice sounded flat, emotionless.

Hyang paused, staring into eyes that were stone cold. They seemed to look right through her. Both his hands were wrapped around the pistol as he crouched down perfectly balanced. As he stood she saw his massive shoulders and thick neck were connected to a large muscular frame. Through the skin-tight clothing his muscles seemed ready to explode. Hyang guessed he easily outweighed her by a hundred pounds.

"I surrender," Hyang spoke softly. "I will come in peace."

"Stand over next to that tree," Callahan ordered. "Put your face in the bark and keep your hands on top of your head."

The lieutenant did as she was told, pressing her nose squarely into the coarse bark of the tree.

"Now spread 'em," Callahan said, kicking at the Korean's legs, keeping his Beretta 9mm pointed at the prisoner's head. "Do you understand me?"

"I understand."

Using his left hand, Michael began to frisk the soldier. First he ran his hand around and up down the legs, working his way up. He felt a lump on the soldier's upper chest and thought he had discovered a hidden weapon until he realized there were two lumps perfectly spaced. Repeating the movement, his hand moved, checking to be certain that they were indeed a woman's breasts.

He cocked his head to the right, realizing the man he had been stalking was a woman. "So your country is sending girls to do a man's work. I guess you can't get the job done either."

Callahan continued his search, barely fazed by the unexpected development. He pulled a six-inch knife from a sheath taped to her belly.

"Isn't this a little big for a kitchen knife?"

The North Korean didn't answer.

"I'll keep it for you until dinner time," Michael needled. He stepped over to the spot where the Korean woman had been lying and picked up her AKS-74, backpack and camera. Peering below he could see the missile site within good distance. She had selected the ideal spot to view the surrounding area. He couldn't have picked a better location himself. He turned back to her. "So you're on a reconnaissance mission, is that it?"

"What are you going to do with me?" Hyang twisted around to face the man.

"We're going to take a hike and go visit friends," Callahan said, his anger rising. "Where did you think we'd go if you got caught . . . dancing?"

Hyang pressed her face back into the tree bark. The image of several South Korean security officers interrogating her filled her mind. She had been told they would strip her naked and use her young body for their enjoyment.

Michael pulled a nylon cord from a leather pouch on his belt. With the North Korean's hands behind her back, he tied them securely together.

"Now, I want you to walk out in front of me going down that hill and into the gully. Don't forget I'm right behind you and if you flinch the wrong way, I'll kill you." The warrant officer paused, wanting his statement to sink in. "Let's get going."

Lieutenant Hyang stepped away from the tree, stopping to look down over the edge.

"I said get going." Michael kept his voice gruff and he jabbed the woman in the back with his pistol.

They began their descent, moving uneasily on the rocky terrain. Callahan began thinking how the guys were going to give him a real ribbing for capturing a woman.

The duo had walked for a few minutes when his prisoner stumbled to the ground. Callahan sighed, rolling his eyes, when suddenly the Korean tucked her body into a tight ball and began rolling down the hill.

Michael watched stunned, losing precious seconds. His big frame then reacted by lumbering down the hill after the woman. Callahan watched the lightweight Korean soldier's body bouncing off rocks and shrubbery as she tumbled away from him. He knew her skin was being ripped to shreds and she might even be breaking bones.

"Damn it!" he shouted for having underestimated the woman's resolve. It was a stupid mistake.

Lieutenant Hyang's body plowed into the trunk of a tree, stopping her escape. Ignoring her injuries, she slid her thin frame backwards through her bound hands. Hands in front, she began to use her teeth attempting to work the rope loose. With her heart pounding in her chest she dared not stop to check the American's position.

In answer to her thought the American's heavy breathing became audible just as she freed her hands. He was only a few feet behind her and closing fast. Not wasting a second she grabbed a fallen tree branch by her side. She turned, swinging it as hard as she could.

Callahan stumbled forward, still shocked by the woman's audacity. He was out of breath, having run down the steep slope.

"Don't move . . ." Callahan muttered, regaining his balance.

In a blinding flash Hyang swung the branch toward the American, shoving it toward his eyes. The warrant officer's free hand flew up to block it. Lunging at the American, she placed her open mouth squarely on his large wrist, biting with all her strength. Her head writhed as her sharp teeth ripped the flesh open. The American toppled backward, falling to the ground.

Callahan let out a loud gasp, struggling to hold onto his pistol. He breathed in deeply, feeling a rush of anger as he pushed the woman away. Jumping to his feet, his face pulsing red, Michael swung wildly at the North Korean.

Hyang's agile body ducked low, the American's giant fist barely missing her head. Stepping back, she placed a swift roundhouse kick inside of the man's leg above the left kneecap.

Callahan cursed, the nerves in his leg protesting.

Hyang scurried to the back of the American. As he turned to face her she gritted her teeth, then breathed out in a yell. Her loud *ki-hap* echoed up the hill as both of her feet landed in the center of the man's chest. The large proud American hit the ground with a hard thud.

# 3

"This is why we need more missiles spread over a greater area." Captain Westport was pointing to the center of the radar screen where several dozen flashing red triangles, hostile aircraft symbols, were making their way successfully south. "When they fly low-level, say below five hundred feet, it is impossible to know each aircraft's exact location. The mountains north of us are steep enough that we lose them from time to time in the clutter. They could literally travel without popping up until they're right on top of us."

Duke moved in closer, watching the computer-generated simulation unfold on the primary screen. Both sergeants tapped their computer keyboards, calling up the targets' speed, altitude, range and heading. A smaller square multifunction display illuminated a three-dimensional image of the mountains north of their position. Bright yellow lines cut across like a miniature topography map depicting the countless valleys, canyons and mountain tops. *Captain Westport is right,* Duke thought, *a dozen aircraft could easily duck below radar coverage before breaking into the open and head south.*

"What's your estimated warning time?" James asked, his mind piecing the information together.

"One . . . maybe two minutes. Of course, that's without the aid of an AWACS. If an E-3C is in the area you could double that."

Duke nodded. "That still isn't very much time."

"Our latest threat scenarios show a ninety percent probability that we will fire all sixteen of our missiles in the first three minutes of conflict," Westport continued. "And you know that over half the targets we take out will more than likely be decoys. Old MiG-21s past their service life that the North have converted to drones."

"What about the SA-5s?" Duke asked. "It's my understanding your primary mission is to counter that system."

"To be candid, sir, that's bullshit. Whoever believes we're going to sit here and let the North send aircraft after aircraft across the border and not make that a primary concern has never been in battle." Westport glanced over his shoulder at Duke. "You give me two dozen more missiles and the North will think twice about sending aircraft this way. Then we can worry about countering the SA-5s if they're launched."

The main radar screen blinked twice and the words END SIMULATION flashed across the top.

"Sir, the simulation's been cancelled. Automatic override sequence," one of the technicians said, his voice officially calm.

"Well what the hell is going on, Sergeant?" Westport's eyes lit up.

"Sir . . . four targets approaching from the north. Speed 520 knots, range 15 miles, altitude 5,300 feet and descending." The sergeant's head maintained a trained eye on his screen. "Bearing one seven niner. They're headed right for us."

## HILL 17, SOUTH KOREA

A swell of panic overwhelmed the anger in CWO Michael Callahan. Lying flat on his back he saw the pale blue sky overhead and was unable to inhale. For the first time in his life the breath had been knocked out of him.

Rolling over he tried to scramble to his feet but the pain in his knee prevented it. He crumpled to the ground, blinking hard trying to clear the sweat and dirt from his eyes. The 9mm was still in his grasp, but he couldn't locate the North Korean. Fighting back a wave of nausea he attempted to focus and get his bearings straight.

His blurry vision clearing, Michael propped up on his elbows catching sight of a shadow to the right of him. Firing only one bullet in that direction he automatically scanned the area to his left. Lying on the ground five feet away he could see the woman's AKS-74 was partly shrouded in snow and dirt.

*No fucking way,* Callahan breathed, realizing she was scurrying to reach it. Digging his elbows into the ground, he brought his good leg up underneath himself. With one loud grunt he sprang toward the weapon.

He grabbed the butt stock of the rifle just as the North Korean grabbed the barrel. Their eyes locked together.

## COMMAND POST KANSAS, SOUTH KOREA

Duke watched two of the targets disappear off the radar scope as they descended through 1,000 feet. They then ducked behind one of the interior mountain ranges just as Westport had predicted during the simulation. The other two aircraft were climbing through 6,000 feet, speed constant at 420 knots, heading 174 degrees.

"What do you make of this, Captain?" James asked, seeing the concern on the man's face.

"From their speed and radar cross sections I'd say they're fighters, probably Fulcrums . . . MiG-29s." Captain Westport pondered a moment, then went on: "They're flying fairly close together. It could be a training flight but they're too far out to know for sure."

"Range . . . seven miles and closing," one of the sergeants chattered.

"Okay, that's close enough. Light 'em up," Westport ordered. "Lock onto both of those lead fighters."

Duke leaned back, looking at Major Erwin to do the same so they wouldn't be in the way. The main control panel blinked a succession of red, green and yellow lights intersecting as the computer-generated lines plotted the course of each aircraft. The senior radar operator tapped the commands on the keyboard of his computer swiftly.

"Radar lock on the lead fighter, sir."

"I've got the other one."

"If you want to play chicken we're ready." Westport's tone remained flat and calm. "Assign a targeting number."

James watched the captain's jaw, then looked back at the radar screen. The lead target was now five miles out, less than a minute away.

## HILL 17, SOUTH KOREA

A mixture of fear and determination filled the North Korean's face. Her dark eyes remained locked onto Callahan's as if probing for a sign of weakness. She was not going to yield possession of the weapon.

The American bared his teeth before yanking on the assault rifle. He felt the wet barrel slip out of the smaller *spetsnaz* officer's hands. Before the North Korean could react Callahan raised the rifle and smashed it over the woman's head. His one heavy strike was all that was needed to knock her out cold.

A stream of dark red blood appeared on the commando's face, running down the side of it. The rifle had torn through her cap, creating a jagged split on her scalp.

*I oughta* . . . Callahan seethed, placing his finger over the trigger of his 9mm. He stopped short, kicking at the dirt and snow in front of him. The woman lay unconscious and he guessed her to be not more than twenty-eight years old. She had been trained . . . hell, she had been well trained. Michael bound her wrists and ankles, connecting them with a rope down the middle.

He then hobbled around on his leg, gathering the rest of his belongings. Keeping his eyes on his opponent, Callahan keyed the mike to his PRC 112 short-range survival radio.

"Goose, this is Mallard. You copy?"

*"This is Goose, go ahead, Mallard. That your gunshot?"*

"Yeah, I have a live one . . . she squirmed out of tunnel nineteen."

*"Did you say . . . she, Mallard?"*

"Affirmative . . . you heard me right. I said she."

*"Ah yeah . . . roger that . . . an easy catch for the Mallard. What's your ETA?"*

"Five minutes."

*"Roger. See you in five."*

After Callahan took a couple of deep breaths he stood tall, putting his weight on the right side of his body. His knee was burning with pain and his head had begun to pound. A large lump was forming next to his left ear. He must have hit a rock when he fell. *Easy catch my ass,* Callahan thought. *You tangle with her next time, buddy.*

"Okay . . . wake up," he grunted, kicking dirty wet snow in the North Korean's face. The 9mm was pointed directly between her eyes. "Let's see you try that again."

"Two miles and closing," called the radar operator.

"Speed?" Westport asked before the man completed his sentence.

"Four hundred thirty knots. They'll cross the border in twelve seconds."

"If they're going to turn they had better do it soon," Major Erwin said.

The two fighters that had disappeared from the scope earlier reappeared. "Two new targets bearing three three four, range . . . four miles."

"Lock them up," Westport ordered, his eyes never leaving the screen.

Duke stood attentively, watching and listening to the ordeal without interfering. The Patriot system had the range, speed and maneuverability to engage and destroy ballistic missiles as well as aircraft over a variety of altitudes. It could easily reach across the border and take out any threat in a fifty-square-mile area. However, rules of engagement stated they couldn't fire until the target had crossed the border. The missile crew would have to wait until the last second to make the right call.

"They just blinked," Captain Westport said.

Duke watched as the two lead targets began their turn north. Within seconds the other two targets followed the lead, making their way back to the northwest.

Westport released a long breath. "Standard procedure. They close to a mile or so from the border then turn back home. They're definitely not afraid to challenge us. We just track them all the way in, then occasionally lock on if they get close enough."

"One of these days they may not stop," Major Erwin added.

"Stand down, men," Westport ordered. "Make a copy of the computer disks. I'm sure the boys in intel will want to take a look at them."

"Excuse me, sir," a baby-faced private said, opening the door to the command van. "Callahan's captured a North Korean commando, sir. He's bringing her in now."

Duke raised an eyebrow, looking back at Westport.

Westport waved the private closer to him. "Get on the radio. I want a chopper in here to transfer that prisoner ASAP." He paused momentarily. "And have someone secure a video camera. Instruct Callahan to take her to the sleeping quarters."

"Yes Sir!"

"Yessir."

"Under the circumstances, General, I hope you don't mind if we end the tour now," Captain Westport said. He expected his two visitors to go on their way.

"Not at all, Captain. Mind if we tag along, though?" Duke asked, knowing the man couldn't say no.

"Ah . . . no, sir," Westport answered.

"It might be a good idea to have me present," Major Erwin suggested. "This involves a woman prisoner. And I am an intel officer."

Westport nodded in agreement.

"Don't worry. We'll stay out of your way," Duke reassured him, holding the door open.

Several soldiers were already gathered around the metal square-shaped camouflaged van used for sleeping quarters. They were whispering among themselves and several were smoking.

"You men position yourselves around this van. I don't want anyone entering unless I say so." Westport didn't stop to look up, taking the black metal steps two at a time. James and Erwin followed.

Inside, the North Korean soldier was seated in the middle of the van. A couple of men had cleared the area, taking everything out of the prisoner's reach. Another man was setting up a video camera on a tripod, pointing it directly at the woman. A red light flashed on.

Duke stood back observing the scene. Dressed in dirty black clothes, the prisoner slumped a little to one side. Blood was beginning to dry on one side of her face.

"Report, Callahan," Captain Westport barked once everything was in place.

The warrant officer had not relinquished his duty to anyone yet and still held his 9mm on the woman. He gave Westport a fairly precise account of what had taken place.

"She's *spetsnaz,*" Callahan concluded. "North Korean special forces."

"Ask her her name," Westport ordered.

Michael looked at the woman and spoke Korean slowly. "What's your name?"

Hyang didn't answer or look up.

"The captain wants to know your name, prisoner."

"Lieutenant Hyang," she answered, ashamed.

"Lieutenant Hyang . . ." Westport repeated thoughtfully. "We've got ourselves an officer."

"I relieved her of this." Callahan produced the knife, remembering how he had made fun of it. Lucky for him when she went after him all she had was a branch or he'd be minus an eyeball—or worse.

"Intel will have to handle the rest," Westport said. "Go ahead and untie those ropes, then take her to the mess hut. Let her clean up before the chopper gets here."

One of the other soldiers came to help Callahan as he limped toward the prisoner to do as he was told.

"Do you need a doctor?" Westport asked.

"It's only my knee, sir."

Lieutenant Hyang sat motionless as the man released her hands and ankles. She knew enough English to understand they had spoken something about a helicopter taking her off the base. Without turning her head she counted the people around her. Six, maybe seven, she estimated, not wanting to arouse suspicion. At least one of them was an officer.

"All right, Lieutenant, follow me." One of the soldiers who had helped untie her spoke in broken Korean. She stood up, and the entire group exited the barracks following behind her.

When they were in the center of the field Hyang lowered her head, putting her hands to her face, pleading: "I do not wish to die!"

Callahan, the last to leave the van, froze at the bottom of the stairs, hearing her false statement. He looked up in time to see Hyang reaching into her left breast pocket while pretending to sob. Before he could speak she pulled on a minuscule round rubber ring.

The ring was attached to a thin nylon cord leading to a tiny battery-charged detonator hidden in the insulation near the back of her jacket. Two strips of metal came together when she tugged on the ring, completing an electrical current. Several sparks flew and heat began to build.

"All praise the Great Leader," Hyang shouted, raising her arms in the air.

"Back away!" Callahan hollered while motioning to everyone around the woman. *"Back away!"*

Within seconds enough heat had been generated to enflame a lead azide booster charge, causing it to detonate. This small explosion immediately ignited a half-inch of C4 plastic explosives sandwiched between the nylon lining of Hyang's black jacket.

Everyone scrambled, taking cover where they could, when a flash of fire, smoke and body parts suddenly blew into the air. James was close enough for the blast to knock him to the ground. He hit butt first, skidding back and bouncing a couple of times before stopping.

The air instantly filled with screaming cries of wounded men and the smell of burning flesh. Getting to his feet, James saw two blotches of fire burning on the outside of his parka. Several other pieces of hot plastic had scorched holes in his pants. The smell of acid filled the air, scalding his nose. He picked up a handful of dirt and used it to kill the flames.

*"Someone help me!"* Major Erwin cried out.

Duke snapped his head around. Through the smoke he spotted Erwin with several blotches of fire burning on the left side of her uniform. He ran straight into her, knocking the woman to the ground.

"Roll, Major. Roll!" Duke shouted, grabbing the intel officer by the legs. He used the force of his own hands to twist her along the ground, trying to smother the flames.

The woman, dazed with fear and shock, wouldn't roll. Duke picked up several handfuls of dirt and snow and threw them onto Erwin's body to extinguish the flames. Her hair was singed and the heavy parka had burned but otherwise she appeared to be physically all right.

Duke turned and saw that the two men who had been escorting the North Korean weren't moving on the ground. Their bodies were spread out, charred in several areas. Next to them James spotted an arm severed at the elbow. The black sleeve attached to it indicated it belonged to the prisoner.

A couple of soldiers appeared with fire extinguishers and began spraying the still-smoldering area with $CO_2$ foam. James searched for Captain Westport and saw the man sitting up, rubbing his forehead. The man's eyebrows and hair were a bit charred and his face was smudged black. He appeared confused.

"What happened?" Westport asked.

"It was the North Korean. She must have been wearing one hell of a booby trap." James helped Westport to his feet. "Are you all right?"

"Yeah, I think so."

"Come on, these men need our help." Duke made his way to Callahan lying unconscious at the foot of the stairs. Lifting Callahan's head the general felt blood from where the man's head had hit the metal step.

# 4

One man against a hundred. It was the battle cry, the solemn vow, and the simple truth Gen. Han Sinchon had lived by his entire adult life—a sacred oath taken by all who had chosen to serve in North Korea's special forces.

For the general, there was more to the special forces than an oath and the promise of an honorable death. His loyalty to the service had become a way of life, the only way of life he knew.

Long ago he had lost his wife and any hope for a family. She had died in childbirth, leaving him a frail baby daughter, a daughter he knew he couldn't care for or raise. He named her WuLee, his wife's name, giving the newborn child up for adoption. His wife's sister had raised the girl and over the years he watched from a distance but never interfered. He had sacrificed everything for the *spetsnaz* and the values it represented to the point of turning his back on his own child.

Sitting alone in his darkened one-room apartment Han Sinchon thought how after forty-three years of service to his country his leaders were beginning to methodically strip everything away. The man twisted his stocky frame, staring at the walls void of any pictures or unnecessary decoration. Deep wrinkles covered his circular face and a double chin hung over the collar of his starched shirt. What hair remained had turned a dull gray, however his eyes, a soft brown, were filled with the glimmer of a man half his age. Above the left breast pocket of his uniform he proudly wore the insignia of *spetsnaz* officer: a lone black wolf's head, its ears pulled back, teeth bared and ready to fight.

In six months the great Gen. Han Sinchon, the commanding officer of the Special 8th Corps, one of the most powerful and feared men in the North, would be forced to resign. To give up his life as a warrior. Sinchon shook his head in disbelief. He controlled three-quarters of a million well-trained and dedicated soldiers. He currently commanded the majority of the North's senior army officers and loyalty to him reached deep into the navy and air force as well. Many of his political allies called him the second most powerful man in the Democratic People's Republic of Korea. But now, at the height of his power and career, he was being forced out. All because a man twenty years younger, Myong Chin, had convinced the leaders that the old should be pushed aside to make way for a new generation of soldiers.

" 'Men with vision and purpose,' " Sinchon snorted. *"I have always had a vision and purpose." I will not allow him to get away with this,* Sinchon thought to himself. *Chief of Staff Myong Chin is a fool. He does not know the power I still hold.*

Sinchon's resolve hardened, thinking of their feeble offer. They would allow him to remain an active member of North Korean society lecturing young officers. His remaining days would be spent like a worthless token collecting dust when he still had plenty of fight left in him.

"A waste. I would just as soon die." His voice drifted through the air.

Sinchon stood and walked to a kitchen cupboard. He grabbed a bottle of scotch and poured a double shot into a glass. Taking large gulps he felt the liquid burn his lips and throat. It was a sensation that revived him.

*The time has come,* he thought, absorbed in his emotion. *The military is at stake and the people are ready. The only man standing in my way is the general chief of staff, Myong Chin. No longer will the Japanese and South think of us as a failed country and backward society. We have lived in shame long enough.*

Needing a clear head, Sinchon put the scotch away. He strode to his desk and removed a pad of paper and a pen. A new surge of energy was sweeping through him as the general slowly began to outline the details of his plan.


THE WHITE HOUSE

"You are certain it wasn't a North Korean trap of some kind . . . someone being captured, then—" Allan Manning stopped short. He leaned over his cluttered desk and spoke again into the phone: "Okay . . . let me know if there are any changes or new developments."

Manning hung up the phone. He scratched a few more notes on a yellow pad before turning off the lights to his office. He grabbed his suit jacket, turned left and headed down the hallway toward the Oval Office.

Physically Manning did not appear to be the stereotypical Washington insider. The press had nicknamed him Mr. Magoo which made reference to his short chubby body, round nose and thick glasses. But any other resemblance to the cartoon character ended there.

Manning, chief of staff to the president of the United States, ruled the White House with an iron fist and thrived on it. Any time there was a crisis, domestic or international, he made sure he was in the thick of things. Organization, he knew, was not one of the president's strengths and Manning used his position to take charge of high-profile situations, faithfully guiding the president to protect his public and political image.

The last twenty-three years, in one way or another, Manning had served the United States. After graduating at the top of his class from Yale he joined a Miami law firm, then hooked up with the CIA, working in the International Law Division advising Special Operations. He resigned after seven years, determined to make money in the private sector.

When two businesses, one a real estate brokerage firm and the other a chain of fast food chicken restaurants, failed within two years, Manning returned to Yale. When all was said and done, he conceded that his strength in life was politics.

Consequently, with his international experience, Yale credentials, well-rounded knowledge of foreign policy and, most of all, insights into the personalities involved, which seemed to change from day to day in Washington, several presidents had depended on him to one degree or another in managing policy decisions.

Being recruited as chief of staff for most career politicians would be a welcome position of power and influence. Paradoxically, Allan Manning had become resentful. He knew he would never go any further. Sometimes his bitterness seemed on the point of overshadowing his considerable talents.

Manning was alone when he entered the Oval Office. Through the far window he could see the morning sun trying to burn through the light gray haze hanging over the city. Checking his watch, he saw it was a few minutes after eight A.M. He turned the portable color television to CNN, took a seat on the couch across from the president's desk and began reviewing his notes.

The president's morning agenda had automatically been cleared through Manning. A news conference was scheduled for 10:00 A.M. Manning liked 10:00 A.M. news conferences. They gave the president maximum exposure on both coasts and fed the information wolves enough detail to last most of the day. His only concern now was that everyone on his White House staff said and did the right thing, including the president.

Looking up he saw the president enter, followed by the national security advisor, Bill Bishop. Bishop closed the door.

"Damn it, Bishop, you are wrong about this one," the president, Louis McEntire, said strolling toward his desk.

"Mr. President, I just got off the phone with the Japanese prime minister. He is disturbed by this incident. The Japanese are concerned this might lead to—"

"I don't gave a crap if Japan is disturbed. I'm not going to make matters worse by escalating a bad situation. I've given the order for our troops to stand down. I'm not changing it."

"Sir, it is my responsibility to advise you on what the best course of action is to protect the interests of the United States," Bishop pressed his point. "The Japanese believe that by not taking more firm action we will be sending the wrong message."

"I know your job description, maybe you didn't hear me. I don't care what the Japanese believe. It's what I believe that matters."

"It's not just the Japanese, sir. Every world leader is looking at how you'll handle this, and in my opinion you're about to make a bad decision. Sending a message of weakness," Bishop responded.

The two men had stopped in the center of the office facing each other. They were each wearing a dark-colored suit, white shirt with a floral silk tie. The president, standing several inches taller than Bishop, bowed his neck and shoulders. Manning could see his jaw set while his face turned pink with conviction.

"Ordering Americans out of harm's way is not the wrong decision," the president said. "That missile site will be moved in twenty-four hours."

"China, South Korea and Japan—"

"*NO!* My decision is final. I want our troops to withdraw until we can piece this thing together." McEntire turned away, stripping off his suit jacket and draping it over a hunter green leather chair, then sat down behind the desk.

He stared at the television for a few seconds. On the screen was a map of North and South Korea and the approximate position of where the Patriot site was located. The picture flashed to a CNN reporter standing near the DMZ. The President clicked the remote, turning the mute off.

"*. . . the U.S. military has confirmed that approximately twelve hours ago two American soldiers were killed by a North Korean suicide bomber. Three other Americans were wounded when a man, believed to be a North Korean defector, blew himself up at a top-secret missile site near the North Korean border. CNN has learned the man came across the border during the night before making contact with . . .*" President McEntire turned the television's mute back on.

"Well, how much of the story is right?" he said, grimacing. He turned to Manning. "Allan . . . do you have any other information?"

"I just got off the phone with Chaniff," Manning answered, referring to the chairman of the Joint Chiefs. "He's been in contact with General James. The general has confirmed that two Americans are dead, two were wounded. Needless to say, the North Korean did not come across the border to defect—and it was a woman, not a man."

"A woman?" The president sighed, not really asking him for an answer. "Well, any reaction from the North?"

"No, sir. The Defense Department and South Korean government are monitoring the situation. Everything is quiet."

President McEntire leaned back in his chair. "Get the State Department on the line. Tell them to contact the Chinese with instructions to communicate our intentions to withdraw the missiles.'' He looked over at Bishop, continuing: "Make sure they understand this was a big mistake and we don't want anyone else hurt.''

"Yes, sir," Manning replied, scribbling on his pad. "What about Congress?''

"Of course . . . how could I forget about Congress. All the appropriate leaders should know what I'm going to say when I go on the air.'' McEntire turned his gaze back to Bishop. "I suggest you get back on the phone and tell your friends in Japan that this president doesn't have any desire to start a second Korean war over a suicide bomber. And when General James gets back in town I want a complete report.''

Bishop stared hard at McEntire before turning away and exiting the Oval Office.

"Allan.'' The president's tone was that of irritation. "Is everything set for my news conference?''

"Yes, sir.'' Manning gritted his teeth at the president's tone of voice. *Shit always rolls down hill and lands on me.* "All the networks are giving us as much time as we need.''

"Great, all the time I need.'' McEntire folded his arms. "How are you coming on my pet project?''

"Pet project, sir?'' Manning asked.

"The *press leaks,* Mr. Manning. Or have you forgotten about my last news conference. Brit Hume embarrassed the hell out of me. Have you talked with the staff about all the crap that's been appearing in the press? For God's sake, the Washington *Post* knows my next move *before* I do.''

"I'm working on it, sir,'' Manning replied.

"You'd better be. You promised to ride every member of my cabinet and your White House staff until we get some discipline around here. I want you to keep them in line. I don't want *any more* leaks. This is your responsibility, Allan.''

"Mr. President, I can assure you I'm working on it. Whoever is betraying your confidence will be caught. You have my word.''

"Good.'' McEntire turned his attention back to CNN. "Get me some coffee and aspirin, please. . . . it's not even noon and my head is pounding like a sonofabitch.''

It was the third time in two days that Col. Khoe Kwang had been called to General Chief of Staff Myong Chin's private office. Located on the second floor of North Korea's Ministry of Defense building, the office was spacious and elaborately decorated. No one ever entered unless they were summoned or had a vital purpose. The fifty-two-year-old colonel was delivering bad news and felt sick to his stomach walking to the office.

It was a little past ten at night and Kwang's clothes were beginning to look worn and smelled of body odor. He stopped outside the door, brushing wrinkles out of his uniform and adjusting the belt over his slim waist. He knocked on the wooden door twice before entering. Kwang closed the door softly behind him, walked to the center of the room and stood at attention.

General Chin sat at his desk, back straight and eyes forward. The man had a handsome square face with extraordinary features. His cheek bones and nose were well sculpted and his skin was unblemished. Only his eyes gave away his true character. They appeared passionately toxic. His right hand curled around a steaming cup of tea. He took a sip, seeming to ignore Kwang's presence.

The giant mahogany desk suited his well-maintained appearance. Everything was neat and in its proper place. Bookshelves lined the far wall behind him and expensive paintings covered the other three. He liked having them where he could admire their value. A fax machine and a row of phones filled an area beside his desk. Finally, after a few minutes of silence Chin spoke.

"What have you learned?"

"The reports are true, sir." Kwang cleared his throat. "Lieutenant Hyang crossed the DMZ by way of tunnel nineteen earlier this morning. It appears she was captured and used the suicide device. Two Americans were killed with her and two or three others were wounded."

"Who authorized this mission?" Chin asked, his voice cracking with controlled anger.

"General Sinchon."

"I will not stand for this." Myong Chin's voice rose.

Kwang tried to swallow but his mouth had become dry.

"Must I remind you once again the old order is dead. Great Leader Kim Il Song is dead. His son, Dear Leader Kim Jong Il, is dead. *I am* the general chief of staff, *only I* give the order to cross the DMZ."

"I instructed General Sinchon—"

"Sinchon had been relieved of that responsibility," Chin said roughly. "I believe that order was clear."

"Yes, sir. Your orders have always been clear." Colonel Kwang's frame stiffened under Chin's gaze. His glasses began sliding down his nose but he was afraid to touch them.

"We have angered the Americans, for what . . . some reckless mission to photograph a missile site." Chin stood and spoke more to himself than to the colonel: "A pointless missile site."

Kwang looked straight ahead, his eyes focused on the massive bookshelves. Out of the corner of his eye he saw the general dressed in a neatly tailored uniform, standing before a painting of Kim Il-Song.

"I assigned you to control General Sinchon," Chin continued. "You have failed me."

"You should relieve me of command, sir," Kwang said.

"Is *that* what this is about?" Chin exploded, turning to face him. "You want to be relieved of command!"

Colonel Kwang didn't answer. He knew the chief of staff well enough to know that no matter what he said it would be used against him.

"How long have you been Sinchon's personal aide?" Chin asked, already knowing the answer.

"Ten years."

"That's right . . . ten years. And is there anyone he trusts more than you?"

"No, sir . . . he believes I am his loyal assistant."

"Then why would I replace you?" Chin quizzed, his tone calmer now. "Or perhaps you have changed your mind about our arrangement."

"No, sir. I have not changed my mind."

"I didn't think so." Chin smiled, showing his teeth. "Your wife and family would be very disappointed if you quit now. Just remember, my friend, in six months I will force that old fool Sinchon to retire. You will be promoted and allowed to live in the best military housing available, as well as having all the benefits of a high rank. Is that not what you have worked for all of your life?"

"Yes, it is, sir," Kwang answered.

"You must not forget that. You must not lose sight of your purpose . . . ever." Chin was quiet for a moment before catching the colonel's eye. "Sinchon is still important to my plans. He is the only man the arms dealer Bandar will contact inside our government. Until I meet with Bandar personally and teach him to respect me, Sinchon must be controlled. Is that not what we planned?"

"Yes, sir. Bandar is a cautious man," Kwang ventured.

"He trusts Sinchon. Why does he trust him?"

"He knows Sinchon. He knows the general is reliable and will pay his price. That is all. Bandar is a businessman. He is loyal to only one thing: profit. He will keep his mouth shut for the highest bidder."

Chin closed his eyes thinking. "I cannot count on Iran and China for everything. Ghaith Bandar has access to the Western-made weapons I need to keep my military loyal. When has Sinchon scheduled his next meeting with Bandar?"

"That is information he does not share with me." Kwang watched

Chin's face for a reaction as he continued: "He is very secretive about certain moves."

"Of course he is," Chin laughed, "paranoia and international arms trading go hand in hand. But you will find a way, Colonel, to get the information I need." He walked to sit behind his desk, indicating the man was dismissed.

"Yes, sir," Kwang replied, pivoting on his heels and exiting the chief of staff's office. Making his way down the main hall and past the security office he took the stairs to the ground floor. Climbing into a waiting staff car, he closed the door.

"General Sinchon's apartment," he ordered.

The colonel lit a cigarette, exhaling the smoke out of his short flat nose. *I never should have agreed to this. Chin is a madman with more power than brains.* He wondered how he could have allowed himself to be put in this situation. *Yet now is not the time to be a coward,* Kwang told himself, taking another drag off his cigarette. He felt his nerves beginning to calm. Looking out the window he watched the lights of multistory apartment buildings streak by. *I have worked under Sinchon for ten years. I have not been promoted and the pay has not kept my family clothed and fed as they should be.* Kwang felt he had become nothing more than an errand boy. He worked long, hard hours and Sinchon expected him to be thankful for the opportunity and even to enjoy it. He didn't owe any loyalty to Sinchon. Six months; he only had to endure this for six more months.

Taking one last drag off the cigarette, he flicked the butt out the window, watching the orange sparks bounce off the road next to the car.

General Sinchon's soft brown eyes stared at the unfinished letter. The flickering yellow candlelight waved shadows across the paper.

Setting the pen down, Sinchon closed his eyes as images of his past ran through his mind like flights of wild geese on a cold winter's day. He recalled the challenges and the victories of his youth, the events that had transformed him from a young boy to a man, from a soldier to an officer.

The years following the war with America were very difficult for his country. North Korea withdrew from the world, only slowly piecing itself back together in order to survive. The responsibility for that survival fell squarely on the shoulders of Korea's military leaders. It was a responsibility he felt even more so today.

Sinchon opened his eyes looking again at the flickering candle. He stared at the wrinkled, twisted scars covering his left hand. The thumb and half a forefinger were all that remained; a bullet from an American machine gun had ripped his hand apart, leaving the other fingers mere stumps.

His reconnaissance team stumbled across an enemy patrol four miles south of the current DMZ. American tracer rounds cut through the air a few feet away from his head. The bullets ripped into surrounding trees, ricocheting off rocks and frozen ground. He shouted the order to return fire but their sidearms were useless against the massive firepower of the US patrol. He had left the bodies of two fallen comrades behind.

Lieutenant Hyang's face suddenly appeared in Sinchon's mind. She too had been trained for the same sort of mission. Only her job was to cross the border alone.

The general pushed out thoughts of the young lieutenant. Guilt for his arrogance and foolishness were forming. He knew if he had not felt threatened by the general chief of staff he wouldn't have tried to prove he was still in control. The order should never have been given for the reconnaissance mission. Hyang died a brave and worthy soldier following his orders and no one else's. For what?

He looked at the words he had just finished writing but didn't read them. For five years he had thought about taking this step, initiating the overthrow of the North Korean government. Sinchon, being a political realist, knew the only way it could succeed was by getting the backing of China and letting the United States know his intentions were peaceful. Sinchon's contacts inside the Chinese government told him they were not happy with General Chief of Staff Myong Chin's militant attitude toward the West and his desire to acquire nuclear weapons. The days of the Cold War were over, like it or not. China relied heavily on US technology, economic investment and hard currency. Privately the Chinese were quite angry at North Korea for not opening up its economy and changing with the rest of the world. North Korea could not even feed its own people, yet it would not change. Sinchon was willing to wager his life the Chinese would assist him if it meant removing Chin from power. It was a risk he would take.

The letter rested on the table before him. It simply summarized his plans. He would deliver it to the Chinese personally, trusting they would be discreet. If they accepted his plan, he would go forward. If not . . .

Sinchon picked up his pen and began writing again. His knobby fingers slowly scratched the last few lines onto the white paper, then signed his name. His hand was shaking unsteadily and a smile came across his wrinkled face. *Funny thing. The older I get the less alcohol it takes to affect me.*

Sitting back in his chair he watched a drop of hot wax roll down the side of the candle, hardening as it neared the base of the brass holder. A second drop followed the bumpy path and stopped halfway down before it too cooled and solidified. Sinchon's eyes shifted from the white flame and focused on the distant wall.

Shadows danced and fluttered as if beckoning him to the wall. He saw himself outside a massive granite building located near the center of Pyongyang. He knew this place, it was the Ministry of Defense. Going through the front doors he was walking down a long narrow hallway. White tile covered the floor, the walls were yellow and water-stained. He watched himself climb the stairs to the second floor and stroll past the security team guarding the entrance to General Chief of Staff Chin's office. They knew his face and would let him pass without question. Entering the lavish office, he saw that the floor of the large rectangular room had been covered with expensive carpets from Iran and the walls were adorned with precious paintings from China and Japan. Sitting at his desk was Myong Chin, the brother-in-law of Dear Leader who had promised to lead his country out of poverty. Sinchon saw himself removing his pistol, cocking the cold steel hammer, pointing it at the man and watching him turn white with fear. He felt himself pull the trigger, the gun jumping in his hands, Myong Chin's head snapping back . . .

From the partially open window a cold breeze suddenly blew in. The shadowy images of the room swirled around him as he became strangely detached from his surroundings. He picked up the government-issue 9mm resting on the table next to him and squeezed the hard plastic grip. Sinchon watched his thumb cock the hammer. The shiny black pistol came up pointing at the beckoning shadows.


## THE WHITE HOUSE PRESS ROOM

"I'll take one last question." President McEntire pointed to a man in the third row. "Brit, go ahead."

"Yes, Mr. President." The man stood. "Earlier this morning an unnamed senior White House official informed ABC that the North Korean Army officer responsible for killing the two Americans had gotten across the DMZ by way of a tunnel . . . tunnel nineteen, and the officer was in fact a woman. If this is true, wouldn't the use of this tunnel be a clear threat to US interests in South Korea? And why aren't you taking a tougher position against the North?"

"I make it a habit *not* to comment on unnamed White House sources, senior or otherwise. As a matter of fact I try to ignore them." The president chuckled, no one else did. "First of all it's a well-known fact that the North has constructed a number of tunnels under the DMZ. Our intelligence sources are constantly finding them and we address our concerns through diplomatic channels. As far as today's events—" he paused, taking a sip of water—"if a tunnel was utilized, I can assure you *and* the American people it will be dealt with properly."

"That will be all for today, ladies and gentlemen." The president's press secretary stepped to the podium as McEntire disappeared behind the divider and into the hallway. ''Thank you very much.''

The president wiped the heavy beige makeup off his tanned forehead and cheeks as he made his way back to the Oval Office. To his relief the news conference had lasted only fifteen minutes and the press had been fairly easy on him, until that last question anyway. It was the third time in two months some unnamed White House source had leaked important information to the press. A gnawing feeling told him if that question had been asked first he could have been in deep trouble. Maybe Manning was right. Someone on the inside was out to get him.

McEntire turned left, his mind searching through his staff. Who could be disloyal to him? A chill ran down his spine. He didn't want to think about it.

Allan Manning, the president's chief of staff, was slouched on the sofa in the Oval Office holding a phone to his ear when McEntire entered the room.

''Thank you, General,'' Manning was saying. ''I need to run.'' Manning hung up the phone and reached for his notes and yellow pad. Glancing at the television he saw CNN was wrapping up its post news conference commentary.

''Well, how'd I do, Allan?'' McEntire asked hopefully.

''Mr. President, may I have a few words with you . . . *privately?''* Manning replied, standing up.

McEntire shrugged, motioning for the rest of his staff to leave.

Manning closed the door behind him and walked back to the president's desk. He folded his arms and looked out the window without speaking.

''What's up, Allan? Your face is red. You're not going to tell me I screwed something up?''

''No, the news conference went fine, sir. You did everything just like we rehearsed.'' Manning sighed softly, trying to calm down.

''Then what is it?''

''Well, Mr. President, it's the leak thing. I just got off the phone with the chairman of the Joint Chiefs. The Defense Department only informed three people in Washington about that North Korean tunnel. You, me, and General Chaniff at the Pentagon.''

''What's your point?''

''My point is . . . Brit Hume specifically mentioned tunnel nineteen.'' Manning held up a fistful of papers. ''I'm holding twenty-some odd faxes that were transmitted to me via the DOD and CIA in the last twelve hours. Not one of them mentions tunnel nineteen.''

''Then how the hell did Hume know about tunnel nineteen?''

''That's just it, sir. I think I know, but you're not going to like it. You remember Gen. Duke James was there when it happened. James told Bill Bishop about the American special forces team watching that tunnel and the code name used to identify it. That's how you and I first heard about it. I think Bishop leaked it to Hume.''

''What? Bill Bishop? I think you're jumping to conclusions, Allan. A hundred people inside the DOD and CIA must know about that tunnel by now. Hell, this thing happened fourteen hours ago.'' The president began to pace. ''Sonofabitch. I don't know, Allan, how can we be sure? I may not always agree with Bill, but he's my friend, too.''

''Sir, friend or no friend, I will not allow *anyone* to put your administration in a negative light. And that includes Bill Bishop.''

''I know it, Allan, and I trust your judgment. Now listen, I want proof. Especially before we go as far as blaming someone.''

Manning examined the president's face. The corner of his lips were pulled back and his square jaw was set, his forehead creased with deep lines. Counting to himself, Allan tried to calm down, remembering that Bill Bishop and McEntire had been friends for twenty years. ''Yes, sir. Now let's go over the rest of today's schedule.''

A sharp rapping sound startled General Sinchon out of his fixation. He blinked, allowing his eyes to come back into focus. The pistol's hammer was still cocked. Carefully he eased it down, setting the gun on the desk. A drip of cold sweat rolled down the side of his face and stopped on the edge of his chin.

''General . . . are you in there?'' A voice sounded from behind the door.

Sinchon pushed back from the table. Someone was outside. *They know, they know about my plan. They have come to kill me.* He wanted to blow out the candle and pick up the gun, pointing it at the door, but he stopped. *I haven't sent the letter. How could anyone know?* He stood, feeling his head spin.

''General . . . General Sinchon. Are you in there?'' His door rattled with several more sharp knocking sounds.

The muffled voice sounded familiar. He folded the letter in half, stuffed it in an envelope and tucked it inside the breast pocket of his uniform.

''General, it is Kwang. Let me in.''

''Colonel Kwang? Is that you?''

''Yes, sir.''

''What do you want? It is late. I did not send for you.''

''General Chief of Staff Myong Chin sent me.''

Sinchon walked to the door, opening it part way. ''I am off duty. What does the bastard want? And what are you doing talking with him? *I* am your commanding officer, not Chin.''

"It has been confirmed, sir. Lieutenant Hyang is dead. Along with two Americans," Colonel Kwang replied, pushing his shoulder into the door, forcing his way into the general's small apartment. "I thought I should inform you personally."

"It is certain then that she is dead?"

"Yes, sir."

"This should *not* have happened." Sinchon stumbled backward. "Why did you let this happen? Why didn't you stop me? You stupid . . . fool. I pay you to stop me from doing such things."

"Sir . . . have you been drinking?" Kwang turned on the lights to see the apartment's cold gray interior.

"I have. What business is it of yours?" Sinchon spit out the words. He sauntered to his chair but didn't sit down. Picking up his pistol, he placed it back in its holster. "Lieutenant Hyang was a brave soldier . . . You and I should die so honorably. But it should not have happened. I am responsible. No . . . no, Chin is responsible. He is evil."

"You're talking foolishness. Come, you need to sleep. You are tired." Kwang took Sinchon by the arm and led him into the bedroom.

The general stumbled a few times before reaching the bed. Collapsing, he rolled over and stared at the ceiling. "Oh . . . oh, my side," he moaned.

"Your side?" Kwang came closer. "What is wrong with your side?"

"The damned doctors. They are stupid just like you." The general closed his eyes.

"What are you talking about?"

Sinchon spoke, rubbing his side: "The doctors . . . they will fix it."

Colonel Kwang began to unbutton the general's coat.

"Kwang . . . you must take me to the Chinese." Sinchon was slurring his words. His eyes opened, bright and filled with anxiety.

"Yes . . . yes, of course." The colonel tried to appease the old man as he pulled off his rancid-smelling socks. "In the morning."

"You must take me to the Chinese. I must see the Chinese," Sinchon murmured, his eyes fluttering heavily.

"Yes, sir. I'll take you," Kwang replied again. "Now get some sleep."

Not bothering to finish undressing him, Kwang threw a wool blanket over the general. Turning off the light, he shut the door and exited the apartment. It was useless to attempt to get any information from Sinchon tonight. He was filled with a mixture of alcohol, guilt and senility, as far as Kwang was concerned. *The old man will be tough to live with in the morning when his head aches from too much drink,* he thought, not realizing it was a mixture of alcohol and medication that caused the general's recent mood swings.

Colonel Kwang turned up his collar and called toward his staff car. The temperature was falling and the low clouds hanging over the city told him there would be snow on the ground by morning. Someday this would be behind him. He filled his mind with the thoughts of his warm apartment and a bowl of hot Ramyon noodles.

# 5

The nice part about being chief of staff, Allan Manning reflected, was that he had the right to know everyone's business, private and otherwise. If they worked in or for the White House, he made sure they reported directly to him. In fact, everything came through him first. The unwritten rules of the White House were simple. Every shred of information fed to the president crossed his desk, and everyone wanting to see the president had to get cleared through him.

*Well, almost everyone,* Manning thought, sitting at his desk. There was one loose cannon and his name was Bill Bishop, the president's national security advisor who, in forty-eight hours, would no longer be a problem. Once the snitch Bishop was gone Manning could get things in proper order. In one triumphant swoop he would become the second most powerful man in the world—and be free from the bondage of his dead marriage when he could turn to finalizing his divorce. Thinking of his wife squirming at his success made him smile. The little bitch only married him because of the access to Washington's elite. He wasn't sure what bothered her most: the fact that he was still in the White House or that he had left her. Either way she squirmed and that made his day.

Manning checked the oak wall clock. It read half-past eight in the evening. He was sure most of the White House staff had left by now. Punching the button on the intercom, he waited for his administrative assistant to answer.

"Yes, Mr. Manning."

"Lindsey . . . you may go now. I'll see you in the morning."

"Thank you, sir. Good night."

Manning got up, locked the door to his office and dimmed the lights. Only the antique desk light remained on. *All right, Mr. Bishop, let's see just how clever you really are.*

The wall behind Manning's desk contained a custom-made cherry wood bookshelf with a number of locked cabinets and drawers running along the bottom. From a distance it didn't resemble anything special with its brass hinges, scrolled woodwork and dark seamless finish. The top two rows contained at least two hundred books and he kept his personal computer on the shelf directly behind his desk. Each of the drawers and cabinets had been reinforced with an inch of tempered steel, enough to stop the blast of a 30-06 rifle bullet fired at close-range. They were also electronically bolted and a backup lock had been placed on each door or drawer in case the electrical system failed.

Manning opened the top drawer of his desk. In the far right corner was a digital key pad. He punched the numbers 4–26–26–4 and hit enter. Several clicks and pops told him the first lock had been deactivated. Inserting a key into the drawer under his computer, he twisted the lock and pulled it open.

The drawer contained a Toshiba TF161 low-profile fax machine and FMS-5000 fax monitor storage system. The fax machine had been connected to the White House's switchboard and the various private lines running into each high-level office, including the president's residence upstairs. It could differentiate between voice and electronic transmissions which allowed the DAT drive to intercept the number of pages being transmitted in real time. This special design could capture the data at any speed from 300 to 19,200 bits per second even if it varied or jumped sequences. The storage system, which wasn't much bigger than a notebook computer, allowed Manning to record every incoming and outgoing fax at the White House even if it had been encrypted.

The red "power" and "record only" buttons were blinking, indicating both machines were on. The digital readout showed 78 percent of the storage space remained. It had been a busy day.

Manning tapped his computer keyboard, calling up a program that allowed him to fax directly from his computer. He scrolled down, highlighted DOWNLOAD FMS-5000 and hit the enter key. It took several minutes for every fax that had been stored that day to be copied onto his hard drive. Now he just had to find the right one.

*If I guess right, James would have faxed his report to Bishop early in the morning, East Coast time, probably before six* A.M. *It would be on standard NSA stationery transmitted over a coded military SATCOM channel.* He instructed his computer to call up every fax starting from midnight to 6:00 A.M. The screen flashed, filling the monitor with a list of 153 correspondences. The menu, located on top of the screen, showed 132 were domestic and twenty-one were from overseas. *Now we're getting somewhere,* Manning thought.

None of the faxes had been encrypted which meant they didn't contain any classified material. Next to each transmission was the name, location, time and phone number. Using his finger he stopped about halfway down.

| | |
|---|---|
| RECEIVED FROM: | MAJOR GENERAL RICHARD JAMES, DEPUTY NSA |
| TO: | WILLIAM A. BISHOP, NSA |
| TRANSMIT LOCATION: | OSAN AFB, SOUTH KOREA |

TIME: 0345 EST

FAX NUMBER: 011–82–333–661–1115/TRANSMIT MODE II

Tapping the word EXHIBIT, Manning watched the yellow LED light flash on as the hard drive dumped the data into memory. A second or two later the two-page report appeared on the screen. Manning read it twice, looking for any reference to the code name—*tunnel nineteen*. He didn't find one.

*Damn it. I should have known James wouldn't be stupid enough to list the tunnel's code name without at least encrypting his message.* Duke James, in Manning's mind, was a dinosaur—a typical military type living by some outdated code of honor that didn't fit in today's fast-changing world of global politics. James, just like Bishop, saw everything in black and white, good and evil. Manning knew things just weren't that way anymore, if they ever were.

Scrolling the cursor left, Manning stopped on the sentence where James mentioned the North Korean had used a tunnel. Entering the program's setup function he matched up the fonts, Courier 10cpi. Then after the word TUNNEL he typed NINETEEN, and hit the print key. The fax machine hummed, spitting out a new copy of the fax with the original date and time it had been transmitted printed on the top along with James's signature. All Manning had to do now was switch it with the original in Bishop's office.

*When the time is right, I'll be sure it's discovered and Bishop's career as national security advisor and chief pain in the ass will be finished.*

Manning smiled, kicking back in his chair. He could soon start concentrating on what he was going to do to end his already lengthy divorce. He just had one more loose end to tie up: who best to serve him as national security advisor to the president.

## THE PHILIPPINES

The 212-foot-long luxury yacht *Van Triumph* barely rocked as the murky water pushed against her steel hull. Moored on the north end of Manila harbor, she dwarfed other vessels in the area. This section was used for interisland shipping, commercial fishing boats and smaller pleasure craft. The casual passerby couldn't help but notice the *Van Triumph*'s stunning clean silhouette. Hers was a flawless white exterior with smoke-colored glass windows. Three large spotlights illuminated the ship's enormous upper deck which included twin communications towers, a spinning radar antenna, swimming pool, whirlpool and wet bar. The ship's sleek lines told anyone that gazed at her she was built for speed and comfort on the high seas.

However, what most people didn't notice were the two smaller eighteen-foot, center-console dinghies slowly patrolling the water on each side of the *Van Triumph*. The smaller boats barely moved, deliberately not calling attention to themselves. The men operating the dinghies carried automatic weapons and had rocket-propelled grenades available at their fingertips. The ship's owner had given them simple orders. If anyone approaches the *Van Triumph* without invitation, give one warning. If they don't stop, do not hesitate to kill.

Ghaith Bandar, the ship's owner, lay motionless in his bed. His unclothed body was covered only by a corner of the red satin sheets. It was one of the rare times the forty-nine-year-old arms merchant could relax. The vaultlike door to the room had been locked from the inside and the internal intercom had been shut down. No one could bother him.

Bandar propped himself up in the bed. The twinkling lights of the high-rise apartments surrounding Manila Bay reflected off the water and through the darkened stateroom's portholes. Bandar threw his legs over the side of the bed and walked to one of the windows. He surveyed the shoreline. Seeing a couple walking hand in hand to the shops that lined the bay, he stared a moment longer.

*Ah yes, to be in love,* he thought. It was something he never had time for.

Bandar turned back toward the interior of the room. The mirror on the dresser reflected his bronze body from head to toe. A personal trainer assisted Bandar in maintaining his physical condition with daily workouts lasting upwards of two hours. Bandar was indeed a handsome man, standing right at six feet tall. His dark blue eyes, short wavy black hair and neatly trimmed mustache made him appear to be more of Lebanese descent than Pakistani. The romantic eyes came from his mother, the bronzed skin from his father. But everything else surrounding him, Bandar had earned himself. At the ripe young age of thirty-two he was one of the wealthiest and most powerful arms merchants in the world.

Bandar had designed the lavishly furnished bedroom himself. It contained an oval-shaped bed carved from European walnut with a matching dresser and nightstands. The walls were fashioned from matching mahogany imported from Brazil. Each plank had been lacquered and pieced together so that the seams couldn't be seen. The light fixtures and door handles leading to the bathroom were custom made, accented with 14-karat gold and sculpted ivory. Along the far wall a glass bar contained only the finest of wines, Champagnes and liquors. He didn't drink alcohol, and he certainly didn't need it for persuasion, but he felt it was an impressive touch when he entertained female guests.

A cool breeze blew through one of the open portholes filling his stateroom with the scent of the sea. Bandar breathed in deeper and a slight smile crossed his face. He savored the smell. It was the smell of freedom, the smell of success for him. He could go anywhere in the world without having to rely on a single person other than himself. He was king on the sea and he indulged in the great pleasures of life without having to answer to anyone. This freedom meant more to Bandar than anything else. More than all his money, women and even more than *Van Triumph* itself.

Bandar glanced at the digital alarm clock. The clock read 4:37 A.M. He walked over and stroked the silky black hair of the young Filipino girl sleeping in his bed. She was sound asleep from too much wine and exhausting lovemaking. He moved the sheets to cover the rest of her naked body. The evening's entertainment was over; he needed a shower and something to eat.

## NGHIA BINH PROVINCE, VIETNAM

"I can't see the damned runway through the fog." The pilot, Bobby Denny, cursed under his breath. "Bring up the gear. I'm taking her around again." Once again he was flying through the rain and fog scarcely a thousand feet above the ground. The steep interior mountains loomed on both sides of the valley, ready to punish him for the smallest mistake.

Denny pulled back on the yoke and added power, giving his Learjet a few extra knots of airspeed. His altitude climbed as he put the jet into a slow banking turn to the southwest.

He ran sweaty fingers through his gray shoulder-length hair, moving the loose strands out of his face. His long thin nose and hollow brown eyes made him appear lonesome and disoriented. He looked more like a rock star who had refused to grow up than a mercenary pilot working for one of the world's most powerful arms dealers.

"Climbing through twelve hundred feet," copilot Craig Bunten called out. "Heading two one six."

Moisture beaded up across Denny's forehead. *This is my last mission,* he told himself. *That bastard Bandar isn't paying me enough for this.* Smuggling AK-47s, rocket-propelled grenades and LAW80 antitank weapons out of Lebanon and into Bosnia was one thing. But flying into the heart of Vietnam at night to smuggle out a load of chemical weapons was something else entirely. Denny liked the money—$5,000 a trip—but he knew the money wasn't any good if he wasn't alive to spend it.

A sudden jolt through the aircraft as the Learjet cut through a rolling air pocket slammed the men back into their seats. White bursts of lightning sliced through the night sky, lighting up the interior of the jet, followed by loud cracks of thunder.

Denny's insides churned. He gripped the yoke tighter, fighting the turbulence. Another burst of lightning erupted in the sky, outlining the huge thunderstorm to the south. His eyes swept the cockpit instruments before returning to the windscreen. Perspiration was building under his beard making it itchy and extremely uncomfortable.

"Heading still at two one six," the copilot called.

"I know what our heading is," Denny said. "Just make sure you keep us out of the trees." The black sky finally gave up just a trace of moonlight, enough to see the broken horizon but not enough to illuminate the ground.

Bandar paused, staring at himself in the mirror. He turned his head from side to side admiring his wrinkle-free face and straight white teeth. He checked his mustache for any gray whiskers; there weren't any. It had been trimmed to his liking, neat and even.

*No wonder women can't resist me. I am better looking than most men half my age.* He splashed a liberal amount of Giorgio cologne on his upper body. Then slipping a tailor-made silk sports jacket over his starched shirt, he adjusted the collar. He glanced again at the young woman asleep on his bed. The lights from the bathroom cast a yellow glow on her tender brown skin. Her elegant manner and passionate lips had nearly touched him, almost made him wish for the comfort of a lady he could call his own.

*Almost,* he told himself. But women have too many needs and take up valuable time. And should he make her angry, she would turn on him with a wrath no man could muster. *You were good, my little flower, but one night will have to be enough.* He would never see her again.

Turning right outside his cabin door, he made his way down the hallway and up the stairs to the darkened bridge. Seated alone in the captain's chair was Carl Hawkens.

"Mr. Bandar," Hawkens greeted him.

"Carl." Bandar strode to the front section of the bridge.

The ship's command center measured ten by twenty feet and was aglow from the main instrument panel, sparkling with red, green and yellow lights. Spread before them was a four-color weather radar, a wide-screen Global Positioning System (GPS), three SATCOM radios, two phones and one laser fax, each showing an array of digital readouts. The walls had been covered with rich dark hardwood paneling and the floor with a floral patterned carpet. The rear section held three large captain's chairs situated in front of the instrument panel. Smoke-colored windows encasing the bridge served to shade and maintain privacy but were also four inches of thick treated glass capable of stopping machine-gun fire or deflecting rocket-propelled grenades.

"Any word from Denny or Tra?" Bandar asked.

"No," Hawkens replied. "Their orders are to report in when Denny lands."

"He was to be on the ground an hour ago."

"He's a good pilot," Hawkens said. "And he's affordable."

Bandar studied Hawkens's face after the last reply. Hawkens had served as Bandar's contact to the West. He was as tall as Bandar, however he weighed fifty pounds more. It was all muscle. The man had large hands and arms leading to a thick chest and neck. He kept his red curly hair short and shaved his face twice a day.

Hawkens's past was shadowy and Bandar knew very little about the man even after five years of working closely with him. It was rumored that Hawkens had been a member of the 82nd Airborne, working as an intelligence specialist, and at some point had also worked for the CIA, working in Operations. He did speak eight languages fluently and was familiar with the customs of a half-dozen different countries. The story was that he had been forced to resign after being arrested for soliciting a prostitute while on a mission in Madrid, Spain.

Hawkens supposedly drifted back to the United States where he was arrested and sent to prison in August, 1992. He served three years in Canon City, Colorado, for the attempted purchase of six ounces of cocaine from an undercover female DEA officer. After his release Hawkens left the country for a short time, returning to purchase a small condo outside Washington, D.C. Bandar was introduced to him at a political party and, being a man always on the lookout for reliable sources, struck a deal.

The men had little in common other than individual self-interest. Unlike Bandar, Hawkens enjoyed scotch and Russian vodka and was known to get drunk from time to time. Bandar didn't mind. He paid Hawkens well for Washington inside information and he had become a trusted informant.

"Money is not my concern," Bandar replied at last. "Denny is starting to get careless. I want you to find someone else after he picks up this shipment." Bandar sat down, looking out at the lights reflecting off the water in the harbor. "The North Vietnamese are difficult to control and I don't need Denny screwing this up. Chemical weapons are much too profitable."

"We have a backup," Hawkens said. "Major Tra gave me his name after Denny's last trip. Tra does not trust him either."

Bandar accepted the glass of mineral water a servant brought to him, then turned back to Hawkens. "You are too trusting, my friend. Tra is only loyal to me because I'm willing to pay for his hijacked bombs. If he finds a higher bidder I become nothing—and so do you."

"Tra is a businessman, he knows your reputation. He would not dare cross you."

"I remind you that Denny is *your* man. You had better control him. I want that last shipment on the ground and ready for sale. After that find yourself a new pilot. We're scheduled to leave at dawn." Bandar sipped his water. "I can't risk staying here another night."

"What about this shipment? If Denny hasn't radioed by then?" Hawkens held up the radio microphone.

"If he doesn't take possession of the cargo in the next five hours I suggest you stay behind. After he returns pay him the money and see to it the cargo is placed in storage." Bandar stood and moved to the back of the bridge. "Let me know if something develops," he said, disappearing below deck.

*I hate this shit hole of a country,* Denny thought, his emotions swirling. When Hawkens met up with him he was flying drugs into northern Arizona and southern Utah. It was near the money he now earned but it had been a hell of a lot easier than this. The skies were clear and he could at least see where he was landing, even at night.

Denny pulled his lower back into the seat, trying to ease the cramping in his legs. Sighing, he tried to revive his numb arms and gnawing stomach. He was nervous and hungry and wanted to be safe on the ground again. *Hot shower and food with a good night's sleep and I'll be a new man.*

It had been thirty-odd years since he had last piloted Medivac choppers out of Da Nang, Vietnam, for the Marine Corps. *At least I don't have to worry about some gook shooting me out of the sky. I just have to find a poorly lit runway and not run this jet into anything in my way.* Even with that reasoning there didn't seem to Denny to be a lot of difference between the two jobs. If he screwed up flying Hueys he was dead, and if he screwed up flying Learjets he was dead. Either way Denny looked at it . . .

"Watch your airspeed," Denny's copilot warned.

"I see it," Denny snorted. "I told those ignorant bastards night landings were a stupid idea. What are they using down there, candles to light that damn runway?" He worked the controls instinctively while his eyes shifted from the lights of the instrument panel to the cockpit windows.

"What do they care when they're sitting safe on a luxury yacht." Denny glanced over at the man sitting next to him.

Craig Bunten's attention didn't shift from the instrument panel. The younger man was drenched with sweat. His short curly blond hair glistened with moisture and his shirt stuck to his upper body.

"Don't worry, *Señor Boonten,* I land in *mierda* like this all the time. Nothing to it," Denny mocked in a Mexican accent.

"Hey, I'm not worried. Have you ever flown into Fayetteville, Arkansas?'' Bunten didn't take his eyes from the cockpit instrumentation. ''Not much different than this.''

*Yeah right . . . no difference at all,* Denny laughed to himself. Bunten's reassuring comments didn't fool him, he knew the man was scared shitless.

# 6

Maj. LeTrong Tra stood hunched over next to the compact two-way radio equipment. The sixty-two-year-old North Vietnamese Army major's neatly combed black hair blended with several strands of gray. Over the years his body had remained thin and his physical stamina was that of a man in his forties. He did, however, have deep lines crisscrossing the corners of his droopy eyes and his angular face was leathery after spending years in the outdoors.

Strapped to his skinny waist was a Glock Model 17 9mm automatic pistol along with three fully loaded magazines. The pistol and ammunition tugged on a black nylon belt. Dressed in green camouflage fatigues and wearing polished black combat boots, Tra looked as if he had just taken command of Vietnam's best-equipped army division.

"He's not responding to my radio calls, sir," a young Vietnamese man said, seated behind the glowing green dials.

Tra put his hands on his hips staring out of the empty hangar. The building, located at the end of the airstrip, had been constructed from sheet metal and wood, making the ceiling and walls fairly thin. He had heard the jet fly over twice.

*Why isn't the American landing?* Tra felt himself grow angrier by the minute.

"I know he's out there, I can hear the engines. Keep trying," Tra grunted, a half-smoked Camel cigarette hanging from his lips. He narrowed his eyes as a spiraling column of blue smoke stung at them.

"Yes, sir."

Tra took one last drag off the Camel and exhaled the smoke through his crooked nose. Flicking the cigarette butt onto the floor, he crushed it in frustration with the toe of his polished boot. *Three hours late. This entire operation is in danger because of one stupid American.*

Denny leveled the Learjet at 2,000 feet, heading due east. He cracked the throttles forward, watching his airspeed increase to 174 knots. Trimming the jet for level flight he glanced at his copilot. "Take her, maintain heading and flight level," he ordered, grabbing a pair of Steiner Firebird binoculars. He began sweeping the jungle below, looking for the faintest spark of light.

Denny swung the binoculars right and left in rapid succession. He didn't feel comfortable with Bunten at the controls of the jet. Night flying at low level in unfamiliar terrain invites disaster. Besides, Bunten was only a fair pilot. Denny hired him because he was dependable and could keep his mouth shut.

He had met Bunten at a bar in Manila. Bunten had been working for Atlantic Southeast Airlines, a small commuter airline flying twin-engine turboprop planes. He was fired after flunking a routine drug test. Unable to find work in the US, Bunten ended up in the Philippines flying small passenger aircraft from island to island. Working for Denny, he could earn in less than ten hours twice what he'd earn in a week on his regular day job.

Denny felt his small, twin-engine Learjet bounce up and down as it cut through a dense cloud of fog. He dropped the binoculars next to his seat and took back the controls.

"Okay, I have her," he said, banking the plane and watching the compass swing around to 268 degrees. This was his third attempt at landing the nimble little aircraft.

If he didn't get the wheels down this time, Denny planned to turn around and head back to Manila without his cargo—his main concern then being whether he had enough fuel to make the return flight. Either way, Ghaith Bandar would have to find another fool to put his neck on the line from now on.

Denny used the back of his hand to wipe the perspiration from his forehead before turning his radio on. "Ground . . . this is Rambo. Do you copy?"

*"We copy, Rambo."*

"Hey, listen up. If we don't catch your lights this time we're outta here," Danny radioed loudly.

*"Rambo . . . ground. Major Tra has ordered you to land. I repeat, land your aircraft."*

"Oh . . . is that right? Well, you tell the major to go *screw* himself."

*"Rambo, this is ground. If you don't land in ten minutes I'll hunt you down. Do you understand me?"* Major Tra's voice was steady over the radio.

"I'm flying this scrap heap, Tra, not you," Denny responded with a defiant tone. "And up here I don't take orders from anyone."

Denny switched off the radio.

Maj. LeTrong Tra folded his arms and began to pace back and forth across the rear portion of the metal building. The structure was located only twenty-five yards from the west end of the runway. It had been designed to shelter the airstrip's equipment, including aviation fuel, to service small twin-engine aircraft. Keeping the planes inside allowed Tra to keep them out of the watchful eye of rebels who combed the hills around the factory and, of course, away from American reconnaissance satellites passing overhead.

The outside walls and roof had been painted several tones of green in an effort to camouflage it. In Tra's opinion it was nothing more than a waste of paint. From several miles away any fool could tell it was a painting. If the green paint didn't give the structure away then the ten-foot-high chain-link fence topped with razor wire surrounding it would. On the inside the aluminum walls and concrete floor were discolored by the humid climate and green fungus which seemed to cover everything.

Major Tra rubbed his eyes in thought. Six months ago during the dry season, a long narrow airstrip had been constructed by Gia Hian Enterprises, a subsidiary of a Japanese pharmaceutical firm. When the weather permitted the landing strip was used during the day to ferry Japanese and European chemical engineers into and out of the area. Tonight it was used for Tra's benefit.

Gia Hian Enterprises had helped the Vietnamese government build four large pharmaceutical factories along the Laotian border, commonly referred to as Hian 1–4. Setting up the factories had been easy. The province's leaders were hungry for investments to help rebuild the region's fragile economy. An average adult male living in the mountains earned less than $300 a month. The new factories offered a way for many people to lift their families out of poverty. Officially, the factories had been set up to manufacture medicines such a diphenhydramine, chlorphreniramine and pseudoephedrine used in antihistamines and cough syrup. Three of the factories did just that, supplying the region with the drugs.

However, Plant 4 had been located away from the others on the back side of a steep sloping hill ten miles from the airstrip. It was surrounded by a high barbed-wire fence with two fifty-foot-high guard towers which were manned twenty-four hours a day. German shepherd guard dogs patrolled the perimeter at night. It was in Plant 4 that the Vietnamese government had secretly set up a chemical weapons assembly line and Maj. LeTrong Tra reigned as chief of security.

*Investment,* the major thought, thinking of the factories. Just another word for the greed that controlled the West. It sickened him when he thought how Vietnam's young people had bought into the Western concept of money and material wealth.

He lit another Camel cigarette. Breathing in deeply, he held the smoke in his lungs. The West had been slowly taking over his country and he didn't like it. China Beach had been transformed into a Western-style resort filled with surfers and fat Europeans browning themselves in the warm winter sun. The streets of Hanoi were filling with high-priced hotels playing country and western music and servicing well-dressed businessmen looking for low-cost labor to fill their factories. Prostitution, once outlawed by the government, was now looked upon as an essential part of Vietnam's return to the plentiful world of business and profit. *A woman selling her body for money . . . capitalism at its finest.* Tra tightened his jaw, gritting his teeth.

Fast-food restaurants were sprouting in every corner of Ho Chi Minh City. The people spoke of money, of the high-paying jobs the West would bring to Vietnam. But Major Tra thought he knew better. The Americans would never allow Vietnam to rise from the ashes of war. His people were slowly becoming servants working in factories, making Nike basketball shoes and Levi's jeans.

Maj. LeTrong Tra had sacrificed enough for his country. He lost his wife, two brothers and his mother and father fighting to unify the country. It was his turn to live the rest of his years in peace. In one year he planned to retire with over a quarter of a million American dollars hidden away in a Swiss bank account. His country could turn to the sewer of profit and greed for all he cared. His war had ended many years ago.

"There! To the left!" Bunten cried out.

Out of the corner of his eye Denny caught a glimmer of light.

"What do you make of it?" Bunten asked, apprehensive.

"I don't know . . . but it's not what we're looking for," Denny answered. The tiny yellow light was coming from somewhere on the mountainside off the port side of the jet. "We're staying on this course for another three minutes, then turning around."

A few drops of rain hit the windscreen of the jet.

*Fucking great, this is all I need.*

A bead of sweat rolled down the side of Bobby Denny's face, stopping at the edge of his thick gray and black beard. The cockpit windows became a blur as streaks of droplets obscured his vision. He strained to see the image of a narrow black runway through the darkness.

"Watch your airspeed," Bunten called out.

"Yeah, yeah, I see it," Denny mumbled under his breath as he worked the throttles and yoke, keeping the older Learjet just above stall speed. The jet pitched up and down, yawing to the right as a gust of wind hit it. The pilot compensated by tapping the left rudder pedal.

"Altitude . . . twelve hundred feet," his copilot chattered.

"Why don't you shut the FUCK up. *I'm* flying this sucker, not you." Denny throttled back, reducing his airspeed to 153 knots. The stall warning sounded so he pushed the nose down, regaining some airspeed. Suddenly in the distance Denny spotted the faint partial outline of a short black runway.

"To the left," Bunten pointed again, his voice elated.

Denny didn't acknowledge him. Through a slight break in the clouds he could see the faint flickering of a half-dozen yellow lights. The same thunderstorm that had delivered the rain had also brought strong winds. The ground fog was breaking up and moving off the runway.

"Get the gear down and turn on the landing lights . . . we're going in, one way or another." Denny adjusted his grip on the yoke and pitched the nose up, reducing his airspeed by a couple of knots.

"Gear down . . . three locked."

Major Tra moved to a table next to the radio and poured himself a cup of hot tea. As chief security officer for Gia Hian he was responsible for setting up a multilevel security network and had access to each segment of the chemical weapons manufacturing process. The sixty-four people employed at the chemical plant were not informed of the true purpose for which the plant was designed. No single person other than Tra knew more than their limited function in the process.

The factory was located five miles from the Vietnamese town of Pham La. A two-lane paved highway had been built through the mountainous terrain allowing trucks to bring in the needed chemicals, storage containers and workers. Seven days a week five-ton trucks arrived with loads of thiodiglycol and hydrochloric acid, along with fifty-five-gallon drums of chlorine, hydrogen cyanide, phosgene, methanol, ethanol, ammonia, and $POCl_3$, all key components in the manufacturing of nerve gas. Four months ago in a secluded section of the factory Tra and a handful of trusted chemical and weapons specialists began to manufacture alkylphosphonates and methylphosohonic. These two chemicals by themselves are relatively harmless and could be manufactured on the same equipment. They are simple compounds that could be used in fertilizer and industrial cleaning solvents. But Libyan engineers had supplied the Vietnamese government with enough manufacturing expertise and technical information to enable them to build weapons. They were also given the precise dimensions and calculations to configure two cylinder-shaped glass containers, each to be filled with specific amounts of alkylphossphonates and methylphosohonic, then placed side by side, separated by a thin perforated strip of copper metal, in a bomb casing. Machined out of solid blocks of 410 stainless steel, the casings weigh nearly 200 pounds each and are not much different in shape and size from a standard MK 84 iron bomb. When dropped from an aircraft at high altitude and airspeed the glass casings shatter on impact, mixing the two agents together. An explosive chemical reaction occurs within a fraction of a second. The resulting detonation forms a dialkyl toxic nerve gas a thousand times stronger than Tabun.

This extremely poisonous and potent vapor lingers in a dense cloud where it can be carried for many miles by surface winds. Once released into the atmosphere it could kill every living creature that inhaled its fumes for up to twelve hours.

The bombs are small, making them easy to hide, remarkably simple to manufacture and powerful enough to make Vietnam's enemies, such as China, take notice. The Vietnamese government had been stockpiling the weapons in the north and leaked word that it now commands enough bombs to stop several Chinese divisions if they ever marched south.

Major Tra stared at the shipment awaiting Denny's arrival. The bombs were so small, in fact, it was very easy to manufacture five or six additional bomb casings each time they opened the production line. With a slight manipulation in the production logs, the retired North Vietnamese Army major could load the extra bombs onto a truck and drive them away from the factory at night. The Vietnamese government had no way of knowing he was secretly selling the lethal warheads to a front company, owned and operated by Ghaith Bandar, for a healthy profit. After each shipment funds were transferred out of Bandar's Hong Kong bank account into Tra's Swiss account via a small investment firm in the Cayman Islands. This was just another of such transactions.

Tra finished off the last of his tea and began pacing nervously. He heard the static of the portable radio equipment and the muffled sound of two portable gas-powered Honda generators.

The major moved to the center of the building. He could hear the faint drops of rain still hitting the metal roof. If it kept up, the roof would start leaking profusely.

*Denny's negligence is throwing everything behind schedule. I don't have time for this.* Tra's insides burned as he looked at his watch. He needed to be back at the plant before the first shift showed up for work at seven o'clock.

Tra walked to the open door leading out of the building. He hesitated at one of the two covered pallets. His hand stroked the corner of the heavy green canvas tarp. He stood for a few seconds before traversing out into the night, letting a few raindrops hit his face. Looking up he could see stars through the broken clouds swirling above his head.

Bobby Denny watched the windshield fill with silver shadows of clouds as he lost sight of the runway once again. He could feel his heart starting to pound as the plane rocked slightly back and forth cutting through the fog.

"We should be breaking out of this crap . . ." Denny breathed and without warning the windshield cleared. The black silhouette of broken treetops fast approaching.

"Six hundred feet," the copilot warned.

*Shit . . . I'm descending too fast.* Denny felt his face turn hot as a shot of adrenalin pumped through him. He inched his throttles forward, picking up a few knots of airspeed. Telling himself not to overreact he gently eased the yoke back, pitching the nose up five degrees.

"Four hundred feet," Bunten warned again. "Airspeed . . . one hundred fifty-nine knots—look out!"

Denny felt the Learjet shudder as the left gear caught the top of one of the trees. A blunt cracking sound filled the aircraft as it swayed left, its wingtip dipping slightly and busting several more limbs. The jet vibrated, yawing back and forth as the gear broke through treetops, snapping the wet wood and stripping the foliage off the branches.

"Pull up! Pull up!" Bunten shouted.

"Hold on!"

A deafening crack filled the flight deck. Suddenly pieces of broken plexiglass exploded into the cockpit, the front windshield of the Learjet was shattered by a large branch.

Denny hauled back on the yoke, forcing the nose up. The fragmented windscreen filled with the sight of rolling gray clouds. In an instant Denny felt the pressure of 3 Gs pushing him back into his seat. The jet snapped into a forty-five-degree climb bleeding off energy rapidly.

*"Warning . . . stall. Warning . . . stall,"* the computer sounded.

"Ah, shit!" Denny's eyes went to the instrument panel. The Learjet had shot up to an altitude of 530 feet in a fraction of a second. His forward airspeed, now less than 120 knots, continued to fall. The jet would shudder again and drop out of the sky like a rock if his forward velocity dropped below 100 knots. He had only one choice. Forcing the yoke forward, he dropped the nose and jammed the throttles forward, adding power. Denny knew it would take at least five seconds for the engines to spool up to give him additional airspeed. This close to the ground, though, five seconds could be too long to wait.

Denny's eyes went back to the front windscreen. He could barely see the ground. Bunten sat stiff in his seat, unable to utter a word. The Learjet's nose continued to push over and Denny caught sight of the runway once again, two miles at his one o'clock. If he could clear the next few hundred feet of treetops he could land the plane.

"Hold together, you bitch!" Denny cursed, pumping the yoke back and forth, hoping to nurse the jet out of the stall. When his airspeed hit 153 knots he banked to the right and throttled back. The Learjet protested, its controls mushy.

"Hold on, this isn't going to be pretty." Denny watched their altitude fall rapidly, 150 . . . 100 . . . seventy-five feet—he didn't have time to line up for a touchdown. He thrust the yoke back to the left, leveling the jet's wings. The black runway loomed in the distance only a half-mile away. In one fluid motion he throttled back and pushed the nose down.

Thirty feet . . . twenty feet . . . ten feet—at the last second he pulled the yoke toward him, allowing the aircraft's rear wheels to strike the pavement first. The jet's nose bounced once, then twice, before all three wheels were firmly on the ground.

"Son of a bitch . . . we're down!" Bunten shouted.

Denny's lips cracked into a thin smile. He added pressure to the brake pedals, waiting for the jet to slow.

The Learjet shook and Denny applied more pressure but she wasn't stopping.

"Shit!" Denny screamed. "We're not going to make it!"

Both men braced themselves. The aircraft swerved left and right as the landing-gear tires skimmed across the wet runway like skates on ice.

Denny used all his strength to jam the brakes forward but the Learjet skidded sideways, hitting the end of the runway. It made an awkward jump across a cleared area, coming to rest at the foot of the trees.

Denny opened his eyes. The beating in his chest took his breath away. He scanned the instrument panel, looking for a fire-warning light. There wasn't one. To Denny's amazement they were still alive and the Learjet was upright. The gear was sinking into the soft soil but it hadn't collapsed. He wiped his entire face with his shirttail and looked at Bunten, who was white as a ghost.

"We're not getting paid enough for this shit," Denny laughed.

# 7

It was useless, Duke James couldn't sleep. Each time he closed his eyes the image of the orange fireball filled his mind. He could hear the men screaming and rolling on the ground in pain, their clothing on fire. The explosion had happened so fast his memory seemed clouded.

Duke couldn't help but wonder what would lead a person to kill herself like that. The young woman must have been highly trained and extremely well disciplined. Or she could have been brainwashed, he reasoned. Probably taught that being captured was worse than dead. All in all, he knew this time he had been damned lucky not to be hurt.

Sitting up, he turned on the desk light next to his bed. The base's VIP quarters were small but comfortable: the room was cold but it did contain a private bathroom. There was a television and CD stereo player in the corner but they didn't look as if they had ever been used.

James could hear a stiff wind blowing outside the window. A cold draft came off the floor, sending a shiver up his spine. The digital clock read 04:18 A.M. local time. He had scheduled himself a flight leaving at 06:30 that morning. That would put him back in the States some fourteen hours later with a short stopover at Hickam in Hawaii for fuel.

The thought of getting back home wasn't making getting to sleep any easier. Whenever things went wrong he had an overpowering desire just to be home with his family. Knowing they were safe somehow allowed him to deal with the anxiety and pressures of any conflict.

James had already missed spending Thanksgiving at home and Christmas was less than a month away. *It never fails,* Duke thought. *I don't know how Katie puts up with it.*

Duke rolled out of bed and picked up the phone. "Sergeant, this is General James. Bring my car around in thirty minutes, please. I'd like to stop over at the base hospital before leaving."

"Ah . . . yes, sir. Thirty minutes," came a groggy response.

"Thank you." Duke hung up the phone and headed for the shower. He turned the hot water on, then suddenly switched it to cold.

PYONGYANG, NORTH KOREA

"Stop there," General Sinchon said, pointing to a dark section of the street. "Pay attention. Are you awake up there?"

"Yes, sir." Colonel Kwang slowed the car and pulled over to the curb. "I don't believe anyone is on duty though, sir. The light in the security booth is out."

"Someone is up," Sinchon responded in monotone.

"Possibly we should sleep some more and come back when the sun is—"

"You just stay here," Sinchon said, looking back at the building. "The Chinese are like ants: they never sleep. Now turn off the lights and wait for me. This will only take a few minutes."

Kwang turned off the car's headlights, put the staff car in park and began to get out to help the general onto the sidewalk.

"I can get out on my own," Sinchon mumbled.

"Very well, I'll keep the car warm, sir."

"You do that."

Twisting his husky body around, Sinchon opened the rear door and climbed out. He didn't bother buttoning his plain gray coat, hoping the cold wind would shake the cobwebs from his mind.

Sinchon lowered his head and walked toward the security booth in front of the Chinese embassy. The booth appeared dark and unoccupied. In a way he was glad the dazed feeling had not left him. It seemed to make things easier. It was like being buried somewhere deep within, looking on while his body went through the motions.

Although he had known the senior Chinese attaché for twenty years and considered him a friend, there wasn't any guarantee the man would deliver the message to the proper authorities.

"Stop and identify yourself," a stern voice sounded while a light suddenly appeared inside the guard post.

The general watched a man scramble to his feet. By his expression he could see the man was embarrassed for falling asleep.

"I said identify yourself," the guard repeated.

"I am here to see Chengji Zheng. Tell him Han is here."

"Han?"

Sinchon stepped closer and spoke in Chinese: "You heard me, soldier. I suggest you do it before I report your performance to Chief of Security Tong."

The guard picked up the phone and, after a few seconds, opened the gate.

Sinchon walked inside. Looking over his shoulder he saw the first colors of the eastern horizon. A new day, he thought to himself.


## NGHIA BINH PROVINCE, VIETNAM

"Get the hangar door open," Maj. LeTrong Tra shouted to several of his men.

As the large double hangar doors came open he walked out onto the taxi way, shielding his eyes from the glaring white lights of the truck towing the plane toward him. The driver raced the engines and swung the nose of the aircraft around, stopping thirty feet from a small metal building just off the runway.

The faint light coming from the hangar was enough for Tra to see mud and vegetation hanging from the landing gear and underside of the jet.

*His plane is probably not even operable now,* Tra thought, checking his wristwatch. Denny was four hours late. The major's contempt for the big-mouthed American simmered inside of him.

Tra's men worked swiftly, cleaning the dirt and mud off the aircraft, whose side door opened slowly before dropping to the ground, exposing the stairs. The interior lights of the jet were off, making it impossible for the major to see anyone inside. *Denny may be rude and arrogant but he isn't a fool,* Tra thought, realizing the man was being cautious. *He's probably concealing a pistol somewhere.*

"You two . . . take up a position in front of the plane," Tra ordered, pointing to where he wanted the men to stand. Each carried an AK-47 assault rifle with thirty-round magazines. *If Denny is thinking about playing games I will be ready.*

After a moment Denny emerged and came down the steps with confidence. He didn't break stride as he approached the major. "Well, if it isn't Major Long Ducks Dong—chief gook and bottle washer of Nghia Binh Province," Denny said, stopping a few feet from Tra. "I've been sitting in that fucking jet for too long. Your men are worthless."

"You are late," Tra answered, boring in on the American's eyes.

"Why didn't you light the runway?" He turned and saw the two men standing ready near his jet. "What are you going to do, shoot me? Or is this an armed escort? I'm flattered."

The North Vietnamese major resisted the temptation to blow the man's head off. Sacrificing his retirement wouldn't be worth the few minutes of pleasure he'd receive in seeing this man die.

"Look, Long Duck . . . I couldn't see the runway through the fog. Not to mention I nearly killed myself." Denny moved closer, stopping a foot away from Tra. "You can understand why I'm a little cranky. Where are the additional landing lights you promised?"

"You will address me as . . . Major Tra."

"Yeah, right," Denny replied. "Now get me to your radio. I have to contact Hawkens."

"This way," Tra gestured after a momentary standoff.


PYONGYANG, NORTH KOREA

It was rumored, and General Sinchon believed it, that being picked to staff the Chinese embassy in North Korea was an extremely desirable assignment. The inside of the embassy was like a lavish hotel. The walls were painted a bright red with large paintings of fruit trees, Chinese landmarks and portraits of the great leaders of China's past hanging every few feet. It had been decorated with the finest Asian furniture. The interior was clean, always smelled of fresh flowers, and when entering one felt warm and welcome.

Sinchon had eaten several meals at the embassy and they had all been elegant affairs. However tonight, with the lights out, the darkened interior appeared shadowy and threatening. The walls and paintings were black and malevolent.

Fumbling with the letter in his breast pocket, Sinchon began to understand the gravity of his plan. The man he was about to meet, Chengji Zheng, had a military career paralleling his own. Their similarities brought them to an ease of conversation that only trusted friends shared. In the last year, during several night-long drinking sessions, Zheng had voiced his country's concern about the North's current leadership. The death of Kim Jong Il, Kim Il Song's son, had left a power void which China felt wasn't being filled. The North's new leaders were young, but they followed the same Soviet economic and military strategy that had once brought the powerful nation almost to a standstill. In recent years North Korea was becoming a large financial burden on China's developing economy.

One of the guards posted in the front lobby grunted for Sinchon to follow him.

Sinchon followed down a long hallway from the chamber used as Zheng's private study and informal visiting room. Sitting alone in a high-backed chair was his friend Chengji Zheng. The large chair made the short man appear even smaller, which almost brought a smile to Sinchon's face. Brown eyes stared out from behind round eyeglasses.

The black robe and droopy eyelids told him Zheng had been awakened by the visit. The guard exited the room and closed the door.

"By the hour of your visit I believe you must be very troubled. Would you like a drink?"

"No, thank you, I do not have much time. So I will get to the point." Sinchon began in a hushed tone: "You and I have been friends many years. I come to you in confidence asking for assistance."

"Go on," Zheng nodded.

"We have discussed the men inside my government that are not worthy to lead. They are corrupt and will destroy my country if they are left in power. I will not allow that to happen." Sinchon reached inside his breast pocket and pulled out the letter. "I therefore place my life in your hands."

Zheng's eyes opened wide with sudden interest. He stared down at the white envelope in Sinchon's hands for a few seconds before taking and opening it. He read it quickly and let out a long sigh. "You are sure," Zheng asked, deep concern on his face, "that you have thought this through?"

"Yes, Zheng. I believe a coup is the only way." Sinchon's voice was soft. "You know my government as well as I do. Tell me if I am wrong."

Zheng's face became rigid. "Giving this to me, you have—"

"I have placed my life in your hands," Sinchon broke in. "If your government is not willing to help me, give the letter back. We can forget I woke you."

The room became still. Sinchon locked his stare on Zheng's face.

"My government will not be surprised at the proposal. However, we did not suspect it would be you. They will want to know which people you intend to remove and which military forces will be on your side."

"General Chief of Staff Myong Chin and President Kim Pyong Il control the country. They must be removed. Once they are out of power the rest of the defense council will fall into place behind me. I can then move my country toward reform."

"What about Defense Minister O Jin U?" Zheng asked. "He is a powerful man."

Pausing, Sinchon glanced away. "You let me worry about him. He is not as loyal to Chin as you think."

Zheng stood and moved toward a tray holding a silver pot of hot tea. He poured himself a cup but didn't drink. "You will have an answer in twelve hours. I suggest you leave before it is light."

"Twelve hours," Sinchon repeated.

The car ride back to Sinchon's apartment was solemn. A heavy overcast hung low over Pyongyang, keeping the streets dark.

Resting his head on the back of the vinyl seat, Sinchon closed his eyes. *Zheng is an intelligent man. He will understand that only a coup will change the course of my country. All will be well.*

The staff car swerved to miss large potholes in the pavement, throwing the general back and forth.

"Slow down, Colonel," Sinchon snapped. "I'm not ready to die just yet."

"Yes, sir," Kwang answered, glancing at the general in the rearview mirror.

Sinchon felt strangely guilty having lied to Zheng. Reforms weren't the only reason for the coup, but he couldn't come out and say it. This was also more personal. If he had to use Zheng's relationship to see Chin dead, so be it. No one was going to force him from his life in the military. If Zheng could convince the Chinese government his motives were sincere, that was all that was needed.

Sinchon looked ahead as the car turned left and headed up a long steep hill toward his apartment. Smokeless chimneys and silent factories lined the roadway—another sign of the disease that continued to eat his country. Sinchon could be content: the first step in his plan to change all this was over now. He just had to wait.

James was heading down the hall of the base hospital at a few minutes after five in the morning. The corridors were just beginning to fill with people. He approached the nurse's station and caught the attention of the nurse on duty.

"May I help you, sir?" she asked.

"Could you tell me where Chief Warrant Officer Michael Callahan's room is located?"

"Visiting hours are from nine to ten in the morning and six to seven in the evening, sir." The nurse glanced at the two stars on the shoulder of James's blue sweater. "Possibly I could take a message?"

"Could I see if he's awake?" Duke asked. "I'm leaving in a few minutes . . ." The nurse's expression didn't change so he decided to try the sympathetic route. "I was with him and the others when the explosion occurred . . . I'd just like to check on him."

"Well, sir—" The nurse looked both ways down the hall to see if anyone else was around and smiled. "You can stick your head in and see if he's awake. If not, please leave quietly. It's room 216."

"Yes, ma'am . . . and thank you." Duke smiled back.

The name plate under the room number, written in bold blue letters, read CWO MICHAEL QUINCEY CALLAHAN JR. The door to Callahan's room was open so Duke entered quietly. The warrant officer was propped up in bed, reading an old copy of *Sports Illustrated*. An empty tray rested next to the bed and every scrap of food was gone.

"Good morning," James said, walking up to the soldier. He noticed a half-inch cut above the CWO's left eye. Three white butterfly stitches were holding the skin together.

"Ah . . . good morning, sir."

"I thought I'd stop in and see how you were getting along."

"Oh, I'm fine, sir. Just a few bumps and bruises. Nothing serious." Callahan put the magazine down. "I think the doctors around here must be bored. I told them nothing was wrong yesterday."

"When are they letting you out, then?"

"This morning, sir, in about an hour."

"Good." Duke pulled up a chair and sat down. "I'm leaving for Washington in a few minutes but I wanted to make sure you were all right first."

"Well, thank you. Are you seeing everyone, sir?"

"Nope . . . just you."

Callahan's expression changed to bewilderment.

"I've heard some talk you're blaming yourself for what happened yesterday," Duke said. "I wanted to let you know that I read the preliminary report. You did everything by the book. It wasn't a screw-up."

"Then the book's wrong, sir." Michael's face was taut.

"Maybe . . . but snake-eaters always take the macho man approach. I'm not going to lecture you, soldier. You know that North Korean did what she was ordered to do. I don't see where you or anyone else could have prevented it."

"I should have stripped her naked. That's what I should have done." Callahan looked away. "I appreciate what you're saying, sir, but it *was* my responsibility. I shouldn't have brought an armed enemy soldier into Kansas. No matter how you slice it, two men are dead."

"Well, next time you'll know better. This was an experience and that's what war is about, the more experienced men leading the new guys. You're a seasoned soldier now and the military needs you."

Callahan dropped his head. He pictured himself frisking the woman, wondering how he could have missed the explosives.

"I know . . . you're thinking you should have found those explosives. Don't underestimate the enemy, Callahan . . . never underestimate the enemy."

"Yes, sir."

"Westport's going to need you back there on the DMZ. What are your plans?"

"If you're asking me if I'm a quitter, the answer is no." Callahan's voice was confident. "General, I'm not a man who has a grand plan. I believe in God and this country, that's about it. But I'll tell you this. If tomorrow I'm ordered back into the field, I'll go and do what I do. It's all I am."

Duke should have known. The special-forces type were a different breed.

From the look in Michael's eyes he could tell the man's conviction might have been shaken, but it wasn't broken. Callahan hadn't gotten this far by being a pantywaist.

"Good luck, then, Mr. Callahan." Duke stood and shook the man's hand. "You ever get to Washington, give me a call. I know a place where the steaks are thick and the beer is ice cold."

"I could use some of that, sir. Thank you."

Duke turned and left the room. He had one more stop to make before heading to his jet.

## THE WHITE HOUSE

The single-edged razor blade sliced easily through the white powder. Allan Manning scraped the finely chopped cocaine into two neat lines atop his glass-covered desk, making sure every last grain was in place. He scanned his office, his eyes shifting back and forth like a little kid stealing the last cookie from the jar. The door was locked, he had checked it twice, and the lights were off, but it didn't matter. Allan was still worried he might be discovered. Not so much, though, that he didn't anticipate the rush of snorting coke and breaking the law. There was nothing like it.

Through each nostril he sucked a full line, using a tightly rolled twenty-dollar bill. Wiping the last few granules off his desk he licked the powder from his forefinger.

"Ahhhh . . ." Manning closed his eyes and sat back in his chair briefly, then picked up his notepad and headed for the Oval Office. It was time for his final meeting of the day with the president.

"We had a good day, sir," Manning beamed, walking into the office. "The latest CNN/ABC poll shows our approval rating is up . . ." Manning stopped midsentence, stunned. Seated across from the president was Bill Bishop, the national security advisor. Bishop looked very relaxed with his tie loosened and suit jacket off. As always his black hair was neatly combed and his face was nicely tanned. Manning wondered why he wasn't at the country club playing tennis with some senator.

"Continue, Allan," the president smiled. "We could all use some good news."

"We were just winding down," Bishop said.

Manning's tone hardened: "I don't remember you being on the president's agenda this late in the day."

Bishop smiled. "I'm not."

"Oh, mellow out, Allan. Bill and I were talking about football. He thinks Notre Dame's going to play Nebraska for the national championship. If they do, I want the Huskers and six points. What do you think? Should he give me six points or not?'' McEntire laughed.

"I don't follow football, Mr. President. Should I come back later?''

"No . . . it's time I go, anyway,'' Bishop said. "Sally has tickets for *The Nutcracker* at Kennedy Center. I don't want to be late. Good night, sir. Good night, Mr. Manning.''

"Good night, Bish,'' the president said. "See you in the morning.''

Bishop picked up his briefcase and walked out of the office. Manning, still standing at the door, closed it.

"Shit, Allan, I know you don't like Bishop but you don't have to make it so obvious.'' The president pulled a cigar out of the top desk drawer. "This job's tough enough without having my top advisors at each other's throats.''

"Like I was saying, sir,'' Manning sat down and began thumbing through his notepad, "the latest CNN/ABC poll shows your approval rating is up 4 percent over last week. The news conferences must have helped.''

"Four percent? That's great.'' McEntire suddenly rolled his eyes. "You have fifteen minutes, Allan. I'm tired, I want a drink and some dinner. What's scheduled for tomorrow?'' He rolled the fat brown cigar between his fingers and held it under his nose.

*Now's your chance . . . do it,* Manning psyched himself up. "You wanted proof. Here it is.'' He handed McEntire the first page of General James's fax. "Your White House leak is Bishop and I want him gone.''

The president's mouth dropped open.

"There it is, on line sixteen or seventeen.'' Manning folded his arms. He watched McEntire's eyes skim across the page.

"I don't believe this . . .''

"Believe it.'' Manning's voice was excited. "I told you it was him. He is disloyal and a sickness inside your presidency. You must get rid of him and you must not waste any time.'' He had stood and was pacing back and forth across the room.

McEntire didn't respond. He just looked at the fax, reading it over and over again.

"Mr. President.'' Manning stopped, forcing his voice to be calm. "I didn't do this, Bishop did. He made a decision to embarrass you because you won't go along with his kick-Korea's-ass policy. Come on, you can see it as well as I can.''

McEntire finally glanced up. His face revealed disappointment and doubt. "I can't believe this.''

"The best thing you can do for this administration is to ask for Bishop's resignation. If you want, the official line can be that he resigned to go back into private business and spend more time with his family. The standard bullshit.'' Manning was now standing over the president's desk. ''Mr. President, you must act.''

''Where . . . where did you get this?''

''One of my aides found it in Bishop's office. Bishop had misplaced it in one of his other files.'' Manning could smell blood, becoming ever cockier. ''As chief of staff I have privileges and one of them is keeping track of everyone's office. Including Bishop's.''

''We've been friends . . . for a long time.'' McEntire didn't try to hide the shocked look on his face. He set the fax down.

''So were Haldeman and Nixon. But in the end it was every man for himself.'' Manning pulled a slip of paper from the middle of his notebook. Several lines were typed on White House stationery. ''This is a request asking for Bishop's resignation . . . effective noon tomorrow. All you have to do is sign it and I'll give it to him in the morning.''

The president hesitated.

''He *stabbed* you in the back, sir. If he did it now, he's done it before and he'll do it again.''

McEntire grabbed a pen and scribbled his name on the document.

''Thank you, sir. You're making the right decision. Without complete loyalty a president can't govern effectively.'' Manning strode to the door. ''I'll see you at seven-thirty tomorrow morning.''

*Yes, yes, yes,* he thought, exiting the Oval Office. He could feel his heart pounding. *I've done it. Bishop, Mr. High and Fucking Mighty, is gone.* His final stumbling block to controlling the president was history. And it had been so easy. Now Manning wondered what had taken him so long.

He entered his office and locked the door. The room was still dark except for the light on his desk. Manning hesitated, his mind was spinning too fast. He needed to think. *What if the president changed his mind? He sleeps on it and decides to confront Bishop . . . he'd deny it, of course. What if that idiot believes him? Everything could fall apart.*

Manning tugged at the back of his hair, walking back and forth across his office. *There's no way I can let that happen . . . not now.* Manning picked up his phone, staring at the speed dialer. *The press are going to eat this up.*

Listening to the dial tone he punched in a local number. It only rang twice.

''At the tone leave a brief message,'' a rough male voice sounded, then one long, sharp beep.

''Bill Bishop will resign as NSA effective tomorrow at noon. You can count on this one.'' He hung up the receiver.

*The story will be in the news tomorrow morning . . . I can tell McEntire I changed my mind and called Bishop rather than waiting to tell him in person. I'll tell him Bishop was angry and he tried to get sympathy from the press. That idiot's not going to be able to back way from this one. I want Bishop gone for good!*

Manning stood in the center of the room, reveling in his triumph.

*This calls for a celebration.* Once more he unlocked the top door to the reenforced cabinet behind his desk. He removed a dark plastic vial. Opening it, he tapped a few small white chunks onto his desk and began cutting them with a razor blade.

# 8

Above the luxury yacht *Van Triumph*'s main deck, just behind the bridge, Carl Hawkens sat in what he considered his overseas office. When he wasn't in Washington lobbying congressmen, bribing congressional staffers or otherwise making certain the right people were taken care of, he used the space to assist Bandar in the purchasing and selling of foreign arms. They would buy whatever they could get including Russian-made T-72 tanks, commando-style hovercraft, high-explosive and cluster bombs, self-propelled artillery pieces, even MiG-29 jet fighters and Foxtrot-class submarines. Hawkens's favorite part was the sell. He enjoyed the bartering and the control it gave him.

Although Hawkens considered Bandar fairly brilliant in his approach to business, he knew the man needed someone like himself before and after money changed hands. It was like being a real estate broker. As long as both sides thought they were getting a good deal everything was fine.

The office didn't contain any windows or portholes, just a hardened steel door at the rear and a hatch on the floor which lead to the lower decks. In contrast to the *Van Triumph*'s other compartments, Hawkens's office was relatively simple. In his opinion it seemed better to appear conservative in business matters. After all this wasn't his home and it wasn't his intention to impress or intimidate the customers.

The front section of the office contained an oak desk; matching paneling lined the bottom half of the walls. Three brown leather chairs blended in well with the sandy beige carpet. Two bronze floor lamps lit the room softly. Large color prints of the *Van Triumph* cutting through the water or in various ports around the world decorated the walls. Located behind his chair, also on the wall, was a brass replica of the *Van Triumph* and above that a wooden captain's wheel.

Hidden inside the ship's hull was a miniature camcorder and microphone surveillance system. It was an easy way to keep track of the clients' demands and make sure there weren't any misunderstandings. Located on the edge of his desk was a Magnavox SATCOM telephone and fax machine linking him into the bridge's communication system. To his right an IBM computer sat with its monitor off.

Hawkens's computer proficiency maintained their inventory, customer orders and general accounting. He also kept a detailed record of his clients' personal lives: their full names, birth dates, the names of their wife or wives and of course their lovers. It was also nice to know how many children they had and even what they called their pets. He and Bandar used the information to add a personal touch or to negotiate terms if necessary.

Bandar had taught him the benefits of knowing customers' preferences. In their type of business it was always best to peel away the fabrications that shielded clients' huge egos. It was much easier to demand top market price for the goods they offered when customers' soft white underbellies were exposed.

"The sun is up. Has Denny landed?" Bandar burst into Hawkens's office.

"Yes. But there is a problem. His aircraft has been damaged."

"Damaged! That incompetent bastard. I told you I have a schedule to keep."

Hawkens swiveled around to face his hot-tempered business partner. "We've been in radio contact. His jet rolled off the runway during a storm. One of the gears could be damaged and the windshield is broken. It can all be repaired."

"I cannot run a business with this type of stupidity. He never should have landed if the weather was bad."

"I agree," Hawkens echoed.

"If he is caught it could jeopardize all my Vietnamese contacts. The entire operation could collapse." Bandar rubbed his face with his hands.

"That's unlikely. The weapons complex is so remote."

"I wish I could believe that, Carl. But you know better than I that the CIA is watching Vietnam. If I'm linked to chemical weapons my days are numbered." Bandar stopped. Placing his hands on his hips he drew closer. "Denny has no loyalty. If someone challenges him, he will talk. I want him dead."

Hawkens took a deep breath and let out a sigh. "I understand."

"And if the CIA should start asking questions, where will you be?" Bandar asked.

Hawkens kept his eyes centered on Bandar's. Refusing to look away, he let the silence build until it was almost unbearable. His face went red with anger. Finally he rose and said, "How much money have you made from the transactions I have set up for you?"

Bandar looked away, not answering.

"Not to mention how you have also benefited from other information I have supplied you with over the last twelve months. How much? Two million . . . three million dollars? And you question my loyalty?"

"Every man's loyalty is to himself," Bandar said, unimpressed by Hawkens's righteousness.

"That's right. And as long as you pay—and pay me well—I am loyal to you, Bandar. We are in this together, my friend." Carl smiled ruefully. Bandar, he knew, was right. In this business it was every man for himself.

"How long to repair the jet?" Bandar asked at last.

"I don't know. At least a couple of days. Tra's going to have to find a new windshield. I'm prepared to stay behind and set up a command center until Denny delivers the bombs. My gear is packed and ready."

Bandar was quiet, his mind racing. "I leave for North Korea within the hour. I have some unfinished business with General Sinchon. You fix this before I arrive there. Then contact me."

"By the time you dock in Nampo I will have the bombs secured and Denny will be dead," Hawkens promised. "I can assure you it will be taken care of."

"That would be best for all involved," Bandar said quietly before leaving the office.

Hawkens waited for the man's footsteps to fade, then let his guard down. *There isn't any future working for a paranoid,* he thought. *It's affecting his judgment. I really don't need him anymore, anyway. I have a gold mine with the orbital times and directions of US spy satellites traveling over Iran and North Korea. That information should add up to a cool five million.*

Hawkens smirked, remembering how he obtained the satellite data. It more or less fell in his lap. He was dating a young redhead who worked for D. Robert Sturdevant III, the senior Republican senator from Alabama. Besides being a conservative judge from the south, Sturdevant was the chairman of the Senate CIA Oversight Committee on covert operations. He and other members of the committee approved or disapproved operations and were therefore provided with all the military's reconnaissance and radar-imaging satellites. Sturdevant also had access to NSA ground base and mobile eavesdropping equipment, making him one of the most informed men on the Hill.

It was no accident Hawkens was dating the woman. It was to his good fortune that she liked to drink red wine and loved to talk, among other things. She willfully spilled her guts about every aspect of the senator's private life. He liked to drink gin mixed with Coke, no ice, even during working hours. The senator slept on the couch, hadn't had sex with his wife in three years, and was deathly afraid of his mother-in-law.

About twice a week, or more if his wife was out of town, Sturdevant dropped by the house of the young woman, who worked as a congressional page for a Virginia congressman. She was very attractive; Hawkens couldn't understand what she saw in the senator. The Sunday Washington *Post* listed what day or days the Senate CIA Oversight Committee planned to meet, so Hawkens simply waited for the senator to park his car behind her townhome in the alley, then picked the Lincoln's door lock and removed the senator's briefcase to photograph the documents. Occasionally, Sturdevant had enough gin-and-Cokes that he even left the doors unlocked.

The only problem was, where to sell the information. It wasn't something that could be advertised in the classified section of the New York *Times*.

Hawkens had made plenty of friends while working with the CIA. Though he had been fired from his position, he still managed to stay in touch with a few of them. Considering his new line of work, it proved to be resourceful. One of the agents unknowingly tipped him off to a fishing-rod salesman, Mr. Nee. He was actually an intelligence spy, Col. Kim Hwan. The fact that he was North Korean concerned Hawkens first, but after several weeks the two managed to trust each other enough for Hawkens to supply the North Korean with the orbital flight patterns of US spy satellites in exchange for money.

Carl Hawkens had enough Middle Eastern and Asian contacts, including several inside the Chinese embassy in Washington, D.C., that his own deals were beginning to flourish. Maybe it was time for Hawkens to step out from behind Bandar's shadow and become a free agent in the world of information and arms trading.

*First things first,* Carl told himself. *I have to take care of Denny.* Opening a small safe located behind one of the *Van Triumph*'s prints, Hawkens reached in and removed a Sig .45 automatic. Working the slide he made sure the pistol was loaded. Next he removed a long black metal cylinder and screwed it on the barrel of the gun. The suppressor, or silencer, made the weapon even more impressive. Gripping the handle he activated the laser site mounted in the trigger guard. He swept the red beam across the room, stopping it dead center on the captain's wheel.

*Bandar is right,* Hawkens thought. *Denny has become too careless. This will be his final flight into Vietnam.* Hawkens climbed down the hatch to the lower deck. It would only take him a few minutes to gather the rest of his gear.


PYONGYANG, NORTH KOREA

The Ministry of Defense building resembled a drab concrete blockhouse, square and plain. The designer, a former Soviet military architect specializing in hardened bunkers, had no intention of making the structure pleasant to the eye. It had been built for one purpose only: to centralize the command of North Korea's massive armed forces and keep them alive and secure when war broke out.

Constructed in the early 1990s, only three of the building's eight stories are located above ground. Each floor contains only six small windows and a single door is located on the main floor. The structure's unpainted gray exterior walls still show the rough ridges where plywood forms were used to hold the tons of concrete. Tests had shown the diamond-shaped roof and sloped outer walls would deflect 2,000-pound smart bombs launched from high altitude. The building's inner structure had been fortified with high-strength fibers including a mixture of advanced polymer composites such as S-glass, boron and carbon. Spectra, an ultrahigh molecular-weight polyethylene sold to the North by Allied Signal, had been used to tether the boron-and-steel rebar reinforcement together, making the building nearly impenetrable.

During normal operations the second floor, housing North Korea's most powerful men, was well protected with elite *spetsnaz* troops. The windows had also been reenforced with thick glass and steel to withstand the blast of a bomb or sniper's bullet. In the event of war, the bottom floors, located 150 feet beneath ground level, would be used as shelter, ensuring the command structure would remain intact. The second floor, or command floor as it was called, had been laid out in the form of a rough wagon wheel. The general chief of staff's main office was located in the center. Each of the military's six commanding generals controlled their branch of the military from corner offices. Other rooms were used for staff, communications equipment and personal effects.

Sinchon's office was located in the southwest corner. Unlike his counterparts, Sinchon had not decorated it with vain tributes to himself. Instead he had set it up to be functional. Two large fluorescent lights hung above his hardwood desk. Three chairs and metal file cabinets lined the wall to the left and the area behind him displayed a map of South Korea and Japan. The top of his desk contained a stack of transfer requests and a hot cup of tea. Sinchon sat staring at the tea and paperwork.

"General Sinchon," Colonel Kwang said, entering the office, "the general chief of staff is requesting your briefing now."

"Chin wants to see me now?" Sinchon raised an eyebrow. "Can't the bastard tell time? I'm not scheduled for another two hours."

"He is requesting to see you now, sir. Should I tell him—"

"You should tell him nothing." Sinchon lowered his head, hoping Kwang wouldn't see his face turn pale. *He knows . . . Zheng has betrayed me. I never should have trusted the Chinese.*

"Are you feeling well?" Kwang asked.

"I am feeling fine," Sinchon snapped. "Now leave me." The general gathered a few notes before taking two long swallows of tea. Each afternoon he was required to give his commanding officer, General Chief of Staff Myong Chin, a brief summary of North Korea's military readiness. It was one of the few responsibilities that hadn't been taken away. Removing a pistol from the top drawer, he placed it between his stomach and belt and buttoned his heavy wool uniform over it.

Sinchon took one last glance at his desk, making sure he hadn't forgotten anything. Then he walked down the long hallway toward Chin's elaborate chamber. He tried to concentrate on the rhythmic beat of his boots hitting the stone floor. *If Chin has learned of my plan why didn't he just have me arrested? Why must he always play games? Chin will use this to disgrace my military career and consolidate his power further. Or maybe, just maybe, it is nothing. I can trust Zheng and my plans weren't compromised. Or possibly . . .* Sinchon looked up and saw the door leading to Chin's office. He paused, knocked twice and entered.

"General Sinchon reporting," he said.

"Good morning, General." Chin didn't look up from his desk. "Sit."

"I prefer to stand," Sinchon said, walking closer.

"Of course . . . I forgot." This time Chin set his pen down and looked at the general.

"North Korean forces are prepared and ready, sir. The Artillery, Mechanized and Capital Defense Corps will complete a week of synchronized training by noon tomorrow. The navy and air forces are scheduled to conclude—"

"Stop. I am not interested in that now." Chin waved his hand through the air. "You are here for something much more important."

Sinchon's body stiffened.

"When is your next meeting with Ghaith Bandar?" Chin asked.

"Bandar?" Sinchon asked, taken off guard.

"Yes, Bandar," Chin said gruffly. "It is time you introduce me to your private and mysterious arms trader."

"Bandar . . . selects who he has contact with. He may not want to speak with you."

"If he wants to continue to do business with this government he doesn't have a choice." Chin rose to his feet. "In six months you will retire as leader of *spetsnaz*. I know the Western-style weapons you and your troops use come from Bandar. I will need access to the same weapons to keep the *spetsnaz* forces ready for battle. Now . . . when will you arrange it?"

*A simple meeting. That was all this was about.* Sinchon felt foolish for doubting his Chinese friend. Zheng hadn't betrayed him. This was just another step in Chin's methodical plan to dismantle Sinchon's control of North Korea's elite forces.

"I meet with Bandar in three days. His ship, *Van Triumph,* will dock in Nampo on Tuesday evening," Sinchon heard himself say coolly. "I am scheduled to leave with him for a five-day business trip. You may meet him when we return."

"A five-day trip?" Chin questioned.

"That is correct." The general spoke in a matter-of-fact tone: "Bandar only conducts business at sea. And he has promised me access to the West's latest night-vision equipment and miniaturized radios. Equipment my forces need."

*"Our* forces, General Sinchon." Chin forced a smile. "Very well. Speak to him about meeting with me while you are at sea. Then report back to me. Is that understood?"

"Yes, sir."

"Very good. Dismissed, General."

Sinchon turned away before his feelings betrayed him. Returning to his office, he closed the door. He could feel the sweat running down his back and the moisture under his armpits. Reaching for a bottle of scotch hidden in the bottom desk drawer, he took a long gulp. Five hours had passed since his meeting with Zheng and he was still alive. *Is it possible my plan will work?* He wasn't sure if he should feel fortunate or not.

Returning the pistol to the top drawer, Sinchon considered how easy it would have been to shoot Chin. *I must be patient and wait for the right time,* he warned himself as he closed the drawer. He took another drink from the bottle before replacing it too. Then, slouching in his chair, he sucked in long deep breaths trying to relax. It would be a few more minutes before he would be able to return to his daily routine.

NGHIA BINH PROVINCE, VIETNAM

Major Tra looked at two of his men and nodded for them to close the hangar doors.

"I repeat that your stupidity and ignorance has—"

Before Tra could say another word Denny reached out and grasped him by the front of his shirt. The American's powerful arms picked the small man off the ground, pinning him against the aluminum wall with a loud bang.

Bunten, the copilot, backed away from the scene, not sure what to expect and not wanting to be Denny's next victim.

"If you ever speak to me like that again, you little gook prick bastard, I'll kill you with my bare hands." Denny pressed Tra hard against his throat and chest, making it difficult for Tra to breathe. He could feel his face growing hot.

"Did you hear me? Or do I have to speak louder?" Denny shouted.

The stench of his foul breath caused the major to wince. But he didn't turn away, keeping his eyes fixed on the American. Denny's expression had turned wild. The powerful fury in his eyes suggested he could probably kill the major with one blow of his fist. Nonetheless, Tra didn't back down. He wasn't afraid of him. Death had been something Tra lived with his entire life and in his mind Denny's threats were nothing more than frightened words.

"Take your hands off me," Tra spoke slowly, forcing the words out of his constricted throat. He felt Denny release his grip, letting him slide down the wall. "I suggest you have some rice and a cup of tea, Mr. Denny. You have had a long flight, and it will take some time to replace your windshield."

"Damn right you're going to replace my windshield." Denny looked suddenly exhausted. "That's all you have is tea? Bunten, get over here and pour me a cup."

Tra reached into his front pocket and pulled out a pack of Camels. The plans had changed considerably. It would probably take him a couple of days to find and truck in a replacement windshield to the air base. Chances were even higher he would have to go to Thailand and that would make it twice that long.

"I will instruct my men you will be staying then." Tra took a deep breath and let it out slowly. He would have to tolerate the American that long. For $25,000 he could tolerate just about anybody for a few extra days. And maybe some day he would see the American dead.


OSAN AIR BASE, SOUTH KOREA

The interior of the twin-engine C-21A transport jet told its age. The eight-passenger VIP aircraft's cabin had worn brown carpet, scratched windows and smudge-covered beige paint. Built to transport high-level military and civilian personnel rapidly between locations, Duke figured the aircraft was pushing fifteen years.

James still preferred taking the jet over standard commercial flights. He didn't have to put up with the hassle of crowded airports, taxis or small talk. The downside was he occasionally had to share the flights with uppity military brass or congressmen coming back from fact-finding trips. If that were the case then Duke would just sit down, keep his mouth shut and read or pretend to sleep.

"Welcome aboard, sir," a sharp-looking Air Force first lieutenant, the copilot, said as Duke entered the jet. The aircraft's engines were at idle, making it hard to hear.

"Good morning," Duke shouted back. The aroma of brewing coffee mixed with sour vomit swirled around him.

"May I help you with that?" the lieutenant asked, reaching for Duke's baggage.

"You can stow this," James said, tossing the man an overstuffed duffle bag.

"And the briefcase?"

"No . . . I'll take care of it."

"Please take a seat then, sir, we'll be leaving in a few minutes. Assuming four and a half hours flying time, plus the time change. We should land at Hickam just before the sun sets—sooner if we catch a tail wind."

Duke took a seat and waited for the lieutenant to disappear behind the forward bulkhead. Placing his briefcase on the seat next to him, he unlocked and opened it. A plain 8½ by 11 brown paper envelope held a package wrapped in tight cellophane, through which Duke could see the words CLASSIFIED MATERIAL TOP SECRET printed across an inner white envelope. Peeling off the cellophane, he removed the contents.

*Shit . . . these are the best yet.* Duke held up a square color photo. It had been taken on a cloudy day after a recent snow. He couldn't tell for sure but it looked like late afternoon. The ground was white which helped contrast a number of large block-shaped concrete buildings. The right side of the photo included two cone-shaped water-cooling towers and in the background an elevated smokestack could clearly be seen.

Duke had seen many pictures of the Democratic People's Republic of Korea's nuclear facility outside of Yongbyon but never from this angle. James guessed the picture had been taken from a mile or so away to the north. It showed a viewpoint of the main reactor buildings that hadn't been observed before. Spy satellite photos were fine, but they could only image a target from the top. The CIA was in constant need of photos from ground level in order to get a clear understanding of just what North Korea was doing and to provide the military with the best targeting options.

Thumbing through several more photos, Duke stopped at one that showed a cluster of five large trees planted in a semicircle. The leaves were off, allowing him to see the bare ground. The light reflected off the snow in such a way it illuminated what looked like a shallow ditch abruptly ending at the side of a hill. He could also make out a slim row of large rocks above where the ditch ended. The rocks were only partly covered in snow and appeared to be in a neat row. Running along the ditch he could barely make out tire ruts under the snow. The ruts cut through the trees and ended at the side of the hill.

Duke paused to think but couldn't remember seeing anything like this in any of the KH-14 spy satellite photos he had studied in the past. Flipping the picture over he saw UNDERGROUND NUCLEAR REPROCESSING PLANT written sloppily in English.

James smiled. This is the place the CIA and International Atomic Energy Agency had been trying to find. Those bastards had done a damned good job of hiding it. If it hadn't been for the snow he doubted he could have made out the crude road leading into the hillside. The North Koreans had allowed the IAEA to inspect their above-ground reprocessing plant but it had long been believed they operated another one below ground. *Mark Collins is going to owe me for this one,* James thought, thinking of his friend at the CIA.

Placing the pictures back in his briefcase, Duke guessed the person who had actually taken the pictures was in the military or possibly a technical advisor of some kind. How else could he get a camera near the complex? Whoever he was the CIA had given him the cryptonym or code name of *Sirhak.*

Thinking of the name, James pondered the reason for the choice. *Sirhak* had been the name of a practical learning school used by a group of eighteenth-century Korean scholars. These scholars focused on finding solutions to Korea's pragmatic social and economic problems. *Obviously he's a reformer and had enough conviction to risk his life for change.*

Normally when the CIA received information of this nature it would be digitized and transmitted to the National Photo Interpretation Center before being passed on to the Pentagon. In this case, however, each batch of photos was being hand-carried, via military transport, to the CIA by a small group of individuals cleared for the operation, General James being the chosen one this time. *It's funny, the CIA doing business the old-fashioned way with all the high-tech computers and instant communications available. They're definitely going out of their way to maintain Sirhak's identity.*

Duke locked the briefcase and slid it under the seat ahead of him. Anything else about the operation was "need to know" and Duke didn't need to know anything more. Settling into the worn vinyl and cloth seat of the C-21A transport jet, he folded his arms looking out the window.

The sun was above the horizon and unlike the last few days the sky looked clear to the east. Duke could see steam rising from the buildings lining the runway and wondered if the temperature would get above freezing. He slid down the shade, covering half the window, then tilted his seat back. Four-and-a-half hours sitting in an airplane was going to be tedious.

Out the bottom half of the window he saw the South Korean landscape.

Modern buildings mixed in with run-down huts and one-room apartment complexes. It was a strange mix of old and new.

"Nice place to visit, wouldn't want to live here," James said under his breath as the C-21A transport jet lifted off the runway heading east.

James glanced at the pink and red clouds meeting the aircraft as she rose up in the air. Katie came to his mind. He slipped his sunglasses over his eyes, then closed them.

NGHIA BINH PROVINCE, VIETNAM

Maj. LeTrong Tra watched the last of his six men load into the back of a one-ton four-wheel-drive truck. He scanned the hangar before punching the button to lower the bulky overhead door. The interior grew dark as he turned to Lai Cai, one of his guards, standing in the back section of the hangar.

The man was large—nearly as tall as Denny but younger and in much better shape. His intense black eyes stood out in contrast to the green camouflage fatigues he wore. Agile movements indicated the AK-47 assault rifle he carried was just another extremity of his body. Two years ago Tra had seen Cai fight and kill four men during a dispute with heroin drug dealers. Weeks later Cai was attacked again, only this time left for dead. Members of the drug cartel had shot him six times and cut his tongue out, leaving it on the ground next to his bloodied face. It was intended as a message for other would-be warriors not to interfere with Vietnam's powerful drug trade. Tra found him before he bled to death. Cai owed his life to Tra and Tra knew he would do anything for him.

The major spoke in Vietnamese, making sure Denny couldn't hear him. "Never let them out of your sight. They must not be allowed to leave the hangar. If Denny gives you any trouble, tie him up but do not kill him. As for the other man, I don't care if he lives or not."

Cai grunted a response, nodding toward the pallet of chemical weapons.

"Keep the Americans away from them," Tra warned. He turned and spoke to Denny across the room: "My men and I will return as soon as we can. It may take some time to find what I need to repair your jet. I suggest you stay inside. There is more food and water in the lockers next to the radio." Major Tra picked up his duffle bag and started toward the door.

"You're leaving only one of your goons here?" Denny asked.

"Cai will keep an eye on you and the weapons."

"I can't believe you, Tra. What if someone comes? Do you think one man is going to do anything? I need more of an assurance than that."

Tra stopped, hearing the panic in Denny's tone for all its bluster. The last thing he needed was for Denny to go crazy on him and do something stupid. "You will be safe here. No one is scheduled to use this airstrip for another two weeks. I recommend you take the time to rest and repair your jet."

"I don't like this shit. I'm a pilot, not an arms expert." Denny pointed to the two pallets containing the chemical weapons. "What do I do with this?"

"Leave the casings alone. They are safe as long as you do not move them."

"Damn you, Tra. I expect you back here when it gets dark tomorrow," Denny barked. "Or I'll fly what's left of this plane out of here without your cargo. And you know what that means . . . no dollars for the gook."

"Cai has clear orders. If you try and move this plane before I return, he will kill you." Tra spoke over his shoulder, exiting the building into the darkness.

Bobby Denny walked around his jet, taking note of every detail. The yellowish glow of the hangar's gas lights made it difficult to see all the damage. The jet was dented in a few places, around the nose section and the leading section of the wings, but the aluminum skin wasn't cracked or pierced. The landing gear didn't appear too damaged, a few broken hydraulic lines, nothing significant. He could probably repair it himself. The more he walked around the aircraft the luckier he felt.

Now if Tra could find a replacement for his cockpit window he'd be set. Actually, Denny knew that could be a challenge. But he also knew Tra was resourceful and well connected with Vietnam's black market. The major would find one because he wanted his money. He turned to Craig Bunten who was standing near the front of the Learjet.

"One of us is going to have to be on lookout while the other sleeps." Denny nodded over at the guard standing next to the wall. "I don't trust Tra's man."

"I'll take first watch," Bunten offered.

"Damn right you will. You know how to use one of these?" Denny pulled a .45 automatic from beneath his shirt, blocking the Vietnamese guard's vision with his back.

"Not really. Guns kind of scare me."

"You pussy, Bunten. Never mind." Denny stuffed the gun back in his pants. "If there's trouble, just yell. Wake me midmorning."

"All right," Bunten nodded. "I think I'll monitor the radio for a while."

Denny strolled to the rear section of the hangar and crawled onto one of the lower bunks. He cocked the pistol, locked the safety and placed the pistol under the dirty yellow sheet covering the mattress. Curling into a tight ball to stay warm, he waited for sleep to come.

# 9

The Chinese embassy is located on Connecticut Avenue in the western part of Washington, D.C. At night the eight-story structure resembles most of the other office and hotel buildings in the area. Older red bricks cover the outer walls, with leafless shrubs and evergreen trees surrounding the lower half. Black cast-iron scrolled rails cover the bottom windows and doors, giving the structure a stockade look. Several large spotlights illuminating the exterior reveal air-conditioning units hanging from a number of the offices on the upper level. All, in short, it appears ordinary except for the red flag flying outside the entrance and the stone lions sitting astride the door.

Mark Collins slowed his silver Acura TL 2.5, steering it toward the circular street. To Collins, a CIA officer working undercover as a State Department diplomat, the building looked menacing and cold. His biased opinion arose from having been to the Chinese embassy on a half-dozen occasions. He couldn't think of a single time when he walked away feeling good about the conversations that took place there. The Chinese were tough negotiators. On diplomatic matters they played hard ball and didn't back down, even to the point of personal attacks. Mark made a conscious effort to stay above all of that. He had to admit, though, he respected the Chinese for their apparently strong convictions.

Collins parked his car several spaces away from the main entrance and checked his watch; he was three minutes early. *Well, at least I'm on time,* he thought, tugging at the collar of his heavy camel hair overcoat. A car drove past and he caught sight of a few snowflakes streaking through the glow of its headlights. The temperature had dropped during his twenty-minute drive. *That's all I need, snow on a midnight rendezvous with the Chinese.* Leaving a warm bed with his pregnant wife sleeping and his little girl tucked in for the night was irritating enough. He considered it the height of diplomatic arrogance for the Chinese to demand a meeting in the middle of the night and refuse to give a reason for calling it.

He still felt slightly uncomfortable with his new assignment although he'd been at it for seven months. Officially he worked for the State Department as special assistant to the secretary of state assigned to Far Eastern affairs. However, as with most matters in Washington, not everything was as it seemed. Collins did carry a State Department ID and maintained an office, along with the other special assistants, that he worked out of three days a week. He never missed an opportunity to show his face on the State Department cocktail circuit yet he avoided the press like the plague. All of this was part of his cover, a well-orchestrated plan by the CIA to let various countries become comfortable with a diplomat before they were transferred to their American embassy overseas.

Collins considered it a solid plan, except for the part about going overseas. He and his wife Christine had a two-year-old at home and they were expecting their second child in a month. He had always heard a career in the CIA was tough on marriages, now he knew why. Exiting the car, he scanned the sky. Low gray clouds reflected Washington's city lights.

Personally, Collins liked working for the CIA. He had been with them for six years. Before joining he received a commission from the army and had risen to the rank of major. After his promotion he worked as a liaison for the army, helping the CIA to understand the special needs of the military. The CIA liked his work and asked him to join as an analyst at the age of thirty-three. A year-and-a-half later he transferred to the Directorate of Operations, or DO. It was a perfect fit. Collins's unique background, combined with his understanding of the CIA's analytical side, made him perfect for the position.

In the last three years he had completed two assignments in the Middle East—one of which was a covert operation in Iran where he nearly got his butt shot off. He was now back in the United States using his experience to help infiltrate the Chinese diplomatic organization. It wasn't as exciting as the Middle East but Collins didn't consider himself the James Bond type anyway.

"Here goes nothing," Collins muttered, clutching his briefcase as he walked up the sidewalk. A blast of cold air whipped around him at the embassy's unprotected front door. A short Chinese man dressed in a black suit with a white shirt appeared suddenly to greet him.

"Mark Collins . . . I'm with the State Department," he said, reaching for his ID.

"It not necessary. Mr. Phon . . . he expect you. Please follow."

Collins entered and was led down a long, poorly lit hallway lined with watercolor and oil paintings of various Chinese landscapes. After making a right and left turn, and passing several other doorways, he followed the man into a small room with an oak table and two chairs. The walls, painted white, were barren. Collins unbuttoned his overcoat and looked around. He had never been in this room before.

"Mr. Phon, he be with you in a minute. Please . . . take seat."

"Thanks." Collins placed his briefcase on the table and took a seat facing the door. The man left the room, bowing graciously.

"Honey . . . it's for you," Sally Bishop said, rolling over. She pushed the hold button and set the phone down.

Bill Bishop stepped out of the couple's bedroom shower, wrapping a towel around his waist. The towel clung tightly to his athletic body. He played tennis at least three nights a week with Philip R. Radford, the secretary of defense, and maintained a regimented workout routine. Sitting on the edge of the bed he dried his hair with a hand towel. "Who is it?" Bishop asked, noticing the call was on his private line.

"They didn't say and I didn't ask." Sally pointed to their alarm clock; it showed 11:23 P.M. "I don't feel well and I want to go to bed."

"I'll make it fast." He tapped the hold button. "Bishop here."

"Yes, Mr. Bishop, this is Marie Esterel with the Washington *Post*. ABC and CNN are running separate reports that you plan to resign effective noon tomorrow. Do you care to comment?"

"What?" Bishop asked. "Where did you get that information?"

"I'm just repeating what the networks are broadcasting. Is it true? Do you plan to resign?"

Bishop took the receiver away from his ear. He couldn't think of anything to say. As a reporter he knew Marie Esterel was well connected inside the beltway, and as far as journalists went, Bishop respected her. Esterel's columns in the *Post* were generally honest; she blasted liberals as well as conservatives. His gut told him something was wrong.

"Bill, what is it?" Sally asked after a few moments of silence. She sat up in bed next to him.

"It's okay," Bishop said to his wife. "Everything is all right . . . Ms. Esterel, I don't have any comment at this time. You'll have to wait until tomorrow. Good night." He hung up the phone.

"Bill, talk to me. What's happened?"

Bishop turned around to see his wife's worried face. Her blue eyes were glassy and wide, her body stiff with tension. Sally was under a doctor's care for heart trouble.

"Nothing important. It's all right, honey," Bishop said calmly, reaching over to turn the answering machine on. He took her shaking hand in his. "It was just some stupid reporter. That's all. Everything is all right."

"There's always something happening." Sally fell gently back on the pillow, her light blonde hair surrounding her pale face. "Bill . . . I'm short of breath. Get my medicine and a glass of water."

"Try to relax, Sal." Bishop scurried off to the bathroom, his mind forgetting about his job.

## HICKAM AIR BASE, HAWAII

Duke James fought off the urge to sleep as the Air Force staff car he was riding in turned left, heading toward the main runway. A hydraulic leak in the C-21A's landing gear had turned his one-hour layover in Hawaii into a three-hour delay. He had used the extra time to shower, get some hot food and call his wife. All that in between briefings with senior commanders at PACAF.

The car headed onto the taxiway toward his waiting jet. He looked out the window at the bright floodlights surrounding the base's perimeter and casting long shadows across the pavement. Duke recognized a number of different aircraft parked on the tarmac including a C-5B and two KC-10 tankers. Letting his eyes close, he began to dream about his wife and kids back in Virginia. They were trimming the Christmas tree and his youngest son, Sean, was running down the hall . . .

"General James."

"Huh?" Duke straightened up.

"I'm sorry to disturb you, sir. Your plane is waiting." The driver, a young pudgy-faced lieutenant, was slowing the car to a stop.

"Thank you, Lieutenant." James blinked hard. The sound of jet engines could easily be heard reverberating against the windows. Through the windshield he caught sight of the C-21A transport jet. The plane's round windows and white exterior became visible with each wink of the wingtip navigational lights.

Duke hoped he didn't look as bad as he felt. Although he kept his forty-four-year-old body in shape with daily runs and workouts, the recently hectic flight schedules made him feel like he was a hundred years old. A quick glance at his reflection in the rear window confirmed his suspicions. His hazel gray eyes were bloodshot and his face, normally tan, looked pale and gaunt. Even his short salt-and-pepper hair was uncombed. *Oh well, at least I'm clean.*

"Let me help you, sir," the lieutenant said, opening the car's rear passenger-side door. The combination of dome light and cool damp air brought James back to life.

"That's all right, I've got it." Duke grabbed his duffle bag and briefcase. "Thanks for the ride."

"You're welcome, General. Have a good flight."

*Yeah, right . . . as soon as I'm home it'll be a good flight,* Duke thought, swinging his six-foot frame out of the car. He could feel the heat radiating off the left engine of the jet as he climbed up the stairs into the main cabin.

"General James, welcome aboard, sir. I'm Captain Norwood, the co-pilot."

"New crew, huh?"

"Yes, sir. Take any seat you'd like and we'll be underway in a minute or two. May I get you some coffee?"

"No, thanks." Duke watched a member of the ground crew push up the ladder door. The copilot locked it in place. Several minutes later they were airborne again.

MANILA, PHILIPPINES

The Manila Diamond Hotel, built on the western edge of downtown Manila overlooking the bay, towered over the city like a symbol of Western indulgence. The twenty-three-story high-rise luxury hotel had been built in stark contrast to the simple one- and two-bedroom wooden dwellings surrounding it. The local people tolerated it only because of the jobs it provided and the promise of Philippine businessmen making contact with Western investors. By Western standards the rooms were simple. A double bed, a table with two chairs, television and bathroom.

Carl Hawkens could care less about the local people. He liked the Manila Diamond for his own personal reasons. It had all the creature comforts he could ask for: fine dining, a great wine list, and most of all, women. He could purchase a night's entertainment for under a hundred dollars and have enough money left over to pay for her cab fare the next morning.

The hotel was also beneficial because it was situated where Hawkens could establish radio contact with Vietnam. He requested a room on the eighth floor, on the southwestern side overlooking the ocean. From these windows there was an unobstructed view of the beach and the horizon.

Hawkens checked his watch. He was due to contact Denny in three minutes. Resting on the table in the corner of the room were several heavy black nylon duffle bags concealing a telephone scrambler, an eavesdropper nullifier, and a long-range radio. Hawkens made the final adjustments on the SC225PXT wireless telephone. The small gray box weighed less than six pounds and resembled a standard portable shortwave radio. He could conduct secure communications from over 7,000 miles away, using a computer chip to hop frequencies over twelve different channels.

There would only be a five-minute window in which to make radio contact. If Hawkens missed that window he would have to wait another twelve hours. Plugging in the antenna, he flipped the TEST button on. He then turned the frequency range to 14.5 Mhz and listened to the radio crackle. Electricity began to flow through its circuits, warming them.

Several sharp knocks on Hawkens's door interrupted his concentration.

"Room service." The voice was female and heavily accented.

*I don't have time for this.* Hawkens quickly tossed the bedspread over his equipment. Grabbing his .45 automatic he tucked it into his belt behind him before opening the door slowly. A large Filipino woman was holding a tray of food and a bottle of red wine. She looked at him smiling.

"Mr. Hawkens . . . room eight two seven. I have—"

"I know what I ordered." Hawkens took the tray and slammed the door closed. He set the tray on the bed and returned to the radio, making sure each of the transmit lights was green.

"All right, Denny, let's see if your head is out of your ass." As the second hand hit twelve on his wristwatch he keyed the mike: "Rambo . . . this is Rocky. Do you copy?" The radio hissed and popped. He adjusted the audio output and noise suppression buttons, trying to eliminate the distortion.

Thirty seconds passed without any reply. Hawkens repeated the call, this time boosting the power level to twenty-eight watts.

"Rambo . . . this is Rocky. Do you copy?"

*"Yeah, I copy . . . Rambo here."*

"I've talked with Major Tra. You'll have your windshield in twenty-four hours."

*"I'm sick and tired of waiting for our gook friend to return, Hawkens. I want to get out of this hell hole."*

"Have you loaded the goods?" Hawkens asked.

*"Hell, no . . . they're still sitting in the hangar, right in front of me. Tra's secur . . . grunt won't . . . near them."*

"Say again. You're breaking up."

*"I can't get . . . them. Get me a new fucking windshield . . . wind . . . shields. So I can get out of here."*

"I'm signing off. Contact me before you take off."

*"Yeah, I'll do that. You just make sure the major doesn't screw things up again. I don't want to be here any longer than I have to—and tell your boss I want more money for this shit. Rambo out."*

Hawkens turned the radio off. A flood of anger came over him. He threw the hard plastic mike against the wall in frustration, denting the plaster. "You'll get a new windshield, Mr. Denny. It will be the last thing you get from me or anyone else."

He poured himself a glass of wine and stared out the window to the west.

WASHINGTON, D.C.

Mark Collins sat picking at a loose thread on his suit jacket. *Why do they always make me wait?* He wanted to get up and walk around the room to see if he could find where they had bugged it. Instead Mark remained seated, thinking maybe that wasn't such a good idea. The room most likely had been wired for sound and probably for video too. From where he sat, though, he couldn't see where they had hidden the video camera.

Collins was an effective agent because of his average-American looks and the fact that he didn't intimidate anyone. His natural mannerisms were along the lines of a docile schoolteacher—practiced and sincere, a trait the Chinese preferred. His light brown hair was thinning a little but it was cut short and accented his round boyish face. He stood not quite five feet nine inches tall and like most men his age had grown a small spare tire around his middle. If the Chinese suspected anything, they certainly wouldn't deal with him.

Mark folded his arms. He stared up at the square white light hanging from the ceiling, trying to fight off the nervous feeling bubbling inside him. He had been sitting in the empty room for fifteen minutes. That wasn't a very long time under normal circumstances but in the middle of the night at the Chinese embassy he had to admit it made him uneasy.

He took a deep breath. The place smelled old and musty. He doubted if they ever opened a window.

"Mr. Collins . . . thank you for coming on short notice," Lin Phon, the Chinese ambassador, said in a hushed tone.

Collins stood, half startled. The thin medium-built man closed the door behind him. An older gentleman with white hair and smooth skin, Lin Phon wore a gray business suit with a black shirt open at the collar. Collins bowed slightly and extended a hand.

Phon returned the greeting, then took a seat at the opposite end of the table and opened a file he had brought in with him, not looking at Collins.

This wasn't Collins's first meeting with the Chinese ambassador. In his opinion Phon was strange, to put it mildly. He rarely smiled and although his English was fair he usually spoke in short soft sentences which forced everyone in the room to listen intently. He wore half-moon-shaped reading glasses that rested on the end of his nose, and sipped hot tea constantly. The State Department's intelligence files reported that before becoming a diplomat Phon had worked his way to the upper levels of China's elite intelligence corps. Over the last ten years he had been assigned to such places as London, Paris and Hong Kong. Phon had a deep and unique understanding of international politics, particularly the politics of economics. He seemed most concerned with how the rest of the world viewed China and how it could affect his country's economic future.

Finally Phon removed a single photograph. He handed it to Collins, then stood and began to pace the floor behind the table.

"Do you know these men?" Phon asked.

Mark studied the photo for a few seconds. It was an eight-by-ten color picture of two men standing on what looked like the bow of a ship. The photo was grainy, meaning it had been taken with a long-range lens at maximum distance. One of the men looked to be Korean. He had a full round face with shadowy eyes and short graying hair. The man was wearing a flower-patterned shirt and khaki pants with a pistol in a black holster on his right side. The other man appeared to be much taller. He had short black hair and a thin mustache. He was well dressed in a dark blue suit jacket covering a collarless shirt. His eyes were covered by sunglasses. It looked as if the two men were talking.

"Sorry . . . can't say that I do," Collins lied. He tried to keep his expression the same, although his insides were jumping. The taller man was Ghaith Bandar, one of the largest and most powerful arms traffickers in the world. Collins's mind raced. He had seen only two other pictures of Bandar and they weren't nearly as clear. *What is Bandar doing with a Korean?* Collins wondered. He normally just prowls the Middle East selling surplus Russian and Chinese weapons. Having him involved with Koreans wasn't good news.

"This picture was taken three years ago. They are traveling onboard the luxury yacht *Van Triumph.* It sailed off the North Korean coast. One of our patrol boats was able to get this shot with a long-range camera."

Collins nodded, waiting to see where the ambassador was leading. He knew *Van Triumph* was Bandar's yacht and he used it as his base of operations, making it nearly impossible to track him.

"The man in the flowered shirt is Gen. Han Sinchon. He is currently the supreme commander of the North's 820th Armored Corps and head of their *spetsnaz* operations." Phon wasn't speaking in his usual soft tone. His words were clear and crisp.

"I'm sorry, Mr. Ambassador, I don't understand."

"Sinchon is one of the most decorated and feared men in the North Korean armed forces. He has nearly a million loyal soldiers under his command, including every artillery tube and tank in the country as well as their elite commandos." Phon stopped pacing at the end of the table. "Sinchon has not only trained but commands the respect of the North's senior army officers. He has loyal connections inside the Navy and the government. He has many political allies. This general has been called the second most powerful man in North Korea. Are you sure you have not heard of him?''

Collins looked at the picture one more time before glancing back at the Chinese ambassador and shaking his head no. He had read a couple of CIA and State Department briefings on Sinchon but off the top of his head he couldn't recall anything outstanding about him. He also knew the CIA's data base on North Korean Army officers was sketchy at best.

''The man standing next to him is Ghaith Bandar. He is an international arms trader. The two are close business associates.''

''What does this have to do with the United States?'' Collins asked, giving his best perplexed look.

''Yesterday . . . General Sinchon contacted one of our government officials in Pyongyang. He and several other Army officers are concerned—*very* concerned—about the new leadership in place in their country. They fear there may be war on the peninsula, possibly within a year if a change is not brought about.'' Phon placed both hands on the back of his chair, leaning forward.

''The United States shares that concern. When Kim Jong Il died it left a power vacuum . . . one that has not been filled. Our position has always been—''

''Let me finish, please,'' Phon stated. ''General Sinchon is planning a coup. Within the next few days. Maybe a week.''

''A coup?'' Collins sat up in his chair, not having to feign surprise this time.

''That is correct,'' Phon said in a muted tone, his eyes growing solid and firm.

Collins shook his head as the Chinese ambassador's words slowly sank in.

''General Sinchon is taking a great risk by coming to us with this information,'' Phon continued. ''If any of this leaks, he will be executed without question.''

''So what do you want from the United States?'' Collins pulled a yellow note pad from his briefcase and began to scribble notes.

''Before the coup . . . General Sinchon wants to meet with a member of the South Korean government and a representative of the United States government. His demands are simple. The United States *must* ensure the South will not attack North Korea during the coup. He is expecting President McEntire to support his new government after the coup is complete.''

Collins swallowed hard as he jotted down several more sentences on his note pad.

''When does this General Sinchon want to meet with us? How can something like this be arranged?'' Collins's pencil was poised over the pad ready to write.

Phon walked around to where Collins was seated. He reached down and ripped off the top page of the notepad. ''If you can't remember what I've just told you, then I suggest you find another occupation.''

Collins forced back a smile. *Well, the cover is working, anyway.* He watched the Chinese ambassador walk back to the head of the table.

''Some time in the next few days General Sinchon will contact our government again. At that time he will inform us of the exact day and time of the meeting. I will contact you at State Department.''

''That's not going to work, Phon, and you should know it. I can't report back to Secretary Weber with this limited information, much less go to the president with a formal recommendation. I need some details . . . some sort of background on this General Sinchon. Sketchy information about something as important as this isn't going to cut it.'' Collins folded his hands, placing them on his lap. Past experience told him he could push Phon, but only so far. He watched the Chinese ambassador look up at the ceiling, then back at him.

Phon picked up the file containing the pictures and tossed it across the table at Collins. ''I will be in touch with you when I have further details.'' Phon looked at Collins, his stare cold and icy.

''I understand,'' Collins replied, happy to have the file tucked away in his briefcase.


## C-21A TRANSPORT JET, PACIFIC OCEAN

''General James. I hate to wake you, sir,'' the copilot said softly.

''I'm not asleep,'' James yawned.

''Chairman of the Joint Chiefs . . . General Chaniff is on the line, sir. He wishes to speak with you.'' The copilot handed him a portable SATCOM phone before ducking back into the flight deck to give Duke some privacy.

*Chaniff,* Duke thought. *Why does the chairman of the Joint Chiefs want to talk with me?* Duke checked his watch. East Coast time was a few minutes past two in the morning.

Duke paused before getting on the line. *This can't be good.* Since Duke reported to Bill Bishop, the national security advisor, he only talked with Chaniff during his briefings or if the chairman needed to clarify one of his intelligence briefings. The only other times were when Chaniff needed to borrow Duke's saltwater tackle to take some high-profile congressman striper fishing in the bay.

"This is James," Duke said at last.

"Duke . . . Chaniff here."

"Hello, Chairman."

"James . . . where are you?"

"A couple of hours out of Hickam, sir, heading east. I'm on my way back to Washington now."

"I've read your preliminary report on the Korea suicide bomber. I want a complete briefing when you return. Do you have the package?"

"Yes, sir."

"Good. Have you talked with Bill Bishop in the last twelve hours?"

"Not personally. We've been communicating like every one else these days . . . by fax."

"What did he tell you?"

*Strange question.* "He instructed me to brief Collins and Staffer at the CIA the second I land. Then he requested I start working on a new North Korean threat scenario now that we know they're still using a tunnel system to spy on us."

"That's it?"

"Well, he did tell me to get some rest. Other than that, nothing unusual. Is something wrong?"

"There've been some rumblings coming out of the press the last few hours. From what I've been able to pick up, the president's asking for Bishop's resignation. You know as well as I do the two of them haven't been getting along lately. I just thought you might want to know before it hits every newspaper in the country tomorrow morning."

"Yeah," Duke replied, scratching his head. "Have you talked with him?"

"No. This all came out late this evening. I thought I should wait until tomorrow . . . when things settle down. You may want to see him after you brief Collins." Chaniff's voice sounded distant and monotone.

Duke let out a long sigh. "What's Manning got to do with this?"

"He's in the middle of it, I'm sure. Manning's never liked the way Bishop spoke his mind. To be honest, I think it bothered him that the two of them had been friends for so long."

"Well, I can't do much from up here. But thanks for the heads up. I'll make sure I see Bish when I land."

"Let me know if there's anything I can do."

Duke locked the receiver into place, setting the phone on the seat next to him. He leaned back resting his head on the fuselage window. *Manning's done it,* Duke's gut told him. *He's managed to push Bill from the cabinet.*

James had watched Manning manipulate people and situations to his benefit for the last six months. No matter who it was, if they wanted to get access to the president, Manning always blocked them. Everything went through Manning and it drove Bishop crazy. In more than one instance Bishop had given Manning a recommendation to be given to the president and Manning changed it before passing it on. The president may be elected by the people but when he appoints a chief of staff that person, as James was discovering, could literally take control of his life.

Duke stared out the window at the blackness. In the distance he could see a flash of lightning. The little jet banked to the right and he heard the engines spool up. The pilot was maneuvering around long stretches of thunder clouds to the southeast.

"You'd better buckle up, sir. There's a large bank of storms ahead of us. It's going to be bumpy," the copilot said as he took the phone back to the flight deck.

"Yeah . . . it's going to get bumpy all right," Duke said, not taking his eyes away from the darkness.


WASHINGTON, D.C.


Collins followed the ambassador down the hallway. As he exited the building into the cold night the air stung his face. He pushed up the collar on his coat and walked to his car.

There was no way Collins would be returning home tonight. His family would have to wait and he hoped his wife would understand. Picking up his car phone, a Motorola Secureline 521 cryptographic portable system, Collins switched the operating mode from CLEAR, normal speech, to PROTECTED for fully secure voice communications. The third mode, PROTECTED DATA, allowed him to send or receive sensitive computer transmissions through the modem on his notebook computer.

Waiting for the LED light located on top of the receiver to flash green, signaling the system was operating in the PROTECTED mode, Collins punched *#214, the private home number of the deputy director for intelligence at the CIA. The phone rang twice before Douglas Brooks picked it up.

"Brooks here," the director said groggily.

"Douglas . . . this is Collins."

"Damn it's late. I didn't think you'd ever call."

"Listen, I just finished my meeting with Phon. You were right. He wanted to talk about North Korea." Collins started the motor and headed for the beltway.

"Where the hell are you?"

"I'm heading back to Langley. I've got some work to do," Collins remarked.

"Do I need to meet you down there or can it wait?" Brooks yawned into the phone, hoping he'd be able to get back to sleep.

"It can wait."

"Okay . . . fine. See you in the morning."

Collins pushed the END and CLEAR buttons and tapped the speed dialer for home, leaving a message on the machine that once again he would be away. Then he dialed Uncle Bruno's all-night Italian eatery. The commercials promised they delivered all night, any night, anywhere, and had the best pizza this side of Chicago. He ordered a medium deep-dish with the works and extra cheese.

# 10

Allan Manning stood several feet away from the president at his desk, next to the darkened window. He could hear the tapping of the raindrops striking the four-inch bulletproof glass. With his arms folded and face locked in a stern glare he ignored the cold draft coming from the window.

"I deserve better than this," Bill Bishop was saying.

"Bill . . . stop," President McEntire said. "I'm sorry. I didn't mean for it to happen like this." The president was wearing pajamas under a forest green robe with the presidential seal embroidered on the lapel.

Bill Bishop sucked in a long breath, looking down at the dark blue carpet. "Louis, I know we don't see eye to eye on *every* foreign policy issue. But I have always strived to provide you with an efficient system to foresee and prevent any disasters. Planning has been—"

"This doesn't have anything to do with planning," Manning cut in. "This has to do with loyalty."

"I've always been loyal to you, Louis. For God's sake, this can't be about not trusting me or my loyalty."

"It's my job to know who is and isn't loyal to the president, Mr. Bishop," Manning stated flatly.

"I should have known you were behind this, Manning." Bishop turned toward the chief of staff.

"Now that's enough!" McEntire shouted. He looked at Bishop. "Bill, this is one of the reasons. I can't have two of my key advisors constantly at each other's throats. Right now I have to do what's best for this administration."

"And I can't have someone with their personal agenda interfering with the decisions of this administration," Manning added.

"Is this your final decision then?" Bishop asked. "Do you at least have someone lined up to take my place?"

"That's certainly not for you to worry about, Mr. Bishop," Manning answered. "But if events come up overseas, we'll respond with measured judgment and timely decisions. This may come as a shock to you but you're not the only foreign policy expert in this town."

"I know this is hard, Bill," McEntire said. "I hope you know it's just as hard for me. Allan and I have discussed . . . it probably would be best for you to hand in your resignation by noon today.''

Bishop stood waiting for McEntire's eyes to meet his, then turned and walked away without saying a word.

''I still can't believe that Bill leaked information to the media,'' McEntire sighed, standing.

''He's guilty as sin. That's why he's squalling so hard.'' Manning checked his watch. ''I've rescheduled your daily intelligence briefing. It's at eight-thirty.''

''Thanks. I'm going to take a shower and get some breakfast.''

''I'll see you in an hour, sir.'' Manning watched the president listlessly exit the Oval Office. He couldn't help but think the man was either incredibly trusting or incredibly stupid.


PYONGYANG, NORTH KOREA

''Slow down! Turn left here,'' Gen. Han Sinchon ordered from the back seat of his private staff car. Glancing at the crude handwritten map, he watched the headlights of the car sweep across the wet blacktop.

Night had fallen and the northern sections of the city appeared calm and quiet. Yellow-green gaslights burned on each corner, allowing Sinchon to read the names of each road, at least the ones that were marked. They had passed only a few cars and bicycles and there weren't any pedestrians walking along the sidewalks. The general understood why Chengji Zheng, the Chinese attaché to North Korea, liked this section of the city. Without any effort a man could easily disappear into one of the hundreds of apartment buildings lining the constricted streets. Various shops were also on every block and several were still open.

''Okay, slow down. I don't want to miss it. Pay attention, I can't waste time.'' Sinchon looked again at his watch.

Colonel Kwang slowed the car and headed down a narrow alley lined with tenants' piled garbage. Most of the windows in the four- and five-story buildings were dark.

''You will see an open garage door to the right. It will be the only one on this block. Enter it and stop the car.''

''Yes, General.''

The realization of what he had done obsessed Sinchon. He was sure Chengji Zheng had notified his country about his planned coup. *China's leaders have made a decision and I will know in a matter of seconds if they will support me. I never thought of dying in a dark alley among the garbage* . . .

The car slowed. Sinchon twisted his head around, half expecting to see an armored military truck overtake his staff car and spray it with bullets. Everything was quiet; they seemed to be alone in the alley. He watched as his aide pulled the car into the garage and stopped.

"Turn the engine off . . . wait here."

Following the instructions he had received from Zheng, Sinchon walked up a short flight of stairs and opened the door at the top. He found himself at the entrance to a long unlit hallway. He waited for his eyes to adjust to the darkness before proceeding.

At the end of the hallway he could make out another door. This one, however, was made of heavy wood and had several locks on it. If the door was unlocked he was to enter knowing Chengji Zheng was inside.

Turning the handle slowly, Sinchon heard the heavy steel locks snap twice. The door opened to the smell of garlic and onions—a kitchen? Sinchon grabbed the grip of his pistol but didn't remove it. The room was sparsely furnished and appeared to be empty. Slowly, placing one foot in front of the other, he moved his stout body to an entryway toward the back of the room. As he moved he noticed several dark bottles, probably alcohol, on a nearby table.


ANDREWS AIR FORCE BASE

"General James, we just received word that a White House staff car is waiting for you," the second officer, an Air Force lieutenant, said from the cockpit.

"Great," James said, waiting for the C-21A transport to swing around and park. He hadn't been on the ground for two minutes and the White House was already calling for him. "Did they say who sent it?"

"No, sir."

Duke used his fingertips to comb through his hair. Seeing Katie and his kids was going to have to wait. He could only guess something was up over Bishop's resignation. *Maybe I'm next.*

The jet came to a stop several hundred feet from the rear of the plain-looking VIP terminal. The pilot locked the brakes and turned the engine off. Duke waited for the sound to die down before unbuckling, grabbing his briefcase and flight bag. The door came open, filling the interior with fresh air. It felt good. James stepped outside as a dark blue Chevy Lumina pulled up next to him.

"Hello, General James," the duty officer said.

Duke didn't respond. He followed the man.

## THE WHITE HOUSE

It was midmorning and Allan Manning was between meetings when he reached his private office. Coming off his fax was the third confidential and "eyes only" State Department memo of the day. He could barely believe his good fortune. In the last twenty-four hours he had gotten rid of his number-one enemy and now a North Korean general was going to attempt a coup against the government.

He couldn't have asked for any better luck. Now the president would have to rely on him for formal national security advice as well as his daily agenda. McEntire didn't have anyone else to turn to—except maybe his milquetoast Secretary of State Weber.

Manning sat down, taking note of the time. At the president's request he had called a national security briefing which had begun ten minutes ago in the chief executive's private study. Manning had intentionally avoided showing up on time. He wanted the president and his secretaries of state and defense to have a few minutes alone. With Bishop's resignation fresh in everyone's mind he didn't want the other cabinet members to accuse him of dominating all the president's time.

Besides, he needed a little pick-me-up. It had been a long night and a little snort of confidence would help him through the next few hours.

"Mr. Manning, President McEntire would like to see you in his study, sir. He is requesting—"

"Yeah, I know what he wants," Manning muttered, hitting the intercom button and cutting off his personal secretary Lindsey Kay. *He wants to talk about this North Korean coup. The idiot is all flustered and needs me to hold his hand.*

Manning inhaled a single line of coke from the top of his desk before making his way to the president's private study located just off the Oval Office.

As Manning entered the room he saw McEntire behind his desk chewing on an unlit cigar and talking on the phone. The president was trying to explain his position on one of a dozen different budget matters, probably to some senator or congressman. His sleeves were rolled up, his tie loose around his neck. The sight of the president on the phone made Allan angry but he quickly calmed himself. *I have to remember to be a realist on some issues. I can't control all the incoming calls and keep him from picking up the phone and dialing one of his buddies in Congress. At least not yet anyway.*

Across from McEntire sat the secretary of state, Irving B. Weber, and

Philip R. Radford, the secretary of defense. Standing in the doorway, Manning tried to sum up the situation. If things were taking their natural course the president was trying to get his two advisors to agree on a common direction regarding North Korea.

Smirking to himself, Manning knew Weber and Radford hadn't agreed with one another on any issue in the last three years. It was one of the main reasons Manning had become so influential. Weber rarely took a stance on any foreign policy issue that might anger the allies—particularly Russia, China or Japan. Members of Congress openly criticized him for not protecting US interests and for the fact that his only foreign policy experience was during the Bush administration as a trade representative. Manning considered Weber harmless, allowing him more access to the president, probably, more than anyone else.

Philip Radford, however, was a different story. Physically Radford was powerful at over 200 pounds. As secretary of defense, Radford had developed a reputation for being tough-minded, fair and candid. He had commanded a navy cruiser during the Vietnam war and retired from the military with the rank of rear admiral. Manning considered Radford a threat to his authority and sided with him only on rare occasions. He knew the president had a great deal of respect for Radford so he made it a point to avoid open debate and only challenged Radford's positions in private. The man didn't hold a candle to the problems Bishop caused, though, and it was easy enough for Manning to keep Radford from seeing the president any time he wanted.

*I better be very careful this morning and not offend anyone. I don't want them guessing I had anything to do with Bishop.*

Manning stepped deeper into the room, then stopped. Seated next to the wall just out of his initial view was Duke James. The Air Force general was dressed in his blues with a sweater, two white stars atop each broad shoulder.

"What are you doing here?" Manning asked before he could stop himself.

"I invited him," Radford answered mockingly. "That okay?"

"I called this meeting," Manning protested. "Just wanted to get things straight." He continued to look at James, who seemed to be staring right back. He moved toward the rear of the study. *You shouldn't have come here, James. You're out of your league in Washington.*

PYONGYANG, NORTH KOREA

The silhouette of Chengji Zheng suddenly emerged from a back room in the tiny apartment.

"Hello, General."

"Did you deliver my message?" Sinchon asked.

"Yes, I did," Zheng answered, pouring himself a drink. "Do you care for some?" He held up a bottle of American whiskey.

Sinchon shook his head.

"You are sure you do not want to drink with me? You should celebrate you are still alive and that you have loyal friends such as myself."

"Did your government agree with my request?" Sinchon asked hopefully.

"My government shares your concern, Han. Your General Chief of Staff Myong Chin is a dangerous man. You are correct to stop him." Zheng swirled the brown liquor in his glass and took a long sip. "Your message has been passed onto the Americans," Zheng smiled, showing his crooked teeth. "We wait for their answer."

"Waiting is a game for the cowardly," Sinchon snarled. "Each minute I delay brings me closer to possible defeat. Tell the Americans this, I will meet them on Langau Island three days from now."

"Langau Island? There is nothing—"

"Precisely . . . nothing but an abandoned fishing village and airstrip."

"I don't . . . how will you get there without anyone knowing?"

"It is best for both of us if you do not know the details. I will arrive after dark and leave before sunrise. I expect to meet with no more than two Americans and one South Korean military leader." Sinchon felt his mouth going dry. "I will be unarmed and prepared to give full details of my plan."

"What if they demand more information before meeting with you?"

"The Americans will have to speak with me personally if they want to know more."

"Okay, Han. But it will take some time to deliver your message. My country sleeps."

Sinchon hated not being in control, not being able to tell people what to do and how to respond. It was as if he had been demoted to a junior officer all over again. He didn't like the feeling. Leaning up against the wall he felt his stomach rumble queasily.

"My friend," Zheng said, "stop looking at me like I killed your mother. I will contact the Americans. Now go home and get some rest. You look tired.'' Zheng put a hand on the general's shoulder, nudging him a little. ''I have guests that wait for my return.''

Through the door to the back room Sinchon heard the light laughter of women. A surge of depression suddenly came over him, nearly taking the breath out of him. *I should have risked going to the Americans myself. Instead I have trusted the future of my country to a man that cheats on his wife. Why did I not know this about Zheng before?*

Sinchon made his way back to his warm staff car. Inside, he felt a stabbing pain deep inside his chest. It wasn't his heart. The pain was lower than that. He had felt it before but never had it been so intense. It made it difficult for him to breathe and was much like a cramp, only there weren't any muscles involved.

''Sir . . . are you all right?'' Kwang asked.

''I am fine. I am fine. Just drive.'' Sinchon looked down at his fingers and wrists. They were swollen and his skin appeared to be discolored. Sinchon closed his eyes. He needed to see his doctor. The medication wasn't working. But right now he craved a drink and his warm bed.

## THE WHITE HOUSE

Duke looked around the president's private study. In the last ten minutes he had heard a rather generalized, inconclusive briefing about a North Korean general planning a coup. Manning was conducting the meeting and the president had for the most part sat back listening. However, James guessed by the president's body language he was about to jump in.

''This is the third memo from the State Department this morning,'' the president said roughly. ''No one seems to know what the hell is going on. Not the CIA, not the D.D. and not the State Department. Irving, what's happening? Who the hell is Gen. Han Sinchon?''

Weber adjusted the round gold-frame glasses resting on his nose. ''I have my best people working on this, sir. Right now we're trying to figure out where Sinchon fits into North Korea's power structure and if he could really make this happen. I would like to know why the CIA didn't predict Sinchon's place in all this.''

''Leave the CIA out of this, Irving.'' The president gathered the fax transmissions resting on his lap. ''Worry about your own department.''

''You better not have too many people working on it,'' Radford warned. ''This thing is supposed to be a Q classification . . . above top secret. We can't allow any leaks.''

Manning said, *''I've* taken care of the leaks. Bill Bishop is gone. Now what are we going to do about this . . . coup thing?''

*What . . . did he just suggest? That Bish was a leak?* James thought he must have misunderstood Manning—or else Manning didn't have his facts straight.

James had only been in a handful of these meetings and each time they ended the same way, with no clear resolution or direction. He had learned they were essentially bullshit sessions and it was best to keep his mouth shut unless asked a direct question. Otherwise Manning would make things very uncomfortable for the unwary person giving what Manning considered the wrong response.

"I stand by my original statement, sir," Weber persisted. "We don't say or do anything until we know who this Sinchon is and what he stands for. Then we confer with our allies, the Japanese and the South Koreans. We should get their opinions before we move forward."

The president turned his attention to James. "Duke . . . you're a deputy national security advisor. Do you agree with Weber? Should we confer with Japan and South Korea before pursuing this?"

"I partially agree, sir," Duke replied without hesitation. "The upper reaches of the South Korean military can be trusted. They'll keep the lid on this. I wouldn't trust their civilian side. As far as the Japanese . . . frankly, I don't think it's any of their business at this point. We can tell them after the fact. If this General Sinchon is serious we don't want him shot in the back before he has a chance to succeed."

"Fair enough. What else?" the president asked.

"Right now we need information." Duke's tall frame sat up in his chair, commanding attention. "We should gather as much data as possible about Sinchon, both personal and professional, as Mr. Weber suggests. I believe we should interview our most reliable North Korean defectors to see if they have any insight into the man. Then we should consider meeting with him. I can tell you that something is going on in North Korea even as we speak. I can't put my finger on it, but they're planning something. A country in poor economic condition doesn't step up border operations the way they have without reason. They have systematically increased reconnaissance of the DMZ and are upgrading their air defenses. In the last six months over one hundred Iranian freighters have docked at Nampo alone—"

"You're getting way off track, General," Manning interrupted. I think you've answered the president's question."

"I don't think this is off track, Mr. Manning," James said simply.

"All right, Allan." The president held up his hand. "I agree with both of you," McEntire said, indicating James and Secretary of State Weber. "Irving, keep this quiet. I want only your two top men involved."

"What about our allies?" Weber asked.

"Keep them out of it."

"I will agree with that," Manning stated unnecessarily.

The president turned to his secretary of defense. "Radford, I want the Defense Department to sit tight. Do not say anything until I give the word."

"What about moving another carrier into the area? We could position it several hundred miles away and they'd never know," Radford suggested.

"I don't think we should do that, Mr. President," James said suddenly. "If the North gets wind of it, things might get very tight."

"I believe you're right, Duke. Let's not do anything hasty." McEntire sighed, looking around his study. "I'm leaving for Europe in a few days for an economic summit. I don't want this to interfere with that trip. Let's make sure nothing falls through the cracks."

"Nothing will, Mr. President," Manning chimed in.

"Well at least we agree in principle that this needs to be acted upon. That's positive." The president stood up.

*We all agree, yeah. Real positive,* Manning thought.

"James, I want you to head up the research on this General Sinchon. Use whatever resources you need." The president extended his hand as Manning looked on.

After the others had left, Manning had the president to himself.

"Well, Allan, as you know I don't have a national security advisor, how am I going to handle this situation?"

"I thought you and I were handling the situation. We clearly decided what to do, Mr. President, and both your top advisors agreed." Manning was cowed for not receiving more credit, not to mention James's intrusion, which still ate at him. With Bishop absent Manning had expected to have more of a voice in the matter.

"I know we did make a decision for now. But once I have more information there will be other things to discuss and more decisions to be made." The president unrolled his sleeves and buttoned the cuffs. "I need a full-time NSA. What do you think of James? He seems sharp. Not afraid to voice his opinion."

Manning stated, alarmed: "As far as a national security advisor is concerned I'm working on finding you another one . . . and believe me, James isn't the man. He's only a two-star and he doesn't understand Washington politics. He's just a washed-up military general Bishop gave a job to. Until I find the perfect replacement . . ." Manning paused, looking directly into the President's eyes, "I'll act as your NSA."

"You?"

"Yes, me." Manning's voice raised as his mind raced. *Why didn't I think of this before?*

McEntire sat back, folding his arms. "But then who would be my . . ."

"Wait just a minute," Manning said, pacing quickly back and forth. "Let's think this through. The CIA is still trying to get a handle on who this Sinchon is and if this thing can really be pulled off. We don't know where this general wants to meet and what the time frame is. As acting national security advisor I would recommend that you send Collins back to the Chinese embassy late tomorrow . . ." He had to pause to swallow, then continued earnestly: "Have Collins tell the Chinese ambassador we are interested in supporting changes in the North, however we need to meet with this General Sinchon before we can determine how much support we'll give, if any."

"What good will that do?" the president asked, puzzled. "It's exactly what this North Korean general wants."

"First and foremost it will let the Chinese know we're not going to let him dictate any terms to us—"

"I'm not convinced this would be the right course of action in any case," the president said. "Right now you have two missions: to advise me on this coup—for the time being—and to find me a new national security advisor within the week. Is that clear, Allan?"

"Yes, sir, it is." Manning spoke to the president's back as McEntire walked out the side door. "It's crystal clear."


PYONGYANG, NORTH KOREA

Gen. Myong Chin stared at Col. Khoe Kwang, standing before him. The man did not look as eager as he to dispose of General Sinchon. Each time Chin noticed he had to send for the man; Kwang never came on his own offering information. This time Chin decided to try a more subtle approach.

"Come, sit down, Colonel Kwang." Chin stood, motioning for the man to take a seat in front of his desk. "Let me pour you some hot tea."

Kwang stepped up to the desk and sat down hesitantly. His hand shook a little as he accepted the delicate china cup from Chin.

"I have been thinking of what position you would serve best once your job with General Sinchon is complete," Chin said, his thin lips curling into a smile.

The colonel remained silent. He sipped his tea feeling uncomfortable in the luxurious office.

"Of course you realize I cannot promote you until Sinchon is out of power. He is a man that does not believe in the benefits that normally accompany power." Chin spoke slowly, stroking his cherry wood desk top. "I have already arranged to have a small token—look at it as a bonus—

delivered to your home. It is in recognition for the extra hours you have devoted to this matter."

"Thank you," Kwang replied.

"Now back to the general. Is there any news to report?"

"In the last twenty-four hours he has had two meetings with Chengji Zheng, one at the embassy, the other in the northern part of the city."

"What were these meetings regarding?" Chin asked softly.

"I do not know," Kwang answered, swallowing hard. "He does not tell me everything."

Chin stood up and began to pace behind his desk. "Has there been any change in the meeting with Bandar?" Chin questioned him coolly.

"No, sir . . . none that I know. But like I said, he doesn't tell me everything."

"Whom do you wish to serve, Colonel Kwang? Me or General Sinchon?"

"I . . . I wish to serve you, sir."

"Listen to me then." Chin placed his hands on top of the large desk, leaning forward. "I suggest you change your tactics. Stop waiting for Sinchon to tell you everything. I want you to go through his desk, files and papers. You have access to his living quarters. Find out what he keeps there. You must take risks in finding out what is going on during these meetings. That is the only way we'll ever be able to reach a speedy conclusion in this matter."

"I can do that, General Chin. I can certainly do that."

"Indeed, I don't see how you could have refused, Colonel Kwang. You will soon see how you will benefit, I promise you. Now go. Report back to me tomorrow night."

As he watched the colonel leave Chin had to wonder if he was doing the right thing. *If Kwang is caught, chances are the colonel will tell Sinchon everything. That is the problem with weak-minded men. They don't believe in anything, just their own hides. Unfortunately that isn't the problem with Sinchon, his convictions run deep.*

Chin had long ago come to the conclusion there wasn't any way to control Sinchon. The man didn't respect the change in the command and that was what made him dangerous. Sinchon did what he pleased without any regard to higher authority. The fact was that if any other officer openly opposed the defense council like Sinchon, they would have been court-martialed and shot by a firing squad, but Sinchon was different, he is a legend.

Chin turned the lights off and entered a room connected to his office. His apartment was only a few blocks away but he decided it was easier to get his rest here. He crawled onto a simple cot set up next to the wall. Looking at his watch in the darkness, the glow of the hands indicated he would get less than the normal four hours of rest his body needed. Wrapping his hand around the grip of a 9mm pistol, he allowed himself to fall asleep.

# 11

"We have been cleared for landing at Pyongyang and should be on the ground in a few minutes," the Iranian transport pilot's voice crackled over the intercom. "Please return to your seats and buckle your seat belts."

"I am not pleased with this arrangement," Salmon Shaqat snarled. The Iranian diplomat sucked the last few puffs out of his cigarette before grinding it into a nearby ashtray. "My government will hear about this. I do not like being treated like some Western businessman."

"Please be patient, Mr. Shaqat," a sharp-looking North Korean Air Force officer spoke apologetically. "There will be no need for you to contact your government. The general chief of staff cannot control the weather. All the air traffic has been delayed by ground fog."

"We have been circling for two hours. I am being treated like a dog." Salmon Shaqat sat down, folding his arms in disgust. The small four-engine jet bounced up and down as the pilot banked to the right dropping the nose.

Shaqat's mood soured considerably as he pictured Chin waiting in the comfort and quiet of his office. He remembered every detail of the room. The fine leather chairs, solid brass lamps and thick wool carpet.

In Shaqat's opinion it was too comfortable and too quiet. Chin lived like a king compared with the military leaders in Iran's armed forces. He wondered if Chin was more interested in trading weapons for gold, diamonds and American dollars than in keeping the scum of Western values from his people. Decidedly, working with Chin was like feeding a child candy. The more you gave the more he wanted and the more spoiled he became.

Shaqat felt bitterness burning inside his belly. He had known Chin for fifteen years. He remembered when the man was nothing more than a meaningless major working in a staff position for North Korean generals and admirals. It was only when Chin started dealing with a Chilean arms dealer named Carlos Cardoen that things changed. Cardoen had become a multi-millionaire selling weapons designed for massive slaughter to Iran during their ten-year war with Iraq.

It had been Chin's job to shuttle between Iran and Chile, securing weapons orders and briefing Iran's generals and mullahs as to what weapons were available on the open market. There wasn't any question in Shaqat's mind that during the war the CIA and Mossad had covertly assisted Iraq, supplying its commanders with technical Western-made weapons, aircraft spare parts and other military hardware in an effort to prolong the war and weaken Iran. What the CIA didn't know, or at least turned a blind eye to, was that whichever country bid the highest price generally received the weapons.

Shaqat recalled when Chin and Cardoen had aided in supplying his country with Chilean-made cluster bombs by sending the shipment of containers through ports in China. The 500-pound cluster bombs were inexpensive compared with the ones being sold by the French but were just as effective at killing.

As Iran's war with Iraq heated up Shaqat found himself dealing more often with Cardoen, Chin and the North Korean government. During the late eighties Iran desperately needed land mines, demolition charges, hand grenades and ammunition. The weapons embargo against his country forced them to buy whatever they could on the world's weapons black market and nearly bankrupted his country.

In the cruel reality of war Shaqat knew that if it wasn't for men like Chin and Cardoen his country would have been defeated, torn apart like a piece of meat between two hungry dogs. It was also inevitable that the two men became rich while assisting his country. Shaqat speculated what had happened when Iraq offered the young Chin a higher price, and wondered how many Iranian men died because of Chin's greed.

Shaqat tightened his lap belt, wishing he had another cigarette to smoke. *Enough of the past,* he thought. Cardoen was dead, killed in a car bombing just outside of Moscow a year and a half ago.

One rumor credited his death to Russian organized-crime leaders, who assassinated him for not paying protection money on a shipment of ZSU-23-4 antiaircraft guns sold to some crackpot general in Bosnia. Shaqat doubted that; Cardoen was much too smart to make such a stupid mistake. Instead, Shaqat believed the rumor that Chin had been behind the killing of his former colleague. Cardoen himself had taught Chin the international arms business, and the ruthlessness that came with it. Chin was close enough to know the players and no doubt had the same connections around the world. It seemed incredibly easy and fortunate for Chin to step in to fill the void left by Carlos Cardoen's death.

The death, however, left Iran with very few choices. If they wanted to acquire enough advanced chemical weapons or nuclear material to construct bombs they had to work with Chin.

"Chin must know I am not a fool," he mumbled to himself as the jet hit an air pocket, causing his stomach to turn over.

PYONGYANG, NORTH KOREA

General Chief of Staff Myong Chin poured himself a cup of tea.

Two hours of sleep had done wonders for his disposition. He felt rested and could think clearly once again. His wall clock showed it was 12:59 A.M. The Ministry of Defense building had become quiet, even peaceful at this hour. *It is a shame,* he thought, *that the most important business has to be conducted in the dead of night.*

Two solid knocks sounded on his door. Chin smiled. Col. Met Lee Kaine had arrived and he was one minute early. The *spetsnaz* colonel was generally exactly on time. Never a minute late or early.

"Enter," Chin said, relaxing in his seat.

He watched the door of his office swing open and a large man enter carrying a leather briefcase. He wore a drab Korean People's Army overcoat without any insignias identifying him as a high-ranking *spetsnaz* military officer.

Chin studied him as he drew closer. He resembled an American football player more than a soldier. Kaine's upper body boasted very broad shoulders and well-muscled arms. His flat face with deep acne scars and wide nose was topped with a head full of short black hair. The forty-three-year-old officer moved with a certainty that only a few people possess. He was also one of a rare type Chin had ever come across in his lifetime: not only was Kaine resourceful but he was loyal and trustworthy.

It was Chin's goal to replace the incompetent Sinchon with Kaine and control the North Korean government with him at his side.

"I trust no one followed you," Chin said.

"No one knows I am here."

Chin didn't try to hide his pleasure. Kaine was as tough mentally as he was physically. His sharp wit and tongue were one of the characteristics Chin liked most . . . and at times disliked even more.

"Sit. Join me," Chin said, pouring the man a cup of tea.

The colonel unbuttoned his coat and took the seat directly in front of Chin's desk where Kwang had sat only hours earlier.

Chin poured the tea thinking of the contrast between the two men. He had followed Kaine's career since he was a captain flying MiG-21s. His potential for greatness was clearly evident even then. Chin had used his influence to move the man up the ranks. Two years ago he had placed him in charge of a secret *spetsnaz* fighter squadron, the most powerful of the DPRK's Air Force. Its existence is only known to a handful of top officers and is simply referred to as squadron two zero. Kaine was personally responsible for keeping the North's most advanced aircraft, a mix of MiG-29s, Su-27s and Su-30s, in top flight condition. He recruited and trained the best pilots his country could produce. In that time he matured and perfected his skills as an officer preparing to take Sinchon's place leading all the *spetsnaz* troops.

In order for Chin's plan to control North Korea to succeed, he needed more military and political power under his absolute control. That power could only be obtained via one device: a nuclear weapon. Chin had devised a plan to produce the plutonium at a secret underground reactor beneath the DPRK's nuclear facility at Yongbyon, but he needed Iran's help to make the bombs. Chin knew the plutonium would also be very valuable to Iran. He could easily trade plutonium fuel rods for completed nuclear weapons. Chin also felt he could secure aircraft, heavy weapons and plenty of hard currency from his Iranian allies.

Recently he had placed Kaine in charge of special security for Yongbyon, North Korea's nuclear facility. Below the facility he had begun an underground operation. The Americans' satellites could not penetrate underground, keeping his plutonium production well hidden. However, Chin needed a *spetsnaz* officer he could trust and rely on to work within the complex, someone who could guard his secret and deal with traitors or spies.

He handed the colonel his tea and took the seat next to him in front of his desk.

"We have accomplished our goal," Kaine said confidently. "The plutonium fuel rods are ready and have cooled enough to transfer. Within twenty-four hours I can have them crated and ready for transport by air or sea."

"The fuel rods are not my main concern," Chin said. "Security is. The United States has a nasty habit of knowing what we are about to do. I don't wish to rush and be a fool. The Americans would undoubtedly stop the transfer of the rods if they discovered our intentions—not to mention the consequences for the underground operation. Are you certain your security is flawless? There must be no chance of betrayal."

"I have installed a new security camera in the cooling chamber and the main reactor control room. Everyone inside this operation will be watched and guarded. My concern is mostly with the engineering team."

"Then get new engineers."

"I already gave the order last week. A new crew will be trained within the week. If you prefer, wait until I approve their performance for the fuel rods to be transferred," Kaine answered, then went on to reassure the general: "Only ten men will know of the transfer. And none of them will know Iran is the destination."

"Ten is too many," Chin objected. "I do not trust engineers. They think too much."

"We are talking about plutonium fuel rods. There are precautions I must take. I need highly trained men." Kaine's jaw tightened. "Of course, I am not convinced we can trust the Iranians, either."

"I will take care of the Iranians. We have the same enemy and will work together to our own advantages. They may not be trustworthy but we need their technology to complete the bombs. What about the American satellites and spy ships? Do we still know their positions?"

"Yes. Nothing has changed." Kaine's stern face showed no emotion. "Col. Kin Hwan sent me the latest satellite documentation from his contact in Washington. The orbits remain the same."

"Very well, then. I will be meeting with our friend from Iran within the hour. Everything is coming together just as we have planned."

Kaine rose and stood at attention. "I will await your orders."


## CIA Headquarters

Duke James walked through the main entrance and approached the first security desk. After his little get-together with Manning and company he had stopped by the Pentagon before going on to his office. It was now 12:24 P.M., just in time for the CIA lunch crowd. James presented his DoD ID and signed in.

"First elevator on the left, seventh floor," the security guard instructed. "Mr. Edwards will escort you."

A minute later Duke exited the elevator onto the seventh floor and followed the middle-aged security guard toward Mark Collins's office halfway down the hall. As always, the seventh floor seemed quietly organized compared to the lower floors where many of the research departments were located. The gray carpet, dark brown paneling and original oil paintings of past CIA directors and founders covering the walls reminded Duke of the Air Force offices in the Pentagon. Everything was conservative and functional.

Duke signed his name once again showing his ID. His badge number was logged into the computer and cross-referenced with a dozen other computers sharing the same network. According to the database the badge number was current and James was employed by the DoD.

"Duke, I didn't expect to see you for another four hours," Collins said, coming out of his office.

"Have tail wind and military jet, will travel," James smiled, shaking Mark's hand. "It's good to see you. How's Christine?"

"Getting bigger by the day. I just hope she delivers before January one. I could use the tax deduction."

"Spoken like a true government employee."

The two men went into Collins' office.

"So I hear you pulled an all-nighter," James turned serious. "This Korean thing has everyone hopping."

"Yeah. I feel like I'm back in college cramming for finals—only back then it didn't matter to anyone else but me if I failed."

Duke took a seat in front of Mark's desk and watched him pour two cups of black coffee. Unlike the other CIA offices and cubicles, Collins operated out of an enclosed room without any windows. It appeared to be slightly bigger than the other surrounding offices, allowing the analyst to keep a small couch, which he used for naps, next to the far wall opposite his desk. Collins used two computers, one on his desk, which was on, and another that was behind him on the credenza. In the corner Duke could see a laser printer, an encrypted Ricoh fax machine and a couple of other gray boxes that didn't resemble anything he'd seen before. As usual, stacked in the center of Collins' desk were files, computer disks, CD-ROMs, a half-eaten submarine sandwich and a can of Coke.

On the wall behind him was a picture of his family, a framed print of a Colorado mountain scene, and an autographed photo of Brig. Gen. Chuck Yeager standing next to an F-20 Tigershark. Directly below that was a black-and-white photo of James and Collins leaning against a special operations MH-53J Pave Low deep-infiltration helicopter. The two men were shaking hands and smiling. James chuckled to himself, remembering the morning it had been taken. They were in Bahrain a few miles from the Persian Gulf and Collins was lucky to be alive. At the time Mark had been working in the CIA's covert division known as the Directorate of Operations, or "the dark side." He penetrated Iranian security by posing as a McDonnell Douglas F-4J engineer and had been stealing military secrets, feeding them back to Langley via an encrypted computer SATCOM link. When Collins' cover was blown James spearheaded a night extraction mission to get Collins out of Iran. They nearly got their butts shot off and one CIA agent was killed. The adventure had created a deep bond between the two men.

The other wall displayed a large laminated map of the world. Collins handed James a cup of hot coffee and sat down.

"Do you have my family portraits?"

"Sure do." James removed the packet from his briefcase and placed it on the desk. "I think they're the best shots yet. And we got an image of what could be an underground reprocessing plant."

"Wow," Collins said, flipping through the pictures. "The International Atomic Energy Agency will love that. We've been trying to find that location for the last two years."

"Well, don't get too excited. We've been disappointed before. The last reprocessing plant turned out to be an underground hospital. A *real* national security threat."

"Be nice, now. We're using a different informant—" Collins stopped short.

"Yeah, I thought these were unusual." Duke sat back, not pushing the point. He could tell by Mark's expression he didn't feel comfortable saying any more. It was one of those unwritten rules of the CIA. When the person in charge shuts up it was time to change the topic.

"Take a look at these," Collins said, handing James a thin file. "These are some of the first shots taken after Atlantis installed the new ultrahigh-resolution IR/Optical cameras on our KH-14. The NRO spotted them and want my opinion."

James removed three photos and spread them out. The pictures were exceptionally clear, the best he had ever seen taken from a satellite. He heard rumors the CIA had developed an IR imaging process capable of colorizing infrared images, turning them into standard color photos with six-inch resolution from 245 miles up. Now he was looking at the proof. The colors were sharp without any of the normal fading or bleeding. Duke was looking at the edge of a taxiway and could see the gray image of a concrete hangar. In the center of each picture was a jet fighter. He guessed the shot had been taken just before sunup because of several long shadows near the bottom of the first picture. The general knew at once what he was looking at—Soviet-designed fighters. Each aircraft had a huge radome, twin tails and square wings. The silvery images in the first two photos were Su-27s; the last was an Su-30.

"So what's your opinion?" Mark asked after a few moments.

"Interesting . . . Su-27 Flankers. Whose are they?"

"North Korea's . . . and without North Korean markings. We got three shots on a KH-14 pass two days ago. My guess is the Chinese sold them several of theirs. We caught them scrambling back to their hangars."

"They didn't get that Su-30 from China."

"What?" Collins asked.

"That's an Su-30." Duke pointed to the last photo. "See? It's a two-seat model . . . the Sovs designed her for air-to-air or air-to-ground. Similar to our F-15E."

"The NRO says it's an Su-27 trainer," Collins said. "Are you sure?"

Duke pointed to the radome of the jet. "See that black ball? That's an infrared search-and-track sensor. They're very expensive and hard to maintain. They don't put them on trainers. This is an Su-30."

"No shit?" Mark stood over the general's shoulder staring at the photograph.

"No shit. How did you guys miss this?" Duke asked, needling his friend. "Aircraft are one of the easiest things to spot. They're big, greasy and can only fly above the ground."

Collins became quiet for a second, then looked up, making certain his door was shut. "Duke, I'll tell you how we missed it. We're not supposed to talk about it, but that picture you're looking at is the first lead we've gotten on anything."

Duke cocked his head to the right. "I'm not sure I want to know this."

"Well, you'll probably hear about it later anyway, so it might as well be from me. It's almost like the North Koreans know when our birds are going to be overhead. The only reason we got these shots was because the range on the new camera is 12 percent further. And look. They were already headed into the hangars. It's the same thing with our Lacrosse flights. We never find anything new. Nothing changes. I think they know the flight patterns of our satellites." Collins' voice was somber and slow. "It's the only thing that makes sense to me."

"What can we do?"

"For starters, I'm trying to get their orbits changed. I'd also like to know how they'd know the orbits in the first place."

"Well," Duke said, "this is going to change a few other things, too."

"What do you mean?"

"An Su-27 is a hell of a fighter. It's an interceptor designed to shoot down other aircraft, but I'd put it up against our F-15 any day. With a good hand on the stick it might even be considered better by some pilots. The Su-30 is a different kind of animal, though. That baby can sneak in at low level below radar and take out strategic targets. South Korea doesn't have anything like it." Duke paused, then added: "Looks like I'm going to be writing up a new Korean threat estimate."

Collins tossed the photos back into the file and placed his foot on the edge of his chair. "Let's change subjects for a minute. I've been given the task of putting together a briefing paper for the president. Do you know anything about a North Korean general named Han Sinchon? He's commander of their *spetsnaz* units."

"I'm glad you asked. Radford asked me to sit in on the briefing at the White House earlier this morning."

"And?"

"And I know about the coup but there isn't a lot of data on the old guy. I guess you know that. I'm in charge of digging up more info on Sinchon too. Actually, I was hoping you could help me."

"Well, I haven't found very much either. He seems to have avoided being included in all of our standard intel briefings. Even the personal data the

South Koreans and Japanese supply us with has come up short." Collins tapped a tall stack of files on his desk. "But I still have this to go through."

"One thing's certain. The man must have guts going to the Chinese asking for help. If any word of this leaks he'll be dead before you can say *kimchi.*"

"Yep . . . but if you were planning a coup wouldn't you like to know if the South and the US were going to support it before putting your neck on the line?" Collins tapped a pencil on his forefinger. "He has guts and he's not stupid."

"Well, I've got to get back to my office and get some work done, then get my butt home. I haven't even seen Katie and the kids yet." Duke walked over and opened the door to Collins' office.

"Oooo! I wouldn't want to be in your shoes. Maybe Katie will be so happy to see you it won't matter if she was last on your list."

"Right," Duke laughed, waiting in the doorway. "I might have to call you later if I'm in the doghouse."

"I'll be here and you can use my couch any time." Mark pushed the intercom button on his phone. "I need an escort, please, for General James."

PYONGYANG, NORTH KOREA

General Chin was not looking forward to his meeting with Salmon Shaqat—or, as he referred to him, "The Iranian Mad Man." Shaqat was fifty-nine years old and a widower. Surprisingly, to Chin, Shaqat didn't remarry when his wife died of heart failure three years previously. *How can a man go without the warmth of a woman,* he wondered, noting that his data showed no mistresses either.

Officially Shaqat currently held the position of deputy interior minister for Iran, a post he had been named to after their prime minister was assassinated two years before. Unofficially Mr. Shaqat served in Iran's government in only one capacity: he was solely responsible for the procurement of weapons-grade nuclear material. Chin knew that Iran was willing to pay up to one hundred million US dollars for enough plutonium or uranium to manufacture a number of nuclear weapons. *One hundred million,* he thought. *They are trying to steal it, not buy it.*

"Send Mr. Shaqat in now," Chin said, tapping the intercom button on his phone.

He stood as the door opened and Salmon Shaqat entered.

"Well, well . . . Mr. Shaqat. Welcome to North Korea." Chin didn't offer a hand or move to greet him from behind his desk.

"Why are my men not allowed to be with me?" Shaqat asked without bothering with Chin's pretenses.

Chin smiled. The man looked a little pale in his tidy black suit. Chin guessed he probably wasn't feeling well.

The last time Chin had worked with Shaqat was three years before in Turkey; he had forgotten how small the man was. He guessed he wasn't more than five feet five inches tall. His gaunt face was covered with a thick beard and the edges of his eyes were yellowing.

"What is said in this room . . . is of no concern to your men," Chin stated politely but firmly. "When you are in my country you follow my rules. Sit down, please."

Shaqat stood staring at Chin for a few seconds, his face set with irritation. He sat down, folding his lanky arms across his chest.

Chin walked over to the bar, filled a glass with ice and poured it full of Jack Daniel's. He smiled, handing the glass to the Iranian.

"Mr. Shaqat . . . Jack Daniel's on ice. I believe it is your favorite." Returning to the bar Chin poured himself a glass of ice water and took his seat behind the desk. "What's wrong, Mr. Shaqat, did I give you too much ice?"

"I am an Iranian government official . . . alcohol is—"

"Well, you're not in Iran," Chin interrupted, holding his drink in the air. "To the glory of Iran."

Shaqat hesitated, then raised his glass. "To the glory of Iran," he whispered, the liquid soothing his parched lips.

Chin took a sip of his water and watched the Iranian down the entire drink in two gulps.

"So . . . how can I be of service to you and your country?" Chin settled into his chair.

"You know why I am here."

"Your country wants the plutonium fuel rods . . . correct?" Chin swirled the ice cubes in his glass.

"Can you deliver them or not?"

Chin's eyes drifted to his glass. He watched the light reflecting off the ice cubes before looking back at the Iranian. He enjoyed this stage in the negotiations. It seemed almost laughable that a man was sitting before him, wanting something that only Chin could deliver, and had the courage to be demanding. Chin had learned long ago that the more demanding a man is the weaker his position. Chin wondered just how weak Shaqat's position really was.

The previous month stories filtering out of Iran had reported their top-secret weapons plant was involved in a major accident. Chin had learned that it wasn't just a single accident but a series of explosions and fires which destroyed nearly the entire complex and killed several hundred of their best engineers. Kurdish rebels, opposed to Iran's ruling defense minister, Sheik Ali Ben Bakhtiar, took responsibility for infiltrating and destroying the weapons plant. It was now obvious that Iran needed help if it was going to be the first Arab nation with nuclear weapons.

"You sound like a desperate man." Chin got up and poured Shaqat another drink.

"If you are referring to my country's recent setback . . . I can only tell you that it will change nothing. Iran will gain the respect that comes with having nuclear weapons. Now either you help us or we go somewhere else."

"Where are you going to go? The Ukraine, Kazakhstan, Belarus? I don't think so. The Russian crime bosses are not that stupid. They will not deal with *Iran,* or anyone remotely associated with you. It would be political suicide." Chin held back his urge to laugh as he handed the glass back to Shaqat.

"Plutonium is like any other weapon. If you know the right people it can be purchased."

"And sold, Mr. Shaqat. It takes 12.1 pounds of plutonium isotope 239, or forty-four pounds of weapons-grade uranium to produce a bomb the size of the one dropped on Nagasaki. By today's standards that is considered small." Chin leaned forward and looked the Iranian directly in the eye. "And when the rest of the world finds out I'm involved in selling nuclear material to Iran, and believe me the rest of the world *will* find out, the number of countries willing to do business with me drops to only one: China. My country cannot survive by dealing only with China."

"What are you telling me, Mr. Chin? *Is your country backing away from our agreement?*" Shaqat sat upright in his seat, spilling his drink.

"Last month two American destroyers forced two of our freighters to return to their port with a shipment of No-Dong-2 missiles bound for Vietnam. Six months before that two of our most trusted engineers defected to the South. They were spying for the CIA. If the United States were to find out about the sale of nuclear material to Iran they would . . ." Chin stopped.

"They would what? Attack? Destroy your weapons complexes?" Shaqat quizzed angrily. "Put a naval blockade around North Korea?"

"The Americans sail surveillance ships off my coast day and night. They fly reconnaissance satellites over our country and any fool knows the CIA could be anywhere. Very few people in the North Korean military can be trusted. You know as well as I do the United States watches every move the North Korean government makes." Chin sipped down a mouthful of water. "Every time I attempt to transfer any weapons the United States knows about it."

"So what is it you want, Mr. Chin? You do not feel one hundred million US dollars is enough for the risk you will be taking, is that it?"

Chin traced the rim of his glass with his fingertip. "I'm glad you understand it is my country's future that is at risk. I have also had to pay high prices for satellite information to coincide with the transfer . . . this of course is an advantage to you that the Americans will not know Iran is the plutonium's destination." Chin again looked directly at Shaqat. "Your country is now manufacturing MiG-29 fighters. What I want is a squadron of MiG-29s . . . twenty-four aircraft, in addition to one of every two bombs your country produces."

*"You are crazy,"* Shaqat said, shocked.

Chin sucked in a deep breath and studied the Iranian's face, letting the room grow uncomfortably quiet. "What would your country pay for enough plutonium to manufacture . . . seven or eight bombs? Bombs that are ten times as powerful as the one dropped by your friends the Americans during World War II?" Chin's face was stone cold sober. He walked over to Shaqat and urged him out of the chair by his elbow. "You think about it. I will await your answer."

Shaqat stood up slowly.

"When your country is ready to talk," Chin said, "you know how to contact me. Good night, Mr. Shaqat."

WASHINGTON, D.C.

It was only a fifteen-minute drive, in light traffic, from the White House to Allan Manning's townhome in Springhill Lake. Located inside the beltway near the Baltimore/Washington Parkway and downtown Washington, D.C. The townhome fulfilled his every need. It was isolated, low maintenance, and cost less than a grand a month to rent.

Manning thought about how he had lived in the two-bedroom, one-bathroom home for the last eight months. His wife, or as he reminded himself his soon-to-be ex-wife, had kicked him out of their three-bedroom house in Georgetown with nothing more than his briefcase and the clothes on his back. He didn't mind living in the townhome, in fact he sort of liked the inconspicuousness of it. What he didn't like was his wife's taking everything he had worked for, including his Mercedes Benz 300E, his summer home in Maine, his savings account, his income mutual funds and half his government pension. Thinking about it made his heart race and he was sure the throbbing in his body was his blood beginning to boil. He glanced up at his driver to see he was still staring straight ahead at the traffic in front of them.

*After twenty-three years of marriage the bitch is trying to ruin me and suck out every single penny she can. It just isn't right.* Manning tapped his hand on the handle of the door, remembering how their divorce came about. *So what if I had an affair with another man for a couple of months? It isn't like we're in love or anything. She just isn't living in the nineties, a lot of people I know are bisexual. I don't deserve this treatment.*

Following the norm, he had dated and finally married a woman. In college there was plenty of experimenting going on. It never revolted him and he didn't understand what the big commotion was all about. Allan was just looking for someone who thought he was as wonderful as he believed himself to be. It didn't make any difference to him if it was a man or a woman. *I don't need a shrink and I'm not going through some mid-life crisis. I just had an emotional hole that bitch couldn't fulfill. After all I've done she still didn't appreciate me, so I found someone who did.*

The Secret Service had protested when he first informed the Treasury Department of his move to the townhome. They wanted him to live in another private residence, preferably a two-story structure with a high wall and iron gate across the driveway, the bottom floor being Manning's private residence, the top floor housing the Secret Service. Such an arrangement allowed easy surveillance and quick escape if needed.

That was the last thing the chief of staff wanted. He had decided there was no way on God's green earth he was going to let the Secret Service keep tabs on his every move. In his view they could protect him during working hours but after that where he went and what he did wasn't anyone's business, particularly the patronizing Capitol Hill cops. In the end he was able to compromise with the Treasury Department. They agreed that a married Secret Service couple could live in the townhome next to him to provide protection.

Manning waited for the black limousine to pull into his driveway before getting out.

"See you at seven tomorrow," he told the driver through the open door.

Turning the lock, he opened his front door and entered the dark living room. It was meagerly furnished with one brown leather couch and a console television set. Flipping on a floor lamp he saw a flashing red light on top of his answering machine. The light displayed the number one.

"Let me guess . . . the *bitch.*" Manning hit the playback button.

"Allan, what is going on with these investments of yours? I just got the quarterly reports and I've lost 3 percent so far this year. I can't believe you were stupid enough to put our money in these things anyway. I'm talking to my lawyer about this. I am not going—"

The sound of her voice grated on his nerves so Manning pushed the off button. He stared at the machine for a few seconds before taking his fist and smashing the top of it. The hard plastic cover shattered into several pieces. The sudden urge to place his hands around her neck and slowly squeeze the life out of her filled his mind.

A moment later, his body shuddering with anger, Manning walked up the stairs, stripping off his suit and tie and throwing them in a pile on his bed. He pulled out a pair of cotton dress pants, a dark wool sweater and a camel's hair jacket. Something brushed against the side of his leg, startling him.

"Oh, there you are," Manning whispered in a soft tone. Reaching down he picked up a fluffy gray cat with dark eyes, long whiskers and black nose. "How are you doing? I'll bet you've been out trying to find some companionship. Just like me."

The cat closed its eyes and began to purr.

Holding the pet close to his chest, Manning paused while stroking the cat's back and gently kissing its head. He had owned the cat for five years, letting it share his bed at night as well as having the run of the townhome. Manning considered him the only real friend he had inside the beltway. For a brief moment the animal's affection allowed him to ignore the pain and despair stewing inside him. The simple animal knew only one thing . . . that it cared for its owner. If only the rest of Manning's life could be so simple.

The cat slid out of his arms onto the bed.

As he changed clothes he again grew angry. *That damn attorney wasn't worth shit! Between him and Rhonda I'm not going to have a fuckin' dime left.* Manning had been the one who had grown tired of the marriage, tired of going through the motions, and most of all pretending to be a stable husband just to further his career in the White House. He refused to get counseling whenever his wife had asked. She had known for quite some time things weren't normal between them. Rhonda didn't want a divorce, either. She enjoyed his standing in the White House, although she frequently complained they didn't get invited to the "right" parties for Allan to meet the "right" people. He needed to do something.

After cutting through all the emotional bullshit Manning *did* do something. He finally realized he just wanted to be left alone to do what he damn well pleased without having anyone criticizing or hounding him. He just got fed up being someone he wasn't. It didn't feel right for him anymore and besides where did it get him? Other people taking credit and moving ahead from his hard work and brilliance.

Allan's face softened into a smile remembering the night when he finally decided he wanted it to end. Allan had simply told Rhonda about the affair. Seeing her revulsion brought him pleasure so he threw in enough details to watch her eyes well up with tears and her face turn white with humiliation.

There had been other affairs with young male prostitutes, too. For the last five years, in fact.

He counted on the truth breaking her spirit and figured she would run away, eager for both of them to go their separate ways. But his wife's spirit turned out to be more malicious than he believed. She immediately hired the best divorce lawyer in D.C., and now controlled the situation. If Manning wanted a quiet divorce, he would have to do things her way. After a year and a half of legal battles, it looked as if she was going to get all the toys and win the game.

Scratching his cat on the head one last time, he made his way downstairs. He turned on the television, making sure the sound was loud enough so his friends next door, the Secret Service agents, would think he was home.

*Yep, just another lonely night watching* "Wheel of Fortune" *and the late night* HBO Movie of the Week, Manning thought.

Quietly he stole outside through the back door. He followed a hedge across his small backyard to the gate. Ducking down into the alley, he turned right, quickening his pace.


## YONGBYON, NORTH KOREA

Dirty brown water dripped off the concrete ceiling of the oval-shaped underground tunnel. In patches of ice covering the floor, the yellowish light of gas lamps lining the walls every ten meters reflected upward. For Capt. Kim Yong-Gil, an army engineer, the poorly lit damp tunnel was the quickest and fastest way to the restricted nuclear research site a mile and a half to the north.

The tunnel had been located one hundred yards underground leading from the water transfer control station to the nuclear reactor cooling towers several hundred yards away. The underground system was also the best way to bypass the security guards roaming every hallway and chamber of the DPRK's sprawling nuclear complex.

The captain's frosty breath hung in the air as he lowered his head. A thin man standing five feet ten inches tall, Yong-Gil sustained himself like most North Koreans. He ate two bowls of rice and a cup of boiled vegetables from his mother's garden each day. His face bared the wrinkles of a man twice his age and this morning, like most mornings, he was dressed in a neatly pressed military uniform, carrying a brushed aluminum briefcase.

Yong-Gil generally worked alone and kept to himself. He lived with his aging mother and a frail younger sister who suffered from the devastating effects of a prolonged battle with diabetes. She was blind in one eye and had lost both feet to infection. His life was very predictable, consisting of work and care for his family. But there was more to this seemingly emotionless nuclear engineer. He spent his evenings reading and learning everything he could about the West, including technical manuals and sporting magazines. And although he rarely showed his feelings, they ran deep.

Before the war his family had been together living as most families expect to. However, now Yong-Gil's father and older brother lived in the south near the small industrial town of Kangnung. They had been separated during the war and the North Korean government refused to let them reunite in either country. But Yong-Gil knew that was all going to change. The North could not maintain their present course forever. And as a patriot he would work to make sure that someday his family would be whole again.

Yong-Gil's uniform was adorned with a bright orange triangle-shaped identification badge. The ID was only issued to a special group of highly trained and trusted engineers responsible for North Korea's secret nuclear program. The plastic badge displayed his picture, two military security numbers and a coded metallic strip running along the back. It allowed him access to all but the top classified areas of the complex.

Located on the banks of the Kunon River, sixty-two miles northeast of the North Korean capital of Pyongyang, the above-ground nuclear research facility was tucked away in a semiforested hilly region. Surrounded by North Korea's most advanced air-defense systems, SA-2 and SA-5 surface to air missiles, Yongbyon facility housed a Russian-built thirty-megawatt, graphite-core, gas-cooled reactor. The compound contained a number of above-ground buildings including a nuclear fuel fabrication and research site, nuclear reprocessing plant, waste storage, air base and housing for security forces.

For Kim Yong-Gil the amazing part of this operation was that at any given time high-ranking North Korean government officials could be escorting a number of Western inspectors, working for the IAEA or International Atomic Energy Agency, through each of the buildings. The inspectors' goals were, of course, to ensure that North Korea complied with each and every regulation outlined in the Nuclear Non-Proliferation Treaty. Captain Yong-Gil and the rest of the engineers at Yongbyon knew it was all part of a well-orchestrated plan to keep the West off balance. "Let them look. Let them find nothing," was what the commanders arrogantly repeated.

*The deceptive plan does work,* he thought. The West keeps inspecting the above-ground buildings and uses satellite-based high-resolution radar with ground-penetrating antennas to look for underground buildings, like the ones at Dimona, but never seem to locate the plutonium. His country built and now operated a sophisticated underground facility right under Yongbyon and America's watchful eyes.

The Yongbyon facility was a perfect decoy to hide the small-scale version of a BN-800, referred to as a BN-880, breeder reactor capable of producing thirty-nine pounds of weapons-grade plutonium a year.

Kim Yong-Gil frowned. *Someday this madness will end. My father and brother will be reunited with us and my sister will get the medical attention she needs.*

Listening to the echoes of his footsteps he guessed he was the only person in the tunnel. Stopping, he turned left and climbed down a cluster of small stairs leading to a steel door. Yong-Gil hesitated before inserting his security badge into the door's magnetic lock. Two LED lights flashed from red to green, the steel locks snapped and he opened the door to the control center.

WASHINGTON, D.C.

"So, Mr. Manning's going out to play," Freddy Cannin whispered to himself. "I thought you would have at least waited until after the nightly news. You must be a real horny bastard tonight."

The burly private detective scratched the greasy stubble of his unshaven face. Wearing a black flannel shirt and a dirty Washington Redskins baseball cap, he shoved the last half of three Big Macs into his mouth. He chewed twice before washing it down with a mouthful of Diet Coke.

Hunching his overweight body down in the front seat of his 1985 Ford Bronco II, he adjusted the 10-CK infrared illuminator, bringing the glowing green image of Manning into focus. The 2.3x magnification night-vision scope permitted his 35mm Minolta X-370 camera to get a good day-quality shot in the middle of the night. He watched as the White House chief of staff moved briskly down the alley away from him.

"Yup, thinking with your little head again," Cannin smirked, stuffing a handful of cold fries into his mouth. This was the second time in the last two weeks Cannin had caught Manning leaving his townhome at night, alone, and without his car. Cannin reasoned Manning was again heading into Georgetown for a little action. This wasn't a surprise. His most common investigations were spouses cheating on each other. "You could have at least tried to disguise yourself. Hell, this isn't even a challenge."

Cannin had honestly thought this job was going to prove to be more difficult. After all, he had followed and photographed some of Washington's best-known people—everything from a senator's cheating wife to a Supreme Court justice taking bribes from a securities firm. He loved his job. Setting up his own schedules, he basically worked when he wanted. Even better, it was easy enough to demand to be paid in cash. No one ever wanted the money to be traced back to them. For the minimal fee of $200 a day, it was well known in the beltway he was the man to catch your worst enemy in the biggest pile of dung to be found.

What he hid from the IRS alone would allow him to spend two weeks a year in Key West, Florida, for the rest of his life. And to top it off, with that kind of dough he could eat as many as he wanted of what he considered to be the finest sandwich ever invented, McDonald's Big Mac.

The muffled sound of his autowind pierced the interior of his Bronco as he clicked off several pictures. Noting the time, Cannin started the engine. Manning was almost at the end of the alley and Cannin figured he would turn left to wave down a cab heading into the city.

The greenish image of Manning rounding the last few garbage cans told Cannin to throw his truck into gear. He drove down the alley and turned right. With only his parking lights on, he carefully navigated around several parked cars and a number of large square dumpsters. Turning left onto the main street he emerged just in time to see Manning climbing into a White Oak taxicab.

"Damn, I'm good," Cannin said, clicking off a half-dozen more pictures. He could hardly wait to see where the man was going for entertainment.

# 12

The black night was giving way to morning. In a half-hour the orange sun would force its way above the horizon and start to burn off the remaining fog hanging in the valley below. Hoe Mie Yan had seen a thousand mornings such as this in his lifetime. In another hour he knew the winter skies would be blue and clear. A short reprieve from the winter rains. He turned his head, listening to each sound. The chatter of wild birds moving from treetop to treetop told him he was still alone and it would be safe to begin his observation.

Resting under a green camouflaged vinyl poncho sheltering him from the night's cool rain and helping to conceal his position from below, Hoe Mie Yan shifted his lean frame and tried to get more comfortable. Even with the added protection of the poncho on his black, loose-fitting uniform, he felt damp and wet. Several drops of rainwater trickled down his face and fell onto the ground in front of him. He had spent the last six hours lying on his stomach amongst the rocks and mud on a narrow ledge overlooking the valley. His fifty-year-old body sent messages saying he was no longer a young man capable of spending days or weeks in the jungle fighting the enemy. His thighs were cramped and numb and he had lost most of the feeling in his feet several hours ago. Turning over on his side, he tried to get the blood flowing back into his legs. His aching legs didn't matter, he reminded himself. There was a mission to be completed and, as in the past, he would accomplish his mission.

Below him he could see a muddy road twisting its way through the thick jungle to the southeast. It was void of any travelers. The wet dirt would be at least eight inches deep after all the heavy rains of the last few days. He knew only oxcarts and people on foot could use the route today and even their journey would be slow.

Glancing over at the Soviet-made SA-16 hand-held surface-to-air missile, Mie Yan looked to see if it was still dry and clean. The five-foot-long weapon lay next to his side covered with black styrofoam and partially wrapped in clear plastic. Double-checking the battery light, he made sure it hadn't been accidentally turned on, draining the weapon's power supply. He would only activate the SAM when he heard the distant rumble of aircraft engines coming from the valley airstrip below him.

Mie Yan reached into a brown leather satchel and removed a pouch containing a handful of boiled rice. Using two fingers he scooped the food into his mouth, not dropping any. He let his mind wander, thinking about his country's future. Mie Yan belonged to a small but growing resistance group that called themselves *Kien Thao*. Theirs was a communist philosophy which uses self-criticism to critique corrupt actions and morals. The company of men considered their mission to correct the mistakes of their government. They were freedom fighters. Most members of the *Kien Thao* lived in the central and northern mountains of Vietnam where they farmed the land and raised their families.

Primarily the group was made up of older men who had fought in the war. Their leader, Tai Ninh Dinh, was determined to keep Vietnam from falling into the hands of the West. The *Kien Thao* had witnessed the trading with the United States, invitations to American and European businesses to open up factories and employ Vietnamese women and children. Not understanding the morals of communism, the younger generation talked only of wealth and status in the business world. The *Kien Thao* considered it their duty to stop the West from poisoning their country further.

In many ways Hoe Mie Yan regretted what he had been ordered to do because his mission meant their thirty-year war against imperialism had failed. The emotion ran long and deep like the white scars covering his body, wounds he received in an American mortar attack during the closing days of the war in 1973. For nearly twenty years the West had left his country alone. He knew it might take another twenty to drive them away once again.

Mie Yan adjusted the eyepiece to his twenty-four-power spotting scope. He meticulously moved it right and left, scanning the valley floor. Fifteen miles to the west a rain-drenched runway came into focus. At the end of the concrete he could barely make out the image of a hangar.

"There it is," he whispered to himself. Suddenly he forgot about the aches and pains running through his body.

Bobby Denny felt like he had spent the last two days and nights in hell. For forty-eight hours he and Bunten hadn't ventured outside the hot, stuffy hangar. He regarded himself a prisoner. His every move was being watched by the overly cautious guard that could only grunt and gesture with his pistol. Even when Denny used the toilet the man stood lurking just outside the door.

Denny and Bunten at least had managed to repair what they could on the Learjet. Once that was completed, they slept and played what seemed like a thousand games of cards. During the height of each day Denny guessed the inside temperature of the hangar reached well over 100 degrees, forcing them to drink the bottled water stored in the back of the hangar. Denny regretted he had. His stomach burned and his insides rolled as if he had eaten glass.

"Bunten," Denny said loudly, "get to the Learjet and start the preflight. As soon as those pallets are secure we're outta here."

"You got it," Bunten said, anxiously climbing inside the Learjet.

*Vietnam . . . it sucked back then and it still sucks now,* Denny thought, taking a sip of hot tea. He watched Tra's men make the final repairs to his aircraft's windshield. Tra had found a windshield for his jet more rapidly than Denny thought possible. It was a used one but it would work. Right now he just wanted to get out of the hangar and into the air. Once he got out of Vietnam this time he swore to himself he'd never return.

"You dumb son of a bitch! I *said* be careful with that!" Denny shouted as one of Tra's men stumbled, dropping the nose section of the last chemical bomb casing. "You want to get us all killed?"

The three men carrying the bomb stopped and looked at him a moment, not understanding the English but getting the gist of it by the tone of his voice. They picked up the bomb, carried it the last thirty feet, and set it on the floor next to the aircraft.

"Do I have to do everything myself?" Denny mumbled in disgust. He walked around the side of the Learjet and grabbed the tail section of the casing. "Well, don't just stand there, *help me.*"

No one moved.

"My men cannot finish if you are in the way," Major Tra said, moving out of the shadows. "Move aside, Mr. Denny . . . let them do their job."

Denny hesitated, staring back at the three soldiers. They were rock solid standing on the ground. Denny gently set the bomb down and walked away to stand near the tail section of the jet.

Tra nodded to his men, signaling they should continue. He then turned to Denny. "Stop interfering with my men."

"Interfering . . . the clumsy fools are going to get us killed!" Denny's eyes were wide as he gestured wildly with his hands.

"The bombs are safe enough. It would take more than a couple of bounces on a concrete floor to break the glass linings."

"Don't try to bullshit me, Tra. Your idiot men may believe you but I know when the military transfers these kinds of weapons they never have both chemicals in the same truck or aircraft," Denny argued. "It's too fucking dangerous."

"You are not an engineer, Mr. Denny . . . and you are not paid to order my men around. If you are afraid of the risks then you should stay at home where it is safe."

"Why you arrogant son of a . . . ." Denny's jaw tightened in anger.

Tra turned away, speaking to his men again.

"Don't turn your back on me, you little slope-eyed gook!" Denny shouted. "I'm talking to you!"

Tra stopped, realizing he should never have turned his back on the American.

## ARLINGTON, VIRGINIA

Duke James handed his White House ID to the bearded night watchman seated in the security house. The man stared at it for several seconds, comparing the picture with Duke seated in the vehicle.

"Are you familiar with the location of Mr. Bishop's house?" the guard finally asked.

"Sure am."

"You may proceed, Mr. James."

Slowing his Chevy Tahoe, James maneuvered the truck through the winding residential street. He stopped at the front entrance of Bill Bishop's two-story house. The living room lights were on, along with the porch light.

Sally Bishop, a tall, distinguished-looking lady with short blonde hair and dark blue eyes, answered the door.

"Duke, I thought you were on assignment," Sally said with a tired smile. "Come on in."

"I was, landed earlier this week. Thought I might see how Bish was doing," Duke explained, noticing the fatigued expression on Sally's face. She didn't look well herself.

"I'm sure Bill would love to see you. The last couple of days have been very hard for him. Nothing like being shot out of the water by a . . ." She stopped, rolling her eyes. "I better shut up. Bill's mad enough for both of us."

"Can't say I blame him. I thought he might need this to cool the sparks." Duke held up a bottle of Glenlivet scotch.

Sally smiled sadly. "Thanks, Duke. Bill's in the den. I'll put this away for him . . . he's had enough for one day."

The general's mind filled with recollections of Bill and the last year. Bishop was unique in that his nature was honest, uncomplicated and consistently steady. He was the same man whether he was sitting behind his desk or drinking a beer on his patio. Duke noticed Bishop customarily listened more than he talked. Yet he had also seen that Bishop would speak his mind clearly, with candor and conviction, when the circumstances deemed it necessary. It hadn't taken the general long to figure out that the man's candidness on matters of national security wasn't appreciated by certain people inside the White House. Bishop would go nose to nose with any member of the president's cabinet, including the old man himself, if he felt strongly enough about a matter. Unlike most of Washington's hierarchy, Bishop put his country's interests ahead of his own career.

When Bishop appointed James as one of his deputy assistant national security advisors, he took him under an empathetic wing, teaching him how to operate outside the protective structure of the military establishment. More importantly he took the time to untangle the informal power structure of Washington politics which could eat a man up in a matter of days. Without his help Duke would still be fumbling through his maneuvers within the White House—or looking for a new job.

Duke suddenly wondered if Bishop would pack up and move west like he always talked of doing when he retired. Or would he try to find something else for a few years? His instincts told him Bill Bishop wouldn't stay in Washington any longer. In the last six months Duke had watched him become a little grayer and more disillusioned as the president's chief of staff, Allan Manning, took more control and manipulated every situation to fit his agenda. Bishop's inner strength was admirable and Duke never figured he'd give up the fight, but everyone has to draw the line somewhere.

If Bill and his wife did leave, Duke knew his and the Bishops' friendship would endure the transition. He had found a true friend in the man. They were both married and devoted to their families, and each had a love for the outdoors. Duke would definitely miss fishing for bass in the Potomac River or hunting pheasant at Bishop's private club outside of Fredericksburg.

Duke stood in the doorway to the den a moment. Bill was seated next to the stone fireplace with one foot propped up on the hearth. A tame fire filled the room with a warm glow while a portable television set, in the corner of the room, chattered quietly. The room was decorated with a mountain-home ambience. Wildlife prints mixed with relaxed family photos and dried-flower arrangements enhanced the knotty pine-paneled walls.

"You're going to feel like hell in the morning," Duke said, watching Bishop take a drink from his glass.

"I already feel like hell." Bishop didn't bother to stand up. He grunted something inaudible and pointed to an overstuffed chair next to him. "Are you going to sit down? Or did you just come here to piss me off?"

Duke took off his coat, then walked over and took his seat. The warmth of the fire felt good and he stared into the flames a few seconds before looking back at Bill. Bishop didn't look too bad. His face appeared flushed but he didn't seem to be drunk. The hair on top of his head was mussed but his eyes were clear and dry. Slouched in the armchair wearing his light blue warmup suit and white tennis shoes he looked as if he had just had another bad day at the office.

"I figured you'd be sitting here feeling sorry for yourself. So I thought I'd better come over and console you."

"So what do you know?" Bishop asked, his mouth turned slightly upward.

"Oh . . . I have ESP."

"ESP?"

"Yeah . . . *extra* feel *sorry* for yourself *perception.*"

"You're not funny, James." Bishop shook his head, taking another drink. "I'm not feeling sorry for myself, I'm trying to get drunk. But I'm not even managing to get that right. You want one?"

"No, thanks."

"So what have you heard?"

"Not much. Just that you resigned."

"Well . . . I guess that's true. I'm no longer your boss . . . just good old Bill Bishop, private citizen." He slurred his words and finished off the last of his scotch before sucking in the last few melted ice cubes. He set the empty glass down on the hardwood floor.

"I go out of town for a few days and you get your ass fired. What triggered the old man?" Duke asked, knowing there was more to the story.

"I don't know for sure," Bishop stated coldly, his anger sobering him. "I got a call from a reporter, not to mention it was airing on the news. I went into the Oval Office and bang, just like that . . ."

"You know Manning isn't losing any sleep over this . . . can't figure McEntire being led around by the nose though."

"Well, I've gone from the fair-haired boy to the bastard child faster than anyone in Washington politics." Bishop's gaze centered on the fireplace. "You know, I've known McEntire for twenty-three years. I don't know what's gotten into him. After his reelection he went squirrelly. Hell . . . I thought I knew him better than anyone. Just last week we were talking about the first time we met." Bishop turned to look at Duke. "I had just passed the Arizona state bar and couldn't have been happier. After ten years in the army I was finally a lawyer. Sally and I had only been married a few months, she was pregnant with Scott, and we had moved into this run-down one-bedroom apartment a couple of blocks from downtown. I answered an ad in the paper for McEntire Construction Company. I can remember the words in the ad verbatim: *Phoenix, Arizona-based construction business seeking skilled attorney who knows how to work with local officials on preserving the desert landscape around the Superstition Mountain—Salary negotiable.* That morning I went into the office to answer the ad. I walked up to this dark-haired man—it was Louis McEntire, the future president of the United States—and told him I was the man for the job. McEntire was nothing more than a struggling businessman trying to make a buck. He

started me out at $16,000 a year and we've been friends ever since. Well
. . . I thought we were friends." Bishop paused. "Sorry, I guess the booze
makes me want to reminisce."

"That's all right. You never told me that story before. I know what you're
going through."

"Hah! You? You've probably never been fired from a job in your life. Not
Mr. Fighter Pilot Priest," Bishop chuckled, almost breaking out in complete
laughter. "That's what I like about you, James. You just keep lumbering
along believing in black and white, truth, God and country. You really
believe that if you do your job, say your prayers and brush your teeth twice
a day everything will turn out for the best. Well, I'm here to tell you, my
friend . . . that's a crock of shit. Sometimes no matter how hard you try,
people like Manning will end up screwing you."

"Hey, Bill. Why don't we call it a night and you try to get some sleep."
Duke searched his face, not sure if Bill was venting off steam or stepping
over the edge.

"Yep. General Duke James, champion of good over evil. Isn't that what
you tell me, Duke? If the good Lord is willing and the creek don't rise, the
sun *will always* come up in the east . . ."

*"Bill . . . Bill,"* Sally's voice called out from the kitchen.

Both men were silent for a moment as if they weren't sure someone else
had spoken.

"Bill . . . I . . . I need your help," her voice, louder this time,
cracked and they leaped out of their chairs, racing to the kitchen. Sally was
crumpled on the floor, her head resting against the base of the refrigerator
as her shaking hand clutched her blouse.

"Sally, are you all right, honey? I'm sorry . . . I should have been
worrying about you, not myself." Bishop held her in his arms.

Sally whispered faintly, gasping for breath: "Oh, God . . . I love you,
Bill."

Phone in hand, Duke punched nine-one-one, then looked up and saw
Bishop's face, drained of color, fill with fear.


Pyongyang, North Korea

The Kim Il Song Medical Bureau, located on the northern edge of the city
in a heavily wooded valley, had been built to house a vast medical staff.
Their mission had been to keep the former Great Leader of the North alive
for a thousand years.

Now it maintained a staff of over 200 doctors, many of them trained in
Europe and Japan. By Western standards, however, the facility was still

thirty years behind the times. But for the military leaders of the DPRK, the medical services were the best their country could offer. Each high-ranking general or admiral received a personal physician and medical staff ready to meet their needs twenty-four hours a day.

"I'm afraid I have some bad news," the Korean Army doctor said, sitting down next to Han Sinchon. The white-haired doctor looked tired and near exhaustion. He had been friends with Sinchon for over forty years and was one of the few people Sinchon trusted.

General Sinchon sat upright. With his shirt off, his large round belly protruded over his belt, revealing a solid chest covered with hair. A bandage hid the prick mark in his arm where they had just removed another vial of blood.

"Let me guess. I'm old, need to lose weight, I drink too much and I don't exercise, my cholesterol is above three hundred again . . . and I'm going to die some day."

The doctor didn't smile.

"Okay, what is it?" Sinchon asked, slipping off the examination table and buttoning his shirt.

"Han . . . this morning I received the blood tests and biopsy we did three weeks ago. I wasn't certain, but today's tests confirm it." The doctor paused. "General . . . you have cancer of the liver."

Sinchon continued to get dressed. In a way he wasn't surprised. The soreness in his side was getting more intense each week and the swelling around his ankles and wrists continued despite his medication.

"How long?" Sinchon asked.

The doctor didn't answer.

"I said, how long?"

"It's hard to tell. Six weeks . . . ten weeks if we don't treat you." The doctor stood. "Han, I'm going to recommend that you leave active duty. We can start treatment at once. I know of this doctor in—"

"NO!" Sinchon shouted. "That is a direct order. No one must know of this."

The doctor, taken aback, finally nodded in agreement.

"I have one last mission to complete. Then you may do what you wish to treat me," Sinchon lied. "Now leave me."

The doctor moved toward the door but hesitated.

"I want to be left alone."

"What about WuLee?" the doctor asked. "Have you thought of her?"

"What are you talking about?"

"Han, we have been friends for many years. Isn't it time you think about her? WuLee is your daughter. She was raised without a father. She should be told." The doctor stopped, seeing Sinchon's face turn more somber.

"I think of her," Sinchon replied, not looking up. He finished putting his boots on before sliding into a heavy winter overcoat. He then stood gazing at the yellowing cracked plaster wall a few feet away. His friend was right. WuLee was his daughter, the one he had given up for adoption after his wife died delivering the child. After all these years Sinchon still remembered every detail. The baby was frail and underweight. He could almost hold her in one hand as she cried, struggling for life. He recalled coddling the infant girl, hating her and loving her at the same time. She was a gift from his wife but she had also taken his wife from him. The girl had been raised by his wife's sister. Sinchon had made sure his personal doctor was involved to take care of her medical needs throughout her life. To this day WuLee did not know that the powerful general was her father.

"Where is she now?" Sinchon asked finally.

"She is here. At this hospital."

"Here? Is she sick?" Sinchon's voice was soft.

"No . . . WuLee is a healthy, beautiful young woman. Just like her mother. She became a doctor a year ago. She helps heal children."

Sinchon's eyes drifted to the floor. He felt them fill with tears. "She still does not know of me?"

"Now would be a good time," the doctor answered with a slight smile.

"I have one more mission. When I return I will meet my daughter." Sinchon brushed his eyes and straightened his back with resolve. "Have my car brought around."

# 13

One of the men, dressed in jungle camouflage carrying a model 92F Beretta, walked up to Major Tra. His face was dirty with sweat and smudged with grease and oil. "The aircraft is ready, sir," he reported, looking over his commander's shoulder at Denny.

"Good. Open the hangar door and fuel it," Tra answered, turning back slowly to confront Denny, but instead he saw Denny was storming back to the bunk area. "Your aircraft is ready, Mr. Denny."

Tra's softly spoken words barely echoed through the hangar. As the doors came open the interior filled with early morning sun. Tra squinted, the bright light hurting his eyes. Looking back over his shoulder he saw Bobby Denny emerging from the shadows into the light. The American was juggling his and Bunten's flashlights, backpacks and thermos bottles in his hands. He looked pale and sick.

"I hope you do better at landing this time . . . considering the cargo you are carrying." Tra's tone was laced with disgust and sarcasm.

"Yeah, well if I don't have to depend on you or your men I'll do just fine." Denny spoke calmly, handing some of the collected gear to Bunten to put aboard the aircraft. The reality that they were finally getting to leave had eased some of his tension.

Tra ignored the American and watched his men connect the fuel hose to the jet's wing tank. He stepped away from the open hangar door.

Denny smirked seeing him make the move.

"Aren't you coming aboard?" Bunten asked, returning for the rest of the gear.

"I'll be there in a minute," Denny answered, not able to resist a chance to needle Tra one last time. "What's wrong, Major, afraid to stand in the open?" he asked. "Your government still having problems with communist rebels? Scared one of your comrades is out there waiting to blow your head off?"

"You are mistaken, Mr. Denny." Tra reached for a cigarette, then remembered that jet fuel and open flames don't mix. "We do not have any such problems."

"Oh, I heard about the mayor of Quang Tri, all right. When they cut his throat and hung him from a flagpole in the center of town he might have considered that a problem. The way I hear it, they're targeting all government officials . . . come to think of it, maybe you *should* stay away from the door.'' Denny was enjoying the glint of discomfort in the major's eyes.

Tra didn't respond but kept his eyes straight ahead, watching his men complete their task. He knew the rebels occupying his country were calling themselves *"new"* communists and they were causing much more trouble than the government had let on. Being frequently out in the field himself, Tra had learned of several key roads to the south being shut down because of rebel activity. Bridges had been blown up, military and civilian supply trucks raided and burned. It was another reason Tra just wanted to earn his money and get out of the country.

''You should board your plane, Mr. Denny. I am sure if there were such rebels that it would probably give them just as much satisfaction to shoot an American.'' Tra turned and walked into the shadows in the back of the hangar.

Denny started to shout a retort but his stomach rumbled with pain and a wave of nausea suddenly passed over him. *What the . . . ?*

Standing a few feet outside the hangar he watched in discomfort as the fuel hose was pulled from his jet, coiled and stored. Tra's men then attached a small gas-powered, hand-held truck to his nose gear and began pushing the Learjet in the direction of the runway.

*It's amazing how fast the little bastards can work when they want to.* Denny peered up into the sky. It was hazy white and the thought of flying in daylight added tension to the rumbling in his stomach. He made a swirling motion with his finger, telling his copilot to start the engines and warm up the aircraft's avionics.

*Son of a bitch!* Denny forced back the urge to double over. His insides now felt as if they were about to explode. The feeling could only be from food poisoning. *Damn food was rotten,* he thought, remembering the shredded pieces of fish mixed in with the rice he ate the day before.

As the engines came on line Denny heard Major Tra yelling at his men to get to their vehicles. Wrapping his arms around his middle, Denny walked toward the jet and climbed up the stairs.

''Doom on you and your men, Major Tra,'' Denny said aloud, holding up his middle finger, then closed and locked the door. ''Did you double-check the cargo?'' he asked Bunten, strapping himself into the pilot's seat.

''Yes, sir. Those babies aren't going anywhere . . . You feeling all right?''

''I'm fine. Let's get this bitch in the air.'' Denny slipped on his radio headset and watched the hangar doors close. Suddenly it was as if no one had ever been at the airstrip. The place looked completely abandoned.

"Oil pressure in number two is a little low," Bunten reported as he surveyed the instrument panel.

"It's always low." Denny ran through the preflight checklist.

He pushed the throttles forward a half-inch and released the brakes. The Learjet shuddered as he swung it around to the very end of the runway, lining up the nose. Denny knew he would have to use every inch of the concrete to get his bird into the air.

"I hope our gook friends didn't load us down with too much gas," Denny said suddenly. He saw Bunten nervously check the fuel gauge.

Nudging the throttles forward Denny felt the rpms of the engines start to build. A swell of cramps caused him to tighten every muscle in his lower body. Breaking out in a cold sweat, he felt moisture bead up on his face. He waited for it to pass before pushing the throttles to the stop. The Learjet slowly began to move down the runway.

MANILA, PHILIPPINES

Carl Hawkens fumbled in the darkness before finding the light switch next to his bed. Sitting up, he realized the ringing sound wasn't part of a dream. Rubbing his throbbing head he remembered he was still in the Manila Diamond Hotel and that he had consumed a half bottle of vodka the night before.

*Shit, who the hell is calling me?* He reached for the phone. "This better be good," he said into the receiver.

"Hawkens, this is Bandar."

"Yes, Bandar," Hawkens said, sitting up a little straighter. He could hear the hissing static telling him his boss was using the secure microwave marine telephone link on board *Van Triumph.*

"Where is my merchandise?" Bandar asked.

Hawkens blinked hard trying to clear his mind. Looking over at the alarm clock he calculated the difference in time zones.

"Denny should be taking off by now. I'll have the shipment by this afternoon."

"You'd better be right." Bandar paused. "Have you seen the CNN this week?"

"No," Hawkens answered, rubbing his head. *I'm still in bed, you prick.*

"Get out of bed and watch it. Bill Bishop has resigned as President McEntire's national security advisor."

Hawkens ran his hand over his oily face, wondering what this had to do with him.

"Allan Manning is going to take over the position of NSA until the president appoints a new one. How much do you know about Mr. Manning? Have we had dealings with him before?''

"Manning? The national security advisor?'' Hawkens cleared his throat, then added: "I know him, okay. I haven't had any contact with him for awhile.''

"Well, I think it's time you did, don't you? He could prove useful for future operations.''

"Right.'' *For me, maybe.* "I'll let you know when the shipment arrives.'' Hawkens set the phone down, his mind beginning to spin into activity. *So Manning is acting as the NSA . . .*

Climbing out of bed, Hawkens headed somewhat unsteadily for the bathroom. He recalled the years working with Manning at the CIA. They had worked together before Hawkens transferred to Operations. Hawkens never thought of Manning as a particularly crafty political animal, but he always knew Manning was interested in climbing up the ladder, even if that meant stabbing a buddy in the back.

Hawkens snickered, thinking how fate sometimes brings old friends together.


NGHIA BINH PROVINCE, VIETNAM

Hoe Mie Yan unwrapped the moist plastic protecting the nose section of the SA-16 surface-to-air missile. He struggled to be careful not to get any water or dirt on the ball-shaped thermal battery. His thin, bony hands manipulated a sharp knife as he cut away the remaining plastic and tape. Mie Yan again let his mind wander as he inspected the SAM.

Tai Ninh Dinh, his former commanding officer with the 324B NVA Division, came to his hut one night several weeks after America normalized its relations with Vietnam. They talked and drank rice wine into the early morning hours, speaking in hushed tones of the growing resentment among the people. They talked of the many men, women and children that had died at the hands of the Americans during the war. They talked of taking up arms once again to stop their country's drift toward capitalism and the evils that came with it.

At first Mie Yan resisted joining the group, telling Tai Ninh Dinh that Vietnam was tired of war. Besides, Hoe Mie Yan had fought his war; he had risked his life in Vietnam's jungles for nearly fifteen years. But when his friends began dying in the hills fighting the government, he didn't have any choice but to join the rebellion.

Mie Yan slowly sat up on his knees, not making the slightest noise. Picking up the SAM he placed it on his left shoulder. Weighing right at thirty-nine pounds, the shoulder-fired surface-to-air missile resembled a long slender bazooka with several odd-shaped black boxes randomly wired together at one end—only there wasn't anything random about the construction. The missile, based on American Stinger technology, had been supplied to the *Kien Thao* by the North Korean Army only three weeks earlier. The lettering on the graphite side plate told Mie Yan the missile had originally been shipped to Iran. He had heard rumors that Iran was allowed to purchase a large quantity of the missiles from Kazakhstan in return for loan guarantees and hard currency. *Amazing,* Mie Yan thought, *how weapons find their way around the world when we fight the same enemy, the United States.*

The missile felt cool against the side of his face. He flipped on the arming switch, activating the SAM's argon gas cooling system. It only took a few seconds for the system to come on line. Sweeping the SAM left and right he heard the faint murmur of the infrared seeker head trying to acquire a heat source.

Mie Yan adjusted the odd-shaped ball containing the battery and coolant protruding just ahead of the trigger guard. He heard the tone changing as he moved the seeker head.

The low rumble of the jet engine could be heard coming from the valley below. A cold shiver went down Mie Yan's spine as he snapped his head around to the right scanning the sky. For the first time who might be on the aircraft crossed his mind. He wondered if the men he was about to kill were married and if they had families . . . if they even really cared about what was happening to his country.

The image of fat Western businessmen in double-breasted suits using the local Vietnamese women for pleasure and lying to town leaders about jobs and money swept over him. Thoughts of Coca-Cola billboards lining the highways into Ho Chi Minh City turned any feelings of regret into anger.

Shielding his eyes from the sun, Mie Yan scanned the valley for the aircraft.


ARLINGTON, VIRGINIA

Standing in the driveway outside of Bill Bishop's house, Duke watched the paramedics swiftly load Sally's limp body into the back of the ambulance. It had taken them less then five minutes to reach the Bishops' home and another ten to assess the situation and stabilize her enough to transport her to the hospital.

Duke had performed CPR, trying to keep her alive until they arrived. Bill, kneeling beside them, held her hand in his, not letting go until the paramedics insisted. All the color had drained from her skin and the lines in her face seemed to erase in her unconscious state.

"Grab a jacket and I'll take you to the hospital," Duke said, zipping up his own coat.

"I'm riding with my wife."

"I'm sorry, sir, we can't allow that," one of the paramedics said.

"Try and stop me."

The man sighed, allowing Bishop to climb inside.

"I'll see you at the hospital," Duke shouted but doubted Bishop heard him as the doors closed. The ambulance pulled away, its siren blaring and lights flashing.

Climbing into his truck Duke thought of the look on Sally's face with her husband at her side. He was determined to call Katie to meet him at the hospital. He'd managed to get through the day, and most of the evening, waiting to see her but couldn't wait any longer, knowing she was in reach.


NGHIA BINH PROVINCE, VIETNAM

"Gear up," Denny said as the jet streaked over the end of the runway. He pulled the yoke back, pushing the nose up seven degrees and clearing the tree line by a good hundred feet. His airspeed increased rapidly and he watched the dark green jungle fast becoming a blur beneath his aircraft.

*Shit . . . I feel like I'm going to die from this shit,* Denny thought. His head was beginning to pound. He needed to get to the restroom to relieve himself and drink some clean water to flush out his system. He was angry at himself because he knew better. This wasn't the first time he had suffered food poisoning by sampling Vietnamese cuisine.

Leveling at 2,000 feet, Denny turned to his copilot. "Maintain a heading of zero eight seven for the next fifteen minutes. I feel like I'm going to explode."

"Got it," Bunten said, taking the yoke.

Denny climbed to the back of the jet and burst into the rest room.


A flash of light caught Mie Yan's attention. It lasted only a few seconds before disappearing. He swung the SA-16 to the right, hoping the heat-seeking sensor in the missile's nose section would acquire the target before he could see it.

A soft low-pitched hum told him the missile-tracking system had detected a distant heat source but it wasn't strong enough to lock on. The sound of jet engines grew closer. Mie Yan stiffened his arms and back, concentrating. His eyes suddenly focused on a white speck. It grew slowly larger until the distinct silhouette of an early model Learjet came into view. He recognized the long pointed nose and twin jet engines just behind the wings with the high T-tail at the end.

*Just as I thought, a Western business jet heading for the coast.*

He estimated the aircraft was several miles away but rapidly approaching him. Mie Yan was not surprised the plane wasn't gaining altitude. The pilot obviously didn't want the air traffic controllers at Da Nang to know he was in Vietnamese airspace.

Mie Yan tightened his grip on the hard plastic handle of the SA-16. He lowered it slightly, waiting for the tone to change. The instruction manual said he should wait until the signal became even, shifting from a low growl to a high-pitched hum, and the aircraft was directly in front of him or angling slightly away for the best shot. If the SA-16 didn't lock up when the aircraft was exactly ahead of him Mie Yan figured he had a three- or four-second window in which to get the missile off before the jet disappeared behind a group of trees to his left.

Sucking in a deep breath, Mie Yan held it while trying to keep the missile steady.

Craig Bunten twisted around, searching the rear section of the aircraft for his pilot.

*Denny must really be sick,* he thought. This was Craig's second trip into Vietnam and Denny had let him take command of the Learjet for this length of time in only one other instance. That had been at 35,000 feet when the jet was on autopilot. Bunten figured Denny wasn't the type of man that liked other people controlling things, particularly airplanes and business deals.

Bunten leveled the Learjet at 1,200 feet, staying below the mountain ridges and away from the watchful eyes of Vietnam's civilian and military air traffic control radars. He swept the instrument panel with his eyes and saw that the jet was functioning perfectly. In two hours he would be eating breakfast with his sweetheart in Manila, $500 richer.

Hoe Mie Yan listened to the SA-16's acquisition tone fluctuate between a low and high frequency. The IR tracking system had not found the target. He unconsciously readjusted his grip on the SA-16 in frustration. The Learjet was now cruising through the valley a little below him, a mile or so away.

He cursed under his breath for not spending more time studying the training manual. There had to be a reason the missile wouldn't lock up. *Maybe the engine cowlings aren't hot enough to detect or maybe the missile's battery isn't at full power.* His eyes stayed fixed on the aircraft. It was now close enough so that he could see the hot smoky exhaust streaming from the jet's twin engines. The Learjet looked to be angling away from him slightly, following the valley floor. He would lose it in the trees in a couple more seconds. In desperation Mie Yan stood up as the jet banked southeast away from him.

"AWWW . . . I can't believe this." Denny hunched over sitting on the toilet in pain. Holding his stomach he rocked back and forth. He wiped the cold sweat off his face and forehead and reached for more tissue paper. His body was shaky and weak; he wondered if he could stand.

Cutting through an air pocket the Learjet bounced up and down. Denny hardly noticed. Right now he only wanted one thing and that was to get rid of his stomach cramps.

Mie Yan swung the SAM to his left, pointing it directly at the aircraft. The rear section of the engines came into view. If the SA-16 had any chance of acquiring its target it would be now. But the tone didn't change.

"*Lock up . . . lock up!*" he pleaded. Out of the corner of his eye he saw the thick branches of the trees coming into view. The jet was soaring away.

The tone varied somewhat before suddenly changing from a low growling to a high-pitched shrill in a fraction of a second. Mie Yan knew he should wait for the sound to remain steady and even for at least five seconds before sending the missile into the air. But he didn't have time.

Closing his eyes Mie Yan held the missile steady and squeezed the trigger. The metal trigger snapped, his heart skipped a beat, and in a flash of sparks and smoke the graphite missile casing lurched in his hands, nearly knocking him off his feet. He opened his eyes to see the four-foot-long black missile gaining speed. A bright white smokeless flame shot out from the back section. After a second or two he lost sight of the missile as it snaked its way toward the valley below.

Bobby Denny flushed the chemical toilet, pulled up his pants and buttoned them. He felt a little better but the insistent rumbling in his stomach told him he would be visiting the rest room several more times before the flight was over.

*I swear . . . I will never ever go back to that damn country again.* As Denny reached for the doorknob he heard a loud bang followed by several turbulent vibrations. The Learjet quivered, the tail section yawing back and forth, knocking him against the wall.

"Oh, shit!" Denny shouted. The aircraft lurched forward and Denny's forehead smacked the inside of the rest room door, cutting deep into his skin. He fell to the ground, blackness surrounding him.

\* \* \*

Hoe Mie Yan watched a bright burst of fire and smoke envelop the rear section of the jet. The explosion lasted a split second and was followed by a larger ball of black smoke. The missile had found its mark, impacting the left rear of the aircraft just behind the engine.

Only it wasn't what Mie Yan had expected. The jet didn't explode, breaking apart in the air and tumbling to the earth in a twisted sphere of fire and smoke. In fact, it looked as if the jet's course hadn't been affected. He wondered if the pilot knew he had been hit by a heat-seeking missile.

Mie Yan had no way of knowing the SA-16 had been developed as a defense against NATO helicopters. Its two-kilogram warhead wasn't powerful enough to blow off the tail section of a well-made jet. However, if the warhead impacted the right part of a high-performance aircraft it would catch fire or cause enough damage to force a crash landing.

Mie Yan set the smoking missile casing down, not taking his eyes off the target. The jet continued its southeasterly heading for several more seconds before Mie Yan noticed anything unusual.

It was the sound. The jet's engines weren't making the same noise as before. Resting on one knee he watched the left engine begin to spit smoke. A few bright red flames appeared on the underside of the jet. He saw an explosion a second before he heard it. At least one of the jet's two engines was not functioning now.

It had happened. Hoe Mie Yan was sure the jet, full of fat American businessmen, was going down. As he watched it begin to lose airspeed any questions about killing the plane's occupants vanished.

Lying down, he covered himself with the green vinyl camouflage and returned to his spotting scope. He would know exactly where the plane crashed. Tai Ninh Dinh would want to know who was on the plane and what it was carrying. The other members of the *Kien Thao* would want to leave a message at the wreckage for the Vietnamese government. Mie Yan smiled, showing his crooked teeth. He had accomplished his mission and could be pleased.

*Shit . . . I'm cut,* Bobby Denny thought, using his shirtsleeve to wipe his forehead. Looking around Denny tried to remember where he was. He felt cold and his vision was blurry. The foul smell of human waste combined with the stinging pain from the slash above his right eye started to bring him slowly back to life. He gazed around and saw he was lying next to a stainless-steel toilet. He picked himself up and started toward the front of the plane.

*"Shit . . . what the hell happened?"* Denny shouted ahead to Bunten. Examining the left side of the fuselage he saw several dozen holes. Sunlight was poking in, along with the high-pitched shrill of wind whistling through the punctures.

*"I've lost the left engine! I'm having a hard time controlling her!"*

Denny could barely hear Bunten shouting from the flight deck. When his copilot turned around he could see the man's face, wild with hysteria.

"Hold on!" Denny called up, making his way through the interior of the Learjet, using the fuselage walls to keep his balance. As he reached the flight deck he saw the instrument panel lit up like a video arcade, yellow and red warning lights flashing everywhere.

The Learjet abruptly banked to the left, its nose pitching up several degrees. Denny grabbed the yoke, sliding into his seat.

"I have her," he shouted. "I have her."

Bunten had already shut down and cut off the fuel supply to the left engine. A large fire-warning light flashed in the center of the control panel. Another yellow light, a few inches to the left, indicated the jet was losing hydraulic pressure.

Twisting the yoke to the right, Denny felt the aircraft quiver, feeling heavy and unresponsive. He kicked the left rudder, forcing the jet to stop yawing and come wings level. Then he pushed the nose down to pick up a few knots of airspeed. Denny worried that if the plane didn't stop losing hydraulic fluid the controls would freeze solid.

"Drop the flaps twenty-five degrees," Denny instructed Bunten, who was staring wide-eyed at him. "We're going to need the added lift."

"It's no use, man, we've lost an engine. We're going *down!*"

"You stupid son of a bitch—*listen to me.* I got us out of one jam and I'm going to do it again if you do as I say . . . drop the flaps twenty-five degrees *NOW.*" Denny took his hand and slapped Bunten in the face.

"Okay . . . okay. Flaps down twenty-five degrees." Bunten worked the controls as uncontrollable tears ran down his face.

"We've got to turn her around and get back to the airstrip. Get on the radio. See if you can contact Tra."

Bunten mumbled, trying to get the radio headset over his ears.

Bobby Denny saw they were losing forward velocity fast. They needed altitude and airspeed. Nursing a few more knots out of the jet, he turned her 180 degrees.

"Fall . . . come on, fall from the sky," Hoe Mie Yan cursed under his breath. Why wasn't the jet going down? He had seen the missile impact the left side of the fuselage. Smoke was now pouring out the side.

Grinding his teeth Mie Yan watched the jet continue down the valley. If the jet traveled too much farther it would cross into a part of the country controlled by government troops. No doubt they would then come looking for him and the rest of the rebels. All he could do was wait and hope.

"Come on you bastard, climb," Denny moaned. But it didn't work. The aircraft wasn't responding. Instead of gaining airspeed the Learjet was losing it. The controls were becoming more sluggish.

"155 knots . . . 150 knots . . . 145 knots. We're going to stall," Bunten called out, his voice again filled with panic.

Denny knew he didn't have a choice. He was going to set her down somewhere in the valley.

"Brace yourself . . . we're going in," Denny said. He pushed the nose down to keep his airspeed above 145 knots. It took his every muscle straining before the Learjet would respond. As the Learjet pushed over, a green ocean of trees came into view. A wave of panic shot through Denny. He wiped away the blood streaming into his right eye. The jet began to shake, on the edge of a stall.

"Speed . . . 139 knots . . . altitude . . . 700 feet." Bunten tightened his lap belt.

*"Hold on . . ."* Denny saw a break in the thick forest, about a mile and a half to his right, running along the base of a steep incline.

With all his strength Denny twisted the yoke right. The jet protested, wanting to stay straight and level.

"Come on . . . turn . . ."

The jet vibrated, the right wing tilting over slightly as the stall warning sounded.

Denny watched the nose swing right as the top of the trees grew closer. Unconsciously he covered his face with his arms and could hear himself cursing with the sounds of the Learjet's wings and fuselage being ripped apart by the thick foliage.

The jet hit the ground with a violent bang.

Focusing the spotting scope on the region where he had seen the jet disappear into the trees, Hoe Mie Yan waited. He was looking for black smoke to signal a kerosene fire. But he didn't see anything. The plane had gone down but it didn't explode.

*So much the better,* he thought. They would be able to display the bodies much easier. And if any money had been onboard they could use it to finance other missions against the Americans.

Mie Yan estimated the Learjet had gone down sixteen or seventeen miles from his position. He made a mental note of the mountain ridge before stowing his spotting scope and gathering his equipment. It would take him six or seven hours to walk back to camp, avoiding the roads and trails. After that he would lead the other members of the *Kien Thao* to the crash site.

# 14

It was 7:30 in the evening when Allan Manning leaned back in his chair and lit his pipe. Using a hand-held remote, Manning flipped on the television set in front of him.

CNN's *Crossfire,* one of his favorite programs, was about to start. He loved watching the two idiots argue.

"Mr. Manning." Lindsey, his administrative assistant, entered the room after one brief knock.

Manning looked up with a hard stare. He had forgotten to lock the door.

"Sir, this arrived a few minutes ago via special courier." Lindsey hesitantly handed him a large brown envelope. "It's from your wife."

"Why doesn't that surprise me?" Manning grunted.

"I've finished everything you had listed for me to do today," Lindsey spoke softly. Her dark brown eyes were red from another long day.

"Go home." Manning waved her away, watching the slender brunette leave his office.

He turned his attention to the envelope. His insides began to twist with resentment, his thoughts drifting toward his stash of cocaine hidden away in the cabinet behind him. He decided he would need a boost to deal with whatever his wife had delivered. It couldn't be good news.

Manning ripped open the envelope and pulled out ten black-and-white photos. His mouth dropped open, the pipe falling to the floor. The hot ashes put a smoldering hole in the carpet.

Written across the top of the first photo in white grease pencil were the words: YOU STUPID PIG—THIS WILL COST YOU FIVE HUNDRED THOUSAND DOLLARS OR I'M TAKING THEM TO THE PRESS.

WASHINGTON, D.C.

The cold vending-machine sandwich and warm Coke Mark Collins had for dinner just weren't cutting it. He still felt pangs of hunger; he needed a big home-cooked meal. In order to keep his mind off it he watched the streetlights streak by on both sides of the road.

"What kind of a mood do you think the president will be in?" Collins asked his boss, Douglas Brooks, seated next to him in the front seat of his Acura.

"Can't say." Brooks was reading the briefing paper Collins had prepared. "The old man's hard to predict. Kind of like trying to predict the weather . . . all the equipment's there to watch but it does what it wants to anyway."

Collins chuckled. Brooks's country-boy manner eased Collins' trepidation.

As the CIA's director for intelligence it was Brooks' job to lead the analytical, bookworm side of the CIA. In standard CIA mode Brooks was dressed in a dark wool suit, light blue button-down collar shirt and striped tie.

Twenty years older than Collins, Brooks had only half a head of black and gray hair which he kept combed straight back in a hopeless attempt to cover bald spots. He wore wire-framed bifocals on his round chunky face and walked with a slight limp, an old college football injury.

"I wish we had more on General Sinchon," Brooks said finally as Collins turned left.

"You got that right," Collins agreed. "I'm glad it's not *my* decision to make."

Collins made another left turn. They were on Executive Boulevard approaching the west wing of the White House. He removed his ID and rolled down his window, slowing the car to a stop.

Lin Phon, the Chinese ambassador, sensed the Lincoln Continental change lanes as it traveled north on Interstate 295 toward the city. Sitting alone in the roomy back seat, Phon watched the red taillights of the traffic directly ahead of them. He counted seven cars including one semi-tractor trailer. In the distance low winter clouds hung over the city.

For the last half-hour they had traveled the beltway. He ordered the driver to take a variety of exits and side streets before getting back on the highway. All in all he guessed they had covered thirty miles. By now the traffic had died some, making it easier for his driver to weave in and out of the cars and trucks speeding toward the capital. It gave Phon time to decide if anyone was following him.

"Stay in the center lane and slow down to thirty-five miles," Ambassador Phon ordered.

"Yes, sir."

Phon twisted his head around to the sound of honking horns and flashing headlights. He counted five cars that sped past him on the left and right.

*"Now* . . . eighty-five and change lanes," Phon exclaimed.

He felt the car's powerful V8 engine accelerate, pushing him back into the soft leather seat. The driver swerved in and out of traffic. Phon's attention stayed toward the rear of the car. After a few moments he tapped the driver on the shoulder.

"Okay. Now drive the speed limit and take me to Pentagon City Mall," he commanded, satisfied no one was following them.

## THE WHITE HOUSE

With his hands trembling from anger, Manning thumbed through each of the photographs one more time. Someone had been following him. *Damn it, I should have known that bitch would do something like this. How could I have been so stupid!* Manning's mind began to spin. He jumped up, running to lock his door.

Going back to his desk he studied the top picture. The edges of the photo were a little fuzzy—whoever had taken it used a telephoto night-vision lens from a distance—but the center of the photo was crystal clear, capturing every detail.

There wasn't any question about it. It was him. Allan Manning, chief of staff, the president's top advisor and confidant, with his arm around the waist of another man, walking out of Rusty's, a gay bar off of M Street in Georgetown. The other pictures were more graphic. One showed him in an embrace with a younger well-muscled man dressed in a tight T-shirt and bicycle shorts. The two men were on the dance floor surrounded by other men. This picture was fuzzier but there was still no mistaking the face.

## PENTAGON CITY MALL

"Drop me at this entrance and park over there." Lin Phon pointed to a dark section of the Pentagon City Mall parking lot. I'll return in one hour."

Phon put on a Colorado Rockies baseball cap and climbed out of the car into the frosty night air. The cold bit his face, tightening his skin. Before walking away he surveyed the area around him. The mall parking lot remained full with late-evening shoppers. Everywhere he looked Phon could see people walking, their arms full of brightly colored boxes and shopping bags.

Jamming both hands into his pockets and lowering his head, Phon entered the mall. The crowds of people moving in and out of the six double-wide doors made him feel comfortable. The more people in the area the easier it would be for him to blend in, disappear in the crowd.

Phon walked swiftly, turning past the Disney Store. He made his way in and out of the groups of people milling about, looking occasionally over his shoulder. No one was paying attention to him. He reached the escalator, took it to the lower level and stopped to buy the latest *USA Today* in one of the vending machines next to Dorothy's House of Donuts. He checked his watch and saw he was running a few minutes ahead of schedule.

Stopping at the counter, he ordered a cup of hot tea and took a seat facing the wall.


QUARTERS SIX

"Thank you, Helen. As always, dinner was great," Duke James said, sipping the last of his Cabernet. Seated next to him was his wife Katie, and directly across the round dining room table sat Gen. Howard Chaniff, chairman of the Joint Chiefs of Staff. On the table before the two couples were the remains of an expansive meal which had included lamp chops, broiled salmon, new potatoes, steamed asparagus and three different types of dessert.

"Everything was wonderful, Helen," Katie added, enjoying the chocolate cheesecake. "I'm going to have to work out at the gym an extra day, though."

"Well, I can't take the credit. Our chef and his staff do all the work, I just pick the menu," Helen Chaniff, the chairman's wife, smiled modestly. "Every once in a while I make him let me in the kitchen so I don't forget how to cook."

"You can come to our house any time you get desperate," Katie said cheerily. "I can't seem to keep up with feeding my bunch."

Everyone laughed, then Chaniff and James stood up to leave.

"You ladies will have to excuse us. The general and I have a few issues to discuss." The chairman kissed his wife on the cheek.

"Let me guess—pheasant hunting in Kansas and fly-fishing in Montana," Helen said happily. "Or is it that Christmas Island bonefish trip you've been talking about? Or maybe . . . something Duke discovered while he was away?" Mrs. Chaniff smiled coyly at her husband.

*"Hmm,"* Chaniff frowned. "Now that you mention it, fly-fishing in Montana doesn't sound all that bad."

James followed Chaniff into the den. Decorated modestly with a mixture of Ansel Adams's black and white works and one or two small bronze sculptures, the chief of staff's private office appeared quite humble compared to his second-floor Pentagon office. It didn't contain any of the impressive ornate memorabilia collected over a twenty-seven-year-long career in the army. The deep maroon carpet as well as two walls lined with dark maple shelves gave the room a striking contrast.

Howard Chaniff's lean body equaled James's height. He looked like the typical hardass army four-star: short cropped black hair, wiry frame and face with a large Adam's apple protruding from his throat. Duke had seen the man chew up and spit out lower-ranking officers when they didn't do their job to his expectations. Chaniff, however, also had the analytical and political ability to rise to the number one position in the military. One thing was for sure, he always got the job done.

Chaniff walked over to the bar, poured himself and James a drink, and sat on the edge of his desk.

"It's a real pisser about Bishop's wife," Chaniff said honestly. "Hell, the man has to deal with getting pushed out of the White House and then something like this happens. I feel for him."

"Yeah, it's bad. I told him he should go to my cabin in the Black Hills after the funeral." Duke shook his head. "I'm not sure he's decided what he's going to do."

James knew this wasn't the only reason Chaniff had invited him and Katie over to dinner—to talk about Bill Bishop. Chaniff didn't make a habit of having people to his McLean residence just to socialize. Chaniff wanted or needed something.

"Duke, I read your report on South Korea's and Japan's Air Force readiness levels. Japan's got their head up their ass if they think we're always going to be there to back them up."

"What did Radford say?" Duke asked, referring to the secretary of defense.

"I didn't pass it along. As you know we've just learned the North has eight or ten operational Su-30s and Su-27 Fulcrums. So your briefing paper is already outdated."

"Well, Collins showed me the satellite photos when I got back. I didn't know it had been confirmed."

"I received a confirmation from the CIA late this afternoon. What you saw in those photos were Su-30s and they're fully loaded. Langley thinks they've been operational for a month or two."

"Now we know what those North Korean pilots were doing at Russia's Zhukhovskii test facility," Duke added. "Our friends were training them."

"Yeah, Fulcrum training." Chaniff swirled his cognac. "I'm recommending to the Secdef and the National Security Council that the air force do a complete bottoms-up review of our defenses and tactics for Korea. What I need from you is a detailed analysis of how this new threat is going to change the balance of power. I also want you to brief both US and Korean forces on how these new aircraft will change tactics and how we're going to counter them. I want a clear message sent to the North that we're not going to sit back and let them expand their Air Force without us reacting.''

''Sounds like *Operation Eradicate* is taking on a whole new meaning.'' Duke suddenly realized with Bishop gone and Manning left posing as NSA there was a very big gap that needed to be filled. He did not hesitate to speak his mind to Chaniff. ''I think we should send that message now and it needs to be clear.''

''I agree. What do you have in mind?''

James looked down and gathered his thoughts. *''Operation Eradicate* needs to become a full-scale training mission, one that the North will definitely interpret as our real intentions if they ever plan to use those Su-30s. I'd recommend we send in a mix of our best fighters to Osan. We can transfer F-16s from the 354th at Eielson and F-15Es out of Elmendorf for starters.''

''Good. I want plans drawn up immediately and I want you to help everyone understand what we're up against.'' The general leaned forward toward Duke a little more. ''Then I'm going to need your help with Congress. They need to understand most of all.''

The room fell silent as Chaniff seemed lost in thought.

''You're worried about F-22 funding again,'' Duke said at last.

''You bet your sweet ass I am. We still haven't convinced enough congressmen to keep the current funding intact at present levels. They don't understand that F-16s and F-15s are no longer air superiority fighters. They're air equality fighters.'' Chaniff finished his drink. ''You may want to make another trip to Korea.''

''I'll be ready whenever you need me, sir.''

''You'll be the first to know,'' Chaniff answered somberly. ''I meet with the president Monday. Clear your schedule and be ready to go any time after we have our initial conference.''

''Yes, sir,'' Duke smiled and finished off his drink as well. ''Good thing I like Korean barbecue.''


THE WHITE HOUSE

Allan Manning tapped the speed dial button on his phone, the one programmed for his attorney. Fingers tapping on his desk, he waited impatiently for someone to answer the phone. ''This is Allan Manning. I want to speak with Boyle.''

''I'm sorry, Mr. Manning, Mr. Boyle isn't in. He'll be back in around eight-thirty tomorrow morning. May I take a message?''

"Let me guess. This is his answering service, right?" Manning asked. "Boyle doesn't work late evenings like the rest of us."

"Have you tried Mr. Boyle at home, Mr. Manning?"

"I've tried him at home, I've tried his car phone and I've tried his private fucking number at the office. Boyle's at some hotel sipping a double martini with his bimbo girlfriend," Manning snarled.

"I don't know, sir. May I take a message?" the woman questioned politely. No doubt she was used to it.

"Tell the lazy slob it's regarding the same thing it's always regarding— and if he doesn't get her off my back, I'm going to fire his ass and get a lawyer that can handle the situation. Tell him that. I'm going to fire him." Manning slammed the phone down, his heart pounding inside his chest.

*Calm down, you're going to have a heart attack,* he told himself. He set his pipe in the ashtray and took a deep breath. Just the thought of his wife turned his blood hot. She had already taken just about everything. Now she was after the last of his savings, threatening him with his job and reputation. *No way,* he thought. *No way is that bitch going to get away with this. I've worked too damn hard to get where I am. If I have to hire every damn attorney on the East Coast, I will. Where in the hell does she think I'm going to get half a million dollars?*

"Mr. Manning?" one of Manning's administrative assistants' voice sounded over the intercom.

"Yes?"

"Mr. Brooks and Mr. Collins just arrived. They apologize for being late."

Manning took a deep breath. *Shit, I forgot about those two stooges from the CIA.* His first thought was to cancel the meeting because they were late, but then thought better of it. He didn't want the president to talk with Brooks directly.

"Give me a minute, then send them in." Manning shoved the photos into his top drawer and locked it. Shuffling the scattered papers on his desk into a neat pile, he sighed. *This is the last thing I need, two stuffed-shirt goons from spooksville central.* As far as Manning was concerned the CIA had about as much credibility as the assholes in Congress. He considered them just another bureaucracy trying to interfere with the power and duties of the White House.

Manning sat back in his chair getting into his chief of staff mode. He lit his pipe and told himself to relax. He knew he'd find a way to deal with his wife so she wouldn't screw everything up, it was just a matter of going about it the right way.

## PENTAGON CITY MALL

As Chinese ambassador it would have been difficult for Lin Phon to have a clandestine conversation in his own embassy. Although he was the man in charge, it would be foolish of him to think he wasn't being watched like everyone else in the building. As word spread of an impending North Korean coup attempt, divisions were clearly being made.

It had become evident to Phon that China's political leaders were more interested in economic gains than in preserving the truth for the people. It wasn't right and it made him angry. In reality it would be political suicide not to do his duties as ambassador, but that would not stop Phon from fulfilling another obligation. Very few people in his government, particularly the younger members of the embassy staff, would understand his motivations. But North Korea, one of China's strongest and most loyal communist allies, could not be permitted to fall the way the rest of the communist block had.

Phon sipped his tea nervously, checking the time. In the thirty years he had served his beloved China his conviction had never waned. Communism could still provide the best way of life for China's billions of people.

Phon took one more drink of his tea and exited the small donut shop. A moment later he entered the Metro subway system entrance in the mall. He inserted his fare card into the beveled front slot of the gate console. Picking up the card on the other side, he walked down the stairs to the subway station.

In the distance he could hear the reverberation of the train. Now all he had to worry about was whether his contact would show up on time, if at all.

## THE WHITE HOUSE

"Mr. Manning, sorry we're late," Douglas Brooks said, entering his office. Mark Collins followed, closing the door. "How are you this evening?"

"Just fine. Take a seat and we'll get started."

"I thought we were meeting with the president," Brooks said in a surprised tone.

"Change of schedule. The president's asked that you brief me on this North Korean coup thing. I'm acting NSA so I'll be advising him as to how this situation should be handled."

*That's interesting,* Collins thought. *The president is the one who called this meeting and now Manning's running it.* Sitting in a leather chair across from Manning's giant desk, Collins removed several files and a yellow notepad.

"Have you been briefed by the State Department?" Brooks began.

"I've read a fax or two from Weber. It's mostly bullshit. I hope you have better information." Manning took a puff off his pipe, exhaling the smoke out the corner of his mouth.

Brooks looked at Collins and nodded for him to speak.

"Chinese ambassador Lin Phon gave me this additional information," Collins said. "General Sinchon is prepared to meet representatives of the US and South Korean governments on the island of Langau in two days. At that time he will give us a detailed briefing of his planned coup."

"What a minute," Manning sat up in his chair. "You're moving way . . . way too fast. Do you have any information on this so-called general?"

"Frankly, not as much as I would like," Collins admitted. "But I do have something . . ."

"Let's see what you have. I don't have a lot of time."

Collins handed him the file, raised his eyes at Brooks, then sat back quietly.

The first two pages of the three-page background were on North Korea. Manning jumped to the section dealing specifically with Gen. Han Sinchon.

| | |
|---|---|
| NAME: | HAN SINCHON |
| BORN: | FEBRUARY 1934—CHOSAN, KOREA |
| EDUCATION: | 1) CENTRAL SECURITY OFFICERS SCHOOL |
| | 2) HOERYONG CADRES SCHOOL |
| | 3) GRADUATE—UNIT 940 NORTH KOREAN SPECIAL PURPOSE FORCES, SPETSNAZ |
| CURRENT POSITION: | SUPREME COMMANDER 820TH ARMORED CORPS—RESPONSIBLE FOR TRAINING ALL ARMORED UNITS. |

SINCHON IS THE OLDEST OF FIVE CHILDREN. HE IS THE ONLY MEMBER OF THE FAMILY TO FOLLOW HIS FATHER AND JOIN THE MILITARY. SINCHON'S FATHER HAD BEEN A KOREAN ARMY OFFICER AND HAD BEEN INSTRUMENTAL IN ORGANIZING AND RECRUITING KOREAN SOLDIERS TO FIGHT THE JAPANESE DURING WORLD WAR TWO. HIS MOTHER DIED WHEN HE WAS EIGHTEEN YEARS OLD, SIX MONTHS BEFORE THE OUTBREAK OF THE KOREAN WAR.

NOT KNOWN TO BE MARRIED. LIVES A RECLUSIVE LIFE WHEN NOT IN UNIFORM. IT HAS BEEN REPORTED, AND CONFIRMED BY SEVERAL DEFECTORS, THAT SINCHON MAINTAINS AN EXTENSIVE LIBRARY INCLUDING THE WORKS OF MACHIAVELLI, DOSTOYEVSKY, LENIN AND THOMAS JEFFERSON. IN RECENT YEARS SINCHON HAS TRAVELED OUTSIDE OF NORTH KOREA, PRIMARILY TO RUSSIA AND CHINA. HE HAS DEBRIEFED RUSSIAN AND UKRANIAN MILITARY LEADERS AND VISITED HONG KONG. HIS

ONLY INTEREST OTHER THAN THE MILITARY IS COLLECTING WESTERN-MANUFAC-
TURED SHOTGUNS FOR BIRD HUNTING.

SINCHON IS MISSING THREE FINGERS ON HIS LEFT HAND, LOST WHILE FIGHTING U.S.
MARINES. SINCHON HAS WORKED HIS WAY THROUGH THE RANKS AND IS CONSIDERED
TO HAVE CONSIDERABLE INFLUENCE WITH HIGH MEMBERS OF THE NORTH KOREAN
GOVERNMENT.

After a moment Manning looked up at Collins. "This is all you have? Give
me a break." He tossed the papers on his desk and shook his head at
Brooks and Collins, his faced hardening again. "I want to make sure I
understand this. You're telling me we're dealing with a philosophical army
general who is as old as my father. He controls a fairly large part of the
North Korean Army, but for all we know he is just someone going through a
late midlife crisis, having delusions of grandeur before he kicks the
bucket." He tapped his pipe full of fresh tobacco and relit it.

"We may not have a lot of background on Sinchon," Collins replied, his
face tight. "But this man could be dead serious . . . are you willing to
take the chance that he isn't?"

"Don't get smart with me, Mr. Collins. The fact remains the CIA doesn't
know anything about this general's political motives except what the Chinese are reporting," Manning said icily. "All you know is that he wants to
reunite the North and South and is insisting that he meet with high-ranking
members of the US and South Korean military before he overthrows the
North Korean government. Well, b . . . f . . . d! Why should we stick
our necks on the line?"

"That's it in a nutshell, Mr. Manning," Brooks cut in. "Like it or not,
sometimes that's all you get."

"How the hell can we make a decision with only three pages of information?" Manning exhaled a puff of smoke. "Now, what about the South?
Have you asked their intelligence service about him?"

"No, we haven't. And I don't think that would be a good idea. It's
enough that we are going to have to contact key members of the government. The fewer people that know about this the better." Brooks scratched
his head, holding his surprise at Manning's suggestion in check.

"So what's the CIA's recommendation for meeting with this General
Sinchon?" Manning asked, turning to Collins. "Or don't you have one?"

"First of all, when it comes to reliable information about the North
Koreans, the Chinese have always been credible. To my knowledge Ambassador Lin Phon has a clean track record." Collins spoke as evenly as he
could, as if he were trying to calm a spooked horse. "Lin Phon and his
government are the only ones that have a handle on what's going on inside
Pyongyang. This may be the break we've been waiting for to turn the tide

with the North Koreans.'' Collins couldn't help adding: ''We'd be stupid not to act on this and at least meet with General Sinchon.''

''Act on what, a Chinese rumor?'' Manning was tapping his pencil on the edge of his desk. ''All I want is your fucking recommendation.''

''Rumor? I told you I believe the Chinese are a reliable source. This is not just a whim or a social get-together.'' Collins was stunned. ''Have you been *listening* to what I've been saying? The CIA is—''

''You're right, Mr. Manning.'' Brooks interrupted, trying to forestall Manning's reaction before things got out of hand. ''We don't know a lot about this general and he could be a crackpot. But it's very unlikely that a man could rise to this level in the North Korean military unless he has some political savvy and at least half a brain. Of course, there is only one way we can evaluate this. So the CIA is recommending, to you, that we send someone to meet with General Sinchon.''

''Very well, then. And who do you suggest we send?''

Brooks turned toward Collins for that answer.

''I suggest you send General James,'' Collins said. ''He has a military background and is someone Sinchon would respect.''

''Duke James?'' Manning questioned, feigning a moment of not recollecting who the man was. ''Oh, yes, he is one of my deputy security advisors. Well, I will pass that suggestion on to the president; he's going to have to make the final decision.''

''In the time being, the CIA will continue to dig up what we can on Sinchon and the situation,'' Brooks reassured him.

''Anything else?'' Manning asked, his eyes locked on Collins. He knew the man was stewing and wanted to have a final word.

''We'll wait for your decision,'' Brooks said, sure that Collins would take his lead and end the discussion. ''And Mr. Collins will be heading back to the CIA to work *all night* if need be to make sure he hasn't missed anything on General Sinchon.''

''Excellent. It's good to know the CIA director understands the importance of thoroughness when it comes to briefing the national security advisor.'' Manning glanced at his watch, smiled and stood. ''I'll discuss this with the president. Contact me when you have more information. I assume you two know the way out.''

''Yes, sir,'' Collins smiled back, a bit sourly.

Manning followed the two men out the door of his office, closing and locking it behind them. Without another word he turned left, walking toward the Oval Office.

This was better than anything he could have planned. Brooks and Collins were right, of course, this was a no-brainer. The United States would have to send someone to meet with the North Korean general and Duke James was the perfect choice. Besides, it would get James out of the picture. The president would again have to rely on him solely. If the meeting turned out to be a false alarm, he would tell the president it's always better to be on the side of caution in natural security matters. And if something more important came out of the meeting, Manning would be credited for guiding the president not only domestically but now with foreign policy as well. *Yes, that's it,* Manning thought suddenly. *The president will see that I'm his best choice for his new national security advisor. I can do both jobs better than anyone else.*

Manning felt his stomach burn with excitement. He opened the Oval Office door, smiling broadly at President Louis McEntire who was seated at his desk.

Collins buckled his seat belt before letting out a long sigh. Flipping on the heater, he turned and looked at Brooks. "I know . . . I screwed up," he said. "I need to keep my mouth shut more and listen for what he wants to hear."

"You're damned right you screwed up," Brooks shot back.

"He's a jerk, Doug. He didn't listen to a word I was saying. He's acting like he knows everything and we're a bunch of grade-school kids. You know I'm right."

"Mark, I don't give a shit if you're right or not. Manning is McEntire's number one advisor. If you piss him off, that's going to hurt your credibility. After that, even if your briefings are 100 percent accurate, he's not going to listen to you. That's beltway politics. So cool it. You hear me?" Brooks barked. "Cool it."

"Yeah, yeah. I hear you." Collins pulled out into traffic heading toward Langley. "I'm ready for a beer and bed."

"Too bad. I want your ass back at the office. I wasn't just blowing smoke. Manning was right about one thing: the president's going to want all the information we can get about Sinchon, and I want it before 6:00 A.M."

"Great just friggin' great," Collins said under his breath.

"Consider it penance for bad judgment. Besides, I do have some good news I haven't told you."

"Well, go ahead and make my day."

"Your satellites. They're being retasked."

"What! No shit?" Collins looked over at Brooks.

"No shit. The DCI agrees with you. There is a leak somewhere in the system and it may be in the Senate Oversight Committee. So, your KH-14 and Lacrosse-C will be boosted to a higher orbit at noon tomorrow *without* informing the committee. The North Koreans shouldn't have a clue . . . if that's where the leak is.'' Brooks was pleased and didn't try to hide it.

"What about the Senate and the House?'' Collins asked. "They're not going to like this.''

"You let me deal with the Hill,'' Brooks said, his tone easing up on Collins. He had schooled him enough on White House etiquette for the night. "Now take me home.''


WASHINGTON, D.C.

"The Blue Line . . . Addison Roooad!'' the subway driver's voice broke over the intercom.

Lin Phon sat down in the center seat of the car as the train pulled away from the platform. It picked up speed heading northwest toward Arlington Cemetery. The Metrorail, or Metro as the locals called it, was the quickest and cheapest way to get around downtown Washington, D.C., and the outlying suburbs in Maryland and Virginia.

The system impressed Phon not only for its comfort and safety but because the subway cars were clean and ran on time. And people from all walks of life rode the train. Phon had seen everyone from street people to four-star military officers and visitors from various countries traveling in the cars. Of all the areas he had surveyed in Washington it was the best place to blend in and disappear. When riding the Metro, very few people talked; they generally looked straight ahead, read newspapers or books or even nodded off for a short nap. No one was interested if you appeared different or a little out of the ordinary.

Phon was in the last subway car. Opening his newspaper, he stared over the top of it and scrutinized the people around him. Sitting across the aisle was an older couple holding hands, with several packages at their feet. To Phon's right a young Army officer was dressed in a neatly pressed uniform. Phon guessed he was on his way to the Pentagon.

He pulled out the sports section and placed it on the seat next to him. His eyes returned to the newspaper and he didn't look up at the Korean man who picked up the paper and sat down next to him.

"Mind if I read this?'' the man asked in perfect English.

"Not at all.''

The man crossed his legs and unfolded the paper.

*So you made it,* Phon thought. He felt a rush of relief come over him. He should have known better than to worry. Sitting next to him, the small-faced man with dark eyes and a stringy black mustache was known to him as "Mr. Nee.'' Phon, being a wise man, knew the man probably worked in what he considered the most disciplined and lethal branch of the North Korean military, the intelligence and special forces branch of the *spetsnaz*. Mr. Nee's real name was Col. Kin Hwan, though Phom was careful not to make his knowledge public—especially to Hwan himself.

Hwan was dressed in a poor-quality wool blend suit with a tattered overcoat. The baggy clothes hid his well-muscled body and the coarse black toupee on his head made him look harmless. He resembled a struggling Asian businessman. Looking quite ordinary, Phon wondered how long Hwan had been following him.

"Arlington Cemetery . . . the Blue Line . . . Addison Roooad!" the muffled driver's voice announced the next stop.

Phon waited for the subway car to halt before getting up. He placed the paper under his right arm and the two men exited the train.


MANILA, PHILIPPINES

"You are absolutely certain about this?" Hawkens asked. "It was Denny's aircraft?"

"Yes . . . I am certain," Major Tra answered. "When I have more information I will contact you again."

The line went dead.

*"Son of a bitch!"* Hawkens shouted, slamming down the receiver. "How in the FUCK did something like this happen!"

He paced back and forth across his hotel room floor. The merchandise they might lose would be a financial setback, but even worse were the problems that might be caused by the discovery of the chemical bombs on board the plane. The future of the operation could be in jeopardy.

Sitting on the edge of the bed, Hawkens ran his fingers over his shaved face. His other hand touched the test button on his secure line 455EX voice and data encryptor still connected to the telephone in his room. Twin red LED lights flashed on, telling him the system was up and running. He plugged in the phone line and waited for a dial tone. The system's RS-232C data port allowed him to code voice or computer-generated data, making it nearly impossible for any foreign country to decipher any conversations. A small portable variant of the encryptor was often used by CIA field agents. The 455EX resembled a hand-held pocket calculator and easily fit into any briefcase.

If Hawkens guessed right, Bandar should be rounding the southern tip of Korea.

WASHINGTON, D.C.

Mark Collins rubbed the back of his neck in frustration. Sitting at his CIA desk on the seventh floor of the old building, he gazed at the blue computer screen. He was beginning to hate this part of his job. *Life as a CIA officer, this is real excitement.* This wasn't exactly the stuff Hollywood films were made of.

Resting on the desk next to him were several stacks of papers, folders, computer disks and CD-ROMs, along with two Baby Ruth candy wrappers and half a can of Coke. From the safe in the CIA's Analytic Support Department he had retrieved most of the CIA's personal profile files dealing with the North Korean government and its military. The information had been compiled over the years from a variety of sources, ranging from personal meetings to electronic surveillances.

However, Mark had still only been able to find a few sentences referring to Gen. Han Sinchon. There weren't any pictures of the man, other than what they received from Ambassador Phon, or a specific file detailing him and his career. Mark knew that the difficulties in retrieving the info stemmed from the fact that North Korea remained a tightly closed society, very suspicious of outsiders. A close-knit group of individuals controlled almost every aspect of the country and military, making it nearly impossible to infiltrate. The CIA's covert side, or Directorate of Operations, had limited success and most of the information they learned came from South Korean sources.

Collins ejected the CD-ROM he had been viewing the information on and inserted another laser disk. The opening sentence on the screen now read: NORTH KOREAN MILITARY STRUCTURE 1982 TO PRESENT.

*Maybe this will have more than just the old guy's vital statistics.* Mark was beginning to grow impatient. Unlike the individual data he studied on other world leaders, such as Middle Eastern or African dictators, the North Korean information appeared unorganized. It increased his work load and meant he had to pay close attention to pinpoint the info he needed. Adding to his irritability was Collins' unhappiness at leaving his wife alone another full night. He was tempted to pick up the files and take them home.

Using the computer mouse, Collins scrolled the document to a list of young army lieutenant colonels. He typed in the name SINCHON and tapped the search button. The screen flashed and nothing happened. *NOT FOUND* appeared at the bottom left corner.

Collins took a mouthful of flat Coke and swallowed it. *No doubt about it, it's going to be another long night.*

## ARLINGTON NATIONAL CEMETERY

Ambassador Lin Phon took the stairs to the upper level. The walkway, a combination walking, jogging and bicycle path, ran along the boundary outside Arlington National Cemetery. At night it was quiet, relatively devoid of people and, in Phon's opinion, the ideal place to discuss the future of his country. Phon spoke first, turning to the Korean man walking next to him.

"How long will you be in Washington, Mr. Nee?" Phon asked as a couple walked past them.

"I leave tomorrow morning," Kin Hwan replied, lighting a cigarette.

"Still selling fishing rods?" the ambassador asked coyly.

"Yes, I am still a broker for a South Korean fishing rod manufacturer, Mung Sun-Moon. Business is good." Hwan exhaled smoke through his nose.

"I only have a few minutes, so listen carefully," Phon said once the couple was out of earshot. "I received a personal fax from Beijing. It was encrypted and coded for my eyes only. The fax came from our chief of internal security . . . It describes a conspiracy to overthrow your government. There will be a coup attempt against your country very soon. Are you aware of this?"

Hwan kept walking. "There have been rumors," he said at last. "But there are always rumors. What makes this different from other times?"

"General Sinchon," Phon stated coldly. "Do you know of him?"

Hwan hesitated. "Yes. Everyone in the military knows of General Sinchon. He is a very powerful man."

"Two days ago Sinchon had a meeting with our attaché, Chengji Zheng, in Pyongyang. It is no secret your country is on the verge of economic ruin and the current government policies will not change that. General Sinchon has seen the reforms and prosperity in China. He believes he can change the North and unite it with the South without war. He also believes that Chin is a fool and needs to be removed from power. We understand he wishes the coup to be without bloodshed but he is prepared to kill people if they get in his way."

"You know this for certain?"

"Sinchon has outlined his plans to Chengji Zheng. He is to have a corps of high-ranking officers from each branch of the military that are loyal to him. His strategy is to capture and if need be kill the top government officials of your country . . . including General Chief of Staff Myong Chin."

"Hmmmm," Hwan murmured, recollecting that a meeting of the supreme council was scheduled to take place during the first week of January in Pyongyang. *General Sinchon is scheduled to address the council on the readiness of the North's ground troops. It was to be his last speech as an army officer. That would perhaps be a perfect opportunity to strike . . . when all the top officials are gathered.*

Phon saw Hwan's eyes flicker in the streetlights.

"Why would Sinchon give your country this information?" Hwan's tone was suspicious.

"The general is requesting our help. He wants the South and the United States to know his intentions before he moves forward. There is to be a meeting with a representative from both countries." Phon walked slowly, then turned back toward the Metro station. Hwan followed.

"When . . . when will this meeting take place?" Hwan asked eagerly.

"Two days . . . Langau Island."

"You have the numbers to my offices in Washington and New York . . . you may contact me at one of them if you learn of anything else." Colonel Hwan took one more drag off his cigarette before flicking the butt on the rocks along the path.

"I am not doing this for your country alone. I do it for China. My country cannot . . . *will* not lose another ally."

"I understand," Colonel Hwan replied, not really caring why the man was divulging the information. He turned away from the entrance to the Metro and disappeared into the darkness.

Ambassador Phon walked down the stairs back into the warm interior of the subway system. He only had to wait a few minutes for the southbound train to carry him back to Pentagon City Mall.


MANILA, PHILIPPINES

The malice in Bandar's voice caused Hawkens to grip the phone tightly. He closed his eyes and listened to every word, trying not to lose his temper.

"I told you Denny was a worthless son of a bitch! This is your responsibility, Carl. Denny was your man. My entire operation could fall apart because of this."

"Nothing is going to happen to the operation," Hawkens said evasively. "The plane went down in a mountainous region about ten miles southwest of the air base. It is nearly impossible to reach on foot."

"Impossible . . . nothing is impossible!" Bandar roared into the phone. "I want Tra to put a group of men together. Have him locate the aircraft and destroy everything . . . including Denny."

"Let things cool down first, Bandar. We don't need any more stupid mistakes. If someone did spot it going down we don't want to get caught making a beeline for the merchandise." Hawkens kept his tone calm as he tried to reason with Bandar. "Besides, what if the casings broke? Tra and his men couldn't get near it if they wanted to."

"That's all the more reason for us to get there first. Offer Tra more money. I want the merchandise and Denny disposed of as soon as possible," Bandar ordered irrationally.

"Bandar . . . listen to me," Hawkens argued. "Money isn't the issue anymore. If the Vietnamese government finds out Tra was responsible for that shipment of chemical weapons, he's a dead man. He doesn't want to go anywhere near that wreck. Give him some time until he can be certain there will be no risks of being caught."

"I want it done immediately, Carl. Do you understand me?"

There was a long pause. Hawkens listened to the electronic hiss as he thought it over.

"Okay, okay. No worries," Hawkens said finally. "I'll take care of it."

He heard the line go dead. Glancing out the window at the low-hanging clouds, Hawkens mind drifted toward the jungles of Vietnam. Bandar had never been in the jungle when it rained. At times the water came down so hard it was impossible to stand on a hillside without being swept away or to see farther than fifty feet in any direction. *That's Bandar's biggest problem. He won't listen to anyone, even when he doesn't know what the hell he's talking about. No one else is going to be trekking through that mess to get at a bunch of wreckage. That ASSHOLE always thinks he knows what's best, especially when he doesn't have to do any of the dirty work.*

Hawkens grabbed the vodka bottle, pouring the last of it into a smudged glass. He needed to fly to Washington, D.C., tonight. If the Americans found out about this, there would be a good chance it would turn up in the press within the next few days. Either way, he still had a few friends in the agency that might tell him something.

# 15

The stern look on Col. Met Lee Kaine's face revealed only a hint of surprise. He reread the encrypted fax transmission from Col. Kin Hwan, his Washington intel agent. The message was short and to the point, outlining his meeting with the Chinese ambassador and Sinchon's coup plans. Shaking his head, Kaine wondered why Gen. Han Sinchon, who had never seemed interested in power and control, would now be plotting to overthrow his own government at this late stage in his career.

And the question that burned even more inside the colonel was how this could be happening under his watchful eye. He was one of the top-ranking *spetsnaz* officers and special advisor to General Chief of Staff Myong Chin. This kind of detail should not have to be discovered through the Chinese.

Kaine read the fax a third time. In certain ways Kaine was envious of Hwan. The man was cunning and knew more about Western society than any of Kaine's other foreign operatives. He learned things easily and managed to retain a variety of information. However, there was a dark side to Hwan. He could be hotheaded and unpredictable. He was valuable but difficult to control, and Kaine knew the day would come when the man would become expendable.

"I need a car," Kaine said, punching the intercom next to his phone.

Walking swiftly he exited the building into the dark night. At the edge of the curb he climbed into the waiting staff car.

"Chief of Staff Chin's quarters," Kaine bellowed to the driver.

Kaine showed his security clearance badge to the guard as he exited the elevator. The sharply dressed guard saluted. This was the third and last checkpoint before reaching the chief of staff's personal quarters which occupied the entire fourth floor of Pyongyang's finest apartment building. Kaine found it odd that a man who occupies an entire floor of a building with lush furnishings normally slept in his office.

He stood in front of Chin's door and knocked several times.

"Who is it?" a gruff voice sounded through the door.

"Colonel Kaine to see Chief of Staff Chin, it's urgent." Kaine stood rigid, waiting. After what seemed several minutes, the door opened. A man dressed in a silk robe and slippers escorted the colonel to a sitting room off the foyer.

"Well, what is it?" Chin asked immediately once Kaine entered the room. "Is there a problem with the fuel rods?"

"No, sir. I just received a transmission from Kim Hwan. It's information I didn't think could wait until morning."


## NAMPO, NORTH KOREA

The sickening sweet smell of crude oil and rotting sea life swept over Gen. Han Sinchon as he sat in the back seat of his staff car. The window was cracked just enough to allow the rancid air to pour in over him. The general tried to ignore it. He concentrated on the calming effects of the bay's rolling black waves. For an instant they permitted him to forget about the pain simmering inside of him and the deception he was about to commit.

Sinchon checked his watch. It showed 4:28 A.M. He was two minutes early.

"Keep the lights off. Drive to the edge of the dock," Sinchon whispered.

Col. Khoe Kwang eased the staff car to the end of the weathered wooden wharf and turned off the engine.

Grasping a small soft-sided bag, Sinchon exited the car and peered into the darkness overlooking the inlet. The north side of Nampo harbor was nearly void of cargo ships and transport ferries. Most of the heavy sea traffic took place in the south part of the port. This section was reserved for military ships and a few private yachts, mostly from foreign countries, sailing dignitaries into and out of the area.

A chilly wind blew out of the northwest; another cold front was on its way. Several hundred yards away Sinchon could see two men walking away along the road behind him. A small skiff, its running light blinking, was making its way across the harbor several hundred yards out. Everything else appeared quiet. *Now is my chance,* Sinchon mused. *To walk away and forget about my plan.* His mind filled with thoughts of returning home to the warm comfort of his small apartment and dying a peaceful death.

Bandar's men had orders to remain in the area for thirty minutes. If they didn't get a signal by that time they would leave, returning to the *Van Triumph.*

*All I have to do is walk away,* Sinchon repeated to himself.

He edged closer to the water. He set his bag down and removed a small metal flashlight from his pocket. He tilted his wristwatch back and forth, catching the glimmer of reflecting moonlight. His watch read exactly 4:30 A.M. Bandar's men should be in position for his signal. Sinchon pressed the on/off button three quick times before sweeping the beam across the water. He waited for a response.

It only took a moment. A few hundred yards to the west, hugging the jagged rocks of the breakwater, he caught sight of three red flashes. The signal repeated itself. *That's it,* he thought, returning to his staff car.

"I will return in five days," Sinchon repeated. "You have your orders."

"Yes, General," Kwang replied.

Sinchon stared at his aide through the open window. In the darkness he could barely make out the outline of the man's face.

"I have not thought to thank you very often, Khoe. You serve me and your country well."

With that the general walked back to the edge of the pier and down the narrow set of stairs to the water. He could hear the hum of a small engine and the splash of a dinghy coming his way.

Kwang backed the car away and turned onto the main road heading back to the ministry building. "Your thanks are too late, old man, and are of no value to me and my family," Kwang said aloud, pressing on the accelerator. Soon Sinchon would be retired and Kwang would be basking in the glory and benefits of a promotion.


YONGBYON, NORTH KOREA

"Where are your authorization papers for this sector?" the guard asked.

"This is it here," Capt. Kim Yong-Gil said politely. He removed the written orders from his briefcase and handed them to the middle-aged man.

"I do not know you," the guard grunted as he studied Yong-Gil's face. His eyes shifted from the photo back to Yong-Gil's face in rapid succession. "And it's my responsibility to know all the engineers in this department."

"Then you will need to remember my face from now on," Yong-Gil stood his ground.

"When were you assigned here?"

"I was assigned a week ago. My orders, you will see, are signed by Colonel Kaine." Again Kim Yong-Gil kept his tone low and even. "I believe he controls the security in this sector."

"I know that."

"If you have any questions, I suggest you contact him." Yong-Gil kept his dark eyes fixed on the man.

"Wait here," the man said, turning to call the security office.

Yong-Gil surveyed the room. It was well lit and much warmer than the tunnel. He guessed it to be about ten feet by ten feet. The low ceiling met rust-stained walls that were lined with steel rebar. An iron cage surrounded the metal door leading to the reprocessing and computer rooms. Everyone going into and out of this section of the complex passed through this check point. If anyone entered without authorization they would be shot without warning—the bullet-pitted wall testified to it.

A security guard, he guessed this one to be a senior *spetsnaz* noncommissioned officer, sat behind thick bulletproof glass. Leaning in gun racks against the wall were five loaded AK-47s and two rocket-propelled grenade launchers. Above the guard were six surveillance cameras showing various sections of the complex. Each flashed a different picture every few seconds.

"Why are you here so early?" the guard asked, replacing the phone.

"Colonel Kaine requires that I complete my work. Do you want to tell him I wasn't allowed to finish it . . . or should I?" Captain Yong-Gil took his authorization papers back from the man and stuck them into his briefcase, adding an appeal to the guard's sensitivity, if he had any. "You know how it is. I must prove my worth or I will be replaced with someone that can do the job."

The guard grunted something unintelligible before hitting the button to release the door. The metal cage came open and Yong-Gil walked inside.


MINISTRY OF DEFENSE, PYONGYANG, NORTH KOREA

"So the old man thinks he can kill me and get away with it," Chin laughed. "Sinchon is a crazy old man. This simple act will not change the direction of our country. No one can change what is right." Sitting in a high-backed hunter green leather arm chair, sipping from a hot cup of tea, Chin's eyes were bright and clear. "The man has lost his mind."

"Maybe so," Kaine said. "But he is powerful. If he did kill you Sinchon could very possibly take control. He has officers in top positions that are obedient and would follow him. You must remember Sinchon has trained a good number of them. They look at him as a teacher and a loyal leader."

"Sinchon is an old, silly man."

"In your eyes he is old and silly. But he commands the respect of each branch of the armed forces, including the *spetsnaz*. No one else can say that, not even you. If anyone could do this . . . it would be Sinchon. Sir, Sinchon is more dangerous than you think."

Chin folded his hands, his face burning with the insult. He didn't like this young officer's impudence, but for the time being he would put it aside. He knew the man was making sense. "So what are his plans? His so-called *business* trip is actually a cover to meet with Americans?"

"Yes, sir. That is what I believe."

Chin looked away from Kaine. *The old man isn't as smart as he believes himself to be. Trusting the Chinese with this type of information will prove to be unhealthy for someone his age. Every soldier in North Korea will know that Sinchon is nothing more than a common traitor.*

"When is Sinchon scheduled to leave with Bandar?" Chin asked quickly.

"This morning."

"I want you to find him before then and have him arrested at once."

"Yes, sir. Of course, sir. I will handle this personally."

"I am planning to meet with our Iranian contact again later today. It is imperative that we stay alerted to the American satellites' orbits during the transfer."

"Colonel Hwan knows to stay in touch with his contact. He is doing everything possible to ensure we have the latest data," Kaine replied, then added: "The Americans will inevitably catch a glimpse of the plutonium during the journey, but if we time it right, they won't know where it came from or where it went."

"Your new security cameras have not detected anything unusual?" Chin asked, the impending transfer weighing on his mind.

"Nothing. One of my best men reviews the tapes every six hours. In fact, I will examine the latest set of tapes myself this morning."

"I want to make certain this matter with General Sinchon does not interfere with our plans." Chin stood, agitated. "Nothing will be moved unless you can provide the proper security, do you hear me? We have worked too long and have spent too much on this project to have it discovered by the Americans. I am not ready to lead this country to war . . . yet."

"I understand, General Chin."

"It is vital that you find Sinchon. You are right that he could prove to be dangerous and you shall be rewarded. We cannot allow that meeting to take place."


ARLINGTON, VIRGINIA

"In Jesus' name we pray," Fr. Francis O'Higgins said, making the sign of the cross over the brushed aluminum casket. A cold November breeze forced his long gray hair to flutter up beyond the neatly combed part running down the center of his head.

"Amen," Duke James whispered under his breath as he blessed himself. Duke put his arm around his wife Katie, holding her close to him.

James felt a gust of wind cut through his overcoat, sending a shiver down his spine. The late afternoon sky had turned a deep gray with low rolling clouds churning overhead. The season's first major winter storm lurked just over the horizon. As soon as the wind stopped blowing the snow would begin to fall.

James watched Father O'Higgins close his black leather-bound Bible, tucking it neatly under his right arm. The priest folded his hands and let out a long breath, not taking his eyes off the casket of Sally Bishop.

"We'll miss you, Sally," Duke heard a female voice whisper from somewhere behind him.

"Rest in peace," someone else said in a hushed tone.

James' eyes swept across the thirty or so people gathered around the gravesite. They all looked cold, with red cheeks and solemn faces.

After a moment or so Father O'Higgins nodded toward Bill Bishop. Dressed in black with dark glasses covering his eyes, he moved stiffly to place a single red rose on top of the casket. He bowed his head as he said goodbye one last time. After a few seconds Bill's oldest daughter came forward and took him by the arm, leading him away. The crowd slowly broke up and made their way back to the vehicles.

"Duke . . . wait a second."

James turned around to see Mark Collins and his wife moving toward him.

"Hello, Mark . . . Christine." Duke's lips turned up, never quite reaching a smile. The two couples walked together to the parked cars.

"Are you and Katie planning to attend the reception back at the church?" Collins asked.

Duke looked at Katie before answering. "Yeah . . . we thought we'd stop in for a few minutes."

"Good. I'll talk with you there." Mark nodded and picked up his pace to his silver Acura TL.

"What was that about?" Katie asked.

"You know Mark. Probably company business," Duke said as they reached their Chevy Tahoe four-wheel drive. "He's been working hard on a project that hasn't been too successful so far."


MINISTRY OF DEFENSE, PYONGYANG

"You were correct in being cautious, Colonel Kaine," the stout fifty-year-old security officer said, placing a video tape into the VCR. "We recorded this surveillance tape five hours ago at Yongbyon. I rushed it here immediately."

Col. Met Lee Kaine stiffened his back at the news. Several veins protruded from his thick neck as he placed his large forearms on the desk.

"Why wasn't I notified sooner? Why did you wait?" Kaine's expression was dark.

"I thought it was best to let the tape run to its entirety, then I had to get background information on the traitor. I did not want to come to you unprepared, sir." The man's face showed his apprehension.

"Yes, of course," Kaine answered, letting out a long breath. "Continue."

"Seven days ago, Capt. Kim Yong-Gil was cleared for nuclear operations in the BN-880 reprocessing room. His main responsibility is to assist in the maintenance and construction of a new cooling system for the reactor," the security officer began.

"I personally signed his transfer papers," Kaine barked. "Are you telling me Captain Yong-gil is a spy?"

"Yes, sir. When the decision was made to recover the plutonium fuel rods and ready them for transfer we installed three new cameras as you instructed." The guard prepared to turn the tape on with the remote. "Yong-Gil is in the tapes of the other monitored rooms; in those he follows every security rule. There is no question about his actions in this tape, however."

The security officer pushed the play button. A black-and-white picture appeared on the monitor. At the bottom of the picture Kaine could see the date and time. The screen showed a wide-angle shot of a long narrow room with a low ceiling and barren white walls. A steel crane supported by several I-beams ran down the center of the room, along with a block and tackle holding a number of thick cables. In the center of the floor was a pool of liquid several feet deep, and protruding from it were a number of round metal cylinders. The security camera panned left, showing a man standing next to the iron rail overlooking the water. He held a briefcase, resting it on top of the rail.

"This is the cooling chamber, of course, where the plutonium fuel rods are stored to be cooled," the guard stated.

"I know what I'm looking at," Kaine grunted. "Just show me your evidence."

The security officer held the fast-forward button down. "This is the sequence here," he stated and froze the picture. "In his right hand you can see a small black box. You can see it better in the next pictures."

Kaine exhaled hard, watching Yong-Gil each time as the camera, scanning back and forth, came back to him. Sure enough the young captain held a tiny rectangular object to his right eye as he appeared to snap four or five photos of the room.

"I do not know how he was able to get into the cooling chamber without an escort." The security officer stopped the VCR to look at Kaine. "That is one problem we need to fix."

"Perhaps he has an accomplice . . ."

"There is more." The security officer had his back to Kaine as he placed another tape into the machine. "This is the computer design room where Yong-Gil works."

Kaine's face grew hot with anger as he realized Yong-Gil had done more photographing. It appeared he could walk freely about the complex without any restrictions. The picture jumped several times before focusing on a cramped room with several computers. In the back corner of the room was a filing cabinet.

Colonel Kaine watched as the engineer methodically went through several drawers and files before stopping to take pictures of specific files.

"What are in those files?" Kaine asked.

"The reprocessing schedule and the amount of plutonium fuel we have in storage."

"Where is Yong-Gil now?"

"I have put him under twenty-four hour surveillance, as you instructed should this occur." The security officer remained standing, his body rigid.

"Very good. You have done well. I want you to return to Yongbyon. Keep Captain Yong-Gil under surveillance but do not arrest him until you have orders from me." Kaine stood, removed the tape and took the other tape as well. "Do you have any copies of these?"

"No, sir."

"Do not speak of this to anyone else. I don't want Yong-Gil to become suspicious. Find a way to ensure that he is not allowed to take any more photographs without alarming him unnecessarily." Kaine's stare bore in on the man as he continued: "Keep your eyes open, for he may be working with someone. I will not tolerate failure."

"Yes, sir." The security officer came to attention and saluted before exiting the colonel's office.

Kaine closed the door, still holding the tapes in his hand. His hand tightened around them as he wondered how much information had already been supplied to the South and their American allies. More importantly, he wondered how this would affect Myong Chin's plans.

ARLINGTON, VIRGINIA

Duke James gently took Katie's hand as they walked up the pathway to Saint Joseph's Church. He could see a few flakes of snow starting to swirl in the air above him.

"Let's not stay long. I'd like to get home before it's dark," Katie said as they reached the stairs leading to the back reception hall.

"Matt's twelve . . . he can handle it," Duke replied with confidence. "I started baby sitting when I was twelve."

"You were fifty when you were twelve, Duke. Besides, I'm not concerned about Matt. I'm sure he's parked in front of the television with the phone. It's what Pam and Sean are getting into while he's not paying attention."

Duke laughed under his breath, knowing his wife was right. Pam turned eight last month and Sean was now three. Duke pictured the scene in his mind: Matt would be glued to the television set watching all-Star Wrestling or a Chicago Bulls game, totally oblivious to his brother and sister torching the living room couch or having their fill of cookies and ice cream.

"Okay . . . fifteen minutes." He didn't need any more convincing.

Duke opened the door for Katie, then helped her with her coat, hanging it next to his on the rack along the wall. In her late thirties, Kate could pass for a woman ten years younger. Her dark brown hair hung softly around her shoulders. She was in beautiful shape. Duke didn't consider Katie the standard military wife. She was strong-willed, even impossibly so at times, depending on the situation. But it had been just that quality that attracted Duke to her in the first place. When he was gone Katie James stayed tough.

"Would you like some coffee to warm you up?" Duke asked, rubbing her cold hands in his.

"Yes, I would," Katie whispered.

They entered the church's reception hall and headed for a long covered table along the wall. A dozen or so people were milling around the table, eating and drinking. He walked up to an older woman serving from a silver coffee pot and glass bowl filled with red punch. He asked for two coffees and the older woman smiled indulgently. Glancing at the table Duke saw several plates of sandwiches, breads, cookies and cakes. He guessed them all to be homemade from the Ladies Auxiliary Club.

Like many older Catholic churches, the Saint Joseph's reception area was nothing extraordinary. The black-and-white tile floor was scuffed and worn and the metal gray chairs were scratched and rusty. Drawings and banners, created by the children in the religious education program, lined the walls. Duke spotted Bill Bishop talking with Father O'Higgins, Mark and Christine Collins.

"I never know what to say, Duke." Katie stood close, taking the cup of coffee and holding it in both hands. "I'm glad you were home this time . . . I hate coming to these things by myself."

Duke lowered his head and then smiled at her. "I know." He took hold of her arm and leaned over, kissing her lightly.

## MINISTRY OF DEFENSE, PYONGYANG

Myong Chin stared at the last video as it came to an end. In a flurry of emotion he picked up his tea cup and threw it across the room. The china shattered and long lines of brown liquid rolled down the wall.

"How long?" Chin asked Kaine, furious. "How long?"

"Capt. Kim Yong-Gil has been stationed at Yongbyon for eighteen months. However, he has only had access to the reprocessing area for the last seven days." Colonel Kaine stood tall, his burly shoulders squared out.

"Long enough to compromise the entire operation," Chin said, his hand shaking. "Only an idiot would believe he has not supplied the West with information. This will make it impossible to proceed with the transfer of the fuel rods to Iran." Chin stood as he started for the tea cart next to the far wall.

"I do not believe he is working alone," Kaine said evenly. "Sinchon is involved in this. That is why he is meeting with Americans. It is all part of his plot. I will arrest Capt. Kim Yong-Gil for treason, then see that he reveals how much information has been supplied to General Sinchon and the Americans."

Chin, his jaw set, finished filling another cup of tea. His face was deep in thought as he returned to his desk. In the last twelve hours he had learned of two high-ranking officers betraying his country. It seemed possible that they were indeed connected.

The predominant problem lay in whether the Americans had been supplied with details of the underground nuclear facility. There was also a good chance other security staff were involved. The only way to uncover them was to allow everything to continue as normal.

"What of Sinchon . . . have you arrested him?" Chin asked, checking the time.

"General Sinchon boarded the *Van Triumph* four hours ago," Kaine answered reluctantly. This was news he regretted having to report. "I have an intelligence trawler shadowing the yacht."

"So he left earlier than we expected." Chin sighed, somewhat uncharacteristically, and remained calm at his desk, thinking. "He has managed to stay ahead of the game. Kwang did not inform me of his departure as I had hoped. I can only assume he has chosen to side with Sinchon."

"Captain Yong-Gil is under surveillance. It is only Sinchon we have to worry about."

"Yes, it is General Sinchon and the Americans we must worry about, not a simple spy.'' Chin paused as a plan began to take shape in his head. ''What if we transferred the fuel rods right under the Americans' noses?''

''Under their noses?'' Kaine asked, perplexed.

''Shaqat has agreed to the terms I have given him and is awaiting details of the transfer.''

''Yes . . . but I do not understand. How will we transfer the rods if the Americans know about the facility?''

''We do not know for certain the Americans have been given that information yet. If Yong-Gil worked for Sinchon then the photos were delivered to him. It is very possible that our operation has not been compromised.'' Chin suddenly smiled. ''It is a risk we must take. We will also take care of the general at the same time.''

Kaine could only sit and wait for Chin to continue. He was not following Chin's reasoning at all.

Chin continued: ''One day from now the *Van Triumph* will dock at Langau with Sinchon aboard the yacht. The Americans do not know we are aware of this meeting. I will send word for the Iranians to position one of their freighters close to the area.'' Taking a pad from the corner of his desk, Chin drew a sketch of the island. ''Colonel Hwan reported that Sinchon has demanded the Americans keep their military out of the area—for his own safety, I'm sure, as well as not to arouse suspicion. After the *Van Triumph* docks you will order one of your Su-30s to blow her out of the water. When that happens I want a cargo plane carrying the fuel rods to land at Langau. The Americans will not have any ships or aircraft in the area to react.'' Chin sat back in his chair, relieved at having devised a counteraction.

''The fuel rods will be transferred to the freighter under the American noses,'' Kaine repeated, giving what appeared to be a smile on his stony face. It was a simple plan.

''Do not make any arrests now or they will know we're onto them. Contact Colonel Hwan. We must know the precise time Sinchon is to meet with the Americans. In one blow we will take care of transferring the fuel rods and eliminating General Sinchon.'' The general chief of staff looked directly at Kaine. ''There cannot be any mistakes.''

''I will prepare at once.'' Kaine turned abruptly to put the plan in action.

ARLINGTON, VIRGINIA

Duke and Katie stood by themselves in the center of the reception hall. People were still trickling in from outside but the conversation remained low and muddled. The solemn mood was beginning to overwhelm Duke, but he didn't want to leave without talking to Bill Bishop. He checked the large round clock on the wall. It had already been twenty minutes.

Bishop still stood talking with Father O'Higgins and Collins, until he saw Duke and Katie. He excused himself from the group and walked toward them.

"Thank you for coming, Katie," Bill said, giving her a hug.

"Oh, Bill . . ." Katie began. Duke could see her force tears back as she blinked hard, then continued: "Sally was such a special person and I know you're going to miss her. Please come visit any time you get too lonely."

They held each other a moment longer in silence, then Bill's face broke into a slight smile. He spoke haltingly, shaking Duke's hand: "Thank you both. Sally kept saying we needed to get together more with you. Now . . . well, she enjoyed your company."

"I meant what I said," Duke assured him. "You can go up to the cabin if you want. If any of the kids want to go with you too, there's plenty of room."

"Thanks, I appreciate it." Bill's smile grew a little. "I might take you up on that. Dixie said she might want to go with me. You haven't met my youngest daughter from Hawaii, have you, Katie? Let me introduce you."

"She's the artist, isn't she?" Katie asked, following Bill to a small group of people seated at a table.

*Damn, that felt awkward,* Duke thought, getting a refill of coffee. He was preparing a plate of sandwiches when Mark Collins came up behind him.

"How's the food?"

"Not bad if you like cream cheese and pastrami sandwiches without any crust."

"How do you think he's doing?" Collins asked, nodding his head toward Bishop.

"Seems okay. Probably handling it better than I would . . . I don't think it's really hit him yet. He's talking to Katie about going up to our cabin with his daughter." Duke stepped away from the table toward a section of the room that was void of people. "So what's up?"

"You really haven't heard?" Collins asked, giving Duke an inquisitive glance.

"Heard what . . . you've been promoted to Director for Operations?" Duke smiled, sipping his coffee.

"Yeah, right. The president's called a classified national security meeting. It's scheduled for 9:00 A.M. tomorrow."

"Classified? How do you . . ." Duke stopped, remembering he was talking to an analyst for the CIA. "Shit . . . why wasn't I told?"

"I don't know . . . but your name is on the agenda."

"Really. And who set the agenda?"

"Your new boss." Collins, grinning, raised his eyebrows at Duke.

"Manning." Duke shook his head.

"That's right . . . everybody's buddy, Manning." Collins suddenly grew serious: "I still can't figure out why McEntire's letting him do it. I don't care what qualifications Manning thinks he has, he's not qualified to be national security advisor."

Duke finished off the last of his coffee. "Well, I'm beginning to understand it. It's called politics and men have been doing it for years. Manning's hungry for it and he must know what he's doing."

"He's a doorknob . . ."

"Maybe so, but he's hungry for power. And from where I sit he'll run over anyone who gets in his way. Case in point . . . Bill Bishop."

Duke knew that Allan Manning, without question, pulled more weight with the nation's chief executive than any other cabinet member. Now that he was national security advisor, Manning could guide the president's every move on domestic and foreign issues. And with Bishop out of the way he had open road.

"Hell, everyone on the Hill is power hungry," Collins said, still not putting much stock in Manning.

"Well, Manning's in a class by himself."

"Hope we're not interrupting anything important." Katie came up beside Duke, taking hold of his arm.

"Nope, we were just trying to figure out how they get the crusts off these sandwiches," Duke replied, smiling.

Katie squeezed Duke's hand. They had stayed long enough.

"We've got to get going. Matt's baby-sitting," Duke said quickly.

"I'm heading over to the agency later tonight," Collins said. "If anything important comes up I'll give you a call."

"Sounds good." Duke and Katie waved a quiet goodbye and made their way to the door.

Twenty minutes later they pulled into the driveway to find their townhome still standing and the kids looking out the living room window, waiting for them.

WASHINGTON NATIONAL AIRPORT

"Do you have anything to declare?" the customs agent asked Carl Hawkens.

"No."

"What is in the bags?"

"Dirty laundry and some books."

"Was your trip business or pleasure?"

"A little of both. I did some fishing and met with a real estate developer." Hawkens was silent for a moment. "All I can say is God Bless America. It's good to be home."

"You may go," the customs agent said. "Next, please."

Hawkens threw the strap of his leather garment bag over his shoulder and headed for the exit. "Taxi!" he shouted. A cab pulled up to the curb. "Georgetown, but first run me by a liquor store. The fucking airline ran out of vodka."

"Got it. One liquor store and then Georgetown," the cabby said, tossing Hawkens' bag into the trunk.


## STAFFORD, VIRGINIA

"Good night, Pamela. Thanks for being a good girl while Mom and Dad were gone this afternoon." Duke kissed his eight-year-old daughter on the cheek while tucking her in for bed.

"Good night, Dad . . . I love you," Pam said, snuggling. One arm was wrapped around the neck of a white stuffed kitty cat named "Katie" after Mommy and the other arm around a fluffy gray stuffed rabbit named "Hopper."

"See you in the morning, angel." Duke gently moved her brown bangs to the side.

"Leave the door open, Daddy." Pam breathed, then closed her eyes.

"I will . . . and I'll keep the night light on in the hallway for you." Duke turned to see his wife standing in the doorway. He flicked off the Mickey Mouse desk lamp next to Pam's bed, gave her one last kiss on the forehead and left the room.

"Can you believe how fast they're growing, Duke," Katie James said, taking her husband's arm as they walked down the hall together. It was not a question, just a statement about the way time managed to fly by them. She glanced at Duke and thought she noticed his salt-and-pepper hair was getting a little grayer around the sides. Other than that he really hadn't changed much in the last fourteen years. Duke was the same man she loved.

She remembered that summer afternoon they met in Fort Collins, Colorado, as if it had happened yesterday. Katie had just finished enrolling for her senior year at the university. She was walking across the campus, heading toward her MGB convertible in the parking lot, when someone caught her eye. She remembered nearly stopping to watch Duke, wearing a faded pair of Levi's 501s with a denim shirt and cowboy boots, angling toward the same direction. In his late twenties, Duke didn't look like the rest of the university crowd. His square jaw and upright six-foot frame exuded confidence that Kate rarely perceived in a man.

She had no way of knowing he was a captain in the Air Force, staying with his parents while on leave. He had spent the day at Colorado State University visiting some of his old teachers and using the library for an Air Force research paper. Duke had parked his 1977 Chevy 4 × 4 next to her MGB and when Katie's car wouldn't start he offered to help. Four months later they were married.

"I'll take that glass of wine now," Duke said, walking into the living room.

"I already have it poured." She gestured toward the coffee table in front of the television set.

Duke smiled at the familiar sight of two glasses of red wine next to a plate of crackers and cheese. A single lamp in the far corner lit the room.

Duke sat down on the couch, picking up both glasses and handing one to his wife. He reached for the remote control to the television but Katie grabbed it first.

"No television tonight, Duke." She smiled, taking a long sip of her wine and running her other hand along his leg.

"Well . . . what do you have in mind, Katherine?" Duke asked, slyly.

"I say we get to bed early . . . and have a little adult entertainment." Katie let her robe fall open slightly, letting him catch sight of a pretty pink nightie. She smiled at him devilishly.

Duke set his wine glass down and took his wife in his arms. "Now why didn't I think of this," he whispered, moving his mouth over her lips down to her throat.

# 16

The bright flash of a car's headlights flickered across the wall. The silver light and shifting shadows awakened Allan Manning from his semiconscious state. Raising his head, he looked around, not seeing anything familiar.

"Shit, where am I?"

Rolling over, he sat up and glanced at a nearby alarm clock. 3:13 A.M. He sat in the darkness for a few seconds trying to piece things back together. He had gone to the other side of town, taking care not to be followed. One of his friends had told him of another bar where he would feel welcomed. Manning rubbed his pounding head. *The way my head hurts I must have had a good time.* Then he recalled walking by a table and seeing the cocaine and shots of tequila lined up in several tidy lines, a group of men seated around the table smiling up at him.

*It must have been the tequila,* Manning thought, exhaling hard. *I need to get home.* Searching the room in the dark he wondered where his clothes and glasses were. Running a hand over his chest, his skin felt sticky and sweaty. The taste of stale cigarettes made his mouth feel dry. Then it hit him. He remembered leaving the bar with someone. Leaving with someone . . . but he couldn't remember his face. He was younger . . . he was taller and had a bald head.

"I've got to get the hell out of here," Manning breathed softly and finally found his pants.

"Hey, it's okay . . . you're with me," a soft male voice spoke from behind him. "I wouldn't tell anyone. I want to see you again."

Manning spun around, startled. He could barely make out the image of a young man lying naked in the bed. The man reached for the lamp.

"No, no! Don't turn on the light!" Manning's voice was a harsh whisper.

"It's okay, Allan. I took care of you. No one knows who you are but me," the man said, turning on the light anyway. He sported a black goatee and his head was shaved, he looked to be in his late twenties or early thirties. Both the man's arms were covered with tattoos and his chest was shrouded in black hair.

"How do you know my name?" Manning asked, wrestling on his pants and shirt.

"You're the chief of staff, for God's sake. I've seen your picture before."

"Shit, man, I'm not the chief of staff," Manning replied, trying to chuckle lightheartedly.

"Yes, you are. I'd recognize your face anywhere."

"No, I'm not," Manning said angrily. He pulled on the last of his clothes and headed for the front door.

"I want to see you again . . . don't you want my number?"

*Get your stupid ass out of here.* Manning blocked out what the man was saying and ran down the stairs two at a time. He had to get to a phone and call a cab.

Manning stepped outside and realized he was standing in front of a condominium complex on the north side of Georgetown. The cold air felt good. He put his hands on his hips and stopped to take a breath. It occurred to him something was missing. Looking and feeling around his belt he realized it was his message beeper. It wasn't there. He'd have a hell of a time trying to explain that one to the Secret Service. Then startling thoughts entered his mind. *What if the White House called? What if the president is trying to find me?*

Turning left around a corner he picked up his pace, heading toward a convenience store.


NGHIA BINH PROVINCE, VIETNAM

*What . . . what happened?* Bobby Denny thought as he slowly regained consciousness. The memory of the Learjet crashing through the trees filled his mind. He tried to move but a sharp throbbing pain in his left side took the breath out of him, forcing his battered body back into the seat. Instinctively, Denny closed his eyes. He started to take shallow breaths, trying to control the burning sensation, but it didn't do any good. Each time his heart beat he could feel a piercing jolt shoot through his entire body.

"Okay . . . let's figure this out," Denny said, trying to remove his mind from the pain. He knew he needed to clear his mind enough to reason—if not, he would die here.

Denny remembered drifting in and out of consciousness but he didn't know for sure how long. It seemed at least a day had passed, maybe more. It had rained often and gotten dark more than once. There had been a little sunlight and the interior of the jet had remained cold.

Opening his eyes, he looked down to see that his left leg was twisted beneath the pilot's seat. It looked broken, although it didn't hurt . . . very much. Glancing up he barely recognized the instrument panel of the Learjet. Most of the gauges had been broken and the yoke was bent over to the right.

The windshield had shattered again and was blotched with green leaves and twigs. He watched a tiny red ant crawl across the top of the panel.

Glancing around, Denny surmised the worst damage was on the left side of the jet. A large tangled mass of branches covered with moss and mildew had penetrated the front corner of the windshield. Several of the branches had perforated the seat next to his head and shoulder. Looking down, Denny spotted a red blotch on his shirt and tugged at it. A splintered twig's end was sticking into his clothing up under his left rib cage. He gently tugged, pulling an inch-long piece of blood-stained wood from his side. He was sure the jagged twig had punctured his lung.

He laid his head against the seat, wondering what else was wrong with him. Running his right hand over his face he could feel the mass of cuts and bruises. Touching his tongue around in his mouth he felt that his front teeth were gone, others pulled out to the very roots. Sucking in some air he felt the sharp tingle of pain.

*I need to get my teeth fixed,* he thought. *I need to call a dentist.* His mind was confused with the reality of his situation.

"Bunten . . ." Denny coughed, trying to twist his head around. He saw his copilot slumped over face down with his eyes open. In the dim interior light his skin appeared gray. Denny pushed him back against the seat, his head flopping to the side. A deep gash above his left eye had oozed several lines of blood down the side of his face. It was semidried.

"Bunten . . . you shit! Wake up," Denny grunted. "We've got to get out of here. Bunten!"

Nothing happened. Denny, grimacing, reached over and placed his hand on Bunten's neck. There wasn't a pulse and his skin felt cool and damp. Unexpectedly, a large brown spider twice as big as a silver dollar crawled from the opposite side of Bunten's body. The spider paused only a second or two before scurrying straight up Denny's arm.

"Ah shit . . . !" Denny exclaimed, brushing the spider off with one swoop. Pain shot through him as he jerked his body to the side attempting to crush the animal. It escaped out of sight.

Denny reached for the radio and began to turn the dial in both directions. It wasn't working. The plane wasn't equipped with an emergency transmitter. He had purposely removed it before the discreet flights. Smugglers couldn't risk being caught by the authorities even if they did crash.

*Maybe that fuckin' Tra saw the plane go down,* he tried to reassure himself. *Someone will come for me.* Yet, realistically, Denny knew it could take days before help arrived. The terrain he had been flying over was mountainous with very few roads. If he was to stay alive Denny needed the first-aid kit.

Sucking in a long breath and holding it, Denny very slowly unbuckled his lap belt and struggled to get out of the pilot's seat. Using his right leg for support he propped himself up with his right arm and started to drag his twisted leg across the seat and side control panel. He moved a few inches at a time, eventually making his way out of the seat. Dragging his leg he pushed and shoved himself along the floor, inching toward the back of the Learjet, resting every few seconds to catch his breath.

"Ah . . ." he moaned. The pain was too much. Biting his lower lip until he tasted blood, Denny tried to stay conscious but a moment later he collapsed, passing out. His body was stretched out between the two seats on the flight deck.

Hoe Mie Yan used his fingers to scrape the last few grains of brown rice from the wooden bowl into his mouth. He washed it down with some lukewarm water and wiped off the excess with his shirtsleeve. To the east he watched the faint glow of pink turn red as the sun began to push its way above the horizon.

Mie Yan hardly noticed the food was cold and tasteless. His only concern was that the rice would provide him with nourishment and the strength he needed to walk the next five miles or so to the crash site. He could eat again when they returned to the base camp with whatever could be salvaged off the aircraft.

Sitting around a lopsided circle, Mie Yan and three other members of the *Kien Thao* finished their breakfast. They had made camp in a shallow ravine near the end of a steep hill. The area, densely forested, provided ample cover and protection.

The two younger members began to break camp, stuffing four waterproof sleeping bags into their backpacks along with several bottles of water, a two-way radio and plastic bags containing extra food, maps and medicine.

Mie Yan finished filling his own backpack. Before hoisting it onto his back, he strapped on a black nylon mesh military vest. The vest carried three extra thirty-round magazines for his AK-47, a large knife and survival gear such as rope, matches and water purification tablets. If they ran into trouble Mie Yan would drop his backpack, knowing the vest contained everything he needed to survive in the jungle for a few days.

"Let's get moving," Tai Ninh Dinh, the *Kien Thao*'s leader, said, hoisting his own weathered backpack onto his tiny-framed body.

Mie Yan grasped his pack and AK-47. He glanced over at Ninh Dinh, wishing the old man had not come along. In his late sixties, Dinh appeared frail. The man's face was covered with deep wrinkles and age spots. His left eye was clouded over and Mie Yan doubted he could see anything out of it. The man's legs and arms were thin, lacking muscle and strength. Tai Ninh Dinh could motivate his men with his strong will and words, but as a freedom fighter his days were past. Mie Yan believed Dinh's place was back in the village where he could be protected and cared for if need be by the women.

"You men," Tai Ninh Dinh ordered, "make sure there are no foot-prints."

"Yes, sir."

"Hoe . . . come assist me. Adjust the strap on my back."

Mie Yan did as he was instructed, fitting the pack to be comfortable on the older man's back. He admired Dinh for keeping up on the hard-traveled five miles yesterday, covering some very tough terrain. Government troops routinely patrolled the area, so they traversed among the most rugged areas. Today would be the real test, however. They had to walk another five miles through thick jungle while climbing up 2,000 feet to the plane wreck. If he slowed them down it would be an annoyance, but if he died it could mean the end to their cause.

"This way." Mie Yan led the group, pointing to the southwest.


WASHINGTON, D.C.

"That will be fifteen dollars," the long-haired cabby said, twisting around.

"Here," Manning grunted, dropping his head. He tossed the man a twenty and climbed out. Without looking up he rushed up the sidewalk toward his townhome, hoping the agents next door wouldn't spot him.

It was a few minutes before four in the morning. Manning knew he couldn't get back to sleep. First things first, he'd check his answering machine.

Locking the door, he turned on the small lamp next to his couch. The flashing green light was on; only one call had been recorded on his private line. That was good. If there had been an emergency the machine would be blinking several calls. Sitting down and breathing a sigh of relief, he hit the play button.

*Out on the town again? I know you're not at the White House so you must be sleazing around. Well, maybe you didn't take me seriously, Allan. I have a dozen pictures that will end your career. You think the conservatives in Congress will tolerate your type of behavior? HA! If I don't hear back from you by noon tomorrow your career is over. Do you hear me, you filthy bastard? I want half a million or I'm going to the press.* The machine clicked off.

Manning slammed his fist out to the side, hitting the wall. The force left an indentation and the side of his palm red. He had heard that tone before. The vindictive bitch wasn't bluffing.

He swiveled around. Resting on the fireplace mantle was a picture of his wife, kept there for appearances only. He gazed at it a few moments, remembering the day it had been taken, a wintry day in January. They had traveled to Maine on a ski weekend. It had been one of the few vacations they had ever gone on together. The deep blue Maine sky and clean white snow were in the background. Manning had snapped the picture while his wife sat outside on the stone hearth of a burning fireplace at Timber Creek Lodge. She was smiling, happy.

*You damn bitch,* Manning thought. He grabbed the picture and broke it over his knee. *Before this is over I'll get you for trying to interfere with my life. There's no fucking way you're going to blackmail me.*

Manning began to pace back and forth across his small living room. *Where in the hell am I going to get a half million dollars . . . in cash?* Even if he sold everything he had he couldn't come up with that kind of money. *And then what if she calls back asking for more?* Manning sat down, holding his face in his hands, his thoughts drifting. *Why can't she step out in front of a bus? . . . I'm so close, so close to having complete control over the White House . . .* Then I could have the CIA or FBI take her out—a threat to national security . . . Or someone else . . . *Who do I know? Someone to help me.*

Jumping up, the chief of staff ran up the stairs to his bedroom. He opened the locked drawer behind his small computer desk. Pulling out a clear plastic bag he dropped several tiny chunks of cocaine on his desk and started to arrange the white powder into lines. He snorted it and sat back in his chair, letting the drug work through his system and mind. A moment later he felt clear again.

He closed and locked the drawer. Next to the phone was a small metal combination safe bolted to the floor, used to store classified documents and other top-level papers. Turning the knob swiftly he opened it and removed a small black phone book.

"Okay, Mr. Hawkens. Let's see if maybe you and I can do a little business." Manning smiled, dialing Hawkens's Washington, D.C., number.

NGHIA BINH PROVINCE, VIETNAM

"Tra . . . Tra, you gook asshole," Bobby Denny murmured to himself. He opened his eyes and realized he was lying on his back staring into the grayness of an empty fuselage. He blinked several times trying to get his vision and mind focused. *How long have I been here?* Struggling from the cockpit into the main section of the Learjet he must have passed out again.

*Now I remember . . . the pain. Each time I move the damned pain takes*
*too much out of me. Where was I going . . . the first-aid kit.*

Denny lifted his head to see several blood-soaked bandages covering his
right arm, left side and legs. He must have put the bandages on himself but
he couldn't remember doing it. He lay his head down, the exertion making
his head spin.

Hoe Mie Yan held up a fist, telling his men behind him to squat down where
they were and not make a sound. He turned his head right and left, listening
carefully to every sound around him. In the distance he heard the low
rumble of helicopter rotor blades cutting through the thick humid air. Mie
Yan held his breath, straining to determine if the choppers were moving
closer to their position or moving away.

For the last two days Hoe Mie Yan and the other members of *Kien Thao*
had worked their way to the crash site. To his surprise government troops
had not yet arrived to investigate the crash. However, Mie Yan knew they
would not stay away for very much longer. Fortunately the jet had not
burned after it went down—partly, he was sure, because of the heavy rains
and clouds that had shrouded the mountainside. If there was anything of
value on the downed jet his team would have to recover it quickly.

Mie Yan dropped down, squirming slowly out onto the point of a steep
drop-off some yards away. As he neared the end of the tree-covered ridge he
crouched down even further. Crawling the last few yards on his belly he
inched his way forward, coming to rest on a large moss-covered rock. He
spotted a giant spider's web and inched away from it, not disturbing a single
strand. Peering through the branches of the trees he could see the valley
below and the mountain ridges around him.

Mie Yan estimated they had climbed more than 1,000 feet in the last two
hours.

When everything appeared to be in order and the birds began to chirp and
sing again, Mie Yan removed a pair of binoculars from his nylon vest. He
surveyed the mountain valley below, looking for hints of other movements,
such as smoke from a fire, exhaust fumes or even a flash off a rifle scope.
He scanned the dense green forest for several minutes. To the east he finally
spotted the dark black specks of two Vietnamese Army choppers flying
away from them. He wondered if they were searching for the downed jet.

Mie Yan swept his binoculars back toward the crash site, studying the
landscape for the best way to ascend to it. Through the trees he could see a
slight opening which didn't appear to be natural. It crisscrossed up from
below, running all the way to the top. Mie Yan knew this area had been
logged for quite some time before the government put a stop to it five years
before. He guessed it to be an old logging trail that had been cut into the

mountainside. It made its way up the side of the mountain, leading to within a few hundred yards of where he believed the jet went down.

He pushed himself from the rock ledge, stealthily making his way back to his men.

"One hour," he said in a hushed tone. "We will be there in one hour."

WASHINGTON, D.C.

Carl Hawkens had just closed his eyes when he heard the faint hum of one of the three answering machines in the next room. The distinct tone of the machine kicking in told him someone was trying to reach him here in D.C.

"Who in hell could that be at this hour?" Hawkens, curious, got up and walked into his office. Flicking on the lights he stared at the stacks of communications-control equipment lining the far wall.

The office, actually a spare bedroom, contained three cheap walnut-veneer computer desks with several black and gray boxes on each of them along with an old outdated Packard Bell Pentium/133 MHz PC. Hawkens used the room as a mini command center, enabling him to send secure faxes and computer transmissions anywhere in the world. The heart of his system relied on two commercially available voice and data encryptors that were nearly impossible to decode or copy.

The communications control was a Secure Liner Level III 450 with a built-in RS-232CX encryptor, allowing him to send or receive twenty-four mbps of data in a five-second burst. He had the option of using his computer or scanning the document manually. His computer operated in conjunction with a CCTA 1000 telephone analyzer, the same model FBI field offices used when on assignment. It allowed him to know if anyone was monitoring his incoming or outgoing calls. The sixty-four-bit system automatically swept fiber-optic, electronic and radio-based transmissions and alerted the operator to the presence of any outside electronic sweep. Hawkens could confidently transmit voice or fax transmissions with little worry he would ever be discovered.

Hawkens watched the caller ID number flash across the tiny display screen under his phone. His computer automatically blinked on, scrutinizing the source of the electronic transmission. The software picked up the number of the incoming call and began comparing it with what was on the hard drive and making sure the incoming phone call wasn't being recorded. He watched the orange light flash on; the software was cycling. Several seconds later his computer screen flashed: ALLAN MANNING/WASHINGTON, D.C.

"Well, well . . ." Hawkens said, grinning. "I guess I don't have to contact him after all. He needs *me* for something.'' Hawkens reached for the volume control on the side of the machine and turned it up.

''. . . call me when you get in. You know the number.'' The line clicked dead and within a second the whir of the machine indicated the message was ready to be replayed. Hawkens hit the playback button.

*''Serpent, this is the Man.''*

Hawkens laughed quietly, remembering how opposite Manning was from his CIA nickname . . . the Man.

*''Haven't talked to you in quite a while, it's time we checked up on each other. Call me when you get in. You know the number.''*

Hawkens stroked his forehead. *The Serpent . . . my cryptonym on my last CIA assignment.* It was the assignment that ended his career. He never should have screwed that blonde DEA agent.

Hawkens sauntered back into his bedroom and crawled into bed. He would call Manning but didn't want to jump right on it. Better to wait a little. No matter what he wanted, Hawkens was sure the only benefit to him would be that Manning owed him one.


NGHIA BINH PROVINCE, VIETNAM

Hoe Mie Yan walked along the edge of the old logging road, the other men following in the same fashion. From the looks of the overgrowth it appeared the road hadn't been used for a number of years. Mie Yan could still see a few deep ruts which had been cut into the earth where heavy equipment had traveled to remove the trees and truck them to the road below.

As he rounded a sharp bend Mie Yan stopped. A shiny object rested in the center of the trail ahead. He walked closer and saw it was a jagged piece of tangled aluminum about six feet in length. Mie Yan ran his hand across the cool metal. He looked at his hand and saw chips of white paint covering his fingertips. From the looks of it, the strip of metal hadn't been in the jungle for very long. It wasn't covered with moss, just the morning dew.

Twenty yards to his right he spotted a large broken branch which had fallen to the ground. He looked up to see a half-dozen busted treetops. Mie Yan spun around and signaled that the others should split and search the surrounding area. Tai Ninh Dinh would follow him.

Mie Yan adjusted his backpack before stepping off the edge of the road into the jungle. Up ahead he could see the thick brush begin to thin out a bit. He glanced over his shoulder, checking on Ninh Dinh's progress.

The two men worked through the thick underbrush, gradually making it to the edge of a clearing. Mie Yan hadn't spotted the clearing from his vantage point below. It wasn't a large clearing—not more than two or three hundred yards along. He could see the cut stumps of several dead trees where the undergrowth hadn't entirely covered them.

A whistling sound cut through the air. Hoe Mie Yan stopped, listening. The sound repeated. One of the men had found the wreckage or something else that needed his attention.

"Can you keep up?" he asked the old man, seeing he was winded and stumbling a little.

"Go . . . go. I will find you."

Mie Yan didn't argue. He dropped his backpack and took off rushing toward the sound as quietly as possible. Jumping over rotting tree stumps his feet landed between the undergrowth as he raced up a small hill. When he reached the top he stopped. Fifty yards away, resting on its belly, was the wreckage of the Learjet. He could see that the nose section had been smashed and one of the wings was completely ripped off. The fuselage was dented and buckled with large tree branches covering the top of it. The tail section of the aircraft was intact. He wondered why the aircraft hadn't caught fire, then realized it was resting in a bog. It was as if someone had placed it there to be perfectly camouflaged.

Mie Yan worked the action on his AK-47 to put a live round in the chamber. He clicked on the safety and motioned for his men to surround the jet as he edged toward it slowly.

The chilled morning air seemed more than Bobby Denny could endure. His light clothing gave him little protection from the damp cold that had settled into the valley. He was beginning to shake uncontrollably, and he realized his hands and feet were numb. He tried to hold his arms closer to his body for warmth but the pain was too much.

The sun was up and it was light enough for him to see through the broken windows of the Learjet's cargo section.

Denny didn't know if he should say something or keep his mouth shut when he heard footsteps making their way around the aircraft. They came from all around; his muddled mind couldn't distinguish if it was real or an illusion.

He listened, closing his eyes to concentrate. Through one of the shattered windows he spotted shadows falling across the ground.

Denny felt his heart beating fast in his chest. His mouth and throat had long ago dried up and he wasn't sure he could speak even if he wanted to. He decided not to say a word. They would find him soon enough.

Hoe Mie Yan pointed his AK-47 at the ground as he approached the wreckage. His eyes scanned the ground as he looked for booby traps and footprints. The other two men were walking around to the rear section of the jet.

Mie Yan approached them after surveying the front section.

"What have you found?" Tai Ninh Dinh asked from behind. He seemed to have regained his energy.

"We have checked the immediate area. There are no booby traps or footprints," one of the men answered. He shifted his stare from Ninh Dinh to Mie Yan, then to the ground. Mie Yan was responsible for the mission and the man had spoken out of turn.

"Set up a perimeter, one of you at each end of the aircraft. If anyone approaches . . . shoot them," Mie Yan ordered. Two of the men nodded and moved into position.

"They are young . . . full of spirit. Much like you were," Tai Ninh Dinh said softly, walking up to Mie Yan.

"I was young once . . . but I was never so bold and stupid," Mie Yan replied, turning his attention toward the jet. He could see wires and cables sticking out of the wing root. The thick grass had an oily sheen from the jet fuel that had leaked from the aircraft's fuel tanks. The left side engine was nearly gone, the metal melted and charred black. He could see where his missile had impacted the jet, destroying the compressor section which in turn ripped the rest of the engine apart. Mie Yan still wondered why the jet hadn't burned more and exploded.

"Wait here. I will check the inside and tell you if it is safe," Mie Yan said, leaving a man with the leader.

He walked carefully around to the front section of the plane, running his hand along the side as if it were a giant beast he had slain. His boots were sinking several inches into the sour-smelling mud. When he reached the cockpit Mie Yan saw the windows were completely shattered where a large tree branch had pierced its way through. He peered inside and saw the empty pilot's seat and the dead copilot, his eyes opened wide.

*I wonder where the pilot is?* Mie Yan stopped and glanced around, thinking maybe his body was thrown from the craft. He walked around to the side door of the jet. He examined it, looking for the smallest indication it had been opened and possibly rigged with explosives. The seal around the door appeared wet and dirty; he doubted anyone had opened it.

He turned the latch and unlocked the door. Using all his strength, with the help of another member, they pulled the door open. The warped fuselage allowed it to open only twelve inches or so, just enough for him to squeeze through.

Someone was attempting to get inside. Bobby Denny could feel them shaking the aircraft. He used his right leg to push against one of the wooden pallets. Inching along, he tried to get his body out of the opening behind one of the bombs.

Clenching his teeth to help tolerate the pain, Denny pushed his broken body around the back of a pallet until he could stand it no longer. He felt himself teeter on the edge of consciousness as he used his last bit of strength.

Lying on the rear bulkhead, he struggled to raise his head to look over the pallet containing two chemical bombs. The pallet was still strapped to the floor, but the bomb casing nearest to him had been jarred out of place and lay twisted in the nylon rope used to secure it. The bomb next to it Denny couldn't see as well.

Denny set his head back down, breathing deeply to keep the oxygen going to his head. It was then he smelt it. The odor was faint and sweet, almost like that of spearmint candy.

Denny's heart began to race. One of the bombs had ruptured. The sweet smell of candy was one of the warning signs Major Tra had spoken of during a prior mission. He felt around with his right hand. First he touched the outside of the bomb casing, then the pallet and finally the floor of the aircraft. He could feel it, a thick sticky substance like syrup.

Denny's body stiffened as he heard someone drop into the front section of the aircraft.

Mie Yan hit the metal floor of the jet with a light thump. He dropped down swinging his AK-47 left and right, prepared to fire at the slightest movement. But everything was still and quiet.

The interior looked gray and shadowy with just a few streams of light filtering through the rear windows and the cockpit. He sucked in a deep breath and stood listening for any type of sound. All he heard was the dripping of water as the morning dew ran off the top of the jet and hit the edge of the door behind him.

Mie Yan moved up to take a closer look at the copilot. He was an American. The man's skin had turned a pale gray. Mie Yan estimated he had died when the plane went down.

Lowering his AK-47, he slowly turned back and surveyed the jet's interior. He saw it was filled with three tarp-covered pallets which were fastened to the floor with black nylon ropes. There were two empty seats next to the bulkhead behind the flight deck, but other than that the jet was empty.

*A cargo jet . . . this is nothing more than a cargo jet!* Mie Yan's anger erupted after his long wait to discover what Western evil he had shot down from the sky. He didn't see any plush carpet. No leather-covered chairs and bottles of Champagne. There weren't any fat dead businessmen strapped to their seats, no briefcases filled with business documents and money he could use to further their cause. This wasn't a high-powered corporate jet, it was a flying truck. A damned jet filled with . . .

Mie Yan spotted smears of fresh blood across the floor. It looked as if someone had dragged a body from the flight deck to the rear section of the jet. He put his finger back on the trigger of his rifle, bringing it up to waist level. Possibly the pilot was hiding somewhere in the rear section of the plane; he could still be alive.

Mie Yan took several soft steps, entering the main cargo section of the jet. He removed his knife and cut the nylon ropes that held down the tarps covering the pallets. Lifting one corner, he saw the shiny silver metal of a casing.

*What do we have here?* he asked himself, recognizing the type of casing. *It looks like some sort of bomb.* Mie Yan reached out and pulled the tarp back further, seeing another of the long cylinders strapped to the same pallet.

"Where are you hiding . . . I will soon find you," Mie Yan said in Vietnamese. He waited for a response but didn't get one.

Then he repeated it in broken English.

Bobby Denny felt the blood rush to his face. He knew sooner or later the man was going to find him. It could be one of Tra's men. If he spoke out now maybe nothing would happen, maybe the man would help him.

"Back here . . . I'm back here," Denny muttered in a weak voice.

Mie Yan shouldered his AK, pointing it toward the back of the jet. Taking short steps he made his way to where he heard the faint voice. As he reached the rear section of the jet he saw the open first-aid kit. Sticking out from behind the last pallet was a black boot. Someone was lying down, hiding between the cargo and bulkhead.

"Don't shoot me . . . I'm unarmed," Denny said, seeing the man standing over him with a rifle. He decided it was best not to mention Tra's name. "I am hurt."

"Where you hurt?" Mie Yan asked. It had been many years since he had spoken English. The words felt awkward and strange in his mouth.

"Yes . . . my leg and my lungs," Denny coughed his reply. "I am very thirsty."

Mie Yan looked at the man's face. He was dirty and covered with bruises and scratches. His lips were dried and cracked. It was obvious he was in pain. *So much the better,* Mie Yan thought. "Who you are . . . American?" he asked, thrusting his rifle toward the man.

"I am an American cargo pilot," Denny said. "I need your help."

"I no help. You kill my country."

"I didn't kill anybody." Denny tried to get up but couldn't.

"What you carry?" Mie Yan pointed to the tarps.

"Medicine," Denny lied, trying to look innocent. "This is medicine."

"This no medicine. To me . . . look like bomb. What is?" Mie Yan felt his temper starting to bubble inside of him. He was not going to allow the American to lie to him.

"You have to believe me. I don't have anything of value." Denny held out his right hand in a gesture of friendship.

"You lie." Mie Yan raised his rifle. "I want to know . . . what you carry?"

"You help . . . I will tell you."

*I will make you tell me the truth, you American scum.* Hie Yan squeezed the trigger. His arm jerked as the AK-47 fired a single bullet through Denny's hand. The 123-grain bullet sliced into Denny's hand, then hit the nearest bomb casing, splitting the stainless steel outer covering.

Denny yelled out and instinctively closed his eyes, snapping his head to the right. The sound of the firing rifle and the bullet ripping into the bomb casing shattered his eardrums. He could feel the hot pain in his hand and hot metal fragments impacting his face and neck.

When Denny opened his eyes he realized what had happened. Every muscle in his body tensed with fear.

"You stupid slope-eyed asshole . . . *you just killed both of us!*"

Mie Yan, startled, stepped back as the air suddenly grew white. He heard the unmistakable hissing sound of a leak from the casing. The air turned hot around him and he knew he had to get out of the jet. It was Mie Yan's last thought. He bent over and at once lost control of his bodily functions. Vomit poured out his mouth and nose. His skin felt like it was on fire and he couldn't breathe. He stumbled backward before he hit the floor of the jet, convulsing. Dying.

# 17

Mark Collins rolled over, feeling a muscle knot up in the back of his neck. He blinked a couple of times before his eyes focused on the round clock above his desk. It took him a few seconds to remember he was in his office and not at home in bed where most normal people are at 5:32 A.M.

"Oh, that's just great," Collins mumbled to himself, knowing Christine would be furious when she awoke this morning. "I need a better job . . . even waste management has regular hours." He turned on the lamp next to the small couch his aching body had been stretched out on. The couch, located against the wall in the rear section of his office, wasn't much larger than a love seat.

Collins straightened up, scratching the back of his head. His forty-five-minute catnap had turned into a three-hour sleep session.

*Brooks won't be happy,* Collins thought. He still hadn't completed his threat survey of Langau Island. The Pentagon's diplomatic envoy would need to know everything they had on the terrain, and weather patterns as well as details of the structures that had been built on the island. So far the latest computer files and satellite imagery showed a desolate finger of land with rocky ridges providing very little cover or protection. Collins would need more data for the president to make a decision at the NSC meeting scheduled for later in the morning.

He yawned and walked over to turn on his computer. He had a sour taste in his mouth and felt like warmed-over death. In another hour or so the building would begin filling up with staff members and other personnel. Collins figured he could work until 6:30 A.M., take a quick shower in the men's locker room located in the basement, and be ready for Tom Staffer, director for operations, and Doug Brooks, director for intelligence, before they arrived around 7:00 A.M.

*Okay, Mark, you have one hour. Make the best of it.* Collins forced himself to sit down and wake up. He scratched his day-old beard and the thought of a cup of hot coffee and an Egg McMuffin crossed his mind.

STAFFORD, VIRGINIA

Duke James listened to the crunch of fallen leaves as he jogged the last quarter mile along the road leading to his townhome. His breath, puffs of white frosty air, shot out in front of him.

Duke jogged past several parked cars. He turned right, headed down a street lined with oak trees, and onto the sidewalk leading to a small cluster of townhomes. Ahead of him he could see the local paperboy making his way from house to house, slipping and sliding as he tried to maneuver his bike through the snow. To the east the glow of a new day told Duke he had better hurry.

Duke grabbed the paper from the slot beneath his mailbox and walked the last twenty yards to the house. Climbing the stairs, he entered the kitchen to the smell of brewing coffee and frying bacon.

"Good morning, General," Katie said, standing over the stove and turning her cheek for a kiss. She was dressed in a red robe with her hair pulled up on top of her head.

"Good morning. Mmm . . . blueberry pancakes, bacon and scrambled eggs. Just what a hungry runner needs to start the day."

"Sorry, flyboy . . . it's for the kids. I have a toasted bagel and banana for you." Katie smiled and patted Duke's middle before pouring him a glass of orange juice.

"Yeah . . . that's what I need. A no-fat . . . no-cholesterol . . . no-taste breakfast. Thanks, honey, you must really love me," Duke joked, finishing off a glass of cold water.

Their three children were seated at the round tiled table eating cereal from small bowls. The older ones, Matt and Pamela, had the boxes turned so they could read the backs. Sean was pushing his spoon down on his Honey Nut Cheerios, watching them sink and rise up again before taking a mouthful, milk running out of the corners of his mouth.

"Looks to me like they *are* eating breakfast," Duke complained.

"The boys couldn't wait for me to finish but don't worry . . . they'll still be hungry, even after the bacon." Katie rolled her eyes.

"I thought they were eating the cereal after school for a snack now," Duke said, puzzled that they could eat so much.

"We do," Matt, his oldest son, answered without looking up.

"Duke, why don't you let me worry about what the kids eat and you just read the paper or something," Katie spoke up, hoping to stop the lecture that was sure to follow. The one about how food just disappeared around this house and we should buy stock with the cereal companies.

"Well, my brother and I—"

"Yes, we know, Duke," Katie interrupted, putting down a plate of steaming pancakes in the center of the table.

"Everybody sure is up early this morning," Duke said, staring at the blueberry syrup Pamela was pouring over her pancake.

"No, they're not. You're running late . . . it's zero six ten."

"What—" Duke glanced over at the microwave clock and raced up the stairs, shouting "Why didn't you tell me? I'm going to be late."

Twenty minutes later, his hair still damp from the shower, Duke snatched the bagel, banana and mug of hot black coffee off the counter. He kissed his wife and kids goodbye and went out the door. He backed the Tahoe out of the driveway and exited onto I-95, traveling north toward Washington, D.C.

## THE WHITE HOUSE

Allan Manning stood in front of his desk trying to run the president's schedule through his mind. He was having a hard time concentrating. His right hand held a large insulated cup of coffee doused with sugar and cream. In his left hand he held a white piece of computer paper, the president's agenda for Monday, November 16. The list included a register of phone calls the president needed to make and a brief summary of questions he should be prepared to answer at the next press conference.

The bottom half of the paper listed what Manning called "Three up and three down." This included three issues in the last forty-eight hours that had gone right for the president and three that had not. The list also included any new crisis that might supersede what was important yesterday. Luckily for Manning there wasn't any new crisis staring him in the face. By using this method Manning found he could predict with 90 percent certainty which stories the nation's newspapers, radio talk shows and D.C. reporters would likely focus on during the day.

Manning adjusted the knot of his patterned maroon silk tie. He felt the bite of his collar, telling him he needed to lose a few pounds. He was just glad his head only felt slightly hungover. In a strange sort of way he felt guilty for what he had done. Not for what had happened but for losing control. He had promised himself when he went out he would only dance and have a couple of drinks to relax. Last night it felt like power not worrying about his ex-wife's threat, but this morning it felt like impending doom. Just because he was on the other side of town didn't mean he could be careless. Rhonda was teaching him that lesson very well.

*Okay . . . if I can get through the National Security Group meeting, everything else will be a breeze.* Manning; took several more swigs of coffee, hoping the caffeine would kick in soon.

"This just came off the satellite," Douglas Brooks, the CIA's director for intelligence, said as he entered Collins's office unannounced. He handed Collins a sheet of computer paper. The words FLASH TRANSMISSION were written across the top in bold print. The message had received a high-priority computer classification at the National Security Agency.

"Who's it from?" Collins asked.

"Lei Nook," Brooks replied, taking a seat.

Lei Nook was the name the CIA used for their top man stationed in Hanoi. A FLASH TRANSMISSION meant trouble. Collins didn't know the exact number of CIA officers and agents operating out of Hanoi but he figured there were at least ten men and women. Nook supplied Langley with a variety of intelligence ranging from drug trafficking and troop movements to economic growth indicators. Collins' face went hard as his eyes skimmed the sheet.

SATCOM TRNSMTTR *.*QXCECKO/CHARLIE/CIA FLASH
PRIORITY ONE RELAY 11/21/0534/98
TRNSMTTR:      HANOI STATION
RECVR:         LANGLEY

1]   EIGHTY-TWO PEOPLE, INCLUDING WOMEN AND CHILDREN, WERE FOUND DEAD SOUTHEAST OF THE VILLAGE PHOM-KEW LATE THIS AFTERNOON.

2]   APPROXIMATELY HALF OF VILLAGE, POPULATION 180, HAVE BEEN WIPED OUT. MORE DEATHS ARE EXPECTED. THE DEATHS ALSO INCLUDE CATTLE, DOGS, CHICKENS AND GOATS. ALSO REPORTS OF DEAD WILDLIFE, PRIMARILY BIRDS, SCATTERED AROUND THE REGION.

3]   CAUSE OF DEATH IS NOT KNOWN. EARLY REPORTS PEOPLE ARE DYING AFTER VOMITING AND SUFFERING VIOLENT CONVULSIONS. REPORTS OF EXTERNAL BLEEDING AND BLINDNESS IN SURVIVORS. AT LEAST TWO SURVIVORS REPORTED A WHITE CLOUD SETTLING OVER THE VILLAGE A FEW MINUTES BEFORE DEATHS OCCURRED. END TRANSMISSION.

Collins' eyes returned to Brooks. "Eighty-two people dead."

"This is only a preliminary report," Brooks commented. "Chances are it will go higher. What do you make of it?"

Collins looked at the paper a second time. "Phom-Kew . . . Phom-Kew. Where do I . . ." Collins stopped.

"What is it, Mark?"

"Phom-Kew . . . it's the only village in a twenty-mile radius of Vietnam's Gia Hian pharmaceutical factories.'' Collins got up and walked to the wall map next to his desk. "It's here . . . near the Laotian border.''

"You think they had some kind of accident?''

"This is the area I've been watching for the last six months,'' Collins began, pointing to the area. "We have strong reason to believe the Vietnamese government is manufacturing chemical weapons right here and this sure sounds like some type of a chemical leak. People throwing up with convulsions, dead animals. I'll bet that's a nerve gas.'' Collins sat down and exited the computer program he had been working on. Calling up another file, he tapped the print button and waited for the report to come off the laser printer.

"You're talking about the cough syrup report.'' Brooks raised his eyebrows recalling Collins's report. The Vietnamese had suddenly become a major supplier of cough syrup.

"Yeah . . . The Vietnamese told the UN they were using thiodiglycol, hydrochloric acid, and fifty-five-gallon drums of hydrogen cyanide and methanol to make Nyquil.'' Collins looked up at Brooks. "This could be the proof we've been after.''

"Any way we can verify it?''

"Well, first thing I'm going to do is review the latest satellite photos. Maybe they'll turn up something new. Other than that we'll need to get a team in there if you want any solid proof.''

"I'm going to put this on top of the president's daily intelligence briefing. You need to be prepared to discuss this during the NSPG meeting at 9:00.'' Brooks started to leave the room, then turned back, looking Collins over. "Better take a shower and get cleaned up first.''

"Damn!'' Collins exclaimed, seeing it was already 7:30.


YELLOW SEA

Four 2,500-horsepower turbocharged diesel engines pushed the 212-foot-long steel hull of *Van Triumph* through the dark night. Running at five knots with her navigational lights burning, the luxury yacht turned northwest, putting her bow into the wind. The half-moon and stars lighting the sky reflected off the calm seas.

Sinchon stood upright in the back of the bridge with his arms folded. He watched the dancing red and blue navigational lights on the ceiling and smoke-colored glass. The lime-green radarscope swept methodically back and forth. The ship barely rocked as he listened to the hum of the engines and chatter of the marine radio.

"How much longer?'' Sinchon asked.

"About twelve hours," Gaith Bander said, turning around. "I'm planning to bring us around to the north side of the island."

Dressed in a white silk sports jacket and dark blue pants, Bander reminded Sinchon of a spoiled rich playboy, not a businessman. His well-manicured hands, neatly trimmed hair and white teeth only amazed the North Korean general. Never had his life been so easy. Bandar had made a fortune buying and selling weapons. If this arms trader was indebted to anyone it was Sinchon. Now he flaunted his wealth to him like it was something he had won in battle.

"Is there anything on the surface radar?" Sinchon asked.

"There is a small return ten miles to the north. It's probably a trawler. To the west we are picking up what looks like a large tanker."

Sinchon was quiet for a moment and then burst out bitterly, "Who is following us?"

"One of your intelligence ships. They always shadow me in these waters. When the time is right we'll make a high-speed run toward the island. They will not be able to keep up," Bandar answered with confidence. "Why don't you go below, I'll have a bottle of my best scotch brought to your room. When you awaken we'll be at the island. If the Americans are on time you will be out of the area in no time at all."

"I don't want your liquor," Sinchon said. "Just tell me when we arrive."

Sinchon disappeared below deck, locking the door to his oversize guest room.


"I replaced the fuel filter to the number two engine," the greasy-faced mechanic said, emerging from below deck. He held a long cylindrical filter which looked rusted and corroded. "The fuel line was also clogged. You should be able to start it now."

"Do it," Capt. Yang Jyong-Sop commanded the helmsman of the North Korean trawler. "We have already wasted enough time."

"Aye, Captain," the helmsman replied, striking the start button for the boat's number two engine.

The trawler's second engine sputtered for a second or two before coming to life with a blaring roar. Bluish gray smoke poured from the back of the boat.

"Increase speed to twenty-five knots," Capt. Yang Jyong-Sop ordered. "Take a heading of two three three."

"Twenty-five knots . . . heading two three three," the helmsman responded, jamming the throttles forward.

Jyong-Sop, the captain of the fifty-foot North Korean fishing trawler, braced himself as the ship's powerful diesel engines shuddered, pushing the boat forward. He raised his binoculars to the night sky. The moonlight mirrored in the water made it difficult to see the *Van Triumph* as she sailed northwest away from him. Using his left hand to shield the glasses from the glare of his instruments he finally caught sight of the thin dark outline of the ship.

*You fool. This shouldn't have happened,* he cursed himself for allowing them to get away. *Why didn't I have those filters changed before this?*

"Captain . . . naval headquarters is requesting the exact location of *Van Triumph.* What do I tell them?" the radio operator asked.

"Confirm our location."

"Our location?"

"You heard me . . . our *location.*"

There was a pause. "Yes, Captain."

Standing in the pilothouse Jyong-Sop listened as his radio operator transmitted his ship's location, heading and speed to the North Korean mainland. He fought off the nervousness starting to boil inside of him. Jyong-Sop had allowed his target to get too far ahead of him while his vessel drifted under repair. If he lost sight, his naval commanders would not understand no matter what the excuse or reason. The captain envisioned his next assignment scraping barnacles off the sides of barges ten hours a day for nothing more than a bowl of cold rice.

"Headquarters is requesting the exact location, sir, of the *Van Triumph,*" the radio reporter reported.

"Damn it!" Jyong-Sop grunted. "Why can't they think for themselves?" He grabbed the radio headset and placed it over his ears. "This is Captain Jyong-Sop. You have our location. *Van Triumph* is approximately fifteen miles northwest, estimated speed . . . five to six knots."

*"Understood . . . channel is clear."*

"Give it all she has but don't get too close." Jyong-Sop picked up his binoculars again.

THE WHITE HOUSE

Relighting his pipe, Chief of Staff Manning checked his wristwatch. 7:30 A.M. The president normally didn't arrive until a quarter to eight so he had some time to think and enjoy the solitude and power of the Oval Office.

Strolling over to the window, Manning peered outside. Through the leafless trees he caught sight of the early-morning traffic as it passed by the White House on West Executive Avenue.

Obsessed with finding a solution to his wife's demands, he couldn't keep the thoughts from emerging. *If the press gets word of those pictures, I'll be through.* Manning knew that inside the beltway he was known as Mr.

Magoo. He deeply resented the slight. Now vivid images of cartoonish caricatures plastered in all the papers and magazines with humiliating captions about his secret life haunted his mind.

Manning's shoulders drooped as he added more tobacco to his pipe. His belly protruded slightly over his belt, making his chest look rather sunken.

*That's all right,* he told himself. *I'll get through this like I have everything else. I just need to be calm and wait for the right opportunities. I hope Hawkens calls me back soon.*

"Good morning, Mr. President," he said, seeing McEntire enter the Oval Office. He glanced at his watch: exactly 7:45 A.M.

"Good morning, Allan . . . sleep well?" the president asked.

"Yes, sir. How about you?"

"About the same . . . three, maybe four hours." McEntire walked over to the coffee pot. "I need some caffeine to wake up."

Manning walked over to his favorite chair by the president's desk, watching as he poured a mug of coffee, adding a few sweeteners but no cream. McEntire had turned fifty-four two weeks earlier, and for a man his age he appeared to be in fairly good shape. In fact McEntire took great pride in the fact that he never had a hair out of place, even in private. The president was rarely seen in public wearing anything other than a suit and tie and he paid meticulous attention to every detail of his image.

McEntire's tanned skin, from regular trips to a tanning booth, had the look of soft leather and his thick black hair had grayed only slightly around the edges. Manning wasn't sure but it seemed as if the president had managed to lose a few pounds recently, making his clothes fit better. In Manning's opinion the man's dress and stature resembled that of a retired golfer more than a president. As with most things concerning the president's image, he assumed it was deliberate.

The president walked over to his desk, taking a sip from his coffee mug. Manning didn't notice the dark circles under his tired bloodshot eyes or the frown cutting into his brow. Manning was too preoccupied with himself.

"How are things progressing?" McEntire asked, sitting down in his chair and leaning back.

"Are you referring to the budget-cut proposals?" Manning asked, jolted from his thoughts.

"No, I'm referring to the man in the moon."

*I'm not a mind reader, you idiot.* "Of course . . . I've made several phone calls already . . . yesterday . . . trying to get a pulse. So far there haven't been any surprises," Manning replied, glad to focus on the tasks at hand. "The only trouble we're going to have is from Senator Branson, but we expected that."

"Branson. That bastard fights me on everything I do." McEntire swiveled around, facing the window, then back to Manning. "We could be talking about nominating Abraham Lincoln to the Supreme Court and Branson would oppose that, too."

Manning chuckled.

"You'd damn well better be right about these cuts, Allan. I'm taking a lot of heat from this Bishop incident—especially since Sally . . ." McEntire paused, seemingly unable to acknowledge that Bishop's wife died after he asked for Bishop's resignation.

"Mr. President, have I ever let you down?"

"No, I guess not. But there's a first time for everything."

The two men were quiet a moment.

"So tell me, Allan, how are things progressing with your divorce?"

"Well . . ." Manning cleared his throat nervously. *Does he know something?* "We are scheduled to go to court for the final time in six weeks. That should be the end of it . . . I hope."

"God, how long has this been going on now? Thirteen . . . fourteen months?" The president didn't look too pleased.

"Just over a year, yes, sir."

"Oh, yes. Rhonda and you broke up right after the election last year. I don't mean to pry into your personal business, Allan . . . but I wish you'd get it over with. I don't need something like that reflecting poorly on this administration."

Manning didn't reply. His face flushed with embarrassment.

"Allan . . . are you listening to me?" McEntire was looking at him steadily. "I want you to wrap this divorce up. There're all sorts of rumblings going on inside and I've been damned lucky this mess of yours hasn't blown up in the press. I hope you understand what I'm getting at."

*I'll take care of the bitch, you don't have to worry about that,* Manning thought wildly.

"Now, what's on my schedule for today?" McEntire asked, turning back to the window.

Manning hesitated, then looked at the computer report and recited stiffly: "Your security group meeting is scheduled for 9:00 A.M. At 10:00 A.M. you are to have breakfast with congressional Republicans to discuss your crime bill. That should be easy enough." Manning was getting back into the flow.

"What else?"

"At 11:00 you will meet with members of the American Association of Retired Persons. They're going to hit you hard on your proposal to limit Social Security cost-of-living increases." Manning waited for McEntire's reaction.

"Let's see, I'll give them twenty minutes to whine. That should satisfy them," McEntire said, getting up to pour himself another cup of coffee.

Manning continued. "Right at 11:30 a scheduled lunch with a group of fifth graders from one of the local grade schools. You're discussing their concerns about crime in the schools. I've scheduled the press to attend . . . you always look good around kids," Manning chuckled.

"Okay. We'll go over the questions I'm prepared to answer . . . let's touch base again before lunch. I don't want to screw anything up."

"Of course, Mr. President. I'll be close by any time you need me." Manning was feeling relieved things were back to normal. "Okay . . . let's meet back here at . . ."

"I'll decide where and when we meet," McEntire said harshly.

*It's going to be a long fucking day,* Manning thought. "Yes, sir."

The vice president entered the Oval Office, and Manning took the opportunity to escape and take care of his queasy stomach and aching head. He was feeling better before his meeting with the president but his ailment had just returned with double vengeance. "I'll talk with you again before lunch, sir."

Manning wondered briefly if the vice president was putting McEntire up to this new aggressiveness. Some new image thing about taking charge, or whatever the polls were saying, was needed.

Duke James pulled into the main parking lot behind the White House off of West Executive Avenue, taking the first available spot. He made sure his parking pass was hanging from the rearview mirror, clutched his briefcase, and locked his Chevy Tahoe.

James's official office was located on the third floor of the Old Executive Office Building, or the OEOB. Located west of the White House, the OEOB had been constructed just after the Civil War. The architecture was French Renaissance. Large carved granite blocks had been fitted together to form the outside of the building, making the slate gray exterior extremely impressive. The interior offices of the OEOB had been remodeled several years before, bringing them up to the standards of the Pentagon and State Department—not that it kept people from making jokes about the OEOB being the only building in the United States without hot water, electricity or telephones.

Today Duke was headed to the cubical he occupied in the west wing of the White House. It was used when he was working on special projects or just as a place to regroup before or after meetings with the president.

Duke pinned his White House staff badge to the lapel of his overcoat upon entering the west wing. Before heading to the situation room he wanted to check his E-mail. He was running a few minutes ahead of schedule—just enough to check the E-mail and dump his coat and briefcase in the "White Office," as he referred to it.

"Good morning, General James," the morning receptionist, a retired Army sergeant, greeted Duke in the White House basement.

"Good morning," Duke replied, signing in.

"Have much trouble getting in this morning, sir?"

"A little . . . there's a big accident on I-395," Duke answered, walking toward the stairs to the subbasement.

"Stop by on your way out. I'll tell you about the striper I caught last week. She was a beaut."

James entered his cubical, took off his coat and hung it behind the door. The walls were a pale white and the floor was covered with worn gray carpet that needed to be replaced. Located behind his desk was a computer workstation containing an IBM PS/1 computer. It was Duke's link to the outside world. From his desk he could access files at the Pentagon, the State Department, even the CIA with the tap of a couple of buttons.

The door took up most of one wall, but one wall displayed a Colorado first-of-state duck print and an eight-by-ten picture of his B-2 bomber with the name *Nightstalker* handwritten across the bottom. Another wall was covered with photos of his family and special notes—at least the ones that weren't too private—from his wife and kids. Unlike most of the staff at the White House, James didn't maintain an "I-love-me" wall filled with plaques, awards, commendations and pictures of himself aboard Air Force One. James preferred to stay focused on getting his job done with the least amount of distraction.

The large wall space behind him had several large paper maps of the world above a series of short file cabinets. Three coded fax machines and a safe to store any current classified projects sat on top of the cabinets. In the corner stood a portable electric heater.

James flicked on the computer and began to look over his notes from the day before. He kept two yellow notepads going at the same time: a general one, listing calls he needed to return and low-priority projects; the other notepad he kept locked in the safe behind his desk, containing a brief listing of high-priority projects that were normally classified.

Accessing his E-mail, Duke called up the highest-priority message. It was from the chairman of the Joint Chiefs, Army General Howard Caniff. They were to meet in the White House Situation Room at 9:00. Duke exited the system and dropped the notepad back on his desk, then headed for the coffee room. He had time for one quick cup.

## Yellow Sea

*Van Triumph*'s twin white radar domes and array of communication antennas gave the vessel a strange appearance through the awkward night-vision goggles. Capt. Yang Jyong-Sop watched the greenish silhouette of the yacht grow larger as his North Korean trawler closed the distance.

The captain seriously doubted the ship's crew had been fooled into thinking he was fishing. The nylon gill nets hanging on the long outriggers and wooden storage boxes stacked on the bow and transom were added to his cover, but trawlers generally didn't make a habit of following private yachts. He figured the deception might have worked for awhile but after trailing the ship for a day the masquerade was more than likely over.

Jyong-Sop felt the ship's powerful engines vibrate, forcing the bow through the calm water at over thirty knots. The wheelhouse shook with a deafening roar as he breathed in the aroma of diesel exhaust. Jyong guessed he had seven hours of darkness to hide behind, during which time it would be difficult for the ship's crew to track him visually. His plan was to stay within eight miles of *Van Triumph* until first light and then back off, using his radar to track her.

The thought of being punished by Colonel Kaine in the event he failed because of a simple oil filter flashed through his mind again. He should have been more prepared. He grasped the rail in front of him as a swell of seawater exploded over the bow, spraying the window.

"Ten miles, closing," the helmsman reported.

"Faster," Jyong-Sop commanded.

"We're at maximum power—"

"Let me have the wheel." Jyong-Sop pushed the man out of the way, shoving at the throttles, making sure they were all the way forward.

He turned the trawler to port hoping to cut the distance to the ship. As he did the number-two engine surged suddenly out of control and then ceased. The trawler immediately cut to starboard and slowed.

"Fire! Fire! Shut down the engines!" someone shouted from below.

Jyong-Sop turned and saw black smoke billowing up out of the engine compartment.

"Get the fire extinguisher . . ."

Jyong-Sop swiveled to his right, jamming the throttles to neutral, cursing himself. The unacceptable had happened to him: his ship was on fire, a captain's worst nightmare.

## THE WHITE HOUSE

Duke entered the Situation Room located in the basement level of the White House's west wing below the Oval Office. Built during the early years of the Cold War, the room wasn't the high-tech marvel a lot of people believed it to be.

The room was only forty feet long and thirty feet wide, with a low ceiling and mildewy smell. The forward section contained a big-screen television tuned to CNN. The only things that would be considered high tech were several fax machines and three computer terminals along with SATCOM communications equipment for each branch of the military, which all filled one corner. The left wall had been covered with a ceiling-to-floor map of the world. A massive hardwood table, a gift from the Canadian government, hogged the center of the room, surrounded by brown leather chairs.

President McEntire liked using the room for two things and two things only: to hold his weekly National Security Planning Group meeting, and for the occasional Saturday night poker party with senior members of Congress.

For Duke, the National Security Planning Group, or NSPG, remained something of an oddity. It consisted of secretaries of defense and state, director central intelligence, chairman of the Joint Chiefs of Staff, the vice president, and national security advisor. The group didn't fit into the standard Washington mode of protocol and executive etiquette. The gatherings were informal and general in nature, and normally didn't last over an hour.

Duke had seen many decisions come out of the encounters, but he didn't know the procedure in which they were made. Notes were never taken, leading him to believe there was a free flow of ideas. Everyone in the room seemed to say what they thought without having to worry about so-called political consequences. Bill Bishop, who was known for his frankness, must have been particularly outspoken here. Duke wondered what impact his sudden resignation would now have on the flow of the meetings—and on the nation's foreign policy.

James took a seat next to Howard Chaniff, the chairman of the Joint Chiefs, and pulled out his North Korean briefing files. The seat next to Chaniff, reserved for Secretary of Defense Philip Radford, was empty. Radford had left the day before on a scheduled tour of overseas bases and wouldn't be returning for another week.

James nodded toward Mark Collins, who was seated across the table next to CIA director Vance Edleman. Not unexpectedly to Duke, the room was relatively quiet, everyone keeping to themselves. Except for Secretary of

State Irving B. Weber. Weber was pacing back and forth, mumbling to himself about China. Duke stole a glance at Collins, who raised his eyebrows at Weber's odd behavior.

"Sorry about the short notice, Duke," Chaniff said, leaning over. "How are you coming with *Operation Eradicate?*"

"No problems, sir. The first eight F-15Es are scheduled to leave Elmendorf for Osan Air Base in twelve hours," Duke answered, feeling fresh and prepared. "I've given the order for three C-17s to back up the air and ground crews with supplies, spare parts and weapons."

"You've set the scenario?" Chaniff asked.

"Yes, sir. I've washed it through the simulation computer several times." Duke twisted around, pointing toward Korea on the map behind him. "Over the next two weeks F-15 Echoes will act as bad guys coming in low at high speed, just like enemy fighters. They've been told to imitate North Korean Su-30s on a low level target run. The F-16 Viper drivers will be vectored to intercept."

Chaniff nodded.

"Those Viper drivers will have their hands full," Duke continued, "but they'll have help from the AWACS."

"And the North Koreans? You'll make sure they know what we're doing?"

"I've already briefed General Foster. The Navy's been tracking several North Korean intelligence trawlers. When we're done there won't be any questions as to our intentions. They'll know we're practicing to take out both their Su-27s and Su-30s," Duke answered, trying to ignore the smell of cinnamon rolls as a tray was brought in. Fresh, hot cinnamon rolls were his favorites. When he was younger he could eat three or four and they wouldn't hang around his middle the way just one did now.

"Good, let them sweat a little for a change," Chaniff said, taking a bite from a big one. "Do you have any concerns or anything we need to discuss?"

"Yeah . . . what can I expect to happen during this meeting?" Duke asked, wondering how much responsibility was going to fall on him with Bishop gone. He wanted to be prepared.

"Stay tuned, sports fans," Chaniff said. "These meetings are always one of two ways. Fast and furious or drop-dead boring."

The president entered the room followed by the vice president and Chief of Staff Manning. Everyone stood.

## YELLOW SEA

"Contact Naval headquarters. Let them know we are on fire and unable to pursue the *Van Triumph*," Jyong-Sop ordered. His trawler was dead in the water.

"But Captain, the fire is—"

"Do it!" Jyong-Sop barked angrily.

His ship wasn't moving. He could see a few licks of fire making their way from the engine compartment, but the thick black smoke had disappeared. He couldn't tell for sure, but he hoped the fire was under control. The crew had acted swiftly, dousing the flames with several $CO_2$ fire extinguishers.

Jyong-Sop wasn't taking any chances, though. He knew the trawler was made entirely of wood and fiberglass. If a few flames managed to get inside the bulkheads it could spread to the main fuel tanks. Then all he could hope for was to be thrown clear of the wreckage by the explosion.

"It's done, sir. We're to check back in once the damage is assessed," the radio operator said, looking up from his seat.

Jyong-Sop grabbed the man by the back of the uniform and pushed him down. "Now get down there and help them put out that fire." He rubbed the sides of his head, thinking, *I am through. Kaine will never forgive me for this failure.*

## THE WHITE HOUSE

Allan Manning walked to the head of the long table. His face looked pale and his eyes were puffy and red. Duke wondered if the man had slept the night before. Certainly, Duke noted, the president's chief of staff appeared older and more out of shape than ever.

Duke glanced at McEntire, who looked relaxed, as always, wearing his standard dark suit. He had to admit he didn't feel comfortable around the president. McEntire was a complicated guy. At times he came across as analytical; other times as emotional, almost childish. It was like dealing with different personalities and it was difficult to know which would emerge next. Duke had decided to use a couple of simple rules when dealing with the president: rule one, when asked a question state the truth, no matter how bad it is; rule two, keep your voice even and calm. So far he had avoided any real confrontations with the old man. James wasn't looking forward to the first one.

Manning began the meeting once everyone was seated.

"Gentlemen, the president has a full day. This meeting will be short and to the point. Everyone's been briefed on the situation surrounding the North Korean coup attempt. The purpose of this meeting is to decide what action, if any, to take." He looked around the room. "Secretary Weber, what's the State Department's response?"

"I recommend we stay out of this," Weber said matter of factly. "We've discussed this before, Mr. President. There is no way a coup can succeed in North Korea, not today. If the Chinese want a change of government, let them handle it. If we get involved the rest of the world will say we somehow precipitated it out of some imperialist self-interest. The whole thing stinks. We don't even know who this Sinchon is."

"Good point." Manning turned to DCI Vance Edleman. "Has the CIA learned anything more about this General Sinchon?"

"Mr. Collins, have we?" the DCI asked.

Duke watched Collins swallow hard and couldn't help but smile. Mark looked about as comfortable as Duke felt.

"Well, the only new data we've obtained is this KH-14 satellite photo showing the yacht *Van Triumph* leaving Nampo harbor. I also have these photographs given to me by the Chinese ambassador." Collins held up the color prints and passed them around. "The general is wearing the flowered shirt. The man standing next to him is Ghaith Bandar, one of the world's most mysterious arms dealers. It is my opinion that Sinchon is hitching a ride to Langau on Bandar's yacht, the *Van Triumph*. This yacht is well armed and equipped with the latest technology. It's also built to outrun anything most navies can put in the water."

"I agree with Mr. Collins," the DCI put in. "Sinchon will use the *Van Triumph* in order to get to Langau."

"Well, now we know how he's getting there. We still don't know if he's a kook or not, do we?" Manning stated, then turned to Chaniff. "General, what's your opinion?"

"In *my* opinion," Chaniff sat forward, tapping his forefinger on the table as he spoke, "anything we can do to rid ourselves of North Korea will be in the best interests of the United States. The military is ready and able to help the South Koreans if they choose to aid in the coup attempt."

"You're saying we should meet with General Sinchon?" Manning asked bluntly. "Is that right?"

"The president should consider it, yes."

Manning looked around the room before turning to President McEntire: "So, we have one nay and one yea. As your national security advisor, Mr. President, I advise you to—"

"Just a minute, Mr. Manning," the president held up his hand. "General

James is present as a deputy national security advisor. I'd like to hear what he has to say about this.''

"Sir, I thought we agreed that I will be handling such matters. James is—''

"I *know* what James' position is, Allan. He did work under Bill Bishop as his chief advisor for this region and I want to hear what he has to say.'' McEntire was clearly irritated as she turned to James in the hushed room. "Duke.''

Duke felt Manning's icy cool stare. He turned to look at Manning and for a brief moment saw the eyes of a frightened, angry man. Duke didn't blink, turning his attention to the president. "Whatever you decide, sir,'' Duke spoke evenly, "you should make sure it's consistent with your long-term strategy for the region.''

McEntire nodded vigorously.

"I concur with Secretary Weber that if we back General Sinchon and the coup fails it could hurt our relations with other nations. However, if you position this as the United States being asked to help—help a people shed a tyrannical outlaw government—that's an entirely different story.''

"Go on, Duke,'' the president urged.

"Mr. President, I suggest we keep things in perspective. History tells us that no president can expect to accomplish more than one or two important foreign policy goals in a term. There is no question that meeting with General Sinchon and supporting him is a risk, but it *is* consistent with your policies. I don't believe that in this situation we're reacting to random events; rather we're trying to make the most of an opportunity. My recommendation is that we, at the very least, meet with this man.''

Again Duke felt Manning's stare on him. He continued: "If he's legitimate we offer to help him. If not . . . we back away.''

"That's easy for *you* to say,'' Manning said, reasonably. "You're not the one that has to face the press if this fails—or the American public. This all sounds very good to you, I'm sure, and I'm sure you'd love any excuse to get up there and shoot down some bogies, wouldn't you, in your Mach-10 fighter plane.''

"All right, Allan,'' the president said calmly. "I asked for James' opinion and he gave it. Thank you for your well-placed concern.'' The president looked back at James. "Duke, I understand what you're saying, but how do we minimize the risk of failure? If I send a high-level person on this type of a trip, the press will have their noses in the middle of it.''

"Well, that's easy enough,'' Chaniff cut in. "Send a low-level advisor, someone that knows the area and has a military background. I think Duke would be a prime candidate.''

"Of course." The president turned to Manning. "Isn't that what you recommended to me earlier—to send James to meet with this general?"

Everyone looked at the chief of staff, wondering why Manning was arguing the point only moments ago if he had already made private suggestions on who should be attending the rendezvous.

"Yes, sir. That was my exact recommendation," Manning was happy to admit. "But the decision is yours, sir."

McEntire looked back at James. "Any disagreements? No? Well, then, you're the man for the job, Duke. I want you to meet with General Sinchon. Have you given any thought to a plan for the meeting?"

"No, not yet, sir." Duke hadn't been able to gather any more information on Sinchon since he finished stepping up *Operation Eradicate* to respond to the discovery of the North's Su-30s.

"Our primary concern now should be that no one discovers we're involved in this," Manning piped in abruptly.

"Any ideas on how to avoid that?" the president asked.

Chaniff offered: "James was already planning to fly back to Korea to check up on how the North was reacting to his training operation, so his arrival wouldn't be seen as anything out of the ordinary. I also agree with General Sinchon's request that we scale back any military operations in the area until after the meeting. If all is quiet around Langau Island, the North Koreans shouldn't suspect anything. I'll give the order to withdraw any naval war ships and make sure our aircraft stay well clear of the area." Chaniff looked at Duke, pausing. "For security I want a minimum of men and equipment involved. That means if something goes wrong, Duke, it could take some time to put a recovery plan into action."

"I understand," Duke said. "That's the way it's got to be."

"Very well, then," the president turned to Collins. "I have one other order of business, Mr. Collins. My intel briefing this morning contained some data on a Vietnamese village. Do you still believe chemical weapons are involved or is it possible it could be a virus of some kind?"

"If the reports are accurate, and I have no reason to believe they're not, chemical weapons killed those villagers."

"I'd love to nail those suckers. How can we get proof? I want something we can take to the UN and present to the rest of the world."

"There is only one way, sir. We'd have to send in a ground team to collect soil, water and air samples. I believe we can come up with an airtight case with that kind of evidence," Collins said excitedly.

"Do it," McEntire said. "I'll sign two National Security Directives by noon. One for James's rendezvous, the other to authorize a . . . let's call it an *environmental* intrusion into Vietnam."

"Wait a minute, sir. What type of mission are you talking about?" Manning complained at the sudden decision, which he hadn't anticipated. "We have diplomatic relations with Vietnam. I want to know what—"

"I'll brief you on the mission," Chaniff said disgustedly.

"I want maps, details . . . I want to know everything."

Chaniff nodded, "You'll have them, Mr. Manning. I'll send copies to your office as soon as the details are squared away."

"Everyone knows to keep me informed of your progress," Manning stated boldly, then smiled directly at Duke. Their eyes locked one more time. "You'd better be packing your bags, General. Looks like you're going to be gone for a while."

"Who the hell does James think he is, trying to take over the meeting in there," Manning muttered, slamming the door to his office. *Did you see the looks on their faces when they realized I had already recommended James for the rendezvous! They're beginning to see why I should be the permanent national security advisor—not James. Damn, he pissed me off in there.*

Manning stormed over to his desk and fell into his chair, exhausted. Going over the meeting in his mind, he realized why James bothered him so much. He had sounded just like Bill Bishop. Every response had been measured, every answer properly thought out. Well, it wasn't going to happen again. No more Bill Bishops were going to challenge his position as the president's primary advisor. No way was he going to let James step in. *No way!*

"Mr. Manning, I have a call for you on line five," Lindsey's voice rang out over the intercom.

Line five was his private line.

"Okay." He took a breath and picked up. "Hello."

"Mr. Manning—well, Allan—after all these years you've made quite a name for yourself. I always knew you had the know-how."

"Carl? Where are you?"

"I'm in my apartment," Hawkens answered, "here in Washington, D.C. But don't worry, this call can't be traced. I didn't forget anything the company taught me."

"I want to meet with you." Manning played with a pencil on his desk, trying not to sound too anxious.

"Name where and when."

"The Denny's on Riggs Road in Lewisdale. Tonight." He paused, then finished hesitantly: "How's three A.M.?"

"Three A.M. it is." Hawkens' voice was smooth, difficult to read.

"See you then." The line went dead and Manning hung up the receiver.

"Mr. Manning, I have your wife on hold . . . she insisted on waiting for you."

Manning, breathing a sigh, didn't respond right away, taking a minute to decide if he wanted Lindsey to say he just stepped out. *Maybe if I talk to her she'll back off a little.*

"You want me to tell her I must have missed you?"

"No, I'll take it." *Shit.*

"Line three, sir."

"Rhonda, how are you?" Manning said, then sat back in his chair, trying to stay calm. "I was going to call you—"

"The hell you were. You have one week, you bastard . . . one week! You and your filthy friends will all be exposed if I don't get what I want." Her voice was even and firm. "And I'm not bluffing, Allan. I'll ruin you."

"You'll get your money, Rhonda. But on *my* terms. You don't need to threaten me, I know you're not bluffing." Manning put his head down in his free hand. "Listen . . . you may not like it but it's going to take some time to get that kind of money. Anyway, how do I know this will be the end of it?"

"That's just a chance you're going to have to take, isn't it?" There was a pause as the phone line crackled. "I can't stay here anymore, that's how you know. I can't even show my face anymore because of you. Just get me the money and I'll get out of town."

"You'll get your money. Now leave me alone, so I can take care of business."

Manning gently set the receiver down in the cradle. His face and armpits were dripping with cold sweat. *I need a fucking drink.*


STAFFORD, VIRGINIA

"I just don't understand why you have to go back so soon." Katie spoke with her back to Duke as she helped him pack his bag. "This was going to be the first Christmas holiday you'd spend with us . . . I thought we were going shopping for the kids together." Her voice cracked as she held back tears.

Duke came up behind her and locked his arms around her waist. They stood silent for a moment, their legs pressed against the bed, then he kissed the top of her head. "I'll be home for Christmas. I promise. If you want, wait and we'll do the shopping late." He jiggled her a little, trying to make her laugh. "Isn't that when you get all the good deals anyway?"

"It's not the same and you know it."

"Please, Katie, don't do this." Duke sighed.

"I know, Duke. I'm the general's strong wife." Suddenly she turned to face him. "I *might* be here when you get back," Katie blurted, her eyes pooled with tears. She placed her hand behind his neck and pulled him down to kiss him passionately. "Just remember what you'll be missing."

Duke stared after her as she closed the bathroom door and locked it behind her.

"Dad, where you goin'?" Matt had entered their bedroom doorway and was looking at the duffel bag. "You're not goin' on another trip are you?"

"Well, I was coming to tell you kids . . ."

"What's going on? Where's Mom?" Pamela joined them, jumping up on the bed.

"I was getting ready to tell Matt . . ."

"Daddy going on the plane?" Sean stood next to Matt, leaning against his leg.

Duke spoke up before he could be interrupted: "Yes, I'm going on another trip. And, yes, I'll be home for Christmas . . . any more questions?"

"Geez, I was just askin'. Come on, Sean, let's go play." Matt placed a hand on Sean's head and pushed him away from the door to follow him.

Zipping the bag up, Duke stood, not moving. Pamela sat on the bed looking at him and the closed bathroom door.

"Don't worry, Dad. She won't stay mad long." His daughter's brown eyes were sympathetic and full of understanding. "She'll miss you as soon as you're gone . . . she always does."

"Thanks, angel," Duke said, picking her up off the bed with one arm and carrying his bag with the other. He gave her a big slobbery kiss on the cheek while she giggled, then wiped it off. "Give that to Mommy for me when she comes out, willya?"

# 18

Duke James felt the hydraulic motors as the C-21A's landing gear retracted with several loud bumps and pops. The 18,000-pound jet banked to the northwest, climbing at 1,500 feet per minute to its final cruising altitude of 45,000. Built for the military by Learjet, Inc. the twin-engine aircraft had been designed to transport time-sensitive material, and people, anywhere in the world. It was fast, quiet and comfortable. It would be Duke's home for the next ten hours as it skirted the Canadian coastline on its way to Elmendorf, Alaska, and then on to Osan Air Base, South Korea.

James leaned back in the seat trying to relax. The last six hours had been filled with a whirlwind of activity and he could use the rest. To maximize time the chairman of the Joint Chiefs of Staff, Gen. Howard Chaniff, had flown with him from Andrews AFB to McChord AFB in Washington State. Having the cabin to himself now, Duke looked forward to the travel time to sort things out. The strategy was straightforward, uncomplicated. However, experience taught Duke that he should always try to anticipate anything that could go wrong during a mission. Because if it could, it would.

Opening his briefcase, James removed a laptop computer and called up the file he and General Chaniff had put together. Six hours ago Chaniff had given the order to withdraw US Naval warships operating in the area. All military flights near the Langau region were canceled and commercial flights out of South Korea were instructed to alter their flight paths. The two men had discussed the possibility of a recovery plan if something went wrong. As a precaution Chaniff had alerted the commanders of the 31st Special Operations Squadron 'Black Knights' to up their state of readiness. Two Air Force Special Ops MH-60G Pave Hawk choppers, capable of transporting two dozen Rangers, could fly at a moment's notice out of Osan AFB if ordered to do so. James knew they would be supported by F-16Cs and an E-3C Sentry AWACS also flying out of Osan. However, Duke was realistic enough to know that if his team needed to be extracted it could take as long as twenty-four hours before everything was ready to go. He preferred to concentrate on the mission and not waste brain power on something he had very little control over.

The plan called for his arrival at Osan Air Force Base in South Korea at 1400 hours local time. He would meet up with Maj. Helen Erwin, again.

She had recovered fully from the suicide blast with no long-term injuries and insisted on an immediate return to her work as the army's intelligence officer on North Korean affairs.

South Korean Army general Don Kimp would also be there. Duke knew of the general by reputation only. Reading through Kimp's file, James understood why Chaniff requested that he attend the rendezvous with Sinchon. Kimp was one of the South's best strategists and had a brilliant military mind. One of his current duties was to set up complicated computer war games, using both nuclear and conventional weapons, in simulated future wars with the North. The only flaw in his file was that he had been disciplined for routinely dressing down younger officers in front of their peers, and occasionally he clashed with civilian leaders. Duke imagined Kimp's poor judgment in this area was probably why he hadn't gotten to the top ranks of South Korea's military.

After touching down at Osan, Duke planned to take a quick shower and grab a hot meal. He would then hop on an army chopper, along with Major Erwin and General Kimp, for transport to the navy's most modern surveillance ship, *Observation Island*.

The CIA had requested *Observation Island* to be stationed off the Korean coast to record flight telemetry from any missile tests. They had been watching the development of a follow-up version of the Koreans' Scud-Cs called No-Dong. The No-Dong had a 680-mile range and preliminary reports considered it to be three times more accurate than the Scud-C. Latest reports indicated the North Koreans were also developing two more missiles which were to be more powerful and advanced versions of the No-Dong. The telemetry data to date indicated the North Koreans were only testing standard Scud-Bs and Scud-Cs.

Currently the *Observation Island* continued to cruise off the North Korean coast with choppers routinely bringing in supplies and crew members. So it was probable that when General James's diplomatic team chopper showed up on the radarscopes, the North Koreans wouldn't suspect anything.

The meeting with Sinchon was scheduled for after dark around 2300 hours, or 11:00 P.M. local time. The chopper would land on the north side of an abandoned fishing village of an unpaved airstrip, near where Bandar's *Van Triumph* should be moored in the harbor. At the request of General Kimp and senior members of the South Korean government, the encounter was to take place onboard the ship. Duke suspected that if something went wrong and China became involved, South Korea wanted to be able to deny that the secret rendezvous was held on Chinese soil. James didn't know but he speculated General Sinchon was thinking the same thing. If all went well the State Department estimated James and his team could be off the island in a couple of hours. Duke didn't believe it. Hell, it would take half the night for Kimp and Sinchon even to begin to trust each other, let alone talk in detail about a coup. James figured they'd be taking off by first light—if they were lucky.

Duke removed a satellite photo of Langau Island and studied it for a couple of minutes. The photo had been taken a year ago by an older KH-12 satellite and was computer-enhanced. The island sat by itself 173 miles southeast of Weihai, China, almost in the northern part of the Yellow Sea. Both China and Korea claimed it, because of its strategic importance, but neither country currently had any operations based there.

Looking at the photo he could see why the place had been abandoned by the Chinese nearly fifteen years ago. The island, the core of an ancient volcano, was nothing more than a desolate body of jagged rocks two miles wide and ten miles long. The land rose straight up out of the ocean and appeared to be covered with boulders of all sizes, devoid of any plant life. Duke didn't see a single tree or bush. The shoreline appeared very steep with broken cliffs and sheer rock bluff. Duke guessed that several ridges reached into the air at least 100 feet or more. Large boulders broke up the surf, making the shoreline dangerous for any ship passing too close.

There was only one natural harbor, a lagoon located on the north side of the island. Collins had circled the area with a black grease pencil. The *Van Triumph* would certainly anchor there. The cove was less than half a mile in diameter. In the late 1970s it had been converted into a fishing village by the Chinese. Duke learned the village was abandoned in the mid-eighties after a series of Chinese military nuclear accidents wiped out the normally large schools of herring and cod. There were still several buildings standing, along with a jetty and ramshackle dock. The northern end of the harbor also accommodated a lighthouse, although intelligence reported it wasn't in operation.

South of the village there appeared to be a short unpaved airstrip. By its appearance Duke guessed it was made by hand and wasn't more than 3,000 feet in length. The runway was littered with rocks and looked uneven. It had probably been designed to handle light, single-engine aircraft for emergencies only.

James returned the picture to its plastic sleeve. Sinchon had chosen well; Langau was the perfect rendezvous point. Looking out the window he watched as several white clouds floated by, and thought of Katie. A moment later he drifted off to sleep.

PYONGYANG, NORTH KOREA

"Our intelligence trawler lost one of its engines last night," Colonel Kaine reported to General Chief of Staff Chin. "The captain was unable to continue following the *Van Triumph*. However, he has made emergency repairs and is staying in radar contact with her."

"Where is Sinchon now?" Chin asked as his eyes narrowed.

Kaine pointed to a map spread out on Chin's desk. "Last report put them here, five miles off Langau Island's northern coast. The ship is not anchored but sailing in a large circle at less than three knots. My guess is they'll stay out of the fishing harbor until the Americans arrive some time later tonight."

"Yes, of course." Chin momentarily forgot the trawler's problems. He was happy as long as they could keep track of the *Van Triumph*'s whereabouts. "Have your surveillance aircraft picked up any US warships patrolling in the area?"

"No, sir." Again Kaine traced his finger over the worn map. "Two US destroyers were spotted one hundred and twelve miles south of Langau just before dark. However, they turned south and are heading out of the area. There is only one other ship in the region. It is here, seventy miles off our coast and heading northwest at eight knots. It's the American spy ship that has been sent to watch us. *Observation Island* is her name."

"That is the ship they will probably use to transport their contact for Sinchon. Clever . . . very clever." Chin shook his head, piecing together the American strategy.

"I've ordered a second surveillance trawler to follow the American spy ship," Kaine continued solemnly. "We will know their every move."

"Don't count on it," Chin replied. He glanced out one of the windows along the wall. Red streaks of sunshine were pushing through the clouds, the first traces of the coming day. By this time tomorrow he would no longer have to worry about the famed Gen. Han Sinchon fighting his every move. He would no longer have to doubt the loyalty of the troops under his command. With Sinchon out of the way Chin would consolidate his power and move toward the presidency.

"I have begun plotting the times to avoid the coverage of the satellites when we transfer the fuel rods," Kaine said, breaking the silence. "We will have to schedule phase one and phase two of the operation between each satellite pass. Sir, when will the Iranians arrive?"

"The Iranian freighter *Allum Bacar* is already anchored in the area, approximately thirty miles north of Langau. It will only take them two hours to reach the fishing port.'' Chin placed a colored pin on the location of the Iranian ship.

"I will contact the freighter captain when I know what time he needs to be in the harbor.''

Chin smiled. He was happy with his choice of successor to Sinchon. Kaine would serve him well. "I want the rods placed onboard the transport aircraft and ready to fly as soon as Colonel Woong has successfully destroyed the *Van Triumph* and the Americans' aircraft. We will not move until we are certain it is safe. By the time anyone knows what is happening the *Allum Bacar* will be anchored in Iran.''

"I have an Il-76 transport standing by.''

"Good, my friend.'' Chin paused, then added: "It is ironic, is it not, that even in Sinchon's death he will help his country.''

"He would serve his country better if he had chosen to retire admirably,'' Kaine stated, his disappointment obvious. Sinchon had once been a great general in his eyes.

"And what about Captain Yong-Gil?'' Chin asked.

"I believe he is working alone. He has not attempted to contact anyone else. I believe our suspicions are correct that the information was given to General Sinchon.''

"Then arrest him,'' Chin said, as if he were asking for a cup of tea.


YONGBYON, NORTH KOREA

"You may proceed,'' the security guard said, handing Capt. Kim Yong-Gil his ID badge.

Yong-Gil tucked the badge into his front pocket and rolled up the window of his cramped Chinese-built car. Waiting patiently he watched the red and white steel security pole lift up out of the way. Putting the car into gear, he headed down the gravel road toward the small village where he and most of the other North Korean engineers lived.

Unlike most days, Yong-Gil had finished his assignments early, and rather than take on another project he decided to leave. His mother hadn't been feeling well so he could use her illness as an excuse also to visit the shops in the village. *My mother needs tea and herbs,* he thought. If any of the security forces stopped to question him, he would be prepared with that simple explanation.

Yong-Gil turned right, shifted into second gear and started up a steep hill toward the village. The single-lane road was filled with deep ruts, dried brown vegetation lining the roadside. The village was built at the base of a long, sloping mountain and many trees had to be removed to make room for the single-story shops and stores which now lined the main street. One side of the roadway contained grocery stores, tea houses and restaurants. The other was lined with government buildings and military clubs. Yong-Gil, his mother and sister lived in one of the whitewashed apartment buildings several blocks away from the main street.

As the captain approached the top of the hill he caught sight of a white security truck traveling toward him. From the dust billowing up behind it, he could tell the vehicle was traveling at high speed. The truck's red and yellow caution lights were flashing, warning other vehicles that it had the right of way.

Yong-Gil swerved to the right, barely missing the box-shaped four-wheel-drive truck. His heart skipped a beat for a moment as he looked up in the rearview mirror. The vehicle wasn't turning around to stop him. He lowered his head and pushed down on the accelerator. He needed to hurry and get on with his business then get home.


VAN TRIUMPH

The hot tea tasted good and warmed his tired body. Han Sinchon took another sip, hoping the soothing liquid would somehow ease his troubled mind.

Sinchon couldn't allow himself to second-guess his decision now. What he was about to do was more important than himself, or a handful of men that would inevitably die. Most of all he knew he couldn't become too emotional. Unreliable and changing as the seasons, feelings were the last thing he needed to consider in a time that called for lucid thinking. Sinchon *knew* what he must do if his country was to survive. He had no other choice.

Walking out onto the weather deck he let the salt air hit him squarely in the face. The cold breeze felt assuring. It was the only kind of feeling he could trust. Taking another sip of his tea, he looked to the south. He could clearly see the formidable cliffs of Langau Island, only three miles away, silhouetted against the gray sky. The base of the rocks was hidden as the ocean waves struck them, turning the water to foam and spray.

"A change of heart?" Ghaith Bandar asked, seeing the general's serene expression. "I am sure you have many questions and only a few answers."

"There are no questions," Sinchon answered, knowing that Bandar knew nothing of the conflict boiling inside of him. He was a man whose only concern was his own well being.

"Maybe some hot food would calm your nerves," Bandar offered.

"No. I am not hungry," Sinchon shrugged. Bandar's pretentious hospitality was beginning to irritate him. No doubt he was thrilled at the prospect of Sinchon's plan succeeding, and his reward for helping it along.

"You will be happy to know the trawler stopped following us last night."

"I want you to stay alert just the same," Sinchon ordered quietly before finishing his tea.

Bandar and the general stood in silence, looking out over the vast waters, each man keeping his thoughts and worries to himself.

YONGBYON, NORTH KOREA

Capt. Kim Yong-Gil parked his car in front of the modest tea shop. He was fortunate. The storekeeper was still open for business and the shop appeared empty. The owner swept the floor, not bothering to look out the window when the car stopped in front.

Yong-Gil sat quietly for a few minutes trying to get a feel for the situation around him. To his left he could see a pair of government troops walking away from him. Their assault weapons were slung across their backs and he guessed they were just getting off duty. To his right was a group of women and children carrying books, no doubt on their way home from the library. He didn't see any other security trucks or anything else that looked unusual. *I have already waited too long,* he thought thinking of the truck that sped by him. *I am just being too careful and in the process becoming fearful.*

The captain knew the owner of the shop only by the name of Moon. It was a common name on both sides of the border. Moon was a thin man and looked to be in his midsixties. Whenever Yong-Gil had been in the shop he chain-smoked Western-style cigarettes. Yellow teeth and stained fingertips testified to many years of the tobacco habit.

Two days a week Moon closed his shop so he could travel to the port city of Haeju, an hour to the south. It was there, Yong-Gil speculated, that Moon made contact with a member of the CIA or South Korean Security Forces. That was where Moon would hand over the film canisters and classified documents Yong-Gil provided.

Stripping off his lab coat, Yong-Gil stuffed it under the passenger seat of his car. The evening sun was setting and the air was cooling.

"Hello," Yong-Gil said, entering the shop. The aroma of fresh tea leaves enveloped him.

The shop owner nodded casually then continued his sweeping. "May I help you?" he asked finally.

The captain sauntered toward the far wall without making eye contact. He surveyed the many wooden boxes holding the dark green and brown leaves. "I am looking for some jasmine. Do you have any?"

"Yes, I just received a new shipment. The large bin on the left." Moon paused then went back to sweeping his floor.

Yong-Gil made his way over to the tea bin and picked up one of the brown paper bags. Pulling two rolls of film out of his pocket, he placed them under the leaves then filled the bag. He walked back to the center of the store and waited for the owner to come to the counter.

"Will that be all today?" Moon asked.

"Yes."

Without warning three *spetsnaz* officers burst in through the front door. They spread out evenly, sweeping AK-47s right and left.

"What is the meaning of this?" Moon shouted, his eyes wide in his wrinkled face.

"Shut up, old man," the tallest soldier said, taking a step forward. He pointed his rifle at Yong-Gil then asked, "Capt. Kim Yong-Gil?"

The young man's body stiffened in fear.

"Don't answer him," Moon replied instantly. "This is a mistake."

"There is no mistake." The soldier pointed his rifle at Moon then at the captain. "You are to come with us."

Yong-Gil looked at Moon helplessly then turned back to the soldier. There were two ways out of the shop: the front door and the rear door next to Moon's cot. If he went for the back door all three men would probably fire. There was no way he could get to it without getting shot. He could run straight at them and in the confusion possibly escape unharmed. He knew that would take a miracle. The courage he felt when beginning his espionage had vanished. Suddenly he couldn't control the tears that streamed down his face. His mother and sister would be alone.

Yong-Gil sprinted forward, heading straight for the front door.

A burst of orange flame shot out from the ends of the rifles. It was the last thing Captain Kim saw as the fully jacketed bullets impacted his body. One hit his head above the right eye, exiting just above the brain stem. He was dead before he hit the floor.

Moon backed away, his hands trembling. He picked up the broom, shaking the straw end in the air at the soldiers. "Why you do this? He was only buying tea!"

"I told you to shut up," the soldier jeered coldly. He walked over and kicked Yong-Gil in the head. "You coward. You took the easy way out. Pick him up. Take his body away."

Moon looked on in silence as the young captain's limp body was carried away. A dark red blood stain smeared across the floor as they dragged him out into the street.

Moving closer to the front window, Moon watched the security truck pull away from the curb, puffs of blue smoke erupting from the back of it.

The old man took a couple of deep breaths. *They had been watching and following the captain,* he thought. *How else could so many of the soldiers know he was here?* But it was only Yong-Gil they were after. The fools had acted in haste. They did not bother to investigate where the information went; they were only concerned with stopping the source. As with every job, though, there were others waiting to fill the need. The CIA would merely replace the captain and the tea-shop owner with another source.

Locking the door, Moon placed a CLOSED sign in the window, then turned off the lights. When he had calmed down enough he retrieved the film canisters. He placed what money he had saved in a leather pouch along with a worn black-and-white picture of his deceased wife. Everything else he owned was on his back. Walking to his motorcycle, parked in the alley, Moon climbed on and started the engine. Within seconds he was gone, before anyone could return to search his shop or interrogate him.

## USS *NASSAU*, SOUTH CHINA SEA

Cutting through the silvery ocean at eight knots, the 39,300-ton *Tarawa*-class amphibious landing ship headed due west into the fast darkening night. A steady breeze pushed the ocean spray along her dull gray sides. *Nassau*'s escort, the guided-missile frigate *Samuel B. Roberts,* maintained the same course a half-mile off her port side. The two warships rocked gently as they steamed toward the eastern coast of Vietnam.

CWO Michael Q. Callahan Jr. sat with the other three members of his special operations reconnaissance team in the first two rows of *Nassau*'s briefing room located on deck three. The room had been sealed off and two armed Marine guards stood as the declaration that no unauthorized personnel would enter. Callahan was still amazed that just six hours ago he had been seated in his office at Osan Air Force Base in South Korea making plans on how to spend two weeks of leave. The next thing he knew his ass, his gear, and his team of highly trained Green Berets were on their way to the South China Sea with orders to infiltrate Vietnam.

Callahan used the tips of his fingers to massage the sensitive skin around the recently healed cut above his left eye. The fresh scar made it difficult to force the memory of the North Korean suicide attack from his mind. He still blamed himself for not being more cautious and downplaying the fact that he had captured a woman. Being careless was not going to happen this time, Callahan said to himself.

Callahan's attention returned to the Naval Intelligence officer standing in the front of the room. The lieutenant was explaining how their mission would be carried out. Callahan smirked, listening to the "by the book" rundown from a man who had never been out of a briefing room.

"Early yesterday the boys at Langley located the wreckage of an aircraft in this area, approximately eight miles north of the Vietnamese village of Phom-kew. The CIA believes this aircraft—" the lieutenant held up a fuzzy black-and-white satellite picture of a downed Learjet—"was carrying a load of chemical weapons when it crashed. Your mission is to locate the aircraft and confirm whether it was carrying chemical weapons. After the drop you'll have twelve hours to collect water, air and soil samples and return to the landing zone."

"Where's the LZ?" Michael asked, referring to the landing zone.

"Hold on, I'll get to that," the intelligence officer said, moving to stand between two large color satellite photos of Vietnam's central highlands. The officer held a pointer which only added to his academic appearance. "If you don't get what you're after and are not back at the LZ by 0500 tomorrow we can't guarantee a safe extract until it gets dark again. That means you'll have to spend another twelve hours minimum in hostile territory."

Callahan cocked his head to the right, hearing the words. Typical military warning . . . or threat. If anyone dropped in the zone wasn't smart enough to haul ass and get his job done, they deserved to be left behind, as far as Callahan was concerned. He sure didn't want them on his team.

"The LZ is located here . . . approximately five miles from your target area. This long flat area here is capable of handling a Harrier. We've programmed your GPS receivers so you'll be able to make it to the crash site. However, the terrain is very rocky with thick underbrush and plenty of tall trees. The weather has been rainy so I'd expect mud and probably fog . . . but not anything you can't deal with."

"A Harrier?" Michael said, interrupting. "I thought we were scheduled to go in with Pave Lows."

"Change of plans, Mr. Callahan. The Pentagon doesn't want us any closer to the Vietnamese coast than two hundred and fifty miles and time is very important. It's been decided your team will be transported in an AV-8B. It's faster, can still come in under radar and the pilot will supply close-air support if you and your men should need it."

"Oh man . . . you talkin' Spam in a can. I don't like this already," Sgt. Steve Pope, the team's communication specialist, murmured under his breath.

"Knock it off, Pope," Callahan ordered, glaring at him.

"You're scheduled to take off at 1800 local. Any questions?" the lieutenant asked, searching the faces in the room.

"Yeah," Pope sounded off again. "If the LZ is five miles from the primary target, that means we have to hike five miles first then collect the samples. You're only giving us twelve hours to get in and out."

"That's correct, Mr. Pope. Your question is?" The lieutenant was repacking his briefcase.

"Is there any way we can get closer to the primary?"

"There's only one place for the Harrier to land. If this was going to be an easy mission we'd be sending in the Marines, now, wouldn't we, Mr. Pope? Maybe you should be thinking about a transfer."

The snickering and jeering in the room caused Pope to slide down slightly in his chair. Callahan shook his head, thinking only Pope would complain about walking a short five miles.

"Anything else?" the lieutenant asked, ready to leave the room. "Okay. Your call sign for this operation will be Tango, as in Tango Team. Get some sleep. I'll wake you an hour before takeoff."


CIA HEADQUARTERS

"Mark . . . I have bad news," Douglas Brooks said uneasily.

Collins looked up, his bloodshot eyes opening wide. He hadn't expected to see the director for intelligence at this late hour. The clock read half-past one.

"*Sirhak* is dead. He was shot about three hours ago at the contact point."

Collins rolled his eyes. *Sirhak* was the CIA Operations' cryptonym for Army Engineer Capt. Kim Yong-Gil, the agent operating inside North Korea's Yongbyon nuclear facility.

"They found him at the tea shop," Collins said, "didn't they?"

Brooks handed him a single page of green computer paper.

"How?" Collins asked.

"We don't know for sure. But one of our border listening posts recorded a two-second computer microburst about twenty minutes ago. The NSA decoded it and this is it." Brooks pointed to the computer paper. "It's from Moon. He's on his way to the South right now."

Collins let out a long sigh. "Sirhak was our best asset in Yongbyon. It could take us years to replace him." He scratched his head as he read the page. "Did you read all of this?"

"Yeah, I did," Brooks said. "But hold on. I don't like that look in your eyes."

"He found the fuel rods. He found the extra fuel rods. I knew it. I knew those bastards had a separate reactor. From this report it sounds as if they're getting ready to move the rods."

"Slow down, Mark, you're not thinking this through." Sirhak is dead,

dead as in compromised. Consider this operation over. And must I remind you . . . you're back to being an analyst. Leave the covert stuff to operations. I don't want you involved in it.''

Collins picked up the pictures that were included in the electronic microburst. ''This is what we've been waiting for. This is the proof.''

''We can't take this to the White House and you know it. This is just the first step. And now that the North Koreans know about Sirhak everything will change. Officially your part in this operation is over.''

Collins eyes continued to scan the computer paper. ''I've analyzed every shred of data that Sirhak has supplied us over the last year. You're not taking me off this . . . I have too much invested.''

''Mark, we're repositioning two satellites for continuous coverage of the North just like you requested. Until operations can position another agent inside Yongbyon . . . if you want to continue looking over operations' shoulder, be my guest, but right now I want this North Korean coup attempt front and center,'' Brooks said to Collins, looking concerned. ''You have to learn to let these things go when it's time . . . it's not healthy to hang on to them, it'll wear you out. These things happen.''

''I understand.''

Brooks turned to leave and then stopped.

''Oh, and Mark, better not let one of those cut-the-CIA-down-to-size congressmen find out you're sleeping in this office. They'll want to charge you rent.''

''I'm putting in for overtime,'' Collins said without a smile.


## OSAN AIR FORCE BASE, SOUTH KOREA

Duke James stepped off the C-21A Learjet into a cold, wet, driving rainstorm. Rolling gray clouds hung over the air base reducing visibility to less than 500 feet. By the temperature James guessed it could be snowing in a few hours. Parked 200 feet away he could see the dark silhouette of a Sikorsky MH-60G Pave Hawk special forces chopper. Its engines were running, the navigational lights flashing, however the chopper's four rotor blades weren't turning.

''This way, sir. There's been a change of plans,'' an Air Force major shouted over the noise of the Learjet's idling engines. ''You're leaving right away.''

''You mean a change in the weather,'' Duke said, lowering his head. He raised his collar and followed the younger officer across the tarmac to the waiting chopper. It wouldn't be the first time he didn't get his hot shower and meal.

James studied the exterior details of the MH-60G as he came closer. Dark green in color, the Pave Hawk was unique, featuring a long sloping nose and tricycle landing gear. He could see two cylindrical external fuel tanks hanging off pylons on each side of the upper fuselage. A long refueling probe extended from the nose section of the helicopter.

Duke had a great deal of respect for the MH-60G and the men and women that flew it. The chopper had been designed for a tough mission, to penetrate hostile territory by flying low-level at night or in adverse weather. The Pave Hawk was large enough to carry a load of special forces troops and was equipped with enough electronics and firepower to challenge most anything that got in her way. *Even with all this technology it still takes guts for these air jocks to fly in alone with no one covering their backsides,* the general thought.

"Good luck, sir," the major said, snapping a quick salute.

"Thanks," Duke nodded, climbing into the Pave Hawk. The sliding cargo door slammed shut and he heard the pilot engage the engines. Within a few seconds the chopper started to shake as the twin turbines spooled up.

"Welcome aboard, General James." Maj. Helen Erwin, US Army intelligence officer, shouted. "Strap yourself in, sir. We need to get underway."

James sat down and wiped the rainwater away from his eyes. The interior of the chopper was warm, that was good, but other than that it wasn't much different than every other military helicopter he had been in. The Pave Hawk might look like a futuristic starship on the outside, but on the inside she was bare bones. The typical row of green nylon-web jump seats lined the metal floor that was scratched and pocked with dents. Wire mesh cover guards protected the light bulbs that lit the passenger compartment. Nylon ties held bundles of cable, insulation and electrical filament together along the ceiling.

"Sorry you didn't get any time on the ground, sir, but when this storm rolled in an hour ago we pushed things up a bit to be on the safe side." Major Erwin leaned back, indicating to her right: "Gen. Richard James, I would like you to meet Gen. Don Kimp."

Duke extended his hand. *"Annyong ha-simnikka.* Nice to meet you, general. Call me Duke."

Kimp bowed his head. "You may call me General Kimp."

Duke bit his tongue as he shook the man's hand sizing him up. Kimp didn't appear to be more than five feet five inches tall. Unlike most senior officers he wore a standard military haircut, short on the side and one inch long on top. To Duke's surprise Kimp didn't cast off a particularly commanding presence. However, his dark eyes and thin face were filled with a deep confidence.

"Good to see you again, Major," Duke said to Erwin as quietly as he could but still loud enough for her to hear. "I'm surprised to see you back on duty."

"Thanks to you, General. I never had a chance to say it officially." Erwin gave what Duke guessed to be one of the few smiles she ever bestowed.

"Not necessary . . . I was just doing the army a favor. How are your men doing?" Duke asked, referring to the other victims of the North Korean suicide bomber.

"Everyone is doing quite well, sir. In fact, Chief Warrant Officer Callahan is back on active."

"Glad to hear that. He's a good man."

"One of the army's best, sir," Erwin grinned. "You might want to get out of that wet jacket. We have a two-hour flight to the *Observation Island*. I went ahead and packed you a parka."

"Thanks," James laughed, thinking of his last trip and the oversized parka he had almost refused to wear. Not this time.

There wasn't any use in trying. CWO Michael Callahan and the rest of his recon team wouldn't be able to sleep. Instead they applied the last bit of green, olive and beige camouflage to their faces and hands.

Callahan used the tips of his fingers as he gently massaged the grease-paint around his eyelids and into the crevices next to his nose, making sure he covered every bit of shiny skin. Next he placed a black watchman's cap over his head and snapped a nylon web mesh vest over his camouflaged green and brown tiger-striped uniform. The vest contained four extra thirty-round magazines for his CAR-15 assault rifle, an eight-inch survival knife, two aluminum flashlights and six fragmentation grenades. Callahan prefered the compact 5.56mm NATO Colt Commando known as a CAR-15. It had a telescopic butt and a short 10.2-inch barrel earning it the nickname of "tunnel sweeper." Designed as a survival weapon for use during the Vietnam War, the rifle had gained favor among special forces troops for battles in close quarters.

Tucked inside his left side under his arm was a US Navy Model 22 type 0 9 mm silenced pistol. The Smith and Wesson had been specially designed for special forces. Constructed of stainless steel to prevent rust and corrosion, the pistol was nicknamed "Hush-Puppy" for its effectiveness at killing guard dogs when penetrating sensitive areas.

Callahan turned around and checked the three other members of his recon team as they readied their equipment. Each man was dressed in a clean camouflaged uniform without unit or rank insignias. Anything that could cause an enemy to identify them as Americans had been removed, right down to the tread on their boots. Michael felt comfortable with the men he had selected for this mission. Each had gone through special forces training at Fort Bragg in North Carolina and was proficient in at least two specializations including demolitions, intelligence, light weapons, and communications. Ranger school was tough and the training adequate, but in Michael's opinion only the hard-ass commanders at Bragg gave a man the full background of training needed to complete a mission in hostile territory. The CWO knew he was somewhat prejudiced, but Callahan figured if it was his life on the line he'd call the shots and select men that thought and acted the way he did.

Seated on the bench to his left were Corp. Todd Ingram, a light weapons specialist, and Sgt. Gary Barnes, the squad's medical specialist. The two men were seven years apart, Barnes being the oldest. Identical in height and weight at five feet ten and 160 pounds, both were from the Midwest. Ingram had grown up in Appleton, Wisconsin, the son of a mailman, while Barnes spent his formative years in the projects of eastern Chicago. Callahan had worked with these two men for the last six months.

Barnes was extremely cool under pressure and Callahan couldn't remember if he had ever seen him break a sweat even when exercising. Besides knowing how to sew up bullet wounds, Barnes knew a dozen different ways to kill an enemy soldier in his sleep. Ingram, on the other hand, was pure soldier. He had the instincts of a mountain cat and the street-smart brains of a drug dealer. There wasn't a weapon invented, American or foreign, that Ingram couldn't handle. In a firefight Callahan couldn't think of anyone he'd rather have on his side.

Sitting directly to his right was S. Sgt. Steven L. Pope, the communications specialist. An E6, Steve was only two years younger than Callahan, but he was still the least mature member of the team. Pope was tall for a special forces member at six feet two and slightly overweight, although it didn't slow him down. He had a sharp wit, complained more than he should and harnessed a lot of hyper energy. Michael was confident Pope could get the job done but in the back of his mind he knew that he was unproven in combat.

Callahan checked the batteries on his night-vision goggles before stowing them in his gear bag. He had packed a gallon of water and several candy bars but figured he wouldn't need them. They were only going to be in the bush for twelve hours and the Vietnamese jungle was full of water. After the suicide bomber, though, he vowed never to take anything for granted again.

"I'm going topside, men. I need fresh air," Callahan said, grabbing his weapons bag. The other three members of his squad followed.

It was 3:15 A.M. and just a handful of customers were still inside Denny's Restaurant. Carl Hawkens had parked his car near the rear in the darkest part of the parking lot. He watched Allan Manning climb out of his late-model car and stand out in the open.

"Manning . . . you always were a dumb shit," Hawkens murmured. "No wonder the CIA wanted to make you an analyst." He watched the chief of staff walk across the parking lot. Manning was recognizable to him a block away, even when he tried to blend in with a crowd. A ball cap and sunglasses completed the picture.

Hawkens put his pearl-colored SC400 Lexus into gear and pulled up next to Manning as he was about to enter the restaurant.

"Get in," Hawkens ordered.

"Uh . . ." Manning, taken aback, stood dumbfounded a moment.

"It's Hawkens . . . I said get in."

Hawkens barely waited for Manning to close the door before he turned left out of the parking lot and back into the north-flowing traffic.

"Were you followed?" Manning asked seriously.

"Followed? Why would anyone want to be following me?" Hawkens asked nonchalantly. "Besides, you were the one that was going to sit inside and wait. If we are being followed, they got a couple of good shots of you in the parking lot," he added, smiling at Manning.

"Well, I'm not the fucking arms dealer," Manning retorted.

"Hey . . . I'm a respected Washington lobbyist and an international business consultant." Hawkens, irritated with Manning's lack of caution, flipped on his ANG 2000 acoustic noise generator. The device filled the car with inaudible high pitched frequencies designed to distort microphones, transmitters and laser/microwave reflections from the windows.

"Turn right at the next intersection . . . slow down," Manning instructed, looking all around them for signs of a tail. He seemed awfully shook up.

Hawkens did as he was told.

"Stop here. Turn off the headlights."

"Are you paranoid or—"

"Just do it."

Hawkens came to a stop behind a Dodge Minivan. He put the car in park and killed the headlights. "Now what?"

"We wait," Manning said, looking out the back window.

After a few minutes, when no one else had traveled down the side street, Manning turned to Hawkens. "You can drive now. No one knows we're together."

"Well, that's good." Hawkens smiled to himself, pulling back onto the main street. They were traveling north, away from the center of the city.

"So how have you been, buddy?" Hawkens glanced over at Manning.

"You and Rhonda ever have any kids? Got a big family to go with your big job?"

Manning removed the sunglasses. His face looked thin and sunken. Several large red veins were clearly present on the surface of his nose and his eyes looked watery and irritated with dark rings circling beneath them. "I'm not in the mood for any bullshit, Carl. I called this meeting to discuss business, not get together with someone who was never really a friend." Manning paused as he looked out the passenger-side window. "I have some information your clients might be able to use."

"What do you mean by . . . use?"

"Let's say what I have to offer could further or possibly protect their investments."

Hawkens' mood turned professional immediately. Keeping his excitement to himself, he could hardly believe what he was hearing. *Allan Manning, the dweeb of the CIA, is now the chief of staff for the president of the United States. And here he is seated next to me, offering to sell me information. This has got to be better than dating a virgin.*

Maybe Manning had flipped out. The man definitely looked like hell and he never was very trustworthy. It was possible he was nothing more than a glorified secretary with a big ego.

"You're coming to me with information?" Hawkens shrugged, acting uninterested. "I'm retired. Besides, what kind of stuff could you supply me?"

"The type of stuff people die for," Manning said, looking out the window.

Sitting in the center of the USS *Nassau*'s flight deck, her engines screaming, the ghost-gray AV-8B Harrier jump jet looked out of place. Its color seemed to blend into the broken late-afternoon clouds hugging the surface of the ocean. The deck had been cleared except for a few sailors wearing different colored vests, preparing the aircraft for flight.

Michael Callahan approached the jet with caution. Anything that looked like an airplane but landed like a helicopter couldn't be trusted. The Harrier might have been a marvel in modern aviation, a small stubby-winged aircraft with incredible maneuverability, but to Callahan it was just another high-tech toy used by pansies called pilots that did their dirty work in the comfort of a cockpit at 20,000 feet. Not quite the same danger as being in the mud facing the bad guys eye to eye.

"I have an idea, Callahan. You be the sardine this time and I'll be the cracker," Steve Pope broke up. "Or maybe we could play peas in a pod. Hey—what happens if I have to take a pee? Has anyone thought about that?"

"Knock it off, Pope. I don't want this to be any more painful than it's got to be," Callahan was carrying his gear bag, backpack and assault rifle. The feel of thick ocean air and heavy humidity swept over him.

Located under each wingtip was a long fiberglass-reenforced pod roughly the size of a large external fuel tank. The nose section of each had been cut away and replaced with clear plexiglass. A square door was open on top of each pod allowing for two of Callahan's crew to climb inside along with their equipment. The pods were lined with thick insulation and came equipped with an internal radio receiver, several canteens of water, and safety belts. Michael didn't like this method of operation. It was uncomfortable for his men to lie flat on their stomachs for the entire flight, then difficult to be limber jumping into action when the time came. The pods were also noisy, leaked and didn't ever warm up even with the heaters turned to maximum. However, when a special forces team needed to penetrate enemy air space at 500 miles an hour at treetop level, it was the only way to fly.

"Barnes, Ingram . . . right side. Pope . . . you're with me. See you on the ground." Callahan looked up, giving the pilot a thumbs up.

Michael crawled inside and strapped the safety belt around his large 220-pound frame. Wiggling back and forth he tried to get as comfortable as possible for the hour and forty-minute flight to the LZ. He plugged in the radio receiver and keyed the mike.

"Two, this is one . . . you ready?"

*"Yeah . . . ready as we'll ever be,"* Barnes' voice crackled over the radio.

"Let's get airborne, captain. We have a date and don't want to keep her waiting," Callahan radioed up to the pilot.

*"Roger that. We always deliver on time."*

Callahan slid on a pair of dark sunglasses and watched as the Harrier pilot swung his bird into the wind. He felt the engine spooling up and a moment later the Harrier lifted off the flight deck, heading west at 200 feet.

"This is a copy of the president's daily intelligence briefing," Manning said, pulling a folded five-page document out of his overcoat pocket. "If you were to get regular access to this, how much would it be worth to you?"

"What are you doing this for, Allan?" Hawkens asked, still suspicious.

"Wasn't it the CIA that taught us everything had a price . . . everything and everyone?" Manning said dully. He didn't appear to be desperate, but he did look pathetic. "Let's just say I also have a price. Now if you want to pay for this information, it's yours. If not . . . I'll find someone else. Someone that doesn't want to play fifty questions."

Hawkens looked straight ahead, not saying anything as he drove. *So this is all there is to it. Manning needs money. Well, that makes sense, the idiot's gone and gotten himself into some kind of trouble. Geez . . . couldn't be another woman.* The fact that Manning was willing to sell out his country for a few bucks made Hawkens feel better. He understood that kind of motivation. But it also meant he'd be in a vulnerable position with a man that was, to say the least, a bit flaky. Hawkens preferred to work with men that didn't mind being evil and corrupt for their own rewards. He knew where they stood and what to expect of them. Like Bandar, Hawkens was unwaveringly selfish and predictably greedy. But there was honor among them in that they both knew each other was guilty. Manning, on the other hand, would consider himself a victim, or of a higher level of corruption. However, Hawkens was operating a business, and maybe if he was very careful he could make a lot of money from what Manning had to offer.

"Are you interested?" Manning asked, his voice strained.

"It depends on what it contains," Hawkens replied cautiously. "My clients have special needs and I have to be selective with the data."

"How *much* would this be worth to your clients?" Manning asked holding up the pages in front of him.

"Ten thousand a week," Hawkens answered. "If it has any pertinent information, that is."

"Bullshit! I'm talking about the president's fucking daily intelligence briefing—the one put together by the CIA and DIA. It's some of the most classified information in Washington. Hell, Congress doesn't know half the shit in here." Manning stared hard at Hawkens, sweat beginning to bead up on his forehead. "It can't get much more pertinent then that!"

"Allan, you're asking me to give you a price without even knowing the contents—"

"This is what I want," Manning demanded. "Twenty-five thousand, in unmarked twenties and fifties, delivered to me each week. In return I'll supply you with a minimum of three DIBs per week. But I need the twenty-five thousand up front now for this info."

Hawkens continued to drive. Realistically he should be jumping for joy, but he took some time to consider the pros and cons of dealing with Allan Manning. If the info supplied turned out to be worthless, he'd know how to take care of Manning. After a while he pulled the car over to a curb, parking on a deserted side street. Looking at Manning, he finally got out of the car and opened the trunk. When Hawkens returned he handed a thick white envelope to him. "How will you get the—"

"I'll fax them," Manning said, wiping his forehead with a tissue and talking rapidly. "That's right. I'll fax them to your office. No one will ever know."

"And the money?" Hawkens asked.

"I'll let you know how to deliver the money later." Manning replaced the glasses over his eyes. "Now take me back to my car, please."

When Hawkens turned into the Denny's parking lot two cars were parked near the entrance, but Manning's Towncar still sat alone in the back. Several young adults were standing on the corner smoking cigarettes and laughing, but everything else appeared quiet.

"I'll be in touch," Hawkens said, stopping the car.

"No . . . I'll be in touch." Manning exited, discreetly leaving the papers on the seat. Hawkens didn't wait for the chief of staff as he merged back into traffic. Anxious about the papers lying on the seat next to him, he stopped at the first McDonald's he came to. He parked and unfolded the papers. Scanning the document, he hesitated at the bottom of page two.

VIETNAM

LATE LAST NIGHT CIA ANALYSTS LOCATED WHAT THEY BELIEVE IS A DOWNED AIRCRAFT WHICH COULD HAVE BEEN RESPONSIBLE FOR THE TRANSPORTATION OF CHEMICAL WEAPONS OUT OF VIETNAM'S CENTRAL HIGHLANDS. IT IS BELIEVED THE AIRCRAFT CRASHED ON TAKEOFF CAUSING ITS LOAD OF CHEMICAL WEAPONS TO EXPLODE AND DRIFT DOWNHILL TOWARD THE NEAREST VILLAGE. CURRENT CIVILIAN DEATH TOLL FROM CHEMICAL POISONING STANDS AT 102 WITH MORE DEATHS EXPECTED.

IT IS THE CIA'S RECOMMENDATION THAT WITHIN TWELVE HOURS, SPECIAL FORCES TROOPS BE AIR-DROPPED INTO VIETNAM APPROXIMATELY TEN MILES NORTHEAST OF PHOM-KEW VILLAGE TO COLLECT WATER, SOIL AND AIR SAMPLES ALONG WITH SEGMENTS OF THE AIRCRAFT. A COMPLETE ANALYSIS WILL BE CONDUCTED AFTER THE TEAM IS EXTRACTED AND SAMPLES RETURNED.

CIA ESTIMATES PROBABILITY OF DETECTION AT LESS THAN 06.123%.

"Oh, shit!" Hawkens said aloud. Manning didn't know how valuable this information was.

*When the CIA figures out that Americans were working with the Vietnamese to sell chemical weapons to North Korea . . .* Hawkens's mouth went dry and his palms grew sweaty with the thought of being discovered. Looking at his watch, Hawkens calculated the time change—it was 4:30 in the afternoon in Vietnam. He had to contact Major Tra immediately.

Hawkens floored his SC400, squealing the tires as he tore out of the parking lot.

# 19

USS *Observation Island*

Duke James leaned toward the window of the Pave Hawk, feeling the chopper bank to the east just below a thick ceiling of clouds boiling with rain. Off to the right side he could clearly see each feature of the 563-foot-long 16,000-ton intelligence-gathering ship. She steamed at six knots heading toward the northern portion of the Yellow Sea.

Duke had been on board the ship for five hours, just long enough for the weather to clear for takeoff and landing and to advise Captain Bliss of his mission.

While waiting Duke had discovered the *Observation Island* wasn't like any other ship in the US Navy. The exterior resembled a mass of communication and microwave towers. The top of the deckhouse contained two bulging round white radomes, one behind the other, housing two Raytheon navigation radars. Bolted to the midsection of the bow were two forward antenna masts reaching into the sky over one hundred feet. The masts, with cross rails dividing the upper one-third in sections, accommodated various electronic gathering instrumentation including antennas for Communications Intelligence (COMINT), Electronics Intelligence (ELINT), and Telemetry Intelligence (TELINT).

The aft section of the ship was equipped with a large four-foot-square rotating box-shaped platform. One side had been fitted with a flat paneled phased-array radar, code named Cobra Judy. This radar was used to track the faint radar images of ballistic and tactical missiles as they streaked across the northern Pacific.

Duke had learned the ship was converted from a Mariner-class merchant vessel. It had been modified originally to supply the National Security Agency with test-flight and impact-accuracy measurements on Soviet and Chinese ICBM missile tests over their Pacific test ranges. Besides tracking the warheads as they reentered the atmosphere, the ship also listened in on coded telemetry, allowing the US to know if any arms-control treaties were being violated.

In more recent years the *Observation Island* found herself patrolling the waters off Iran, India and, now, North Korea.

A few drops of rain started to impact the side of the chopper as it was rocked back and forth by several violent gusts of wind.

Duke tightened his lap belt. The chopper pitched forward as the pilot dropped the nose. The Pave Hawk vibrated rapidly picking up airspeed.

James looked at the South Korean general. They had sat across from each other on the two and a half hour flight from Osan and only made eye contact once. He had heard the Korean officer speak less than a dozen words and James was beginning to wonder if the man knew very much English.

"General Kimp, we really haven't discussed General Sinchon yet. What do you think of him?" Duke questioned.

"He is a North Korean military officer . . . what else is there to know?" Kimp answered simply.

"I understand he commands the respect of many of their best forces."

"I have heard the same rumors. But I will not be tricked by good intentions. The thirst for power is what compels men to act and take great risks. History is filled with men that talk of great ideals but want nothing more than to control the people." Kimp paused then added, "I have heard nothing to suggest he is a man of honor. Nothing that tells me I can trust him."

"So your mind is made up."

"During your country's long struggle against the Soviet Union did you trust any of their officers?" Kimp asked with a straight face. "Why should I trust a man I've trained my entire life to kill?"

James looked into the man's eyes. They were dark, showing little emotion. It was almost a decade since the Soviet Union had dissolved. James had nearly forgotten what it was like to have the constant threat of attack hanging over his own country. It was obvious that General Kimp had not had that pleasure. His emotions were high-strung and he appeared very much on edge.

"General Kimp . . . believe me, I understand what you're saying. However, this could be the breakthrough your country has been waiting for." Duke spoke earnestly. "You could be the one that lays the first stones in the path towards a reunited Korea."

"Or this could be an insane man that wants to embarrass my country," Kimp stated. "I am here only because of the pressures from your government . . . and I am following orders. My recommendation was to let this general come to us, to South Korea, if he was serious. It was your government that agreed to meet him under his own terms. Not mine."

"Maybe your government sent the wrong man," Duke said at last. "We believe attitude makes one successful or a failure in our country . . . and I'd say right now you're not even in the game, general."

"You Americans are all alike. Everything is fun and games to you. This is my country's future at risk, not yours. When we meet with Sinchon I will know his true intentions . . . you may observe his attitude all you want." Brow furrowed, Kimp turned away.

Duke made eye contact with Major Erwin. He could almost read her mind. If General Kimp wasn't kept under control the entire mission could be blown. *Keeping him under control could be Erwin's job,* Duke thought, raising his eyebrows at her and smiling.

The female intelligence officer knew more about Korea's military and its history than anyone else Duke had come in contact with. Not only that, Erwin had proved herself to be a persuasive soldier. Over the course of the last year Duke had come to know her as very smart and no-nonsense, the perfect formula for her current role in military intel.

The only child of a twenty-four-year career Army NCO serving in the special forces, Major Erwin had lived in Europe, Southeast Asia, Japan, Korea and Central America as well as the United States. After high school she applied to West Point and was accepted. Erwin made it clear she wanted to follow in her father's footsteps and not sit behind some desk shuffling papers.

Duke had learned her father was forced to retire from the army for medical reasons. Records stated that Sgt. Maj. H. Melvin Erwin developed arthritis and had trouble walking. The truth was classified. The sergeant major had actually been captured during Desert Storm while on a recon mission into Baghdad to rescue two downed Navy flyers. He escaped and was recaptured a day later. The Iraqis broke both his knees.

"All right, gentlemen," Erwin replied in an upbeat tone, raising her eyebrows back to Duke. "Next stop is Langau Island . . . and hopefully a rendezvous with history."

## KIM IL SONG AIR BASE, NORTH KOREA

Lt. Col. Kaine shielded his eyes from the small stones being kicked up by the rotor wash of the Mi-8 transport chopper as it hovered a few feet above the tarmac. He watched the landing gear hit the ground and heard the pilot power down the engine. Kaine guessed the temperature was a few degrees above the freezing mark and knew it would get much colder during the long hours of the night.

Located twenty miles southeast of Pyongyang in a secluded mountainous area, the air base had been named in honor of North Korea's late leader, Kim Il Song. Colonel Kaine used the base to house North Korea's most advanced equipment and best trained pilots. He liked to think of them as the *spetsnaz* of the air force: men and women who had honed their war-fighting skills to equal those of the West. On the surface the base appeared crude and outdated.

Surrounded by several rolling tree-covered mountain ridges, a single

10,000-foot runway filled the valley floor. Constructed in the mid 1990s with the help of Iranian engineers, underground bunkers had been designed to protect the North's military commanders from the West's best smart bombs. The majority of the base's command and control personnel also operated from below ground. Thirty-six concrete reenforced aircraft hangars dotted the rugged landscape and only one large above-ground structure could be seen from the air.

The hangar's ground radar positions and maintenance areas were well camouflaged using a mixture of nylon netting, natural shrubs and trees to hide the site from the prying eyes of American reconnaissances satellites. Still, Kaine seriously doubted the base was a secret.

Colonel Kaine watched his superior officer, General Chief of Staff Myong Chin, step off the chopper. He lowered his head and walked toward him. The general was dressed in a dark olive uniform and carried a leather pouch under his right arm. It was most unusual not to see four or five assistants following the chief of staff.

"Are your pilots and aircraft ready?" Chin asked, coming within earshot.

"Yes, sir. The jets will be armed and fueled within the hour."

"Very well."

"There has been a change in plans," Kaine said as the two men walked to the main building.

"What change?" Chin barked.

"The weather. Visibility at the target area is less than one-half mile and deteriorating rapidly. We will have to send two jets . . . not one."

"I agree. And the *Allum Bacar,* the Iranian freighter, is it moving into position?"

"Yes, I have a complete briefing prepared for you. This way, please." Kaine strode ahead, leading the way.

The two men entered a long windowless concrete-block structure set 200 yards off the main runway. The building was surrounded by leafless trees and brown camouflage netting. From the air the structure appeared to be a sloping hill dotted with dried brush and rocks. Once inside they turned right and followed a long corridor to a set of stairs leading to a cluster of command rooms 150 feet below the surface.

The main command operations center (COC) was a low-ceilinged chamber reenforced with steel I-beam struts and wire mesh suspending from the ceiling. The center had been equipped with a backup electrical system, fresh water reservoir, ninety days of food and medical supplies. When war came with the South, Kaine was determined his country would not make the same mistakes as the Iraqis. His country would survive a prolonged air assault from the United States while keeping its command and control structure intact.

The operations center was filled with eight functioning computer monitors, each linked directly to one of eight remote command/operations centers (SCC/SOCs) placed strategically on the edge of North Korea's border. These outlying sites transmitted radar/radio data to the command operation center. Computer stations were occupied by technicians and the room was filled with the chatter of radio transmissions and the continuous clicking of computer keyboards.

In typical Chinese style, the control center had been laid out in the shape of a large T with three primary computer screens located on the far wall. Data collected from the North's elaborate radar-warning network was displayed on the screens showing the movement of both friendly and enemy aircraft. The center display exhibited a green blue background with red lines showing the Korean peninsula bordered by China to the north. The screen on the right was South Korea with yellow and orange dots marking the locations of US and ROK military bases. The last display on the left showed a 200-mile radius around the island of Langau. From here they could control and communicate with the North's most elite and best-trained pilots.

Kaine led Chin into his office, closing the door behind him. The office, actually an eight-by-eight windowless room resembling a prison cell, was located off the main floor. It contained a desk, two chairs and a cot. A large map of the Korean peninsula was the only wall decor. Several telephones sat atop the desk, linked to the Ministry of Defense building in Pyongyang. The room was nothing more than an area where Kaine could retreat to evaluate his troops' effectiveness during an exercise or an actual battle.

"The data shows there is a satellite pass every six hours. That means we have a six-hour window where there is no satellite coverage. The Americans will be blind for that amount of time." Kaine stood next to his desk, pointing at the map. "Latest communications place the Iranian freighter fifteen miles north of Langau."

Chin, his elbow on the chair, ran a finger over his lips contemplatively not taking his eyes off the map. "You have finalized your attack?"

"I have," Kaine answered. "The intelligence trawler keeping watch on the *Van Triumph* is just over the horizon. It is using its radar-warning receivers so *Van Triumph* should not know we are still tracking her. Just after dark two Su-30s, armed with antiship missiles, will take off and head straight for Langau. The trawler will begin to broadcast a ground-to-air radar signal. The fighters will pick it up and follow it to their target . . . the *Van Triumph.*"

A slight smile came across Chin's square face. "And the fuel rods?"

"Once Woong has returned to confirm his mission is completed we will have four hours in which to transfer the rods. While the transfer is taking place my men will find Sinchon, or what's left of him. When everything is secured the *Allum Bacar* will sail and we will return home with the general's body. The Americans will think the coup attempt and their meeting was discovered and we retaliated. By the time they determine something is amiss, it will be too late.''

Chin cautioned the overzealous Kaine: ''The Americans are not stupid. They will likely have a communications link with the team or be expecting them back by a certain time. What will happen when that link is broken?''

''They will of course send out some type of rescue. But I estimate it will take twelve to eighteen hours before they could get into the area.''

''You have done well, Colonel Kaine. I am glad you will be recovering General Sinchon's body. I want it displayed as a warning to anyone that wishes to challenge my authority.'' Chin lowered his eyebrows. ''I want you to accompany the fuel rods to Langau. You should be on-site when the transfer is made.''

''Yes, I will be there,'' Kaine responded, having already made that decision.


## LANGAU ISLAND

Gen. Han Sinchon watched *Van Triumph*'s anchor slide into the dark waters of the harbor with a giant splash. Checking his watch he calculated it had been dark for five hours. Sinchon felt his self-confidence ebbing. He was beginning to wonder if the Americans and South Koreans would come.

The general allowed his stocky body to rest against the ship's side rail. The burning pain in his side had turned to numb sensation. He coughed occasionally, spitting up reddish bile into a handkerchief.

Raising a pair of night-vision binoculars Sinchon surveyed the dark island and surrounding area. He could now see why the harbor had been built at the end of an oval-shaped bay. In its natural state the bay was much like the rest of Langau Island, surrounded by vertical rock outcroppings which reached out of the ocean ten to twenty feet. Chinese hard-rock miners had blasted away the steep rock in an area approximately 300 yards wide allowing for construction of the fishing village and wharf.

At the entrance of the bay the Chinese had used the broken rock to create a long breakwater to shield the harbor from the open sea.

Sweeping the heavy glasses back toward the main island it was evident the harbor had not been used in several years. The wood and concrete pier *Van Triumph* anchored next to was cracked and splintered. Part of it had fallen away and was covered by the sea water, barnacles and underwater plant life. Several weathered, run-down buildings were clustered at the base of a sloping hill a hundred yards away. The largest structure was nearly the size of *Van Triumph,* 200 feet long. It had a narrow slanted roof covered with age spots and gull droppings. There weren't any windows.

Sinchon guessed the building had been used to process the fish after the catch had been pulled in from the nets. The other smaller buildings he assumed would have been used for crew quarters and storing equipment. The windows and the doors of the other structures were no longer intact, either broken or gone completely.

To the left of the structures a rusted truck lay wretched under a large metal crane. Its tires had been removed and it sat covered halfway in the ground. He couldn't make out the model or type, but it resembled a Russian design. There were several rolls of what looked like rusted wire and one large pile of partially burned debris.

To the right he could make out the island's rough unpaved runway stretching to the southwest. It was still in relatively good shape, considering it was made by hand, though there were several water-cut ruts angling across it in different directions. The remains of a sun-bleached wind sock were flapping in the breeze. *The Americans will be landing there,* he thought. In a few hours this would all be over. He would either have won their trust . . . or return to North Korea to die a resentful, meaningless death.

"The Americans will be coming soon," Bandar said, joining Sinchon at the rail. "I have instructed the crew to keep the ship's lights off except for our navigational lights. I want to keep those on."

"I do not want any light. No lights should be seen from the air," Sinchon said.

"Very well. I guess you have informed your friends of our whereabouts?" Bandar didn't want to anger the general but was finding it increasingly difficult to deal with his brusque manner.

"The Americans will be landing there," Sinchon stated, pointing to the edge of the runway. "They will know we are here. If your ship is dark it will not be such an easy target . . . should anything go wrong."

"I assure you, general, we are alone in this forsaken place. And the Americans will not want to spoil their reputation as the peacemakers. I am certain we will be safe." Bandar stared directly at Sinchon. He turned in silence and walked back to the bridge.

Sinchon allowed himself to slump slightly against the rail. The binoculars dangled from his thick neck as suddenly he gasped for air. He imagined he could feel the cancer growing, gnawing at his insides. It was like a worm getting larger each day while it slowly, painfully ate him from the inside out. His own inevitable death was before him in his mind; it would be long and painful.

*Don't waste time thinking of events that can't be changed,* he said to himself. The general slowly lifted himself from the railing. He needed to get to his quarters and take more painkillers. Perhaps he would have a drink of Bandar's scotch as well.

## NGHIA BINH PROVINCE, VIETNAM

*Son of a bitch,* Michael Callahan thought as his face was pressed against the hard clear plexiglass nose cone of the cargo pod. The nimble little Harrier jet banked back to the southwest as the pilot dropped the nose and came wings level a hundred feet above the water.

The Green Beret pushed himself away from the pointy window, breathing in deeply to relax. Gripping the handrails he concentrated on the dark rolling sea below. The small of his back was stiff and sore, and if the pilot made anymore Top Gun moves he was going to puke. He had only trained with the Harrier pod one time before and now everything about that experience was coming back to him. Being cramped up in a noisy space with little room to move and having to breath stale air was one fast recipe for airsickness. And when Michael got airsick it wasn't a light headache and a little indigestion. It was a splitting head and projectile vomiting.

Callahan watched the white sands of the Vietnamese coastline flash beneath them. The pilot added power and dropped the nose. He rotated his head right then left, seeing that they were flying through a sparsely populated area to cross into Vietnam. There were, however, several fishing boats to the south and he could see flickering fires coming from small villages to the north.

*"Feet dry,"* the pilot radioed. *"ETA to the LZ . . . forty-three minutes."*

"Good thing. I can't take much more of this fun," Pope complained from behind Callahan. "At least you have a window. All I can see is—"

"Don't push it, Pope. You're not in the best place to be pissing me off." Callahan rolled over on his side for a change of positions. The landscape turned to heavily wooded forest with an occasional road cutting through the jungle. He estimated they were cruising over the trees at less than fifty feet now. The Marine pilot guided his jet between the rolling hills toward the interior's mountainous terrain.

"By this time tomorrow I'll let you buy me a beer back at Osan," Callahan quipped.

"Bullshit," Pope shot back. "After this ride it's going to be tequila, and the boss is buying. That means you, José."

"Tell you what, Pope, I'll buy as many as you think you can . . ."

Callahan stopped midsentence, feeling the jet pitch up then come level to clear a hill.

*"I'm picking up a search radar to the northwest. Hold on—we're heading for the deck,"* the pilot's voice cracked over Callahan's headset.

"Shit, I love this job," Callahan mumbled, swallowing to push down the bitter liquid moving up his throat.

Outside it was completely dark but the flickering red cabin lights of the Pave Hawk cast off just enough illumination to see the mission clock. They were running behind schedule because of the bad weather at Osan. They should have been over the island ten minutes ago. James picked up the headphones next to his seat and slipped them on. "What's our status?" he radioed the chopper's pilot.

*"ETA five minutes, sir. We just picked up the coastline on the FLIR."*

"Roger . . . keep me posted." Duke reached into his duffle bag and pulled out a pair of night-vision goggles.

"What are the pilots saying?" General Kimp asked.

"The forward-looking infrared sensors just picked up the coastline. We'll be landing in about five," James shouted back, placing the awkward device over his head. Twisting around, he stared out the side window of the Pave Hawk trying to orient himself to the area.

In the distance he could make out the southern tip of the island as the chopper continued its northwesterly heading 200 feet above the ocean. The greenish glow of the shoreline came into view as the pilot maneuvered the chopper in an effort to stay parallel with it.

*"Secure the cabin. Two minutes to touchdown,"* the pilot's voice boomed over the intercom.

Duke slipped off his NVGs, placing them back in his duffle bag before zipping up his parka. He stuffed his belongings under the seat and returned his attention to the window. The fishing bay was coming into sight. He could see the breakwater and the slender outline of what had to be the *Van Triumph* moored in the harbor next to a cluster of buildings. She was completely dark.

Several hundred yards away he picked out the broken profile of a runway. The Pave Hawk banked to the west. The pilot was going to circle the area once before landing.

KIM IL SONG AIR BASE, NORTH KOREA

"She's fueled, armed and ready sir," the chief maintenance sergeant reported after snapping a sharp salute.

Lt. Col. Krung Woong completed his walkaround. He stood in front of the younger sergeant, pausing a brief moment. Then he signaled his approval by gesturing for the ladder to be pulled into position.

Wearing a black insulated flight suit, the colonel climbed the paint-chipped aluminum ladder. Stepping into the gray and black front cockpit of his tandem-seat Su-30 fighter, his compact, well-muscled body fit comfortably into the ejection seat. Woong ran his fingers through his short black hair before placing the heavy fiberglass helmet on his head. He began the process of securing himself into the ejection seat with the numerous nylon straps.

"No . . . I'll stow that myself," Woong told the sergeant who had been helping to strap him into the fighter. The colonel grabbed his nylon flight bag, placing it next to his left leg under the ejection seat.

The sergeant didn't speak as he climbed down the ladder and pulled it away.

Woong swiveled around, watching his weapons officer, Capt. Park Seo-won, climb into the rear cockpit and begin to strap himself in place.

The man was ten years younger than Woong, very thin with a balding head. He sometimes seemed to be on the edge of hyperactivity and ran six miles a day to burn off added energy. Seo-won had recently reached the rank of captain. Out of the eight weapons officers qualified to fly in the Su-30, Woong considered Seo-won the best trained. He had completed two years of training at the Russian test center in Krasnodar and finished first in his class each year. Most of all, Woong liked flying with Seo-won because he kept his mouth shut, followed orders and did his job.

"Bring up the weapons systems. I want a complete check before we take off," Woong ordered.

"Yes, sir," Seo-won replied, continuing his preflight checks.

"Do you hear that?" Ghaith Bandar asked, turning his head back and forth. In the darkness overhead the muted sound of a helicopter cutting through the night air became louder.

"Yes," Han Sinchon said, standing outside *Van Triumph*'s bridge. "It is the Americans."

"I will order my men to the landing strip. They will bring the Americans to us." Bandar moved to the door.

"No," Sinchon ordered. He moved closer to the rail, trying to get a fix on the sound. The temperature had fallen since the sunset and he watched his frosty breath float off into the distance as he scanned the night sky.

"What do you mean?" Bandar asked, puzzled.

Sinchon didn't answer. The dark water appeared calm, the sky deep black. Sinchon could barely make out the silhouettes of the buildings only a few hundred yards away. *I should be feeling pleased,* he told himself. Everything had fallen into place, just as he had planned. The Americans were here and he was still alive to carry out the mission. North Korean security forces had not tried to intervene, reassuring the general his plans were still secret. Yet there was a nagging at his instincts, a strong sensation of apprehension, perhaps self-doubt. He was not so worried about the Americans. He was concerned more about his own country and, of course, the South Koreans. He turned slowly and caught Bandar's eye.

"The plan was for the meeting to take place aboard *Van Triumph,*" Bandar said, interrupting the general's thoughts.

"I paid you only for transportation, Bandar. You need no explanation for my change of plans," Sinchon answered, not wanting to reveal that it was only a feeling that caused him to react.

"I will send several of my men with you . . . for protection."

"No, again. I will go alone . . . unescorted." Sinchon looked back at the arms trader, his stare hard and steadfast. "Bring me a gas heater and lantern. That is all I need."

*You are a foolish old man,* Bandar thought. He was becoming concerned for the vested interest he had in the general. "It would be safer for you on my ship," he repeated.

Sinchon ignored him as he walked to the gangplank. A gentle breeze had come up out of the north and he could now see a few stars breaking through the clouds. The general could no longer feel the pain in his stomach, his medication and several shots of scotch keeping it at bay.

"The lookout is reporting that a chopper has touched down on the edge of the runway." Bandar handed Sinchon a rusty metal lantern and a small kerosene heater. "If you are not back by daybreak or there is gunfire I will leave without you."

"I would expect nothing more from you, Bandar," Sinchon answered calmly, unshaken by the man's threat. Taking the lantern and heater, he headed slowly down the steep gangplank. "I will return by first light."

# 20

Lt. Col. Krung Woong watched the heavy steel reenforced-concrete bunker doors slowly begin to open, exposing the interior of the hangar to the night air. The runway lights cast a blue glow onto his aircraft, highlighting its long sloping nose, two-tone blue and gray camouflage, large dual air intakes and twin vertical tails.

Woong had only been stationed at Kim Il Song for the last eight months after being transferred from North Korea's elite MiG-29M squadron based at Sinanju. He had commanded that squadron for three years, but he asked to be transferred the day after learning his government was to purchase the advanced Su-27 and Su-30 aircraft from China and Russia. The transfer request was approved by the minister of defense and Colonel Kaine surprisingly quickly.

Soon after three check rides with a Chinese test pilot and six months of flying, the colonel had been chosen to be the base's wing commander officer, and was the North's first pilot to be assigned to fly one of the sleek Russian-designed jets. He was a short, solidly muscled father of one who had learned many years ago that a pilot was only as prepared as his training allowed. He made sure the pilots under his command received the best training his country could offer and continually pushed them to the limit. They flew a minimum of three times a week and were rigorously trained in both air-to-air and air-to-ground tactics. Eight of the sleek Su-30 aircraft, roughly the size and weight of an American F-15C, had been delivered to Kim Il Song air base ten months before. The pilots were only allowed to train at night, away from the meddlesome eyes of American intel satellites.

Outside of Russia and Iran, North Korea was the only other country to operate the Su-30 interceptor. Woong had read a number of intelligence reports explaining why the West considered the tandem-seat fighter one of the most potent adversaries in the sky—although, he reminded himself, he had read the same reports about the MiG-29M and then had watched as American pilots plucked them from the sky over Iraq like lost, blind birds.

Woong studied the instrument panel for a moment or two, double-checking everything. The cockpit was similar to a MiG-29M if a little roomier, with a larger canopy giving him more room to move and watch the sky. Unlike the single-seat MiG-29M, the Su-30 had more powerful engines and could carry up to ten air-to-air missiles, or a mix with air-to-ground. To-night, however, cradled between the twin engine nacelles was a single Kh-35RE antiship missile along with two rocket pods and two R-27AE long-range air-to-air missiles under each wing.

The colonel lowered and locked the canopy before being towed from the hangar. He started the left then the right engine, watching as the gauges and dials came to life. He waited for the avionics to warm up, including the bright green symbology on the HUD (Heads Up Display) before plugging in his radio and snapping the oxygen mask into place.

"Weapons check," Woong called out.

"Weapons ready," Seo-won answered.

"Radar and ECM."

"Systems up and ready. Fuel at eighty percent."

"Tower . . . this is Flight Leader two seven three. Ready to taxi," Woong radioed.

*"Copy Leader Two Seven Three. Proceed to runway three niner and hold."*

"Copy tower . . . Two Seven Three."

Colonel Woong advanced the throttles a half-inch, releasing the brakes. Activating the nose wheel he guided the Su-30 to the edge of the runway. He waited for the second Su-30, his wingman, to line up behind his fighter.

*"Two Seven Three . . . tower."*

"Copy Tower."

*"Cleared for take off. Maintain runway heading to flight level three zero zero."*

"Tower . . . Lead Two Seven Three, understood and rolling."

The throttles in his grip, Woong pushed them forward just short of the afterburner groove. The Su-30's engines roared to life. In a blur the runway lights flashed past the cockpit windows. Watching his groundspeed on the HUD Woong waited for it to hit 145 knots before gently pulling back on the center stick. The heavy fighter eased into the air. Looking over his shoulder, Colonel Woong watched his wingman come even with his jet as he cleaned up the gear and banked to the northwest.

THE PENTAGON

Chairman of the Joint Chiefs General Howard Chaniff walked into the Spe-cial Technical Operations Center, commonly referred to as STOC. At 0846 in the morning the fresh cup of black coffee he was sipping tasted better than normal. Chaniff let his tall frame rest against the nearby wall as he watched the darkened operations center.

Located in an out-of-the-way classified section of the Pentagon in room 2C865, the STOC had become the US military's nerve center for black operations in the post-Cold War military world. Approximately the size of a grade-school gymnasium and shaped in the form of a moderately sloped amphitheater, it held eight large $48 \times 72$-inch computer-generated color screens arranged in a half-circle on the far wall.

Each screen displayed separate sections of the world and was linked into the military's SATCOM communications network, NORAD, early warning satellites and Global Positioning System. Three Digital VAX 6610-1A computers, capable of 890,000,000 instructions per second, processed command/control information, radar data, weather conditions and weapons assignments, and linked encrypted SATCOM communications to a variety of black-world tasks which were in progress. If one computer failed the other two automatically reconfigured to handle the entire load.

Below the main screens were ten Sony twenty-by-twenty-inch color touch-sensitive multipurpose consoles (MPCs). These high-resolution monitors, comprising $3,486 \times 3,486$ pixel resolution, could be used as mini command screens and included communications, tabular data and text and moving map displays. An air force technician sat behind each screen operating a computer keyboard in order to constantly update the info on each display.

The back of the room contained an array of specially built technical equipment allowing Chaniff, top Pentagon brass and civilian leaders to keep track of every covert military operation on a twenty-four hour a day basis. Chaniff could communicate in real time, using satellite and ground-based transmissions, with Green Berets, Air Force Special Operations, Ranger Black Commando teams or Navy SEAL units anywhere in the world.

In addition a new *Force Strike* SATCOM data system had recently become operational, giving STOC the ability to transmit intelligence directly off satellites to combat aircraft. This system allowed B-2As, B-1Bs, F-117As and F-15Es to process down-link data, enabling the crews to see real-time radar and optical images of a target area as well as threat locations and current weather. Not only did this allow the Pentagon to watch over and protect the teams in the field, it also made it possible for each team to be extracted from a hot zone if its mission became compromised. The STOC also had the capacity to update the White House on enemy troop and aircraft activity as well as foreign submarine and ship movements.

Chaniff took another gulp of hot coffee, stepping further into the center of the room. The large displays cast off a blue hue and the flashing green, blue and red symbols on the computer display screens reminded him of the Edwards Air Force Base's state-of-the-art air traffic control center. He knew the data shown was in fact transmission codes from teams already in the field and intercepted radio transmissions decoded by the CIA and NSA.

The general liked the way the operations center was set up. In a world of ever-changing political loyalties the STOC permitted him to update civilian leaders with real-time intelligence from the military's best-trained and educated soldiers. When a situation became hot the information provided by special operations forces wasn't slanted like the standard CIA intel briefing and was generally a lot quicker than CNN.

"Lieutenant, what's the word from *Observation Island?*" Chaniff asked, walking up next to the communications officer. He could see the yellow outline of Langau Island on the man's display screen. The American intel ship was approximately 100 miles to the southeast.

"General James' chopper dropped off radar about ten minutes ago. No word, sir . . . so we're assuming all is well."

Chaniff rubbed the stubble on his face, calculating the difference in time zones. It would be dark on Langau. If all went well James would be taking off again by first light, or 6:00 P.M. Washington time.

"What about Tango Team, are they on the ground yet?" Chaniff asked, referring to the Vietnamese operation.

"No, sir, the lieutenant answered, tapping on his computer keyboard.

"ETA?" Chaniff leaned closer to the screen. He didn't like the idea of sending a recon team into Vietnam. If something went wrong, which was a real possibility, the press would jump all over it.

"ETA for Tango touchdown twelve minutes. The pilot is reporting smooth sailing. Only scattered radar contact."

"I'll be in the detail office," Chaniff said, finishing his coffee.

"Yes, sir."


## LANGAU ISLAND

"There . . . to the right," Major Erwin said in a whisper. "It's a light coming up from the buildings."

"Can you see how many people?" Duke asked at the chopper's window.

"I see only one . . ."

"This is not right," General Kimp broke in. "We are to meet on board the yacht. There was no word of someone greeting us at the chopper. I recommend we take off at once. Our lives are at risk."

"That's our contact," Duke said. "Maybe he feels safer out in the open."

"Do you hear me?" Kimp grabbed James' arm. "The North Koreans would like nothing more than to kill a top officer of the South."

"I hear you and take your hand off me," Duke replied, still not looking at the general. "If they wanted to kill us we'd be dead already."

"You trust too much, American," General Kimp chided. "I will not vary from the original plan, he could be one of their special forces. If we do not meet on the boat then we will not meet at all."

"Yeah, right," James mocked. "A North Korean special forces officer . . . walking this way . . . holding a lantern. I don't think so. Listen to me, General. We have a mission and I intend to complete it. If you want to stay here, that's fine."

Duke stood and moved to the Pave Hawk's flight deck, hoping the general would either shut up or lighten up. He didn't care which one. "What do you guys pick up on the FLIR?" he asked the pilot.

"Nothing unusual, sir. Just like you said in preflight, there's a ship moored in the harbor. Its profile is a yacht. We ran its heat signature through the computer and it matches that of the *Van Triumph*. There were three men standing on the deck, although we couldn't tell if they were armed." The pilot paused a moment. "There are no other vessels in a ten-mile area and we're not picking up any radio transmissions. There doesn't appear to be a welcoming committee, if you get my drift."

"Good. Can you tell me how long the ship's been anchored?"

"Not for sure. There is still a lot of heat radiating off her engine compartment, but I'd say she's running her engines to generate electricity. The RHAW is picking up her surface radar . . ." The pilot pointed to the radar homing and warning display on the instrument panel.

"Well, then," James said, letting out a long breath, "looks like we've spotted our contact. If we're not back by zero six hundred hours your orders are to return to *Observation Island* without us. Do you understand that?"

"Yes, sir."

James nodded. "See you in a few hours, Captain."

Duke grabbed his duffle bag and climbed out of the chopper into the cold night air. Scanning the sky he could see the thin clouds allowing a slight amount of gray moonlight to hit the island sporadically. Out in the open it was easier to make out many details, including the ship moored in the back section of the bay. He turned back to the interior of the chopper.

"Looks clear," Duke waved to Major Erwin, motioning her out. Erwin climbed out fearlessly, followed by a reluctant General Kimp. They stood next to the chopper, watching the single figure make its way toward them.

"I have ten bucks that says we're looking at General Han Sinchon," Erwin whispered.

Duke didn't reply. He just stared at what appeared to be a stout man dressed in a heavy military overcoat. He thought that whoever it was must be somewhat apprehensive, but the man walked bravely, advancing without hesitation.

"This is too big to trust to anyone else," Duke finally said to Erwin, watching her tighten the hood of her parka. "Sinchon would be reckless to trust too many other people at this point. What do you think, General?"

Duke turned to see Kimp pulling a Beretta 92 9mm from under his uniform jacket. "Until I meet this man and look him in the eye it doesn't matter what I think." Working the slide, he cocked the pistol, stepping away from the chopper. "I will find out soon enough who this man is and what his true intentions are . . ."

"Bullshit," Duke breathed, stepping forward as the general strode past him. He reached out and grasped the man's arm with the gun. Pulling him back toward the chopper, James knocked the gun from his hand as his feet stumbled along the ground.

Kimp spun around, ready to challenge the American but Duke picked up the gun and spoke first: "We need to get something straight, General. This is an American mission and I'm in charge. You have a simple choice. You can either follow my orders or keep your ass in this chopper. And the gun stays here."

"Don't be an idiot, General James. We are dealing with the North Koreans."

"Do as I say or stay here." James nodded that he had everything in control to the two pilots looking on.

"Your State Department will hear about this," Kimp threatened. "You will pay for being an arrogant American."

Duke looked at Erwin who was waiting patiently. "Let's go. Kimp, you follow the major if you're coming."

NGHIA BINH PROVINCE, VIETNAM

"Tango Team . . . secure your NVGs," Callahan said over the secure radio link connected to his entire team.

*"NVGs secure,"* came a response from the other pod.

"Darth Vader ready for action," Pope replied from behind him.

Michael adjusted the head and chin straps making sure his night-vision goggles were in place. The last thing he wanted was to lose them during the drop. Flipping the "on" switch he activated the two AA batteries, transforming the black night into glowing green daylight.

If the Harrier pilot followed standard procedure he would hover about five feet above the ground for fifteen seconds. That was all the time Callahan and his men would have to clear the aircraft. He felt the AV-8B decelerate. The ghostly green image of the jungle floor came into view. The pilot had found the LZ, or was checking an area that resembled the LZ. Callahan listened closely, preparing for the drop.

*"Thirty feet . . . twenty . . . ten . . . five feet,"* the pilot called off.

"Go . . . go . . . go!" Callahan yelled into his headset as the Harrier jet seesawed above the dark jungle.

He twisted around as Sgt. Steve Pope opened the pod's upper hatch. The sergeant tossed his backpack onto the ground and grasped his M16A2 before jumping from the pod under the aircraft's wing. Michael followed, hitting the ground a couple of feet away from his communications specialist. The ground was soft and wet with a thick layer of plants to cushion his fall. Thick, moist smells of the jungle instantly swept over him.

Callahan picked up his backpack and adjusted his grip on the CAR-15 assault rifle. He looked up as the other two members of his team dropped out from beneath the opposite wing.

Michael motioned for his men to move out of the immediate area. Grabbing their equipment the three men, heads ducked low as the Harrier's hot exhaust blasted around them, scrambled into a nearby clump of bushes.

Shielding his NVGs Callahan gave the AV-8B two hard thumps signaling the pilot that everyone on the ground was safe. He backed out of the way watching the jet wobble up into the air. The Harrier, lingering, spun around to the east gaining altitude, then the engine blared back to life with a shrill cry. The jet appeared to move in slow motion before disappearing into the darkness, the roar of its engine fading.

Callahan joined his team. He looked around to see the members hunkered down in a tight circle, weapons at the ready.

"Barnes . . . clear."

"Ingram . . . clear."

"Pope . . . clear."

As the team's leader, Callahan scanned the jungle in front of him. There wasn't any movement, flicker of light, or anything that didn't seem natural. "Callahan . . . clear. Area secure," he said, hoisting his backpack onto his shoulders. "Welcome to Vietnam, gentlemen. Let's clear the LZ before checking in with Cheerleader."

"Just follow the yellow brick road," Pope said, looking at the tall trees and thick brush surrounding the landing zone.

Callahan led them in the thick underbrush toward a line of protective dark trees. He could just barely make out the sound of running water.

Lt. Col. Krung Woong leveled his Su-30 fighter at 5,000 feet, keeping it a few knots shy of Mach 1, heading due west. The moon had faded to a low glow, yet he could see its light reflecting off the small ponds and buildings spread out across the frozen countryside below him. The broken outline of the Korean coast was fast approaching.

Woong wasn't a stranger to this type of mission. He had encountered American F-16s and Japanese F-15Js during night-training missions over the Sea of Japan on several occasions while flying single-seater Su-27s. One night he had locked up his long-range radar on an American C-5B making its way from Japan to Seoul. The huge aircraft, largest in the American fleet, was easy to identify on radar and made the perfect target. That confrontation had triggered an American response of four F-16s chasing his Su-27 to the edge of North Korean airspace. The encounter was the first lesson that taught Woong the Americans weren't afraid of a fight. He grew a deep respect for the West and its military power. Believing any pilot that thought differently was a fool, he would wash them out of his ranks.

Woong had become a student of the West's high-tech approach to defeating enemies with lightning-fast force using advanced weaponry to gain the upper hand in the first few minutes of a battle. He reasoned that if he could understand their tactics he could counter and also defeat them.

At thirty-nine years of age he had already amassed over 7,000 hours in the cockpit of high-performance jet fighters. His father, Lee Kim Woong, had flown MiG-15s against the American F-86s during the Korean war. Woong, not born until after the war, relished the pictures of his father standing next to his MiG with three blue stars painted on the side standing for each of his F-86 kills. It was known in the military that Woong's father had ruled the skies whenever he took to the air.

*Nothing had changed,* Woong pondered. *The Americans and the South were still the enemies.* He was determined to carry on his family's honor by serving in the military. Someday, Woong knew, his young son would also take to the sky.

The colonel scanned the cockpit instruments looking for yellow caution or red warning lights. There weren't any. He twisted his head right and saw the other Su-30 tucked neatly in formation behind his jet.

Woong throttled back, watching the HUD click off his airspeed, altitude and heading. Two miles out in front and 1,000 feet above him the blinking navigational light of a transport lumbering to the south caught his attention.

Woong keyed his mike. "This is Lead. Drop to 500 feet, increase airspeed."

*"Copy, Lead."*

The North Korean coast flashed under his jet as he pushed the nose down, heading for the ocean.

*  *  *

General Sinchon stopped at the base of the long sloping hill. The terrain was much tougher than he had judged and his breath had become shortened. He did not wish to be winded when he met up with the contacts.

The island was nothing more than a giant rock with loose gravel and boulders of all sizes dotting the landscape. The general suddenly had a flash memory of what it was like going through his basic infantry training fifty years ago.

Sweeping the lantern across the ground in front of him, Sinchon struggled to see the outline of a chopper. He couldn't see anything other than darkness and more rocks. He knew his vision and depth perception were particularly bad at night but someone had to be out there. Sinchon raised the lantern, swinging it back and forth three quick times.

"This way," James called out behind him, holding a firefly—a luminescent emerald-green chemical glow stick—in front of him. The stick cast just enough light for him to see the ground around him.

"What do you make of it?" Erwin asked, seeing the light swinging below.

"Looks like he's come as far as he's going to. The rest is up to us." James waved the firefly in the air in response and quickened his pace. He gauged the light was about a hundred yards away down the slope.

"You still with me, Erwin?" James asked, worried he was maybe moving along too fast.

"General, if we had time I'd race you down this hill and back up just for asking me a question like that," Erwin said lightly, coming even with James. Kimp was lagging behind.

"Major, when this is over we might just have that race. And the loser gets to sit next to General Kimp on the way home."

For the last twelve minutes Colonel Woong had maintained a two nine eight degree flight pattern, heading northwest, flying 500 feet above the choppy ocean. He scanned the Su-30's instruments. The fighter-bomber was operating perfectly, although its high wing-load design made the low-level ride less than comfortable. The aircraft bounced and jostled about in the air.

"Colonel, we just lost the missile on the starboard wingtip," Capt. Park Seo-won reported from the rear cockpit. "The turbulence must have broken the electrical connection."

"Shut it down," Woong ordered, thinking he would severely discipline the weapons sergeant after they returned to base.

Woong ran the mission details through his mind for the tenth time. Intelligence reported the American spy ship *Observation Island* was 110 miles southeast of his position and the only military vessel in the area. North Korean intel had learned many years ago that *Observation Island*'s radar tracking system had been designed to plot the footprints of high-flying nuclear reentry vehicles during Soviet ICBM tests. After years of monitoring the spy ship's operations, North Korean and Chinese intel officers also learned this same high-altitude radar system became distorted when attempting to track targets below 1,000 feet. As long as Woong stayed below 1,000 feet and ninety miles away he could sneak in under the ship's long radar coverage.

Twenty-five miles from the island, the North Korean Intelligence trawler would send out a radar pulse. Woong's fighter's radar warning equipment should pick up the friendly surface radar and he could then correct his course to fly straight toward Langau Island. At ten miles out he and his wingman would pop up to 3,000 feet, sweep the island with power radar, lock onto the *Van Triumph* and destroy it. *It will be easier than a training mission,* he thought. The only trick was to make one pass while staying above 1,000 feet for a minimal amount of time. Otherwise there was a high risk the *Observation Island* would spot them first.

If the mission planners were correct, Langau Island was now twenty-seven miles directly ahead of him and he should be in range to pick up the surface radar of the North Korean trawler.

With a flick of his thumb Woong turned his radar warning receiver (RWR) from standby to active, trying to acquire the weaker radar sweeping the surface. In a few seconds a faint high-pitch pulsing tone in his helmet told him the trawler was below in the darkness.

"Contact, sir, bearing two niner four," Seo-won confirmed from the back seat.

"I see it." Woong's eyes glanced at the flashing round RWR display before returning to the HUD. He let the fighter drift upward, his eyes studying the instruments. The directional indicator inside the RWR now showed the surface radar four degrees off his nose, range fifteen miles. The colonel unconsciously allowed himself to smile under his oxygen mask.

Woong continued to watch the HUD as he broke through 800 feet, climbing at four degrees nose high. He flipped off his navigational lights, signaling to his wingman the mission was a go. He eased back on the stick, feeling the jet pitch upward.

Breaking through 3,000 feet Woong leveled the jet while activating the Su-30's powerful J-band pulse-Doppler radar.

"Radar active . . . find the target."

*  *  *

Duke James paused fifteen feet from the older man dressed in heavy dark clothes. The greenish glow radiating off Duke's firefly gave the man a spooky appearance but his uniform was definitely North Korean.

"General Sinchon?" James asked.

"I am Gen. Han Sinchon," came the reply in thickly accented English.

Duke walked closer, peering at the man's round face. Deep wrinkles spread out around his eyes. James figured him to be in his mid to late sixties.

"I am Gen. Richard James, US Air Force, currently serving as deputy national security advisor." He held out his hand and bowed slightly.

Sinchon returned the gesture, shook James's hand and remained silent.

"This is Gen. Don Kimp and Maj. Helen Erwin, a North Korean liaison, Army Intelligence. They are here to assist me." Each one nodded briefly at Sinchon. "You have something of great importance you would like to discuss."

Sinchon lifted his lantern higher to look them all over more closely. After a brief moment he spoke again.

"Yes, we have much to talk about. Follow me."

"No. We discuss it here," General Kimp protested immediately. "You have already varied from the original plans once."

Sinchon smiled. "I am honored that your country would send General Kimp. He is a powerful man and I know of his reputation as a strong leader. The night is dark, the wind cold and I am not so young. We will discuss this in one of the abandoned buildings, out of the night air." Sinchon didn't wait for any argument. He turned, lowered his lantern and started to walk down the trail back to the harbor.

"I'm going to follow him," James stated, looking at the South Korean general. "Major Erwin."

They left General Kimp standing alone on the windswept hill.

Colonel Woong watched the CRT on the right side of the cockpit as a solid white line scanned across the screen. It took just fifteen seconds for an unprocessed black and white image of the island to appear. Woong studied it and saw the broken image of a bay on the north end of the island. Somewhere inside the bay the *Van Triumph* floated unsuspectingly.

"Weapons check," Woong said, keeping his jet under 3,000 feet.

"Guidance system up and ready. Radar data is being downloaded." Seo-won punched a series of buttons on the top display above his back-seat radar display. The fighter's air-to-ground weapons computer began to download the stored data into the guidance system of the Kh-35RE antiship missile strapped under the fighter.

"Get me a radar lock," Woong ordered roughly.

"I'm working on it, sir."

The colonel watched two thin white lines sweep across the radar screen. His backseater was trying to find the radar signature of a 200-foot ship in the midst of all the ground clutter reflecting off the water and rocks of the island.

"More altitude . . . up to four thousand feet," Seo-won requested, not wanting to anger his pilot for not locating the target fast enough.

"No. We are already risking detection." Woong allowed the fighter to climb through 3,300 feet before leveling, then ordered again: "Find the target."

A break in the cloud cover allowed Duke to see the half-moon. He could barely make out the outline of the yacht. A yellowish glow reflected off the water around the exterior before more clouds rolled in, making it impossible to see the ship at all.

James, Erwin and Kimp, who chose to accompany them, followed Sinchon down the hill into the first building. The structure, made of weathered plywood with a rock foundation, was approximately ten by ten feet square. The only window had been broken but the lopsided door was at least still attached to the hinges. The North Korean general entered, set the lantern down and put a match to the small gas heater. The element cast off a warming orange glow and managed to produce a fair amount of heat.

"This will do," Sinchon said, kneeling down. Setting his lantern on the cracked floor he began rubbing his hands together.

"Enough of this!" Kimp bellowed suddenly. "You asked for us to come here. We are not here to watch you set up house."

Sinchon straightened his body then got up, taking his time. "My country . . . *our* country needs your help. You can either assist me or turn me away. But change will come. How that change comes is partly your choice."

Duke said quickly, "The president of the United States has agreed to listen to your requests. And if possible we will help you. We understand you have taken a great deal of risk to come here. What is your plan, general?"

Sinchon's eyes were studying James' face, then fleetingly glanced at Kimp and Erwin. James could see his narrowed expression open as if he had decided, at that very moment, to trust them. Sinchon reached inside the breast pocket of his heavy coat and removed several folded papers.

"Let me explain."

*  *  *

Woong estimated he was now less than two minutes away from Langau Island and the *Van Triumph*. The black water below his fighter blended into the night sky wiping out any distinguishing marks of the horizon.

His attention went from the HUD to the glass CRT on the right side of his instrument panel. He watched the two white lines moving across the screen before centering on the midsection of the harbor. An uneven electronic outline of a ship came into view. Woong could see the V-shaped bow and jagged edge of the top of the ship.

"I've found it. Bottom of the screen to the right," Seo-won called out.

Woong began to slew the round targeting cursor over the electronic profile of the ship. Depressing the castle button on top of the control stick, he instructed the fighter's targeting computer to lock onto the ship's radar return.

"Eight miles out," Seo-won informed.

"Lock up, lock up," Woong whispered into his oxygen mask. He tapped the button a second time.

Within five seconds the Su-30's targeting computer located the ship through the electronic clutter. The blinking square box on the HUD told Woong the target had been acquired. The box stopped flashing and turned a solid color, indicating that the target's range and electronic profile had been down-loaded into the Kh-35RE antiship missile's guidance computer. A wave of exhilaration came over the colonel.

Woong clicked his mike twice, signaling to his wingman he had acquired the target. A split second later he received the same response. His wingman had also locked onto the ship. Inching the nose up, Woong let the Su-30 drift to 3,400 feet above the waves.

"Seven miles out. Closing fast," Seo-won called updating the target's range.

Woong lowered his clear night visor and watched the HUD as his fighter slipped past Mach 1. His Su-30 shuddered slightly as it accelerated due west. He sucked in a deep breath.

"Six miles out. All systems on line."

"Fire one," Woong shouted into his radio. He pushed the red oval-shaped button on the control stick. His fighter barely vibrated as a glowing light appeared below it.

The Kh-35RE's rocket motor came to life, filling the sky with fire. The twelve-foot missile spit out in front of the Su-30 spewing bluish-white flames as it climbed away, gaining speed.

*"Fire two,"* his wingman radioed.

Woong looked away from the bright rocket motor cutting through the dark night. Out of the corner of his eye he saw his wingman's Kh-35RE rocket head in the same direction. Two good missiles were in the air.

They listened as Sinchon continued to explain why he was ready to risk his life in a coup attempt.

"It is critical that the United States send a clear message to the rest of the world once we have removed General Chief of Staff Myong Chin. It must be announced your country has no intention of attacking my country and that your president wants to work peacefully with the new leaders . . . to *re-unite* our country." Sinchon paused, looking briefly at General Kimp. "Only then will I have a chance of controlling the rest of the military and government. Once everything has stabilized I will turn the power over to a group of younger . . . more capable leaders. I know I am too old to be running a country."

James stared into the man's eyes. The light glow from the heater softened the old man's expression and he definitely sounded rational. In all truthfulness he seemed almost too rational for someone taking the risk he had already embarked on.

"And if my government refuses to help?" Kimp asked, his arms folded across his chest, his legs rigid.

"Then I go ahead with the coup . . . alone," Sinchon answered resolutely.

"We would like a moment, please, general," James asked politely.

"Of course." Sinchon nodded and went outside.

Jamming the stick left, Woong forced his Su-30 into a steep diving turn. He watched his altitude click off on the HUD, 2,000 . . . 1,500 . . . 1,000 feet. Pulling back on the throttle and the stick he reduced his airspeed to below Mach 1 and leveled the fighter. The abrupt bite of 4 Gs swept across his compact body. In the distance he followed the two glowing fire-trails of the missiles as they gained speed and altitude heading for their target.

"Missiles now three miles from target," Woong's backseater reported.

The colonel keyed his mike three quick times. Without breaking radio silence he watched his wingman's jet kick into afterburner, heading back to the mainland. Woong was now flying in the area alone with just his backseater. Their flight would continue over the island to make certain their target had been destroyed.

"No . . . no," Woong shouted instinctively.

Without warning the second missile began to pitch wildly up and down. Woong knew what had happened. He had seen it before while testing the Kh-35RE on targets in Korea Bay. The missile's guidance computer had lost its lock on the target. The computer was now trying to reacquire by forcing the missile into a snakelike search pattern.

"Reacquire," Woong demanded a heartbeat before the Kh-35RE pushed over like a falling star. It only took a few seconds before the 1,060 pound ship-killer hit the surface and exploded into a bright fireball. Woong pulled back on the stick to gain some altitude.

"Second missile is dead," the backseater called out.

"Update . . . missile number one," Woong ordered.

"Ten seconds to impact. Missile has internal lock."

The semiactive radar seeker-head on the first Kh-35RE missile scanned right and left before obtaining an electronic radar match to the target. Its internal guidance computer automatically compared the reflecting radar returns with that of the Su-30's larger J-band. Two miles from the target, the missile was now on its own. One mile from impact the missile slipped past Mach 1. The front-mounted angular canards steered the nose toward the center of the ship.

"Seven . . . six . . . five . . ." Seo-won called out.

"What was that?" James shouted, exiting the building to see the fading orange glow of an explosion a mile or so away. Duke stepped next to Sinchon who was standing motionless, staring in the direction of the explosion.

"Did you see that?" James asked.

The general did not respond.

Duke was looking at Sinchon as he turned to face him. The men's eyes met for a brief moment.

A bright flash of light appeared a split second before the roar and concussion of the explosion knocked James and Sinchon off balance. Duke's head snapped back as he hit the wall behind him with a loud thump. A giant fireball rose from the ship as the entire harbor lit up. Duke scrabbled to his feet to see large pieces of metal and fiberglass flying through the air before the churning inferno subsided, leaving the ship broken in two and on fire.

"Let's get the hell out of here," James shouted, grabbing General Sinchon by the arm.

# 21

Capt. Frederick H. Bliss III popped open a cold can of Coke. Standing in the Combat Information Center (CIC), he took a long drink before making his way back to the worn leather captain's seat elevated three feet above the other technicians. From this position the captain had an excellent view of the ship's electronic displays and instrumentations.

A Navy veteran with twenty-six years of experience under his belt commanding both naval combat ships and special warfare craft, Bliss didn't take his responsibilities as the ship's commander lightly. The crew referred to him as "the iron duck." He was a hardass who loved the water. Thick black frame glasses covered bright blue eyes, thinning gray hair topped a stern narrow face and a growing midsection poked out from his short stout frame.

Burned into Bliss's mind was the fact that *Observation Island* didn't carry any offensive weapons, which made it all the more critical he maintain a well-disciplined ship and not break any international laws. Their orders were uncomplicated and stringent: snoop around the western Pacific gathering information while staying in international waters. It sounded much simpler than it was.

In the last five months the North Koreans had taken an active role in watching them. They were generally shadowed by a naval intelligence ship disguised as a fishing trawler, and at least twice a week a reconnaissance aircraft of some type would fly directly over the *Island*. The actions were never threatening and the crew was under strict orders not do anything that might provoke any of the North Korean crafts, like locking on with a radar. Bliss was in a constant state of worry about overzealous fighter pilots or rogue sub commanders attacking his ship in a moment's notice just to bloody the United States' nose.

"Sir, the radar emissions I was picking up are gone," the electronics watch officer said, spinning around from her station.

"Did you get a fix on it?"

"No, sir. I've been picking it up intermittently but it's too weak to get a location. Somewhere to the northwest. Eighty . . . maybe a hundred miles out."

"Could you tell the type of radar?" Bliss asked, adjusting his glasses.

"No, sir," CPO Janis Owens said, turning back to her computer station.

"Well damn it . . . what type *wasn't* it, then?" Bliss asked impatiently.

"I've ruled out ground-control intercept and early warning . . . the standard stuff. Our computers show a Soviet-built Back Net operating on the North Korean coast."

"So what does that leave?"

"Airborne, sir, or it could be atmospheric skip."

"It could be a Chinese sub transmitting to mainland," another officer sitting close by warned.

"Keep an eye on it," Bliss ordered. "Maybe one of our commie friends is getting ready to drop his shorts."


LANGAU ISLAND


Duke James topped the hill and saw the Pave Hawk chopper still sitting on the ground a hundred yards away, its rotor blades churning and nav lights flashing. A sense of relief came over him. The pilots were ready to take off. They would be off the island in a matter of minutes.

James glanced back over his shoulder to see both generals charging up the hill. The older Sinchon was managing to keep up with Kimp. Major Erwin, proving her earlier challenge, was ahead of Duke.

"We're almost to the chopper. Come on, move your asses," Duke shouted to the men behind him.

"Go . . . go, without me." Sinchon waved for Duke to continue on. "I'm out of breath." Sinchon, his face flushed and his chest heaving, dropped to one knee.

"Leave him here." Kimp stared down at the general. "If we had been on that ship—"

"Shut up, Kimp!" Duke shouted, rushing to aid Sinchon. "Now's not the time." He looked up to see that Major Erwin had come back down.

*"Ne . . . ne,* leave me. This was my fault. I never should have trusted . . ." Sinchon started to cough, his body going limp.

*"Anio.* We're not going to leave you, General, so you better help us get you to that chopper," James said as he and Erwin placed an arm around Sinchon's waist, straining to lift him. Duke looked up at Kimp. "Are you going to help us or not?"

Kimp didn't bother to reply. He turned his back and ran for the waiting aircraft.

Sinchon had managed to get his feet under himself when Erwin cried out. "Oh, no!" she said, twisting her head around. "Do you hear that?"

"What?" Duke asked, hesitating just as the low rumble of turbofans filled the air.

"That's a military jet," Erwin declared, searching the skies.

"Yeah . . . and it's not one of ours." Duke grabbed the arm Sinchon had placed around his neck for support. "Come on, General, we've got company."

Colonel Woong turned his radar off. With a flip of his thumb he activated the Su-30's infrared search-and-track system. The IRST, a round basketball-sized glass sphere located on the right side of the nose, contained a laser rangefinder and passive IR tracking system. The liquid nitrogen-cooled ball was sensitive enough to pick up the heat signature of a man twenty miles away on a hot desert night. Woong could now get a clear picture of what was happening on the island without the use of radar. The American spy ship still wouldn't know he was in the area.

Colonel Woong watched his airspeed drop below 240 knots. He lowered the leading edges and flaps, giving his fighter more lift, then pushed the nose down two degrees. The HUD showed he was 300 feet above the ground. In the distance he could see the reddish orange fires still consuming the twisted hull of the *Van Triumph*.

"Whoever was on board is dead, sir," Captain Seo-won stated. "No one could have survived that."

"I've got one more target," Colonel Woong said, leveling the Su-30 at 200 feet. He banked to the west, planning to circle the island. The Americans had probably arrived using a small aircraft, most likely a chopper, he reasoned. There was no way they could have taken off without his noticing.

"To the left—I'm picking up the IR signature of a helicopter. Its blades are turning," Seo-won said.

Woong looked at the IR screen below, to the left of his HUD. The Su-30's IRST had locked onto a heat source 200 yards away from the burning ship. As Woong came wings level he could see the blurry green image of an American chopper sitting on the ground. Its greenish white rotor blades were spinning. The center of the scope glowed a bright white, telling the pilot the turbine had been running for a least a minute or so. They were trying to take off.

"Stupid Americans," Woong said under his breath. This would be as easy as fishing cabbage from Mongolian barbecue. He moved the side-switch on the throttle from the air-to-ground missile mode to rockets. Next he slewed the IR targeting cursor over the center of the target and tapped the lock button. A round circle appeared on the HUD indicating where to point the unguided eighty-millimeter rockets.

"Come on, we're almost there," James said as the burly general shuffled his feet along. The chopper was only fifty yards away, the whine of its engines pleading for them to hurry. General Kimp was just climbing inside the Pave Hawk. *I'm going to kick your ass,* Duke thought.

"I can't believe that jerk left us out here," Erwin said breathlessly under Sinchon's weight.

"We don't need him . . . come on, we can do it." James' voice was calm, encouraging Sinchon and Erwin to give it all they had.

"Leave me . . . I am . . . an old man . . . a foolish old man. Leave me," General Sinchon responded, unable to help anymore.

"Sorry, that's not going to happen," Duke said, grunting, taking most of the weight on his shoulder and urging the man's body closer to the waiting chopper.

Opening the air brake Woong slowed the Su-30 to under 200 knots. Keeping the huge fighter on the edge of a stall he dropped the nose and centered the HUD's aim-point on the chopper. The laser rangefinder illuminated the target and the words RANGE: 1,342 METERS appeared under the aim-point.

Woong knew the S-8KO rockets could travel up to 1,000 meters in a straight line. The chopper would be an easy kill.

One quick glance told him the Su-30's video camera was operating properly. He would proudly use the video for future training on how to make a low-level attack on a ground target.

RANGE: 981 METERS flashed under the aim-point.

Pressing the trigger on the stick two times, he fired forty rockets, twenty from each pod. They streamed toward the ground below in rapid succession. Resembling pearly white streaks of string, the rockets seemed to twist and curve as they gained velocity. Their deadly beauty painted the dark night sky.

Woong blinked, watching the first salvo hit in a blur just short of the chopper. In a matter of seconds the rest of the rockets had engulfed the helicopter. The area became consumed in fire and flying debris. Woong's IR screen was dazzling white, forcing him to look away. Cleaning up the flaps he banked to the southeast while jamming the throttles into afterburner heading back to base. The fighter responded, shoving him back into his seat. Looking over his shoulder Woong saw a burning circle of fire. Right in the middle was the coiled wreckage of the chopper.

A smile emerged across his tired face. The colonel had been wrong. Killing the chopper was much *easier* than fishing cabbage from Mongolian barbecue.

"Play it back again," Captain Bliss ordered, sitting on the edge of his seat.

*"This is Beagle we're under . . ."* A loud cracking sound ended the radio transmission.

The mood in the *Observation Island*'s CIC had changed from routine to tense. The random chatter had stopped and every person remained at his or her post.

CPO Janis Owens, a radar expert from St. Louis, Missouri, rubbed the back of her neck trying to relieve some of the tautness caused from sitting behind the radar and communications screens for the last eight hours. She felt her stomach growl, telling her it was time to eat, and the sting in her eyes suggested quitting time was near. Yet right now her personal needs didn't count.

Something was happening out beyond the horizon. She could sense it along with everyone else in the room and she wanted to be a part of the action.

Bliss stood alert in front of his captain's chair. Beagle was the code name he had assigned the chopper carrying Deputy National Security Advisor James and the other members of his team. He waited as patiently as he could for a confirmation while wild thoughts ran through his mind. He checked his watch. *Maybe James had finished his assignment early and they were headed back. Maybe that's what the transmission meant. But why would the pilot break radio silence for that? Shit, something's gone wrong . . .*

"I've confirmed it, sir. It was Beagle," Owens was finally able to report. "Shall I try contacting them?"

"No. But keep an open channel," Bliss answered gruffly, sitting back in his chair. The entire mission had a Q classification, under the strict control of the Pentagon. Bliss knew he would have to relay this information to them first and they would make the call.

"Copy the transmission and send it to Cheerleader."

He stared at the main $48 \times 48$-inch display showing the western coast of Korea outlined in bright yellow lines. A small blue rectangle showed the position of the *Observation Island,* 102 miles offshore. A pulsing red dot indicated the location of an operating North Korean radar station.

*Observation Island*'s CIC was nearly twice the size of a combat ship. In many ways it reminded Bliss of the television showroom of his local department store back in San Diego, California. Ten large display screens filling the walls in front of the captain, each with a different picture. The floor and ceiling were decorated with flickering red, green and yellow lights as the symbology changed.

The $30 \times 30$-foot room remained dark at all times and the only background noise was that of muffled communication radios and hushed whispers of the operators talking with each other. Each screen served a specific function. It was monitored by one or more technicians seated behind computer terminals. The two center display screens were the most critical, keep-

ing the captain and the crew aware of the ship's exact location at all times.
Linked directly to the ship's Global Positioning System (GPS), the display
on the left showed a computer-generated aerial view of 300 square miles.

"Update," Bliss grunted, trying to keep his cool.

"No change," the watch officer reported as he looked at the data appearing on the main screen. "I'm still tracking that North Korean trawler ten
miles to the south of us. It's maintaining our heading but speed has increased to twenty-five knots."

"If that's a fishing trawler then I'm Jimmy Hoffa," Bliss blurted out.

"Sir, I'm picking up coded radio transmissions coming from the
trawler."

"Record it," Bliss said, hoping this might be an answer to all the
questions.


KIM IL SONG AIR BASE, NORTH KOREA


Col. Met Lee Kaine watched the fuel truck back away from the darkened
hangar as a dozen men scurried around the T-tail Il-76 transport. Kaine
walked to the front of the hangar, inspecting the four engine swept-wing jet
transport.

They were running fifteen minutes ahead of schedule. He was pleased but
his face didn't show it. There would be no rewards until the entire mission
was complete.

Armed security forces encircled the area, warning any nonessential personnel not to get near the plane. For the last three hours Kaine's men had
been methodically transferring the cooled plutonium nuclear fuel rods from
three specially designed trucks to the interior of the transport. If all went
well Kaine and the rods would be in the air in sixteen minutes.

"The fuel rods are secure," the chief flight engineer informed him as the
rear cargo door of the Il-76 Ilyushin began to close.

"Are you detecting any radiation?"

"None. And I've scanned the area twice . . . personally."

"Good."

"Colonel Kaine. Flight leader two seven three has just reported in. Colonel Woong reports his mission was successful," one of Kaine's aides reported from behind him.

"Very well. Tell the pilot to warm up the engines and run through the
preflight checks twice. I don't want anything overlooked," Kaine ordered,
preparing for the second phase of their plan.

"Yes, sir."

Kaine walked out of the hangar and climbed into a waiting staff car. In twenty-four hours he would be a general commanding among the most ruthless killers on the earth, North Korean *spetsnaz* troops, making him the second most powerful man in North Korea.

"General James, are you alright?" Major Erwin asked, wiping the dirt out of her face and eyes. She was trembling on her knees next to Duke, her body covered with dust.

"What the hell happened?" Duke stared out but could only see fuzzy images.

"I'm not sure, but . . . I think the same bird that got the ship must have . . . gotten the chopper," Erwin stuttered slightly, then asked: "Are you hurt, General?"

"No . . . no I'm all right. I think," James said, using his fingertips to brush the rocks and dirt away from his eyes, mouth and ears. He looked over his arms and legs, not seeing any dark spots indicating he had been cut. It felt like someone had kicked him in the stomach and twice in the head. His ears were ringing and his legs felt sore and numb. There weren't any broken bones, so he guessed he'd be okay.

"I don't think I need to tell you we were the targets of that air assault." Duke shook his head to get his bearings. "Where's Sinchon?"

Not more than sixty feet away was the burning wreckage of the Pave Hawk. Through the flames Duke could see the charred body of the pilots still in their seats. The intense heat was overpowering and he backed away with Erwin at his side. The ground was littered with pieces of wreckage from the chopper. James looked behind him to see a dozen small fires still burning on what was left of the *Van Triumph*. Her bow was now under water and he could see the oil, leaking from her engine compartment, burning on the surface of the water.

"There he is," Erwin said casually. She was in a daze.

Duke turned to see the man's crumpled body on the ground. "I've got two dead pilots, a South Korean general that's well done, and one North Korean general in a heap. I don't need you to flake out on me now, Erwin," James said harshly, staring her straight in the eye. "I'm going to need your best army attitude until help arrives."

"I'm starting to think Kimp was right. This whole thing was some type of a setup. And Sinchon was in on it."

"Don't be trying to plot some perverted conspiracy . . . they tried to kill him, too." Duke wouldn't let the woman look away from him. He grabbed her by both arms, forcing her to face him. "Just think . . . everyone thought we were meeting on the yacht. No one but us knew the plan had changed. Why would Sinchon destroy his own way off the island?"

"Right," Erwin said at last.

Taking Erwin by the arm, Duke walked to the spot where Sinchon was lying on the ground. The dancing flames cast enough light for them to see a dark line of blood dribbling out of the corner of his mouth. His eyes were open and blinking. He appeared to be conscious.

"So much for our secret meeting," Duke said to the man lifting his head up.

"I . . . I thought I had everything planned well. I don't know how anyone could have known," Sinchon muttered as Erwin dabbed at the blood with a tissue.

"It's hard to keep something this big a secret, General," Duke soothed the beaten-looking soldier.

Sinchon nodded, his eyes not leaving Duke's. They spoke his appreciation for him.

"I think his right arm is broken and his pulse rate is pretty high. Let's get him to one of the buildings before he goes into shock," Erwin suggested.

"No," James said, helping the general to his feet. "Whoever did this wants us dead. They may be back to take out those buildings next. We need to find cover away from here."

"But where? This is nothing more than a rock pile. There's no place to hide."

James searched the area in the darkness. "There's got to be something. Maybe on the other end of the runway."

Erwin shook her head, feeling the desperation of the situation returning. "How are we going contact the *Observation Island?* How will they know we need help?"

"Let's worry about that after we find cover. Our first concern is to stay warm and out of sight. That will give us some time to think, too." James placed Sinchon's arm around his neck. "Once we're overdue they'll come looking. Our job is to stay alive until they get here."

Erwin relented. Pressing Sinchon's broken arm close to his body she tried to help support him by his waist. The North Korean general moaned slightly at the movement.

The fires were beginning to die down as James scanned the area in a 100-yard radius. On the sloping edge of the runway, to his left, he spotted a deeply cut ravine.

"This way," Duke said, heading out of the light into the dark toward what he hoped would prove to be sufficient shelter.

THE PENTAGON, SPECIAL TECHNICAL OPERATIONS CENTER

"General, I'm receiving a transmission from Tango," the communications officer, a young lieutenant, reported from his post.

"Put it on the speaker," Chaniff ordered.

*"Cheerleader . . . Tango. Do you copy?"*

"Roger that Tango, this is Cheerleader. Authenticate transmission."

Chaniff leaned over the black and gray computer console. A pulsing blue dot showed Tango Team's position in the center portion of Vietnam approximately twenty miles north of Da Nang.

*"Cheerleader . . . Tango. Authentication . . . November, Charlie, Romeo, Lima, Echo, November, Bravo."*

The lieutenant checked the code words on a computer list next to his monitor. He glanced at Chaniff before responding: "Confirmed, Tango . . . Go ahead."

*"Cheerleader . . . we're down and approximately three miles from LZ. Situation clean with no hostiles. Proceeding to primary and will advise one hour before extract."*

Chaniff listened to the confident voice crackle over the SATCOM radio. From the mission orders he knew he was listening to a special forces Green Beret. He closed his eyes, wondering what it was like for the young soldier in the darkness halfway around the world.

"Roger that, Tango. You're good to go."

*"Tango out."*

Chaniff straightened up. "Any word from General James?"

"No, sir. They're not scheduled to check in for another four and a half hours."

"All right, you know where to find me," Chaniff said then once again disappeared into the back of the special operations center.

"The first Kh-35RE malfunctioned a mile from the target. It impacted the water and exploded," Lieutenant Colonel Woong explained, standing next to the Japanese-made television in the briefing room. Still wearing his sweat-stained flight suit he talked his way through each series of black and white IR images captured on his Su-30's videotape camera.

The room was dark, with only him and Kaine present. The two men stood around the podium at the front of the room next to a large wall map of the region.

"And the second missile?" Colonel Kaine asked.

"The second missile performed perfectly. It impacted the midsection of the *Van Triumph* ripping it in two. No one could have survived." Woong pointed to the television screen. "As you can see the warhead penetrated the interior of the ship before exploding. The fuel onboard also caught fire. In a matter of seconds the entire vessel was consumed in flames. By now it has sunk to the bottom of the harbor."

Kaine nodded his approval. Knowing that Sinchon was finally dead caused his stomach to turn with gratification.

Woong pressed the fast-forward button advancing the video. It stopped on a blurry black and white image of the American chopper resting in a barren stretch of terrain.

Kaine moved closer. "Where was this taken?"

"About three hundred yards south of the ship, on the edge of the runway. It is the helicopter that transported the Americans." Woong tapped the play button. "It will make a fine training film on the art of precision ground attacks at night."

In a haze of white streaks the rockets weaved toward the ground. Seconds later the chopper exploded on the screen. Black and white specks of debris mixed with fire filled the screen.

"Stop. Back up the tape," Kaine ordered.

"Yes, sir."

"Stop it there. Right before the rocket's impact." Kaine's giant finger reached out to touch the monitor. "Do you see that . . . on the bottom of the screen?"

Woong walked up closer to stand shoulder to shoulder with the colonel. He squinted to see what his commanding officer was concerned about.

"Those are hot IR spots . . . three of them. What are they?"

It wasn't a question that needed to be answered. Woong knew what they were and so did Kaine. The spots were small and they were faint, but there wasn't any question as to their source. Three people could be seen moving toward the chopper just before it was hit. Woong knew what the next question was going to be.

"Are those people dead?" Kaine asked, turning to stare down at the shorter man.

Woong tapped the play button again and the screen suddenly filled with the white IR color of fire.

"Those people are dead," Woong said, not taking his eyes from the screen. "They were too close to the chopper. Those rockets have a kill radius of one-hundred meters. The concussion alone would—"

"How do you know for sure?" Kaine asked, looking concerned.

"Sir, you are looking at the proof," Woong pointed to the screen. "Look at the circle of impact. It was wide enough to kill everything around . . . the heat signatures disappear in its path."

The room fell quiet as Kaine studied the screen. Woong rewound and replayed the scene one more time. Kaine rubbed his chin, considering the possibilities. The pilot was correct. The fire from the multiple explosions did consume the IR images of the people. The chances of someone living through that attack were very slim. Nevertheless he decided he couldn't risk it. He would have to make certain.

"Operations places the Iranian freighter *Allum Bacar* here, fifteen miles northwest of Langau. She is headed toward the island," Kaine stated, strolling over to the large wall map and pointing to the location. "I will have six of my best security officers on this base accompany me to Langau with a highly classified cargo. I will not take any chances that you are mistaken." Kaine checked his watch.

"I understand, sir." Woong said, standing at attention.

"For your sake you'd better be correct, Captain Woong," Kaine said bluntly as he exited the briefing room.

"This will do for now," Duke said, crawling out of the steep ravine. Waiting for him on the edge of the runway were Major Erwin and General Sinchon. A cold biting wind was blowing out of the northeast kicking up dust and pebbles as it swept across the unpaved runway. They were far enough away from the fires that their heat could no longer be felt. Duke was sure the temperature had fallen several degrees. The low clouds hinted at snowfall.

"What'd you find?" Erwin asked, her teeth chattering. She clasped her hands together then put them up to warm her chapped pink cheeks.

"There's a concrete drainage pipe that runs the width of the runway. It's about four feet in diameter . . . big enough for you two to take shelter for a while." Duke took hold of Sinchon's arm. "It will get you out of the wind, General."

"I can walk," Sinchon growled, struggling to stand upright. "I can walk."

The three of them traversed down the steep ten-foot-deep ravine using half-buried rocks as makeshift steps where possible. The soil was sandy, making it unstable and difficult to maintain good footing. At the bottom Duke stood at the entrance of the drainage pipe.

"I want you to crawl in there, stay quiet and stay put until I return," James instructed.

"What are you going to do?" Erwin asked as she slid the last few feet to the base of the gully. She peered into the concrete drainage pipe, then looked questioningly at Duke.

"It's safe. I already crawled inside."

"Right. Okay," Erwin said, nodding.

"I am going back for the heater and anything else I can find." Duke pulled up the hood on his parka and tightened it around his face.

"I think you should stay here. We need to stick together," Erwin protested. "You were a pilot . . . aren't you guys told not to ever leave your wingman?"

"If I don't leave my wingman and get that heater she's going to end up like Frosty, the snowman," Duke replied, smiling. "Besides, you've still got General Sinchon here . . ."

"I will do my best to take care of her," Sinchon interrupted.

Erwin nodded ruefully, knowing that Duke meant she had to look after the general, not the other way around. She bent down to crawl into the pipe and Sinchon followed. James checked that they were well enough inside so as not to be seen from above.

"Now stay close together, it will help conserve body heat. I'll be back as soon as I can."

"Be careful, James," Erwin said, omitting the formalities of rank. He had already turned to head back up the ravine and gave a wave of his hand in acknowledgment.

The flight deck of the Il-76 medium-range transport resembled a standard Soviet design: simple almost to the point of being crude, and built to endure years of mistreatment. The instrument panel contained only the bare essentials for flight, navigation and communications. Years ago the interior had been painted a puke green and the seats were covered in a light gray vinyl. They were now worn and cracked, metal supports protruding through the back of each chair. The black paint on the Y-shaped control yokes was evident only at the bottom of the Y, the rest bare metal. Even the plexiglass windshields were scratched, the dirt imbedded in the grooves.

Col. Met Lee Kaine didn't particularly like flying in any type of transport aircraft. As he stepped farther into the cockpit he wondered how many hours the Il-76 actually had on it.

When his country purchased six of the four-engine Ilyushins three years ago, the aircraft reportedly had less than 5,000 hours on each airframe. Kaine doubted if that was true. The Russian government needed hard currency and they would have said anything to make the sale.

Like it or not, though, Kaine knew that North Korea's fleet of Il-76s were the most modern transports in service and if he was to complete his mission it would be in this jet. In addition this specific transport had been specially modified, with the help of Russian technicians, and incorporated an IR navigation screen allowing it to fly and land in total darkness or in poor weather.

Kaine strapped himself into the jump seat positioned a few feet behind and between the two pilots. From this location he had a clear view of the instrument panel and cockpit windows. The seat was normally used for instructor pilots but he would use it to command the mission. Besides, it gave him a sense of control. He also preferred being separated from the cargo hold with the fuel rods and security forces.

Watching the two pilots continue their preflight, Kaine slipped on a pair of headphones going over last-minute details in his mind.

The mission would be much like that of the first phase. They would fly below 1,000 feet over the water, then the Il-76 would land at Langau Island. The Iranian freighter *Allum Bacar* should be in the bay, ready to take possession of the fuel rods. It would take less than two hours to offload the cargo. Then Kaine and the rest of the crew would fly back to North Korea. He relished the thought that the arrogant Americans would never know what happened. The latest intelligence reports put *Observation Island* 112 miles southeast of Langau.

"Ready to taxi," the pilot radioed to the tower.

*"Copy . . . cleared for takeoff at your discretion."*

"Understood, tower. We're rolling."

Kaine watched the pilot nudge the four throttles forward. The engines spooled, the flight deck began to vibrate, and the 300,000-pound transport started toward the runway. The pilot killed the landing lights and darkened the cockpit and cargo bay. He lined the jet up and pushed the throttles to the stops. Forty seconds later the jet lifted off on a westerly heading.

Duke was starting to think that returning to the buildings next to the harbor was a bad idea. There was the possibility that a commando team had landed and he knew those guys got their jollies when they had a target to kill. *A warm body moving across the cold landscape would make the perfect bull's-eye for a sniper's bullet,* Duke thought.

Breaking into a slow run James kept his head low as he skirted the edge of the burned-out chopper, continuing south. The terrain was fairly flat. He had only to watch out for rocks jutting out of the ground. Most of the fires from the rocket attack had burned themselves out, leaving two large black chunks of charred metal that no longer resembled a chopper. Duke tried not to look at the remaining fires. The brighter light made it more difficult to see in the darkness.

James decided to skirt the back of the wreckage, keeping it between him and the harbor. If an enemy special forces squad was out there it would be harder for them to see him. As James came around the rear edge of the runway he nearly tripped over a jagged pile of debris. Lying in the dirt a hundred or so feet away from the chopper's hull, the clump was a tangled mass of wires and aluminum. It appeared to be about half the size of a computer desk. In the darkness James didn't know what it was at first. Then he saw a shattered piece of plexiglass. He realized on the ground at his feet was a section of the Pave Hawk's cockpit.

*It must have blown clear when the first rockets ripped into the front section of the chopper,* James deduced. A strip of metal about three feet long contained several of the instruments. Behind it were a maze of black boxes, broken circuitry and a tangled mess of wires. Another section contained two rows of dials and switches, but without any light Duke couldn't tell what they were.

Using his shoe Duke kicked away some of the wires covering the main section of the instrument panel. He could see several more black boxes, some dented and broken apart. However, one had what looked like a round speaker protruding out the front with what appeared to be a hand-held microphone connected with a coiled cord. Duke ripped away the loose wiring being careful not to cut himself on the sharp metal edges.

It took several minutes for James to work most of the wires, insulation and broken plastic away from the still-warm black box. It seemed that two mounts were used to hold it in place. One of the mounts was broken and the other nearly twisted off. Duke grasped a piece of splintered metal and used it as a wedge to break the other mount loose. He then slowly removed the box and turned it over.

*Hot damn,* he thought. In Duke's right hand was a four-by-six-inch metal square box. Turning it over he could see a set of knobs and digital displays. It was the Pave Hawk's backup radio. It was dented and two of the plastic dials were broken off but it was a radio. James tucked it under his arm and moved on to his original destination, the old building on the harbor.

"We'll clear the coast in three minutes," the pilot said, twisting around in his seat to face Kaine.

"Take her down to one thousand feet. We need to stay clear of the Americans' radar."

"Understood." The pilot pushed the yoke forward forcing the transport into a shallow dive. The jet shuddered in protest as the pilot backed off on the throttles trying to maintain a steady speed.

CPO Janis Owens had left her mother and three sisters to join the navy. At the age of eighteen she had wanted to see the world. She never dreamed that ten years later the career of a scope dope, tapping away on a computer keyboard in the center of the ocean, would be so rewarding. There wasn't any other place in the world she'd rather be.

Pounding on the computer keyboard, Owens was getting the most she could out of the ship's complex equipment. On the upper-right edge of the radarscope she watched a red triangle, a hostile aircraft, making its way to the northwest. She had begun tracking it at 5,000 feet when it suddenly appeared south of Pyongyang, the North Korean capital. From the bird's speed, heading and straight-as-an-arrow flight path she guessed it was a military transport, probably on a night-training mission. Or it could be a civilian cargo jet.

The aircraft was on the edge of her sensors and she hoped the readings were accurate. The *Observation Island* had been built to track suborbital Soviet reentry vehicles, not to watch low-flying aircraft. Modifications and updates were performed on the ship's instrumentations; however, as Owens had learned over the last year, not everything on the screen was gospel.

She blinked hard, seeing four more targets grouped in close formation ten miles to the north of the first contact. She watched them for a few seconds before they disappeared behind one of the interior mountains. *No doubt fighters,* she thought.

"So where do you think you're going?" Owens whispered under her breath, looking back at the red triangle. She watched the data change as the single contact descended through 2,000 feet.

"Two thousand feet . . . fifteen hundred feet," the Il-76 pilot called out, at the same time easing back on the transport's yoke.

Kaine looked out the cockpit windows. The Korean coastline flashed by in a blur. Ahead of them was nothing but darkness and the lights of a few ships making their way up or down the shoreline.

The colonel felt the Il-76 quiver as it cut through several low clouds. The pilot banked to the left, avoiding more of the feathery white haze, before leveling the wings and throttling back. The altimeter read 950 feet and a compass heading of two eight nine, speed 310 knots. Kaine was not a man who enjoyed being in a passive position, but there was nothing for him to do but sit back and wait.

Brushing a lock of golden brown hair from her eyes, Owens forced her eyes to stay focused on the four-color radar screen. *So are you going to play around or do you have the guts to try for the big prize?* she thought. The target had dropped below 1,000 feet and disappeared from her dark scope.

"Shit." The petty officer gritted her teeth in frustration. She knew her radar wasn't configured to track anything below 1,000 feet. Hell, she could locate a grapefruit-sized target fifty miles up or a reenter vehicle traveling at Mach 20 but not an aircraft below 1,000 feet at 160 miles away. So much for rocket science.

Owens sat up in her chair. Swiveling around, she faced the captain. "Sir . . . radar contact lost on target descending through one thousand feet

. . . last bearing two niner one. Range one hundred sixty-five miles, speed steady at three hundred and ten knots.''

"Opinion, Ms. Owens," Captain Bliss grunted.

"A military transport, sir."

"That heading places it on a possible course for Langau Island. Is that not correct?" Bliss asked coolly.

"Yes, sir, it does."

Captain Bliss acknowledged Owens with a nod. He changed positions in his chair, his face hard in thought. Finishing off his third Coke he stood and tossed the empty can into a nearby trash can.

"Commander Noel . . . what the hell do you make of this?" he asked the ship's intelligence officer.

"Of which situation, sir?" Noel asked, raising his eyebrows.

"All of it. The whole damn situation starting with General James's transport sending us a message that's cut off, that trawler transmitting and now we've got a military aircraft flying under the net heading for Langau Island . . ." Bliss paused to rub his forehead. "My gut's telling me something is brewing out there. What do you think?"

"It could all be coincidental, of course . . . except the piece that doesn't fit is General James. I know he wouldn't want to break radio silence unless it was vital." Noel kept his voice low. "So the main question is, why did he?"

"Where's that trawler now?" Bliss turned to ask Owens.

"Bearing one seven three, ten miles behind us and shadowing our every move."

"Bastard," Bliss grunted. "All right, I don't want them to think we're doing anything unusual. Owens, you have a mission. Try and realign that radar of yours and see if you can track the military transport . . . and anything else that might be going to or coming off that island."

"Yes, sir, but it will take some time. If it can be done at all." Owens had already begun to manipulate the keys on her board.

"Well, get it done and fast. If something did go wrong and James is in trouble . . ." Bliss stared at the scope, wishing it could show a definite picture of what was happening on Langau Island.

# 22

CWO Michael Callahan held up his fist, signaling the other three members of the recon team to hold short. They were crouched in the darkness at the end of a tiny box gulch not more than ten feet wide.

The gully walls surrounding them were twenty feet high and covered with tangled vines and large-leafed plants. A thick column of trees reaching into the sky about fifty feet lined the top of both sides of the ridge. Cascading down at the end of the gully, a waterfall filled the air with the sound of rushing water. Callahan could just barely see the moss-covered rocks on each side of the falls. Looking up, he could no longer make out any stars; a thick blanket of clouds had rolled in, covering the mountainside with low fog. A sprinkle of rain began to tap on his face and forehead.

Staying on the trail they had been following for the last 500 yards, Callahan walked ahead of his squad. In the four hours since touching down he estimated they had covered roughly 4.5 miles. The warrant officer was glad he had taken the time to study several satellite maps before taking off. Even with an NVG strapped to his head, the dense jungle became obscure beyond twenty or thirty feet. The gradual, changing terrain hadn't been a surprise, though, since he had memorized several landmarks to know precisely where they were. It felt good not having to refer constantly to his GPS.

The only setback was that the trek to the downed aircraft was a lot rougher than he had anticipated. They had crossed two open rice patties, one several hundred yards long, wading through waist-deep water and mud before starting their ascension into the steep hills. The jungle ground, covered with its normal obstacles, was wet and slippery.

Callahan stopped a few feet from the end of the gully. Methodically he turned his head left and right, listening and watching. With the loud roar of the water he depended more on his eyes as they shifted back and forth. He soaked in every detail around him. There weren't any footprints, no branches or plants were broken and he didn't see any trash such as cigarette butts or food wrappers. It didn't appear as if any humans had been in the gully for a very long time.

"Psst," Callahan hissed, signaling the squad to come even with him. So far he couldn't have been more pleased. His men were handling it well considering they hadn't trained in dense cover for over a year. He shouldn't have expected anything less. The men he was leading were well disciplined, and although they liked to cut up and make light of things they were dedicated and professional.

Squatting down, Callahan circled his men around him and began talking in a hushed tone: "Okay, listen up. This is where we get real serious. Once we climb over the end of this gully the crash site should be about five hundred yards to the southwest on the edge of a small clearing." Callahan looked directly at his medical specialist. "Barnes, I want you to collect water samples from this stream and soil samples every one hundred yards until we reach the aircraft. When we get to the site you get what samples you need while the rest of us provide cover."

Each man, listening intently, nodded while maintaining their vigilant watch. The night-vision goggles covered their faces.

"Once Barnes is done, buddy up and take turns collecting pieces of aircraft debris and vegetation from around the plane. Put anything you collect in the pouches Barnes gave out earlier. Don't get picky . . . this shouldn't take us any more than a few minutes. Any questions?"

"Yeah. Did anyone bring along extra candy bars? I'm starving," Pope said, looking dead serious.

"Shit, man, is that all you think about—your stomach?" Barnes handed Pope two peanut butter cups.

"No way," Pope said, placing the wrapper in a pocket. "Do you have a beer in—"

"Hey, listen up you two. I'll take point," Callahan announced. "Stay ten feet apart and keep your eyes and ears open."

"We'll be right behind you, sir," Pope mumbled, stuffing one of the peanut butter cups into his mouth, then exaggeratedly licking his fingers.

Callahan shook his head. Standing up, he started up the back of the gully, being wary not to slip on any of the mossy rocks.

LANGAU ISLAND

"Let's move it," James said, appearing at the end of the culvert. He had his NVGs strapped to his head. In his right hand was the duffle bag he had taken to the building with him from the helicopter. Under his left arm there appeared to be a roll of what looked like ripped and torn canvas with loose strings hanging off it.

"Don't scare me like that," Erwin jumped. "I was just getting comfortable. I see you found your gear."

"Sure did. Now let's move it." James helped the two crawl out of the drainage pipe.

"Did you get the heater?" Erwin asked hopefully.

"Yeah," Duke said, pointing to the bag. "And a few other things. But right now I want to get away from this runway. Come on, I found a cluster of large rocks to the west. We can hide there."

## THE WHITE HOUSE

"Did you get it?" Manning asked in hushed tones.

"Yeah, I got it. But it's only twenty-five thousand dollars, Allan. Is that all your career is worth . . . twenty-five thousand dollars?" his wife said over the phone.

Manning cupped his hand over the phone receiver so his wife couldn't hear his labored breathing. Brushing the beads of sweat off his head, he closed his eyes and clenched his teeth. He could barely control the tension in his chest. A surge of depression came over him while his body began to scream for another rush of cocaine.

"Are you listening to me, Allan? I said, is your career only worth a lousy twenty-five thousand? I know you're hiding more from me. You and your sleazy lawyer friend. All you did was buy yourself time. I want half a million, Allan, not a cent less. Do you hear me?"

"Listen, Rhonda, listen . . . I don't know where you got the idea that I have that kind of money. Remember, if you ruin me now, you'll get nothing."

"Don't you threaten me, Allan! You're the one that shot off your mouth about how smart you are . . . how could I have been so stupid!" Rhonda's voice wavered, then broke. "You're such a pig! You disgust me, Allan . . . if you just hadn't told me . . . and those pictures . . . how could you!"

Manning lowered his head, feeling his face grow hot. His emotions were flashing between anger and hatred as if someone was playing with a light switch. Why was Rhonda doing this? He'd already given her enough. Was she stupid enough not to realize who he was now . . . the second most powerful man in the world? She could go ahead and turn the pictures over to the Washington *Post*—or better yet, the New York *Times*. He didn't care any more. No one in D.C. would care if he was gay, straight or a virgin. Hell, this is *Washington,* not fuckin' Utah. He could always say it was a setup and sue her for slander. He had access to the best legal advice in the world. She wouldn't have a chance. Everything would work out, Manning reassured himself.

He felt his confidence swell and then suddenly sink. A rush of dread shot through him. What if McEntire did something stupid? That was the wild card. *If the president didn't have the backbone to support Bishop, why would he support me if the media got hold of the pictures?*

"Allan, are you listening to me?" Rhonda asked. "Do you really want to deal with this? Its easier just to give me the money. How long, Allan?"

Manning's insides jumped. She's right, he thought. I've got better things to do right now. I'll tell the bitch what she wants to hear. When this thing's over and I've pushed James out of the way I'll deal with it. "A couple of months . . . that's all," Manning said, gripping the receiver more tightly.

"A couple of months! Are you back on the dope again? Is that the problem . . . spending all your money on nose candy and gay bars?"

"No, no . . ."

"I know what you're thinking, Allan. That the people in D.C. might not care about what you do away from the White House—but don't forget, there are others who will."

"What do you mean?" Allan asked, rubbing the side of his head.

"Don't play stupid with me. It's Main Street USA, the president and Congress you worry about. McEntire won't tolerate anyone on his staff creating a disturbance. And after the big deal the press made out of Bill Bishop being forced to resign and then his poor wife dying, don't tell me you didn't have something to do with that."

Manning held the phone away from his ear and rolled his eyes. She was hollering loud enough that he could still hear every word she said.

"But that's fine by me . . . maybe I'll just send those closeup shots of you directly to McEntire. Bye-bye Allan."

"Rhonda, wait," Manning said, bringing the receiver back to his head. "Don't hang up. I'll get it for you. You'll have it by the end of the month."

There was a long pause. Manning listened to the dead quiet of the phone line, waiting for his wife to respond.

"Are you there? Did you hear me?" he asked.

"I heard you. You have until the end of the month." The line went dead.

Allan's hand shook as he unlocked the drawer behind his desk. Removing the dark brown glass vial, he spilled out the contents. Just the sight of the white powder made him feel better. If I had the guts I'd blow her fuckin' brains out, he thought.

## CIA Headquarters

A slight frown came across Mark Collins' face as he opened a sealed brown envelope from the National Reconnaissance Office. The padded envelope contained a fresh set of CD-ROM disks packed in several layers of clear plastic. Typed across the top of one set of disks on a white computer label were the words: KEYHOLE*.*LACROSSE DOWN-LINK/YONGBYON, NORTH KOREA.

Collins slipped the CD-ROM into the D-drive of his desktop computer. Tapping the keyboard he watched the yellow "busy" light flicker on. The screen flickered once before slowly displaying a high-altitude KH-14 photo. From the shadowy screen Collins guessed the picture had been taken a few hours after dusk. However, Mark could see by the orderly specks of light that the satellite had been directly over Yongbyon, North Korea, when the first picture was dumped to the Pine Gap receiving station in Australia. The shot had been taken from directly above the nuclear facility and the weather had been clear. Clicking the mouse twice he called up the next photo to see if the perspective would change.

Collins' frown turned to a tight-lipped grin. The second photo showed Yongbyon from a slightly different angle, indicating that the satellite's orbit had changed. The question now was, how much and when? Tapping the mouse button three quick times, a series of bright green digital numbers appeared on the bottom of his computer monitor. The numbers told Collins the KH-14's orbit was now in an elliptical path varying between 185 and 284 miles above the earth. It also told him the KH-14 satellite data on this CD-ROM disk had been transmitted twenty hours ago. The picture he was looking at was nearly a day old. *Shit, I can't believe this.* With each click Collins's blood pressure rose until he could stand it no longer.

Grabbing the phone, Collins dialed the direct line to his contact at the National Reconnaissance Office inside the Pentagon.

"Ronald here."

"Give me Jack Spinner," Collins said.

"Jack's out. May I help you?"

"This is Mark Collins at CIA. I *need* Jack."

"Mr. Collins . . . Jack's mother passed away yesterday morning and I'm filling in for him."

Collins' face went hot. *Of all the times,* he thought.

"I'm not sure when he'll be back. Is there something I can help you with?"

"Check your imagery distribution chart. I'm on it. Make sure I get a copy of the KH-14 and Lacrosse-C CD-ROMs for my area in a reasonable amount of time. That means within *one hour* of transmission." Collins suddenly exploded, late nights and lack of sleep overruling his sense of tact. "Do you understand? *One hour!*"

"Yes . . . I understand."

"Good. And tell Jack I want a phone call when he gets back." Collins hung up the phone.

His eyes returned to the computer screen. The upper corner of the twenty-four-inch monitor contained a rectangular menu box. Collins centered the mouse pointer and clicked the icon box for the Lacrosse-C radar-imaging satellite. The screen flashed again, this time turning from black to dark blue with a yellow outline of North Korea. Data on the bottom of the screen confirmed that the Lacrosse-C's orbit had also been moved but not as much as the KH-14. Mark estimated the Lacrosse's orbit had been changed by three hours and it now trailed the KH-14 rather than leading it.

Centering the cursor over the nuclear facility at Yongbyon, Mark tapped the mouse and called up a radar picture of the ground from 100,000 feet. Waiting for the CD-ROM to cycle he watched the picture slowly clear. From experience Collins knew the synthetic-aperture radar could only penetrate the ground up to thirty feet in soft soil. It was, however, powerful enough to penetrate wooden structures with metal roofs, unless there were more than four inches of steel-reinforced concrete—and unfortunately the North Koreans knew it. In the last six months Collins hadn't gotten any worthwhile data from the Lacrosse. Each time the satellite passed over the area everything looked the same.

Mark instructed the computer to zoom into an altitude of 10,500 feet. This time when the screen cleared, he stared hard. He could see the outline of each building in the Yongbyon complex along with the network of criss-crossing roads, pipelines, water-filled reservoirs, and open areas. The majority of the dark blue structures were hardened buildings the radar wasn't able to penetrate. The outer perimeter included several rows of yellowish buildings, wooden structures, and light blue spots which Collins knew were trucks or cars.

At first glance nothing looked out of place. The Koreans were still working on a new building to the south but it appeared to be made out of wood and was probably some sort of barracks for troops. But in the right-hand corner Collins noticed a series of faint red spots. *What have we got here?* Red wasn't a normal color to be seen on these photos. It meant dense material, extremely dense, like lead, gold—or unshielded uranium.

Collins clicked the mouse several more times zooming into 1,000 feet. Slewing the cursor over the first red dot, he enlarged the picture. He could see the blurry outline of a truck. Behind the cab, in the cargo bay were several long red lines. *Those sonsobitches are moving plutonium fuel rods.* Collins tapped the print button and reached for the phone.

Duke was the first one to reach the other side of the runway. Approximately 100 yards off the airstrip a group of large rocks were piled together in a rough U-shape pattern. The largest rock in the center was four feet high and about six feet wide. A number of smaller rocks were piled around it. Several dried bushes were in front adding to the cover.

"In here," James said, helping both Erwin and Sinchon around to the back side of the boulders. He unrolled the canvas tarp he had been carrying. Draping the ends over each side of the largest rock, he secured it with dirt and rocks to create a crude shelter. Then he crawled inside and joined the other two. They were squatted down on their knees trying to stay out of the wind.

"Get that heater going," Erwin said, shaking, both her arms crossed and moved up and down to keep warm.

"Hold tight." James pulled the small kerosene heater out of his duffle bag. Pumping the pressure valve several times, he struck the start button. A moment later the area began to glow as an orange flame brought warmth into the primitive hideout.

"Look at this," Duke smiled, removing the radio. "I found it in the wreckage."

Major Erwin grasped the black box and held it next to the heater. "It's a radio!"

"It's the back-up radio for the Pave Hawk," James said, holding his hands over the heater.

"Does it work?"

"I don't know," Duke shrugged. "I didn't stop to check it out."

Erwin turned a couple of the switches, listening for some static. There wasn't any. Flipping it over she saw where the wires from the backup battery had been cut.

"General, was there a battery connected to it?" Erwin asked, her eyes wide.

James turned to the major, attempting to hide the fact he was feeling a little silly. "Let me guess. There isn't a battery inside the radio. I disconnected it when I yanked it out of the wreckage."

Erwin nodded unhappily.

"Never send a general to do a grownup's job," James rolled his eyes, sighing at his blunder.

"Well, if this is going to work I'm going to need some electrical current."

"I will go this time," Sinchon said suddenly.

"*Anio* . . . You stay here. It was my mistake." James grabbed his NVGs. With his broken arm, Duke didn't think the general would be able to do much anyway.

"You'd better hurry," Sinchon stated seriously, moving closer to Duke. "Whoever attacked us will want to make sure we're dead. That means they make another pass with an aircraft or land a ground team—maybe both, depending on how badly Chin wants to dishonor me."

Duke looked at Erwin knowing she was a North Korean intel expert. "Major . . . should I wait for the cavalry or go for it?"

"I don't know," she answered, looking at Sinchon. "I'm not sure who we're dealing with here. How do you know it was Chin, General?"

"This had to be *spetsnaz*. There is no other explanation. Chin has wanted me out of his way for a long time. He has been guiding a younger man, Colonel Kaine, to take my place. Some of the troops have already been placed under his command. Somehow he must have learned of this meeting."

"This was an air attack, General. I thought the only *spetsnaz* troops were airborne or amphibious," Erwin said, her face questioning.

"My country has a squadron of aircraft dedicated to the most secret and special missions," Sinchon replied. "I believe Chin used these aircraft to attack me . . . us."

"The Su-30s," Duke said to Sinchon's surprise.

"Indeed," Sinchon said.

For the first time since the attack Duke had a chance to think. If Sinchon was right, then they wouldn't make it to first light. They were unarmed, with no food, and the kerosene heater would run out of fuel within a few hours. If North Korean commandos did land on the island they could easily sweep the area before the Americans sent a rescue party. This being a covert mission, it could even happen before the Americans realized they needed rescuing. Their only way of surviving, Duke realized, would be to contact the *Observation Island,* and that meant getting the radio working.

"I hope you're wrong, General," James said at last. "But if not, there're three charred bodies in the chopper and the ones in the harbor with the boat. Let's hope they'll be happy with that."

"We need a battery, General James," Major Erwin pressed.

"I'd prefer a gun . . . a big one," Duke said bluntly.

"The battery is going to be about half the size of this radio. Probably square and black, with several wires coming out of one end . . . and it will be heavy."

"You just happen to know all this?" Duke asked.

"As a lieutenant I was a communications specialist in West Germany. We could make a radio out of a shoe box and string," Erwin said proudly. Duke didn't think she was exaggerating. "If you find me the right pieces, I can make a radio. I'll need extra wire for the antenna. Copper works best."

"All right, Major. I'll get that shoe box and string, then it's up to you to do the rest."

"I should go with you," Sinchon spoke again, starting to rise.

Duke placed his hand on the man's shoulder. "There is nothing you can do out there. It would be better for all of us right now if you stayed here."

Duke turned into the cold night, then stopped. "If I don't return . . . I would like Major Erwin to have a chance at being rescued, General."

"I am defeated but I am still a soldier, General James. Do not worry, I will give myself up before I let them take her."

Satisfied, James turned, leaving the warmth and safety of their makeshift shelter.

## IL-76 ILYUSHIN TRANSPORT

"Fourteen miles, sir," the pilot called out. "I'm taking her up to two thousand feet. We need the altitude to get an IR picture of the island."

Kaine nodded his approval. The IR screen, located in the center of the transport's instrument panel, remained black. At fourteen miles the colonel knew the jet's long-range IR sensors should be picking up the faint heat signature of Langau. It would be on the horizon, placing it on the bottom of the screen.

"Breaking through nineteen hundred feet. We should be seeing something," Kaine said.

"There she is," the copilot blurted out, pointing to the image of Langau Island on the screen.

The transport rocked back and forth as it was hit by another strong gust of wind. The Il-76 pitched up before the pilot nosed over, leveling at 2,110 feet.

Colonel Kaine sat upright to see the display. On the bottom of the screen he could see a dull greenish-white image about an inch long.

"Stay under two thousand feet," Kaine instructed as the return slowly grew larger.

"We have a problem, sir," the pilot said, pointing to the instrument panel. "The number four engine is losing oil pressure."

Kaine's eyes went to the flashing red warning light next to the pilot's right knee. "Shut it down."

The pilot throttled back, killing the engine. The transport yawed to the right.

"Number three is running hot," the pilot warned.

"Get us on the ground, NOW!" Kaine shouted, then stole a quick glance behind him, thinking of the plutonium fuel rods.

## USS *OBSERVATION ISLAND*

CPO Owens could feel a thin layer of grease covering her face and neck. She hadn't showered or slept in twenty hours and was starting to feel stressed sitting behind the radarscope and communications gear. For forty-five minutes she had attempted to realign the ship's radar in an effort to track low-flying targets below 1,000 feet, on the edge of the ship's range. So far she had been unsuccessful. Rubbing her eyes, Owens thought maybe it was time to grab a burger and hit the bunk. If there was anything out there, it was gone by now.

*I'll give it one more try,* she thought. Owens tapped her computer keyboard, focusing her attention back on the screen. She could see the west coast of Korea, a jagged yellow line, on the right side of the monitor. The scope was clear of any aircraft in an eighty-five-mile radius.

Looking right, Owens spotted an unknown aircraft symbol appearing. She tilted her head to the right, waiting for her equipment to get a fix on the new target.

"I'm showing an unknown aircraft heading two niner fiver. Altitude 1,950 feet, speed 285 knots," Owens called out.

The ship's intel officer, Commander Noel, appeared by Owens's side. "Where's it headed?"

"It looks like Langau Island." Owens looked at him with her tired eyes. "It's thirteen miles out."

Noel checked the digital clock above the computer screens to his left. "Could it be General James's chopper?" he asked.

"No, sir. I'm sure it's heading toward the island, not away from it, and its speed is more like that of a transport or very large turboprop."

"Get Captain Bliss back up here," Noel ordered. "We have a situation."

It is an awareness, or more accurately an instinct. The men that had it referred to it as *the Force.* It put them on the very pinnacle of the food chain. It's something that can't be taught in sniper or special-forces school and was certainly not written into a text book as a "how to" course for some washed-up military professor to teach. Callahan knew it definitely couldn't be communicated with any degree of precision or even talked about openly with the men that had it. You were just born with it or developed it at a very young age when you needed it in order to survive.

In Callahan's opinion a point man, particularly for a recon team, had to be someone with this special intuition. It meant the difference between keeping his squad alive or getting them killed. Some men with fast reflexes tried to fake it, but not for long; they always ended up dead along with the rest of their team. Michael considered himself the best point man in the Green Berets. The fact that he was still alive proved it.

Hunching down, the CWO stopped halfway up the gently sloping hill heading toward the aircraft wreckage. Callahan methodically swung his head gracefully, even with the cumbersome NVGs, left to right. The heavily foliaged landscape had cleared up some, allowing him to see the leveling terrain. He could see a number of broken branches on the ground where he figured the jet had sheered the tops of trees. The grass and brush looked natural, lying in various directions. There weren't any animal trails or human footprints and he couldn't smell anything unusual, just the moist damp mold of the jungle. A few birds were chirping and the sound of insects buzzed through the thick night air. The sounds were a reassurance to him. Birds and insects were like a natural tripwire. As long as they were buzzing and singing there wasn't anyone in the area.

Something didn't seem right, though, and Callahan couldn't put a finger on it. Everything seemed to be in place. Maybe he just had the willies because they were in Vietnam.

Callahan looked straight ahead, trying to get a fix on any debris. He estimated the downed aircraft was now 200 yards away, at the back of an open field his team had just entered. He had decided it was best if they skirted the field to the right of the wreckage and come in above the jet. They would approach slowly, evenly spaced out, ten yards between each man.

Callahan placed his finger on the ribbed trigger of his CAR-15 assault rifle, keeping the weapon pointed forward. Standing up, he took several steps. The ground was turning hard and rocky, making it difficult to remain noiseless.

Sucking in a deep breath the CWO tried to shake off the feeling of apprehension. *If anything was wrong I would see it or smell it,* Callahan reassured himself. After all, *the Force* was with him.

Duke checked his watch as he reached the back side of the burned-out Pave Hawk chopper. It was a few minutes past two in the morning and the wind had picked up out of the northwest, kicking up a great deal of dust and making it difficult to see. He calculated there were gusts up to thirty-five or forty knots. The added chill was enough to cause the tips of his fingers to feel numb.

By now the fires had died out, leaving several glowing red chunks of metal scattered around the area. Using his NVGs, Duke spotted the twisted bundle of chopper wreckage where he had found the radio. The greenish images in the night-vision goggles were starting to fade. The cold was beginning to affect the batteries. He would have to work fast in order to save the remaining power.

Reaching inside the bundle of wires and metal, James used his hands to feel for a square box resembling the one Erwin had described. He tried to remember where he had found the radio in the pile of junk. *Was it behind the broken instrument panel or underneath it?* He couldn't remember.

"Come on . . . where the hell are you?" James said under his breath, not feeling the box.

"How long have you been tracking it?" Captain Bliss asked, looking over Owens' shoulder.

"About four minutes. The radar picked it up flying out of the east. If it stays above 1,800 feet I can track it."

Bliss rubbed his eyes and looked back at the screen. The unknown aircraft symbol showed the target approximately eight miles east of Langau Island. It appeared the aircraft was circling around to the back of the island.

"I need some answers, people. What is it and what's it doing out there heading toward that island? Could it be General James' contact coming in late?" Bliss wished he would hear from someone ASAP. Whether it was the Pentagon or James, it didn't matter, just so he didn't feel like an expectant father just waiting.

Owens was quiet for a few seconds, her eyes following the target. "Sir, I'd say it's not a chopper . . . I repeat it could be a large transport of some type."

Commander Noel, the ship's intel officer, shook his head. "The North Korean contact was to arrive on a private yacht. I don't think it's them."

"From the flight path I'd say it's lining up to land," Owens said, still watching the screen for any changes.

"Land?" Bliss' face turned to disbelief. "This is bullshit! There shouldn't be anyone else in the area."

"But that doesn't mean—"

"Damn it, Noel, just be quiet." Bliss began giving fervent orders. "Open a channel to Washington." *I'm not waiting for those molasses assholes any more,* the captain thought, taking his place in the elevated chair.

"Secure the cabin. We're on final approach," Colonel Kaine's voice boomed over the speakers into the cargo section of the Il-76. The four-engine transport banked to the south as the pilot lowered the flaps.

Kaine examined the darkness out the left side of the cockpit, in the direction of the abandoned fishing village. He could make out several shimmering fires burning in and around the yacht. The flames were bright enough to illuminate some of the bay. He showed no emotion. The once luxurious *Van Triumph* was nothing more than an incinerated chunk of debris.

The colonel felt his stomach turn over as the cockpit crew made one more banking turn. The pilot intended to come in low, without using the landing lights. By watching the runway on the IR screen he could touch down, reverse the engines and taxi to the end of the runway without overly exposing their presence. There would only be dust and noise. It was a risk worth taking. If the Americans had smuggled any ships or submarines into the area they would have a hard time seeing the transport.

"Two miles out." The pilot turned the yoke, leveling the jet. "Keep me in the center," he told the copilot.

Kaine's attention went from the black windshield to the spooky-looking IR image of the runway. They were rapidly descending.

"We have a fire in number four," the copilot announced calmly. Hitting the fire-suppression switch, he flooded the engine with halon gas.

Kaine leaned forward. He could see a few licks of orange fire coming from the left side of the transport. Then he heard the engines surge as the pilot tried to keep the jet level.

"Recommend we return to base. I can't land her on this airstrip in this condition," the pilot suddenly called out to the colonel behind him.

Kaine watched the flames die before looking back at the pilot. The flashing of three red warning lights reflected in his eyes and a line of sweat trickled down the side of his face.

"You have your orders," Kaine commanded. "Get us on the ground."

"It's gone, sir," Owens stated matter-of-factly. "It just dropped off the screen."

Captain Bliss didn't reply. He opened another can of Coke and drank half of it before pulling the can away from his lips.

"Sir, I have the Special Operations Center at the Pentagon on the blue line," one of the backup communications officers said over his shoulder.

"It's about time." Bliss picked up the bright blue-colored phone, keeping his eyes on the computer display. "Cheerleader . . . this is Guard Dog. We have a problem."

James felt a shiver go down his spine from the frosty wind cutting through his parka. He wrapped his hands around what felt like a square box near the base of the rubble pile. It was about the size of a Spam can and appeared to be heavy like a nicad battery. But he couldn't be sure it was the battery. He pulled hard several times and it finally broke loose.

Duke flipped the black box over, looking for a set of wires. The metal housing was dented in several places and an oily fluid covered the outside.

He placed it in his pocket and turned away from the howling wind. The low rumble of jet engines echoed to the south of him.

*Aw, shit!* Falling quickly to his knees, James crawled around to the back of the wreckage. Scanning the sky, he braced himself for the crushing force of a bomb blast to knock the breath out of him.

A rage of wind rocked the Il-76. The nose pitched up and the engines surged.

"Warning . . . stall. Warning . . . stall," the computer sounded.

The pilot pushed the yoke forward and back, struggling to keep the giant jet level. "She's unstable. I can't . . . can't control her."

The ground seemed to rush up at the aircraft on the IR screen. The white gravel runway was free of the larger rocks and looked to be flat and even. Colonel Kaine watched in silence. He could see the uneven edges of the airfield on either side of the screen as the jet rocked back and forth in the changing wind. Again the pilot pulled the yoke toward him before pushing it rapidly away. His efforts didn't seem to be helping.

"The crosswinds . . . I can't hold her," the pilot called out, hoping for a response, then added: "I'll bring her around again."

"Put this aircraft on the *ground!*" Kaine shouted. "We don't have time to waste."

The pilot tightened his grip. The Il-76 shuddered as it yawed right and left. The floor vibrated as the gear came down and the jet began to slow. Again the pilot pushed the yoke forward, forcing her toward the ground. Kaine checked the green back-lit altimeter, which showed they were at 300 feet and descending at ten feet per second—only they were already over most of the runway. They were coming in too fast, using up too much of the short, rough field.

"One hundred feet," the copilot called out. "Fifty feet. Down to one hundred thirty-nine knots. She'll stall at one hundred thirty-five."

Without warning a gust of wind caught the left wing of the jet, forcing it up. The sudden draft dropped the airspeed to 134 knots. The faltering transport banked right several degrees before the pilot could compensate. Forcing the throttles forward to gain airspeed, he pitched the nose up and retracted the air brakes. The Il-76 didn't respond. On the edge of a stall, the aircraft came down with a heavy thud on the right-side gear. The right wingtip skimmed the dirt, slamming the nose section forward. With a loud pop the nose gear snapped, causing a shower of sparks to explode from under the transport. The starboard gear cut into the dirt runway and buckled under the fuselage.

Kaine's head jerked forward as the jet decelerated and angled toward the edge of the runway. A cloud of dirt boiled up, making it impossible to see out the windshield. At the same time the IR screen went dead. His shoulder straps cut into his arms while the jet skidded sideways.

Turning on his NVGs James sat up in time to see a T-tailed four-engine transport hit the runway a half-mile south of his position. He watched the jet skip back into the air and then come down hard nosefirst. A barrage of sparks exploded from beneath the aircraft. For a moment he thought the jet would explode, but it didn't. The aircraft veered to the right and then back to the left as pieces of metal ripped from its belly, cartwheeling through the air.

Duke scrambled up to a group of rocks near the edge of the runway as the transport slowed. The jet came to a halt about a hundred yards away from him. He waited, covering his eyes, for the dust to clear. James could now see what he thought was an Il-76 Ilyushin. He couldn't tell if it had North Korean markings or not. It appeared to be completely dark inside and out.

Duke waited. There wasn't a fire and he couldn't see any smoke. He heard the engines shut off, which meant at least one of the pilots was still alive. Then he saw the cockpit lights come on.

*Okay . . . time to get out of here.* Duke ducked down and ran across the runway several hundred yards behind the jet.

"I heard it." Major Erwin shook her head, glancing darkly at Sinchon. The North Korean general was standing outside, looking toward the runway. "What do you make of it?"

"I don't know," Sinchon said, bending back down. "It's too dark to see anything. But it looks large. Maybe a transport."

"Can you see *whose* it is?" Erwin asked. "Is it American?"

Sinchon turned to face her sadly, shaking his head no. He climbed back into the makeshift shelter. The canvas covering was doing a good job of preventing the wind from entering. The kerosene heater rattled as it labored to keep the shelter warm. Crawling up to the heater next to Erwin, Sinchon looked at the American officer.

"What is your duty for your country?" He asked after a few seconds.

"Duty?" Erwin gave the man a wary smile. "I specialize in North Korean political and military affairs."

Sinchon nodded. "So that is why they sent you here."

"You could say that."

"You are a brave woman," Sinchon said, speaking slowly, remembering the young female *spetsnaz* officer that died doing her duty at the tunnel. "Do you understand how my country works or how this could happen?"

"Your country understands only one thing: strength." Erwin wasn't timid about speaking her mind. "Do you agree?"

*"Ne,"* Sinchon nodded yes, looking back into the warmth of the heater.

"We know that after Kim Il Song's death there has been a lot of turmoil and shifting of loyalties, much like the former Soviet Union. I don't think any American could totally understand," Erwin said.

"Then why are you here?" Sinchon asked, curious. "Why risk your lives to meet with me?"

Erwin was quiet for a moment, then answered: "We want what you want for your country . . . peace and unity. We are not the ogres some make us out to be. Our CIA didn't have much information on you but we knew you controlled one of the most powerful elements of the military. If there was a chance that you were on the level, then it was a chance worth taking."

"I have failed. Not only my country but yours as well." Sinchon hung his head.

Erwin moved over to the canvas opening and peered out at the aircraft on the runway. It was too far away to see any details or if anyone was around it.

"I must leave now," Sinchon said, coming up behind the major. "If I turn myself in they will not continue searching the island. You will be rescued. Tell General James I thank him and you . . ."

"Shhh. It's too late now, I hear someone."

Sinchon unexpectedly stepped in front of the major, placing his large body in the opening and pushing Erwin to the back of the shelter.

General James emerged from the darkness.


NGHIA BINH PROVINCE, VIETNAM


As CWO Michael Callahan rounded a stand of trees he could see the primary target. Resting at the base of a rock ledge sloping away from him a hundred yards to the west was a broken aircraft fuselage. Its tail section had several vines draped over it and for about fifty yards the ground appeared to be torn up where the jet had skidded across it. Through his NVGs the white fuselage appeared a dark dull green and the vines were lighter in color. One of the wings was broken off and the nose section was badly damaged.

Callahan began to think about why he was standing in the jungle. Over a hundred people had been killed by some sort of nerve gas or biological agent. The CIA must have pretty good evidence the chemical came from this aircraft to have sent them in for samples. He wondered just how much danger they were in being this close to the jet. The specialist assured them that the chemical had dissipated by now and the air was safe. He did recommend they wear gloves when collecting the samples and be careful not to put their hands to their eyes or mouth.

Realizing they were dealing with an enemy he might not see made him want to complete the mission and head back to base in the shortest possible time.

Holding up his hand, the CWO stopped in his tracks. Turning around he could see all his men behind him. S. Sgt. Steve Pope, the squad's communication specialist, stood hunched over ten feet away.

Pope's thin six foot two-inch frame was loaded down with equipment, including the squad's only link to the outside world: a Motorola URC-200 VHF/UHF ground-to-ground/ground-to-air AM/FM radio tucked away inside his backpack with only the stubby antenna exposed. Callahan watched Pope swing his weapon right to left covering his position. Behind Pope stood Corp. Todd Ingram armed with an M16A2 fitted with an M203 grenade launcher. Ingram was on one knee, his M16 at his shoulder and ready. Sgt. Gary Barnes brought up the rear. Barnes had his weapon pointed to the side. He was using his NVGs to absorb every detail around them. Knowing his team was alert and ready made Callahan feel somewhat better.

Callahan turned around to face the open field. He knew he needed to get a *feel* for the situation before proceeding any further. Basic recon training 101 stated that any primary target about to be infiltrated on foot should be considered hostile. In other words, proceed with caution and don't do anything stupid. And right now Michael couldn't think of a place much more hostile than the jungles of Vietnam on a dark night.

A light rain continued to fall as Callahan methodically surveyed every possible detail surrounding him. His eyes stopped on each branch along the path, making sure none of them were broken or stripped of leaves. Everything appeared normal.

Looking down he began to scan the ground. Twisting the objective lens on his NVGs Callahan focused on the vegetation ten feet in front of him. Suddenly his instincts took control. Every nerve came alive like small radar detectors. His nostrils flared and the hair on the back of his neck stood on end. Resting on a flat rock several yards in front of him were two rectangular lumps of mud—it looked like fresh, wet mud. Crouching down, he crawled closer to pick up the small square pieces of dirt. Grinding them between his thumb and forefinger, Callahan could tell it was fresh, not more than an hour old.

The wet mud had come from between the lugs of a boot sole. By its shape he knew it was a Russian military design. Looking carefully, Callahan could now see several impressions in the wet grass. There were footprints evenly spaced apart. To his right was the remains of a spider's web hanging from a branch a few feet off the ground. The milky white threads were torn and covered with drops of water.

Propping himself up on his knees, Michael swept the NVGs in a wide arc.

The night air was still; tilting his head he realized the sounds of the jungle had ceased. He wasn't sure how long the air had been quiet.

Callahan's face turned hot with anger and fear. Holding up his hand, he signaled his team to be ready then slowly snapped his weapon's safety from on to off.

Without warning a stream of yellow tracer rounds came out of the tree line behind him. The jungle exploded with the echoes of rifle fire as bullets impacted the ground and the trees around Michael and his men. Leaves and branches splintered off the trees as a dozen projectiles flashed past his head a few inches away.

*"Ambush!"* Callahan shouted.

# 23

In the warming light of the kerosene heater General James watched Erwin twist two copper wires together. Using the tips of her fingers she connected a third wire, the antenna, to the back of the radio transmitter.

"Feed this out on top of the rock," Erwin advised, handing James the other end of the wire.

James did as he was told, pushing the thin antenna wire outside their canvas-covered shelter. He secured the wire on top of the rock and pointed it to the east toward *Observation Island.*

Major Erwin placed the radio and battery adjacent to the heater before looking up at James.

"I don't know, General," Erwin said, shaking her head. "They're both fairly beat up and the battery is losing fluid. I think we should let the pieces warm up for a few minutes before we check to see if the battery has any power."

The three stared silently at the odd-shaped boxes, hoping they would work. Thoughts of men unloading from the transport that landed filled Duke's mind. After only a few minutes he said impatiently, "We don't have time to wait any longer. What's the call sign for *Observation Island?"*

"Guard Dog," Erwin answered.

"Here goes nothing." Duke flipped the radio on and grabbed the plastic hand-held mike. Three of the four back-lit dials flashed on. It was operating. The needle on the power-level dial surged to maximum before coming to rest a fraction of an inch from zero. They had battery power but not much.

"Good job, major," James said. "Your hot-wire job seems to be working."

"Try frequency 669.9," Erwin instructed. "It's an emergency military frequency reserved for reconnaissance aircraft coming out of China."

"I'd say this is an emergency," James said, clicking the frequency dial and keying the mike. "Guard Dog . . . this . . . this . . ." He let off on the mike seeing the power transmit light hadn't flashed on. "It's not working."

Erwin patiently took the wires and scraped more of the plastic coating off with her fingernails then reconnected them. She held the battery box away from the radio so the wires were taut instead of bunched up together. "Try it again."

Duke keyed the mike. The power needle jumped. "Guard Dog, this is James. Do you copy?" The red transmit light blinked on and off.

There was no reply.

"Guard Dog, this is James. Do you copy?"

*"You're breaking up. Say again."*

"Guard Dog, this is James. Do you copy?"

*"Aw, James . . . Guard Dog. Stand by,"* Came the crackling response.


USS *OBSERVATION ISLAND*


"Captain, I'm receiving a transmission from General James," Owens reported from her station—then with uncertainty she added, "At least I think it's General James."

"What?" Captain Bliss came out of his chair to stand next to the communications expert. "Are you sure?"

"Well, that's who he says he is." Owens glanced up at the captain, her eyes wide and alert. "He's on the emergency egress channel reserved for recon aircraft."

"Are you picking up anything on radar?" Bliss checked the tracking screen and slipped on a headset.

"No, sir. I can't verify the transmission's authenticity without an IFF transponder code."

There was a short pause while Bliss came up with a way to verify the caller's identity and location: "Caller, this is Guard Dog . . . state what type of jet transported you to the primary?"

*"A Pave Hawk with whirling blades. Now can we cut the crap? We're in deep shit out here, Guard Dog."*

Bliss nodded. That was James, all right. "Roger that . . . use call sign Beagle. Repeat . . . use Beagle. What's your current status?"

*"Our mission has been compromised by an air attack. There are only two other survivors besides myself. Another transport just landed on the runway . . . need transport out of here ASAP."*

The signal's fading, sir," Owens said, twisting the gain knob on her console.

"Beagle . . . have you found shelter?" Bliss asked hurriedly.

*"Roger, Guard Dog."*

"Okay, Beagle, your transmission is breaking up. I'll start working on something to get you out of there. Hold tight for now, then check back in four hours . . . and keep your asses out of sight."

*"Roger, Guard Dog . . . Beagle out."*

Bliss pulled the headset away from his ears. "Owens, get CINICPAC and the Pentagon on the line right now."


## CIA HEADQUARTERS

"Sit down, Mark, you're making me nervous," Brooks said as Collins paced back and forth. Brooks was studying the satellite photographs.

"If you hadn't changed the orbits I never would have caught this." Collins ran his fingers through his hair. He paced the floor several more times before taking a seat in front of his boss. "Those bastards *did* know when our birds were overhead."

"Well, don't get too excited. I'm still not convinced we're looking at plutonium fuel rods." Brooks took off his reading glasses and leaned back in his chair. "If we take this to the president and the Joint Chiefs they're going to want some definite proof it's plutonium. And a couple of photos doesn't mean—"

"Tell me what else they could be," Collins almost shouted.

*"No,* Mark, *you* tell *me* what else they could be. You're the one making the claims."

Collins sucked in a deep breath, knowing Brooks was right. The president wouldn't take action against the North Koreans for breaking the Nuclear Proliferation Treaty unless he was convinced they were indeed plutonium fuel rods.

Collins cleared his throat. "Originally the Lacrosse's radar was designed to see through clouds. From orbit the radar returns bounced off the ground to locate tanks, ships or aircraft at night, in bad weather, ground fog, whatever. During the Gulf War we discovered it could also see inside buildings, aluminum hangars and even penetrate soft bunkers . . . say, not more than five feet deep."

"Okay, what else?" Brooks said. "We already know this."

"We found that by changing the software and color coding it could reveal the density of wood, metal or concrete. Since then the software's been refined even further. In the past the radar could pinpoint a vehicle moving on a highway, but it couldn't decipher what kind. This new software can distinguish the density of metal, which helps indicate whether it's military or not. High grade materials are generally used in military equipment. Some of the computer nerds at the NRO say they can even tell the difference between a T-72 and T-54 tank just by the shade of color from the radar return."

"And . . . ?" Brooks waved his hand in the air, urging Mark to go on.

"The colors white and gray mean something is made out of aluminum or brass, green and yellow mean steel. Red or maroon means heavier metals such as lead, uranium, gold or . . . plutonium."

"So . . . it's your opinion, judging by the color of the red lines, that these are plutonium fuel rods."

"That's right. And these colors indicate trucks are parked at the North's Yongbyon nuclear facility. We were supplied information by Sirhak, our North Korean agent, that the underground reactor was located here. The lines could in theory be lead or gold, but I don't think so. Especially given their dark red color. I believe these trucks are carrying fuel rods and they're going to be transported."

Brooks thought it over. "You could be right. In any case we can't take these photos lightly. Now, where are the rods being transported to?"

"That I don't know yet. These were the last five photos of the pass. We're going to have to wait for the next overflight. I've got the NRO working on tracking the trucks. They'll send me a new set of CDs if anything shows up." Collins rubbed his forehead in thought: "If we can relocate the trucks, we can track the fuel rods. The only problem is there are six hours between the two satellite passes."

"Okay, I'll get things rolling with the Pentagon and White House," Brooks said. "I'm with you 100 percent on this, Mark. I don't like it, but I think you're onto something."

The sour smell of jet fuel swirled in the air around the Il-76 Ilyushin transport. The crew evacuated the four-engine jet moments after it skidded to a halt. The emergency access doors were open and debris from the cargo bay and cabin was scattered around the area.

Once Col. Met Lee Kaine was certain there wasn't going to be an explosion, he gave the order for the pilots and crew to return to the jet.

He walked around the entire aircraft sweeping his flashlight beam across the dull gray, windowless aircraft. The fuselage was buckled behind the cockpit and fuel was dripping out from the wing roots. Black soot from the fire covered the number four engine and the engine next to it appeared damaged as well. Kaine cursed under his breath at the older plane.

The right wingtip left a gouged trail where it had skidded across the ground during the landing. He looked up, seeing how the jet had veered off the edge of the runway and came to rest near a cluster of rocks. Kaine peered underneath and couldn't tell if the main gear had collapsed or dug into the ground. One thing was certain, there was no way to move the giant jet.

In his eagerness to complete the mission, Kaine realized, he had been foolish ordering the pilot to land in the crosswind with an engine out. It was no matter to him now, though, his priority was to transfer the fuel rods.

Turning to face the area around the jet the colonel used the flashlight to scan the barren terrain and rocky ridges. Glancing up at the sky's blackness he saw low hazy gray clouds moving in. A strong gust of wind kicked up dust, causing Kaine to shield his eyes. To his right was the bay. He took a moment to grin at the glowing red embers of a fire smoldering on what was left of the *Van Triumph*. The entire mission wasn't a failure.

Kaine walked back to the main cockpit door and pulled himself up. Entering the flight deck, he flipped the radio switch on and waited for the electrical equipment to warm up before keying the mike.

"Red Crown . . . this is Red Star. Respond, Red Crown."

*"This is Red Crown. Go ahead, Red Star."*

"One of our engines caught fire and the transport was damaged when we landed. I need another transport flown here at once with a team of aircraft mechanics and cutting torches to assist me."

*"What about the cargo?"* General Chin's voice suddenly came over the speaker.

"Cargo intact," Kaine assured him. "If we can cut the bay door off there will still be plenty of time to complete the transfer."

*"Very well, I'll send it at once. Report back when the transfer is complete."*

Kaine turned off the radio. He was a man accustomed to overcoming obstacles and he wouldn't waste time worrying about any mistakes. Stepping into the cargo area, his eyes slowly adjusted to the shadowy glow from the red emergency lights.

His large hands placed on his hips, he surveyed the interior damage. The thirty-foot-long wooden boxes lining the floor of the jet had been tossed about in their restraints. Looking to the rear of the jet, Kaine noticed the forklift had broken free of its tie-downs and had crashed into the cargo bay door. It too was damaged beyond repair.

"You men . . . secure those crates," Kaine shouted. "And be careful."

Several armed men scurried around to the wooden boxes and began slowly restacking them.

"I have found three fuel leaks. My men are patching them now," the pilot said, coming to stand next to the colonel. "We are very lucky."

"We are not very lucky," Kaine fired back angrily. "We need to get those crates off this aircraft. Have you tried the bay door again?"

"The door is jammed. If I try it again I could cause a short. With all that fuel leaking this entire jet could explode."

"Then I suggest you have some men cover the spilled fuel with dirt. A team of engineers will be here to assist us shortly." The pilot didn't realize just how big an explosion it would be with the plutonium fuel rods on board.

Exiting the aircraft, Kaine spotted a man already using a hand shovel in an effort to dig the jet's nose gear from the rocky runway.

"You, come here." Kaine's stout body stood stiff while he waited, but the soldier only stopped to look up. He wasn't sure the colonel was speaking to him.

"Yes, that's right. I'm talking to you, soldier," Kaine shouted.

The man jogged over to stand at attention in front of the colonel. Their statures were similar, and looking into the man's eyes Kaine could see they were rock solid, evidencing a great degree of confidence.

"Your name and rank."

"Jae Hyun. First Sergeant, sir."

"Can you be trusted, Sergeant Hyun?" Kaine asked, knowing that every man on the jet could be trusted—otherwise they would not have been selected for the mission.

"Yes sir, I can."

"Get your equipment. You will come with me."

"Yes, sir."

Kaine covered his nose as he moved away from the jet. The cold wailing wind was a blessing. It would help dissipate the fuel's fumes.

"Our mission is to find a dead man," Kaine said once the soldier had rejoined him in the darkness.

"A dead man, sir?"

"You will help me find Gen. Han Sinchon."

"General Sinchon, sir? *The* General Sinchon?"

"Yes . . . *the* General Sinchon."

In the distance the soldier saw for the first time the wreckage of a ship burning in the harbor.

NGHIA BINH PROVINCE, VIETNAM

*"Rock'n' Roll! Rock'n' Roll!"* Michael Callahan shouted at the top of his lungs above the enemy fire. Crawling as fast as he could, the CWO made it to the edge of a fallen tree thirty feet away. With his rifle cradled in his arms he leaped over it, hitting soft wet earth. He slithered up to the nearest tree and peered over it, using the dried branches as cover.

Swiveling around, he caught sight of his men lying on the ground, their faces down. They were pinned down by the gunfire. Bullets were impacting the ground all around them. Callahan scanned the area to determine which direction the tracer rounds were coming from. As soon as he concentrated his fire on one area the rounds changed origins. Callahan knew his team wasn't going to last long if they didn't move out immediately.

Glancing back at his men in their shallow depression, a wave of panic overwhelmed him. A few well-placed grenades could kill his squad in a split second.

Callahan watched as tracer rounds continued to explode out of the tree line. He counted six maybe seven areas of concentrated fire. Checking his CAR-15 assault rifle, he made sure it had a full thirty-round magazine.

"Gather upon my mark," Callahan shouted to his team. "Respond."

"Pope."

"Barnes."

"Ingram."

He allowed himself a sigh of relief knowing his men were alright. No one had been killed.

"On three. One . . . two . . ." the chief warrant officer called out, shouldering his weapon.

*"Three."* Callahan began pumping the trigger. The force of the fifty-five-grain bullets blasting from the muzzle caused the short-barreled assault rifle to climb up. Fire leaped from the flash suppressor. Callahan's massive arms kept the weapon steady and pointed toward the enemy positions along the dark tree line.

The enemy fire stopped abruptly. Callahan continued to spray the area, watching his men run toward him, jumping headfirst behind the log next to him. Then the jungle fell silent. All Michael could hear was the beating of his heart.

"Pope . . . get Cheerleader on the horn. Ingram, pump some grenades into that tree line."

"Give me a six-hundred-mile aerial view," Captain Bliss ordered from his chair. "I want any aircraft approaching within one hundred miles of Langau tagged as hostile unless it's displaying a friendly IFF or comair code."

"Aye, captain," Owens said tapping on her computer keyboard.

Bliss watched the main display screen change. Outlined in yellow he could see the eastern coast of China and the Shantung Peninsula. The Korean Peninsula was displayed on the right side. Flashing yellow triangles pinpointed the location of three large surface ships one hundred and fifteen miles southeast of *Observation Island.*

"Anything else moving out there?" Bliss asked.

"No sir . . . just our shadow the trawler."

"Sir I'm picking up one . . . no, make that two airborne targets just off the Korean coastline," another radar officer reported. "Heading zero fiver three. Range two hundred ten miles, altitude 4,000 feet and climbing. They're staying close to the North Korean coast.''

"Keep an eye on them," Bliss commanded, rubbing the bridge of his nose. Two hours of sleep wasn't cutting it.

Slumping back in his chair, Bliss reviewed his handwritten notes on the yellow pad next to him. As always his conversation with Chaniff had been short and to the point. He didn't like his orders but he knew there wasn't much he could do about them. He was to sit back and wait. Chaniff had also instructed him not to get any closer than 100 miles to Langau Island. At least he'd agreed to have the destroyer *Paul Hamilton* steam toward his position. *A little added firepower never hurt anyone,* Bliss thought, glad to have some type of reenforcement on the way.

Bliss's watch beeped. Looking down at the time he noticed the date. It was his anniversary. Twenty-five years ago today he was married in Las Vegas. He allowed himself the luxury of thinking about his wife for a moment and hoped she was thinking of him at this very moment, too. The older he grew the more he thought about being at home with her. *Maybe it's time for the iron duck to dock and try dry land for a while,* he speculated.

"Captain, the *Paul Hamilton* just radioed. They're six hours south and heading this way," the communications specialist called out, interrupting his thoughts.

"Owens, it's time you get some rest," Bliss said, seeing her weary face. "You're relieved for six hours."

CPO Janis Owens was on her way out when she hesitated at the captain's chair. "Sir, I'd like to be here when General James radios again."

Bliss could see the seriousness of the woman's expression and couldn't help but feel proud that she was part of his crew.

"Very well. But first get an hour or two of sleep then get down to the galley and have them fix you some ham and eggs for breakfast. And tell'em I said they'd better not use any of those fake egg-beater things, either.''

"Yes, sir. No egg beaters," Owens repeated, smiling broadly as she turned, leaving the CIC.

"Cheerleader . . . this is Tango. Do you read, Cheerleader?'' Steve Pope spoke into the mike.

The SATCOM radio only hissed in response.

"Cheerleader . . . this is Tango. Come in, Cheerleader," Pope radioed fervently again. "Someone answer me . . . we're getting our asses shot off out here!''

"Tell'em we need an extract now!'' Callahan shouted, firing over the log.

"Nothing . . . I'm not getting a thing." Pope's voice was high-pitched and strained as he held the mike out, frustrated.

Keeping his head down, Callahan twisted around, surveying the area behind them. The cloudy image of a rocky hill appeared about fifty yards away. It was to the right of a broken column of trees with long grass and knee-high weeds covering the ground. If his team could reach the back side of the hill they would be clear of the area. At the very least they could regroup and come up with a plan to make it back to the LZ. He turned his attention back to the front. "Ingram, get boomer ready."

"She's ready and willing," Sergeant Ingram responded. Attached to the bottom of his rifle was an M203 grenade launcher. The short black tube could thrust a grenade over 400 yards.

"Put one there," Callahan pointed in the direction of the most intensive fire, "at about one hundred yards."

"You got it." Ingram placed his M16 solidly to his shoulder. Then, pointing the rifle at a thirty-degree angle to the ground, he figured the range.

Callahan watched him close one eye and tighten his grip. He braced his NVGs as the sergeant squeezed off the grenade. It arced through the air and exploded into the ground a little short of where Callahan had intended.

"Two more," Callahan shouted to the sergeant as return fire blasted noisily. "One left, one right."

Ingram reloaded as fast as possible, this time sending the fist-sized projectiles to the left and right of the first.

Callahan watched the tree line blow up into balls of boiling fire. Screeching birds shot up into the air as the shrapnel splintered branches from the trees. After a chaotic moment the jungle once again fell silent, with only the sounds of popping and hissing from the fires being heard.

"No response from Cheerleader," Pope whispered, looking to Callahan for suggestions.

"Pack it up. We're going to blow this fruit stand." The CWO turned to Ingram again: "You have to lead the team out of here. Go straight back toward that hill over there . . . I'll cover you. Wait for me on the other side."

"Got it." The sergeant faced the other two men: "I'm point on this one, you guys follow me."

Callahan rolled onto his side, dropping an empty magazine from his weapon and replacing it with a loaded one. Raising the weapon, he fired several bursts into the quiet darkness to keep the enemy occupied.

"We're outta here," Ingram called once the firing had begun.

Callahan didn't take time to look back at his team moving away to the northeast, following a string of dense trees.

THE PENTAGON

"Try it one more time," General Chaniff demanded urgently.

"Tango . . . this is Cheerleader. Come in, Tango," Lt. Frank Fontano, a dark-haired New Yorker, radioed from his console.

The split monitor showed the outline of central Vietnam and a fifty-mile perimeter around Langau Island. *Nothing like having two operations getting screwed up at the same time,* Chaniff thought.

"No response, sir."

"Damn it!"

"I only had the signal for a couple of seconds before it faded," Fontano said, manipulating his equipment to regain contact.

The Special Operations Center had become hushed with all heads turned to Chaniff and Fontano.

"Where were they broadcasting from?" Chaniff asked.

"Just a second . . ." Fontana's voice trailed as his computer flashed a new set of numbers. "The primary target area. It looks like they were right on top of it."

"I'm on my way to the White House. Phone me there if you reestablish contact," Chaniff ordered, already halfway across the room.

"Yes, sir," Fontano said, letting out a long breath.

Michael Callahan hugged the ground as several bullets whisked over his head and ripped into the trees behind him. Others impacted the log he was lying behind, showering the CWO with wood splinters and bark.

"Come on out where I can see you, chickenshits!" Callahan shouted, firing in the direction of the shots.

Glancing back he saw his team fading into the cover of the dense jungle. It was time for him to clear the area.

Once they regrouped and reloaded their weapons Callahan would try to find an open spot to contact Cheerleader. Then he would make the decision either to retreat or try and outflank the bad guys. Foremost on his mind was getting his team out alive, but running out of ammo in a prolonged firefight was also an immediate concern. His team wasn't equipped for a long battle and he knew things would get worse if the enemy called in reenforcements.

Snapping another fresh magazine into his weapon, the CWO crawled up on his knees. He pivoted on his feet, turned and began running to rejoin his men.

THE WHITE HOUSE

Allan Manning sat alone in his darkened west wing office. A single brass desk light cast just enough light for him to see the paperwork scattered about. Piled to his left and right were file folders containing CIA and State Department briefing papers outlining each agency's concerns on the Democratic People's Republic of Korea's current leadership. Manning had spent the last few hours reading several of the files, and the stone-cold reality of being the president's national security advisor was beginning to sink in. There wasn't any question as to the threat North Korea posed to peace in that region of the world. North Korea was becoming more and more unstable. Its economy was geared for war. The leadership thrived on obtaining high-tech weapons and trading arms with Iran but couldn't feed its people. The power shift from Kim Il Song to his son Kim Jong Il and now to General Chief of Staff Myong Chin and President Kim Pyong Il had made their military more powerful and paranoid than ever before. The CIA believed the DPRK processed enough plutonium to produce a half-dozen dirty nuclear bombs—bombs that were low-tech but nuclear weapons nonetheless. With help from Iran it was only a matter of time before Chief of Staff Chin could threaten Seoul or Tokyo with nuclear blackmail. Manning was now convinced that if things didn't change, and change soon, there would be war on the Korean peninsula.

Manning stroked his forehead before relighting his pipe. The meeting with Sinchon gave the United States its first real opportunity since the Korean War to remove the communist threat with little or no bloodshed. *It's just too bad Duke James has to be involved,* Manning thought. *Because there isn't any way I'm going to let this mission succeed as long as his name's on it.*

"Mr. Manning, may I speak with you, please?" a tall naval officer said, walking into Manning's office. The man was holding a piece of white fax paper.

"It had better be important. The president and I are leaving for Europe in a few hours and I don't have time to waste," Manning said, glancing up. He was packing his briefcase.

"It's about General James, sir. Captain Bliss onboard the *Observation Island* is reporting a radio transmission. Their mission has been compromised."

"Really? Is James dead?" Manning feigned concern as his heart jumped at the possibility.

"No, sir. General James is the one who made the contact. There are also two other survivors."

*That stupid James. Can't he do anything right?* Manning sighed, putting his briefcase on the floor next to his desk. "I assume Chaniff knows about this?"

"Yes, sir. He's on his way over from the Pentagon right now. He's instructed Captain Bliss to hold tight until he can talk with you and the president."

"Fine. I'll give this to the president and let him know." Manning took the paper from the officer and indicated that he was dismissed.

*Great . . . just fucking great.* The chief of staff sank discouraged into his leather chair. *Why couldn't they have waited until I was gone?* He was looking forward to climbing onboard Air Force One and flying to Brussels with the president for a few days. It would do him some good to get away from Washington and his malicious ex-wife, not to mention the idiots he had to deal with at the White House. Most of all, though, he had been looking forward to dining on Air Force One and hobnobbing with members of the press. It made him feel important.

*Well, shit! Now I get left behind to oversee this damn mess while the president is out farting around with a bunch of dignitaries.* Allan slammed his fist on the top of his desk. Thinking about his bad luck, it suddenly occurred to him this was what he had wanted in the first place. The president would be out of the country and he would be in charge. Everyone would have to go through him. Sitting upright, Manning quickly jotted down a few notes before heading to the Oval Office to inform the president.


Sergeant Ingram looked right and left as he approached the base of the hill. The popping sound of gunfire had faded behind them. Callahan was right. This would be the ideal place to recover.

Hunched over, Ingram kept his M16 pointed directly out in front of him. Running in short bursts, he ducked behind the next available cover. As he ran to a cluster of bushes and flat-leafed plants, he didn't notice the drops of sweat and rain dotting his greasepainted face.

Ingram paused. All they had to do was cross a small opening before they reached the safety of the hill on the other side. He tried to ignore the stinging sensation of his tired and irritated eyes blinking hard under his NVGs. Inspecting the ground, he searched for footprints and others signs of intrusion made by humans. He didn't see the broken branch next to him. The sergeant raised his right hand, signaling the other members of the squad to follow his lead.

*   *   *

Michael Callahan heard another volley of gunfire and hit the ground flat. His team was only twenty yards ahead of him. Lifting his head, he looked behind him to get a fix on the gun site. It took only a second to realize the shots were coming from in front of him, not behind.

The unique sound of large projectiles cutting through the night air hit his ears. This wasn't a chance meeting with another Vietnamese patrol, the enemy had been waiting for them.

Turning back, he saw the heavy cannon rounds pounding the ground. Mud and rocks were shooting up into the air from the force of the rapid shots. *Fuck!* They had been herded into a classic ambush, boxed in on both sides by heavy brush and steep terrain with concentrated fire raining down onto their position. There was no way out. The enemy had both ends sealed off.

Straining to see through his NVGs, Callahan spotted Ingram caught out in the open trying to make his way to a large tree. Callahan picked up the heavy gun's position fifty yards away. He saw Barnes jump up, holding his M16 at his waist, his mouth open wide yelling, "Go, go, go!"

Callahan immediately shouted a warning but Barnes was already up and firing three-round bursts. The green image of Ingram's head exploded as a volley of 30-millimeter cannon rounds sliced through his position. The man's body fell limp, crashing on the jungle floor. Callahan dropped his head, the sight taking the breath out of him.

"Callahan! Get your ass over here!" Pope's voice screamed for support. Instinctively the chief warrant officer picked himself up on his elbows and with his knees going out to the side, crawled wildly toward his men.

Approaching them, he could see Barnes was on his back. The medical specialist's mouth was distorted, his teeth clenched in pain. Callahan looked down and saw his leg had been severed below the knee by the cannon. A pool of thick blood was forming as Barnes's heart pumped the red liquid from the stump.

"Barnes is all fucked up, man, and Ingram . . . they got Ingram," Pope cried out to Callahan. "What's going on here? I think they knew we were coming!"

"Shut up, Pope!" Callahan shouted, crawling closer to Barnes. He peeled off his NVGs. In the starlight he could see the man's face had hardened with pain. His eyes were glazed over and his body had begun to tremble. He was going into shock.

"Hold on, buddy. We're going to get you out of here," Callahan said, trying to calm him while tying a tourniquet around his thigh.

"I can't believe it, man . . . we've been had, Callahan," Barnes coughed in short breaths, grasping Callahan's wrist. "Get those assholes for . . ."

Barnes didn't finish the sentence. Callahan saw his eyes go dull, then roll back in his head.

"Don't worry, Barnes, I'll get 'em for you." Callahan reached inside Barnes's uniform, grabbed his dog tags and stuffed them in his pocket.

Mark Collins sipped lukewarm coffee while scanning the computer screen. Shuffling the computer mouse on the pad, he clicked on different icons, searching the latest Lacrosse data available over North Korea and the Yellow Sea.

This was the part of his job he liked least. Collins called it "fishing." He knew what he was looking for, he just hadn't found it yet.

The interior mountains and vast number of secluded roads in North Korea made it difficult to track anything on radar for any length of time, particularly from space.

Collins tried to put himself in a North Korean intelligence officer's place. *Would I ship an important cargo by air or by ship? And who would be my customer? Probably a country looking to build a bomb. A country that had the money and I considered to be somewhat friendly. Well, Iran fits that scenario and their freighter isn't in Nampo harbor where it usually is.*

Clicking the mouse, Mark zoomed in on the port city of Nampo. He would start at the northern section of the harbor and work his way south.

"What was Ingram's position?" Michael asked, rolling over next to his communications specialist.

"I don't know. It's over there somewhere," Pope answered, pointing, his eyes wide.

"Look, it's just you and me. If we're going to get out of here alive we've got to work together. It'll be just like training back at Bragg." Michael's voice was calm and stern.

"I'm all right, man," Pope lied nervously. "Just tell me what to do and I'll do it."

"Help me find Ingram's rifle. We need that grenade launcher."

The two men slowly raised their heads above the narrow rock outcropping. They both tried to remember where Ingram was standing before he got hit.

Callahan's camouflaged uniform was soaking wet, covered with mud and rotting vegetation. To the left was a thick row of plants and bushes obstructing their view. The right side was an opening which allowed the large cannon that had them pinned down a clean line of fire.

"I see it. It's about ten feet from his body . . . to the right," Pope said suddenly.

Callahan strained to see the weapon. He could see Ingram's dark forearm half hidden in the grass. Starting there he estimated ten feet away.

"Okay . . . I've got it." The dark image appeared in his NVGs.

Without warning another volley of cannon fire shredded the ground in front of them. Large pieces of mud and chunks of rock showered down on them. Callahan listened to the chainsaw-like sound of the 30-millimeter cannon cutting through the jungle. There weren't any tracer rounds and peering up he spotted the white muzzle flash of the gun firing. He guessed the gun emplacement to be just inside a slight V-shaped indentation of large trees and memorized the location in his mind.

"Get down." Callahan dropped his head, instructing Pope to do the same. "Make them think we're dead."

They lay motionless, not returning fire, waiting. After a minute or so the jungle fell silent. Faint shouts of Vietnamese voices echoed down from the trees.

"This is bullshit," Pope whispered. "If we stay here we're dead meat."

"How fast can you run the fifty?" Callahan asked, devising a plan.

"With someone shooting at me . . . in three seconds," Pope replied, still not moving.

"Okay . . . they think we're dead or they'd still be shooting," Callahan said softly. "We'll have a few seconds of surprise before they figure it out."

"A few *seconds?*"

"I'm going for the launcher and grenades," Callahan said, ignoring Pope. "I'm going to need a diversion. Can you handle that?"

"Yeah, I ain't no wuss, man."

"When I get the launcher and fire the first round you keep firing your weapon and run directly for the far tree line."

"And what about you?" Pope asked, suddenly not wanting to be left alone—or the last to die.

"I'm going to blast those sonsabitches to hell and back," Callahan grinned, then rolled over on his belly. "Ready?"

"Yeah," Pope said, shaking his head, feeling psyched.

Callahan crept like a cat twenty yards away. Pope readied his M16.

The barrel of Ingram's M16 was within Callahan's grasp. Moving a few more feet he eased his left arm out, reaching for the gun. He inched it toward him with his fingers, then, having a firm hold, pulled it to his chest. It was still warm. Not wanting to look at Ingram's splattered head he rolled up to his lower body, thinking to use it as cover. The Vietnamese voice stopped.

*Oh, Jesus, don't fail me now,* Callahan thought, not moving. He held his breath.

In the last few minutes a light fog had formed and was hanging above the ground. *No wonder they aren't firing,* Pope thought. *This fog is degrading their night-vision equipment. They can't see us anymore.*

Pope caressed the trigger of the M16 cradled in his arms. *Come on, Callahan, I'm ready to get the hell out of here.*

The eerie silence was interrupted by the voices again. Keeping his head down, Callahan ripped four grenades off Ingram's ammo belt.

Holding the grenades in his cupped hands, he loaded the weapon silently. He signaled to Pope he was ready.

When Pope started firing his weapon Callahan came up on one knee, shouldering the grenade launcher. He picked out the V in the tree line and aimed directly for it. *This one's for Ingram and Barnes you prick gook bastards.* He pulled the trigger. A flash of fire told him the projectile was on the way. He watched a stream of yellow sparks arcing up then down toward the area. The big cannon began to fire before the grenade impacted.

"Now, Pope . . . run!" Callahan shouted, shoving another grenade into the breach. Slamming the launcher closed he fired a second round into the trees. The sharp sounds of Pope's rifle firing moved away in the distance.

In a flash of white and red fire the second grenade struck home. Callahan leapt to his feet, running as fast as he could toward the tree line.

# 24

Howard Chaniff entered the Oval Office, closing the door behind him. Seated on each side of a green and gold plaid couch in the middle of the room were President McEntire and Allan Manning. The two men faced each other with several faxes in the middle of their laps. On the table were the scattered remnants of a hasty breakfast.

The chairman of the Joint Chiefs cleared his throat and moved between the two men, taking a seat in an armchair across from them.

"Sounds like we have a problem," the president said, looking up.

"Yes, sir, we do." Chaniff opened his briefcase and removed an inch-thick notebook. Four white stars in a neat row were on the leather cover.

"I've read the faxes from the Pentagon. Is there anything new to report on James' situation?" McEntire asked worriedly.

"No, sir," Chaniff replied. "It appears the North Koreans are reenforcing the island with ground troops. James' only hope of surviving is playing hide and seek until we can mount a rescue."

"Why would the North Koreans be landing planes and men on the island?" Manning questioned.

"I don't know." Chaniff took a guess: "It could be they want to be sure General Sinchon was killed in the attack, or possibly they want to retrieve something before it gets into our hands."

"I recommend we go to the Chinese. Hell, it's their island too. Besides, they're the ones that came to us with the message from General Sinchon," Manning suggested.

"What do you think, Chaniff? Should we go to the Chinese and lay the cards on the table?" McEntire asked.

"This is what concerns me about that type of approach. If we spill our guts and ask the Chinese for permission to land a military team on the island they will *have* to say no. Armed American troops on their soil isn't going to cut it with the hard-line communist leaders. Of course, they'll also have to deny any knowledge of the coup and will have to openly support the North." Chaniff shook his head. "It's a no-win for us."

"How the hell did they find out?" Manning asked. "That's what I'd like to know."

"Well it wasn't Bill Bishop, now, was it?" President McEntire said out of the corner of his mouth. "So, what can we do?"

"There's not much else." Manning said resignedly, ignoring the sarcasm. "James knew the danger when he took this assignment. Maybe he should surrender and we could work it out diplomatically afterward."

"What are you saying?" Chaniff couldn't believe his ears. "We should leave James . . . and the other two survivors on the island?"

"Yes, that's what I'm saying. They're all military people and these are the consequences of their jobs." Manning paused, not wanting to appear too eager to get rid of Duke. "What I'm saying is the situation is too hot. We need to wait a few days for everything to cool down. North Korea and China are already involved. If we react too fast it could suck in the South Koreans and maybe Japan, too. Are you willing to risk a second Korean War over a few people? I don't think so."

"Those military people are paying the consequences of a job we sent them to do. In my book that makes us responsible for their lives, Mr. Manning. I want James and the others off that island as soon as possible." Chaniff turned to look at McEntire. "Mr. President, the decision is yours."

McEntire stood and moved to his desk. "I may not have the right answers all the time. But I don't think it would sit too well in my conscience if we didn't at least try to rescue General James. I can't allow the military to believe we won't support them when they're out there doing their duty. I want James and the two other survivors brought back to US soil." He sat down. "General Chaniff, you've been my chairman of the Joint Chiefs for four years now. I know you didn't just walk in here without a plan."

"No, sir," Chaniff answered. "I have everything right here."

The president checked his watch. "I'm scheduled to leave for Europe in six hours. So start talking."

"It's going to take some planning but we can do this in less than eighteen hours. First let me give you some background to the assets already in the theater . . ."


LANGAU ISLAND


Colonel Kaine stood staring at the burned-out hull of the once mighty *Van Triumph* yacht. Most of her sleek white paint had melted or was covered with black soot. The front section of the bow had broken off and lay half submerged in the black water. Columns of black smoke curled into the air from the smoldering fires. A small oil slick kept flames licking upward.

Kaine turned his attention to Sgt. Jae Hyun, who placed a weathered two-by-twelve-inch piece of lumber across the water connecting the dock with what was left of the bridge. Walking across the makeshift gangplank, Kaine stepped onto the distorted remains of the ship's control center. The hot smoldering fiberglass and aluminum warmed the night air around him.

The weather cover for the bridge was floating upside down in the bay. Control panels once lining the room were no longer recognizable. The computers, radar and weather monitoring equipment were nothing more than piles of melted plastic and wiring. Fine leather seats had been incinerated, producing a sharp smell.

Kaine walked to the edge of the bridge. Moving his flashlight's beam across what remained of the bow, any doubt he'd had about survivors vanished. The back section was cracked in many places and smoke curled out of two large irregular cavities. Whoever had been below deck had either burned to death or perished from the thick smoke and intense heat.

Turning away he began to inspect the rest of the ship's upper section. The small swimming pool, located twenty feet behind the bridge, had been shattered and was dry. Directly in front of Kaine was a sitting area with a demolished bar and unoccupied lounge chairs.

Moving his flashlight beam near the floor the colonel froze. Curled in the corner was the blackened body of a man. The sight made Kaine's stomach turn slightly.

"Sergeant Hyun," Kaine called to the man checking a burnt body lying across the room. "There is another body here."

"Yes, sir. That man could not be General Sinchon," Hyun stated, attempting not to breath in the acrid odor.

Kaine shook his head focusing his flashlight beam on the dead man in front of him. "Search this body."

"Yes, sir." The first sergeant knelt down and began probing the body with his fingers.

Kaine looked to the east. The Iranian freighter still hadn't made port. He stood for a moment trying to keep his anger in check. His entire mission was beginning to come undone.

NGHIA BINH PROVINCE, VIETNAM

The shallow craters were side by side. Most of the vegetation in a ten-foot circle had been shredded and scattered everywhere. Branches dangled from nearby trees and large pieces of splintered wood littered the ground.

Michael Callahan thrust his CAR-15 right and left, searching for any movement. Every sense in his body was tuned to maximum. He listened for the slightest bit of motion or sound, ready to answer with a hail of bullets from his weapon.

The gray light of the ground fog cast long shadows over the sniper's mutilated body. Callahan stood between the two craters then crouched down trying to find a spot that looked man-made. Looking up, he saw tattered camouflage netting hanging from a broken branch. Glancing directly beneath it he saw an army boot and canteen.

Then his eyes rested near the center of the closest crater. Lying on the ground, the barrel bent and covered with dirt, was a black 30-millimeter cannon. A distorted tripod lay next to it. Knowing he had destroyed the weapon that killed Ingram and Barnes gave him a morbid satisfaction.

Swiveling on the balls of his feet he saw that the ground was covered with brass casings and unspent ammo belts. Callahan scanned the area, wondering what happened to Pope.

"Oh . . . Oh . . ." Callahan's body snapped around in the direction of the moan, ready to fire.

"Oh . . ." the moan sounded again.

Creeping to the general area, following the voice, Callahan examined every inch of ground around him. Suddenly ten feet away, lying sprawled in the dirt, was the outline of a man's body. The CWO edged closer, keeping his rifle pointed at the man's head.

At last Callahan stood studying the Vietnamese soldier before him. The man was dressed in jungle green and black tiger-stripe camouflage. It was clear, with his arms and legs twisted in odd positions, that the soldier wasn't going to make any sudden moves. Half his head was covered in blood and his dark black eyes stared up at Michael.

The man's suffering was evident but Callahan couldn't control the vengeful emotion surging through him.

"Oh . . ." The soldier's mouth was moving but only the moaning emerged from his throat.

"I ought to kill you," Callahan mumbled out loud. He raised his rifle and pointed it at the soldier's head. The man looked at Callahan, his expression staying the same.

Slowly the wounded Vietnamese attempted to raise his right arm. It plopped to the ground. Grimacing, he tried it again, pointing a broken finger to his pocket, mouthing faint slurred words.

"You want something in there?" Callahan asked, lowering his weapon. He squatted down next to the soldier, taking notice of the leather pouch strapped around his waist. With his fingertips he felt the outside to be certain it wasn't a trick. Then after feeling under the flap for any wires to a booby trap he reached in and removed a pack of Marlboro cigarettes.

"You want one of these?" Callahan asked, shaking one out of the package.

The man barely nodded his head. Pulling out a cigarette, the American placed it in his mouth then found the lighter in the pouch. He lit the end and watched him puff and cough a few times.

"Let's see what else you have." The CWO searched the other pockets on the man's chest. He thought the man's eyes flickered when he reached the right breast pocket, but wasn't sure if it wasn't just from smoke. Callahan pulled out the contents.

A water-stained black-and-white picture with a lot of people huddled together was the first thing he looked at. *Probably his family,* Callahan thought. Next he flipped through six or seven documents. The paper had been treated with a wax to keep them dry in the wet jungle.

Studying them more closely, Callahan's jaw tightened and his mouth went dry. He couldn't read the Vietnamese writing, but looking at a roughed-out drawing of the valley, he didn't need to. An X marked the spot of the downed aircraft and scribble marks indicated the tree lines. Round circles disclosed the areas where the two sniper nests had been set up. Running up through the center of the paper was a dotted line. It was the path *his* team had taken to the crash site. Callahan looked at the next page. The location of the LZ was marked, along with another dotted line marking their path from the crash site.

They had been sold out. *Some motherfucker is going to pay for this shit.* Callahan was resolved to make it out of the jungle alive. The ambush wasn't just a precaution on the part of the Vietnamese—it was set up by someone in the States.

"You bastards were waiting for us, weren't you?" Callahan grabbed the soldier's collar. "You knew we were coming."

The half-smoked cigarette fell from the man's lips as his eyes glassed over and he stopped breathing.

Callahan let go of his collar when a snapping twig sent a renewed rush of energy through his veins. Staying low he raised his weapon in the direction of the sound.

## CIA HEADQUARTERS

The phone rang twice before Collins heard it. Without taking his eyes from the computer monitor he picked up the receiver.

"Collins here."

"Mark, I found them," A familiar voice filled the receiver.

"Jack, is that you?" Collins asked, surprised.

"Sure is," Jack Spinner at the NRO replied.

"Hey . . . I'm sorry to hear about your mother," Collins said, embarrassed at his earlier behavior. ''I thought you were going to be out a few days.''

''I was taking a couple of days, but it's kind of hard to just hang around the house after a while. I needed to get out and do something . . . but listen. I think I found your fuel rods.''

''Let me guess—Nampo harbor,'' Collins said, excited. ''I knew it. They're shipping them by freighter.''

''Nice try, but they're sending them by air. Pull up Il Song air base.''

Collins tapped his mouse, changing screens. ''What imagery digit?''

''Sixty-three B,'' Jack instructed, then continued: ''Now look right over the left runway at fifty-six hundred feet. It looks like an Il-76.''

Collins waited for the screen to flash. He centered the pulsing, cross-shaped cursor over the runway and tapped 5600 on his keyboard.

''Hold on, it's working.'' Collins waited for the software to cycle. On the bottom of the screen the outline of a fuzzy T-tailed transport aircraft came into view. The radar had hit the aircraft at an angle. He didn't care about the blurred image anyway; he was staring at several thin red strips resting inside.

''That's it!'' Collins shouted. ''Thanks, Jack. I would have been here forever searching for that plutonium.''

''No problem. Now you just have to figure out where they're taking them,'' Jack said modestly. ''Talk to you later.''

''Thanks again,'' Collins said, hanging up the phone. ''That's the million-dollar question all right . . . where the hell are they going?''

''Hey, it's me,'' Pope said mockingly, holding up his hands. ''I'm one of the good guys.''

Callahan let out a controlled breath and took his finger off the trigger. ''You scared the dog shit out of me, Pope.''

''Well, you don't see me jumping for joy either,'' Pope limped closer to his commander.

''Are you all right?'' Callahan looked down at Pope's leg. A grazing 30-millimeter-wound was just above his kneecap and was wrapped with gauze. The dark, rich blood was soaking through.

''I'm okay. The assholes got a lucky shot,'' Pope smiled. Then he spotted the dead soldier behind Callahan ''Your plan worked, man . . . we nailed these suckers!''

''Let's get moving. We need to find a clearing and contact Cheerleader. Our LZ's been compromised.''

''Shit, man, don't nothin' go right in this man's army,'' Pope complained, falling in behind Callahan.

The chief warrant officer grinned to himself, glad to hear Pope sounding like himself again. Then he grew serious once more as he took point out of the area.

## THE OVAL OFFICE

"So you think you can pull this off without having to transfer any other equipment into the area?" President McEntire was leaning over his desk, listening intently to Howard Chaniff.

"Yes, sir, I do. Eight F-15Es from Elmendorf landed at Osan six hours ago. When you combine their firepower with the F-16s already stationed there, everything is in place."

"Okay . . . we have the men and the equipment. What's your plan?" Manning asked. A pencil poised over his yellow pad, he crossed his legs, prepared to take notes.

Chaniff took a small color map of the region from his notebook and covered the top of the desk with it. "In twelve hours it will be dark again on Langau Island. I will give the order for Duke and the others to make their way south toward the midsection of the island. There's a small cove surrounded by high rocks that should provide enough cover. We need to get them away from the airstrip and bay." Chaniff pointed out the areas on the map as he spoke of them. "At zero five hundred local time tomorrow morning, two Ranger teams will take off from Osan AFB aboard Air Force Special Operations MH-60G Pave Hawk choppers. The Pave Hawks will skim the water to avoid radar detection before landing on the cove, code-named Delta Point. Their mission will be to secure a quarter-mile area and to find James and the others. I don't expect the Rangers to be on the ground for longer than a half-hour."

"What if General Sinchon is one of the survivors?" Manning asked curiously.

"What if he is? I don't suspect James will leave him there to die. He'll probably let him tag along," Chaniff answered, glancing over at Manning. "An E-3C AWACS will patrol the skies in a tight orbit approximately here—" Chaniff pointed to the map—"which will be able to monitor any air traffic in the region out to about three hundred miles. An RC-135 electronic-surveillance jet will go in before the mission to intercept and record any radio traffic coming off the island. It will clear the area once the AWACS is in position. I've also ordered a naval destroyer into the area to counter any surface threats but I'm not too worried about that. The North Korean Navy is almost nonexistent. The entire mission should take less than two hours."

"Are you sure you have the right aircraft for this mission? What about the Navy's F-18s?" Manning challenged.

"Mr. Manning, those F-15 Eagles have enough power to set the sky on fire if the North is stupid enough to put anything into the air. That's why I'm calling this operation . . . Eagle Fire."

"What's your biggest concern," the president asked.

"That they make it another twenty-four hours on that island," the chief of staff answered, glancing over at Manning, who leaned forward to take a drink of his coffee.

On his notepad Manning had written the exact details of the mission as well as the aircraft involved. He had even sketched a map of the Korean peninsula and circled the flight path of the AWACS. Next to that was a rough diagram of Langau Island with the words DELTA POINT written in large letters.

"I have a few questions," Manning said after setting his cup back down.

"Fire away," Chaniff replied.

"Tell me again what this E-3C AWACS will do? It's a command and control aircraft, right?"

"That's right. An Airborne Warning and Control System," Chaniff said, thinking. *And this guy is the president's NSA.* "It's basically a converted Boeing 707 with an enclosed spherical radar located behind the wings. It has an all-weather, long-range, high-low radar with range in excess of two hundred miles. In other words, it's a flying command post, filled with technicians that tell our pilots where to fly and who to kill. Put simply, it's the quarterback of the air battle. With it we control the sky. Without it our pilots will be hard pressed to figure out what's going on around them."

"I see," Manning said, rubbing his chin.

"It will orbit at forty thousand feet, keeping watch on the entire area. Like I said, if the North Koreans send any aircraft to counter our Ranger team, the radar operators on board the E-3C will spot them and our fighters will be vectored to intercept."

"How will you know if an aircraft is hostile or not?" Manning asked, continuing to jot on his pad. "The last thing we need is one of your hot-shot pilots shooting down a civilian aircraft."

"We know the location of every North Korean air base, Mr. Manning. Hell, in most cases we can watch their aircraft taxi out of the hangars onto the runway. Plus the system uses an IFF system . . . Friend or Foe. Believe me, Mr. Manning, if an enemy fighter comes off the ground from one of those North Korean air bases, we'll know it. As far as civilian aircraft are concerned . . . well, there will be a few flights in the area but the airlines won't know what's going on and the AWACS will keep our fighters clear of them."

Chaniff studied Manning for a moment, watching him write something before speaking again. "Anything else?"

"Yes." Manning referred to the map: "This AWACS . . . it can cover the entire country of North Korea?"

Chaniff pondered the question for a second. "Not the entire country. From where it will orbit the cities of Najin and Unggi will be out of its range." He pointed to the northernmost tip of North Korea.

"I see." Manning shook his head and sat back.

"There isn't any need to monitor that region. There aren't any air bases located that far north," Chaniff added casually.

"Well, I think that's enough information for me," President McEntire said at last. "General, I'm prepared to sign an executive order to authorize this mission."

"I agree," Manning echoed, folding his hands on top of his pad.

"Allan, you'll need to stay behind to monitor this while I'm in Europe," McEntire said, then stood to shake the chairman's hand. "Good work, Howard. You have my authorization to do whatever is reasonable to ensure the safety of all the American lives involved in the operation." He glanced at his watch and picked up his suit jacket from the back of his chair. "Air Force One takes off in four hours and I plan to be on it. See you when I get back, gentlemen."

Once the president exited the Oval Office, Manning stood to stare Chaniff in the eye. "I want you to keep me posted on everything that happens," he demanded. "And I mean everything."

Chaniff spoke coolly gathering his notes. "You'll be updated . . . as always, Mr. Manning."

Duke crouched next to the opening of the shelter. It had been three and a half hours since he had made contact with *Observation Island.* The faint hint of the sunlight on the eastern horizon told him morning was on the way. He turned his night-vision goggles off and ducked back into the warm shelter.

"What's going on out there?" Major Erwin's voice was filled with anxiety.

"It looks like they're preoccupied with trying to repair that transport jet," Duke answered, crawling next to the heater. "I wish we knew what they were up to."

"When it's light they will begin to search the area," General Sinchon, who had been silent until now, replied solemnly. "If they find our footprints they will track us down. It is best to keep moving."

"Where to?" Major Erwin asked, frustrated. "In case you haven't noticed we're on a rock in the middle of the ocean. There aren't a lot of places to run and hide.''

''He's right, major. I'm going to have to go back out and find someplace better than this.'' Duke looked at Erwin, imploring her to remain clear-headed. Puzzled by the aircraft, he said: ''If they just wanted to kill you, General, why didn't they land helicopters with ground troops? That aircraft out there looks like an Il-76 to me, a transport jet, and I didn't see anything resembling a search party climb out of it.''

''I wish I could give you an answer,'' Sinchon said simply. ''General Chief of Staff Myong Chin is the only man who could be responsible for this attack. And I know that if he had other plans as well, he would not have confided in me.''

''Of course not,'' James nodded, sighing. ''I'm going to scout around, Major. Maybe I can locate another place for us to hide. When I return we'll contact Guard Dog. You stay with the general.''

''Don't worry, I'm not going anywhere,'' Erwin replied, pursing her lips together.

''This will work,'' Steve Pope said, sitting down and looking east. Opening his pack, he pulled out the radio.

Callahan estimated they had traveled three miles north of the crash site. He had intentionally stayed on the rougher terrain knowing it would be harder to track. The ground was filled with slippery rocks and large-leafed plants dotted the landscape. Fast-moving streams rushing down the mountainside enabled them to move without worrying about making a little noise.

From his vantage point Callahan doubted they were being followed. Looking down, he could see a dirt road winding through the valley. No one was traveling on it. Callahan's senses went to the sky. It was still pitch black. If they couldn't get an extract before daylight they needed to locate a secluded hide-out until the next nightfall.

''We should have a clear line to the satellite this time,'' Pope said, drawing the chief warrant officer's attention.

''How's your leg?'' Callahan asked.

''I could use a doctor or a nurse.'' Pope removed his radio and snapped the stubby five-inch antenna into place. ''Female, of course. I'm not a male chauvinist . . . I believe in equal opportunity. I'll give every woman an equal opportunity with me at any time they want.''

Michael shook his head, wondering how Pope could be so goofy-headed.

''It's ready,'' Pope called out at last. Welcome words.

## THE PENTAGON

*"Cheerleader . . . Tango. Do you copy, Cheerleader?"*

"Roger you, Tango. This is Cheerleader. Where the hell are you guys?" Lt. Frank Fontano radioed, waving his hand to General Chaniff. "I have them, sir. I have Tango."

Chaniff quickly slipped on a headset.

*"We were ambushed at the primary. I've lost two men and have one wounded. Request immediate extract."*

"What's your location, Tango?" Fontano asked, ready to plot their position.

*"Approximately three miles north-northeast of the primary. We can't use the LZ, the area has been compromised and is hot. Request new extract."*

Chaniff touched Fontano on the shoulder, his expression bewildered. "Ambush? Find out what he's saying . . . they were waiting for them or they just cut the area off?"

"Tango, Cheerleader requests details of ambush and compromise." Fontano's dark eyes went back to his console, waiting for a reply.

*"Retrieved documents from dead Vietnamese. Maps with LZ, primary and path marked. We were boxed in on both sides. CIA is written all over it, Cheerleader. Somehow we got screwed."*

The CIA was always the first organization to be blamed when something went wrong. It wasn't always the case. At any rate, Chaniff was unsettled by the news. "Ask if they can sit tight until we can locate a safer extract. We need to make certain we're not sending another chopper into a hot zone. Tell them to radio back when they can."

"Tango . . . Cheerleader. Negative on immediate extract. Keep low and on the go. Radio when you're clear. Cheerleader out."

*"Roger, Cheerleader. We're on the go. Tango out."* The SATCOM transmission went dead.

"I hope they make it, sir."

"Yeah . . . me too," the general agreed. "Contact the *Nassau* and update them on the situation. Tell the captain to stand down until he hears from me."

"Yes, sir." Fontano said, changing radio frequencies.

Chaniff turned away calmly, his stomach rolling over. How did the Vietnamese know about their mission? The Harrier pilot reported not a single radar had tracked him going in or out. And what did Callahan mean by maps of their entire mission? Only a handful of top people knew Tango had been ordered in to retrieve evidence of chemical weapons. Chaniff started to run through his mind all the people who had been briefed about the mission. *There are generally two reasons information gets leaked: money or political motivation, or both. Two missions in one night compromised? That can't be a coincidence.*

Duke crawled along the ground, looking occasionally over his shoulder. He was about fifty feet from the eastern edge of the runway and close enough to the ocean to see the dark, boiling waves.

By now it was light enough that he could make out the soldiers milling around the damaged jet. It appeared they were taking a break. So far there was no sign of any foot patrols. When it got light, if the soldiers were still on the island, it would only take a little luck and skill for them to discover the shelter where he had left Major Erwin and General Sinchon.

Duke angled his way toward the coastline, then began ducking in and out from behind the large granite rocks. Ocean waves sprayed him as they crashed into the shore. The cold water kept him alert but with the added breeze his feet and hands were feeling swollen and numb.

Duke stopped, propping himself up next to a round boulder.

"What the hell?" he whispered, staring out into the bay, where what was left of the *Van Triumph* filled the innermost part. Sailing around the breakwater on the northern tip of the island was a large freighter. The ship made a wide turn before heading into the bay. Black diesel smoke billowed out of its dual smokestacks; tall masts, cables swinging from them, rose from the bow. The bridge was located in the rear of the ship leaving plenty of room for containers to be loaded in the midsection. It was clearly a cargo ship of some kind.

In the low moonlight Duke could make out a mixture of colors along the side of the ship. Its gray background was uneven, motley with rust and dull blue-black patches. The ship didn't appear to be in the best condition. He strained to see signs of its country of origin. Large black letters were printed on the bow. Duke focused his eyes out over the bay, barely making out the letters.

"*A . . . l . . . l . . . Allum . . . Allum Bacar,*" James read under his breath.

Things were starting to make more sense to Duke. First a transport lands, then a freighter comes into the harbor. *For being a deserted, worthless piece of rock this place sure manages to get its share of visitors.*

James stepped down toward the water. He needed to find a better place to hide. Somewhere along these rocks there had to be a cave or deep ravine.

"I found a fourth body," Sergeant Hyun said, walking up the ladder from the lower deck. "In the largest stateroom on the floor."

"Is it General Sinchon?" Kaine asked as they continued their search aboard the burned out yacht.

"No, sir, I don't believe so. The man was tall . . . about six feet . . ." The sergeant held up a gold medal. "He was burned badly like the others. All I could find was this."

Kaine took the medal out of the sergeant's dirty hand. Examining it the colonel knew the piece and the chain from which it hung were solid gold. Etched on the front of the medallion was a yacht—the *Van Triumph*. Turning to the back he saw the name Ghaith Bandar engraved with a date. Kaine shoved it into his pocket.

"There may be more bodies below deck. But there is no way I can get to them," Sergeant Lee said, wiping the sweat and ash from his face. "The passageways were incinerated and have collapsed. I will need help if you want me to go below."

Kaine thought for a minute. Only four bodies had been found and none of them had been Sinchon or American. It didn't make sense. They should have been on the upper section of the ship.

Kaine walked up the charred steps to the bridge. Sergeant Hyun followed. *Maybe Sinchon isn't dead. Could he have gotten off the ship before the attack?* He thought of the three heat signatures on Colonel Woong's video during the attack on the chopper.

"Colonel Kaine . . . a ship," Hyun called out when they were topside.

Kaine spun around to see the Iranian freighter coming into port.

Duke had crawled on his hands and knees the last twenty yards so he couldn't be seen.

"It's about time," Erwin almost shouted when he entered behind the rock.

"Shh . . . I found a cave about a hundred and fifty yards from here. It's small but it will be safer than here. Come on, let's get a move on it," Duke demanded, turning the heater off, preparing to stuff it into his duffle bag.

"We'd better check in first."

"Okay . . . get that radio warmed up," Duke said, checking his watch. They were twenty minutes late already.

## USS *Observation Island*

"Get the Captain. I have Beagle." Owens keyed her mike: "Copy you, Beagle. This is Guard Dog."

*"Guard Dog . . . confirm transport jet has landed. It is an Il-76. It was damaged in landing, believe they're trying to repair it."*

"Copy you, Beagle . . . confirmed aircraft is Il-76 Ilyushin," Owens repeated, writing it down.

*"We have more company, too. A freighter pulled into port."*

"Roger Beagle. A freighter." She added that information to the sheet. "North Korean?"

*"I don't think so. It's not flying a flag. The name on the ship is* Allum Bacar.*"*

*"Allum Bacar* . . . Middle Eastern?" Captain Bliss suggested, standing next to Owens. He had appeared quietly and read the notes on her pad. "Ask him if there are any other markings on the ship."

Owens repeated the question.

*"Negative, Guard Dog. Just the name."* The radio signal started to break up and fade.

Glancing at the captain, Owens shook her head. "Any instructions, sir?"

"Not yet, tell him to . . . hell, I don't know what to tell him." Looking up at the clock, Bliss saw it was now 6:30 A.M.

"Beagle, orders are for you to stay out of sight and check back in with discretion," Owens said at last.

*"Roger, Guard Dog. Beagle out."*

"Good thinking, Owens. Don't make it any tougher for them than it already is . . . you didn't make any promises we couldn't keep," Bliss said, his mouth set in a tight grin. "Now get a fax off to the Pentagon. Tell Chaniff about that freighter." He moved up to his chair. "Who the hell sent out invitations to this party."

# 25

Mark Collins followed Brooks into Chaniff's second-floor Pentagon office. The chairman of the Joint Chiefs' face said he didn't have time to waste.

Collins waited for the door to close before opening his briefcase.

"Thanks for seeing us on such short notice," Brooks said, starting the meeting.

"Make this fast, I'm juggling ten different things." Chaniff sat back, stretching out his legs and crossing his size elevens at the ankles. "I assume you've been briefed on General James' current situation?"

"Yes," Brooks answered. "I've got three of my best men working with the Air Force planners on threat scenarios for the rescue mission."

"Good," Chaniff replied, then looked at Collins. "Your recon mission into Vietnam was also botched."

"What?" Collins said in disbelief.

"As of the last report we've got two dead Green Berets and two stuck in the field."

Mark glanced over at Brooks. "Why didn't you tell me?"

"It just crossed my desk," Brooks turned to him calmly. "Look, kid, there's nothing you can do about it now."

A lump moved up Collins's throat. *It should have been a simple mission,* he thought. He had checked the area. There weren't any Vietnamese troops around the crash site. The LZ was only five miles away and it was a clear shot to the downed bird. Collins sighed and shook his head, trying to focus on his more immediate task.

Removing several enhanced Lacrosse satellite radar images, he handed them to Chaniff.

"Will someone please tell me what I'm looking at?" Chaniff said, turning the pictures in all directions. "I never could understand these damn things."

"We . . . I mean I—" Collins glanced at Brooks before turning back to the general—"believe the North Koreans are trying to smuggle plutonium fuel rods out of the country. We've suspected for quite a while they've been operating a secret reactor. What you're holding is the proof."

"This satellite data might mean something to you, Mr. Collins . . . but it means diddly to me," Chaniff exhaled hard, tossing the pictures on his desk. "Please explain to me in clear language, without any techno babble, what your proof is."

Collins spent the next few minutes explaining everything as he had to Brooks. Chaniff waited until Collins was completely finished before asking any questions.

"You say you're sure this is an Il-76 transport these rods are being loaded onto?" the general said.

"Yes, sir. Four engines . . . high T-tail . . . Soviet design. Look at the stubby nose. I've washed it through the computer twice. It's an Il-76 Ilyushin parked on runway thirty-two left, Kim Il Song air base," Collins repeated confidently, pointing to the outline of the jet. "I'm sorry I can't tell you where it went, though."

Chaniff leaned forward to study the picture, then looked back up. "How many bombs could they make out of this?"

"It's hard to say . . . depends on how it's processed."

"Take a guess."

"Five . . . maybe six. But the North doesn't have the facilities to process the fuel, General Chaniff. I'm not sure you understand what I'm saying . . ."

Brooks kicked Collins' foot under the desk. "I'm sure the general understands, Mark. He knows there are other countries who have the engineers with the technology and equipment to build the bombs."

"Mr. Collins, you can relax a little. I received a fax from the *Observation Island* that General James reported a transport landed on Langau Island—" Chaniff glanced at his watch—"four and a half hours ago. He confirmed it's an Ilyushin." The general paused, then referred back to the fax. "I need someone in your office to run a name through one of your electronic brains, one that knows about ships. We need to know what country the *Allum Bacar* is registered in." He jotted the name down and handed it to Collins.

Collins took the paper enthusiastically and grabbed the general's phone.


LANGAU ISLAND


Colonel Kaine stood at the edge of the dock as the Iranian freighter edged her way into port. The rust-stained ship floated, allowing the stiff wind to push her hull into position before slipping in behind the broken hull of the *Van Triumph*. Kaine watched her crew scurry around the deck before the heavy anchor smashed into the water.

The Iranian captain appeared on deck. He was wearing a dark blue overcoat and a white cap with the ASICS logo across the front. The captain stood on the bridge as his men hoisted a heavy wooden gangplank connecting the ship with the island. He shouted several orders, then made his way down the wooden plank.

"Colonel Kaine. I am Farajolla Rassai, the captain of *Allum Bacar,*" the man bowed his head, speaking in perfect Korean.

Kaine merely nodded at the man, studying his features. His face was cleanly shaven with a neatly trimmed mustache.

The tall Iranian smiled and placed his hands deep into his pockets. "I was ordered to pick up a cargo from you here."

"You are late."

"Allah controls the weather," Rassai said, looking up to the sky. "We are here now and I suggest we start loading the cargo . . . before the Americans arrive."

"There is a delay. The cargo cannot be transferred yet."

"Perhaps my men could—"

"No. You and your men stay aboard the freighter." Kaine answered curtly.

"Very well. My orders are to remain here until my country receives what it has purchased." The Iranian wasn't riled by the colonel's abruptness. He calmly turned around and headed back up the gangplank.

It was taking longer than he had planned. Every second they were out in the open increased the odds of being seen. Erwin was keeping up but General Sinchon couldn't move very fast. Cradling his broken arm to his chest, he stumbled along the rocky terrain behind them.

"We're almost there," Duke coaxed the older man. "Step on the rocks, not the dirt."

James led them up a shallow hill, staying low and using the shoreline as cover, rounding a sharp gap between two large rectangular rocks. Skirting the edge of a twenty-foot-high cliff, Duke slowed the pace, making sure everyone could make it safely. Occasional waves hit the rocks below, sprinkling them with salt water.

Duke waited for Sinchon and Erwin to catch up before stepping down into a five-foot-deep ravine. The cut in the rocks ran east and west about thirty feet back toward the end of the runway. The edges of it were clustered with broken stone and dead bushes. At the back of the shallow galley was a hole not more than four feet wide. Duke crawled up to the opening and stopped.

"After you," he said, placing a hand in front.

"Wow. I hope this place takes credit cards." Erwin made a face as she crawled into the hole.

## The White House

"Meet me at six o'clock tonight . . . Union Station's off the mall," Manning's voice cracked. "I want twice as much this time. This stuff is hot and I'm taking a big risk."

Hanging up his desk phone, the chief of staff checked his Rolex. He had an hour to kill before collecting fifty thousand more dollars. *Easy as pie. I should have done this years ago.*

Manning ripped the front cover off his notepad, checking it one more time. He wondered what other questions the North Korean government might want to know about Chaniff's Eagle Fire operation.

"Lindsey . . . get Chaniff on the line," Manning said, tapping the intercom button to his private secretary.

## The Pentagon

"Thanks, Maddie," Collins said, hanging up the phone. he turned back toward Brooks and Chaniff. "The *Allum Bacar* is an Iranian freighter. The last port we spotted her in was Libya."

"Libya?" Chaniff asked curiously.

"One of our agents in Tripoli photographed three T-72 main battle tanks and four Scud-B launchers being off-loaded along with several hundred tons of wheat and rice. That was eight months ago." Collins looked down at the notes he had taken while on the phone. "Iran uses that ship to carry sensitive military cargo. She looks like a death trap but it's all a ploy. She's fast and the captain and crew are top-notch. The computer file says she can steam at thirty-two knots in calm seas—and she's well armed with both heavy machine guns and hand-held surface-to-air missiles."

"The Iranians . . . Well, Mr. Collins, now you know where your plutonium fuel rods are going." Chaniff let a slight smile emerge on his face. "James also reported a freighter had pulled into port at Langau Island. It was the *Allum Bacar.*"

"Looks like Eagle Fire has another mission," Brooks said uneasily.

"Yes," Chaniff nodded. "When can you get me some satellite photos of Langau Island?"

"In a couple of hours we'll have a live shot," Collins answered, gathering the satellite photographs from the general's desk. "If that's the same transport, the fuel rods will show up easily."

"I'm going to give the order to move up the operation," Chaniff said to Brooks. "James can keep us informed of any changes."

The phone rang and the chairman picked it up. "Chaniff here."

"Howard . . . this is Allan Manning. What's the latest?"

"Mr. Manning, I'm finishing up a meeting with Collins and Brooks. I'll—"

"A meeting! Why wasn't I informed?"

"It wasn't a formal meeting, but they have come up with some information pertaining to the mission," Chaniff answered, tapping a pencil on his desk.

"The president left me in charge while he was away and I should have been informed immediately, General."

"Yes, I know that, Mr. Manning."

"Well . . . what's happened?" Manning seemed to calm down.

"The CIA is convinced the North Koreans are transferring plutonium fuel rods to an Iranian freighter at Langau Island. I'm moving up the mission by twelve hours," Chaniff answered, his face hot.

"By twelve hours? Can you be ready in time?"

"I believe so. You understand the urgency of the matter, now, don't you?" Chaniff's tone was disgusted. "We can't allow the transfer to take place."

"Of course I understand that, General. It's my job to insure the safety of this country, isn't it." Manning said brutally. "I want a full report from you in half an hour on any changes made to Eagle Fire."

The phone went dead.

Chaniff replaced the receiver. His face had turned a deeper red.

"What was that all about?" Brooks asked.

"I really don't know." Chaniff stood, all business. "If anything else comes up you can reach me in the Special Operations Center."

Collins let out a long breath. *The next twenty-four hours are going to be a bitch,* he thought.

"Look at this . . ." Sergeant Hyun pointed to the ground around the burned hull of the American chopper. "These are footprints. I count three, maybe four sets."

Kaine reached down to touch the dirt. "Can you tell who made them?"

"No, sir," the sergeant replied, walking toward the front section of the Pave Hawk. The charred remains of the two American pilots were still strapped into their seats. Their helmets had melted into black plastic balls around their heads, their eye sockets empty and dark. He saw where their lips had been burned away to expose what were now black charred teeth, as if they had clenched their jaws at the moment of death. The sergeant moved around to the side, seeing the black body of a man lying half in and half out of the blackened frame.

Kaine inspected the chopper walking to the front. The right side of the nose section was missing a large piece of the instrument panel. Scanning the rest he saw the plexiglass windscreen was melted and the refueling probe was lying on the ground, warped from the heat.

"There are only the three bodies," Sergeant Hyun stated. "The two pilots and another smaller man."

Kaine could see the man's body. He doubted it was Sinchon. His clothes were burned beyond recognition but his frame was too small to have been the general's.

"Colonel, I've found a Korean footprint," Hyun shouted to his commanding officer. "This is an older special forces sole print . . ." He circled the print with his finger as Kaine joined him.

"How do you know this?"

Hyun turned his boot over to display the tread design. "See these ridges? This makes it different. That one is about a size larger, that's all. It could be a North Korean officer's."

Thoughts raced through Kaine's mind. If Sinchon's body wasn't on the ship, it must be on the island. Could he still be alive after both the ship and helicopter were destroyed? Again the three images from Colonel Woong's video came to his mind.

"I count three sets of footprints leading off in this direction . . . toward those abandoned buildings." Hyun pointed to the end of the runway.

"Get a team of men together," Kaine ordered. "Search the buildings. If you find proof someone is still alive, bring it to me."

Putting his head into the wind the colonel started back toward the transport. If Sinchon was alive, he would find him.


WASHINGTON, D.C.


It was dark when Manning walked into Union Station. The main hall stayed open twenty-four hours daily but the other shops, restaurants and movie theaters maintained normal business hours. He strode to the information booth, stared casually at the visitor pamphlets and flyers. It was 5:58 P.M.

The top of a white envelope stuck out from his overcoat pocket on the side. He hadn't entrusted the details of Chaniff's rescue mission and the morning's briefing to his fax machine this time. They were too valuable. Lighting his pipe, Manning walked around the booth studying the doors. An old couple walked inside, practically leaning on each other for support. A group of young adults walked noisily down the corridor, their laughter echoing. He didn't see anyone or anything out of the ordinary.

Sucking in a long breath full of smoke, he exhaled through the side of his mouth. *It's finally moving,* he told himself. *My life is coming together. The president is halfway to Europe, leaving me to oversee the White House. Soon Rhonda will have what she wants and get out of town. Then I can make a couple more deals and have some money for myself, and forget this ever happened.*

Manning puffed again on his pipe and spotted Hawkens. He too was wearing an overcoat with the top of a white envelope sticking out the side pocket.


LANGAU ISLAND

Maj. Helen Erwin rested her tired body against General Sinchon. The cave was dark, cold and not much bigger than the interior of a small car. The three survivors huddled close against the back wall. At least there was enough room for the three of them to sit up comfortably with their legs stretched out in front.

Duke brushed the dried roots hanging from the ceiling away from his face. The entrance was low, sheltering them from the wind and easy discovery. He saw the general's droopy eyelids and felt drowsy himself.

"We should take turns standing watch," Duke said. "I don't want someone to stumble across us unexpectedly."

"I'll take the first watch," Erwin volunteered. "You've already done most of the work."

James was thankful she offered. Folding his arms, he tried to get comfortable. "Wake me if you need me."

Before he could doze the low rumble of turbofans shook the cave.

"General, do you hear that?" Erwin whispered.

Duke opened his eyes and scrambled to the opening of the cave. Staying low, he scanned the skies until he caught sight of an odd-looking Soviet aircraft.

"Erwin," Duke muttered before going to peer over the ravine. "Bring the radio."

The plane hit the gravel runway a quarter-mile away. He could hear the twin engines of the jet reverse as it slowed to a stop near the Il-76 Ilyushin.

## USS *OBSERVATION ISLAND*

"It just dropped off the screen, sir," Owens reported from her radar station. She touched the glass monitor, showing the last location of the aircraft. "I'm showing four comairs to the south, one to the east. No other military air traffic."

"What about surface ships?" Captain Bliss asked, shifting positions in his chair. He hadn't realized just how big this party was going to get.

Owens tapped her keyboard. The *Island*'s surface radar only swept an area out to fifty-five miles. To the west of their position she saw a fast-moving ocean ferry carrying businessmen from Seoul to Qingdao, China. To the east were two large freighters—one appeared to be an oil tanker—making their way south. And fifteen miles south, following their every move, was the Korean trawler, which Owens referred to as the shadow. No matter where they sailed the shadow went with them.

"No change on the shadow, sir."

Captain Bliss didn't respond. He was sitting in his command chair in the center of the intelligence ship's CIC. Blue and green lights danced off the ceiling. If Owens was right, and he believed she was, that was the second transport to land on Langau Island. Combine that with an Iranian freighter and the entire situation was beginning to stink.

"Owens, what's our position?" Bliss asked, rubbing his eyes.

"Ninety-four miles southeast of Langau. Heading two five three, speed sixteen knots."

"Radio Cheerleader. Let them know about the new aircraft," Bliss said, sighing.

"Shut them down," Kaine shouted. "Shut them down." The piercing sound of the AN-72 Coaler's engines made the colonel place his hands over his ears. The smaller transport was about half the size of the Il-76. She had been designed for short hauls and short runways, hence the odd shape with two large turbofans mounted high on each wing. The aircraft swung around, blowing clouds of brown dust into the air.

Kaine heard the engines power down before the pilot locked the brakes. He walked around to the back of the AN-72's high T-tail. The cargo ramp came open, hitting the rocky ground with a hard thud.

"Secure that aircraft immediately," Kaine shouted pointing to the Il-76. Some of the men jogged down the ramp carrying tool boxes and shovels while others untied a mobile fuel pump from its restraints. Behind the pump were four more armed soldiers. Kaine turned to them. "Set up a perimeter around that aircraft and keep your eyes open. Don't let anyone else near it."

"Yes, sir," the senior sergeant shouted back. His men fanned out to surround the jet.

"Get that pump over here!" a soldier shouted.

Staying out of the way, Kaine supervised the beginning process of pumping the fuel out of the damaged Il-76. Once that was completed they could cut the bay door off and remove the fuel rods.

"How much longer?" Kaine asked, walking up to one of the engineers.

"This pump is the best we could bring, but it is not very large. At this rate it will probably take an hour to offload the fuel. After that it will be safe to start the torches and cutting saws."

Kaine's eyes went to the skies. He listened for any sounds of aircraft approaching the area. The Americans would be here soon, he knew.

Climbing into the Il-76, he noticed the smell of jet fuel had subsided. It was time to report their progress to General Chin. Entering the flight deck he turned on the radio and let the electronic circuits warm up.

Carl Hawkens sat alone in the computer room of his two-bedroom townhome. The room's lights were low, enhancing every electronic dial and LED. He had just finished reading the last of the two briefings Manning had passed to him. They each contained enough data to make him one of the most valuable traders in the world. Who else had access to such sensitive information?

*Manning was right,* Hawkens thought, *this is worth every penny of that fifty thousand dollars.* He picked up the yellow paper containing Manning's handwritten notes. *Especially this. This will give me the clout I need to make it on my own.* Hawkens looked over the details of a military operation code-named Eagle Fire. He grinned at the name, knowing F-15E Strike Eagles were the favorite jets of many top generals.

Seeing that the mission involved the North Koreans, he wondered if Bandar was aware of the situation. It didn't matter. Hawkens wasn't going to include him. He was going solo on this deal. He had his own contact and Bandar had taught him all he needed to know to deal with the military of other countries—particularly the North Koreans. They placed trust and honor at the forefront of business, reserving the right to lie and cheat for themselves, of course.

Hawkens scooted the desk chair out and bent down. Placing a hand along the wood on the side panel underneath the desk, he felt along the molding. The secret compartment came open when he pulled a section of the molding down. It was only a small five-by-five-inch hinged drawer, but it was large enough to hold computer discs. He pulled them out and selected the black one, inserting it into his hard drive. The computer cycled, then stopped, not displaying anything without the password. He typed: NEXUS. Within moments a list of contacts and numbers appeared on the screen. Scrolling down, he stopped at Mr. Nee.

Placing half the papers upside down, his coded fax machine grabbed at the first page as he dialed the number. Hawkens hit the send button and the line rang the North Korean intelligence officer's Washington apartment. The pages started feeding through when the receiving fax machine answered.

Smiling, Hawkens went into his living room. He'd get a call soon to arrange an exchange for the rest of the papers.


Chairman of the Joint Chiefs Howard Chaniff ran his security card, magnetic strip down, through the computerized door lock. The check light flashed green and he typed in his nine-digit clearance number. The lock snapped open. He turned the knob and entered the Special Technical Operations Center without anyone noticing.

Everyone was attentive at their station. He blinked, trying to get his eyes to adjust faster to the dark light of the command operations center.

"Any word from Tango?" he asked.

"No, sir," Lieutenant Fontano replied. *"Observation Island* is reporting a second transport landing on Langau Island. We're waiting for James to confirm it."

"Damn!" Chaniff muttered, filling his coffee cup and taking a sip of the bitter brew.

The red and yellow lights flickered on Fontano's screen. Chaniff's mind wandered to his last conversation with Manning. *Why was that man incessantly wanting to have the exact details of every mission? Is he just some control freak . . .* Chaniff stopped suddenly, remembering that Manning had asked the same type of questions about Tango Team's mission. He had even taken notes. The general sighed, thinking he was just wishing Manning was the explanation for the two missions' getting blown. As chief of staff Manning was hard enough to deal with; now that he was acting national security advisor he was unbearable. It would give Chaniff greater personal satisfaction to catch Manning red-handed than the North Koreans with the fuel rods. Chaniff pondered the possibilities.

"Sir, should I radio the *Island* and request an update?" Fontano turned.

"Ah . . . yeah," Chaniff said abruptly. "Let me talk to Bliss. I wonder if James can see plutonium fuel rods from his location."

"Fuel rods, sir?"

"You heard me. After we've talked to them, put me through to Colonel Conrad at Osan."

LANGAU ISLAND

The antenna wire was spread out behind Duke, pointing to the southeast. He wondered how the beat-up electronic contraption continued to work.

Duke watched the power needle flutter near zero as he keyed the mike. Crouching down, he peeked over the top of the rocks so he could keep the transport and men in sight.

"Guard Dog . . . this is Beagle. Do you copy, Guard Dog?"

*"We copy you, Beagle."*

"Guard Dog, a second transport has landed. Repeat, AN-72 Coaler is now on the ground. Count eight . . . maybe ten soldiers. A few white coats came in with the second transport," Duke added, referring to the engineers.

*"Copy Beagle . . . one Coaler joining the party."*

James listened as the transmission faded in and out.

*"Need confirmation of plutonium fuel rods aboard the Il-76 Ilyushin."*

"Are you guys nuts?" the general breathed into the mike. "I'm trying to stay as far away as possible."

*"The freighter* Allum Bacar *is Iranian, Beagle."*

Duke shook his head, understanding. "Roger Guard Dog," he answered, "I'll see what I can do, but I'm no Steven Seagal."

*"Co . . . tha . . . agle."* The signal broke up.

James turned the radio off. He had used most of the battery's power. "Erwin," he whispered, beckoning the major to join him outside.

"What's up?" she asked, settling next to James.

Without speaking James moved his eyes back to the direction of their hide-out.

"He's sleeping. I don't think he's doing very well."

"Follow me."

They scooted along the ground until they could both get a view of the airstrip. Lying on their stomachs, they used a large boulder as cover and peered out opposite sides.

"Guard Dog thinks there might be plutonium fuel rods on that Il-76," Duke nodded to the aircraft. "There's an Iranian freighter in port, too."

"Iranian freighter?"

"That's right," Duke said as sand blew into his eyes. He closed them tight until they watered.

"North Koreans and Iranians . . . what a bad combination," Erwin mused. "If there are fuel rods on that plane, you know they're transferring them to the freighter.'' Erwin looked at James, frustrated: ''I think we've just been had.''

''Yeah, me too,'' James agreed, peeking back out from behind the rock. ''And I'd be willing to bet your friend down there knows about this. What a great excuse for ordering all our military equipment out of the area.''

''I don't know about that,'' Erwin countered. ''Why doesn't he just walk out there and wave his hands saying, here I am? Go ahead and unload your cargo. The Americans will never know.''

''I guess you're right,'' James answered. ''But let's be cautious about what we say around him. You go back and stay out of sight. I have to try and get closer to see what they're doing.''

The general didn't wait for Major Erwin to argue. He moved out from behind their cover and crawled quietly toward the runway.


## KIM IL SONG AIR BASE, NORTH KOREA

Myong Chin wiped the cold rice from his lips. He cradled a hot cup of tea in his hands and paced back and forth across the rear portion of the underground command and control bunker. The tea tasted good and helped calm his nerves. Everything was quiet. The Americans had discovered something was amiss by now, he knew that. It was just a matter of when they would respond, and how.

''General, I have Colonel Kaine,'' the senior radio operator said. ''He is transmitting on channel five three.''

''Five three,'' Chin repeated, placing a set of radio head phones over his ears. Dialing the proper radio frequency, he opened the channel. ''This is Red Crown. Go ahead.''

''Red Crown . . . Red Star. The second transport has landed and the freighter is now in port.''

''We are behind schedule,'' Chin stated, a torrent of anxiety coming over him. ''You don't have any time to waste. The Americans will not wait for you to finish before they come looking for their team. They could be on their way right now.''

''The men will be finished securing the aircraft shortly and we'll be able to cut the bay door from the Il-76. We should still have plenty of time to transfer the cargo before the Americans arrive.''

''Let's not waste time discussing it. Just do it . . . You have found General Sinchon's body?''

The radio hissed several seconds before the response came: ''We have searched the wreckage, but . . . he is not there.''

"What? Have you checked in the Americans' transport?" His heartbeat increasing, Chin's voice bellowed through the room.

*"Do not worry, I will continue searching for it."*

"Dammit! Do not fail me, Kaine. You have two missions. First, make sure the Iranians get their cargo. Second, find Sinchon, dead or alive, and bring him back to me."

There was no doubting the implications of the general chief of staff's seething words.

*"Understood. Red Star out."*

Chin slammed the radio mike down.

"General Chin." A carrier entered. "I just received this coded transmission from Washington, D.C., in the United States. It is marked urgent and addressed to Colonel Kaine.

*It must be from Colonel Hwan.* Chin took the envelope, wondering what the *spetsnaz* intelligence officer had to report that was urgent. He did not want to hear any more bad news. "How was this transmitted?" he asked, uncomfortable with Kaine's spies faxing sensitive documents around the world. He didn't care how well they had been encrypted with the powerful American and Japanese computers; the codes could be broken if the transmissions were copied. It had better be extremely important.

"I don't know, sir," the courier answered, standing at attention.

Chin returned to his office. Opening the envelope, the general held a two-page fax with the breakdown of the Americans' planned rescue and attack on Langau Island. It included the number of aircraft, the AWACS flight patterns, routes of the aircraft, along with target and threat assignments. The general smashed the intercom button on his desk. *Hwan will be rewarded for this.*

"Get Colonel Woong in here at once," Chin shouted angrily.

## 26

OSAN AFB, SOUTH KOREA

"Agreed. We'll be good to go in six hours," Lt. Col. Miles Conrad said, hanging up the telephone, ending his conversation with General Chaniff. Seated alone in a tiny rundown office in the back of hangar seven, the thirty-nine-year-old F-15E squadron commander typed a few more notes into his IBM ThinkPad notebook computer.

He tried to shake the jet lag from his body then sat back, reflecting on the mission Chaniff had outlined. It seemed straightforward enough. He would lead a group of eight F-15Es and four F-16Cs providing air cover for two Pave Hawk choppers tasked to recover an American diplomatic team. Their job would be to keep bad guys away from Langau Island and, if the order came, drop a couple of smart bombs on an Iranian freighter docked at the northern end of the island.

Conrad's compact, well-conditioned frame and commanding presence were every bit the fighter-pilot stereotype. He stood at five feet eight inches and kept his G tolerance up with daily workouts in the base gym. The deep-seated wrinkles around his blue eyes gave testimony to long days in the bright sun on the flight line.

Growing up in the Western town of Casper, Wyoming, Miles had often watched B-52 bombers practice refueling over his grade-school playground. The skies were so clear and blue he could actually see the jets' refueling probes as they flew overhead.

After high school he was awarded an appointment to the United States Air Force Academy from his congressman, Dick Cheney, who later served as secretary of defense for George Bush. He graduated with high marks and his career soared. He flew F-111s out of Lakenheath then transferred to F-15Es three months after the Gulf War ended.

As a captain, later promoted to major, he flew with the 336th fighter squadron out of Seymour Johnson, North Carolina. The Fighting Rocketeers bragged that when it absolutely, positively had to be destroyed overnight, they were the ones to call.

He was ordered to a flying staff position with USAFE, stationed out of Ramstein Air Base, Germany, for three years. Now Conrad was stationed at Elmendorf AFB Alaska flying F-15E Strike Eagles again. He had worked his entire life just to have the opportunity to fly the E model, or Echo. It was the only jet in the Air Force's inventory designed to kill hard targets on the ground and fight air-to-air. Conrad considered flying the most sophisticated fighter/bomber in the world his calling as a warrior.

The only thing he would rather do than fly jets, maybe, would be to grab a twelve-gauge shotgun and hunt ducks or geese with his wife, Jamie, and their two sons, Matt and Jake.

Conrad looked at the clock on the far wall and watched the second hand click past the twelve. The chairman of the Joint Chiefs was expecting him to plan, organize and brief his pilots for a mission to launch in six hours. It could be done, but Conrad didn't feel good about it. His squadron of eight F-15Es had only landed eleven hours ago. He figured he could get the jets armed and ready first, giving his men a few more hours of rest.

LANGAU ISLAND

Duke reminded himself never again to leave on a diplomatic mission without bringing a pair of binoculars. The closer he got the more he worried a pair of sharp eyes would spot him if he wasn't careful.

The wind continued to blow a frosty breeze across the island. Staying as far away from the runway as possible and near the shoreline, Duke estimated he had crawled a quarter-mile away from the cave. As he crept along he saw the shoreline beginning to fall off, changing from large boulders to a smooth slope. Looking beyond that Duke could see another rock outcropping. If he could get there without being seen he would have ample cover to sneak up within a couple hundred feet of the transports.

Duke raised his head to study the scene around the aircraft, then dropped his head and began to crawl, slowly, the taste of dirt filling his mouth.

Colonel Kaine checked the sky for any possible signs of American reconnaissance aircraft. Chin was right. The Americans would be coming, and when they did Kaine hoped he was no longer here to face them.

He made his way around to the side of the Il-76. A team of flight engineers was discussing the best way to dismantle the cargo bay door as they stood around the portable fuel pump attached to the left wing tank, still sucking kerosene from the jet. The fuel was pooling in the dirt near the aircraft even though the hose was extended as far as it could reach. Another group of soldiers was using shovels in an attempt to cover it completely with dirt.

Sergeant Hyun approached. "Colonel Kaine, there is no one in or around the buildings," Hyun reported.

Kaine was not surprised. It would be too obvious a place to hide. "What did you find?'' Kaine asked, placing a hand up to hold down the bill of his hat as a gust of wind hit him in the face.

''I found a number of footprints near the closest building. They appear to be the same sets as those near the chopper.''

''And where did they lead?'' Kaine barked impatiently. He was losing patience.

''I have searched the entire area several times, sir. But with the wind it is difficult to determine.''

''Why is it difficult to determine, Sergeant? Either you found the prints or you didn't!'' Kaine roared.

''There are footprints leading away from the building going to the chopper, sir. But I have also discovered a single set of prints coming from the yacht. It appears they joined up and walked back to the first building.'' Hyun spoke with as much confidence as he could muster. He didn't dare tell the colonel it might help if he knew what the circumstances were for the prints to be on the island. ''Another set leads away from the chopper to the other side of the runway. I searched in all directions but each time I found nothing.''

Kaine's body stiffened. ''There are footprints leading away from the chopper?''

''Yes sir.''

''You have wasted enough time. There shouldn't be any footprints leading away from the chopper . . . not if everyone was killed. And there should be several sets leading to *Van Triumph.''* Kaine stared at Hyun, hoping he would say that he might be mistaken. The sergeant stood at attention, not wavering on his report.

Kaine realized now that Sinchon had gotten off the yacht. He had met with the Americans in one of the abandoned buildings. *Why hadn't I thought of that possibility!* He was angry with himself for not planning better. There were not enough men to organize a proper search party. *It will not matter,* he thought, *I am sure they were not armed when meeting with each other.*

Kaine turned to the sergeant. ''I want you to head up a search team with as many men as the engineers can spare. I believe General Sinchon escaped our attack and is alive. He was meeting Americans on this island to discuss a coup against our country. He is a traitor and must be found.''

''Yes, sir!'' Sergeant Hyun saluted earnestly then ran to gather the other men.

## KIM IL SONG AIR BASE, NORTH KOREA

"Kaine has not found General Sinchon's body. I must assume he is still alive," Myong Chin informed the pilot. "He wasn't on the ship when you attacked it."

"I destroyed the ship and the chopper just as ordered, sir," Lt. Col. Krung Woong stood his ground defensively.

"I know you did. Colonel Kaine will have to take care of General Sinchon now," Chin said, pacing across the underground pilots' briefing room and stopping near the wall map of North and South Korea. "You have a new mission."

Woong's ears perked up.

"The transfer of a special cargo to a freighter docked in the bay at the island has been delayed. Your mission will be to make sure the Americans don't interfere with the transfer." Chin's eyes flickered with pleasure.

Woong was silent only a moment, his eyes wide hearing the order. "My pilots are very good, but you are asking my men to commit suicide, to go up against the West's best technology."

"I admire your courage, Colonel Woong. There are few men with the stomach to talk with me this way. That is why you will lead this mission. However . . . you and your men will not be committing suicide."

Woong remained quiet, waiting for his commanding officer to explain.

"I have obtained the Americans' attack plans." Chin circled an area as Woong moved closer to the map with renewed confidence. "Your first objective is to destroy their eyes and ears. We know their AWACS will orbit right about here."

Woong shook his head. "An AWACS has never been destroyed in battle. The Americans assign their best pilots to protect it."

"That is about to change," Chin said, smiling. "I have a plan that will make it possible. Gather your pilots. I will brief all of you in thirty minutes."

"Yes, sir." Woong left the briefing room feeling privileged to have been chosen by General Chief of Staff Chin for this momentous mission.


## NGHIA BINH PROVINCE, VIETNAM

Cradling a large leaf in his hands, Michael Callahan tilted his head back, letting the cool water trickle into his mouth. He picked up another leaf and repeated the procedure. His dried lips and tongue soaked in the liquid before it reached his throat.

He had found a secluded spot between two animal trails in the center of a large clump of bamboo trees. The bamboo was so dense the only way they could enter was by crawling on their hands and knees. Their camouflage blended in perfectly and the overgrowth allowed them to lie on the ground with substantial protection. However, they soon discovered the area was infested with fiery bright yellow ants.

"I don't think I'm going to make it," Pope whispered. The communications specialist brushed ants off the top of his hands. "Six more hours in this hellhole and I'm going to be skin and bones. These frigging ants are eating me alive."

"You're in the special forces, Pope. You've been trained to eat bugs, drink piss and fight twenty-four hours a day," Callahan chided.

"Can I have some of that?"

"Some of what?" Michael moved his eyes to meet Pope's.

"Whatever you've been smoking . . ."

"Shhh." Callahan pulled his CAR-15 closer to his body.

Their bodies froze stiff, hearing the footsteps.

A shallow ravine filled with dried tumbleweeds stopped Duke from slipping any further. He lay motionless, catching his breath. His heart pounded even though no one could have seen since the gully was deep enough to conceal him from the runway. Bringing his hands up, he saw they were raw with pieces of gravel imbedded in his palms.

Looking around, Duke decided he couldn't have picked a better spot anyway. The weeds would help his cover. There was long grass and a few boulders with clumps of dried bushes surrounding them at the top of the bluff overlooking the runway. Behind him was a steep drop-off leading to the ocean below.

Duke had stopped several times when it appeared a soldier might be approaching his position. So far each time they had stopped and turned to take a different direction.

Pushing himself up and peeking over two basketball-sized rocks he had a good view of the Il-76 and AN-72 not more than a hundred yards away.

The AN-72 was the closest jet to him and blocked the front cockpit section of the Il-76. The smaller Coaler appeared to be relatively new. The white paint was clean and the North Korean flag, painted on its high T-tail, was bright. Its rear ramp door was down and Duke figured it had brought the white coats and equipment to work on the other transport.

Checking out the Il-76, he could tell it wasn't new—or in good shape, for that matter. The Ilyushin had a two-tone paint scheme, white on top and light gray on the bottom, and was faded from years of being exposed to the elements. Studying its rear section Duke saw where long strips of gray paint had been scraped off the underside. The landing gear appeared to have dug into the gravel runway and he wondered if it had given way. The aircraft listed to the left and its ramp door remained closed.

He didn't see any sign of fuel rods. *Maybe,* Duke thought, *Guard Dog sent this Beagle on a wild-goose chase.*

He turned his attention to the men around the two jets. He counted them: twelve armed soldiers and five or six engineers. The soldiers were wearing dark green camouflaged winter parkas and carrying AK-47s. Duke couldn't tell who was in charge.

Puffs of bluish-gray smoke shot out of what appeared to be a small mobile pump. Duke saw it was attached to the underside right wing tank of the jet. His eyes followed the long black hose lying across the runway and he could see liquid pouring into the dirt. He realized what the soldiers were doing—spreading dirt over jet fuel.

"The crazy sonsabitches," Duke mumbled. The North Koreans were pumping the fuel out of the Ilyushin. One small spark and this island would see the largest fireworks display this side of Hong Kong.

*There has to be a reason for pumping the fuel out of that jet. And whatever it is has to be worth risking blowing the whole place sky high,* Duke thought, grinning. *Like maybe your cargo bay door was damaged when you crash landed and plutonium fuel rods are stuck inside.*

Michael Callahan smelled the distinct aroma of garlic and peppers mixed with body odor a few seconds before he saw several pairs of black boots creeping along the wet grass and mud. The Vietnamese soldiers were making very little sound. If special forces school had taught Callahan anything it was that sometimes smell was better than sight.

Resting his head on the ground Callahan waited for the soldiers to pass. They crept through the area, stopping every few feet. He strained to see through the thick bamboo the number of boots. By just moving his index finger Callahan readied himself for action, placing it on the trigger of his weapon. It would be the last time he could move unless it was to fight.

*Now where would all of you be headed?* Duke watched six men spreading out from the runway in a wagon-wheel pattern. He watched them for several minutes as they searched the grounds directly in front of them. Occasionally one of them would stop and bend down to the ground for a closer look.

James figured they had to be looking for footprints. Their search had begun sooner than he had hoped. Now he not only had to worry about the two jets, he had to make sure someone didn't sneak up behind him.

Duke grabbed a clump of weeds and pulled them over his body for camouflage. He turned back to see the last of the fuel trickle from the drainpipe. Two men disconnected the fuel pump while the others continued to shovel dirt over the kerosene-soaked ground. The fuel had pooled and was several inches deep. It would take them hours if they intended to cover all of it completely.

Tensing his muscles, he tried to alleviate the numbness in his legs and pain in his lower back. He had been waiting for nearly forty minutes as the Koreans drained the Il-76. Duke wasn't about to leave before he knew for certain what they had in there.

The men in white coats entered the back of the Coaler, emerging shortly thereafter pulling black metal carts containing two long steel cylinders connected with thin hoses and a variety of other tools. James knew at once they were metal cutting saws and plasma-arc torches. His assumption about the mission of the second plane had been correct.

They split up, setting up on each side of the Ilyushin's rear cargo door and one at the center near the bottom of the jet. A few of the men were gathered around holding fire extinguishers.

*Well they do have guts,* Duke chuckled to himself. He guessed 5,000 gallons of fuel had emptied out of the jet. Hand-held fire extinguishers would be about as good as spitting on a forest fire if any of it caught fire.

He watched the men put on metal welder's helmets and light their torches. A moment later they started slicing through the thin aluminum skin of the transport.

*One . . . two . . . four,* Callahan counted to himself as black boots came into view. Four men were searching not more than twenty feet away. The shafts of their boots were covered in dark green cloth, not the standard multitone camouflage used by the Vietnamese government. Looking at the toes he saw their boots were shiny black like new.

It didn't add up. Callahan wondered if these guys were Vietnamese soldiers and if they were the same assholes that had ambushed them. Or maybe someone else was after them?

*Come on . . . just walk on by,* he pleaded silently as an ant crawled across his face, stopping near the edge of his left eye. Blinking slowly, he tried to knock the insect off. It didn't work. Callahan suddenly felt an intense itching pain as the ant bit the soft tender skin. He squeezed the eye shut, struggling to keep watch over the men's movements with the other eye still open.

"Bring it up slowly," Colonel Woong shouted. The sound of large diesel engines roaring to life vibrated the interior of the hangar as columns of black smoke shot into the air. A series of pulleys began to spin and the steel rope connecting the crane to a two-ton blue and gray Su-27 fighter tightened. The crane moaned and cracked in protest. While the engines continued to power up the crane operator slowly eased the fully loaded interceptor off the hangar floor.

"Be careful . . . do it slowly," Woong cried out loudly, trying to be heard over the sound of the engines.

The colonel had inspected the placements of the nylon cradle used to lift his jet off the concrete floor, making sure the weight was distributed evenly. He didn't want to risk losing any of the ten air-to-air missiles or damaging the delicate flight controls during the transfer. Even one missile or instrument could make the difference between life and death.

The single-seat jet revolved a few degrees as the nose and landing gear came off the concrete. The crane operator let the jet hover six inches off the ground for a moment to insure that the restraints would hold the jet. He then powered up the engines, lifting the giant bird fifteen feet into the air.

"Back the truck in," Colonel Woong ordered, waving his arm.

He watched a semitractor-trailer back in under his fighter. The driver locked the brakes before shutting off the truck's motor.

"Bring her down . . . slowly . . . slowly," Woong instructed though the driver was too busy to hear what he was saying.

Five flight engineers climbed on top of the trailer, helping to guide the Su-27 into place. The fighter rocked gently as its landing gears touched the bed of the trailer. Flight technicians immediately began to secure the jet in place.

The colonel nodded his approval as he walked around the back of the jet. He watched the men throw several canvas tarps over the top of the fighter and tie them to the edge of the trailer. The next time he would see the interceptor it would be parked on a stretch of highway north of the coastal city of Najin.

Woong had spent the last hour listening to General Chin's briefing of his pilots. Their objectives were clear. Blind the Americans by bringing their AWACS down, make sure the Iranian freighter cleared the port with the fuel rods and keep any other Americans from interfering. The success of the operation depended on Woong's completing his mission first.

Placing a pair of American-made Ray-Ban sunglasses over his eyes, Colonel Woong strode back to the base's main building. He felt confident he could accomplish his assignment. When he succeeded he would become a national hero and the rank of general would be his without question.

Woong knew one of the Americans' biggest strengths in air combat was in keeping track of all the planes in the sky. They could control the battle by vectoring their powerful interceptors to the threats entering the area before they even got close to their target.

He also knew the Americans had plotted and electronically stored the location of every North Korean air base, making it impossible to take off without being detected.

However, General Chin had learned the limitation of the AWACS from Colonel Hwan and planned to exploit it. The very northern reaches of North Korea were not covered by the airborne American command center.

Woong's Su-27 would be taken by truck to a remote highway ten miles north of Najin. There he would use a flat two-lane paved highway as a runway. After taking off to the north he would fly at low level into China to avoid radar detection. Civilian flight schedules showed a Chinese A310 Airbus scheduled to take off from Harbin, China, on a nonstop flight to Shanghai. The Airbus would pass within sixty miles of the American AWACS a few minutes after it reached operational orbit.

Chin ordered Woong to fly in a tight formation with the A310 using it as cover. He was to get as close as possible to the American E-3C before breaking away to make a dash toward the jet. Woong only had to get within thirty miles before he could fire a salvo of radar-seeking missiles. The slow four-engine command center wasn't capable of outmaneuvering them.


CIA HEADQUARTERS

Mark Collins clicked the computer mouse two quick times. The 3-D color image on his monitor didn't change. He repeated the procedure a second and third time with the same results. No matter how hard he tried it wasn't going to work.

The western coast of North Korea was on the right side of the screen. Mark centered the cursor on the left side trying to call up the latest data from the Lacrosse-C overflight. Langau Island had not been in the detection range of the radar imaging satellite. There wasn't any way he could verify the North Koreans had flown the fuel rods to the island.

Collins cursed under his breath before picking up the phone.

"Doug . . . this is Mark."

"Did you get it?"

"No, I don't have a damned thing. And it's going to be another six hours before that satellite is in position again. This whole thing could be over by then."

"Cool down, Mark. Remember, James is on the ground and they're hoping he'll be able to verify it."

"Damn it, I won't be the one to see this through, though, Doug. I've been with it from the beginning and I want to help end it.'' Collins sank deeper into his chair.

''Mark, you've done your job. I suggest you take the rest of the night off. Go home with Christine and get some rest. If anything comes up I'll call you.''

Collins was quiet for a few seconds. ''Just be sure you call me when something happens,'' he said then hung up the phone.

He knew Brooks was right. It was his job to sift through the mountains of information that flowed into the intelligence side of the CIA. He had found the fuel rods; now it was up to the military to make sure they didn't get any further—and help James off the island.

Collins thought about James' wife Katie and his kids. Something didn't feel right. It felt like reading a really good book and stopping before you got to the end. You might think you know the outcome, but you'd always be wondering.

Shutting off his computer, he grabbed his coat and headed for the door.


Michael Callahan had stopped counting at ten. Ten little yellow ants with red heads were now biting his face and hands. He blamed himself for not checking the area better. Only an idiot would hide in the center of an ant-infested bamboo growth. And right now he considered himself an idiot. He knew the same thing was happening to Pope. Callahan could feel the emotion radiating from the man behind him.

The four Vietnamese soldiers were still in front of them. Michael could see the broken outline of two men crouched down talking to each other in whispers through the trunks of the bamboo trees. They weren't more than ten or twelve feet away. The soldier facing him had short black hair and one long scar across the top of his forehead. He couldn't see what the other one looked like. Their AK-47s were stretched across their laps and they each wore droopy fanny packs. They didn't look like Vietnamese special forces troops. Their faces weren't covered with black camouflage paint and they carried standard assault weapons rather than M3 submachine guns used by the Death Volunteers of the Vietnamese People's Liberation Army. Both men were pointing to the ground and looking in all directions.

One of them shouted from fifty feet or so away. Whatever he said caught all their attention. Both men jumped up to follow the others.

*It could be a trick,* Michael thought. *One of the men might have stayed behind to see if anything moves.*

## The White House

"Yes sir, I have everything under control," Manning said with one foot propped up on his desk. "Chaniff reports that everything is falling into place and James should be off the island before you wake up in the morning. No need to alarm the Europeans until after everyone is back on safe ground."

"Good work, Allan. Make sure you notify me if anything changes."

"Yes, sir. I'm right on top of it." Manning hung up the phone, disgusted. *I can't believe that sonofabitch just called to check up on me. Don't I always take care of everything for him?*

Manning picked up the envelope containing $50,000 in cash. He stared at the money, enjoying the feeling of possibly having his troubles behind him. The court date was set to finalize the divorce, he would soon be national security advisor and with a couple more deals like this one he could be prosperous again. *Rhonda doesn't need this. I've given her everything I have already. That bitch is bluffing about those pictures. She'd be more embarrassed than I would to have them splattered all over the newspapers. This money is mine. I've worked hard to get where I am and that bloodsucking Rhonda can go find another victim.*

Manning suddenly felt a huge surge of relief. He wasn't going to allow himself to be tormented any longer. Giddily, he picked up the phone and dialed his wife's home number. "I have a little surprise for you, baby . . . go ahead and call the press or whoever else you want. I'm not giving you any more money." He paused briefly, then added: "And if you call to harass me again I'll turn you over to the FBI for blackmail. That's illegal, you know . . . being bisexual isn't."

The wind had died, allowing Duke to hear some of the talking and shouting by the men working on the Il-76 Ilyushin. Even though his Korean vocabulary consisted of mostly greetings and salutations he could tell most of what was being said by their gestures and tones. The final chunk of aluminum from the cargo door fell, hitting the ground. James watched it smolder as the last two men operating the cutting torch took off their helmets and killed the flame. Almost in unison a half-dozen men came running from the inside of the AN-72 Coaler carrying metal ladders.

Duke had begun to study one man more intently than the others. He was larger than the rest of the men, with broad shoulders and thick legs. The soldier shouted orders with a demanding tone and his walk and actions were confident. Clearly he was the officer in charge.

Duke's lack of movement caused his hands to feel numb from the cold. Duke pulled his hands into the sleeves of his parka to warm them. He was eager to get back to the cave and radio Guard Dog, but he knew they would want a visual verification.

So he watched and waited. The Koreans had placed the ladders along the bottom edge of the Il-76's rear cargo door. He could see several men inside pulling on something, trying to move it closer to the edge of the transport. The officer was right on top of them shouting explicit orders, seemingly worried the men weren't being careful enough.

"Use the ladders to slide the crates down!" Kaine shouted as he jumped into the back of the Ilyushin.

For the most part Kaine was pleased. The men had worked swiftly without making a single mistake. With the mobile forklift destroyed, hauling the fuel rods was just a matter of manpower.

"Move them one at a time," Kaine instructed, wanting to be cautious but also anxious to complete the mission. "I want one man at each end, two in the center on each side . . . You men clear this netting out of the way."

Kaine had the engineers helping to move the crates as well. Each crate was being moved to the edge of the transport door then set down like a basket of hen's eggs.

Kaine, checking his watch, turned to the pilot of the damaged jet. "Go and tell the Iranian freighter captain I need his men." This was no time to be proud. They were too close to succeeding.

Duke studied the light green crates, counting thirteen or fourteen stacked in the transport. There didn't appear to be any other markings or numbers on the outside of them—at least, none that he could see from his position. He watched as the Koreans let one slide down a ladder. The crate looked at least twenty feet long but not very wide.

The men didn't allow it to touch the ground as they hoisted it up to their shoulders. He guessed it weighed a lot by the grunts filtering in the wind toward him. They carried it in the direction of the port. Duke looked back to the transport and saw another crate sliding down the ladder. At this rate it wouldn't take them more than an hour to offload and transfer each one to the Iranian freighter.

Duke had seen all that he possibly could. He pushed himself back down into the ravine, away from the top of the bluff. Turning to crawl back across the exposed cliff, the sound of grinding gravel suddenly hit his ears. At once he knew he was in trouble. Someone was walking behind the nearest line of rocks. Looking around him he saw there were only dried weeds and small bushes to his left and right. He was exposed, sitting in the ravine like a kid in a sand box.

Duke had forgotten about the foot patrol. He had been so concerned about the cargo he had lost sight of the men working their way around from the north. He heard the man's steps draw closer. Any second he would see an armed Korean solider approaching the edge of the ravine.

*You dumb shit, James!* Crawling on his hands and knees without looking back, Duke headed straight for the bluff twenty feet away. Peering over the edge he saw the breaking waves hitting the rocks below. He wasn't sure if the water was deep enough for him to jump. It didn't matter. Duke pushed himself over the side into the icy cold ocean.

# 27

The pilot-briefing area at Osan was older than most of the men seated in the smoke-filled room. The wooden floor hadn't been polished in years and the once white walls had turned dirty yellow. Yet because of its age the room possessed a certain personality, with various items once treasured now left to collect dust on its shelves and walls: ceramic wings, sculptured jets, aerial watercolors, faded photographs. Gun metal gray chairs were dented and scratched from years of service. Against the far wall, card tables, with squadrons' names and wing numbers etched into them, dutifully stood the test of time.

Lt. Col. Miles Conrad wondered how many times the room had been used to outline a mission in defense of South Korea.

"Alright, gentlemen, listen up. We don't have time to waste," the colonel said stepping to the podium. Dressed in a green nomex flight suit, he waited for the rest of his pilots to settle down before he spoke again: "You already know why we're here. This briefing is to outline a few recent developments, designate call signs and get your input on how best to do our jobs. I want to be back here drinking beer at twenty hundred. Major Green tells me he's reprogrammed one of the satellite dishes and we'll be able to pick up the Denver-Oakland game. I'm taking Denver and he's giving me six points."

"Leave it to a wizzo to get sucked into a bet like that," someone called out amidst the laughter and jeering.

Maj. Skip "Greeno" Green was Conrad's backseater-weapons systems operator, or WSO. He was also one of his best friends.

The moment dissipated some of the men's tension but Miles could sense they were still nervous. That was good. It meant they were alert and knew what they were getting themselves into.

"I'm not going to tell you this will be a milk run. It's not. The North Koreans are unpredictable and the CIA is reporting they now have Su-27 and Su-30 Flankers in addition to MiG-29 Fulcrums. Langley believes the Flankers are operational."

"Just sounds like more targets to me," one of the F-16C pilots spouted off. "Bring'em on."

"Maybe so . . . but I'm not going to downplay it. We've never faced Su-27s in combat. And I'm not looking forward to being the first." Conrad stopped, letting his words sink in. "The CIA also believes these 27s and 30s are Chinese and could be modified. In other words they're not the standard fighters flown by the Russians. The best intel we have says their radar has greater range than our F-15s and they can carry up to ten air-to-air missiles." Conrad folded his arms and looked straight at his men. "That's a hell of a lot of firepower, gentlemen, and they can turn with any Eagle or Viper driver in this room."

"Death will rain upon them the second they leave North Korean air space," Green said mockingly but loud enough for everyone to hear.

Conrad walked to a laminated map hanging next to the podium. The large ten-by-ten display showed the entire Korean peninsula as well as Korea Bay and part of China.

The pilots had already studied their air-tasking orders so several had their laptops open and used the mouse to review their mission profiles and weapons mix as Conrad talked. Others were puffing on cigarettes as they leaned forward, giving Conrad their full attention.

Glancing back at the men, Conrad saw that Lt. Col. Hank McGiven sat slouched holding a lit cigarette between his thumb and forefinger. His bald head was tilted to the side and his eyes were half closed. He wondered if the man was awake.

There were rumblings that Hank considered himself the best F-16C pilot in Korea and the whole US Air Force, and was making it known he wasn't happy Conrad was placed in charge of the operation. He felt that Osan was his turf and an Eagle driver from Alaska didn't have any business trying to run the show.

Conrad gave McGiven a wild-ass stare, letting him know he wasn't going to tolerate any crap and he had better pay attention.

"Two Pave Hawk choppers, each carrying a Ranger team, will launch at sixteen-hundred hours. The choppers will fly at low level and land here at Langau Island." Conrad pointed to the map then continued: "Their mission is to rescue a diplomatic team and head back to the mainland ASAP. Our job is to take up positions between Langau and North Korea. We'll make sure nothing gets in the way of these choppers and provide air cover for their flight back to Osan." Conrad moved back to the podium.

"What about threats?" Capt. Ned "Red Dog" Ruddy, a chunky F-15E pilot, asked.

"Air to air should be your biggest concern. Besides the Flankers and Fulcrums we know they have at least a hundred operational MiG-21s. They're old but they're fast and hard to pick up on radar. The latest electronic intelligence says the North is now operating an updated Soviet-built Back Net located at Sinuiju. It's a long-range E-band command-and-control radar with over the horizon capability. The Rivet Joint boys say it can detect aircraft flying as low as two hundred feet . . . and out to a range of two hundred miles. So there's a damned good chance they'll be watching our choppers clear the coast before they drop down and head for Langau Island. Immediately after the Pave Hawks are airborne an E-3C will take up station right about here.'' It will keep a watch on everything so there won't be any surprises. Intel is not anticipating any SAM threats, but I want your electronic countermeasures armed and watching each other's backsides.''

Conrad looked around the room. "I'll be leading a four ship, call sign Tacoma. We'll be on guard here closest to the North Korean coast and about ten miles northeast of Langau Island. Red Dog, you'll be my wingman.''

Captain Ruddy nodded acknowledgment as he folded several pieces of gum together in a wad and threw it in his mouth. "Goch ya.''

"Paul, you'll be south of our position heading up another four ship, call sign Intrepid.'' Conrad looked at Maj. Paul Burns, a former hockey player from Minneapolis.

Burns didn't respond. He was too busying taking notes.

"The E-3C will be covering every air base in the region, so if the North decides they want to play games we'll be tracking them before they take off. My guess is they'll leave us alone, though. There will also be a RC-135 Super Snooper on station fifty miles south of Sinuiju until the AWACS is in place. Their job will be to intercept any communications or changes in radar data.''

"And where do my F-16s fit into all of this?'' McGiven asked, still slumped over and looking sideways at Conrad.

"I was just getting to that,'' Conrad answered. "Tacoma and Intrepid flights will orbit at thirty-five thousand. We're fragged for MiGCap. I'm placing your four Vipers at twenty thousand feet, below us and between us and the AWACS. I'm tasking you and your wingman to protect the RC-135 as it exists the area.''

"That's bullshit, Conrad. My men know the Korean pilots better than anyone. We should be tasked for air superiority,'' McGiven protested loudly, sitting up.

"McGiven, your job will be to pick up anything that tries to sneak in out of the south or east and to make sure the Super Snooper comes home. Period.''

"We're better than that, Colonel, and you know it. Our Vipers carry AIM-120s, we can take on any threat out there,'' McGiven said roughly. "Sticking us below your fighters . . . hell, you might as well keep us on the ground.''

The entire room turned its attention back to Conrad, waiting to see who would win the tug of war. Conrad let the silence build a moment, staring directly at McGiven.

"Let me cut through the crap for you. The F-15Es have better radars than your Vipers. We can pick up and lock onto targets before you guys even know they're out there. That's why we'll be above you. This has nothing to do with ego or who's a better pilot. It has to do with which aircraft is the best for the job. Now I've been placed in charge of this operation and if you don't like it I suggest you take it up with PACAF or better yet Air Combat Command." Conrad paused, to see if McGiven was going to object. He didn't. "Then you do it my way or you *will* sit on the ground, colonel."

McGiven didn't say a word.

Conrad went on. "McGiven, you will lead a four ship, call sign Benji. Now, are there any questions?"

"What's the E-3C call sign?" one of the men called out.

"Mentor . . . as in guide," Conrad announced. He looked around the room one last time. "Alright. We launch at sixteen-thirty. Be good."


LANGAU ISLAND

The orange glow of the heater cast just enough light into the cave for General Sinchon to see Major Erwin's brown hair loose around the sides of her hood. He wondered how she came to be on the island only now to be hiding in some cold rock fissure with him.

"Major," Sinchon whispered, not certain she was awake.

Erwin lifted her head. There was no drowsiness on her face or in her eyes. "Yes."

"You are married?"

"Me? No . . . well, I guess you could say I'm married to the military."

"So you do not have children."

"I have two cats. I consider them my children."

Sinchon smiled. In his country cats weren't considered pets.

"What about you, General? Are you married?"

"Once . . . a long time ago," he said, more solemnly. "My wife died and I gave our daughter to her sister to raise. I did not want a family to interfere with my career."

"I see." Erwin replied softly.

"At the time . . . it was the best decision." Sinchon glanced at Erwin's soft eyes. She was silent in the light. He looked down at her hands. Her nails were short, rough and unpolished. The major was very different from his image of an American woman. His thoughts drifted to his own daughter, wondering if he would ever have the chance to look into her eyes and touch her hands. He wondered if she resembled her mother. Had he made a mistake by not seeing her before leaving North Korea?

"You were ordered to come?" he asked at last.

"No. They asked me and I agreed. I felt it was my duty. North Korea is a difficult place for my country to understand and I'm considered an expert, but I don't know that much." There was a pause. "For example, we had hardly any information on you, General."

"Ahh." Sinchon nodded his head, knowing his government wanted it that way. "So why did your government agree to meet with me if they knew so little?"

"We had to take the risk. We hoped you'd be a man of understanding and wanted the same things we want for your country." Erwin was now tracing a twig in the dirt as she spoke sincerely. "I know some people think we're arrogant and always trying to push our ideals on other countries. I guess in a way it's true, but every time I go to vote or whenever I get in my car to drive to the store or to visit friends . . . whatever I want to do whenever I want to do it . . . I think I should be trying to help others enjoy the same freedoms a lot of us take for granted."

"I believe you know a lot more than you think," Sinchon said earnestly.

"Well, the worst-case scenario was you could have turned out to be a fruitcake," Erwin said, grinning. "We didn't anticipate things the way they've turned out."

"Someone betrayed me," the general said simply. "I am sorry you are . . . how do you say? Caught in the middle?"

"Yep. I'd say caught in the middle is a good way to put it." Erwin placed her hands up to the heater and rubbed them together. They sat for a moment, listening to the hiss of the heater.

"Why did you decide the time is right to overthrow your government?"

The question startled Sinchon. The American woman was blunt and straightforward. It was actually a quality he wished more of his countrymen possessed. "A right time? I do not know if there is a right time. It was just time for me. I wanted to live my last days as I wanted and I had grown tired of not seeing any change in my country."

"I do not understand," Erwin said.

"General Chief of Staff Myong Chin is not a man of honor. He believes only in his own power and greed. If Chin were dead, then maybe my country will have a chance to unite and change." Sinchon hung his head, thinking of his failed plan. "I had planned to take the first step. The rest would have been up to the United States—and my fellow countrymen."

"You may get another chance," Erwin said. "Your countrymen will respect your courage."

"*Anio . . . anio.* I do not think so. Machiavelli wrote that it is better to be feared than loved if one must choose between the two. I have always chosen to be feared. Now I have failed. I shall never be feared again.''

Erwin nodded. She could feel the anguish in his voice.


STAFFORD, VIRGINIA

Mark Collins rang the doorbell a second time. He glanced up to see one of the upstairs lights in the townhome flash on. A moment later Katie James appeared at the door's window glass.

Opening the door, Katie stammered, ''Mark . . . what are you doing . . . is there something wrong?''

''Is it all right if I come in, Katie?'' Collins asked, forcing a smile.

''Of course.'' She let him inside, then closed the door. ''Mark . . . just tell me straight out, is Duke all right?''

''Duke's mission has been compromised. We've received communications from him so he's alive, but he's stranded until we can put a rescue mission together.''

''Where is he?''

''I can't . . .''

''Don't give me that CIA crap, Mark. I want to know where my husband is.''

''He's on an island in the Yellow Sea. You have to believe me, we're doing everything we can.'' Collins replied, his voice firm.

''Mom . . . what's wrong?'' Matt appeared sleepily at the top of the stairs.

''Nothing, Matt. Go back to bed.'' Katie turned back to Collins, speaking more quietly. ''Don't make me wait for the official call if—''

''I won't, Katie,'' Collins answered, interrupting her thoughts. ''Don't you worry.''

''Duke promised me he wasn't going to miss this Christmas,'' Katie said, placing a hand to her forehead. ''I should have told him I was going to hold him to that promise.''

Collins stepped out onto the porch and walked in the darkness to his car. He needed to get back to the CIA.


NGHIA BINH PROVINCE, VIETNAM

It was like having to wait until after Christmas to open presents: the anticipation was the hardest thing to endure. Callahan wasn't sure how long he and Pope had been lying perfectly still but it seemed like days rather than hours. He wanted to move just an inch but he couldn't. Being bitten by ants was a hell of a lot better than being hit with 123-grain bullets from an AK-47.

Michael let out a long, slow breath and forced himself to relax. He sensed somewhere nearby one of the Vietnamese soldiers was hiding and waiting. The other soldiers' leaving was only a ploy for him or Pope to disclose their position. But it wasn't going to work. Callahan had already decided they would lie there until necessary with or without the ants. He only hoped Pope felt the same way.

Michael felt another stinging sensation on the back of his neck. Blinking, he tried to stop a drop of sweat from rolling into his eye and in doing so he saw it—a slight movement in the weeds at the base of a large tree about forty feet away. Callahan centered his eyes on the area, half expecting to see a small animal or bird. Instead he detected the blotched outline of an upper body.

The man was dressed in a full-camouflage uniform and appeared to be on his knees. Clumps of plants and tree branches were interwoven into his clothing and his face had been painted in green and black stripes. Callahan watched him blink and wondered how many times he had looked in that area without seeing the man.

It was decision time. Moving his right arm a fraction of an inch at a time, Callahan maneuvered his hand near the handle of the Model 22 Smith and Wesson suppressed 9mm. Wrapping his fingers around the grip, he released the strap holding it in place. Carefully, without taking his eye off the enemy soldier for fear of losing sight of him, he slid the pistol from its black nylon holster. It took him a full five minutes to maneuver the pistol into position for a clear shot.

Callahan kept both eyes open as he drew a bead, centering the iron sights on the man's face. The soldier still didn't move. His attention seemed to be fixed on something to the right of Callahan's position, then his eyes went back and forth to encompass the area. Callahan didn't hesitate.

Taking a full breath he slowly released half of it, beginning to squeeze on the trigger.

First Sgt. Jae Hyun and the group of men he selected had covered just about every inch of the island. He wondered if any of the other soldiers had discovered another set of footprints or anything else indicating someone was alive on the island. Hyun knew some of the men had returned to the transport, but he did not want to tell Colonel Kaine there was no one alive until he was absolutely certain.

Kneeling down, Hyun touched the soft sand between a set of wedge-shaped rocks. He ran his finger across a slight indentation in the dirt. It wasn't a full footprint but it didn't appear natural either. The mark was a half-moon shape and could be the front of a small military boot.

Hyun looked up. The coastline for the next fifty yards or so became progressively steeper and more broken before changing back smoothing out further on. He should have searched this section of the coast first. He counted four deep ravines cutting across the shore with a mixture of rocks and boulders scattered about. There were dense patches of dried weeds and leafless bushes between many of the larger rocks. Some were as high as four or five feet. *Now, if I was going to hide, this would be the place,* he reasoned.

Standing up, the sergeant walked closer to the broken shore. He would search this one last area before heading back to give his report to Kaine.

Callahan felt the pistol jump in his hand. The only sound was the movement of the steel slide ejecting the round and chambering another 9mm hollow point. A hot, spent casing landed next to Callahan's face. Smoke curled up from it.

A split second later he heard a soft splat as the hollow-point bullet impacted on the man's face below the right eye. The bullet mushroomed immediately as it penetrated the soldier's skull and soft brain tissue, destroying all the man's motor functions before he could yell out or even raise his weapon.

Michael quickly drew another bead, placing the sights on the soldier's forehead. His mouth and eyes were open and a trickle of red blood dripped down his face. Callahan waited. The soldier never even flinched.

"Pope," Michael muttered. "Come on. We're out of here."

Callahan rolled over to look at his communications specialist. Pope was curled into a tight ball with his M16 next to his chest. The side of his face was lying directly on the ground with ants crawling in every different direction. Pope was blinking trying to keep them out of his eyes.

"Are you alive?" Callahan asked, seeing the gruesome sight.

Pope ran his hand over his face and neck. There were dozens of red spots where the ants had bitten him.

"Be . . . all that you can be . . . in the army," Pope sang under his breath. "I should have stayed at home and been a rocket scientist like my mom wanted me to be."

"Shhhh," Callahan hissed as the two men stayed low, moving out of the area.

"Shit . . . this is all we need," Major Erwin cursed, lying on her stomach. The intel officer watched as a large bank of storm clouds moved in out of the north. She guessed the front was still ten miles away but the rolling gray clouds were only a few hundred feet above the ocean. The weather would help mask their presence, but it would more than likely inhibit the rescue attempt.

She glanced back to the south, watching as the North Korean soldier slowly made his way toward her and General Sinchon's hiding place. She had been watching the man for some time. He had walked past her position once but was now doubling back. He appeared to be navigating his way back up the coast in a zigzag pattern. His head was down and he stopped occasionally, bending down to the ground. She estimated he was 200 yards away and taking his time.

Sliding back down the gully Erwin meticulously erased her tracks using a dried weed to brush the marks from the dirt. She ducked back into the cave and looked at Sinchon. He was looking worse by the hour.

"Someone is coming," she whispered.

"Foot patrol," Sinchon sighed then looked up at the woman, not wanting to alarm her. "General James has done a good job of hiding us. The soldier will have a difficult time locating our exact position."

"I hope so . . . he keeps coming back to one spot. I think he must have found something." Erwin finished arranging the bushes and weeds at the entrance so they looked more natural and blocked the opening.

"It is me they want, not you." Sinchon held his hurt arm and scooted forward.

"Where do you think you're going?" Erwin asked, putting a firm hand on his shoulder. "You can't go out there now . . . he'll see where you came from. Let's just sit tight and see what happens."

Sinchon shook his head and sat exhausted against the wall as the major turned off the heater. Erwin hoped James was managing to stay out of sight. Looking down at the radio, she decided if he wasn't back after the soldier left the area she'd make contact with Guard Dog herself.


THE PENTAGON

The office General Chaniff maintained in the Special Technical Operations Center was no larger than a broom closet and about as well decorated. The only personal touch was a plastic model of an M1A2 Abrams tank given to him by his ten-year-old nephew. Chaniff only used the room to catch a quick catnap or to take an important phone call. Other than that he believed he should be spending his time on the floor of the operations center.

"General, I just talked with Colonel Conrad," Lieutenant Fontano said, entering the office.

"And?" Chaniff frowned, suspecting it couldn't be good news if the man had come to deliver it straightaway.

"He is recommending the Pave Hawks launch on time and the mission go forward. The weather over the target area is getting worse, sir."

"He's the man in charge, Mr. Fontano. If he says go, we go," Chaniff said as his phone rang.

"Yes, sir."

Chaniff dismissed the man, then picked up the phone. "Chaniff here."

"General, what's the latest? Are the jets in the air? Have they got James yet?" It was Manning.

"No, but you'll be the first to know." Chaniff checked his watch. 12:15 in the morning. *What are you doing up this late, Mr. Manning?*

"I'd better be. I need to know everything the second it happens. I want all information going through me. Do you understand? All information. What's going on in Vietnam? The president's not happy your team got ambushed."

"We're arranging a rescue now," Chaniff answered. *I never said anything about an ambush.*

"Fine. Just keep me updated."

Chaniff hung up the phone. His lower right leg began to twitch with a combination of anger and nerves. Manning had always been difficult but now things were getting worse. Chaniff didn't like having to go through Manning to get to McEntire. The man was acting more like a hyperactive kid than a professional servant to the president of the United States. *What did he mean by saying the team was in an ambush?* Chaniff clearly remembered he hadn't said a damned thing about an ambush to Manning. This was beginning to stink.

You'll be the first to know, all right. What I want you to know, Chaniff thought, wishing he knew how Manning had gotten the information. For now he was tired and needed a short nap to recharge his batteries. Then he'd be able to think more clearly.


LANGAU ISLAND

The cut on Duke's scalp had stopped bleeding. He stood with his back next to a barnacle-covered rock as the ocean splashed below him. Looking down at the front of his parka, he saw it was ripped. Duke grinned, thinking Major Erwin would be happy to know the overstuffed coat helped break his fall.

Checking out the rest of his condition, Duke knew if he didn't get warm soon, hypothermia could set in. He glanced up to see if the soldier had seen him tumble over the edge. There was no one looking down at him.

Duke studied the rock ledge thirty feet above him. He couldn't see anything out of the ordinary, just a few wisps of brown grass blowing in the wind. The sound of the waves hitting the shore was all that filled his ears.

The cliff was straight up with a number of sharp-edged rocks sticking out the side. He wondered how he had managed to slide over the ledge without breaking his neck.

The general stepped away from the breaking surf. He wrapped his hand around close to the roots of dried underbrush, then placed his foot in a small indentation in the cliff. Exerting all the strength he had left, he attempted to climb upward to the right of his former position. He'd worry about the soldier when he made it to the top.

"It is proceeding much slower than I expected," Farajolla Rassai, the Iranian freighter captain, said in fluent Korean. The taller Iranian stood next to Kaine with his arms crossed, a brown cigar hanging from his lips.

Six Iranian sailors were assisting with carrying the wooden crates from the Il-76 to the waiting ship. The crates were then secured below deck, to be covered with bags of corn and wheat seed.

A gust of wind kicked up dust as storm clouds brewed to the north.

"Allah has provided me and my crew with a gift." Rassai took a lusty puff on his cigar. "The Americans will never find me in a storm. Our mission will soon be a success."

"Allah had nothing to do with this," Kaine answered coldly, his tone condescending. "And I would not discount the Americans' abilities to find your ship."

"My crew is seasoned. We have eluded the Americans many times before," the captain boasted proudly. "They rely on satellites and technology while I trust Allah to guide my ship for a safe voyage."

"If the Americans discover what cargo you are carrying they will hunt you down," Kaine warned. The man's arrogance was beginning to wear on him.

"Perhaps they will try. I would be more concerned if I had damaged one of their choppers," Rassai stated, staring over Kaine's shoulder at the wreckage on the island.

Kaine's expression hardened, yet he knew Rassai was right. His men were lightly armed and they would not be a match for a well-trained, heavily armed American assault force. Again he cursed the older aircraft for malfunctioning. He scanned the ominous sky, searching and listening for anything unusual.

"I will be in the Ilyushin." Kaine ignored the smug look on the Iranian's face for having rattled him.

\*   \*   \*

Duke James took the last few steps, reaching the top of the barren bluff overlooking the two transports. He stopped to catch his breath while slowly looking left to right. The horizon was barren as he watched a few whiffs of sand streak from the ground as the wind continued to increase.

Keeping his head down Duke rolled in behind a broken line of rocks. Lying flat he looked over the outcropping. He couldn't see any tracks in the dirt where the foot soldier had walked past his position. He slowly pushed his head up, trying to see over a small hump.

In the distance he caught sight of the soldier walking back to the north. He realized the Korean must have walked to the edge of where he was hiding and turned around.

Colonel Kaine walked toward the Il-76. Far off in the distance he could see the first of Sergeant Hyun's foot patrol returning from their search. They did not have anyone with them and Kaine wondered if Sinchon would be found before it was time to depart. *Maybe his body was on the* Van Triumph, *buried under the lower deck.*

Stepping onto the flight deck, Kaine addressed the Il-76's copilot who was seated alone monitoring the radio: "Go. I need every man moving those fuel rods."

"Yes, sir."

Kaine put the radio headphones over his ears. The channel to Kim Il Song air base was still open.

"Red Crown . . . Red Star," Kaine radioed. In his mind he pictured the darkened command-and-control center at Kim Il Song air base. General Chin would be seated in the center of the room watching the technicians at their posts.

*"Copy Red Star . . . go ahead."*

Kaine keyed his mike. "We are close to completing the transfer. Anything on your radar?"

*"Negative. The skies are clear."*

"I want air support standing by," Kaine demanded, relieved, but still apprehensive. "The Americans—"

*"I have the situation under control, Colonel Kaine,"* General Chin cut in. *"You let me worry about the Americans. Your job is to transfer the fuel rods. I order you to concentrate on that assignment and nothing more."*

"Understood. Red Star out."

The colonel leaned his large head against the back of the copilot's seat. The plan was not going as Kaine had expected and all because of a fire in an engine. He knew the entire plan revolved around timing. Painstakingly he himself had worked out the times to miss the American satellites' orbits. Now, hours behind schedule and Sinchon's body still not found, Kaine pondered things as they were. *I should have been prepared for something like this and loaded the Ilyushin with hand-held SAMs and heavier machine guns.* Kaine at last closed his eyes for a few minutes of rest.

## Najin, North Korea

The Su-27 groaned as the crane operator lifted the interceptor off the flatbed truck and lowered it onto the hard pavement of Highway 23 North. Three miles away the flashing yellow lights told Lt. Col. Krung Woong that the level stretch of highway had been blocked off by military police.

Woong exited the bright blue Chinese-manufactured staff car, dressed in his flight uniform and G suit. He watched the restraints supporting his large twin-tailed fighter fall away as a group of flight technicians stripped the canvas tarp off the jet. A second truck pulled in behind the Su-27 and a second group of men began to pull the safety pins from his missiles. An auxiliary power unit was connected to the jet's engines and the reserve under-wing fuel tanks were topped off.

His mouth set and the Ray-Ban sunglasses concealing his mood, Woong walked with his white helmet under his arm toward the jet as her canopy came open. The Su-27's powerful turbofans came to life as a flight technician activated the interceptor's avionics.

After one quick walkaround, Woong studied the afternoon sky. White broken clouds hung over the mountaintop on each side of the valley. He could see patches of blue sky, and the sun, when it peeked through, felt warm. The wind blew out of the north at six or seven knots. It shouldn't affect his takeoff.

"She's ready, sir," the senior flight engineer said assuredly.

"Tell everyone to clear the area. I'm going to run up the engines." Woong ascended the ladder and stepped into the dull gray cockpit. The canopy closed and locked into place. The high-pitched rumble of the engines was muffled inside the cockpit. Swiveling around, he watched the men and equipment start to pull away.

Colonel Woong's eyes swept the cockpit instrumentation and HUD. Everything looked to be in order including oil and hydraulic pressure, weapons' status and fuel. He adjusted his lap and shoulder straps to get more comfortable. It felt somewhat strange sitting in the middle of a secluded mountain valley without the support of an entire air base on the ground around him. He made sure his radio, IFF transponders and electronic countermeasures were all turned off. He flipped through the notepad containing the mission profile secured to his left thigh.

Taking off to the north, Woong would stay low to avoid radar contact and skirt the North Korean border with China. He would then receive a radio call from Chin giving him the signal to execute the mission. Twenty minutes after that he would be the first pilot to down an American AWACS in combat.

Locking the Su-27's brakes, Woong throttled engines to 50 percent power. Watching the rpms build, he checked the instrument panel for warning lights or broken gauges. There weren't any. He flashed a thumbs-up to the ground crew standing next to the highway. Releasing the brakes, he felt the big jet bounce slightly as it started down the two-lane road.

He waited for his airspeed to hit sixty knots before pushing the throttles into afterburner. The Su-27, loaded with two auxiliary fuel tanks and ten missiles, accelerated, chewing up 6,800 feet of road in seconds. At 183 knots he eased the center stick back, lifting the nose five degrees off the road. He cleaned up the gear while letting his airspeed build past 200 knots.

Woong snapped the jet out of burner as he reached his desired airspeed to conserve fuel. He kept any eye on his altitude as the interceptor climbed to mission altitude.

This time it only took Duke about twenty minutes to cross the barren bluff crawling on his hands and knees. He recalled the path he had taken earlier with no problem. His clothes were drenched from the ocean and the lack of sleep was wearing him down but he pressed on.

Duke hustled up a small hill and ducked behind a group of larger boulders. The cave was 300 yards to the south. He was almost there and hoped there was enough fuel in the heater to dry him.

He positioned himself to take one last look at the Korean transports on the far end of the runway. A group of men pushed another crate from the aircraft. A second group was there to receive it, then it started toward the Iranian freighter. Duke tried to see how many containers were still in the back of the Il-76 but he was too far away. Four men stood guard around the transports now and he guessed them to be the foot soldiers who had returned from their search.

Staying hunched over, he darted from rock to rock, working his way south.

Lt. Col. Miles Conrad strode down the flight line to the last dark steel gray F-15E fighter. His backseater, or WSO, Maj. Skip ''Greeno'' Green, followed one step behind him.

Green had flown with Conrad for six months after making the jump from

F-111Es. Slightly taller at five feet eleven with a medium frame, Skip's head was stopped with sandy blond hair. The major loved sports and it didn't matter what kind. Conrad often joked that if Green was ever captured during war, the worst torture the enemy could inflict on him would be to let him watch television and scramble ESPN. He would break in a week.

"There they go," Skip said, his large brown eyes on the other side of the tarmac.

Conrad stopped. Near the maintenance hangar, two MH-60G Pave Hawk choppers lifted off one after another. The ghost-gray special operation choppers, each loaded with a dozen Rangers, swiveled around before heading to the west and feeding into the low afternoon clouds.

Conrad climbed up the aluminum ladder and into the front seat of his Strike Eagle. Green followed, strapping himself into the ejection seat directly behind the pilot.

## USS *Observation Island*

CPO Owens watched two friendly aircraft symbols appear on her computer screen. The code znc56 appeared under the symbols, telling the radar and communications specialist the aircraft were American Pave Hawks.

Owens checked her flight schedule. The Hawks were right on time. They would clear the coast in two minutes. She took a drink of hot coffee before addressing Bliss.

"Captain. Operation Eagle Fire has started," she said. "I'm showing two Pave Hawks squawking on MODE III IFF. They're on course and on time."

"What's the flight time?"

"They should be approaching Langau coast in forty-five minutes, sir," Owens answered immediately, then added, "If the weather doesn't slow them down."

"Where's the *Paul Hamilton?*" Bliss asked, referring to their destroyer escort.

"She's twenty minutes out to the southeast still heading this way."

"All right, people. Ms. Owens says it's show time. Everybody on their toes."

# 28

Manning nervously flipped through the channels on the television in front of him. CNN was broadcasting its standard late-night format and the other channels were airing old sitcom reruns or infomercials. The nightly political talk shows were focusing as usual on President McEntire's economic policies.

Manning's desk was cluttered with the remains of a Chinese fast-food dinner. He picked at the last few noodles stuck to the bottom of a wax-paper dish.

"Why am I still picking at this crap," he grunted, tossing the carton in his trash can.

Seated in his office alone, Manning felt edgy and uncertain. Chaniff was at the Pentagon watching over the Vietnamese and Langau operations and the president was in Europe with all the other cabinet members. Everything was in order.

Manning tapped his foot nervously on the plastic chair mat under his desk. He was thinking he could go to his townhome and get some sleep, but he wanted to be in the White House in case something came up on one of the operations again. *Well, I know something is going to happen, don't I? That's what I'm waiting for. Why hasn't Chaniff called me yet?*

He looked at the authority phone linking him directly with General Chaniff in the Special Technical Operations Center in the Pentagon. Picking up the receiver, he hesitated. He set the receiver back down. What he wanted was for Chaniff to call him. *I'm not going to call that jerk. He'll have to call me. I'm the one in charge.*

"I just need to learn how to settle down and relax," Manning said to himself, looking in a mirror. "Damn, I look like shit." He took out a comb from his desk drawer and combed his hair.

*I have everything under control . . . I can relax because I'm right where I want to be,* Manning thought, grinning and sitting back behind his desk. He filled his pipe with tobacco and fired it up. The blue smoke lingered over his head as he sank deeper into his chair. He closed his eyes, letting the realization that he had accomplished his goals sink in. A few moments later the chief of staff drifted off to sleep.

NORTH KOREA

The Su-27 broke through 2,000 feet as Colonel Woong banked to the north-west. A solid white line of condensation streaked off each wingtip as he maneuvered the fighter through a narrow valley leading to the Chinese border.

Dark green pine trees, broken up by an occasional dirt road, streaked under the jet in a blur. The farther north he flew the worse the weather was becoming. The clouds were now thick and dark with a ceiling of only 3,000 feet.

Leveling the wings he watched his airspeed remain steady at 245 knots. Woong scanned the airspace in front of him. He had flown over this region several times during training missions. It was free of commercial air traffic, which allowed pilots to mix it up in mock combat. He knew when he crossed the next mountain range he would be in Chinese airspace. The terrain would then flatten out some, allowing him to maintain a constant altitude.

The colonel let the fighter drift up to 2,300 feet before he forced the stick down. The fighter responded a bit sluggishly, hampered by the extra fuel tanks and full load of ten air-to-air missiles.

Woong's attention went to the weapons panel directly below the HUD. The missiles he was most concerned about were the R-77AEs strapped to the fuselage on either side of the engine. The twelve-foot-long Russian missiles were called AMRAAM-skis by the West because they bore a re-markable resemblance to the AIM-120, America's most advanced air-to-air missile.

The R-77AE had been designed to kill highly maneuverable targets such as cruise missiles, SAMs and the West's best fighters from beyond visual range. More importantly it was equipped with a powerful electronic counter-countermeasures system and a passive and active radar tracking and homing seeker head. It was equipped with a solid rocket motor and could be fired from 100 miles out at high-priority targets, such as AWACS and E-2C Hawkeyes, to home in on the powerful radar emissions coming from the surveillance aircraft.

Woong wasn't confident the big missile had the range to kill a target from 100 miles. However, he knew the American AWACS jet was large and slow and Woong felt he had a good chance of killing it if he could only get close enough. His biggest obstacle would be getting past the American fighters assigned to protect it.

Pulling back on the stick, the gentle push of 2 Gs hit Woong's body as the nose came up. The Su-27 pitched over a ridge of pine trees, climbing slowly. His eyes swept the HUD as his airspeed dropped below 220 knots. Woong banked to the east and dropped the nose, his airspeed increasing rapidly as gravity pulled his heavy jet to the ground. Leveling the jet at 3,000 feet, Woong looked to the right. He watched brown smoke rise from the stacks of a cement plant on the edge of a town drifting to the south.

Woong centered his attention back on the HUD. If everything was going as planned, an A310 Airbus should be taxiing in preparation for takeoff outside the Chinese city of Harbin to his north.

## OSAN AFB, SOUTH KOREA

Colonel Conrad adjusted the oxygen-to-air mix, sucking in several long breaths before starting to taxi his F-15E. Ahead of him the E-3C AWACS, its white-paint scheme offset by the rotating black oval radar dome atop the fuselage, turned onto the runway, waiting for clearance from the tower.

"Flight controls . . . check for full movement," Maj. Skip Green, the backseater, said, running down the last few items on the checklist.

"Full and free," Conrad responded.

"Harnesses."

"Check."

"Seats armed and ready."

"Check."

"Visors down and we're ready to go," Green announced.

"Visors down." Conrad nudged the throttles forward and released the brakes. He swung the sleek F-15E to the left, passing in front of the other gray eagles. Looking over his shoulder he watched his wingman, Capt. Ned "Red Dog" Ruddy, pull away from the flight line to follow him.

Conrad heard the message radioed from the tower to the AWACS: *"Cleared for takeoff, Mentor Zero three three. Maintain runway heading flight level two zero. Turn left heading two eight zero. Wind out of the northeast gusting to ten knots."*

"Roger Tower . . . Mentor rolling."

Guiding the big fighter down the taxiway, Conrad watched black smoke pour from each of the 707-320B's four jet engines. His F-15E vibrated as the AWACS roared down the runway and lifted off. The big surveillance jet banked to the left before disappearing in the clouds.

*"Hold short, Tacoma Lead."*

"Roger, Tower. Tacoma Lead holding short," Conrad responded, taxiing to the edge of the runway and stopping.

His eyes studied the three multifunction displays on his instrument panel. He checked his IFF transponder one more time to make sure it was on.

To avoid North Korean radar contact each fighter package would take off to the west, then turn south. They planned to skirt the South Korean coast before banking back to the west. Then they would hook up with the AWACS south of Langau Island.

"How we doing back there, Greeno?" Conrad asked his WSO.

"Peachy keen. You just keep us from digging a hole in the ground and I'll do the rest."

"You have yourself a deal."

*"Tacoma Lead . . . cleared for takeoff."*

"Roger, Tower. Red Dog, you with me?" Conrad radioed as his wingman pulled up next to him.

*"Let's rock-and-roll,"* Ruddy radioed back, pulling his F-15E up even with Conrad's.

"Tower . . . Tacoma Leader. We're rolling."

Conrad jammed the throttles forward, feeling all five zones of his afterburners kick in. Watching the HUD click off the speed, Conrad lifted his jet smoothly into the air.

## KIM IL SONG AIR BASE, NORTH KOREA

"New contact bearing one niner seven. It's out of Osan," the senior radar technician reported from his position in the darkened command and control center. "Range one hundred seventy miles . . . altitude two thousand feet. It's climbing, sir."

"Your opinion, Sergeant," General Chin demanded, standing to watch the screen.

"The radar return is large and solid. It looks like a four-engine aircraft. Possibly a transport."

"Is it changing course?" Chin quizzed.

"No, sir. Course is constant at two eight zero. It's heading west."

Chin folded his arms in front of him. Colonel Hwan's information had been correct. The Americans had just launched their AWACS, right on schedule. Now if the radar picked up two low-flying choppers heading west behind the AWACS, he would know the American rescue plan had been set into action.

"Sir, I'm tracking two new targets. Bearing one eight two, altitude 2,000 feet, speed 230 knots. They just crossed the coast and are descending. Altitude 1000 . . . 750 . . . 550 . . . they're off the screen."

"Opinion?" Chin asked.

"Choppers, sir. They were flying in a tight formation." The senior radar technician hesitated, turning around. "I can't be 100 percent certain, though."

"Give the order anyway. I want the pilots in their jets standing by." Chin moved to the communications console. He felt it in his gut that the information was accurate. "Contact Colonel Woong."

"Yes, sir."

Chin's heart began to beat harder. It was an uncanny feeling knowing the Americans' next move.

Colonel Woong trimmed the Su-27 for level flight at 3,000 feet. There was a slight hum in his helmet. A weak Chinese air-defense radar was sweeping the skies to the north. Checking his radar warning receiver on the left side of the instrument panel, he noted the signal was barely registering. He doubted it was powerful enough to track him.

*"Victory One flight, respond,"* Woong's radio crackled.

He keyed his mike twice confirming the transmission, trying to keep the radio chatter to a minimum.

*"Operation Great Leader is authorized. Repeat . . . Great Leader is authorized."*

The pilot felt a slight twinge move up his spine. He keyed his mike again two quick times before jamming the throttles forward just short of afterburner. Waiting for his fighter's airspeed to build to 300 knots, he pulled the stick back, banking to the north. This time the Su-27 responded more quickly, the increased airspeed adding to its performance. The press of 4 Gs pinned him back into the hard plastic seat and the canopy turned white as he cut into the boiling clouds overhead.

Woong felt Gs bleed off as he gained altitude rapidly breaking through 10,000 feet. The jet bounced and vibrated as it cut through the thick overcast. At 13,000 feet Woong broke into the open. The sky was suddenly light blue, the sun a glowing white ball of light. He could see a slight filmy overcast about him but otherwise the heavens were clear.

He lowered his visor and came wings level at 15,000 feet heading three two five degrees, northwest. Woong estimated he was ten to twelve miles inside Chinese airspace. He throttled back and scanned the sky to the north. If the Chinese airliner had taken off on time, he should be able to see its contrails streaking across the deep sky.

"Come on, where are you?" the North Korean pleaded into his cockpit. His desire to complete the task was overpowering.

## LANGAU ISLAND

Stumbling across a patch of dead branches and rock, Sergeant Hyun hit the ground and tumbled forward down a steep ravine. He felt sharp rocks cutting through his clothing into his elbows and knees as he plunged head over heels.

Hyun came to a stop and cursed out loud. He sat upright and quickly circled the area with his gun. His anger masked the underlying embarrassment he would feel if someone had seen him.

*What else could go wrong today?* he thought. Satisfied no one was around, he picked two splintered rocks from his right knee. He wished he had never been picked for this assignment. No matter what happened he knew he would be blamed for not finding General Sinchon.

Hyun stood and brushed the remaining dust from his pants. He heard the ocean behind him and turned to see how close he was to the shoreline. A few more feet and he would have been in the water.

Turning back, Hyun noticed an area at the foot of the ravine. It was much darker than the area around it and partially obscured with weeds and a dead bush. If it was an opening it wasn't very big but it looked large enough for a person to crawl into.

Sergeant Hyun lowered his weapon, angling toward the side. He didn't want to walk directly in front of the opening. All he could hear was the lapping of the waves at the shoreline.

## F-15E TACOMA LEAD

The South Korean coast paralleled Conrad's southerly flight path 12,000 feet below. Off his left wing, 100 yards away, cruised his wingman Tacoma Seven. A half-mile to the north Tacoma Eight and Nine maintained the same heading and airspeed trailing a half-mile behind.

"Tacoma Lead. Feet wet," Conrad radioed as his fighter drifted over the water. The moving-map navigational display showed another three miles before he hit the first way point. He would then turn right to lead his package to their patrol area.

*"Copy, Tacoma,"* came the final call from Osan.

Changing radio frequencies, Conrad called up the command guard channel used by the AWACS. Colonel Conrad waited for his fighter to pass over the first way point before keying the mike with the toe of his boot.

"Mentor . . . Tacoma Leader. Feet wet. Way point one clear."

*"We have you, Tacoma. Turn right heading three two seven. Maintain air speed and altitude."*

"Roger, Mentor. Tacoma turning."

Conrad nudged the stick right, banking his jet to the northwest. He could see a long bank of cloud ahead of him.

At 23,000 feet Woong broke through the thin layer of haze, still heading north. At this altitude the sky was a deeper blue and totally clear of haze or clouds. It was as if someone had lifted a veil from his canopy. With the deeper-colored sky Colonel Woong reasoned it would be easier to spot the white contrails of the A310 Airbus.

He pushed over, leveling the interceptor at 24,000 feet. Activating the autopilot, he resumed his search scanning left and then right. He focused his eyes to infinity trying to locate his target.

"There you are," he breathed, grinning under his mask. Ten miles to the west and 12,000 feet above him Woong caught a flash of reflected sunlight. His visor allowed him to pick out the twin faint contrails in the bright afternoon sun. Without thinking he instantly shoved the throttles forward, pushing the Flanker into afterburner. Concentrating on catching up to the small white speck, he didn't notice his fighter slip past Mach 1 breaking through 30,000 feet.

Woong knew he couldn't let the pilots of the Chinese A310 see him approach. Commercial airline pilots had all been trained to report any military aircraft coming within a mile of their position. He would have to sneak in behind the airliner and take a position at its six o'clock under the right wing. When the A310 was picked up on the AWACS' radar it would only see one return.

Flying in a wide arc Woong rapidly closed the distance as he swooped in behind the airliner. Staying 2,000 feet below the white A310, he leveled out. The HUD showed he was on a southeasterly heading, altitude 34,000 feet. Hot exhaust blasting from each wing-mounted engine was cooling into white mist a hundred or so feet behind the jet. Using only his fingertips to control the stick, Woong edged the Su-27 up a hundred feet at a time.

The bare aluminum underbelly of the airliner filled the windshield of his cockpit. Throttling back, he opened the air brake, slowing to 550 knots. Then he let the fighter float up, maneuvering it underneath the right section of the A310. He pulled back twenty feet from the wing to position himself between the fuselage and inboard engine. The wing flap was directly above him. Woong concentrated on the airliner's path making sure he didn't get too close. When flying in formation one lapse in concentration could bring both airplanes down.

## E-3C AWACS, Mentor

Maj. Keith R. Tallman, a lanky six-foot-four-inch West Texas cowboy from El Paso, liked being the "Hammer." In flyboy lingo "Hammer" is the officer responsible for all decisions on an AWACS.

Tallman had wanted to be a pilot but his poor eyesight and slightly crooked spine caused him to wash out. Though he was disappointed, his wife was pleased with the outcome. She didn't want him rocketing around the sky in what she believed was a lethal version of a single-engine sports car with wings. So in his opinion he did the next best thing. He told the pilots where to go and how to get there.

He considered himself lord and master of the 335,000 pounds of flying radar station. The only thing he chewed more than his junior officers' butts was Red Man tobacco. Tallman's professionalism and dedication were almost unmatched in the air force. He had checked out as the number one "Hammer" in the AWACS fleet for the last three years. For the last eighteen months he had instructed other AWACS Hammers flying in mock combat over the Nellis Test Range in Nevada. Tallman had been looking forward to getting back into the field, although he missed the dry air and clear blue skies of the high desert.

Tallman waited for the AWACS to level at 42,000 feet before leaving his seat. The interior was dark, enabling the crew to see their computer monitors more easily. Red, green and yellow lights skipped across the walls and ceiling as fans cooling the electronics filled the cabin with a mild hum.

The major made his way down the port side of the jet past the nine Hazeltine high-resolution display consoles. He walked up behind the duty officer at the air combat station. Watching the young second lieutenant manipulate the computer controls, Tallman studied the display. The color screen changed every ten seconds as radio waves from the APY-2 radar swept the area around the jet to 260 miles out.

On the left side of the screen he saw the uneven Korean coast. In the upper center was Langau Island which appeared as a yellow, misshapen rectangle. Near the bottom in bright blue letters were the words USS OBV ISD. A friendly surface ship symbol marked the exact position of the USS *Observation Island* and its escort, the USS *Paul Hamilton,* as they sailed north. On the far right side of the screen just outside of Chinese airspace flew the RC-135 spy plane at 23,000 feet heading east. In twenty minutes the jet would pass fifty miles north of Langau Island on its way back to South Korean airspace.

Tallman's eyes returned to the left side of the screen where friendly fighters were just breaking over the coast. The Strike Eagles in Tacoma and Intrepid packages were flying in a fluid four formation. The loose formation allowed the interceptors to fly a half-mile apart to get the maximum maneuverability for both offensive and defensive actions. The Strike Eagles were thus able to cover a larger portion of the sky with their powerful APG-70 radars.

Tacoma Lead, which he knew was being piloted by Colonel Conrad, was leading the entire package. Conrad's fighter was now five miles offshore at 12,000 feet. Two miles to the south and three miles behind Conrad's position flew the Intrepid package. The four F-15Es cut through the sky in the same type of loose formation 2,000 feet below. The F-16Cs trailed at 8,000 feet in a tighter formation. His eyes returned to the center of the screen. Directly below his AWACS, orbiting at 25,000 feet, was a KC-10 Extender tanker.

"Where are the choppers?" Tallman asked.

"Here, sir," the combat duty officer, Lt. Buddy Klages, touched the screen. "They're thirty minutes out and on schedule."

"Any other air traffic?"

"Yes, sir. I'm showing three comairs. Two to the south and one to the north." The duty officer pointed out the northernmost target. "This one will pass within sixty miles of our position."

Tallman studied the screen for a moment before talking. "Sounds okay. Give the word. This mission is a go."

"Tacoma package, you are cleared for angels three five. Maintain racetrack pattern at zulu."

Tallman listened as his combat duty officer, a brown-haired, blue-eyed Penn State graduate, put the pilots through the paces. The symbols on the screen changed positions as the F-15Es began to climb to 35,000 feet.

*"Roger, Mentor. Tacoma on the way."*

Tacoma flight's green symbols suddenly turned north.

"Intrepid package, climb to angels three five . . . you're at bravo."

*"Copy you, Mentor. Intrepid to the rescue."*

Tallman watched the four-color monitor as the second flight of F-15Es broke formation to make their way to the south of Tacoma package. Sticking a wad of Red Man chewing tobacco in his mouth, Tallman continued to supervise the younger man.

"Okay, Lieutenant, get the Vipers in place." Tallman spit into a paper cup.

## RC-135S, SUPER SNOOPER

M. Sgt. Matthew P. Fletcher took a sip of cold coffee. The taste made him grimace. He clutched his chair's armrest as the RC-135, a large four-engine military version of the Boeing 707, came out of a long banking turn and leveled at 23,000 feet. It was heading west at 230 knots.

On the surface the jet was a windowless airliner with a long nose and enlarged midsection. The aircraft contained two pilots, two navigators and a half-dozen highly trained technicians capable of analyzing every shred of electronic transmissions radiating from miles around.

Off its right wing, ninety-two miles away, was the broken shoreline of North Korea.

Sergeant Fletcher, or Matthew P. as his colleagues called him, was a "Crow," the senior signals intelligence specialist on board the aircraft. The thirty-three-year-old man felt surprisingly alert considering he and his crew had been in the air for eight hours straight. Usually, after being seated in the same place, drinking countless cups of bad coffee and eating cold turkey sandwiches with old cheese, he was ready to climb the walls. Either he had started to like his job or the routine had numbed him.

Sitting behind a wall full of color displays, navigational instruments and recording devices, Fletcher had worked hard to become the most experienced member of the RC-135 crew. After cutting his teeth aboard an E-3C AWACS in the early nineties, Fletcher transferred to the more clandestine RC-135. When his second wife divorced him Fletcher was completing his training at Offutt AFB, Nebraska. He was hoping reconnaissance would be more exciting and looked forward to the change and a new beginning.

He soon learned it wasn't much of a change and in the last few months found himself becoming disillusioned with his air force career. A typical RC-135's mission involved flying ten to twelve hours outside enemy airspace recording radar transmissions, telephone and military radio conversations, and photographing reentry vehicles during ballistic missile tests. The missions were long and tedious. Fletcher counted the days to retirement so he could rejoin his family's grocery store business in northern Miami. His older brother referred to it as "Matt getting a life again."

Fletcher finished off the last of the bitter brew and secured his chipped Miami Dolphins cup into its holder. The cup, a gift from one of his former wives, made him think of south Florida's nearly white sandy beaches and glowing orange sun. He pictured himself drinking an icy beer checking out an array of bikini-clad women.

"Sergeant Fletcher, are you still with us?" Capt. Lawrence McQuire, the spy plane's electronics commander, came up behind Fletcher's station.

"Oh . . . ah, yes sir." Fletcher shook himself out of his daydream. "I just received confirmation the E-3C AWACS is orbiting. Nothing from our friends to the north."

"Any word from the *Observation Island?*"

"No, sir. Everything's quiet."


## THE PENTAGON

"Eagle Fire has started, sir." Lt. Frank Fontano's athletic frame stood in the doorway of Chaniff's office.

General Chaniff was lying on a sofa with his back to him.

"What's in the air?" Chaniff asked, rolling over to face the lieutenant.

"The Pave Hawks crossed the coast ten minutes ago. The AWACS is on station and Colonel Conrad's fighters are forming up. They'll be on station in five minutes."

"So why are you waking me?" Chaniff stretched his arms out before bringing them in across his chest.

"You asked me to, sir." Fontano's dark eyes flashed.

"Okay . . ." Chaniff sat up, rubbing his face. His uniform was wrinkled and hair messed up. "Any word from James?"

"No, sir."

"Alright . . . I'll be out there in a minute. Make sure there's fresh coffee, Lieutenant." Chaniff mumbled to himself as Fontano went back to his post, "Can't get any damn sleep around here."


The wind had changed directions and was now gusting from the north. Sgt. Jae Hyun was focused on the opening in the wall of the ravine and hadn't noticed the temperature dropping or the thick layer of clouds beginning to descend over the island.

He worked the action on his AK-47, chambering a round. Holding the metal slide in check with his hand, he let the bolt strike the receiver quietly.

Placing one foot in front of the other, he crept the last ten feet toward the cave. Inspecting the ground, he saw where the dirt had been replaced around the bush.

Hyun remained to one side of the hole, not wanting to be directly in front. He knew someone was inside.

NGHIA BINH PROVINCE, VIETNAM

Callahan and Pope were huddled together next to a puddle of muddy water overlooking a rice field. Behind them was a stand of trees covered with dried vines. They provided cover as well as shade from the sun.

The men had covered themselves with wet mud and green foliage stripped from the trees. Besides providing a natural camouflage the mud also soothed their ant bites.

Callahan was lying on his stomach using a compact pair of binoculars to scout the area. Vietnamese farmers were on the other side of the rice field using oxen to plow. A mile away was a dirt road. Every few minutes a bicycle or motorcycle passed along it. He kept close watch to their right. There, parked next to a grass-roofed hut, were three military trucks. Callahan couldn't tell for sure but they looked like troop transports to him. The rear sections were covered with green canvas tarp and the wide deep-lug tires were designed to cut through the thick muddy roads when it rained.

He estimated that if each truck had been filled with men there were probably eighteen or twenty Vietnamese soldiers searching the area. He didn't like the odds.

"Clear," Callahan dropped the glasses, glancing back.

"Clear," Pope whispered, telling his commander no one was at their six.

"Pope, get the radio."

"They won't do it, man . . . it's not dark." Pope removed the hand-held radio and snapped the antenna in place. Switching it on, he passed the unit to Callahan. "Give it a try but I think your dream'n'."

Callahan ignored him, adjusting the volume so the static was barely audible. "Cheerleader . . . Tango. Come in, Cheerleader."

*"Go ahead, Tango."* the Motorola URC-200 SATCOM radio crackled.

"We need evac in here now," Callahan demanded quietly.

*"No daylight extracts, Tango."*

"That's bullshit, Cheerleader. The Vietnamese are crawling all over the place. I've already got two dead men. Why don't one of you desk jockeys get your asses down here and see how long you'd last!"

The radio hissed as Callahan waited for a reply.

*"Tango . . . Cheerleader has authorized an immediate extract. Give us a GPS location."*

Callahan removed his GPS-117 SATCOM and SAR radio. Using a six-inch rubber-coated wire as an electronic bridge, he connected the two compatible systems together. His SAR radio contained an integrated communications and positioning system, allowing him not only to talk but send a short LPI/LPD satellite data burst giving their exact position to the Pentagon with the push of a button. The electronic data burst could be stored or, in the case of a search-and-rescue mission, relayed to an aircraft entering the area. The GPS system was accurate to within three meters.

Callahan hit the transmit button and waited for the red light to flash before removing his finger.

*"Got it, Tango. Hold tight."*

Callahan picked up his binoculars and again scanned the area in front of him. Everything looked the same. The farmers were still plowing their fields and the trucks remained empty.

*"Tango . . . Cheerleader."*

"Copy you, Cheerleader." Callahan kept his voice low.

*"Cavalry on the way. Be ready to move. It's going to be a single."*

"Roger, Cheerleader. Tango out."

"Did you hear that?" Major Erwin tilted her head to one side.

Sinchon shook his head. "No. I don't hear . . ." He stopped as the sound of moving gravel filtered into the cave.

"It must be General James," Erwin said, dropping forward to a crawling position.

Sinchon grabbed her leg. She turned to face him as he held his finger to his lips.

Erwin realized the man could be right. She moved warily back to the rear wall next to Sinchon.

"I am a Korean solider. Identify yourself." A voice came from outside.

Erwin looked at Sinchon, not knowing what to say. She really hadn't believed they would search until they found them.

"Identify yourself or I will fire into this opening and see who you are after you are dead."

"You must stay here," Sinchon ordered, whispering. "Do not move or say a word."

"I can't let you," Erwin answered, grabbing his arm. "They will kill you."

"They will kill you as well if you are found with me. Do not make me carry the burden of your death to my grave."

Erwin removed her hand as Sinchon turned away toward the opening.

"I am not armed. Do not fire," he said, crawling out the opening. Placing his hand on his knee, Sinchon stood proudly. Looking to the left he saw a Korean soldier in a squatting position. The man's cheeks and nose were red from the cold. His expression was hard and unemotional. Sinchon saw the *spetsnaz* insignia on his shoulder, the head of a black wolf with the ears turned back, teeth exposed and ready to fight.

"I am not armed," he repeated, holding his hands up slightly and turning to face the man.

"General Sinchon," Sergeant Hyun said uneasily. He dropped the tip of his AK-47 toward the ground. "It is you."

"Who sent you to search for me, Sergeant?" Sinchon lowered his hands, keeping his gaze steady.

"Colonel Kaine, sir. He was looking for your body . . . ." Hyun stammered not sure he should repeat what the colonel had told him. "I . . . I am following his orders."

"Ahh . . . I should have known it was Colonel Kaine."

Hyun cleared his throat and again raised his weapon. "Colonel Kaine has given me direct orders to bring you to him."

"Under these conditions?" Sinchon challenged, sounding offended as he stared at the AK-47. "I suggest you drop your weapon before I have you arrested for assaulting an officer."

"Put your hands back in the air, General," Hyun demanded, his tone growing more confident. "I do not know what has happened here, but I do know there is a ship and a helicopter on the island that were destroyed. Colonel Kaine said you were meeting with the Americans and I found you hiding in a . . . in a hole." Hyun paused, looking at the opening. The situation was becoming clearer in his mind. "Is there anyone else with you?"

"No, I am alone." Sinchon winced with pain, his arms still raised in the air. It felt like his insides were being ripped apart. "Take me to Colonel Kane and I will straighten this matter out."

The general stepped away from the opening to walk down the ravine.

"Stop!" Hyun shouted. "Or I will shoot you first, then fire into your hiding place."

Sinchon stopped and sighed.

"You in the cave, come out or I will fire my weapon."

Sinchon turned around to see Major Erwin emerge from the cave. She looked up at him briefly and kept her hands in the air.

Duke rounded the back side of several large boulders and caught sight of three people making their way out from the farthest ravine.

"Shit!" he breathed, watching as a Korean soldier held a rifle on Major Erwin and General Sinchon.

James heard the soldier shout. Their hands went to the top of their heads as they walked toward the runway. He took a deep breath and let it out slowly, trying to suppress a surge of anger. *I shouldn't have left them alone.* Ducking toward the shoreline, he continued toward the cave. With any luck the soldier hadn't found the radio.

# 29

KIM IL SONG AIR BASE, NORTH KOREA

General Chin paced behind the main radar tracking console. The underground command-and-control center was now buzzing with activity. Echoing through the darkened chamber he could hear the radio conversations of the pilots as they chattered with the tower awaiting takeoff clearance.

Several other technicians were communicating with the ground-control-intercept (GCI) radar operators at Sinuiju, advising them on the efficiency levels of the Soviet-built Back Net. To his left Chin watched another communications officer receiving the latest data from the trawler shadowing the USS *Observation Island.*

Chin struck a match and lit a Camel cigarette. He inhaled deeply and exhaled through his nose. He walked back to the radar console and stood over the operator. The symbols on the screen changed every few seconds as the radar fed the tracking computers a continuous stream of new data.

Right now his mind was on the American fighters circling the skies outside his country's airspace. If his plan to keep the Americans off Langau Island was to work, Colonel Woong's attack must succeed. Chin would then launch fighters to keep the Americans occupied until the Iranian freighter and Kaine were a safe distance from Langau Island.

"Any change in the airliner's heading?" Chin barked, sucking on the white filterless American cigarette.

"No change in heading or altitude. Two minutes from breakaway." The radar technician pointed to the red triangle on his radar screen. "The airliner is here. I can only speculate that Colonel Woong is still in position."

"I know that," Chin blurted out. "How far is the American AWACS from the airliner?"

"Sixty-two miles. Radar shows it at an altitude of forty-two thousand feet. I'm tracking a second large aircraft at twenty-three thousand feet heading west."

"It's the RC-135 spy plane." Chin shook his head and folded his arms, recalling the Americans' plans. "That will be our next target."

Cigarette smoke swirled around his face as he studied the radar screen. The red symbol representing the airliner continued on a southwesterly heading. It was flying at 38,000 feet, speed 490 knots. On the bottom portion he watched the AWACS flying in a circular pattern.

"What else are you looking at?" Chin asked.

The technician tapped the glass monitor again. "There is a group of four fighters. Altitude thirty-five thousand feet."

"American F-15s," Chin said, keeping things straight in his mind.

The radar data on the screen before Chin was being supplied by a Soviet-built Back Net based at Sinuiju. It was sent to Kim Il Song air base via a secure fiber-optic land-link, making it impossible to jam the transmission unless the station itself was attacked. The early warning system had been overhauled within the last five months and many of its computers had been updated with more processing power, permitting them a wider range of 300 miles.

However, Chin had given explicit orders that the radar was not to track anything over 200 miles. He was counting on the Americans' not knowing the radar had been modernized. They would be surprised when he ordered it to go to full range today.

"One minute to breakaway," the technician rattled off.

"Instruct Sinuiju that I want maximum radar power *now.*"


## E-3C AWACS, MENTOR

"Where'd that power surge come from?" Tallman asked, leaning over closer to the screen.

"I . . . I don't know," Lieutenant Klages responded, staring at his computer monitor.

On the right side of the screen two vertical frequency band dials had jumped up before sporadically fluctuating between 3080–3125 Mhz. Klages worked swiftly, searching for the source.

"I have it . . . it's the radar station at Sinuiju. They just boosted power by one-third." The defensive electronic's officer glanced up at the major.

"One-third." Tallman rubbed the bridge of his nose, only a little concerned. "Record it. I want band width and antenna rotation rate. Let me know if you detect any ECM."

"Yes, sir."

"Anything new out there?" Tallman asked, his brow furrowed in contemplation.

"No, sir. I'm still tracking one comair to the north and three to the south," Klages reported throwing in an update on the RC-135: "That Super Snooper is fifty-seven miles north of Langau Island and continuing west at 320 knots."

"Get on the horn and tell them to get the hell out of there. We don't need them in the area gumming things up. Vector McGiven in Benji Lead to cover it on the way out.''

''Understood, sir.'' The communications officer keyed his mike, ''Benji Leader . . . Mentor. Take heading of zero six three. Need cover on Super Snooper exiting the area. Escort at angels twenty-three heading west.'' Angels twenty-three was a fast way of saying twenty-three thousand feet.

*''Roger, Mentor. Benji Lead turning.''*

Tallman watched two blue F-16C radar symbols turn to the northeast increasing their airspeed.

''Good . . . I'm going to get a cup of coffee. Contact the *Observation Island.* I want to make sure they're monitoring all of this,'' Tallman said before disappearing into the back of the aircraft.


## RC-135S, SUPER SNOOPER

''The *Observation Island* is reporting a boost in power levels coming from the radar station at Sinuiju. Do you confirm it?'' Capt. Lawrence McQuire asked Sergeant Fletcher, the ''Crow.''

''Yeah . . . I mean, yes, sir.'' Fletcher rubbed his eyes. His attention had wandered from the instruments a second time. It was time to go home. The reconnaissance aircraft's dark and chilly interior was a stark contrast to his daydream.

''And?'' Captain McQuire raised his eyebrows.

''E-band sir. Operating at the top of the frequency. I've been recording it for the last thirty seconds.'' The sergeant's vision came back to the middle of the computer screen. ''Standard power boost. I'd say they increased their range by 20 . . . maybe 25 percent.''

''Let me know if there are any other changes,'' McQuire grunted. ''When they *happen,* Mr. Fletcher.''

''Yes, sir,'' Fletcher answered, staring at the four-color navigational scope located on the lower left side of his primary instrument panel.

The small round display showed their location, with the Korean coast to his right and the Chinese coast to the left. A blue square revealed the approximate location of the *Observation Island,* 142 miles to the southeast. Ten miles farther south was the *Paul Hamilton.*

Chin watched the radar screen flash several times before stabilizing. Now the American AWACS was in the center of the display. The added power allowed him to see seventy-five miles farther south. It had also picked up one more formation of fighters to the southwest, orbiting at 24,000 feet. If he hadn't boosted the power level he never would have seen them. The Americans had positioned the fighters just outside his radar coverage.

"Clever . . . very clever," Chin muttered. "How many American fighters are in the air now?"

"Twelve, sir. Eight at thirty-five thousand feet to the northeast of the AWACS. Two at twenty-four thousand to the southwest. And two more to the northeast at twenty-eight thousand."

*Just as there should be.* The Americans were following every detail of their plan. Chin watched the AWACS maneuver into a slow banking turn to the north.

"Ten seconds to breakaway," a radar technician announced.

"In one minute that A310 will be at its closest point to the American AWACS," Chin said excitedly. "Launch the MiG-29s and order the Su-27s to start their engines but to remain in the hangars until I give the order."

He watched the A310 radar-tracking symbol inch to the southwest.

"Break now," Chin said hitting the radio transmission switch.


VICTORY ONE, SU-27


One final check told the pilot his radar, radio and electronic countermeasures were off. There was no way the Americans could detect his fighter via electronic emissions.

Chopping the throttles, Colonel Woong let his fighter slowly drift down and away from the A310. The turbulence coming off the tail caused his jet to toss around. Woong gripped the stick tighter to stabilize the interceptor.

Activating the jet's SPO-15 Beryoza radar-warning receiver system, he watched the needle spin to the left to point toward the powerful radar beam of the AWACS sweeping the sky around his jet.

Woong scanned the instrumentation one more time. Yanking a metal lever next to the throttles, he released the twin auxiliary fuel tanks hanging from each wing. The Su-27 quivered as the near-empty tanks broke free and cascaded to the ground like poorly thrown footballs.

Rolling to the left he shoved the throttles all the way forward. They snapped past the afterburner groove, lashing Woong's head and upper body back against his ejection seat. The jet climbed to the southwest, breaking through 35,000 feet in a few seconds.

Major Tallman felt the AWACS come out of the slow banking turn and come wings level. They were on the north side of the twenty-mile radius racetrack flight pattern, heading east. The major sipped a mouthful of hot

black coffee as he strolled to the duty officer's station located in the center
of the aircraft.

"Sir, look at this," Lieutenant Klages said, puzzled. "It looks as if that
comair is breaking up. I'm showing two radar hits not more than a hundred
yards apart."

The symbol representing the commercial airliner had broken into two
parts. They were at slightly different altitudes but the heading and airspeed
were the same.

"What the hell . . ." Tallman said, nearly spilling his coffee. "What's
that comair's flight number?"

Lieutenant Klages tapped his computer keyboard, calling up the Comair
I.D. A menu box appeared on the bottom of his screen showing: CHINA AIR
FLT #316 AIRBUS A310.

"This doesn't make sense." Tallman finished his coffee and threw the
styrofoam coffee cup in a nearby garbage pail. "What's your IFF saying?"

Klages' eyes swept the IFF instrumentation. Inside the AWACS' rotating
radardome an array of high-speed electronics powered the most advanced
IFF system in the world. Designed to identify as friend or foe any aircraft in
a 200-mile radius, the APX-103 IFF/Tactical Digital Data system cycled
through its library of IFF transponder codes to tell Klages it was only
picking up one signal, a civilian airliner.

"Sir . . . IFF confirms one target, one target only. But I'm looking at
two. This return is the Airbus." Klages centered the cursor, a pulsing white
cross, over the new radar contact. The tracking computer locked onto the
return to give him altitude, speed and heading.

"Heading two one three, southwest, speed 600 knots and increasing.
Altitude 36,450 feet and climbing fast." Klages turned around to look at his
commanding officer's stunned face. "Range . . . sixty-one miles. It's
heading straight for us."

"Dragon One Seven rolling."

First Lt. Yun-Kyong Roh guided his MiG-29M out of the hardened hangar to the edge of the runway. He stopped for his wingman to come even
with him, then pushed the double throttles forward and the MiG thundered
down the runway to liftoff.

At 500 feet above the tire-smudged runway Roh pulled the stick back
pulling the nose up ten degrees as the jet gained airspeed and altitude. The
twin-tailed fighter, loaded with a mix of eight air-to-air missiles, flashed
over the end of the runway. He banked left heading west and climbing at
2,500 feet a minute.

Being in the air helped cool his temper. For the last thirty minutes, with
his engines running, the lieutenant had been seated in his fighter concealed

in the hangar. He had burned 10 percent of his fuel. Fuel he might need in the air.

Roh leveled his MiG concentrating on the changing symbology of the HUD. The twenty-five-year-old fighter pilot had recently returned from a five-week training mission in Russia. He had flown three missions a day fighting against some of Russia's best pilots. At the end of the training Roh found himself defeating the Russians about half of the time. His short stocky body could sustain 9 Gs in a fast-turning dogfight, which allowed him to capitalize on the agility of his fighter to kill the enemy.

The oldest son of a North Korean Air Force general, Roh was the lead pilot of eight MiG-29Ms that had been assigned to make a high-speed run at American fighters flying outside his country. Their plans were, to his frustration, somewhat ambiguous. General Chin had ordered them to fly at the American fighters hoping to pull them away from their patrol patterns. After crossing the coast they were to drop down to 800 feet above the ocean and fly at high speed with radars off. Roh knew the ground-control-intercept radar (GCI) at Sinuiju would track their progress and when the situation changed they would be ordered to break into two groups and pull straight up, heading for the American jets. Roh had also been told, because of his skill, that if the operators at Sinuiju spotted a high-value target, such as a spy plane or airborne command center, he would be vectored toward it.

When the order came to pull up and close in on the American fighters Roh had instructed his pilots to use heavy chaff to break the radar lock of the American jets. He had practiced the technique in Russia, using it to break the pulse-Doppler lock of Su-30s and Su-27s attacking from above.

Looking over his shoulder Roh watched the other MiGs lining up behind him as they streaked for the coast forty-two miles away. He forced the nose of his aircraft down, watching his airspeed increase.

"This is bullshit!" Tallman cursed loud enough for every scope-dope in the AWACS to hear. "That bastard is heading this way at over Mach 1."

"Confirmed, sir. Speed 720 knots . . ."

"I can read the data as well as you, son. Mark it as hostile and contact Intrepid. We need fighter support *now.*" Tallman placed another large chunk of Red Man between his cheek and gum.

"Intrepid Leader . . . Mentor. Take heading of three one seven. We're showing a hostile to the northwest approaching fast."

*"Roger Mentor . . . Intrepid on the way."*

Tallman moved closer to the radar screen. There weren't any electronic emissions coming from the target. Just a solid radar return.

"Run it through the targeting computer. See if you can ID that sucker," the major commanded, breathing down Klages's neck.

Klages tapped away at his computer, instructing the radar-targeting software to come on line. It took several seconds for the Westinghouse Modar 5400 X-band radar to find and lock onto the fast-moving target.

Known as MARS or Monopulse Air Recognition System, the X-band electronic identification program was used to distinguish the type of aircraft the E-3C crew was tracking by identifying its electronic radar return. The radio waves bouncing off the target were washed through what the crew called a mini-Cray super computer capable of processing five billion bits of data a second. The return was digitized into a mathematical pattern and compared with the electronic returns stored in an onboard electronic library containing more than ten million distinct radar returns. By comparing the radar returns the computer could give the operator a breakdown of probable aircraft identifications.

"Come on baby, work faster." Klages coaxed.

A menu box appeared on the bottom of the screen:

MAX RANGE:      35% FLANKER    28% FULCRUM

"I'll be a son of a bitch!" Tallman shouted.

Light orange flames streamed from the Su-27's twin AL-31F afterburning nozzles. Colonel Woong watched his HUD click off the airspeed and altitude as his jet climbed at a steep seventy-degree angle into the deep blue sky. He let his head rest against the ejection seat as the big fighter rocketed nearly straight up.

The Su-27 broke through 50,000 feet and past 560 knots at the same time. Taking the interceptor out of afterburner, he flipped it over, leveling out upside-down. The quick rush of 4 Gs pushed him deeper into the seat as he struggled to keep his eyes focused on the HUD.

Woong took in a deep breath feeling Gs bleed off. Righting the interceptor, he watched the round radar-warning receiver below his HUD. The black needle inside the dial showed the AWACS' powerful radar sweeping from the southeast. He didn't know the range but could tell the direction. With any luck he was above his target and the Americans were still trying to figure out what was going on.

Dropping the nose three degrees, Woong jammed the throttles back into afterburner. He watched his airspeed build, 600 knots . . . 650 . . . 700 knots. Changing radio frequencies, he opened up a coded frequency-hopping channel.

"Red Crown . . . this is Victory One. Request heading to target."

*"Victory . . . Red Crown. Turn left four degrees to one eight four. Target at forty-two thousand, heading away, range . . . fifty-nine miles. Area is clear."*

"Understood."

Gently pushing the stick left he watched his heading, marked in degrees across the top of his HUD, swing around to 184.

*Beep . . . Beep . . . Beep.* Lt. Buddy Klages heard the warning tone coming from the right side of his display terminal. Swiveling around, he saw the secondary tactical warning and tracking screen light up suddenly.

Klages enlarged the tactical warning screen to make it easier to read. "I'm tracking seven . . . no make that eight new targets coming off the runway at Kim Il Song. They're heading west toward the coast. Looking at their airspeed and rate of ascent . . . I'd say they're fighters."

Tallman spit into his cup, running the scenario through his mind. He had a single fighter flying straight for him and now eight more targets were coming off the runway at one of North Korea's most guarded air bases.

The major straightened his tall, thin frame. In a loud voice he addressed the other officers seated inside the E-3C AWACS. "Heads up, ladies and gentlemen. We have a few things developing that will need all your concentration. I need everyone awake and alert."

Klages touched the screen. "Bandit number one just broke forty-five miles."

"Vector Tacoma Package to go defensive . . . Oscar pattern. I want them ready if those eight bandits break the coast." Tallman knew this much activity shouldn't be occurring this early in the mission. His gut told him somehow the North Koreans were one step ahead of them.

"Tacoma Package . . . Mentor."

*"Copy Mentor . . . this is Tacoma Lead."*

Klages recognized Colonel Conrad's Wyoming drawl. "Tacoma Lead, Tracking eight repeat eight bandits at zero niner four. Fan out to defensive Oscar formation."

*"Roger that, Mentor. Tacoma going Oscar."*

Klages and Tallman watched as the four F-15Es of Tacoma package banked to the west, beginning to disperse. The Strike Eagles would spread out in a basic defensive formation, a four or five mile-wide line, widening the coverage of the E model's powerful radar and allowing them to target with their long-range AMRAAM missiles.

"Bandits breaking one hundred ten miles out. They're crossing the coast," Klages called out. The tactical warning display showed the eight hostile aircraft symbols flashing over the coast. "They're staying low. Altitude eight hundred feet . . . speed four hundred twenty knots."

"Give me an update on the Pave Hawks," Tallman said, referring to the Ranger team heading toward Langau Island.

"Twenty-eight minutes out, sir." Klages touched the screen at the location of the choppers.

Tallman knew if those North Korean fighters got within fifty miles of those choppers they would be falling from the sky like lead pigeons.

General Chin's shoulders had turned hard with tension as he watched the pulsing radar returns on the scope in front of him. The Americans had detected Colonel Woong sooner than he had hoped. He watched two red hostile aircraft symbols moving toward the colonel's fighter. He guessed the odds of Woong downing the American AWACS were now less than fifty-fifty.

"Give him the range one more time," Chin ordered.

"Victory One . . . Red Crown. Range . . . fifty-one miles. Altitude forty-two thousand heading one eight five."

*Click . . . Click.*

Chin felt his insides rumble when the colonel's only response was the clicking of his mike. He knew the man was intent on acquiring his target. "Come on, Colonel Woong. Don't let me down."

A sharp warning tone sounded inside Woong's helmet. He winced as the pulsing pitch generated by his radar-warning receiver told him an American radar was sweeping his jet.

Woong watched his airspeed flicker past 730 knots. His Su-27 was descending at 1,000 feet a minute heading 182 degrees. He flipped the metal radar switch from "off" to "standby" to warm the electronics of his jet's RLPK-27 pulse-Doppler.

The colonel studied the weapons panel. All ten of his air-to-air missiles were functioning. Right now he was only interested in the two long-range R-77AEs. Moving the weapons select button on the stick, he activated the R77AE radar-guided missiles located under his fuselage. His eyes went to the HUD and back to the weapons panel again. Everything appeared normal.

Tugging on his shoulder restraints Woong flipped his radar from "standby" to "active." The glass CRT below his weapons panel came to life. A yellow line representing the radar beam swept across the CRT. The radar was working.

"Come on . . . find the target," Woong said into the empty cockpit. He knew that every second he closed on the AWACS the chances of an American fighter firing at him increased. The yellow line moved across the screen two more times before it stopped. A low rhythmic tone sounded in his helmet, telling him the radar had acquired the target.

Woong pressed the oval button on his throttle to lock the radar. The data on the bottom of the CRT return was that of the AWACS: RANGE: 45 MILES   CLOSURE 412 KNOTS.

Dropping the nose of the jet, Woong changed the angle of the radar. He watched the flashing yellow square air-to-air targeting cursor move across the HUD screen, then it stopped and turned a solid orange in the lower right corner as his jet's radar dumped the target's speed, range, altitude and radar frequency into each of the R-77AEs' computer guidance systems. Without hesitating Woong tapped the launch button twice, sending the first then the second missiles on their way.

The Su-27 barely vibrated as the solid-rocket motors lit up, kicking out a trail of blue fire and silver smoke.

Lt. Buddy Klages sat in his chair hunched over, yelling out, "Threat! Threat! Missile launch . . . I'm showing two missiles coming this way bearing three one seven."

"Jam the sons'a bitches," Tallman ordered, placing a hand on the back of Klages's chair.

"I'm trying, sir, but no response." The defensive electronics officer's voice was high-pitched.

"Where the fuck is Intrepid?" Tallman demanded.

"Fifty-three miles out, heading straight for the bandit."

Tallman stared at the two short yellow lines moving toward his AWACS. The symbols under them read 90 SECONDS TO IMPACT.

"Sir, that bandit just lit up his radar. I'm showing a powerful J-band."

TACOMA FLIGHT, F-15E

"Let's move it, Red Dog," Conrad radioed his wingman.

*"I'm with you, Cowboy."*

Coming out of a long banking turn, Miles moved the throttles just short of afterburner, feeling his Strike Eagle accelerate to the east. Drawing the stick back, he allowed the fully loaded fighter to climb slightly as his airspeed increased to 490 knots.

Conrad routinely checked the cockpit instrumentation. Everything looked good. He was flying with his F-15E's radar turned off, allowing the AWACS to guide him. With his radar turned off he wasn't broadcasting his position to any enemy fighters in the area. Once his fighter got into range the AWACS would instruct him when to activate his radar to lock onto a target for the kill.

"What do you have back there, Greeno?" Conrad asked his wizzo seated behind him.

Spread across the top of the rear cockpit were four multifunction displays known as MFDs. Maj. Skip ''Greeno'' Green checked the left MFD showing the electronic data-link being broadcast from the AWACS' tactical display screen. It showed a single target converging on the AWACS at a high rate of speed and eight more targets to the east crossing over the North Korean coast. The data was used for situational awareness only and didn't give range, heading or altitudes.

''Mentor's got company alright,'' Green said. ''I am showing two missiles heading for her and closing fast.''

Conrad took a deep breath of cool oxygen. Intrepid had been vectored to cover Mentor. There wasn't anything he and the other half of Tacoma Package could do from their positions. As much as he wanted to go help protect the men in the AWACS from the immediate threat, it was best for them to stay on course and do their own jobs.

Silently to himself he said a quick prayer for them then pushed his throttles past the afterburner groove. Both pilots were slammed back into their seats, continuing east.

''Forty-five seconds to impact. They're still tracking.'' Klages was on the edge of his seat.

''Shut her down,'' Tallman ordered.

Lieutenant Klages's fist hit the automatic shut-off button, turning the AWACS' powerful radar off. Tallman picked up a headset connecting him with the flight deck.

''Get us out of here, gentlemen. Head for the deck.'' The jet nosed over in a steep dive. ''More chaff,'' Tallman instructed, holding himself steady by gripping the handrail.

Woong lost sight of the missiles as they disappeared into the gray-blue haze below him. Looking at the radarscope he watched the R-77AEs descending through 45,000 feet picking up airspeed as their rocket motors pushed them past Mach 2.

The colonel knew at thirty miles from target each missile would go autonomous using its dual active and radar seekers to home in on the AWACS. Throttling back he took the jet out of afterburner and nosed over. The sting from two negative Gs caused his eyes to water.

Blinking, Woong saw a flashing asterisk. The missiles were now independently tracking the target. Woong waited a few more seconds before he shut down his fighter's radar. The radar symbology faded from his HUD.

''They're active, man. I can hear them sweeping us,'' one of the defensive electronics officers warned.

"Fifteen seconds to impact," another officer called out. "They're coming out of the northwest."

Tallman watched as the data flight on the screen next to him continued to change. The pilots had the AWACS in a steep banking turn heading for the deck at 500 knots. He could feel the thirty-year-old airframe shuddering from the added stress of the high-speed turn. They had dropped 10,000 feet as the pilot corkscrewed the jet toward the deck trying to break the radar lock of the missiles. Tallman knew it was a vain attempt. The AWACS was too big and slow to outturn any missile. Their only chance would be to fill the sky with chaff to break the radar lock. In his mind he pictured a steady stream of radar-fouling chaff streaming out behind the AWACS.

"More chaff!" Tallman shouted again. "More chaff!"

"Five seconds to impact."

Tallman sat in his seat and buckled his lap belt. Taking a look around at his crew, he braced himself.

The lead R-77AE made a midcourse correction 3,000 feet above the E-3C. Pushing over it made a tight 10-G turn heading for the tail section of the AWACS. The guidance computer, located just behind the radar dish in front of the warhead, automatically triggered the electronic counter-countermeasures. The software filtered out the weaker return of the chaff boiling behind the jet, instructing the guidance computer to stay locked onto the denser return of the jet itself.

Swinging right and left, the R-77AE closed in on its target at over two-and-a-half times the speed of sound. Making one more course change it exploded a dozen yards behind the AWACS. The sixty-six-pound warhead sent shrapnel into the tail section of the enormous jet.

Tallman flinched as the first missile exploded behind the jet. The sound of cutting metal filled the air as pieces of the missile's warhead sliced into the 707's outer skin. He expected the aircraft to depressurize but nothing happened.

For a split second Maj. Keith R. Tallman thought, hoped, the worst was over. The jet seemed rock-solid as the pilot throttled back the engines and began to pull the nose up.

"All aircraft . . . all aircraft," Tallman radioed. "This is AWACS on guard. We're hit. Switch to frequency November. Repeat switch to frequency Novem . . ." He didn't finish his sentence.

The inside of the fuselage lit up in a flash of bright white light and a fireball rolled through the cabin. Tallman felt a sensation of fire and icy air coming across his body as he watched the plane seemingly come apart. The bold blue sky surrounded him before he was ripped from his seat.

*   *   *

"It is gone, General Chin," the senior technician said, amazed.

Chin's face betrayed no emotion as the AWACS' radar symbol faded. He stared at the dark screen waiting for the symbol to suddenly reappear. It didn't. A wave of disbelief and elation came over him as he realized he himself hadn't expected Woong to succeed in destroying the American command aircraft.

The command center was silent and all eyes were turned toward the general chief of staff. The only sounds Chin could hear were the computer-cooling fans and static hiss from the nearby communications console. His plan had worked and the faces before him were filled with respect and awe. It was as if he had conquered the giant and the game was over.

Chin, seeing the blinking lights reflecting off the nearest man's eyes, snapped him out of his daze. Radio calls were going unanswered, everyone was ignoring their assignments. The real test was about to begin.

"Get back to work," Chin stated evenly. "We have MiGs in the air. This is not over."

In unison heads dropped as the men and women turned back to their screens.

"Vector 1st Lieutenant Roh to the American RC-135. That will be the next target." Chin stood proudly. "And after that we will destroy what is left of the American fighters."

## 30

Langau Island

Duke James crawled on his belly to the edge of the ravine and stopped. He was now about forty feet from the cave's entrance. Peering over a pile of rocks he spotted Major Erwin and General Sinchon 300 yards away walking toward the AN-72 Coaler with the North Korean soldier following them, his weapon at the ready. James could make out a group of North Koreans standing near the back of the jet awaiting the two prisoners.

His body still wet and shivering uncontrollably, Duke scooted down the back of the ravine. Fearing another member of the foot patrol had been left behind, he scanned the area. Dried grass and dirt were disturbed where he guessed the soldier had led Erwin and Sinchon up toward the runway, but the rest of the area looked clear.

Rolling over on his side Duke picked up an apple-sized stone. He lobbed it in a high arc. The stone smacked the wall next to the cave with a loud thump. Pebbles and dirt tumbled slightly down the side of the gully. His body stiffened as he waited for any movement or sound.

All Duke could hear was the wind rustling through the dried weeds. Sliding down the rest of the way, the general made his way to the entrance of the cave and went inside. Blinking to adjust his eyes, he felt around in the darkness, then stood quiet. There was no one there.

Breathing a small sigh of relief, he spotted the radio and heater. He shook the heater and guessed it contained ten or fifteen minutes of fuel. He hoped it would be enough to dry his clothes.

"First things first," James said, pumping the primer knob, then hitting the quartz starter button. Adjusting the heater he waited for the burner to glow bright orange before picking up the radio.

Colonel Kaine jumped out from the Il-76 Ilyushin and moved toward the rear. Stopping midstride he saw a group of men gathered near the loading ramp of the AN-72 Coaler. They had their backs to him facing the runway.

"What is this?" he shouted. Kaine walked closer to see two figures, their hands on their heads, followed Sergeant Hyun.

He breathed deeply when he recognized Sinchon.

"Clear out of here," Kaine ordered. "Get back to your posts, *now.*"

The other soldiers scattered back to their assignments as Kaine's eyes locked with the approaching general's. Sinchon's face was tired, dark rings around his eyes. His cheeks were puffy and his lips were light with a bluish tint. Kaine thought to himself that the man didn't look like he commanded the most disciplined and well-trained troops in North Korea. The sight reassured the colonel that the old man's time was up and it was his turn to fulfill that role.

Kaine glanced quickly at the other prisoner, a woman. The skin on her face was tight and red from the cold and under the hood of her coat he could see her hair was cut short. She was small but appeared strong. The oak leaf clusters told Kaine she was an American Army officer.

"Where did you find them?" Kaine asked Sergeant Hyun.

"In a cave near the ocean. They were hiding like frightened animals."

"Frightened animals? General Sinchon may be many things, but a frightened animal he is not." Kaine looked into the general's eyes. "You found no one else?"

"No, sir. These were the only two. I searched the area thoroughly."

"I will decide when the island has been thoroughly searched," Kaine said harshly.

"There is *no one* else," Sinchon declared in a rough voice. "Your attack killed the others."

The two men's eyes locked in an unwavering stare. Kaine's faced hardened as he tried to force the general to look away in humiliation. Sinchon's eyes remained fixed, rock solid.

"I had hoped it *wasn't* true, General. I had hoped you weren't a traitor to our country." Kaine's eyes were cold. "You could have retired with an exemplary military record, but you have foolishly attempted to hold on to your command."

"I am not a traitor," Sinchon answered. "You have—"

"Do not insult me with lies," Kaine interrupted, his voice filled with contempt. He looked at Erwin, then back at Sinchon. "She is proof you were meeting with the Americans to plan the overthrow of our government. You are a traitor and a spy."

"No. You are following the wrong man," Sinchon persisted, ignoring the pain that shot through his body. "Chin is not the future of our country. He is a self-centered bureaucrat grasping for power."

"Bind their hands and place them in the transport. I do not have time to waste now." Kaine turned to leave then looked back to Sergeant Hyun. He would talk to Woong about the three heat sources on the video of his ground attack when he returned. "Have the other men go out and continue the search. I believe there is one more person alive on this island."

"Yes, sir." Hyun nodded. He motioned for one of the men at the Ilyushin to come help him.

Using pieces of electrical wiring, the soldiers bound Major Erwin's and General Sinchon's hands behind their backs before leading them into the AN-72's cargo hold.


## Tacoma Lead, F-15E

Colonel Conrad leveled his fighter at 30,000 feet heading due east. Throttling back to 50 percent power he placed the horizontal situation indicator on top of the skyline and trimmed the jet for level flight. Sucking in a deep breath he tried to think things through.

"Mentor . . . Tacoma Lead. Do you copy?"

Conrad waited for a response.

"Mentor . . . Tacoma Lead. Do you copy?" The radio hissed with static.

He waited a full five seconds before looking over his shoulder. "Greeno . . . I have a sick feeling about this."

"Shit, man . . . I'm about ready to puke."

"Are you seeing anything at all?"

"It's gone. Mentor is gone," Green said incredulously from the rear cockpit. "My data link is dead and I'm not showing any radars to the southwest."

"Osan control . . . Tacoma Leader. Mentor is down. Repeat Mentor is down."

*"Copy, Tacoma. Stand by and go autonomous."*

"Roger that, Osan."

Conrad wiped the sweat from around his eyebrows. He had heard the last radio transmission from Mentor. The code word November was used to instruct all pilots to switch to an emergency guard radio frequency known as "Navy common." The frequency was only used in the case of extreme emergencies such as the downing of a command aircraft or loss of a key air base or carrier. *Tallman must have known they were going down,* Conrad thought.

As senior pilot in the group it was now Conrad's responsibility to sort things out and take control. The colonel would have to formulate a new game plan using his F-15E as the provisional command aircraft. He would assign the targets then get all his men back home . . . alive.

Conrad turned his radar from "standby" to "active." It took just a few seconds for the APG-70 to power up. He watched the solid white line move across the six-by-six-inch monochrome MFD on the upper left side of the instrument panel. Moving the radar method switch on the throttle, Conrad triggered the APG-70's vertical scan mode. Scanning 140 degrees a second, the powerful I-band pulse-Doppler swept right to left and back again.

*Okay, think, Conrad, just think this through,* he told himself. He had twelve aircraft in the sky around him. Benji package, consisting of four F-16Cs, had been readied for air-to-air with a mix of four long-range AIM-120B AMRAAMs and two short-range wingtip mounted AIM-9M Sidewinders. The eight F-15Es making up Tacoma and Intrepid packages had been configured for both air-to-air and air-to-ground. Each fighter carried four AIM-120B AMRAAMs, two AIM-9M Sidewinders, and two 2,000-pound smart bombs for taking out ground targets or ships.

Conrad began recalling the last instructions Mentor had given his pilots. There were eight bandits somewhere out in front of him hugging the deck. Mentor had vectored Benji Lead and his wingman to cover the RC-135 exiting the area. And the two Pave Hawk choppers were making their way toward Langau Island. That was it. At least he hoped that was it, he couldn't remember anything else.

The colonel looked at the threat list strapped to the right thigh of his flight suit. The list had been supplied by air force intel before takeoff. Halfway down the page he saw GROUND CONTROL INTERCEPT RADAR—BASED AT SINUIJU. Conrad knew if he was going to regain control of the skies he would have to return the deed and blind the North Koreans.

The only way to do that was to knock out their ground-control-intercept radar to the north.

"Greeno. Where's the range to that North Korean GCI?"

"Intel places it east of here on an island south of Sinuiju," Green answered immediately. "About one hundred eighty miles."

*All right, here we go.* Conrad changed radio frequencies using the toe of his boot to key the radio mike. "All fighters . . . all fighters. This is Tacoma Lead. We've lost the AWACS. Your orders are to go autonomous. Repeat . . . go autonomous. Leads check in."

*"Benji Lead . . . heading toward Super Snooper. I'm in."*

"McGiven, stay on target. That RC-135's going to need the cover."

*"Roger, Tacoma. Benji element will stay on escort."*

"Intrepid Lead, you copy?"

*"Copy Tacoma, Intrepid Lead in."*

"Burnsie, what's your heading and altitude?"

*"North at zero one two. I'm at thirty-nine thousand."* There was dead air and Conrad knew Burns was keeping the channel open. *"I couldn't get there in time . . . I lost the radar data-link when the AWACS went down."*

"Now's not the time for that, Burnsie. I need you in . . . we've got to get that GCI radar out of the picture. That's your target."

There was only a short pause.

*"Leave it to me, Conrad, and they'll be blind as bats. Intrepid Lead turning to engage."*

Conrad signaled his acknowledgment then closed his eyes as he tried to picture the position of each fighter package. Two F-16Cs were below him and to the south. He would need to pull them out of their orbit to help intercept the bandits flying in from the west.

"Benji three one and three two . . . Tacoma Lead. Head east at zero niner zero, increase speed to four hundred knots and climb to twenty-eight thousand. Tacoma's going to make one pass through these bandits. You're fragged to pick up any stragglers."

*"Roger that, Tacoma. Turning to engage,"* Maj. Darryl Schaal replied.

Conrad placed his right hand back on the stick. Pushing the nose over he put his F-15E into a shallow dive.

"Okay, Greeno, it's time to earn our pay," Conrad said, feeling his aircraft descend. "If those bandits close within forty miles, they're toast."

"I am right behind you Colonel . . . I am right behind you." Green grabbed the handrail as the Strike Eagle pushed over.


## DRAGON LEAD, MiG-29M

"Understood, command. Dragon Leader turning to engage." First Lt. Yun-Kyong Roh pulled the MiG's stick right, banking his fighter to the north. Adding power, he pushed the nose up and broke through 1,000 feet.

*"Range to target fifty-three miles. Heading east at zero eight four. Altitude twenty-eight thousand. Intel advises you're looking at an RC-135 spy plane."*

"Confirmed target heading east at zero eight four," Roh responded. Out of the corner of his eye he noticed his wingman coming even with his MiG.

The six other MiG-29Ms making up Dragon flight had crossed the coast two minutes ago and were now streaking for Langau Island 1,000 feet above the rolling ocean. The lieutenant estimated it would take him and his wingman six to seven minutes to reach their new target, the RC-135.

Roh pushed the twin throttles forward to afterburner letting his jet climb. The acceleration made him smile.


## USS *OBSERVATION ISLAND*

"I am not picking up any coded radar or radio transmissions," Petty Officer Owens said as she manipulated her computer keyboard. "I'm afraid the AWACS is gone, sir."

"Gone? You mean it's been shot down?" Captain Bliss' hands went to the arms of his chair. He sat upright in the center of the darkened CIC.

"Yes, sir. I'm picking up some chatter from the pilots. It seems they're trying to carry on the mission without the AWACS."

"Give me the location of the Pave Hawks," Bliss demanded.

"Sixty miles out . . . twenty-four minutes from Langau Island, sir."

Bliss looked at the main display screen. It showed a 200-mile aerial view of the area with the *Observation Island* in the center. His first impulse was to call Chaniff at the Pentagon to recommend that the entire mission be called off. The Pave Hawks filled with the Ranger teams were halfway between the island and the mainland. They would need fighter coverage whichever direction they traveled. The problem with canceling the mission, Bliss realized, was more than General James and Major Erwin being stranded on the island at the hands of the enemy; it was the United States' credibility.

Captain Bliss walked up behind Owens and put his hand on her shoulder. "Owens, we're the only surveillance ship in the area. Those fighters are going to need some help sorting things out. Think you can do it?"

He felt a slight twinge of guilt seeing her face tense up before she answered. "This system wasn't designed for command and control, sir. It's used only to track missiles streaking across the sky up to two hundred thousand feet . . . or to watch satellites on a clear night." Owens pointed to the screen. "I can't see anything below one thousand feet and sometimes I can't even tell the good guys from the bad guys."

"What do you mean?" Bliss asked, his face scrunched up in disbelief, not fully understanding the equipment's capabilities.

"It's the software." Owens cleared her throat. She swiveled around in her chair to face the captain. "Occasionally when I tag a target hostile and try locking the range radar on it the frequency will jump and I can't maintain a solid lock. I'll lose the track and three times in the last two months the targets have disappeared from the scope. The technicians at Pearl said it has something to do with our current IFF transponder software."

"I'm not talking about locking the radar onto a target and tracking it. If you could supply our jets with altitudes, headings . . . that sort of thing, they might be able to figure out what's going on themselves."

Owens nodded, her eyes staring straight ahead. Bliss could see the wheels turning as he continued. "This system can track ten targets reentering the atmosphere at one time. Why can't it target twenty or thirty fighters in a dogfight?"

"It could, but . . ." Owens stopped, her voice breaking with excitement. "The new IFF software . . . wasn't scheduled to be installed for another three months." She swiveled back around and opened the metal cabinet under her computer terminal. She removed a stack of papers and thumbed through them.

"What are you looking for?"

"The last systems update fax I got from Raytheon," Owens answered without looking up. "It says the technician back at Pearl could download the program over a satellite by remote. If I can find our authorization number I could radio them and see if they could update the software now by dumping it directly into the computer. Then I can track *our* fighters by using IFF signals . . . the enemy aircraft would show up as default red hostile symbols."

"Hell, don't worry about the damn authorization—tell those rocket scientists this is a priority-one order." Bliss caught the pile of papers Owens thrust at him as she cleared her cramped station to reach for the radio.

"I'm looking at six bandits right, two o'clock low," Green conveyed from the rear cockpit. "It looks like they're heading toward us."

Conrad's eyes went from the HUD to the radar screen located on the upper left side of the instrument panel. He set his APG-70 radar to the vertical-scan mode. The long-range scan could detect a target out to 120 miles, even farther if he was above 50,000 feet, however it couldn't detect their speed, closing rate, or altitude.

"Tacoma two, three and four, this is Lead. Bandits right two o'clock low."

*"Two's in."*

*"Three's in."*

*"Four's in."*

"Follow me down. We'll engage at angels twenty. One pass . . . shoot'em in the face. Regroup on the back side," Conrad instructed. "If these are MiG-29s or Su-27s I don't want anyone in a furball. Is that understood?" Furball was fighter-pilot slang for a dogfight.

*"Copy, Lead,"* the other three Strike Eagles echoed.

"Hold tight, Greeno, I'm taking her downtown fast. I want to be a moving target."

"Yeah . . . me too. And I also want to make it home in time for dinner," Green answered.

Conrad flipped his jet over and headed for the ground in a diving turn. He was careful to keep the F-15E's nose pointed toward the targets.

Flying upside down he could see the rolling gray clouds 20,000 feet below. Looking back at the HUD Conrad watched the symbology as his airspeed passed 550 knots, heading east at 087 degrees. His glance shifted back to the radarscope and he watched the targets' range closing in.

Descending through 25,000 Conrad righted the Strike Eagle, pulling the nose up in one fluid motion. The F-15E responded as the stab of 4 Gs pushed him and his WSO back into their seats. Conrad grunted, feeling his spine snap and pop from the stress of leveling the fully loaded fighter.

He let the big jet continue to drift down, descending at 1,000 feet a minute. Pushing the throttles forward he kept his airspeed above 500 knots not wanting the Strike Eagle to bleed off energy.

"We need a range to target, Colonel," Green warned from the back seat as he looked at the radar screen.

"You watch our back side. I'll get this lead asshole." Conrad replied. "Alright. We'll see what you bad asses are made of."

Not taking his eyes off the radarscope, Conrad switched from vertical scan to super search. The radar would now automatically lock onto the nearest bandit. Watching the screen, he waited for the radar beam to move across the nearest three round dots several times. On the third sweep the beam stopped and the lead contact's dot began to flash. Conrad's jet had acquired the target. The Strike Eagle's IBM CP-1075C, using a bank of very high speed integrated circuits known as VHSIC, instantly gave him range, heading, closing rate and altitude. A second later the radar steering cue appeared on the HUD showing Conrad which way to turn his fighter to engage the target.

"Lock up, Greeno. Range . . . forty-three miles. Heading two-five three closing at 930 knots. Altitude . . . eight hundred feet."

"Shit, they're in the dirt."

Conrad keyed his mike. "Tacoma two, take the pair to the left. Three and four you've got the pair on the right. Lead has the center guy and the trailer."

*"Roger, Lead."*

"Follow me down to ten thousand feet, Tacoma package," Conrad called out, pushing the nose of his F-15E down as he banked five degrees right."

*At least the cargo hold is warmer than outside,* General Sinchon thought as he rested his tired body on a canvas jump seat next to the fuselage wall. His hands were tied behind him. The pain in his broken arm was becoming unbearable.

The Coaler's bay door was open, allowing him to see the runway stretching to the south. He could also see two guards positioned on either side of the door. The strong odor irritating his nostrils, he realized, was jet fuel fumes being blown in from outside.

Sinchon inspected the cargo bay. The windowless interior was a dull gray with nylon ropes and straps hanging from the ceiling. The metal floor was scraped and scarred from freight being transferred into and out of the air-craft. Along the side of each wall was a row of jump seats. The only cargo inside were two carts loaded with metal-cutting saws and other equipment secured to the ramp floor next to the open bay.

Directly across from him Major Erwin sat leaning over staring at the ground. He wondered if she wasn't feeling well.

"Major," Sinchon whispered.

"Yes?" Erwin looked up. Her face said she was exhausted.

"Stay alert. I need you to help me count how many armed men are guarding us." Sinchon glanced out the bay door.

"I've counted twelve," Erwin responded immediately. "Eight of them are armed. The rest must be some type of engineers."

"I count fourteen. You're right . . . only eight are armed." Sinchon smiled at the woman's tenacity.

"I'm trying to get my restraints loose," Erwin said in a hushed tone, leaning forward again. "Are you having any luck?"

"No." Sinchon didn't want to tell her it hurt his broken arm too much to move. He watched Erwin moving her shoulders up and down as she attempted to slacken the tight wire restraints.

"If I could just . . ."

"No talking," one of the guards shouted. "Colonel Kaine said no talking."

"Shove it," Erwin said under her breath.

"You are brave, Major, no longer afraid," Sinchon said, seeing her eyes filled with determination.

"Brave? It's more like pissed off." Erwin smiled. "Or scared stupid . . . one or the other."

The rhythmic crackling of electricity told James the radio scarcely had enough power to transmit. Moving the heater closer to the radio he hoped would keep the battery warm and make it last a little longer. Duke twisted the volume knob to maximum and keyed the hand-held mike. "Guard Dog . . . Beagle. You still out there, Guard Dog?"

*"Beagle . . . where the hell have you been?"*

"Playing cloak and dagger as ordered." Duke shivered as a draft of wind swirled in from outside. "I can confirm the North Koreans are transporting some type of cargo to that Iranian freighter. Whatever it is they packed it in long wooden crates and it must be heavy. It takes six or seven men to carry one crate to the ship. Could be fuel rods, but without X-ray vision I can't say for sure."

*"Okay . . . I'll contact Cheerleader and let them know. The choppers*

*are twenty-seven minutes out to the east. They'll be landing on the south
end of the island. Can you make it there?''*

"Negative, Guard Dog. Two other companions were captured. They've
been taken aboard the Coaler." James watched the power meter fluctuate
near zero.

*"Understood, Beagle. We'll leave that call to the Ranger commanders.
Start broadcasting in another fifteen minutes. The choppers will pick up
your signal and you can guide them in. Chopper's call sign is Doberman.
Repeat . . . call sign Doberman.''*

"Roger that, Guard Dog. Beagle out." He switched off the radio.

He rested his back against the rock wall and rubbed his face. Attempting
to sort things out in his mind, he thought of Erwin and Sinchon. He didn't
want to leave them in the hands of the North Koreans. Duke looked toward
the opening. They probably didn't see the soldier coming. Or by the time
they discovered he was out there there wasn't anything for them to do but
hope he'd pass them by.

*Well, the same thing's going to happen to you if you don't get your
ass out of here,* Duke thought. He was still wet, but he'd rather take his
chances with hypothermia than North Koreans. He stuffed the radio and
heater into his duffle bag and crawled out of the cave back into the cold
afternoon air.


"Electronic sensors picking up four I-band radars sweeping the area west of
our MiGs," the defensive radar officer called out.

"American fighters descending through fifteen thousand feet," another
technician reported from his station.

Chin listened to the chatter as he watched the symbols on the radar
screen.

"Fourteen thousand . . . they're beginning to level off."

Lighting another Camel cigarette, Chin watched the triangle-shaped radar
symbols representing the six MiG-29Ms cluster into a small group. The
numeral digits under the symbols revealed that the pilots were following
their orders precisely. The MiGs were flying below 1,000 feet thirty-six
miles away from the American jets.

"Thirteen thousand . . . still descending."

"The American jets are spreading out. Preparing to launch their missiles.
At thirty-five miles, call it," Chin ordered.

"Yes, sir."

"Twelve thousand feet. Closing fast . . . thirty-six miles . . . thirty
miles."

The radar operator keyed his mike. "Dragon flight. Break formation."

*   *   *

North Korean captain Lee Chung, a tall Korean with short dark hair and a deep acne-pocked complexion, looked right and left at the two MiG-29Ms in formation off each wing. Averaging fifty yards away, the fighters floated up and down making their way west at Mach .95. A sixth fighter trailed Chung three hundred yards to the rear and a little above him.

The captain adjusted the sensitivity of his SPO-15 radar warning receiver. He listened to the distant *pong . . . pong . . . pong* of the American radar sweeping his fighter from above. The RWR flashed yellow, indicating the Americans had locked on his jet. Chung had been trained to disregard the yellow warning light. However, in this real-life situation it was hard to pretend he didn't care when he knew if the light changed from yellow to red the system had detected a missile coming toward his jet.

Flying as lead in a six-ship formation, Chung gently fingered the stick as he guided the jet over the rolling ocean 800 feet below him. Once again he checked his radar and IFF to make sure they were off.

"Red Crown . . . Dragon Flight. Turning to engage," Chung radioed.

*"Understood, Dragon Flight. You are cleared for intercept."*

Changing radio frequencies, the captain made contact with the other five pilots.

"Dragon Flight, this is Dragon One Seven. Targets straight ahead . . . follow my lead."

Chung tightened his stomach muscles before pulling back on the stick. Jamming the double throttles forward he put the MiG into afterburner and watched the nose come straight up. Instantly the bite of 6 Gs drove him back into his seat as the twin-tailed fighter rocketed straight up toward the cloud cover.

"Chaff now," Captain Chung grunted under the strain of the pressure.

*What the hell?* Conrad scanned the radar targeting cursor on his HUD. It flickered on and off sporadically as if someone was teasing him. His Strike Eagle's radar was losing radar lock on the target below.

"Greeno, what's going on?" Conrad asked as he leveled the jet a few hundred feet below 10,000.

"The signal's breaking up. We're losing it in Doppler shift."

Conrad looked back at the radar screen. The targeting computer showed the lead bandit at twenty-nine miles, altitude 3,000 feet and closing at a speed of 510 knots. Looking back at the HUD Conrad saw his airspeed was 507 knots. The bandits were flying straight up from below.

"We've got to get closer," Major Green warned.

"Yeah . . . I know." Conrad thumbed the weapon select button on the throttle to call up his AIM-120B AMRAAM air-to-air missiles. Just then the steering cue on the HUD faded as the radar lost its lock on the target.

The radar warning clamoring in Chung's helmet diminished as he pumped the chaff button three more times. Jinking his MiG in a corkscrew spiral, he sliced through 8,000 feet and broke through the thick gray clouds.

Watching the HUD, Chung lowered his visor to block out the sun. Rolling the MiG over, he swung the nose west. His MiG responded, going into a banking turn. Long trails of black smoke poured from the engines as he continued the steep climb.

*"Dragon flight . . . Red Crown. Radars on. Continue west heading two seven zero degrees. Targets at ten thousand . . . range . . . twenty-nine miles."*

"Copy, Red Crown. Dragon flight going active."

Righting the MiG, Chung came wings level at 9,400 feet heading due west at 410 knots. Concentrating on the deep blue sky with the sun hanging low on the horizon, he looked for the twisting white smoke trail of a missile heading toward his jet.

Methodically he rotated his head right and left and noticed the other MiGs taking up formation on each side of his MiG. They were again strung out in a long line two miles wide and a little behind him. Activating the MiG's powerful NO-193 radar, Chung watched the CRT screen positioned below and to the right of his HUD. The scope displayed a superimposed electronic beam moving up and down in a jerking motion.

As the system warmed up he caught sight of two radar returns approaching head on, range twenty-eight miles, closing at 953 knots.

"Hostile radar straight ahead," Green shouted from the back seat. "It's an air-to-air sweeping from the east."

"I see it. Start the music and jam the sucker," Conrad ordered.

Green toggled the switch triggering the F-15E's electronic countermeasures. An instant later the Strike Eagle's ALE-45 chaff/flare dispenser began to spit out a steady stream of radar-confusing foil. At the same time the ALQ-135 hostile signal jammer went active, filling the sky with J-band radio waves.

*All right, sucker, you're mine.* Using his forefinger Colonel Conrad manipulated the radar-tracking castle switch on the inside throttle handle. Watching the black radar screen, he moved the twin yellow cursors, centering them over a bright solid circle in the upper section of the screen. Depressing the button he locked the APG-70's powerful I-band onto the lead bandit.

"I have him. Range twenty-five miles and closing. Altitude angels ten. He's heading straight for us," Conrad announced.

"That's one. Where's the second?" Greeno complained.

"I'm working on it." Conrad repeated the radar lock procedure. This time he slewed the cursor over the second target trailing the first and pressed the lock button. The second target began to flash.

"Range . . . twenty-one miles," Greeno called out anxiously. "Are you going to shoot these guys or kiss them?"

Conrad checked his IFF transponder. It was clean. There wasn't any electronic clutter. He would fire one missile at each target.

"Range . . . eighteen miles . . . closing at 985 knots," Greeno yammered.

Conrad checked the HUD one more time. On the lower left side, below the airspeed scale, 4-MRM flashed, telling him four AMRAAMs were ready. The APG-70 radar had automatically dumped the target's range, heading, and speed into each of the AIM-120Bs' flight computers. The shot cue appeared on the HUD signaling the missiles were ready to go.

"Tacoma Lead. Fox one . . . Fox one." Conrad punched the weapon's release button on his stick.

*"Tacoma Two. Fox one. . . . Fox one."*

*"Tacoma Three. Fox one."*

*"Tacoma Four. Fox one."*

Conrad listened to the other pilots as he pulled his Strike Eagle up two degrees nose high and watched the missiles streak away. Out of the corner of his eye he caught sight of the silver smoke trails as the other missiles curved their way toward the distant targets.

Captain Chung banked his MiG four degrees right, adding power. The pulsing tone in his helmet became steady as the MiG's powerful NO-193 burned through the American jamming radar and locked onto the closest American jet.

Chung concentrated on the radar screen. He glanced at the flashing red warning light below the HUD. It would take forty-five to fifty seconds before the American missile closed the distance. Enough time to fire his own missiles.

Moving his left thumb, he manipulated the inverted radar missile control button on the stick. Stirring the targeting symbol over the closest return, Chung locked the radar beam. The HUD flashed a square targeting cursor and it began to move across the display, signaling a hostile fighter was in range of his missiles.

The captain's thumb rested on the launch button. Counting to three, with the tone staying constant, he punched the button once and then a second time sending two long-burn, active-radar semi-IR guided R-27AE missiles toward the lead American fighter.

''Two missiles away,'' Chung shouted into his face mask.

*''Missiles away . . . Missiles away,''* the other five fighters called out.

The captain felt his mouth go dry as he kept his fighter on course heading west.

# 31

The chairman of the Joint Chiefs of Staff, Gen. Howard Chaniff, rubbed his bloodshot eyes. The darkened Special Technical Operations Center had become dead quiet. There wasn't any unnecessary chatter as each person continued to do their job.

Chaniff looked over Lieutenant Fontano's shoulder and stared at the black computer monitor. Just minutes ago it had shown an exact electronic duplicate of the tactical operations screen Tallman was observing on the E-3C AWACS.

He picked up the authority phone linking him with the White House. As much as he didn't want to, Chaniff knew he had to inform Manning of the lost aircraft. The phone rang four times before Manning answered.

"Manning."

"Allan, this is Chaniff. I have some bad news."

"Let me guess. The military has fucked up again."

Chaniff fought the urge to lash out at the NSA. *Now's not the time,* he told himself. "We lost the AWACS a few minutes ago. I've given the order to get another one airborne." Chaniff paused, forcing his voice to remain low and even. "At this time we can't say exactly what happened, but there is a hell of a lot of North Korean activity."

"So who is commanding the operation there?" Manning asked.

"Right now . . . no one. The fighters are operating independently and the Pave Hawks are still flying toward the island."

"That's a pile of crap and you know it. We have fighters and helicopters fluttering around the skies over the Korean Sea with no command and control."

"Mr. Manning, this is not something to panic over. The crews in those jets are trained for this type of thing to happen and we do have two surface ships in the area. My recommendation is to continue with the mission. That new AWACS will be in the air in a half-hour at the most."

*"My recommendation* is to retreat . . . pull back," Manning said. "You are not only putting more lives at stake, you're—"

"And what about the rescue mission?" Chaniff interrupted, no longer able to contain his frustration with the man's apparent lack of fortitude.

"Screw the rescue mission." The line went dead.

Chaniff stared at the receiver in disbelief. He couldn't believe Manning would leave Duke James, one of their own, to the dogs, or see the bigger picture.

"Lieutenant Fontano."

"Yes, sir."

"Get Osan on the horn. Tell them I want that AWACS in the sky in two minutes." Chaniff sat quietly, thinking to himself.

## OSAN AFB, SOUTH KOREA

Lt. Col. Warren W. Reader ran up the aluminum stairs and entered the cold dark interior of the E-3C AWACS. The white jet, displaying the colors of the 964th Airborne Warning & Control Squadron, sat on the south end of the runway. Two fuel trucks worked in unison, pumping JP-8 into her wing tanks. A dozen other maintenance personnel strived to get the jet ready for takeoff in record time.

"Secure the cabin. Get the engines running," the short, lean colonel, with white hair and a black mustache, shouted. Wearing a blue wool sweater with silver oak leaves on each shoulder, Levi's and running shoes, there was no doubt the AWACS "Hammer" had been snatched away from his living room. He surveyed the interior and saw that most of his crew was already in their seats. Several were, however, milling about their stations.

"Get your asses in those chairs. Those computers need to be warmed up," Reader shouted, staring hard. "In case you haven't figured it out, ladies and gentlemen, this is an emergency situation."

It normally took thirty minutes to launch an AWACS from a cold start. Reader knew he needed to do it in ten minutes or less.

"Sir, I have Cheerleader. They want to know our ETD," one of the communications specialists shouted.

"Tell Cheerleader . . . we're moving," Reader shouted back. *I don't have time for chitchat.*

The colonel took the seat normally occupied by the tactical duty officer. He slipped on a headset and watched the computer monitor coming to life.

"Sir, the front office is saying another few minutes before she's fully fueled."

"Flight deck, this is Reader. This aircraft was on standby. It should have been fueled," Reader howled after slamming his thumb on the intercom button. "Get this bitch in the air now!"

TACOMA LEAD, F-15E

"They're active, man. Turn this baby," Maj. Skip Green advised, referring to the AIM-120B AMRAAMs. The missiles were now tracking the two targets independently, using their internal radar located in the nose section to remain locked onto the enemy fighters.

Conrad banked his fighter left, and dropped the nose. He watched his airspeed increase to 530 knots as the jet dropped through 9,000 feet. The radar warning receiver filled his helmet with a steady high-pitched whine as the MiG's J-band radar continued to pound his F-15E from the east.

"Threat . . . threat. I'm showing a launch. One, maybe two radar-guided missiles." Green's voice was an octave higher than normal.

"Watch for it, Greeno. Give me some chaff."

The colonel came wings level heading east at 093 degrees heading straight for the enemy fighter. He was trained to defeat a radar-guided missile by coming across its beam in order to get lost in the Doppler shift. His plan was to swing his jet around and begin flying perpendicular to the radar locked onto his F-15E. He knew the North Korean J-band was a pulse-Doppler which relied on a changing radar return to lock onto a target. By design it could only find a target if it was moving toward or away from its radar beam. Any object that flew in a perpendicular course, or directly in front of the beam, would show little variance. It was then automatically filtered out of the radar picture as clutter. Conrad reasoned if he could stay on a steady course in front of the MiG the Doppler shift wouldn't change and the missile would lose its tracking ability.

"Chaff . . . chaff . . . chaff!" Green yelled, hitting the chaff switch on the controller.

"Slammers eight miles from impact. They're tracking. Hold tight." Conrad grunted, referring to the AIM-120B AMRAAMs. "I'm bringing her around again."

The colonel cranked the stick hard right pulling a steady 5 Gs. The symbology on the HUD changed direction as the fighter looped back 180 degrees.

"More chaff," Green said pumping the button.

"Find the missiles," The colonel grunted to his WSO.

Traveling at Mach 4, the first AMRAAM pushed over at 12,000 feet gaining airspeed. The front canards moved in unison to keep the nose pointed toward the target.

For the last twelve miles the missile had been following the reflected radar energy of the F-15E's I-band as it raced toward the closest MiG-29. As a backup, to counter enemy jamming, every ten seconds the Strike Eagle's computer sent an electronic data burst updating the missile's heading. The flight computer made course corrections, keeping the missile pointed in the right direction.

Six miles out, thirty seconds from impact, the first missile locked its internal radar on the reflecting radio energy coming off the lead MiG. Pushing the nose down it headed for its target.

## DRAGON ONE SEVEN, MiG-29M

Captain Chung let his MiG drift up to 11,000 feet. The HUD showed his first R-27AE was fifty-two seconds out and climbing. He watched the American move across his radar screen maneuvering left to right. This told the captain the American pilot didn't need his radar to guide the incoming missile.

A wave of panic shot through him. If the American fighter was maneuvering that could only mean one of two things. One, he hadn't fired any missiles or two he had fired AMRAAMs and they were actively tracking his jet. Only an idiot would risk option one.

"Dragon One Seven. Breaking right," Chung shouted into his oxygen mask. At the same time he jacked the stick right, putting his MiG into a 7-G turn. Hitting the chaff button, he strained to look over his shoulder. As his vision began to narrow from the G forces he spotted the streaking white blur of an AMRAAM coming toward his jet.

The lead AIM-120B turned left, still locked onto the nearest MiG. Descending through 11,500 feet the twelve-foot-long missile's rocket motor burned out letting gravity and forward momentum carry it to the target.

At three seconds from impact the targeting computer began to overload. The balls of chaff churning behind the MiG caused the radar homing-head to shut down because of the varying electronic returns. The software automatically rebooted, switching back to scan-mode and locking the radar onto the nearest and strongest radar return. Banking three degrees left it headed for the chaff cloud boiling below it.

*"Tacoma One. Break left."* Conrad heard his wingman's panicked voice over the radio.

"Break . . . break!" Green roared from the back cockpit, hitting the chaff button again.

Conrad's head snapped around to see his wingman in a body-crushing left turn a half-mile away. White hot decoy flares were spiraling from beneath the fighter. As the jet came around Conrad noticed the fighter was in afterburner.

"Ned, you're in blower. Take her out of blower!" Conrad screamed at Capt. Ned "Red Dog" Ruddy.

Above the long slithery curl of white smoke the colonel could see two enemy missiles nosing toward the Strike Eagle below. It happened so fast Conrad couldn't get off another warning. The first missile struck the back section of the F-15E enveloping it with red fire and black smoke.

"Punch out, you guys . . . punch out!" Conrad shouted at the sight.

The second missile entered the fireball, blowing the rear of the jet into several pieces. His wingman's jet decelerated rapidly before going into a tumbling spiral. The colonel waited for chutes to appear but didn't see any. Looking back at his radar screen he saw his two AMRAAMs merging with their targets.

"Greeno, call Osan, we need SAR choppers out here," Conrad heard himself say, not knowing how he got the words past his heart pounding in his throat.

Chung grunted as he pressed the stick left, this time putting his MiG into a reverse 6-G turn. His airspeed fell to 289 knots as the MiG came around to the northwest. He tapped the chaff button one more time.

Using all his strength Chung looked right just in time to see the first American missile hit the chaff cloud nearest his jet. The missile exploded in an orange fireball peppering the tail section of his MiG with slivers of hot metal.

The captain leveled his MiG, feeling the Gs fall off. One scan of the HUD told him he had dropped 2,000 feet while evading the first missile and his airspeed was now at 260 knots, too slow to outmaneuver another missile. He didn't notice the radar warning light was no longer flashing. The American had lost radar lock.

Pitching the nose up and adding power, Chung started to climb, when he saw white flashes over his fighter. Cranking his head around, Chung watched two AMRAAMs hit their mark. Two MiG-29Ms to the northeast exploded at the same time. They each came apart in yellow-orange balls of fire. Only one pilot ejected.

Instinctively Chung threw the MiG into afterburner, turning to the northeast and keeping his interceptor level. Watching the radar screen Chung centered his MiG on the closest American and watched his airspeed climb. A third and fourth missile flashed by his fighter to the southeast. These two also hit their marks.

One exploded directly in front of the cockpit of his wingman, killing the pilot instantly. The next snaked right and pushed over before taking out the MiG trailing Chung. The clear blue sky was now black smoke and bursts of fiery orange dotted with parachutes and chunks of aircraft descending all around.

"Tacoma Lead . . . Splash one MiG . . . Splash one MiG," Conrad called out to the other pilots. He watched the second target disappear off his screen.

*"Tacoma Three . . . Splash one MiG."*

*"Tacoma Four . . . Splash one MiG."*

"Shit hot. That's four," Green counted.

"Stop celebrating. We've still got work to do," Colonel Conrad warned.

"Two missiles coming in from the east. Range two miles . . . closing fast," the WSO rattled off immediately.

"Okay, I see them."

Looking to the east Conrad could make out the white smoke trails of two air-to-air missiles snaking toward his jet from several thousand feet above. They looked to be in a search-mode, turning in long S-shaped patterns trying to acquire a target.

"It's time for some of that teamwork bullshit," Conrad told Green.

"I'm on it. Break right on three."

Conrad adjusted his grip on the stick and throttles as he leveled his Eagle at 12,000 feet, speed 340 knots. His RWR was no longer signaling a hostile radar locked up on his jet. Conrad was now concerned with outmaneuvering a pair of radar-guided missiles with backup infrared tracking.

"One . . . two . . . three. Break right," Green called.

Conrad snapped the Strike Eagle into a hard ninety-degree angle. Watching the HUD, his airspeed decreased as he kept a steady 6-G pull on the stick. 320 knots . . . 300 . . . 280 . . . 240 . . . Below 240 knots he knew the Strike Eagle was a sitting duck.

"Talk to me, Greeno," Conrad called out under the force of the Gs.

"Flares . . . chaff . . . flares," Green moaned to his pilot letting him know what he was doing. "Give us more airspeed."

Conrad dropped the nose and saw his airspeed increase slightly. He knew he couldn't put the jet into afterburner for fear an IR guided missile would find its mark.

"You got it, man . . . more stick," Green acknowledged.

The F-15E had turned in an almost complete circle. Conrad saw several magnesium flares floating toward the ground when the first R-27AE went stupid heading for the nearest heat source, a single flare. The second missile locked onto a cluster of flares a hundred yards away. It blasted through the center, failing to explode.

Conrad brought his fighter around, pointing its nose to the east again. In a sudden burst the radar detected a target seven miles out heading straight for them.

"New target bearing zero eight seven," Conrad relayed the new data. "Range . . . seven miles, altitude 12,000 feet . . . we're closing at 840 knots."

"Yeah, I see him. It's our first target. We missed!" Green exclaimed.

"Range . . . six miles . . . closing 890 knots." Conrad's eyes swept the HUD. He listened for a radar warning. The MiG's radar was sweeping his jet but it wasn't locked up. Both jets were closing at the same altitude and speed. Conrad couldn't turn away. If he did the MiG would pull in behind him and stick a heat seeker up his tail. His instincts and training told him the only way to attack this guy was to merge, go vertical and try to shoot him with a Sidewinder from above.

"Three miles . . . tally-ho! Left, eleven o'clock. He's above us," Green shouted.

Conrad looked up as a flash of sunlight reflected off the MiG's canopy. He thumbed the weapon's select button on the throttle to call up AIM-9M Sidewinders. As he did the MiG-29 streaked 300 yards above his jet heading to the west.

"Here we go," Conrad warned his WSO to hold on. Putting his jet into afterburner he pulled the stick back rocketing straight up. His airspeed increased as the Gs crushed both Conrad and Green. Clear open sky filled the HUD.

"Now," Chung moaned to himself. He felt the piercing pain of 7.5 Gs as he turned the MiG-29M to the right and nosed up thirty degrees. Out of the corner of his eye he saw the American climbing away with afterburners glowing orange.

*Stupid move,* he thought. Chopping the throttle and extending the airbrake Chung let his fighter roll over losing airspeed and altitude. Not taking his eyes off the American he rolled the stick around and pointed his nose at the glowing orange tailpipes of the F-15E. Jamming the throttles forward, he closed the distance.

"Shit, he's right below us," Green shouted.

Conrad pulled the stick straight back again, bringing the Strike Eagle out of its vertical climb and pushing over at 14,000 inverted. Hauling the throttles back he took the jet out of afterburner and let her nose over toward the ground.

At once his HUD filled with the gray MiG 1,000 yards below him heading straight at him.

"Flares . . . Greeno . . . Flares," Conrad shouted.

If he could get the first shot off the American was dead. Chung switched from R-27AEs to R-60T Aphid short-range heat seekers. The weapons data symbology on the HUD flashed and a throbbing tone sounded in his helmet as the Aphids began to detect heat radiating off the F-15E above his jet. Listening for a solid launch tone Chung kept the nose of the MiG centered on the dark gray American jet.

*Errr . . . errr . . . errr.* The R-60T wasn't locking up. Chung suddenly saw the white flicker of several decoy flares tumble out from behind the American jet.

The tone instantly became constant. Chung hesitated. He knew his missiles had just locked up on the flares and not the American jet. Switching to guns, he waited for the MiG's rangefinding laser to lock up. It didn't. He pulled the trigger.

The MiG vibrated as forty-two 30-millimeter rounds blasted from the right wing root of his MiG.

"Oh, shit!" Conrad exclaimed.

He blinked once as a burst of cannon fire exploded from the MiG. A dozen yellow tracer rounds flew by the cockpit windows. The even high-pitched tone sounding in Conrad's helmet confirmed the magnesium-fluoride-cooled seeker head of the AIM-9M Sidewinders had locked onto the hot leading edges of the MiG's wings.

"Do it," Green shouted.

Conrad tapped the weapons-release button, sending one and then a second AIM-9M Sidewinder off the rails on each side of his fighter.

"Fox two . . . Fox two," Conrad declared.

In a blur of white fire and smoke the projectiles rushed to their target.

Captain Chung couldn't react fast enough. Drawing the stick right and popping three decoy flares, he tried to outturn the missiles. The ploy didn't work. Chung watched an AIM-9M corkscrew toward his jet and hit his left wing, exploding in a blaze of fire. The canopy cracked and the controls instantly froze as the second missile impacted his tail section.

The MiG's instrument panel lit up with red and yellow warning lights. The stench of burning plastic and white smoke filled the cockpit. Pulling the ejection handle between his legs, Chung armed the seat. He straightened his back, closed his eyes, and pulled the lever up. In less than three seconds the captain had rocketed from the stricken fighter and was floating away from the jet under a parachute.

Conrad banked left trying to avoid the pilotless MiG. Rolling his F-15E he watched the canopy fly off as the enemy fighter broke into several pieces before exploding in a burst of red fire.

The colonel banked to the north, slowly bringing his fighter out of its dive. The last MiG-29 was turning to the east bugging out. For an instant he thought about trying to lock up a missile but instead turned west.

"Splash one MiG," he radioed, wiping the sweat from his forehead. "Tacoma Flight . . . Tacoma Leader. Regroup."

*"Copy, Leader. Two approaching your left wing."*

*"Three's to the right a mile away."*

Conrad listened, knowing he would not hear from his wingman.


## LANGAU ISLAND

Duke James didn't make any quick movements. Resting on his side on a small mound of dirt he overlooked the south end of the runway. He had pressed his body next to several flat rocks to blend into the landscape. Behind him, twenty feet away, was a sheer jagged cliff extending down to the ocean. He could hear the waves breaking over the rocks below.

There was a small crack between the boulders allowing him to see most of the bluff to the right and the sharp ravine below him. In the distance Duke could make out the two transport aircraft including the men around them. A light fog was beginning to cover the island and he could no longer see the *Allum Bacar* docked in the bay. A few minutes earlier he had watched several armed men moving toward the south end of the island. They were weaving back and forth in a search pattern. He lost sight of them as they moved through the fog or disappeared behind many of the rock outcroppings.

*I hate this damn waiting,* Duke thought. *By now Erwin and Sinchon could be dead.*

James made a fist and ground it into the dirt next to the boulder. His emotions told him to do something . . . anything. Yet his brains and military training told him to sit tight. No matter how bad he wanted to act, he knew it would be suicide trying to get Erwin and Sinchon off the AN-72. He was unarmed and there were at least a dozen armed men around the transports.

He had set up the radio between himself and the rocks. The black antenna wire was on the rocks allowing him to transmit or receive. He checked his watch and saw that twelve minutes had passed. Close enough. It was time to contact the choppers.

Turning the radio on, Duke waited for the power dial to move and tell him how much electricity was left in the battery. The dial didn't move. Duke held the radio to his ear, hearing it crackle with static. This conversation was going to be short.

"Doberman . . . Beagle. Do you copy, Doberman?"

*"Say again, Beagle, you're breaking up."*

"Doberman . . . Beagle. What's your ETA?"

*"ETA . . . eleven mi . . . utes. Bea . . . wha . . . wea . . . c on . . . ons?"*

"Say again."

*"ETA . . ."*

The channel went dead. Duke looked over at the transmit light. It was out and the battery power dial showed zero. He slammed the mike down and sighed. He turned the radio off, hoping he could nurse a few more minutes of power if the battery was shut off for a while.

Looking back at the transports, the fog had grown thicker to the point where he could barely see them. The temperature was falling and he guessed his pants had gotten as dry as they could in the cold. Duke zipped up his parka, wondering what was happening to Erwin and Sinchon.

Major Erwin sat with her hands bound behind her back. The interior of the AN-72 had cooled and her feet and hands had grown numb from the cold. With the rear cargo door still down she could see a heavy fog rolling over the island. She knew poor weather would hinder the rescue attempt the Americans were planning.

Seated across from her, General Sinchon didn't move. His breathing was shallow, his face pale. The ordeal was taking its toll on him.

Erwin looked to the left at a sudden commotion going on outside the jet. The guards were all facing the other direction intently watching the scene beyond her view.

Closing her eyes the major leaned forward and thrust her shoulders together in front of her. The wire stretched a little. Concentrating with all her strength, her fingers extended, Erwin squeezed her palms tightly together.

She pulled with all her strength, feeling the skin around her wrists beginning to tear from the restraints. The cord slipped down a tad and she tugged harder.

*Come on, Helen, you can do this.* In one final thrust she pulled one of her hands free, feeling the skin rip. Resisting the urge to cry out in pain, she sat upright gritting her teeth. She closed her eyes and breathed in deeply.

As she opened her eyes, Erwin saw Colonel Kaine walking up the back of the cargo ramp.

Duke keyed the radio mike one more time. The transmit light flickered a couple of times before fading completely away.

"Damn it," he whispered. Playing with wires on the back of the radio, he tried to transmit one more time. Nothing worked.

Duke tucked the radio into a small crevice near his feet. He would have to listen for the choppers. With a little luck they might land near him. *Maybe this fog is a blessing,* Duke thought. *If I can't see the North Koreans then they can't see me either.*

# 32

The green software cycle light under COP Janis Owens' computer monitor told her the download procedure was in process. She watched the light flicker on and off as the hard drive whirred accepting the data. At last her computer monitor read, SATCOM DATA LINK TRANSFER COMPLETE.

"That's it, sir. The software's loaded."

"Well, what are you waiting for?" Bliss bellowed. "See if it works."

Owens tapped on her computer keyboard feverishly. "Going to a two-hundred-mile aerial view. If this works the American fighters transmitting the correct IFF codes will show up as blue triangles along with their call signs. Everything else in the sky will show up as a yellow triangle."

"And if it doesn't work?" Bliss asked.

"Then we're back to square one." Owens made several more key strokes. "I'm just not sure how long it will take for the two programs to interface. Here goes nothing." She tapped the button. In the center of the screen the words appeared, SOFTWARE DOWNLOADING, PLEASE WAIT.

"Aw, shit," Bliss said out loud, turning away from the screen.


BENJI LEADER, F-16C

"Stay with me, Benji three three. I have the target on radar bearing three four seven degrees," Lt. Col. Hank McGiven instructed his wingman.

*"Roger, Leader. I'm above you . . . to the right."*

Flying to the northwest at 420 knots, 18,000 feet in the air, McGiven watched the flashing dot on his radar screen representing the RC-135 ten miles out. His eyes went to the HUD and back to the radar as he tried to spot the four-engine spy plane flying above him in the late afternoon sun.

McGiven considered himself part of the new "Fighter Mafia," a group of hot-shot pilots determined to forge the future of Air Combat Command and the United States Air Force. An Academy grad, McGiven had been flying Vipers since the Gulf War. Many of his superiors considered him potentially one of the best all-around F-16C drivers in the air force. In practice, however, personal problems and an overly pushy personality were keeping him from advancing.

McGiven's goal had been to become an instructor at the Fighter Weapons School at Nellis. Unlike most pilots, McGiven had been through two well-publicized divorces—political suicide for high-profile officers. In McGiven's mind the US Air Force wanted poster children, not pilots.

At thirty-nine years of age the colonel knew his days in the air force were numbered if he didn't make the jump to full bird colonel within the next year.

"Tally-ho! Twelve o'clock, six miles out," McGiven said, seeing the dark silhouette of the RC-135 floating out in front of his fighter.

SYSTEM READY. HIT ANY KEY. The phrase blinked across the top of Owens' radar screen. She felt her heart rate jump. Of all the times she needed a computer program to work the first time, this was it. *Come on, you silicon wonder, don't fail me now.* Closing her eyes she hit the space bar.

"Captain . . . I've got it!" she exclaimed.

Bliss appeared behind her again.

Owens' screen filled with blue triangles showing IFF codes along with call signs under them.

"Good job." Bliss squatted next to her. He studied the screen trying to get a feel for what was happening. Mixed in with the blue triangles representing the American jets were four yellow triangles showing the position of each enemy fighter.

One of the enemy jets was heading to the east and had just crossed over the North Korean coast. Another was flying to the southwest and appeared to be circling around to the south end of Langau Island. The last two radar blips caught Bliss' attention. They were flying in tight formation toward the northwest and appeared to be heading for the RC-135. Bliss touched the screen.

"Zoom in on this area," he ordered.

Owens did as she was told, going to a fifty-mile aerial view. In the upper part of the screen the blue radar symbol of the RC-135 appeared along with two F-16Cs to the southeast. Under the F-16Cs' IFF codes Bliss saw Benji Leader and Benji Three Three. A slight grin came across his sweating face. He could tell the good guys from the bad guys. To the southeast two yellow triangles were moving toward the RC-135 head-on at a high rate of speed. By their flight paths Bliss wondered if anyone knew the enemy jets were close by.

"Change radio frequencies. You need to talk with those jets."

*Me?* Owens looked at him, her eyes filled with doubt. "Sir, I don't—"

"Ms. Owens . . . there are two enemy fighters to the east closing on the RC-135. Those F-16s need to know that."

"Yes, sir." Owens answered, swallowing hard. She switched radio frequencies.


## DRAGON LEADER, MIG-29M

First Lt. Yun-Kyong Roh was flying heads down. He wasn't using his MiG's radar, knowing the RC-135 could detect it. Instead Roh watched the IR scope in the center of his instrument panel. The five-by-five-inch screen was blackish green and free of targets. Roh knew that on a clear day the IR system had a range of twenty miles. A blank screen told him there weren't any aircraft out in front of him.

Without the AWACS to track him and with his radar turned off, Roh's MiG was essentially invisible. By using the Fulcrum's advanced passive electro-optical Infra Red Search and Track (IRST) system he planned to sneak up on the American RC-135 and kill it with a single heat-seeking missile.

Roh tapped the computer buttons below his HUD, activating the laser rangefinder and helmet-mounted targeting device. A pair of electronic-magnet sensors placed on each side of his helmet and the HUD began to detect the movement of his head. Each motion was fed into the targeting computer, allowing Roh to instantly shoot at off-boresight targets simply by rotating his head and squeezing the trigger. The system allowed him to fire his Russian-made Vympel R-73M2 heat-seeking missiles at a target while in a dogfight, at an angle of sixty degrees off the center of his nose in a high G turn.

Roh touched the computer buttons two more times, linking his R-73M2 heat-seeking missiles and 30-millimeter cannon to the helmet targeting system. Looking back at the IR screen he noticed a bright orange dot. The IRST had picked up the first heat emissions of the American spy plane. Roh keyed his mike twice and his wingman returned the signal. They were both tracking the target.

*"Benji Leader . . . This is US Naval ship* Observation Island. *Do you copy, Benji Leader?"*

"Aw yeah . . . this is Benji Leader . . . Say again," McGiven answered.

*"US Naval ship* Observation Island. *We are tracking you. Enemy fighters approaching from the east. Turn right heading zero seven three."*

McGiven checked the radio frequency. The transmission was on the Navy Guard channel Conrad had ordered all fighters to monitor. It was a secure channel which randomly hopped from frequency to frequency and couldn't be jammed. It had to be authentic.

"Roger, *Observation Island*. Benji Leader turning." McGiven moved the side-stick control to the right, sweeping his radar to the east. "Let's move it, Benji Three Three."

## RC-135S, Super Snooper

"Roger that, *Observation Island*. We understand." Matthew P. Fletcher looked at his commanding officer, holding one side of his headset.

"How many enemy fighters?" Captain McQuire asked.

"Two. They must be flying totally passive. My instruments aren't detecting a thing." Fletcher pointed to his radar warning receiver and communications intercept console. It didn't show any electronic threats in the area.

"Tell the flight deck," McQuire ordered and took a seat. He buckled the lap belt. "It's going to get bumpy."

"Flight deck, take us down. We've got two enemy fighters closing fast from the east." There was a certain thrill with the impending danger, but Fletcher wasn't sure this was the kind of excitement he had in mind. He braced himself as the big jet rolled to the right and nosed over toward the water, gaining air speed.

RANGE: 14 MILES came across the MiG's IR screen. At the same time the faint humming of a distant radar grew stronger. Roh's radar warning receiver (RWR) seesawed to the left, showing the direction of the threat. By listening to the threat warning generated by the RWR, Roh could tell two pulse-Dopplers were trying to acquire his jet. With each beat of the RWR Roh knew the enemy jets were getting closer.

Lieutenant Roh had a choice to make. He could announce his presence, and his position, by activating his radar in order to learn the jets' range, heading and altitude. Or he could stay passive to close the last few miles silently and get his IR missiles in range. Either plan was risky.

Looking at his IR scope, Roh watched the RC-135 in the center of the screen. On the lower right edge he observed two new targets flying from the southwest. By their speed he knew at once they were fighters.

"Dragon One Five, this is Lead. We have company to the southwest. Looks like fighters."

*"Confirmed. I'm tracking."*

"Break left. See if you can draw them off," Roh ordered.

*"Understood, Leader."*

Lieutenant Roh kept his nose pointed at the RC-135. Pushing the throttles forward, he watched his airspeed climb to 425 knots. Out of the corner of his eye he saw his wingman bank to the left.

"Come on, sweetheart, find the target," Colonel McGiven whispered under his breath. His eyes shifted from the HUD to the radar screen and back again in quick succession. Swinging his Viper around, he took an easterly heading at 093 degrees. Scanning the sky he searched for signs of a target.

The HUD revealed his F-16C was level at 18,500 feet, traveling at 415 knots, and the sky was void of any aircraft.

McGiven looked back at the radarscope. The Westinghouse APG-68 radar was in BORE or SCAN/LOCK mode, configured to lock onto the first target coming into range.

"There you are," he said into the cockpit as two radar blips showed up on the screen. The IFF transponder was clean. They weren't broadcasting any type of identification signals. The colonel watched them for a few seconds before the trailing aircraft banked to the right, taking a heading toward the southwest.

"Benji Three Three, Benji Lead."

*"Go ahead, Lead."*

"Targets are splitting. I've got the one to the left, you take the trailer."

*"Roger, Lead. The trailer's mine . . . breaking right."*

McGiven looked right and saw his wingman rocket away in a hard turn, gaining altitude. The exhaust nozzle glowed orange as the jet kicked into afterburner, accelerating.

Returning to the radar screen, McGiven watched the APG-68 lock up on the nearest target. The targeting data appeared on the bottom of the screen: range eighteen miles, altitude 24,000 feet, closing at 835 knots.

Lieutenant Roh pushed the nose of his MiG-29M down, picking up a few more knots of airspeed. The IRST showed the American spy plane was now twelve miles out. In thirty seconds his missiles would be in effective range. It would be impossible for the lumbering four-engine monster to escape.

*BUZZZZZZZ.* A radar warning lock tone sounded inside the cockpit. Roh's eyes went to the RWR. The lead American jet had locked up on his MiG. It was sixteen miles out and closing fast.

Roh forced himself to stay on course. *Two can play at this game,* he thought. Manipulating the radar missile control button on the stick, he moved the round targeting select cursor over the tracking symbol of the American fighter. He tapped the button, locking the cursor over the tracking symbol. Touching a toggle switch, he activated his MiG's radar.

With any luck the American would hesitate, giving him a few seconds before any missiles were launched. A few seconds was all he needed.

*So you think you're Mr. Cool,* McGiven thought, watching the symbology on the HUD change rapidly. He was climbing through 20,000 feet and gaining airspeed at the same time. What surprised him was that the target hadn't changed course. The MiG driver either didn't have his radar warning receiver turned on or the jerk didn't think McGiven had the balls to fire.

The colonel leveled his Viper at 22,000 feet, keeping the square targeting cursor in the center of the HUD. The letters IN RNG flashed under the HUD's altitude indicator. The four AMRAAMs were "in range" and the targeting data had been dumped into their guidance computers.

*"Fox one,"* his wingman radioed.

McGiven didn't look away. Staying focused on the HUD he rested his right thumb on the weapons-release button and began to add pressure.

"Threat . . . Radar . . . Threat . . . Radar," a soft female voice sounded. At the same time his threat panel lit up, signaling a hostile radar had locked onto his jet.

Without thinking McGiven forced the side stick back and throttled forward just short of afterburner. His Viper responded instantly, shooting straight up. The thrust of 6.5 Gs came across his body. The nylon G-suit inflated to keep the blood from being pulled from McGiven's head. Climbing through 25,000 feet, he leveled off and banked to the east. As the Gs faded the Viper's Loral ALQ-178 electronic countermeasures kicked in, alternately spitting out chaff and flares to the right and left of his jet. His eyes went to the radarscope. The target was now ten miles out and the radar warning was no longer sounding.

Flying just above a small bank of clouds, Roh spotted a faint white speck. It was the American RC-135. The jet was turning to the southeast and descending. Watching the HUD he saw the fire-when-ready symbol flash onto the screen. The round tracking cursor was centered over the target. He estimated the big jet was eight, maybe nine miles out.

"One . . . two." Lieutenant Roh counted to himself as he hit the fire button on the stick twice. Two R-73M2s rocketed off their rails located under each wing. They seemed to hesitate for a split second before each solid-rocket motor kicked in, sending them toward the American RC-135.

Roh watched them briefly before pulling his MiG up and away from the smoke trails. The IR-seeking missiles were now tracking on their own. The liquid nitrogen and fluoride-cooled seeker heads had already locked onto the distant heat radiating from the four engines of the spy plane.

Looking back at the IR screen, he noticed the second target to the south-west. It was still coming towards him.

"Now it's your turn," Roh said confidently.

"Threat . . . Threat," McGiven shouted. "RC-135 to the northeast. Break right. You have two missiles tracking you."

The colonel rolled his Viper to the east once again, this time dropping the nose and leveling out. He watched the radar screen. Scanning in a 120-degree arc horizontally and 1.5 degrees vertically, it only took the APG-68 X-band pulse-Doppler radar a few seconds to lock up on the MiG. He punched the weapons-release button twice, sending two AMRAAMs on their way.

"Fox one . . . Fox one," he radioed. "Slammers away." McGiven watched the smoky trails of his missiles as they accelerated away from his Viper.

*"Threat . . . threat. I'm hit!"* McGiven's wingman shouted over the radio. McGiven's helmet suddenly filled with hissing static.

A surge of adrenalin shot through the colonel's body. Banking his F-16C back to the north, he saw a bright flash in the sky about five miles out.

"Eject!" McGiven shouted. "Eject!"

The flash was followed by a larger explosion. A trail of black smoke and debris caused McGiven's stomach to drop. His wingman had been mortally hit. Looking to the northwest he saw a dark fast-moving object streak past his wingman a half-mile away. He couldn't tell for sure but the jet appeared to have twin tails. He was either dealing with a MiG-29 or an Su-27.

"You're butt's mine, asshole." McGiven grunted as he put his jet into a hard 8-G turn. Coming around, he jammed the throttle into afterburner, turning in behind the MiG. Dropping the nose of his jet, McGiven stayed in the MiG's six o'clock, behind and below him.

Lieutenant Roh let his MiG float up to 22,000 feet and swung the nose to the southwest. In the distance he could see the twisted smoke trails of two missiles cutting across the sky. He estimated they were five miles out and closing on him faster than anything he had ever seen. His next move had to be timed perfectly.

Gripping the center stick with all his strength, Roh straightened his back, placing his head squarely on the ejection seat. Dropping the nose, he let his airspeed build to 426 knots. He would need the speed to make his turns.

*BUZZZZZZ.* The radar-threat warning sounded again. This time, how-ever, the signal was weaker. It was the missiles locking up on his jet.

The white smoky trails grew nearer. Roh tightened every muscle in his body.

*  *  *

Sucking in a breath of cool oxygen, McGiven let the Gs fall off. He came wings level and checked the HUD. Shutting his radar off, the colonel saw he was now heading to the west at 430 knots about a half-mile below a dark gray MiG-29. A thin trail of black smoke flowed from the two engines, making the MiG very easy to track. Breaking through 450 knots, he closed the distance. He switched the weapons-select button on the throttle from AMRAAMs to heat-seeking AIM-9M Sidewinders. The HUD weapons cue changed from AMA to AAM.

"Don't you know . . . smoking engines are bad for your health," McGiven said as he slipped in behind the enemy fighter. Staying under the MiG, he doubted the pilot knew he was there. The MiG went into a banking right turn, heading back to the west.

"Come on, talk to me. Talk to me," McGiven coaxed the AIM-9s. He listened to the rattling sound in his helmet as the heat seekers struggled to lock up. He maneuvered the jet so the midpoint of his HUD was centered on the two black engine nozzles. He let the Viper drift up a little closer as the rattle turned to a chirping then to an even, solid tone.

*Now you'll really be smokin', asshole.* McGiven hit the weapons-release button once. "Benji Lead . . . Fox two."

"Break," Roh grunted. With all his strength he pulled back on the stick, shooting his MiG-29M up and to the right. Using fifteen kilograms of force he overrode the G limiter, putting the fighter into a 9.5-G vertical climbing turn.

As the jet pushed up and over four bundles of chaff exploded from behind, causing the first missile's guidance computer to lose its radar lock. The software instantly instructed the seeker head to lock onto the strongest radar in the missile's narrow thirty-two-degree field of vision. The lead AMRAAM snaked back and forth before it veered off course and headed for the ground. The second AMRAAM stayed locked onto the jet. It turned, pulling 12 Gs as it closed the distance.

Roh topped out of the climb upside down, heading back to the east. As the Gs fell off he stole a glance over his shoulder. He could see he only had a fraction of a second to react.

Hitting the chaff button again Roh pointed the jet's nose straight down. He let his airspeed build for just a few seconds before thrusting the nose up again. The HUD read 278 knots, altitude 24,560 feet. He had just enough airspeed for one more frantic maneuver.

Roh wasn't prepared for the stabbing penetration of 8 Gs ripping into his body. He felt his neck pop and crack as the G-forces pinned his arms and upper body in place.

The AIM-9M didn't vary its course one degree as it tracked toward the heat source. The warhead automatically armed 750 feet in front of the Viper. Colonel McGiven glanced away as the missile slammed into the left engine nozzle of the MiG. A bright flash lit up his cockpit.

The second AMRAAM hit the chaff cloud a hundred yards behind Roh's fighter. The radar-sensing fuse detected a solid target and instructed the computer to activate the warhead. The missile exploded, sending shrapnel through the air. A few pieces of hot metal impacted the rear section of Roh's MiG-29M without causing any real damage.

Roh dropped the nose again, suddenly aware of two negative Gs. At the same time he looked to the southwest. A burning flame caught his attention.

"What . . ." He stopped short, realizing his wingman had just been hit by an American missile. He could see an F-16C flying behind the exploding MiG in a perfect six-o'clock position.

Forcing the throttles into afterburner, Roh banked to the south descending through 23,000 feet. Keeping the American in the center of his HUD he rested his finger on the weapons button.

McGiven looked back at the MiG in time to see the left tail fin and horizontal stabilizer separate from the fighter in a ball of churning red fire and black smoke. A heartbeat later the rear section of the Fulcrum exploded, showering the sky with flying pieces of hot metal.

"Benji Leader . . . Splash one MiG," McGiven radioed. "Splash one MiG."

The MiG pushed over, going into a long spiral turn. The colonel watched the canopy separate and the pilot eject from the stricken fighter upside down.

McGiven pulled the stick back to level his Viper. He noticed his knees were quivering and his flight suit was soaked in sweat. Out of habit he took in a deep breath and looked over his left shoulder in time to see the second MiG darting toward him from the north.

"What's that idiot pilot trying to do?" M. Sgt. Matthew P. Fletcher groaned, clutching the sides of his chair as the RC-135 lurched downward. "This airplane's not designed to take this."

"He's trying to save our lives," one of the other technicians shouted back from the front section of the jet.

Looking back at the radar data on his screen, Fletcher watched their altitude continue to drop rapidly. He nervously called it out. "Five thousand feet . . . forty-five hundred."

The RC-135 began to bank to the right. The jet vibrated, propelling a dozen unsecured operators out onto the floor. Open notebooks spilled loose pages throughout the cabin. Matt closed his eyes. *Our Father who art in Heaven* . . .

The lead R-73M2 snaked over, accelerating into a fast dive pushing past Mach 3. The supercooled liquid nitrogen and fluoride seeker head had locked onto the right outboard engine. Only seconds away from impact, the missile's front canards moved in unison, guiding the projectile to within fifty feet of the American spy jet.

The first missile exploded in a bright sphere of flame. The second missile, only a half-mile away, banked to the left. The flash of white hot heat from the exploding missile confused its sensors, causing it to veer right. The missile flashed past the RC-135 failing to explode.

A sudden loud bang made Fletcher's heart skip a beat. The lights inside the RC-135 flashed on and off several times and the jet began to roll and push over toward the water. The console to the left of him shorted, filling the cabin with the smell of burnt plastic.

Pinned in his seat, Fletcher clenched his teeth as the four-engine spy plane was in a steep forty-five-degree dive. They were heading for the water at 580 knots, forty knots faster than Boeing authorized in their flight manual. Fletcher listened to the fuselage snap and pop with the added strain of flying right at the speed of sound. He opened his eyes wide and glanced reluctantly at his screen.

"Thirty-five hundred feet . . . three . . . thousand. Pull up, man, pull up."

Almost on cue he felt the jet come level. Another surge of vibrations raced through the jet as she strained to bring her hefty nose up. As the pilot throttled back Fletcher felt several Gs push at his body. He didn't take his eyes off the radar screen.

"Call it, Fletch," the senior officer called out.

"Fifteen hundred. One thousand . . . it's going to be close." Fletcher sensed the Gs beginning to fall off as the jet was beginning to level. "Five hundred . . . brace yourself . . . three hundred . . . two hundred. Come on, baby, level out. One hundred."

Watching the radar data flicker at ten feet above the water, the master sergeant swallowed hard. The RC-135 was screaming just over the water at 530 knots with its number-four engine trailing black smoke and fuel streaming out from several dozen punctures in her right wing.

"This is the flight deck. Secure the cabin for emergency landing," the pilot radioed as some of the crew were picking themselves off the floor and into their seats.

"Secure my pants for an emergency pair of underwear," Fletcher said, sweating.


## LANGAU ISLAND

First Sergeant Hyun backtracked along the same trail where he had lead the prisoners. As he walked toward the coast Colonel Kaine's words burned in his mind. He had captured two prisoners, and for what? To be shouted at like a new recruit. Kaine's actions and his temper were demoralizing not only to Hyun but to the other men as well. The sergeant tried to shake the feeling. He was a *spetsnaz*-trained soldier. He had orders and he would follow them.

Cresting the top of the bluff, Hyun stopped. It would be senseless to check the cave a second time. If there were other Americans out there they wouldn't be stupid enough to be hiding in it again. *However,* he thought, *there may be other caves near the ocean.* He tried to place himself in the position of having to hide on the island. *Where would I hide if I knew troops were searching the area . . .*

Hyun scanned the rocks on the edge of the shoreline. Some of the boulders were very large and could easily shelter a man . . . or woman. He could hear the waves crashing into the side of the coast. *It would be there,* he thought. *There has to be another cave somewhere along this coast.*

Checking the action of his AK-47, Hyun saw that it was loaded. He stepped down into the ravine and made his way toward the coast.

*"Benji Leader . . .* Observation Island. *Tracking a hostile to the northwest of your position. Closing fast."*

McGiven didn't respond to the call. He kept his eyes fixed on the enemy MiG and saw two glimmers of light come from each side of the enemy fighter. The MiG had just launched at him.

"Damn it." Inching the throttle back, the colonel made sure he wasn't in afterburner. One sweep of the HUD told him he was flying level at 19,800 feet. The RWR was quiet, confirming no hostile radars were locked onto his Viper. McGiven reasoned the MiG pilot was attempting to kill him with heat seekers and that meant only one thing. He needed to turn and turn hard.

Looking back in the direction of the MiG, he saw the silver smoke trails winding toward him. He estimated the missiles were two miles out. Keeping the Viper out of afterburner, McGiven banked right and pulled the stick back slowly. The fighter responded gracefully. He waited, watching the missiles fly in closer.

"One thousand one . . . one thousand two. Now." He grunted and heaved back on the side stick control. In the same motion he pushed the stick down, allowing his fighter to use gravity to maintain its airspeed.

He watched the G-meter on the HUD shoot up to 7.5 . . . 8 . . . 8.5 . . . 9. Grunting, he kept his leg and stomach muscles tightened. McGiven tapped the IR decoy button, sending a dozen hot magnesium flares out behind his jet.

As the Viper came around to the right the first missile flew past. McGiven caught sight of the MiG trying to break away from him. The Korean pilot had made the wrong choice—he too banked right, not counting on how fast and tightly a Viper driver could turn.

Keeping steady pressure on the stick, McGiven continued to slice through the sky in a diving turn, speed 340 knots, altitude 18,400 feet. He heard a loud boom—the second missile exploding fifty feet behind his jet.

*"Over G. Over G,"* the female-sounding computer tone sang out.

McGiven leveled the jet and forced the nose to stay on the MiG.

"You stupid fool," Roh shouted to himself. Snapping his head around, he watched the American fighter slide in behind him. Roh realized his mistake. He had underestimated the quickness of the F-16 in a tight turn and should never have tried to turn away. It would have been better to shoot past the American into a vertical climb.

Roh knew he only had one choice left now. Jamming the twin throttles to the afterburner groove, he pointed the MiG's nose straight up. If he could keep his airspeed up he might loop in behind the American and get a quick missile shot.

*No way, asshole.* McGiven yanked the throttle back, opening the air brake. The Viper slowed to 317 knots in an instant, throwing McGiven against the ejection seat's shoulder restraints.

He watched the HUD. He was climbing slightly at 19,850 feet to the north. If his airspeed dropped below 250 knots, he couldn't turn with the MiG. The 29's double engines and twin tails made it more maneuverable at lower airspeeds.

The colonel watched the dark gray MiG seemingly float above his jet. The enemy fighter was slowly accelerating away. McGiven pushed the jet into afterburner, keeping the center of the HUD on the enemy jet. It was too late. The MiG was already pushing over.

*   *   *

The Korean turned around and checked the airspace between the tails of his jet. He couldn't see the American below him.

"Where are you?" he shouted, applying more pressure on the stick. The MiG-29M pushed over at 24,700 feet. The fighter hung in the air for a split second before its nose arced toward the ground.

McGiven's Viper shot past the MiG-29 just 200 yards away in a vertical climb breaking through 24,500 feet. In an instant the colonel knew what to do. He threw the throttles into neutral and flared the air brakes. His Viper, her nose pointed straight up, decelerated. Watching the HUD, McGiven waited for the airspeed to bleed off . . . 360 . . . 300 . . . 260 . . . 200 knots. It only took a few seconds for his jet's airspeed to fall below 150 knots.

"Come on, baby . . . don't stall on me," McGiven coaxed. Moving the stick to the right, he pushed her nose down. The F-16C's fly-by-wire control system responded by rolling the fighter over in less than a half-second.

The MiG should be right below him. He blinked once and saw the dark outline of the enemy fighter in the upper section of the HUD. His last AIM-9M heat seeker began to chirp. It acquired a heat source.

Lieutenant Roh had both hands on the stick. Using all his strength he pulled back, trying to bring his MiG out of its steep dive. The Fulcrum responded by slamming the young lieutenant deep into his seat.

The sudden G forces were more than he was prepared to withstand. His vision rapidly narrowed and without knowing what was happening Roh blacked out.

"Fox two," McGiven radioed. The remaining AIM-9M Sidewinder raced from his right wingtip. In a blur of fire and smoke the missile impacted the MiG-29 just behind the canopy.

The colonel pulled back on the stick as the enemy fighter came apart in a churning explosion. Coming level at 21,000 feet, he scanned the skies around him. He didn't see any other jets.

"Bingo fuel . . . Bingo fuel," the computer sounded.

McGiven keyed his mike. "Benji Leader . . . splash one MiG. I'm at bingo fuel heading for the tanker." The colonel breathed in, feeling as drained as his fighter, as he banked to the southeast.

## 33

LANGAU ISLAND

Duke watched the thick blanket of fog coming out of the northwest as it skimmed over the ocean to cross the island. Within minutes he could only see fifteen to twenty feet ahead of him. Cocking his head right and left, he listened for the low rumble of helicopter rotors cutting through the air. The choppers should be coming into range but he didn't hear a whisper of sound.

James raised his head to see over the rocks. To his right the sound of grinding gravel caught his attention. The sound was even and paced—footsteps.

Ducking back down, Duke caught sight of a North Korean soldier cresting the rocky ridge. A moment later the man walked into plain view coming directly toward his sheltered position. The man was only fifteen feet away.

Duke forced every muscle in his body to remain still. He guessed the soldier must have traversed the back side of the ravine or followed the shoreline. The rocks along the coast had hidden his approach.

Duke studied his features. The soldier appeared to be about five feet ten, a little shorter than he was, dressed in a dark green North Korean combat uniform. His long wool coat was cinched tightly around a trim waist. Broad shoulders indicated he was probably in good physical condition. The man carried an AK-47 assault rifle with at least two extra magazines clipped to his belt. If he continued in his current direction, the North Korean would pass within a few feet of Duke.

Propping himself up on his elbows and knees, Duke readied himself.

First Sergeant Hyun drew in some air to catch his breath as he came to the top of the ravine. He had skirted the coastline searching for additional hiding places or any other signs of someone else alive on the island. The fog was now an obstacle and his gut told him to return to the aircraft. It was a waste of time wandering around in the fog.

Hyun walked several more steps and stopped. Ten feet in front of him were two long rocks about two feet thick. There were several dried weeds in front of them. He could see where some of the dirt around the rocks had been scuffed and there were several footprints in the sand. Looking closer, he spotted what looked like a black cord or wire of some kind resting on top of the largest rock.

Snapping off the safety of the AK-47, he crept closer to the area. Hyun couldn't believe how skilled he was becoming. If he brought the final prisoner in to Colonel Kaine, there would be no denying him the respect that was due him.

Duke froze. Watching the man's eyes through the crack between the rocks, he knew he had screwed up. He glanced up at the black antenna wire of the radio hanging down from the side of the rock.

He grasped a handful of dirt. The pounding in his chest seemed to beat with the Korean's steps. He was only five feet away.

In one quick movement Duke sprang from his hiding place and hurled the sand at the soldier's face. Hyun, blinded by the dirt, stumbled backward. Duke grabbed the rifle by the barrel and jerked it free of the man's grasp. Taking the palm of his other hand, he shoved it up under the soldier's chin and followed with a punch to the stomach. The soldier fell to his knees. Duke grabbed the rifle in both hands by its barrel and forestock and swung it, striking the man across the temple. Duke watched him fall to the ground with a hard thud. The Korean lay on his side and moaned once in pain before his eyes rolled back in his head and he blacked out.

Duke waited several seconds to make sure the soldier wasn't going to move. He knelt down and searched the soldier's clothing. Going through his pockets James removed a large knife, two matchbooks, a pack of cigarettes, a 9mm pistol and a water bottle. He removed the extra AK-47 magazines and tossed them next to the rocks.

"All right, buddy, let's tie you up," James said, reaching for the man's boots.


## E-3C AWACS

"It's about time," Lieutenant Colonel Reader said, feeling the 707's nose pitch up. The main gear left the runway and the big jet banked to the west, gaining altitude as fast as the lumbering four-engine jet could.

Reader stood up and leaned against his console. "We have a code-blue situation," he announced. "There are a dozen American fighters over the Korean Sea without any command and control. Last reports have them engaging North Korean fighters. Two of our jets may have already been shot down." Reader paused, looking around the darkened cabin. "When we cross the coast I want every one of you at your stations giving me one hundred and ten percent of all you've got to give."

"Yes, sir," several officers responded.

Reader sat down and buckled himself back into his chair. The radar screen showed they were still five minutes from the coast.

KIM IL SONG AIR BASE, NORTH KOREA

"How many MIGs are left?" Chin asked the technician nearest him. His earlier delight vanished as the Americans wiped out seven of his most advanced pilots and jets.

"One, sir. It is returning to base."

Chin fought back the urge to lash out at the radar controller. Only two American jets had been downed in the battle. *The Iranians will pay for this,* Chin thought. *They will replace my MiGs.*

"Where is the American RC-135 now?" Chin was wondering how the Americans knew the two 29s were on course to attack the spy plane. The fighters had turned to engage the MiGs as if they knew they were in the area. How could they know? The AWACS was gone.

"It's heading east . . . toward South Korean airspace." The technician went on, "I'm tracking two targets fifty miles to the south of Sinuiju heading straight for the station. Altitude twelve-hundred feet."

Chin ran his fingers through his oily hair. The Americans were targeting his radar station.

Leaning over, he looked at the radar screen. Near the bottom he saw the symbols for two surface hostile ship symbols. His face went hot with anger. *How could I have been so careless? The Americans are using their surveillance ship to control the fighters.*

"I want four Su-30s and four Su-27s airborne at once. Vector the Su-30s to the American spy ship and the Su-27s at the American fighters. Instruct Colonel Woong it is time for him to kill the American choppers," Chin ordered.

"Victory One . . . Respond, Victory One," the communication technician ordered. "This is Red Crown."

The general chief of staff folded his arms and stared at the ground. Myong Chin knew he should not be feeling defeated. Colonel Kaine had not let Sinchon escape death and the fuel rods were successfully transferred. He was sending eight more of his most advanced pilots and fighters into the air. They might not be as skilled, but they would hopefully wear the Americans down and permit the *Allum Bacar* to leave the area unscathed.

VICTORY ONE, SU-27

"This is Victory One. Copy you, Red Crown," Lieutenant Colonel Woong responded to the radio call.

*"Turn southeast heading one five four degrees. Your orders are to shoot down two American special forces helicopters entering the area. They are flying below two hundred feet . . . approaching the south end of Langau Island."*

"Understood, Red Crown. Victory One turning to engage."

Woong banked his single-seater Su-27 to the southeast and leveled at 8,000 feet heading 154 degrees. Woong had been flying his fighter electronically quiet. When he fired up his powerful radar to target the low-flying American choppers his Su-27 would show up on a hostile radar sensor like a flashlight in a dark room.

Pushing the throttles forward, Woong watched the HUD as the jet broke through 435 knots. He hit the "radar on" switch located next to the throttles, activating the Flanker's RLPK-27 radar. He moved his eyes from the HUD to the radar screen to watch the targets appear.

USS *OBSERVATION ISLAND*

"Confirmed, sir. The RC-135 was hit by one missile. She's lost one engine and is leaking fuel," Petty Officer Owens reported. "The pilot radios she's limping but will make it back to base. They're not reporting any casualties."

"Good." Captain Bliss stood beside her. "When's that new AWACS going to get airborne?"

"It's on the way. Should be in position in ten or fifteen minutes."

Bliss continued to look at the radarscope. He could see two enemy targets on the screen. One was twenty miles west of Langau Island, heading east. The other was heading toward the North Korean coast and was almost out of the area. The top of the screen still showed a powerful enemy ground control radar sweeping from the north.

Bliss' attention went to the blue triangles representing the American fighters. The three F-15Es of Tacoma package were orbiting to the east of Langau at 28,000 feet along with a KC-10 Extender tanker. It appeared on the screen that one of the Strike Eagles was taking on fuel. The four Strike Eagles of Intrepid flight had split up. Two F-15Es had taken up position to the northeast, altitude 24,000 feet, while Intrepid Lead and his wingman,

Intrepid One Four, were flying to the northeast toward the radar station at Sinuiju. The two remaining F16Cs of Benji package were flying in a tight orbit to the southeast.

"Sir, I'm tracking eight new targets. Speed 540 knots . . . altitude 5,000 feet. Heading two four niner. They just cleared the coast," Owens reported.

Bliss checked the mission clock. "Keep an eye on them. Right now I'm more interested in where those choppers are located."

"They're still below two hundred feet. I'm not tracking them. And if they're squawking an IFF signal I'm not picking it up."

"They've got to be near the island by now," Bliss thought out loud.

His eyes stayed on the hostile-aircraft symbol flashing near the south end of Langau. A single North Korean fighter had managed to sneak through the US fighter patrols.

Bliss looked back at the right side of the screen. Eight more hostile aircraft targets were coming his way, 112 miles out. His escort, the USS *Paul Hamilton,* was six miles to the south and closing on their position. If those aircraft had any intention of firing on *Observation Island* the *Paul Hamilton* would be there to defend her with guided missiles.

This time Bliss slipped on a headset. Changing radio frequencies, he spoke into the mike.

*"Paul Hamilton,* this is *Observation Island.* Do you read me Marshall?"

*"Copy you, Island. This is Marshall."* Aldridge Marshall was the commander of the *Hamilton.*

"What do you make of this?"

*"Looks like they didn't learn their lesson the first time. Don't worry, Fred. They won't get within twenty miles of your floating computer."*

"Alright," Bliss replied, feeling reassured. "Keep me informed of anything on your end. *Island* out."

Bliss turned to Petty Officer Owens. "Contact Tacoma Lead. Vector him to intercept that single approaching Langau. And vector four F-15Es to intercept the new targets to the east."

"Tacoma Lead . . . USS *Observation Island.* Turn left heading two three four," Owens radioed with confidence. "We're tracking a hostile to the south of Langau Island."


TACOMA LEAD, F-15E


The Strike Eagle slipped through Mach 1 without Major Green's noticing. The WSO was heads-down seated behind the pilot as the fighter turned to the southwest heading 217 degrees.

"What's happening back there, Greeno?" Colonel Conrad called out from the pilot's seat.

Green didn't answer. He continued to concentrate on the four multifunction displays located across the top of his cockpit. The back seat of the F-15E was set up so Green could manipulate his sensors even while in a high G-combat maneuver.

On each side of the consoles he used two hand controls designed to select the menus on the MFD. The hand controls also permitted him to manipulate the APG-70 radar, allowing him to lock up air-to-air missiles and locate ground targets for air-to-ground operations. Along the sides of the consoles were switches controlling the LANTIRN system, radios, chaff, flares, ECM and emergency canopy release. Each MFD was surrounded by twenty-four buttons to change or call up various data. Right now he was most concerned about finding the American choppers before the North Koreans did.

"Hey, Greeno . . . you alive back there?" Conrad shouted.

"Yeah," Green answered. Using his thumb he manipulated the castle switch on the left-hand controller to change the far left MFD. He was now watching the same information as the pilot.

"Turn left heading two zero five," Green instructed.

"You got it." Conrad rolled the fighter to the left. The jet was five degrees nose down breaking through 19,000 feet and gaining airspeed.

Green waited for Conrad to level the jet. Checking his instruments he couldn't understand why his radar wasn't tracking any targets. With a range of over 110 miles, if there was anything in the air they should see it.

"Ten degrees to the left."

The Strike Eagle responded, picking up additional airspeed as Conrad pushed her nose down.

"Shit, there they are!" Green shouted. "Three targets left bearing two five three degrees."

"I have them," Conrad confirmed somberly.

Green felt the jet bank slightly to the south and push nose down again. The F-15E continued to accelerate through Mach 1.5.

Colonel Woong trimmed the Su-27 for level flight at 6,500 feet above the water. Below him the clouds reflected the low afternoon sun. Occasionally he would streak past a break in the thick haze. He could see the steel-blue ocean speckled with white rolling caps.

Throttling back, he reduced the Flanker's airspeed to 350 knots. He concentrated on a solid orange line moving across the screen in rapid succession. The radar antenna was scanning the sky in front of him. Woong verified the radar was sweeping the sky in SRC/LCK mode so it would automatically lock up on the closest target.

*BUZZZZZZZ.* The Su-27's radar warning receiver (RWR) sounded. An enemy radar was now sweeping his fighter. Turning the volume level down Woong swept his eyes across the instrument panel. The hostile radar hadn't locked up on his fighter.

Banking the jet to the northeast, he kept watching the radar screen. The colonel dropped the nose and floated down gracefully into a bank of clouds.

"Give me an ID," Conrad commanded. "IFF is squawking negative. Are we looking at bad guys or good guys?"

"It's a fader, man. I can't lock up," Green said, referring to a target that appeared on the screen for a short period before being lost. "Switching radar to supersearch."

"Find them, Greeno. I don't want those choppers going down on my shift."

"Give me some airspeed. Turn left five degrees." Green's head remained bent as he stared at the radar screen. "Whatever we were looking at must be flying in the soup. I can't get a lock."

Woong placed his thumb on the weapons-select button, calling up a single R-27AE air-to-air missile. Two targets had just appeared on the top section of his scope. He pressed the RNG-TGT (Range-to-Target) button and the in-flight computer flashed RNG-TGT: 16 MILES across the bottom of the HUD.

The warning tone faded from his helmet. Looking at the warning receiver, he could see the hostile radar was no longer sweeping his jet. He touched the RNG-TGT button again. The lead target was now fourteen miles out.

Woong moved the target cursor over the closest radar return to lock it up. An orange steering circle appeared on the right side of the HUD, instructing him which way to turn the jet. It flickered on and off. The radar wasn't locking up.

Adjusting the J-band frequency from the low to high side of the band width, Woong attempted to fine-tune the radar return. Experience told him the Su-27's radar had problems locating low-flying targets over solid ground. The ground caused the radar waves to scatter and disperse the signal, making it difficult for the computer to distinguish any target below 500 feet. By adjusting the radar to the high side of the J-band frequency the flight computer software was able to filter out most of the clutter. The American choppers were no doubt over the southern section of the island.

Swinging the jet around, he placed the targeting cursor in the center of the HUD. When the target came within ten miles he would fire.

\* \* \*

Duke grabbed the unconscious North Korean soldier around his outstretched arms and began to drag him to a cluster of rocks near the base of the bluff. The man's limp body was heavy and Duke stumbled awkwardly walking backwards.

Duke had only dragged him a few feet when he stopped. The distinct churning of rotor blades piercing the thick air sent a surge of excitement down his spine.

*It's about time,* James thought, letting the man's body fall to the ground. He didn't bother to try to see through the fog; he knew they were flying in from the south. The echo was bouncing off the ground and low cloud ceiling, causing a reverberation from the rotors chopping slowly through dense air. Turning his head toward the sound he guessed there were two Pave Hawks only a mile or two away, moving sluggishly. James reasoned the pilots were having trouble finding the LZ.

RNG-TGT: 10 MILES blinked across the Su-27's HUD. Woong didn't hesitate. With a press of the fire button he unleashed a single R-27AE missile and nosed the Su-27 up several degrees, allowing the missile to clear his fighter.

The short-burn radar-guided missile, equipped with a semiactive radar terminal homing device, disappeared into the clouds heading for the first target.

Woong's attention went to the radar screen again. He repeated the process, locking up the second target. A quarter of a minute later the second missile was on its way toward the trailing chopper.

The number three multifunction display showed the F-15E's radar searching the sky. Conrad and Green were now thirty-seven miles east of Langau traveling at 980 knots, altitude 15,790 feet and descending. Green watched three radar hits appear on the display. A second later IFF symbols appeared under the two targets near the center of the screen. The numbers notified the wizzo they were American choppers. His radar automatically locked up on the hostile target to the west of the choppers.

"There you are," Major Green said from the back seat. "Lock up right three degrees. Range . . . thirty-five miles, heading one zero niner. Oh, shit . . . I show a missile launch."

"At us?" Conrad shouted, easing back on the stick. Sweeping the sky out in front of him the colonel didn't see any bright flashes revealing the launch of a missile.

"Missiles bearing zero nine eight. They're heading for the choppers," Green called.

"Threat Apex . . . Threat Apex!" Green shouted over his radio, indicating a radar-guided missile launch. "US choppers bearing one zero niner. Missiles at your six."

"Shit!" Conrad watched the two missiles on their straight path.

Within a second they merged, one after the other, with the IFF codes on the screen.

Duke listened as the echoes drew nearer. *They have to be close to landing,* he thought. He would have to make contact with the Rangers before they assaulted the transports. The rescue team would need to know which aircraft Erwin and Sinchon were being held in. The picture of some gung-ho trigger-happy Ranger shooting at him entered his mind as he thought about rushing out to meet the choppers. Duke glanced back at the unconscious North Korean soldier, still sprawled out on the ground.

As Duke turned back to face the sound of the approaching choppers sudden loud explosions erupted consecutively. Duke flinched at the sounds, placing his hands over his head. Peering out from the side he saw a yellowish fireball light up the clouds. A wave of compression rolled over the island, pushing him off balance from his squatting position. He heard the high-pitched shrill of metal cutting through the air.

*"Oh, God, no,"* Duke cried under his breath. He knew at once what had happened. *Where's the second chopper?* Looking back at the clouds he could hear the thump, thump, thump of another helicopter heading towards him. This one appeared to be farther away. The tone of its rotors was changing pitch. The pilot was trying to maneuver.

Duke rose and moved toward the sound. The vibration of another explosion froze him in his steps. A second blast flashed through the sky, followed by the sound of wreckage striking the ground.

Duke didn't move as everything went quiet. His mind was spinning. He wondered how many American soldiers had just died trying to get him off some fucking rock in the middle of the Yellow Sea. James turned around and looked at the North Korean soldier. He could feel the rage building inside of him.

He pointed the AK at the man's chest. The low rumble of turbofans roared over the island. The low pitch wasn't a Western design. Duke had heard the sound before. It was a high performance Soviet-designed fighter.

James lowered the rifle. If he was going to get off this hellhole he would have to do it himself.

"I don't believe this shit," Colonel Conrad moaned in protest, slamming his fist against the side of the cockpit. The two radar symbols representing the choppers had faded from his screen in rapid succession.

"Range . . . twenty-two miles," Major Green instructed. "Target is dropping below 1,000 feet. The bastard's descending."

"I see him," Conrad said, taking control of the radar. "You watch our six." He snapped the castle switch on the throttle, changing his radar screen to an 8.5 mile aspect. The left MFD flashed showing the target to the southwest of his position.

Using the quarter-sized target-acquisition button on the throttle Conrad worked the twin radar-lock cursors over the round electronic return. Pushing the button, he locked the radar onto the target. The bandit continued to descend, 500 . . . 300 . . . 250 feet.

"We're going to lose him in the clutter," Green warned. "Range eighteen miles."

Conrad concentrated on the HUD. He centered it, waiting for IN RNG to appear. His finger rested on the weapons-release button, ready to fire one of his last two AMRAAMs. "Come on, baby, give me this one."

"Aw shit . . . he's gone!" Green shouted.

Woong leveled his fighter at seventy-three feet above the water, flying just under the cloud ceiling heading due east at zero nine zero degrees, airspeed steady at 410 knots. The Su-27's radar warning receiver continued to chirp, telling him a hostile air-to-air radar was sweeping from the northeast.

Checking his weapons mix, Colonel Woong saw he had fired a total of four long-range radar-guided missiles. His jet now carried a mix of two short-range R-60T and four medium-range all-aspect infrared homing fire-and-forget R-27TEs. If he was to engage any more American fighters he would have to close within seven or eight miles.

Focusing on the HUD Woong cued his radar up at a forty-five degree angle while banking to the left. He was careful not to break 100 feet. The radar warning receiver showed the enemy radar searching the sky to the northeast.

Leveling the F-15E at 5,000 feet, Conrad pulled back on the throttles and reduced the jet's speed to Mach 0.98. Flaring the air brake, he let the fighter slow to 420 knots before cleaning her up and pushing her nose down once again. The Strike Eagle was now in the clouds heading west, dashing straight toward the enemy fighter with only the radar to guide them.

"Range twelve miles. Altitude . . . eighty feet. Closing at 780 knots," Conrad called out.

"Don't fire, man. That slammer will never find the target. He's too low for a head-on pass. We need to get around behind him, shoot the bastard from behind."

"Bullshit. One pass and his ass is mine," Conrad said, channeling all his energy on getting the bandit. IN RNG flashed on the HUD. The square box on the heads-up display showed the target was to the right and steady.

Looking at the radar data one last time, Conrad saw it showed a single enemy fighter only eight miles out. He tapped the weapons-release button, sending one of his two remaining AMRAAMs toward the target.

The data on the right side of Colonel Reader's display showed the E-3C AWACS was breaking through 20,000 feet heading southwest. In another two or three minutes the command-and-control aircraft would be high and far enough out for him to get a clear picture of what was happening over the Yellow Sea. Right now the only things the colonel could track were a few commercial aircraft making their way into Seoul, South Korea.

Reader sat on the edge of his seat wondering what kind of a mess he would find once the E-3C reached altitude. He had commanded many training exercises that ended up in confusion *with* a trained AWACS crew monitoring the situation. He could only guess what was happening out there without that kind of assistance.

"Damn it!" Reader shifted positions impatiently. "Tell those pilots in the front office to climb faster. I want altitude. Do you hear me? Altitude!"

Colonel Woong barely touched the center control stick. He permitted the Su-27 to float down to fifty feet above the water before bringing the nose up a half degree. Every ounce of concentration he could muster was on the HUD.

He kept the steering symbol and waterline right on the horizon, not letting it bank in either direction. Traveling at 420 knots he knew that one slip up, or the slightest feel of a negative G, and he would be dead.

"It's starting to go pit bull," Major Green said, referring to the AMRAAM.

"Shut up, Greeno." Conrad watched the missile's flight data. The AMRAAM was three miles out and starting to snake back and forth. The missile's internal radar had failed to find and lock onto the target below it. It was now in an automatic search-and-kill mode. Conrad and his pilots referred to it as a pit bull in a meat market. The missile would kill the first solid return it contacted.

"Two miles to impact," Green called out. "I'm not showing a lock."

The constant *ping . . . ping . . . ping* of the American pulse-Doppler radar was starting to wear thin. At fifty feet of altitude there was only one way to maneuver and that was up. If Woong's radar picked up a target above him he could pull straight up, using chaff and flares to evade any missiles.

A square radar targeting box appeared on the upper left side of Woong's HUD. A second later he caught sight of a bluish rocket motor twisting out of the clouds.

Woong's instincts took over. Smashing the chaff button in quick succession, five bundles of aluminum foil strips and carbon fibers filled the sky behind his jet. He watched the missile streak in front of his jet, hitting the water a half-mile away.

Woong pulled back on the stick to gain altitude. The American fighter was above him, only four miles away.

"The sonofabitch didn't even flinch!" Conrad shouted as his missile disappeared from his radar screen. The colonel rolled the big fighter up on its side as they merged with the Su-27 below him. "Where is he, Greeno?"

"Radar threat . . . Radar threat," the computer sang out.

"I don't know. He must be under us," Green shouted. "I hear his radar."

Conrad's eyes went to the threat panel. A yellow caution light confirmed a hostile radar was sweeping his jet. The radar warning receiver was pointed straight down, showing the threat from below.

"Hold on, Greeno." Conrad snapped the Strike Eagle into a tight turn. Watching the G-meter he kept a steady 7 Gs of pressure on the stick. Flying the jet in a half circle, he waited for the target to come back up on the radarscope.

Breaking through 3,000 feet, Woong kept forward pressure on the throttles as he tried to force a few extra knots of airspeed out of the engines. The Su-27's nose was pointed almost straight up as the jet continued to accelerate, 360 . . . 365 . . . 370 knots.

Woong wanted to get above the clouds. If his luck held he could acquire the American visually as he broke through the haze. Then it would just be a matter of getting close enough for a missile shot.

At 5,200 feet Woong broke through the clouds. Leveling off upside down, he let 4 Gs press him into his hard vinyl seat. Coming wings level he pointed his radar antenna forty-five degrees down and began sweeping the clouds below him.

"Where are you?" he shouted into the cockpit.

"He's not below us . . . he's not below us," Major Green grunted as the Strike Eagle came out of her turn heading west at 4,300 feet, still in the clouds.

"This guy is really pissing me off," Conrad growled, checking his radarscope. It was clean. Pushing the throttles to military power, he watched the jet pick up airspeed. The HUD showed he was flying five degrees nose high and climbing slightly.

"He didn't just disappear," Green said, then cursed something inaudible.

The Strike Eagle's radar warning receiver suddenly sounded. The bandit was above them.

"There . . . finally," Lt. Col. Warren W. Reader grunted. The AWACS was still climbing at 34,000 feet but he was high and far enough from the coast to get a clear radar picture.

Reader's tactical information display showed seven US fighters flying in different orbits to the north of his position. Below their blue friendly aircraft symbols were IFF codes, along with the call signs for each package. To the east he saw eight hostile aircraft symbols: four climbing to the west at 12,000 in a loose formation, the other four descending at 1,200 feet, heading over the Yellow Sea—toward the *Observation Island* and her escort the *Paul Hamilton.*

Reader put on his headset and tapped the computer keyboard, splitting the tactical information display into two even sections. The screen on the right showed the IFF codes for each aircraft, however that was the only data it displayed. If he was going to direct the fighters in combat he needed to know the mix of weapons, fuel state and general condition of each aircraft.

Keying his mike, Reader reported, "All aircraft . . . all aircraft. This is AWACS on guard. Mickey . . . Follow Dolly. Repeat. Mickey . . . Follow Dolly."

"Hot damn, Greeno, we have our eyes and ears back," Colonel Conrad announced. He knew what the AWACS Hammer needed. *Mickey, Follow Dolly* was an abbreviated way of saying the AWACS crew wanted—hell, needed—each F-15E and F-16C pilot to reconfigure their Have Quick II radios for a flight data update.

Punching a series of buttons on the data entry panel below the HUD, Conrad rebooted his Strike Eagle's Joint Tactical Information Data System (JTIDS). Two seconds later the Have Quick II radio transmitter sent a newly configured electronic data burst to the AWACS, updating the E-3C's computers as to his fighter's fuel state, weapons load, condition of F-15Es avionics, radar contacts, heading, speed and altitude. The system was basically a flying wireless computer network that allowed the AWACS to act as the central computer or, as the pilots liked to call it, big brother.

"Get ready, Greeno. We're about to kick some ass," Conrad said, tugging on his oxygen mask.

\*    \*    \*

Reader watched Tacoma Lead's data appear first on the right side of his screen. Line by line each F-15E and F-16C flight status materialized. It only took a quarter of a minute for Reader to make his first decision.

Looking back at the far left side of his computer monitor, he noticed two aircraft symbols, a friendly and hostile. He keyed his mike.

"Tacoma Lead . . . this is AWACS on guard. Bandit . . . I repeat bandit is to the east. Take heading of one zero two. He's at angels five and steady. Heading towards you."

*"Roger, AWACS. Damn glad to hear from you guys."*

Conrad didn't pause, feeling a renewed confidence from the new added support.

"Hold on, Greeno."

He pushed the throttles forward and pulled the stick back. The Strike Eagle shot nearly straight up, rolling to the east. Conrad pictured the situation in his mind. The bandit was about a thousand feet above him and probably not more than two or three miles away. If he could blast out of the clouds ahead of the enemy fighter, climb to 8,000 or 9,000 feet and loop over the top, Conrad knew he could kill the guy with a missile shot from above.

"Five thousand feet," Major Green called. "Here we go again."

Woong saw the F-15E blast out of the cloud to his right only a half-mile away. The jet's engine nozzles were glowing orange from its afterburners. Before he could react the jet disappeared into the skies above him.

Woong snapped the stick to the right, bringing the nose up. *If I can follow the American and get around behind him it would be a quick kill.* He felt his oxygen mask dig into his face as six quick Gs pinned him back. Woong strained to switch from R-27TE medium-range missiles to the short-range R-60T heat seekers.

As the Su-27 nosed up he heard a beeping sound inside his headset. One of the R-60Ts was trying to lock up.

"I got him! Left seven o'clock," Green shouted.

"I see him . . . I see him." Conrad pushed the jet over and came down on the back side of the loop. His airspeed was a healthy 450 knots and increasing.

Conrad was close enough now that he could see the wide twin tails of the enemy jet. It was larger than a MiG-29, with a giant radome and long canopy. The colonel realized he was fighting a Su-27 Flanker.

"He's trying to climb with us," Green warned from the back seat. "Quit screwing around with this guy and let's blast him."

"Lock him up, Greeno. You got the radar."

"Bring us around . . . I can't get the beam on him."

Conrad didn't back off. Keeping his Strike Eagle in burner, he completed the loop and came level at 5,800 feet. He let the Gs bleed off for a few seconds before jamming the stick back. The jet pitched up, losing some airspeed. The double-beeper G-warning tone went off, notifying Conrad he was pushing the jet to her limit.

The nose of the Strike Eagle continued to pitch up but the fighter wasn't coming around fast enough. Using both hands, Conrad pulled the stick back with all his strength. The G-meter on the HUD jumped to 9.2 . . . 9.3 . . . 9.5 Gs. A ton and a half of force pounded Colonel Conrad's body. He winced as the G forces pushing him back into his seat made it difficult to move.

"Over G . . . Over G," Bitchin' Betty, the computer, warned.

Conrad ignored the warning as he saw the enemy jet coming into view above him.

*"Just a few more seconds,"* he grunted. Moving his thumb a quarter-inch on the throttle, he switched from missiles to guns.

Rolling his head back Woong saw the American fighter coming at him from below in a tight turn. White trails of condensations coiled off its wingtips. Woong felt his stomach lurch up in his throat. He had made a mistake. He should have fired when he had the chance instead of trying to turn with the American fighter.

Woong tapped the chaff and flare buttons, spewing out a steady torrent of decoys. There wasn't any way the American could lock up a missile.

The flash of fire coming from the F-15E's wing root told Woong he had underestimated the American pilot. He reached for the ejection handle.

The HUD-mounted round gun site floated a fraction of an inch away from the Su-27's nose. Conrad's vision narrowed from the strain of the high-G turn. Without taking his eyes off the enemy fighter he squeezed the trigger once, then twice.

His right wing root erupted with two bursts of ninety 20-millimeter cannon rounds. Conrad saw the first few tracing rounds impact the enemy jet behind the canopy. A ball of fire burst up and engulfed the jet.

"Shit hot . . . you got him!" Green hollered.

Conrad took the jet out of afterburner, coming wings level at 6,400 feet. Shaking his head, he sucked in a deep breath trying to get his bearings.

"You alright, Colonel?" Green asked. He was feeling the frustration of having gotten the target too late to save the choppers.

"Yeah . . . yeah." Conrad adjusted his oxygen regulator from FULL to EMERGENCY. He needed an extra boost to clear his head. The HUD showed he was heading to the southwest at 560 knots, banking slightly.

"Tacoma Lead . . . Splash one MiG," the colonel radioed, then keyed his mike again. "Make that . . . splash one Flanker."

*"Tacoma Lead . . . AWACS on guard. Copy that."*

"Yeah . . . one Flanker," Green echoed.

Colonel Conrad banked to the northeast, keeping the jet out of after-burner. He rubbed his free hand up and down his legs a couple of times as he tried to stop the trembling.


Duke rolled the North Korean's limp body over, stripping off his heavy green wool coat. He saw the man was wearing a flack jacket underneath it.

"Expecting trouble," Duke whispered under his breath. He removed the jacket and tossed it a few feet away.

James noticed the Korean's head was swollen and starting to turn black and blue. He pushed his body behind two long rocks, using several handfuls of dried weeds to cover his black hair.

Looking around, Duke removed his own parka and covered the soldier with it. He picked up the flak jacket and put it on, then put on the soldier's wool coat. It smelled of body odor and stale cigarettes. He wondered how long the man had been wearing it.

Duke tucked the two extra thirty-round magazines into his belt. He slipped the knife into a long pocket on the side of the flak jacket.

Grabbing the AK-47, he made his way into the fog toward the two transport jets.

# 34

"General Sinchon, wake up. General . . ." Kaine said, standing over Sinchon with his hands on his hips.

"I am awake," Sinchon said opening his eyes.

"I do not have time to waste. You know I will use whatever means necessary to get the information I need." Kaine spoke quietly but his voice was filled with determination. "Who else survived the attack?"

General Sinchon met the man's gaze but remained silent.

"I know there is another survivor. Where is he?"

"I told you there is no one else," Sinchon answered steadily.

Kaine's large frame puffed out as he pulled a 9mm pistol from its holster. He held the weapon tightly in his hand.

"If I did not need to know about the other traitors involved in your scheme I would kill you now."

"Why do we wait? Take me to Chin." Sinchon glanced over at the major. "You are a fool to think the Americans are not on their way. Leave the woman. You have what you came for . . . I am your prisoner."

Kaine's laugh echoed through the hull. He stopped and smiled at the general.

"You are the fool, old man. Do you think I came just to take you off this island?" The colonel walked closer, his eyes unwavering. "General Chin was correct in his timing to replace you. You have no sense of responsibility for the growth of our military. You sit there and have no idea what is taking place. I will bring greatness to our country once again. Your days are through."

"The only thing you will bring to our country is destruction. You and General Chin with your lust for power and greed . . ."

"Colonel Kaine." A soldier ran up the ramp, excited. "One of the patrols is reporting two midair explosions to the south of us. They heard one, maybe two helicopters approaching just before the blasts."

"And now?" Kaine asked thinking of Chin's reassurance that the Americans would be taken care of. "Do you hear the choppers now?"

"No, sir. Everything is quiet."

Kaine, convinced that Chin had kept his word, turned back around to look at Erwin. "Your rescue attempt has failed. No one will be coming to take you and whoever is still out there off the island."

Erwin's first reaction was to lunge at him and strike him in the face. But she knew that would be stupid. She would have to wait to make her move.

"Where is the Iranian freighter?" Kaine asked, relieved that their plan was still coming together.

"It exited the bay a few minutes ago," the guard replied.

Colonel Kaine checked his watch. Running at high speed, forty knots or more, it would take the *Allum Bacar* at least thirty minutes to sail clear of the island. The captain planned to sail north and slide into the crowded sea lanes running between China and North Korea. When darkness fell he would steer his freighter south into the South China Sea. The captain should be docked at Bandar Abbas before the Americans could retask their ocean surveillance satellites.

Kaine turned back to Sinchon. "My mission is now complete. You should know that as your replacement I will restore power to our country."

"You will fail because you do not see the future clearly," Sinchon said, clearly unimpressed.

Kaine turned his back to the older man and stepped out onto the ramp. "Secure this cabin," he said to one of the guards outside. "Find one of the pilots to ready this aircraft for takeoff."

"My government will never allow this," Erwin shouted then hung her head low, not wanting to look at Sinchon.


## USS OBSERVATION ISLAND

"We have AWACS support again," Chief Petty Officer Owens reported, not smiling. "That's the good news. The bad news is the four hostiles I was tracking just dropped off the radar screen. Last heading was one niner five, range seventy-five miles. Speed 510 knots and heading straight for us."

"Get on the horn. Tell that AWACS we need fighter coverage at once," Captain Bliss ordered.

"AWACS . . . this is *Observation Island*. Do you copy, AWACS?"


## E-3C AWACS

"Copy, *Observation Island*," Reader responded. "I'm tracking four bandits . . . range seventy-three miles northeast of your position heading one niner five. Vectoring Vipers for the intercept."

"*Roger, AWACS.*"

Reader changed frequencies. "Benji three one . . . Benji three two. Bandits bearing one seven six at angels one. Range . . . seventy-three miles. Turn to engage."

*"Roger that, AWACS. Benji Three One in."*

*"Benji Three Two in."*

Reader's screen showed the radar symbols of two F-16Cs banking to the southeast. The E-3C was now at 42,000 feet swinging to the north in a long oblong circle. Watching the screen, Reader zoomed in on the northern section of the scope. The threat-warning panel displayed a powerful E-band to the north. Air force intelligence classified E-Bands as either long-range command and control or medium-range SAM-2 or SAM-5 acquisition radar. Reader was willing to bet the E-band was part of North Korea's command-and-control system.

Tapping his computer keyboard Colonel Reader instructed the computer to identify the nearest long-range radar threat. Across the bottom of the screen a small menu box appeared:

| | |
|---|---|
| FREQUENCY: | E-BAND |
| NATO: | BACK NET |
| TYPE: | AIR SURVEILLANCE/EARLY WARNING |
| LOCATION: | SINUIJU |

A pulsing red dot materialized, indicating its location. Reader scrolled his target identification cursor over the radar site and pushed the lock button. The computer automatically zoomed in on a twenty-five-square-mile area around the site.

"I'll be damned." A smile crossed Reader's face. Two blue triangles, Intrepid Lead and Intrepid One Four, were thirty miles out flying 500 feet off the deck directly at the station.

*I need to find out who tasked these fighters when this is over. This is exactly what I would have done . . . gouged their eyes out.*

## Kim Il Song Air Base, North Korea

"General Chin, I'm showing another American AWACS taking up a position to the south," a sober-faced radar technician reported. "Altitude forty-two thousand feet."

General Chin lit another cigarette. He took several long puffs, not responding to the information. Spent tobacco fell to the floor of the command center. He wasn't surprised. In fact he felt fortunate the Americans had taken so long to get another spy plane into the air. His gaze left the radar screen as he checked his watch. He only needed another twenty minutes. The Iranian freighter and Colonel Kaine would need at least that much time to clear the island.

Chin began to pace again. Without evidence of the fuel rods it would appear to the world that the Americans had used their military power in an attempt to overthrow the sovereign government of North Korea.

"I'm tracking two targets. Thirty-two miles south of Sinuiju station and closing fast. They'll be under our coverage in forty-five seconds."

Chin took a long drag off his cigarette, his eyes narrowing. "Instruct the radar at Sinuiju to keep operating. Their mission is almost complete."

"What about the American fighters?" the radar operator asked, turning his face up to Chin.

"Twenty minutes!" Chin shouted. "I need twenty more minutes. That cargo is more important than a radar station. Order Sinuiju to go defensive but to keep broadcasting."


SINUIJU RADAR STATION

The Soviet-designed Back Net radar reached thirty meters into the late afternoon sky. Located on a high windswept rocky ridge at the edge of the Korean Bay, the long-range search-and-track radar had been operational for the last ten years.

Developed in the midsixties as an early warning and theater defense against American high-altitude bombers, the Back Net had recently been updated to track low-flying cruise missiles as well as high-speed, high-flying reconnaissance aircraft. The radar site was defended by a fleet of six North Korean Najin-class fast frigates, each equipped with a short-range surface-to-air radar, hand-held SA-16 SAMs and newly installed Russian developed SA-N-4 Gecko surface-to-air missiles.

Rotating six times a minute, the radar station's wire-mesh radar antenna transmitted a steady stream of data to both the North Korean Navy and Air Force via fiber-optic and copper cable. A concrete reenforced blockhouse one hundred yards from the base of the antenna served as the maintenance and communications center.

"Understood, command," the lieutenant in charge of the site responded. He reached over and pulled down two large levers activating a pair of powerful electronic broad-band radar jammers placed on each side of the antenna. The lieutenant picked up the radio transmitter.

"All ships, this is Sinuiju station. Command reports inbound hostile targets approaching from the south. This is not a drill. Repeat . . . this is not a drill."

INTREPID FLIGHT, F-15E

Maj. Paul Burns, commanding Intrepid Lead, noticed the threat-warning panel go black. The E-band sweeping from the north was gone. He blinked several times as the threat panel blinked back on. A piercing shrill-pitched whine filled his helmet, indicating a high-powered radar jammer was now sweeping his jet.

"They're jamming us. Too little too late," Burns said out loud. Weighing in at a solid 210 pounds, Burns had been a goalie for a semipro hockey team before joining the Air Force. The major's neck was as thick as his thighs, and it looked like he had used his head to stop hockey pucks instead of his stick or glove.

"Intrepid One Four . . . this is Lead. I'm losing the target."

*"Roger that, Lead. So are we."*

"Hey, Radar. What do you make of this?" Burns asked his wizzo seated behind him. Capt. Brent "Radar" O'Reilly had been flying as wizzo with Burns for the last six months. The two had begun flying together with the 366th Wing's 391st Fighter Squadron base at Mountain Home AFB, Idaho—the "Bold Tigers." Together they had been transferred to the 11th Air Force, 3rd Wing, at Elmendorf AFB, Alaska. The air force didn't feel it was wise to break up a team that worked well. The men were the same age, thirty-two, and became fast friends even though everything about them was like night and day. O'Reilly weighed 130 pounds and looked more like a Sunday School teacher than a fighter pilot. He had a long pointy nose, light curly hair and the only sport he played was chess.

"They know we're out here. We should have dropped to two hundred feet at fifty miles out."

"It's too late now. Range to target?" Burns asked determinedly.

"Eighteen miles. We're close enough to find it."

"Then do it," Burns ordered. "Get ready, I'm taking her up to angels five. One good patch map should do it."

Major Burns hauled back on the stick. The Strike Eagle came up fifteen degrees, shooting through 3,500 feet in half a minute.

"Level her at five thousand," O'Reilly advised. "This won't take long."

The moving map display on the far right multifunction display showed the Strike Eagle 15.5 miles from the North Korean coast. Gripping the back seat hand controllers on each side of the cockpit, Captain O'Reilly switched the radar from air-to-air mode to air-to-ground. The APG-70 had been designed for high-resolution ground mapping, allowing the pilot and wizzo to call up near photolike black and white pictures of ground targets while the Strike Eagle was still well out of enemy missile or antiaircraft artillery range. Inside twenty miles the radar had a resolution of less than seventeen feet. It could zoom in on a $1.5 \times 1.5$-square-mile area with surprising detail.

"Fifteen degrees right," O'Reilly called out, telling the pilot not to fly directly at the target.

"Roger . . . fifteen off center." Burns moved the stick. His eyes went from the pipper, the aiming designator, to the top of the HUD.

O'Reilly focused his attention on his radar display. He had been trained that an off-center shot was preferred in order for the synthetic-aperture radar to work adequately. Using Doppler-shift returns from the ground, the F-15E's targeting computer automatically calculated the relative speed of the fighter in relation to objects reflecting the radar return. Ground targets with a corresponding Doppler-shift are digitally grouped in an arc around the front of the fighter. The computer senses objects directly in front of the fighter. The computer senses objects directly in front of the Strike Eagle, which have a remarkably higher Doppler-shift, than those out to the sides, where the velocity is lower. The APG-70's wide-angle radar beam, transmitting at least ten degrees off boresight, right or left, at 140 degrees per second then intersects the imaginary points on the computer-generated arc. At the same time the radar's imagery computer recognizes which Doppler-shift coincides with the axis of the beam. This allows the system's computer to clarify raw radar returns into a detailed and organized pattern resembling a black and white photo image.

O'Reilly let the radar paint the target area for several seconds, then made sure the image was locked into the computer. He watched the screen as the computer counted down the seconds while it processed the data . . . 4 . . . 3 . . . 2 . . . 1. An image of the target-area appeared.

"Okay, Major, I've got it. Take her back down." Clicking the castle switch on the left hand controller, O'Reilly enlarged the radar image. The F-15E pushed over, heading for the safety of low-level flight.


## USS *PAUL HAMILTON*

"Mark the targets as hostile and assign tracking numbers," Captain Marshall ordered. His deep Southern accent had a Georgia twang.

"Aye, captain." The ship's identification supervisor immediately changed the four airborne target designations from "unknown" to "hostile." The main display screen flashed as the new data suddenly appeared.

"Increase speed to twenty knots and swing us around to zero eight niner," the captain ordered. "I want us pointed at those aircraft." Marshall took a step closer to the ship's displays.

"Aye, captain. Zero eight niner, speed twenty knots."

A tall man with a slight paunch and thick brown hair, Marshall was pushing fifty and could tell you exactly how many days he had until retirement. The navy had been good to him but he was ready for a change. If all went well this would be his last cruise and the last Christmas he would spend at sea away from his family.

Captain Marshall stood in the center of the ship's command and information center. Unlike the CIC on the ship he had been ordered to protect, *Observation Island,* the command center onboard the *Hamilton* was dungeonlike. Buried below deck, built in the shape of a horseshoe, the gray walls reflected the flickering lights of the destroyer's tactical displays. Everything Marshall needed to evaluate what was happening on the surface could be displayed on four tactical-situation screens which filled the three walls in front of him. A half-dozen technicians sat below the screens, constantly updating the ship's computers and filtering out unwanted data.

Marshall felt the 8,300-ton guided-missile destroyer swing around, increasing speed. The dull purr of four gas turbines grew louder. With each knot of increased speed Marshall sensed the anxiety of his crew building.

"Sir . . . I have Captain Bliss on a secure radio link," the senior communications officer announced.

"Put it here." Marshall pointed to the phone next to his command chair. "Marshall here."

*"What do you make of this?"*

"Don't know." Marshall was unconsciously playing with his bushy mustache.

*"Our sensors show a long-range radar at Sinuiju. Our read is they vectored four fighters our way thinking it could be a quick kill."*

"Could be."

*"I can't track anything below a grand. Are you watching them?"*

"Yep. Picked them up as they cleared the coast." Marshall heard the apprehension in Captain Bliss' voice. "By their speed and altitude they look like fighters. But we can't confirm that."

*"Just make sure you keep them off my back. We're slowing to ten knots to align our instruments."*

"Aye, skipper. You play with your video games. We'll do the talking." Marshall hung up the phone and looked at the main tactical-display screen. He appreciated Bliss' concern. After losing one AWACS, two Pave Hawks and two fighters the situation was critical. If Murphy's Law applied anywhere, it applied to the US Navy.

"Forty-five miles out. They're in our missile range," the offensive-weapons officer reported.

Marshall caught the man's anxious glance.

"Maintaining zero eight niner," the helm reported.

"Bring up the fire-control radar. I want them to know we're looking at them," Marshall commanded, his voice even.

"Aye, Captain."

## USS *Nassau*

"Your Harrier's fueled and ready," Lt. Weston B. Baker, the ship's intelligence officer, announced in the darkened briefing room. "The ship's turned into the wind. We'll be in range for a launch in ten minutes."

"I'll be ready." Capt. Connor W. Tobin didn't take his eyes off the Loral CCTT (Close Combat Tactical Trainer) display.

Seated behind a rough mock-up of an AV-8B Harrier II cockpit, he studied five color computer screens, each arranged at eye level and showing a computer enhancement of the Vietnamese hot zone he was about to fly over to extract Tango Team. Driving the system was an advanced VAGA-II computer software program, using a blend of twenty-five-year-old SR-71 and current KH-14 satellite digital images. The software enabled Tobin to fly on an exact simulated route. He could fine-tune his flight plan, then download the route, way points and landmarks onto a 64K data transfer module (DTM), a fancy name for a computer disk. The captain could then use it to program his AV-8B's navigation, weapons and communication computers.

Tobin moved the computer joystick right and left, banking his Harrier into a long green valley. Flying at 200 feet above the ground, the video gamelike graphics put him above the trees as he jinked right and left. The computer displays showed an open area coming into view ahead of him. The marine captain recognized it from several detailed images he had studied beforehand. At the base of several rolling hills was a series of rice paddies grouped together like a checkerboard. He chopped the throttle, slowing the Harrier. The two center screens showed three long fields with a dirt road on each side. Tango Team was hiding in the southeast corner of the largest rice paddy.

Tobin tapped the SAVE button on the computer keyboard next to him. A light blinked on as the data was dumped onto a disk. The twenty-eight-year-old pilot grabbed his helmet and made his way to the flight deck.

## NGHIA BINH PROVINCE, VIETNAM

CWO Michael Callahan tried to clear some of the brown scum off the surface of the water he and Pope had been hiding in for the last seven and a half hours. The water was dark brown and smelled like a toilet. Slowly reaching into the breast pocket of his mesh vest, Callahan removed a water purification straw. The half-inch-diameter straw contained a charcoal purification filter, which allowed him to drink water from just about anywhere for up to three days. He sucked in a couple of long gulps, then reached behind him and handed the straw to Pope.

Hiding in the waist-deep canal water next to the rice paddy had been a good idea. They were out of the sun and well concealed. Whenever a patrol approached all they had to do was duck under the weed overgrowth. Callahan blinked to stay alert. His body was beginning to go numb and the lack of food and water was making it difficult to concentrate. Every few minutes he would use his knife to scrape the leaches off his forearms. He estimated it would be dark in another two or three hours.

*Click . . . click . . . click.* The muted ticking came from the radio. Callahan picked it up, placing the receiver next to his ear.

*"Tango . . . Cheerleader,"* the radio crackled softly.

"Cheerleader . . . Tango. Where the hell's my extract?"

*"ETA for extraction thirty minutes. Harrier will approach out of the south. The pilot will monitor this frequency. Advise you talk him in."*

"Roger that, Cheerleader. The area is still hot."

*"Understood, Tango. Good luck. Cheerleader out."*

"Looks like we have more company," Pope whispered over his shoulder.

Callahan raised his binoculars. Looking over the ditch separating the canal from the main rice field, he saw four Vietnamese Army trucks come to a stop in the center of the road. One of the soldiers was shouting something at the farmer as a dozen or so armed men piled out of the back of each truck.

"The-e-e-ey're ba-a-a-ack . . ." Pope mocked as the search for them developed.

Maj. Paul Burns, flying Intrepid Lead, felt his jet lurch up and down from turbulence as his heavy fighter-bomber streaked over the ocean at 520 knots. A half-mile to the west Burns caught sight of his wingman a little above him.

"Come on, Radar, we don't have all day."

"Range . . . eleven miles. Give me some altitude," O'Reilly instructed.

Strapped on two separate wing pylons each F-15E carried two AGM-130Cs EOGB (Electro-Optically Guided Bomb). The 130C was fast becoming the preferred air-to-ground weapon of the F-15 "Echo" community. The long-range rocket-powered AGM-130C was known as the "jack-of-all-trades," allowing an air crew maximum flexibility when attacking a high-value target. Attached to the nose section of a standard 2,000-pound BLU-

109B penetrator was a DSU-27 E/O solid-state TV seeker combined with an advanced low-heat IR seeker and INS/GPS guidance system. The AGM-130C allowed an aircrew to locate and attack a target at night or in adverse weather with the best possible accuracy. But, the best part of the AGM-130C, in O'Reilly's opinion, was that he could guide the bomb to the target himself, making any last-second corrections if necessary.

O'Reilly used the castle switch on his left hand controller to change the radar-generated map. The number two multifunction display showed a five-mile section of the jagged North Korean coastline. The radar image was clear enough to recognize the silhouettes of two ships on the edge of the screen. In the center O'Reilly could make out a small knob-shaped image. He guessed that was their target.

Clicking the castle switch three more quick times, he waited for the computer to process the data. The screen flashed, showing a half-mile view of the coast. To the right were several square buildings. O'Reilly figured the structures held the radar's electronics. On the left side of the screen he could see the broken outline of the large radar antenna.

"I have it," he called out.

"Breaking through seven thousand," Burns said in response.

O'Reilly used the cursor button on the hand controller to center the targeting crosshairs over the radar site. The data was dumped into the two AGM-130Cs' guidance computers. The smart bombs would now fly toward the target.

"Range nine miles . . . it's locked up," O'Reilly advised.

"Intrepid One Four, we have the target. Transmitting data now," Burns radioed.

*"Copy, Leader."*

"Do it, O'Reilly."

With a flip of a switch the targeting data stored in O'Reilly's computer was transmitted via a UHF AXQ-14 data link to their wingman. Four seconds later the crew of the second F-15E was looking at the same radar picture.

*"Intrepid Lead . . . Intrepid One Four. We've got the data. We'll follow you in."*

"Launch on my mark," Burns ordered.

"Range seven miles," O'Reilly called out.

"Two . . . one . . . mark. Rifle . . . Rifle." Burns smashed the pickle button on his stick. Both AGM-130Cs separated from the wing pods. A split second later their solid-rocket motors boosted the 2,000-pound bombs to climb away from his fighter.

*"Rifle . . . Rifle. Two away."*

"Aw, shit. Spike right two o'clock near," O'Reilly shouted a radar warning. "It's over the fence."

*"Threat radar . . . threat radar,"* the computer sounded as a hostile surface-to-air radar locked up on their jet.

"I show a missile launch," O'Reilly yelled into his face mask.

## USS *Paul Hamilton*

"What's happening?" Captain Marshall moved up behind the Combat Systems Coordinator.

A husky Iowa farm boy, PO Lance McCoy's job was to sort the information and data gathered by the ship's SPY-1D radar and other electronics. He determined the priorities then projected the data onto the main display screen. This allowed Captain Marshall to make quick and accurate decisions by merely checking the screen.

"Still tracking four targets," McCoy said, touching the dark glass screen above his computer keyboard. "Range . . . thirty-one miles, altitude three hundred-fifty feet and speed 510 knots. By their radar cross section I'd say we're looking at four large fighters. Electronic jamming is messing with some of our equipment."

"Are their radars on?" Marshall asked.

"No, sir. Range now thirty miles, speed 512 knots."

"IFF?"

"Nothing, sir."

Marshall leaned intently over the younger petty officer as he studied the screen. His ship was equipped with enough surface-to-air missiles to handle just about any threat the North Koreans could throw at them. He also knew his destroyer's radar system and missile systems had been designed for offensive use first and defensive second. His crew had been trained for the quasi-war scenario but he didn't feel comfortable about it.

"The *Island* is reporting heavy jamming, sir," the communications officer reported from his console.

"Increase speed to twenty-five knots." Marshall pivoted around.

"Aye, skipper."

"Sir. Range twenty-eight miles. Altitude increasing. Breaking through one-thousand feet. Speed 490 knots." McCoy recited the data as if it were routine.

"Where is it, where is it?" Burns shouted, twisting his head right to left.

O'Reilly was looking over his right shoulder. He watched a bright flicker of light emerge from the haze five miles away.

"It's behind us, Major. Four miles out." O'Reilly scrutinized the sky for a few seconds. The SAM was climbing and accelerating as it banked south toward their position.

"Okay . . . I have it. You guide the bombs and I'll keep this sucker off us."

O'Reilly adjusted his shoulder harnesses then grasped both hand controls. The television image being projected back to his cockpit by the AGM-130C was out of focus. The missiles were still five miles out.

"Intrepid Lead . . . break right," Burns radioed his wingman. "Chaff . . . chaff . . . chaff."

The F-15E rolled up on its side. O'Reilly grunted as six sharp Gs slammed him into his seat.

"Go to twenty-five miles overhead," Captain Marshall ordered.

"Aye, sir." McCoy tapped his computer keyboard, changing the main display screen. The four bandits were now at the top of the screen maintaining their heading to the *Observation Island* and *Paul Hamilton*.

"Captain," McCoy's voice cracked nervously. "I'm picking up a civilian IFF code. Squawking on MODE I. It's coming from that lead aircraft."

"What?" Marshall asked.

"I've confirmed it, sir. It's a MODE-I code . . . civilian frequency on a military channel."

"That's bullshit! There's no way in hell those are comairs." Marshall wiped his runny nose. "They must think we're stupid. Range and heading?"

"Range . . . twenty-five . . . heading one niner five. Altitude . . . five-thousand feet. Speed 400 knots. They're on track for the *Island* . . . not us."

Marshall was quiet in deliberation.

"They could be setting up for a missile launch at . . ." McCoy stopped. "Shit . . . they just activated their radars. I'm showing four J-bands."

"Okay. Lock up the lead aircraft," Marshall ordered. "Let's see just how big their gonads are."

Maj. Haeji Cho, flying in the lead Su-30, heard the high-pitched pulsing sound of his jet's radar warning receiver. The electronic device, not much different than a fuzz buster, had detected an enemy radar.

*"Contact right two o'clock,"* came the call from Haeji Cho's wingman.

"Confirmed. Hostile radar," his back seater advised.

Haeji Cho acknowledged the transmission with two clicks of his mike and banked his fighter a few degrees right, dropping the nose. He squinted in order to see the faint image of the American ship on his radar screen. The American spy ship was almost in range.

Haeji Cho adjusted his grip on the stick and throttles. He and his wingman would make the first pass coming in at 5,000 feet at supersonic speed. When they hit fifteen miles out they would each launch a Kh-35RE antiship missile then split and climb away from the target. A half-minute later the other two Su-30s would follow the same flight path and plan.

"This is Lead," Cho radioed. "Two Seven Four, stay on my wing. Seven Five and Seven Six, stay high and follow as briefed."

*"Copy, Leader."*

Major Cho shoved the throttles forward, kicking his big fighter into afterburner. His body snapped back into the seat as he watched the symbology on the HUD change. He waited for his airspeed to increase to 450 knots on his way to Mach 1.

"Stay with it, O'Reilly," Major Burns urged. With steady pressure on the stick he kept the Strike Eagle in a 6-G turn to the west. Continuing to look over his shoulder, he watched the missile arc above his jet and push over, gaining speed.

"Time to impact . . . twenty-five seconds," O'Reilly cried out. The WSO's head and body were pinned against his seat. All he could move were his fingers. Keeping his eyes on the multifunction display O'Reilly watched the image of the radar antenna come into view. He moved the crosshairs to place them at the base of the radar tower.

"Oh, shit . . . this isn't going to work." Burns groaned, nudging the jet's nose down to gain airspeed. The incoming missile was still tracking his jet.

"Just fifteen seconds, hold her steady," O'Reilly pleaded.

"Chaff . . . chaff . . . chaff," Burns said. Looking back at the HUD he saw his airspeed was only at 320 knots. Barely enough for one more turn.

"Ten seconds," O'Reilly called, watching the pulsing crosshairs. The lead AGM-130C was now diving rapidly for the target. The WSO knew he couldn't budge an inch. If he didn't hold the targeting cursor steady the missiles would miss their mark.

"Hold on, O'Reilly. One more turn." Burns pushed the throttles forward and pitched the nose down in 3-G negative dive.

*"Dammit!"* The negative Gs forced O'Reilly's body up in his seat. The harnesses dug into his shoulders as he felt his left gloved hand slip off the hand controller. The pulsing white targeting cursor moved right, away from the base of the enemy radar antenna.

Tightening every muscle in his body, O'Reilly forced his hand back onto the controller. The multifunction screen was displaying the missile's perfect image of the fast approaching target. O'Reilly slewed the cursor back into position over the target. The display screen flashed white just as several blood vessels burst in his nose from the force of the negative Gs.

"We're hit!" Burns shouted as the F-15E rocked back and forth.

O'Reilly glanced up to see a white flash outside his cockpit. His head hit the side of the canopy and he blacked out.

The *Paul Hamilton* had completed a wide turn and was now headed east back toward the fighters. The CIC was filled with the sounds of humming computer fans and the clicking keyboards but was free of any human chatter.

"Range . . . twenty-three miles and closing. Speed 480 knots, altitude 5,200 feet," McCoy called out.

Marshall didn't move. He waited a few seconds before responding. "Arm missiles. Lock missile onto the lead fighter."

The main display screen changed to show the eight square miles around the *Paul Hamilton*. Marshall could see the two-mile-wide gap between his destroyer and the intel ship. The fighters were heading for the gap.

The ship's missile-system supervisor inserted the firing key into the fire-control box on the console in front of him. He turned it, arming the *Hamilton*'s surface-to-air missiles. Eight square red buttons flashed on, telling him the ship's vertically launched Standard-MR SM-s surface-to-air missiles were ready.

Captain Marshall flipped open the cover of the console next to his command chair. He glanced down at the two primary buttons, "FIRE ASAP" and "HOLD FIRE." He fingered the "FIRE ASAP" button but didn't press it.

"Twenty-one miles out and closing."

Marshall's eyes stayed fixed on the main display screen.

## Su-30 Flanker

Maj. Haeji Cho brushed the sweat off his eyebrow and checked his fuel gauges. His tanks were less than half full. He would have to launch his missile and return to base as soon as possible. Sucking in a long cool breath of oxygen, he tried to calm his nerves.

Turning off his radar warning receiver, he kept focused on the HUD. The high-pitched whine and flashing lights were beginning to get under his skin. He was now less than one minute from launch. His attention went to the radar CRT unit below his HUD. He slewed the round cursor and centered it on the midsection of the spy ship. Depressing the castle button on the throttle, he instructed his computer to lock up the radar on the ship.

"Target now in range," Cho's back seat radar operator reported.

"Lock up, lock up," Cho whispered into his oxygen mask. He tapped the button a second time. It took less than five seconds for the Su-30's targeting computer to locate the ship through the electronic clutter coming off the ocean. The blinking square box on the HUD told Haeji Cho the target had been acquired. The targeting box stopped flashing and turned a solid color, indicating a solid fix on the target. The major could see the *Observation Island* in the center of his screen.

## BENJI THREE ONE, F-16C

"Benji Three One . . . Fox one . . . Fox one," Maj. Darryl Schaal radioed.

*"Benji Three Two . . . Fox one . . . Fox one."*

Schaal squeezed the launch button on his stick twice, sending a pair of AIM-120B AMRAAMs, one from under each wing, rocketing toward the targets approaching *Observation Island.* He watched the HUD click off his airspeed and gently eased the stick back as the two missiles left white snaky trails in the sky ahead of him. The jet's nose pitched up five degrees as the missiles disappeared below into the haze.

"Hold fire . . . Hold fire," McCoy yelled out. "New targets . . . friend-lies . . . F-16Cs. They just fired their missiles."

Captain Marshall moved his hand from the fire-control button. He looked up at the main display screen. On the upper edge he saw the electronic signals representing the F-16s. Four yellow lines, representing the AMRAAMs, were streaking toward the enemy jets.

"Hey, O'Reilly . . . you okay back there?" Major Burns asked for the third time.

"No . . ." O'Reilly protested. He blinked and brushed his gloved hand across his face. There was blood running out of his nostrils.

"Are you hit?" Burns's voice was concerned and panicky.

O'Reilly looked around, trying to remember what had happened. The right side of his canopy had several pockmarks from flying missile shrapnel. His instruments showed one engine out. He realized he couldn't breathe through his nose. Looking down he saw the front of his flight suit was bloodstained. Then he remembered the radar site and missile tracking them.

"It's just a bloody nose," O'Reilly said, clearing his throat. "Did we get it?"

"Yeah . . . *you* got it. A perfect shack," Burns replied, relieved to hear his WSO was fine. "And then *we* almost got it. That SAM exploded close enough to make me piss my pants."

"What's our status?" O'Reilly asked, his senses coming back.

"Level at fifteen thousand. One engine out and heading for home plate." Burns then added, "We have company, too."

O'Reilly's head shifted to the right. Their wingman was fifty feet away giving them the thumbs up.

Maj. Haeji Cho moved his finger to the launch button. With the Su-30's radar warning receiver's volume turned low he didn't hear the American air-to-air radar lock up on his jet fifteen miles away.

A smile appeared on his face. His family would receive much praise and glory for his bravery in combat. His commanding officers would promote him. He would be a great leader in the North Korean Air Force. He would get to choose . . .

The American missile pushed over, gaining airspeed before it collided with the Su-30. Slicing through the aluminum skin just behind the cockpit, the warhead exploded, igniting the main fuel tank. The second missile struck his wingman a half-mile away.

Cho felt a loud explosion vibrate throughout the fighter, followed by a bright burning sensation which engulfed his body. He felt the stick go dead. Instinctively he reached for the ejection handle but he was too slow. The aircraft was breaking apart and the cockpit was now consumed with fuel and fire. He began to scream as the jet pushed over and the canopy ripped from the nose section. The sudden rush of air extinguished the fire for a brief moment, bringing Cho back to his senses.

*Eject . . . eject,* he thought, trying to move. Then without warning the fuel ignited again. He watched his hands, arms and legs begin to burn. His oxygen mask melted into his face. He tried to scream again but nothing happened. Cho blacked out a few moments before the Su-30 exploded into a hundred pieces of flaming wreckage.

## USS Observation Island

Each technician sat at their stations in the CIC in a zombielike state. The steady flickering of blue and red lights and radio chatter were the only indications that the *Island* was functioning.

"AWACS is reporting no radar or radio contact with Pave Hawks. They are speculating they've been shot down," Owens stated somberly. Her eyes didn't vary from the screen.

Bliss' jaw hardened. "There were twelve Rangers on each of those chop-pers . . . plus the pilots. Instruct that AWACS not to give up."

"Yes, sir."

"Anything from General James?" Bliss asked, beginning to feel over-whelmed.

"I've been trying to reach him for the last five minutes. There's no response, sir."

"Keep trying."

# 35

A cold, dense fog continued to shroud the island. It was impossible to see more than thirty to forty feet ahead. General James walked north along the edge of the runway toward the two transport aircraft. He casually pointed the barrel of the AK-47 toward the ground but his finger stayed on the trigger of the weapon. Duke hoped he looked like one of the North Korean soldiers coming off his patrol. Men's voices speaking in Korean filtered through the air.

Duke listened to the voices. They sounded hurried but not alarmed. He guessed they were preparing to leave the island. Walking faster, he knew he had to be realistic about his situation. There wasn't any way he could walk up to the AN-72 and overtake all the armed men. He needed some sort of diversion. Then maybe he would have a good chance of freeing Erwin and Sinchon. They'd have to figure out what to do after that as they went along. Duke knew it wasn't a great plan but as he saw it he didn't have any alternative.

James estimated he was about fifty yards from the aircraft. Every now and then he could see the tail section of the transports through a break in the fog.

Taking a deep breath to calm himself, Duke caught a whiff of kerosene. *That's it,* he thought. *The Koreans pumped out all the fuel from the Il-76 transport. If I could set fire to the fuel . . .* he searched the pockets of the wool coat, remembering the book of matches. He pulled one out, smiling to himself.

Walking off the edge of the runway, Duke stopped next to the pool of jet fuel. It was spread out along the side of the runway for as far as he could see. Some of it had been covered with dirt but it was soaked enough to burn if ignited.

Kneeling down, he paused a moment as another thought emerged. *When the North Koreans offloaded the fuel they let it drain on both sides of the runway. What if I could ignite both sides?* Duke knew that would cause even more confusion if each side went up in flames at the same time.

Reaching deeper into the front pocket, he removed a package of cigarettes. If he could figure out a way for a slow burning cigarette to ignite all the matches in the book at one time it would give him a few minutes to get to the other side of the runway.

Duke's heart jumped as his mind raced, thinking how to make a matchbook bomb.

Turning his back on the jet fuel, he struck a match and lit a cigarette. Duke fought back the urge to cough as he sucked on the filter to get the tobacco burning. He placed the lit cigarette between the folds of the match book. When the cigarette burned down the hot ashes would come in contact with the heads of the individual matches. One or more of the matches would hopefully light and start a chain reaction. Then the book would ignite the fuel.

He set the package down next to the jet fuel then picked up his AK-47 and moved to the other side of the runway.

"Unable to regain radio contact with Sinuiju, sir. Should I keep trying?" the communications officer asked.

"No." Chin stood looking at the blank radar screen. He checked his watch. It was past the twenty minutes he had wanted. "Recall the fighters."

"Yes, sir."

Reaching into his pocket Chin pulled out another cigarette. The freighter should have had enough time to clear the bay, but Colonel Kaine was still out there. Chin had done everything he could possibly do to help him. It would be up to Kaine's own skill and luck to make it home safely.

"I'll be in my office," the general chief of staff said, walking off into the back of the room.

The main radar display screen in the CIC showed six North Korean fighters retreating back to North Korean airspace at 15,000 feet.

*"Benji Package . . . this is AWACS on guard. RTB . . . repeat RTB."*

*"AWACS . . . Benji package. Roger that . . . Benji returning to base."*

Owens checked the five F-15Es patroling the skies to the east of Langau Island. Three were flying in a box-shaped flight pattern at 28,000 feet while the other two were flying behind the KC-10 tanker at 22,000 feet heading south.

"Have the AWACS vector one of those F-15s over Langau. Maybe we can get a visual of what's going on," Bliss ordered.

"Aye, captain." Owens keyed her mike. "AWACS . . . *Observation Island.* Requesting visual."

USS *NASSAU*

Capt. Connor W. Tobin, call sign Terminator, watched the canopy of the
AV-8B Harrier II snap shut, locking out the screeching of the engine. He
inserted the navigational computer disk into the NAV computer's hard drive
and downloaded his flight path, way points and INS settings before calling
up the symbology on the HUD. The multifunction display below his HUD
blinked once before a moving computer-generated map appeared, showing
the east coast of Vietnam. In the center of the screen was the *Nassau*
positioned thirty-two miles offshore. It would only take him eight minutes
to cross over the coast, bank north and head for the LZ. If he played his
cards right he would be back on deck in forty minutes and eating a cheese-
burger with the works in forty-five minutes.

Captain Tobin nudged the throttles, steering the jet to the portion of the
flight deck used for takeoff. Tobin had been flying the little jump jet for
three years and had grown fond of the plane.

After graduating with honors from Arizona State he followed in his father's footsteps and joined the Marine Corps. Upon completion of flight
school, Tobin signed up for his lifelong dream of chopper duty but learned
his commanding officers had other plans for him. He was drafted into the
Harrier corps because of his flight-school test scores and athletic ability.
His medium build, lightning-fast reflexes and high IQ made him the perfect
Harrier pilot.

Manipulating the throttle a couple of times, Tobin made sure the fuel-
control unit was operating properly. Backing off to half throttle, he hit a
switch activating the jet's water injection system to give the engine added
thrust. One look at the instrument panel confirmed the AV-8B was ready to
go.

"Strike . . . Mongoose. Ready to go."

*"Roger, Mongoose. See you on the flip side."*

Designed to take off and land like a helicopter, the Harrier's stubby
wings, bubble canopy and single engine had the ability to turn on a dime in
combat. The little jet resembled a giant porpoise. Regardless of how it
looked, though, the AV-8B was unique and well respected among other
aircraft. The Marines liked the jet because it could hover over a hot zone to
give close air support or swoop in on an enemy stronghold at high speed.
Tobin liked the jet because of its agility, but mostly because of the satisfaction it gave him knowing the men on the ground counted on him.

Pushing the throttle forward, Tobin sensed the jet beginning to skid along
the flight deck as the engine rpms built to maximum. Releasing the brake he

felt the jet lurch forward. Hitting ninety knots in a matter of seconds, the captain pushed the nozzle vector control lever hard up at a sixty-degree angle. With thirty feet of flight deck to spare, the Harrier hopped into the sky. Tobin let the airspeed build to 160 knots before he pulled the stick back to climb at 500 feet per minute, banking to the northwest.

NGHIA BINH PROVINCE, VIETNAM

"I count twenty-three," Pope said. "There may be more to the west but I can't see through the friggin' trees."

"I count twenty-four," Callahan confirmed. Both men peered out from the overgrowth of weeds lining the edge of the rice field shielding their heads. Callahan watched the armed soldiers, dressed in fresh khaki uniforms with beige helmets and carrying AK-47s.

"Pope. These guys aren't Vietnamese regulars. They look like mercenaries," Callahan whispered, wondering who was paying them and what they had to do with the chemical weapons onboard the downed aircraft.

"It doesn't matter who they are. I'm starting to get that nauseated feeling again."

"What feeling?" Callahan asked, glancing at his communications specialist.

"The feeling where defecation is about to hit the rotary oscillator," Pope replied seriously.

"Shit! The bastards are lining up. They're serious about finding us." Callahan peered through his binoculars.

The soldiers began to spread out across the rice field. They were going to walk across evenly spaced to see if they could flush them out of hiding. Callahan used to hunt pheasants back in Nebraska the same way.

"Why do these guys have such a hard-on for us?" Pope asked, dismayed.

"Lock and load," Callahan ordered. "And hope that Harrier gets here soon."

Duke was crouched down on the west side of the runway. Reaching over, he grabbed a handful of dirt and smelled it. The sand was soaked in kerosene. He needed to find a puddle to insure that it would light.

Staying in a crouched position, James quickened his pace, anticipating that the fuel on the other side would ignite at any moment. After fifteen yards he came in contact with a pool of jet fuel an inch or so deep. The area around it was dark and he assumed most of the fuel had soaked into the ground, saturating it. Removing the last matchbook from his coat pocket, he checked his watch. Three minutes had passed. Any second the opposite side of the runway should explode.

"You . . . come here."

Duke heard a Korean command shouted somewhere behind him. Turning cautiously, he saw a guard staring directly at him. He didn't understand what the man had said but by his tone Duke knew it wasn't an invite to dinner.

"What are you doing? Why aren't you preparing for takeoff?" the North Korean soldier spoke again, moving out of the fog toward him.

"Feet dry," Captain Tobin radioed, signaling he had crossed the coast and was now over enemy territory. Glancing down, he saw a white sandy beach flash by 200 feet below his jet.

Throttling back, the captain let the jet slow to 360 knots. The HUD showed he was flying northwest and his warning receiver showed a weak ground-control intercept radar to the north, probably civilian. It wasn't anything strong enough for him to worry about. Looking past the symbology on the HUD he could see a sparse haze over the tops of the dense trees below him. To the left he caught sight of a dirt road but didn't spot any vehicles traveling on it. On his right was a small village with thin bluish smoke curling up from the shacks lining the main street.

Pushing the stick forward, Tobin dropped to 100 feet above the trees and banked to the north. He would follow the shallow valley he was flying in for another two or three minutes before banking again to the west.

"Ohhhh . . . Ohhhh," Duke moaned suddenly. Keeping his head down, he didn't look up at the soldier approaching his position. Instead he listened to the footsteps crunching across the loose sand and gravel.

"What is wrong with you?" The soldier stopped short. "Colonel Kaine will not stand for this."

James doubled over as if he were sick. *"Ohhhh. Maekchu nappumnida . . . Maekchu nappumnida."*

The Korean's expression contorted with confusion upon hearing Duke's response. "What do you mean you drank bad beer . . . where did you get bad beer?"

*"Maekchu nappumnida,"* James repeated, not knowing what else to say.

"Get up before I report you to Colonel Kaine," the soldier stated.

Duke sensed the man's skepticism. He staggered to his feet swaying his head back and forth. He held the matchbook tightly in his grip.

A hissing roar on the opposite side of the runway was accompanied by yellow and red flames shooting up into the air. The fire, which started at the far end, raced toward the transport jets.

Startled, the Korean turned to see the commotion. Duke didn't delay. Swinging the stock of his AK-47 around he hit the man across the face. A sharp crack announced that the man's jaw bone had shattered; teeth popped out from his mouth. The soldier was wobbling backwards as James swung the rifle in the opposite direction, hitting the man across the throat. His face turned red and blood began dripping from his mouth as the soldier let out a slight moan before crumbling to the ground. Duke looked at the man. His legs were barely moving but he was out cold.

"Nice try, sucker," James said under his breath.

Dropping to his knees, Duke struck a match and tossed it into the pool of jet fuel. A blue hue danced on top of the pool before it exploded into flames.

Duke began creeping toward the transport amongst the shouts of panic and confusion coming from the area. He hesitated in order to get his bearings. Black smoke was pouring from the flames on the opposite side of the runway, mixing with the ground fog to create a thick blanket. Heading away from the fallen soldier, James glanced back and saw him rolling over, trying to get on his feet.

Dropping to one knee, James shouldered his AK-47. Centering the iron sights, he watched the Korean soldier wobble somewhat before he pointed his assault weapon at Duke. James knew he didn't have a choice.

Squeezing the trigger, James' AK-47 jumped, sending a bullet into the man's head above the left eye. Keeping his weapon on the North Korean, Duke watched the man sink to the ground.

Kaine spun around. He was certain he'd heard gunfire. Standing next to the open cargo ramp of the AN-72, he took several steps forward before realizing that both sides of the runway were on fire. On the left side the flames roared up the runway's perimeter to come within a few feet of the IL-76 transport. If the IL-76 exploded it would take the AN-72 with it.

"Instruct one of the pilots to get the engines started and move this aircraft from danger," Kaine yelled at one of the soldiers standing guard outside the transport. "We should have taken off five minutes ago!"

Swiveling around, Kaine faced the other guard next to the open ramp. "Gather the troops. Have them keep the fires under control until we take off."

The colonel scanned the area. He couldn't determine which direction the gunfire had come from. There weren't any signs of a struggle or enemy troops coming toward them. He thought possibly one of the men had gotten excited when the fuel ignited.

Major Erwin leaned forward in an attempt to see what was happening outside the aircraft.

"I will have to turn around in order to have enough room to take off," she heard the pilot holler to Kaine.

"Then do it!" Kaine shouted, then ordered, "Leave the bay door open. The men are not to board until we are ready to take off."

The pilot ran up the ramp through the cargo bay, past Erwin and Sinchon to the flight deck. She could see men racing around with shovels and fire extinguishers. Both sides of the transport were illuminated in dancing orange flames. Black smoke was starting to filter into the bay.

"What's happening?" Sinchon whispered to the major, his view blocked by Kaine's large frame.

"I don't know," Erwin replied, "but this might be some kind of a diversion."

With the guards gone, Erwin kept her eyes on the colonel's back as she stripped the ropes off her hands and began to untie her legs.

"They're stopping," Pope said.

"I see them." Callahan slowly moved his 8 × 30 Steiner binoculars, completing a sweep of the rice field in front of them. Less than fifty yards away were a dozen Vietnamese soldiers talking among themselves and pointing in the direction of Pope and Callahan's hideout. To the right were several other men also pointing weapons in their direction.

"I think we've overstayed our welcome, Pope. This is the only place they haven't searched." Callahan shook his head. "I'm surprised it took them this long."

*"Tango . . . Mongoose. Do you copy?"* the radio crackled.

Callahan grabbed for the radio and turned the volume down.

*"Tango . . . Mongoose. Do you copy?"*

"Mongoose . . . this is Tango. We've got bad guys coming straight at us fifty yards to the north." Callahan spoke with the mike up to his mouth. "What's your position?"

*"Three minutes out. Give me a GPS and talk me in."*

"Negative, Mongoose, negative. Area is way too hot," Callahan replied.

The crack of rifle fire caused Callahan to flinch. Three bullets hit the water in front of him, splashing mud into the air. Before Callahan could raise his rifle Pope returned fire, hitting a Vietnamese soldier. His head exploded and he fell to the ground as the rest of the soldiers opened fire on their position.

"Stay down, Pope," Callahan screamed, raising his CAR-15 and squeezing off five quick shoots. Keying the mike he radioed the Harrier. "Mongoose . . . Tango. All hell just broke loose. Get your ass out of here!"

*"Negative, Tango. Give me a GPS point."*

Callahan shook his head. His gut rolled over, glad the pilot was stubborn enough to attempt to pull them out when the area was way too hot for an extract. He punched the POSITION button on his GPS-117 SATCOM and SAR radio, sending an electronic microburst to the Harrier. He waited, knowing it would take a few seconds for the transmission to be relayed off the satellite to the AV-8B.

*"Roger, Tango . . . Mongoose has your position. This snake killer is inbound at one eight seven."*

Several more bullets cut through the air, hitting the embankment above Callahan's head.

Duke broke into a slight jog, holding the AK-47 across his chest. Through the fog and smoke he could see the tail section of the Il-76 transport sixty feet away. Two men ran across his path carrying shovels toward the fire burning near the Il-76's wing. He saw another group of soldiers throwing shovels full of sand and dirt onto the flames.

James kept his head down. Making sure the safety of the AK-47 was off, he paused under the T-tail of the Il-76. He was now close enough to see the area around him clearly. The cargo bay of the Il-76 had been cut away and its landing gear was broken. Twenty yards to his right was the AN-72 Coaler. Its bay door was down and there wasn't anyone standing around it. James heard a muted whine which quickly became much louder and more shrill. Both engines on the AN-72 were spooling up.

*Here goes nothing,* Duke thought. His heart raced as he ran to the edge of the cargo bay, keeping his AK-47 in front of him.

A pulsing white dot on the upper edge of the AV-8B's radar screen pinpointed the exact location of Tango Team. Captain Tobin's eyes drifted to the data on the bottom of the screen. They were two miles north of his position.

Banking the Harrier to the left, he came wings level heading due north. Easing back on the stick, Tobin nosed up to 500 feet. Over the top of distant trees he recognized the area. *This is it.* Several rows of rice paddies stretched north and east for a couple of miles. Tobin's heart beat harder. The special forces team was on the south end. He would have to make one pass to get his bearings before dropping down for the pickup.

Increasing his airspeed to 410 knots, Tobin let the Harrier climb to 1,000 feet. He had configured his AV-8B for both air-to-air and air-to-ground operations. The outboard pylons each carried an AIM-9M Sidewinder. The intermediate pylons in the center of each wing supported the extraction pods used to ferry the special forces troops. The inboard pylons had been fitted with AGM-65A Maverick laser-guided air-to-surface missiles. Housed in two under-fuselage pods was the Harrier's gun system. Consisting of a General Electric GAU-12/A cannon with 300 rounds of HEI or high explosive incendiary, the cannon could spit out 4,200 rounds a minute. Looking at the weapon's display, Tobin made sure the select mode was on the GAU-12.

Streaking over the trees, Tobin banked to the right. Beneath him he saw a line of soldiers approaching the south end of the rice paddies. Several were crouched down, firing toward an overgrowth of weeds.

"Tango . . . Mongoose," Tobin keyed his mike.

*"Tango here."*

"Stay low. It's time to rock-and-roll."

*"Roger, Mongoose. We're not going anywhere until you get these assholes off us."*

Tobin pulled the stick back and broke through 2,000 feet. Working the throttle and nozzle vector control, he pushed over in a tight loop, heading for the rice paddy field below.

"He's coming back," Sinchon whispered, referring to Colonel Kaine, who had only moments ago stepped off the ramp toward the fires.

Erwin sat down again with her hands behind her back. She lowered her head, hoping he hadn't seen her attempting to remove the general's ties.

Walking up the cargo ramp, Duke stopped in the center. The bay was empty except for Erwin and Sinchon seated next to the bulkhead.

"Thank God! It's Duke!" Erwin shouted. "I thought—"

"Shhhh," James hissed, rushing in the rest of the way. The shouts continued outside the AN-72. He nodded toward the flight deck. "How many?"

"Just one," Erwin mouthed.

Duke reached up and ripped a piece of canvas rope off one of the storage tie-downs.

"Cut the general loose then don't move." James handed Erwin the knife from inside his jacket. "I'll take care of the pilot."

Erwin nodded then whispered loudly, "Then what?"

"Then we're going to fly this thing out of here," Duke said, moving toward the flight deck.

"There he is!" Pope shouted then ducked as several bullets hit the water in front of the two men. He reared up, answering back with three quick bursts.

Callahan looked up to see white vapor trails coming off the wingtips of the Harrier. The jet was coming around from the east. Callahan knew instantly what the pilot was going to do. He would line up east of the rice field and let loose with the Harrier's cannons, strafing the line of the soldiers out in front of them.

"Shit, they've spotted him," Pope exclaimed, seeing the soldiers pointing their weapons to the sky and firing at the Harrier.

Callahan keyed his radio. "Mongoose . . . Tango. They see you and are concentrating their fire. Recommend you come off the south. Use the trees for cover."

*"Roger that, Tango. Move after my first pass. I'll pick you up on the back side of the tree line."*

"We'll be there. Tango out."

Callahan looked back at the AV-8B. The two-tone gray jet was coming level. Several decoy flares appeared from behind the jet just as white smoke appeared from the gun pod under the fuselage. A split second later Callahan heard the ripping sound of the cannon shells cutting through the air.

In one fluid motion Duke James wrapped the rope around the pilot's neck. Pulling back on the rope with all his strength he heard the man's neck pop. James waited for his body to go limp before he eased the tension.

Duke locked his arms under the man's shoulders and pulled him from the seat. Holding his AK-47 in one arm, James pushed the door open with his back, dragging the pilot with his other arm.

"Erwin, let's get . . ." He dropped the man and froze.

Standing just outside the door was a North Korean officer. He was holding Erwin around the neck and pointing a 9mm pistol at her head. Sinchon was slumped over with fresh blood running down the side of his face.

The rice paddy exploded in a rain of 25-millimeter cannon rounds and mud. The sound of the projectiles hitting the water was loud enough to drown out the Harrier's engine.

Callahan hesitated for a second as he watched the AV-8B tear up the landscape. Every one of the Vietnamese men stopped firing as they dove for cover into the water and mud.

"Move it," Callahan shouted to Pope. Keeping low, they scrambled out of their hideout to the back side of the tree line thirty yards away.

Callahan looked up to see the AV-8B pull off its strafing run and head back to the south.

James kept his eyes locked on the large Korean officer. The insignia on his uniform told him the man was a colonel in the *spetsnaz*.

"Tell him to drop his gun," Colonel Kaine said to Erwin in Korean. "This game is over. I have won."

"He wants you to drop your gun, General." The major fought back tears welling her eyes. "He'll kill us both anyway. Don't—"

Kaine yanked up on Erwin's throat with his massive arm. "Shut up. Only repeat what I say." He guessed that she was saying more than he had instructed.

James saw Sinchon move out of the corner of his eye but didn't vary his stare. He and the colonel kept their gaze locked on one another.

"Tell him to drop his weapon," Kaine repeated, "or I will shoot you."

"He says to drop the gun or he'll shoot me." Erwin's voice cracked, her hands holding onto the arm around her throat.

James swallowed. He blinked hard as if he was ready to back down and began to crouch slowly toward the floor, holding the stock of his AK-47.

Tobin felt the pressure of three negative Gs as he pushed over, heading for the ground at 280 knots. Rolling left 150 feet off the deck, he caught sight of two men running toward a small clearing behind the tree line. They were all that was left of Tango Team.

Throttling back, he leveled his Harrier at 125 feet. Tobin popped the air brake and slowed to 100 knots, then swung around in a tight arc. He kept the clearing to the right of the jet's nose. Using the thrust vectoring control to hover the aircraft, the captain shoved the stick down, forcing exhaust to keep his jet hovering above the ground. The Harrier was now flying more like a chopper than a jet. The HUD showed he was at fifty feet and coming in way too fast.

Tobin sucked in a deep breath and throttled back again. Using the stick he placed the clearing in the center of his HUD.

Callahan reached the clearing first. Waving his arms, he tried to call attention to his position. The AV-8B was only a hundred yards away. Looking back, he saw Pope hobbling toward him.

Callahan glanced at the AV-8B, seeing it rock its wings. The pilot had seen them.

"Move your ass faster, Pope!" Callahan raced back to help him along. The jet's loud engine made it impossible to be heard.

Several bullets hit the ground around them.

Tobin hovered the jet twenty feet above the ground. Loosening his grip on the controls, he floated toward the ground.

Staring out of the cockpit he gave the two special forces soldiers a thumbs up as the Harrier hit the ground.

"Come on, guys . . . fifteen seconds," Tobin shouted futilely as bullets hit the rear half of his canopy, shattering the plexiglass.

\* \* \*

"Umph," Sinchon grunted as he shoved his black boot into the side of Kaine's knee. With a loud crack the Korean's knee snapped. The colonel faltered, both his arms dropping away from Major Erwin.

Duke instantly brought the rifle up and drew a quick bead with the iron sights. He could see the man's stunned face as he lined up the end of the AK-47's barrel and pulled the trigger.

Callahan grabbed Pope by the collar and pulled him over his back into the top hatch of the nearest pod. Another bullet sailed past him to hit the tail section of the AV-8B.

"I'm in," Pope shouted, going head over heels into the pod.

Callahan felt the Harrier begin to lift off. He jumped with enough momentum to roll in safely without falling back out.

"Fly, baby, fly," Pope screamed, hitting the side to signal they were in and ready.

Simultaneously Callahan lowered the top hatch and locked it into place. The jet swung around, picking up speed. Crawling to the clear plexiglass nose section of the pod, Callahan watched the running soldiers stop to raise their weapons. Tracer rounds shot past the Harrier in all directions.

"Until next time, assholes," he said, flipping them the bird.

The Harrier banked left. In a matter of seconds they were streaking over the treetops at 400 knots, heading for the sea.

Michael Callahan rolled over on his back and removed the zip-lock bag holding the map he had taken off the Vietnamese officer. He stared at it silently. *Whoever supplied this to the Vietnamese was going to pay,* he told himself. *Even if I have to kill the man myself.*

The gunshot echoed through the AN-72's interior as Col. Met Lee Kaine's body hit the floor with a hard thump.

"Don't let anyone inside this aircraft," Duke shouted to Erwin as he tossed her the rifle.

"You got it."

Looking out the left side of the cockpit, Duke saw that the flames of the fire had engulfed the left wingtip of the Il-76 and were heading toward the Coaler.

James quickly dropped into the pilot's seat. "We're next if I don't figure this thing out in a hurry."

Glancing over the Russian-designed flight controls, James attempted to familiarize himself with the system. *No sweat,* he thought, nodding his head. *Flown one plane you've flown them all.*

James found the switch to raise the cargo bay door. He hit it and pushed the throttles forward. The flaps were down and there weren't any warning lights. The AN-72 began to move as he swung to the right, away from the burning Il-76. Through the thick cloud of fog and smoke he spotted several men running toward the jet, waving their arms.

"Sorry, you'll have to catch the next bus," Duke shouted, looking down at the cargo-hold light. It switched from red to green, telling him the ramp door was closed. Watching the compass needle point to the south, Duke shoved the twin throttles all the way forward. The transport began to accelerate down the makeshift runway.

Watching the airspeed, he waited. At 140 knots James pulled back on the yoke. The AN-72 roared off the ground into the gray overcast. He reached for the radio and turned to the navy guard frequency.

"AWACS on guard . . . AWACS on guard. This is Beagle in the An-72 Coaler, heading south and climbing."


## TACOMA LEAD, F-15E

"Roger, AWACS. Turning to engage," Colonel Conrad radioed. Banking his F-15E to the east, he leveled at 12,000 feet and dropped the nose. Off the right side of his jet he saw a Russian-made AN-72 breaking out of the overcast and banking to the east.

Maneuvering his Strike Eagle closer, Conrad came even with the transport. Throttling back to match the Coaler's airspeed, he keyed his mike.

"AWACS . . . Tacoma Lead. I have them."

*"Roger, Tacoma. Stay with them to Osan."*

"Roger, AWACS."

Duke looked out the left side of the jet. He saw the dark gray F-15E a hundred feet away. Both pilots were looking in his direction. The sight relaxed him a little.

"Thanks for the escort, AWACS," James radioed. "Give me a heading. I want to go home."

*"Maintain current heading at zero nine five. Flight level twelve zero, you're halfway there."*

"Roger." James engaged the autopilot. Slumping in his seat, he stared out at the clouds below him. They looked peaceful, like a blanket of fresh snow on Christmas Day.

# 36

General Chief of Staff Myong Chin sat behind his desk, his office dark and filled with the stale smell of smoke. Cradled in his right hand was a cup of hot tea while a cigarette burned in the ashtray next to him. Standing before Chin with his arms at his side was China's North Korean ambassador, Chengji Zheng. The ambassador's expression was that of a schoolboy being reprimanded for breaking the rules.

"Your government's concerns are unfounded, Mr. Zheng. My country did nothing to provoke this confrontation with the United States," Chin insisted. "They violated our airspace and we responded."

"Your attack on the American AWACS and the *Van Triumph*—"

"My attacks were justified." Chin stood up. "The Chinese leaders should be thanking me. General Sinchon is a traitor and you know it. He was dealing with a known arms merchant and I stopped him."

"My government is—"

"Your government is filled with cowards. Where was your military when the Americans violated our airspace? Or did you choose not to confront them?"

Zheng didn't answer.

"With Sinchon gone I am now firmly in control of the military. There is nothing the United States can do about it. Tomorrow I will send a letter to the United Nations protesting this incident. I plan to tell the world the truth. The world must know that North Korea has no plans to acquire nuclear or chemical weapons. It was Gen. Han Sinchon's plan to overthrow this government and obtain these weapons of mass destruction." Chin pounded his fist on the desk. "He is responsible for this . . . *not me*. Now leave. I have nothing more to say."

Zheng stood for a moment before exiting the office.

Chin returned to his seat and allowed himself a slight smile. The Iranian freighter *Allum Bacar* had not been intercepted by US Naval forces. By now it was hiding easily in the vastness of the open ocean as it steamed toward its home port in Iran. In forty-eight more hours his plan would be complete. Iran would have the fuel rods.

Chin took a sip of tea as his confidence swelled. The Americans could do nothing to stop him. It would simply be a matter of time before both Iran and North Korea had nuclear weapons. He could then deal with the United States on his own terms.


## THE WHITE HOUSE, THE NEXT DAY

"General Chaniff is here to see you, Mr. Manning," Lindsey Kay, the chief of staff's private secretary, announced over the intercom.

Allan Manning drummed his fingers on the top of his desk before replying.

"Send him in," he finally said, sighing.

Chaniff entered the room followed by Duke James and two other men dressed in dark business suits.

"What is this?" Manning stood up.

"Shut up and sit down, Mr. Manning," Chaniff replied coldly, coming to stand in front of the desk.

Manning continued to stand as one of the men closed the door and James joined Chaniff's side. Manning's face grew taut and he opened his mouth to protest again.

"Sit," Duke instructed, towering over the desk.

Manning saw the fire in Duke's eyes and did as he was told.

"Mr. Manning, these two men are from the FBI. They have a few questions for you." Chaniff tilted his head back in the dark suits' direction.

"The FBI?" Manning attempted a chuckle. "If this is about Bill Bishop's leaking information you should be—"

"It's not about Bill Bishop." Duke was enjoying seeing the man squirm.

"Well then what is it?" Manning cleared his throat, picking up a stack of papers on his desk. "I have work to do."

Chaniff nodded at Duke who was holding a manila envelope in his hands. Opening it, he removed a file folder.

"What I do in my spare time is my own business," Allan said quickly, glancing at the folder James was holding out to him.

"Unless it has to do with the security of the United States, Mr. Manning." James tossed the file onto his desk.

A couple of photos slid out. Manning stared down to see clear shots of him entering Hawkens' Lexus and then again at Union Station. The edges were fuzzy. It was the same telephoto night-vision lens that had taken the pictures Rhonda had sent him earlier.

"Oh, God" . . . Manning dropped his head. She had managed to get him without embarrassing herself after all. It never occurred to him she would keep the private detective on him after she had gotten the first incriminating photos.

"There are a lot of people who want to know why the acting NSA is meeting secretly with a well-known arms dealer," Duke's firm voice broke the silence.

"I . . . I . . ." Manning stammered.

"How did a map of Tango Team's infiltration route into Vietnam get into the hands of a Vietnamese commando officer?" Chaniff asked, motioning to the FBI men. "And how did the North Koreans know about our Langau operation?"

"I don't know what you're talking about."

"You're a damned liar, Manning," James said, cutting him off. "Twenty-six men and women died when that AWACS was shot down."

"I said . . ."

Manning tried to stand but Duke pushed him back into his chair.

"Two dozen Rangers and four pilots were killed trying to get me off that island," he continued. "You sold out, didn't you?"

"I want to speak with my attorney," Manning stated, not looking up.

"I'm sure you do," Duke said as the two men stood on either side of Manning. "I'm sure you do."


HICKAM AIR BASE, HAWAII

The sun was just breaking over the horizon as Gen. Han Sinchon moved to the window. Looking to the east from his guarded hospital room, he watched as several birds made their way toward the breaking surf. The water appeared a deep blue matching the cloudless sky.

The beauty of the morning helped lift his spirits. The general's mission had failed and he could never return to his homeland. He was sure that in the months to come Chin would discredit his career and rip apart everything he had worked so hard to achieve. It was best not to think about it.

Sinchon walked back to his bed and sat down. He looked at the scars on his disfigured hand, remembering the sacrifices he had made throughout his life. For the first time in a long while a sense of peace came over him. After all, he had tried to change his country. He had risked his life one last time for what he felt was right. Although he had failed, he had tried. He knew he could not do any more.

"I have one last thing to achieve in life," Sinchon said to himself.

Removing a piece of paper and a pen, the general began to write. Somehow, some way, the Americans would get a letter to his daughter.

*My Dearest Wulee,*
*I am your father . . .*

## THE PENTAGON

"We had an opportunity to change the world," Chaniff said to Duke as the two men walked down the hallway toward Chaniff's office.

"I know. But the military can only do so much," Duke said. "Without solid civilian leadership making the right decisions, the military is useless. Allan Manning should never have been allowed to gain so much power."

"I agree," Chaniff said. "The government is only as good as the people in it. That's why I'm recommending that you become the president's next national security advisor."

James stopped in midstride. "I don't think I heard that."

"Why not, Duke? You have the experience and the integrity. You're country needs men like you."

"I'm not ready for Washington. There're too many head games. Keep me on the flight line. I still have a few more planes to fly." Duke held out his hand, not letting Chaniff respond. "General, if you need me . . . I'll be at home."

"Alright, Duke. Have it your way," Chaniff said, shaking Duke's hand. "Merry Christmas."

"Merry Christmas," Duke replied.

## STAFFORD, VIRGINIA

Katie James sat on the plaid couch with her three-year-old son, Sean, on her lap. Pamela was pressed up against her arm, staring down at the hardcover book she held in her hands. Tossing popcorn up into the air, Matt was trying to catch it in his mouth as he lay on the floor with his legs up on the couch.

Katie continued reading from Chris Van Allsburg's book *The Polar Express.* The conductor had just handed the boy up to sit on Santa's knee when he was asked what he would like for Christmas.

"Know what I want, mommy?" Sean said.

"What do you want, Sean?" Katie leaned over to see his face.

"I want a choo-choo train."

"That's dumb," Matt said, the popcorn missing his mouth for the thousandth time. "You should ask for something cool like one of those motorized cars so you can drive around in the backyard."

"He can ask for whatever he wants, Matt," Katie chided her eldest son.

"Yeah, well I hope Santa remembers I'm supposed to get my own computer this year."

Katie sighed, shaking her head. She glanced up at the lights blinking on and off on the Christmas tree. Mesmerized for a moment, her eyes watered as she thought of Duke. She wished she hadn't fought with him before he left.

Sniffling, she blinked away the tears before the kids noticed. Matt got up to poke the fire and Katie glanced down at the top of Pam's head, still leaning against her arm.

"You haven't said what you want for Christmas, Pam."

Her hair was divided into two pigtails and braided with red and green ribbons dangling from the tops.

"I wish . . ."

The door suddenly burst open with a gust of wind bringing in swirling snow. Duke James stood in the entryway, staring at four somber faces.

"I'm home," he said, raising his eyebrows at the silent welcome. "Merry Christmas everyone."

Their faces lit up as the group charged toward him, nearly knocking Duke over with their hugs.